The Atonement of Sasha

Joseph Warren Morris

New Branch
PUBLISHING

New Branch Publishing
7454 Huntwick Trail
Nashville, TN 37221
Email: newbranchpublishing@gmail.com
Phone: 1-615-662-7224

First published by New Branch Publishing

ISBN: 978-0-615-26947-4

Printed in the United States of America
Nashville, Tennessee

This book is printed on acid-free paper.

Printing by Lightning Source

"You are blessed," said Mary Tonka, "given
Talents by your Maker that are reachable only by
A few. The lot of most of us is to struggle slowly
Up hills of little grade; yours is to dash up mountains.
So do not let your sorrow for the girls hinder you. It
Was not meant that they should wear fine clothes, nor
Understand the mystery of arcane medicine, nor play
Wondrously beautiful music. That is your crown to
Wear, not theirs. But you may someday save their
Child's life, or their own."

Acknowledgments

The typing was demanding, the long hours of editing equally so, and for her prodigious effort, together with numerous other contributions, I cannot express sufficient gratitude to my wife Joyce Ann. But I feel them; and go on to say that without her this story would not have turned out nearly so well.

And now an allusion to my friend Kimberly Martin. Kim is a superb formatter and graphic artist. I am indebted to her for her expertise in the publication of *Cowboy,* my latest novel until now, and in *The Atonement of Sasha.* I am fortunate to have had her with me along the way.

Lastly, I call to mind my dear friend Barbara Bowmer Davis for her efforts in assisting me with prior published works.

Foreword

MY MOTHER was old when she died and so was my grandmother and so was my great grandmother. I do not possess an exactness of my great grandmother's birth date, but heard my mother and grandmother often speak in a tone of certainty that she was born some years prior to the 1840's and particularly mentioned that she was a good friend of a Miss Novellus Eastbrook, a lady somewhat older than herself, who lived in a small town near a slave plantation in the western sector of Tennessee. What attracted me most keenly was a manuscript of a sort that Lady Novellus had set to pen which described the habits and lifestyles of the people there kept in bondage. Because of her family's connection and friendship with the owners she often took the liberty to venture onto the grounds, there intermingling with and among the inhabitants, getting to know many by name. At first my curiosity was only mildly struck—I was too young—but upon further maturity I began to listen with unvarying intentness.

Why it was divined that the lady's jottings were to follow my family tree up through the course of years, and eventually land in my lap, I deem unuseful to conjecture, but will offer that they at first simply migrated into the hands of my great grandmother who passed them on to her daughter, my grandmother, who then passed them on to me. One day, at my urging, she retrieved the manuscript from the lower shelving of an armoire she kept as a furnishing in her bedroom. Of inescapable notice was the condition of the pages—fading, yellowing, and frayed at the edges—and that their sum total amounted to a voluminous length.

It came easily to me that the compiler had gone through some several years of sacrifice and toil, meticulously keeping notes and scribbling them into an unfinished essay. The notes that she had set down were logically convincing and appeared to be grounded in fact. I believed that a great portion of them were and as a whole contained much more than a mere transcription of the habits and customs of a slave people. I sensed a prodigy here, a story rare, infused with a mystery that surrounded a beautiful young girl, if I could but piece the fragments together that lay openly at my disposal, inclusive with those I might later discover on my own. True, the language was devoid of finesse and excessively incoherent and jumbled, the sentences refusing to end, running one upon the other without pause or punctuation. Nonetheless, what she had created was commendable, and all things about it simply served to further my intrigue. I knew then that I would pursue to the finish what she had begun.

Chapter 1

IT WAS in the approximate mid eighteen fifties when Mr. and Mrs. George Van Doke were married in the late afternoon in one of the more prominent weddings of the summer in the home of the bride's parents, Mr. and Mrs. John Henry Edom of Chicago. The bride was pretty, very pretty, but not beautiful, yet they all deliberately said she was beautiful when talking to one another about her. One could assume that it was the perception of beauty that compelled their remarks, prompted by the taffeta faille gown of creamy white that blended with the pale rose veil she had borrowed from her mother. In any event, when the bride made her way toward the altar and her bridegroom she radiated a charm that captivated the congregation while the reporters in attendance gaped and busily copied words onto their pads that described what they saw.

So, socially prominent Elizabeth Anne Edom was married on this date, whatever it was, to rich slave owner George Van Doke of the South who presently lived in a mansion that his father, or mother, had named La Belle. After the reception and banquet, arranged and offered by Mr. and Mrs. Edom, the couple left Chicago early the next day bound for New York where on arrival they found passports and other essentials conveniently in place, thereby commencing their departure on an oft traveled and much heralded passenger vessel for England, Germany, France, and a sizeable docket of other ports of call, Austria, Poland, the Balkans, Norway, Finland, and the Port of Danzig among them. They had not ever before seen first hand these sovereignties, but had read avidly of their geography and culture. They planned to spend a full year abroad.

Jim Van Doke, George's brother, was in attendance at the wedding with his wife Lucy. A few mornings after their return from Chicago Jim and Lucy sat enjoying the comforts of their home in Nashville, while Brister and Prunelle, the house servants, were serving Moss

Jim and Miss Lucy their breakfast. Lucy was reading an account of the wedding in one of the Chicago newspapers she'd bought or was extended as a gift from one of the reporters on the scene. Suddenly, as if seized by impulse, she turned to Jim and declared that George's and Elizabeth's wedding was "adorably beautiful" and that "they can say what they please down here about us Yankees but that wedding out shone anything I've ever seen North or South. And the Edoms are wonderful people." At this Jim laughed aloud but it was only mildly released. He laughed because Lucy herself was from the North. She loved his playful bantering. Jim, two years older than George, remarked that she had to be unquestionably right in what she said she saw because he was close by her side seeing it too. He predicted a blessed future for his brother and new wife, further letting out that he thought Elizabeth Edom was a fine girl and also very beautiful, that they were well matched, and moreover that he deeply regretted his mother and father hadn't lived to see the union.

Red haired, reddish cheeked Jordan Van Doke, Jim and George's father, sometimes given to temper tantrums, and drink, but on the surface generally kind to his wife Martha, had died of a stroke some time before. Martha too died within a year or less, succumbing to a bout of influenza. Or cancer. They didn't know which. Lucy pitched in that she was greatly thankful that George's mother was able to meet and know Elizabeth a few years back and that she knew his mother thought quite well of the young lady. She said that she felt he used really good judgment in choosing Elizabeth Edom and that Elizabeth used the same wisdom in selecting him; then exuded a sigh and voiced in an air of excitement, "They are right now on the Atlantic somewhere on their way to England. Just think of it." Jim peeked over his glasses and kind of nodded unaffectedly, then returned to his reading.

By now Lucy was caught up in another attraction that had begun to tug at her fancy. Sometimes she was easily diverted. "Oh Prunelle, bring my soft pink shoes. My feet are killing me. I'm not used to being on my feet like I've been for the last week, and oh how they hurt."

It was as if Prunelle held them in her hands that very minute. "Here Miss Lucy, let me puts these here old softies on yo poor tired feet. After breakfast when you're relaxed and all, I'll rub them with sweet oil, then they'll feel just like new feets."

There was a lull for a second among everyone, no one uttering a word, whereon, Jim's concentration at once left his readings as if he were in fixed contemplation of a matter that was far more engaging than the newspaper lines or anything else recently said; and then brought it to surface, though his words seemed reluctant to come out, but it was clear that he felt a compulsion to speak them. Lucy glanced at him curiously.

He cleared his throat. "It wasn't right, Andre not being there. That tore at me."

"Yes I know dear, and it bothered me too," Lucy enjoined. "Nothing has ever been right about what happened."

That is all they said and nothing more. Brister and Prunelle cut their eyes knowingly at one another, their faces solemn, unexpressive, sad. The matter was seldom mentioned above a whisper in that household, and very lowly and cautiously among the slaves back on the plantation. At this, Jim, changing to a more airy tone, shifted to something else as if the former had not even arisen, with Brister and Prunelle carrying silently on with their routines.

"It was another time of course, Lucy, when George and me and Andre used to tag along to Chicago with our father to buy wagons and harnesses and tools and supplies for the plantation; and little was it in my wildest then that George would now be married to Elizabeth. Still doesn't seem true in a way. Mother always counted on George marrying the young lady from Virginia; I know she did. Let me see, what was her name? It was Sally Ringgould. That was it. Oh sure it was. Why am I cloudy on this? She made a few visits to the plantation with her parents in a fine carriage and she was fine herself; she surely was. Like you'd expect of a Virginia lady. But the trips, as I began to see they would, proved fruitless. I could read George, saw his thoughts without asking him or waiting for him to give them to me of his own accord. For some reason or reasons he didn't suitably warm up to the girl, nor was he impressed with her parents. When he met Elizabeth and fell in love with her he wrote his letter of severance to the young Lady from Virginia and that was the finale. He asked me if I'd proof it and I said no, that that was his own private business, yet assured him that I'd bet any amount he'd expressed himself admirably."

Jim then said the time was nearing nine thirty and that the docket was pretty heavy that faced him, for he had suspended a number of cases until the wedding was over, and that the day which awaited promised to be busy in the extreme. He rose and asked Brister to bring his coat and hat, adding that he felt a pressing need to take up his tasks at the office as soon as he could get there.

"Here you is Moss Jim," said Brister, with a simultaneous movement of helping him slip on his coat and handing over his walking cane. Jim was finicky about his hat, preferring to put it on himself, and after the usual adjustments, angling it to one side then to the other and at last feeling he had exacted it to the best possible fit, smiled self flatteringly that it now closely mirrored the image he had in mind of himself. He wasn't vain. Only likened to any other Southern gentleman of the legal profession. He simply wanted to look his best. Turning to Lucy, who now stood by him on the portico, he kissed her goodbye, and with Brister's assistance, climbed up into the carriage which had been pulled as close to the steps as Brister could manage. After Brister had mounted into the driver's seat Jim glanced over with a countenance which said, "Let's go," then his faithful servant clicked to the horses and began to drive his master downtown.

Very quickly thereafter Lucy left for her room, not in the least forgetting to ask Prunelle to come rub her feet with the sweet oil; and Prunelle, who had begun to carry out that which she was asked, started as well to heap praises on Mr. Van Doke to the effect that since his appointment to the supreme court of Tennessee he had day by day become one of the renowned names of the state. Endowed of clever faculties Prunelle realized that Lucy understood her artful embellishments, much exaggerated, but she loved to hear them anyway; so Prunelle did something of the sort upon every chance. But this morning she would quickly leave off Jim and take up a topic much unlike the former. They frequently talked about everything under the sun and Lucy welcomed it as much as Prunelle, even though at times it was repeated jibber jabber. Besides, the flow between them kept her from being lonely.

"Young Miss Lucy you was talking to Moss Jim about the white folk in the North. Do young Miss Elizabeth's pappy got lots of slaves like Moss George and Moss Jim?"

"No Prunelle. There aren't many slaves in the North to begin with, and it's too cold up there for them to live; and besides, there's no cotton up there, so there wouldn't be much of anything for them to do. Now as you've heard me say over and over, Mr. Edom has a fine business, making all kinds of things, like for instance, carriages, rockaways, and surreys. Oh just lots of things. I don't know what all."

"You don't mean to tell me," Prunelle persisted, "that no cotton is up there. What do the folks do for clothes?"

Lucy laughed and Prunelle laughed with her. "Well, we raise the cotton here in the South and the North people buy our cotton which they use to make clothes and then they build things and sell them to us. It all kinda goes round and round, like the fox chasing his tail."

"I don't think I'd like to live up there," said Prunelle with a plaintive cast. Lucy laughed even louder this time while Prunelle kept rubbing her feet.

"They feel better Prunelle. They sure do. Now will you fetch me my other shoes, the blue softies, and my morning dress and after I've slipped them on I'll read awhile." When Prunelle had done as asked Lucy commented gratefully "What would I do without you Prunelle?" And thanked her.

"Youse welcome young Miss Lucy."

Chapter 2

WITH ACTIONS exacted by their father in his will, with no attachment of codicil then or later, George and Jim Van Doke, upon his passing, were declared owners of one of the largest plantations in West Tennessee, several thousand acres, and an old colonial home belonging to the Van Doke family since near the turn of the century, the patriarch having ruthlessly stripped a great portion of the land from the native Chickasaws and straggling white settlers who held weak and indefensible title to ownership. When the territory was thrown open to public purchase the land outside his claim sold rapidly to settlers in parcels varying in size and price, and he alertly seized upon the opportunity by buying additional ponderous tracts in the Hatchie River bottoms for one cent per acre and choice adjacent tracts for not a sizeable margin more.

He was British by origin, but served as a soldier, a Captain, under the American flag, a fighter, prone to dueling, and once cashiered out of the army returned to England but soon thereafter set sail to return to American soil where he put down roots, buying a part of this exact piece of soil with money secured largely from English investors whom he later swindled, paying them nothing as profits and keeping the principal for himself. In the fullest sense of the word he was a clever business scoundrel. He had learned a great deal about the South during his military occupation, and especially the acreage he now claimed as his own. With the use of axes and cross cut saws and wagons and under conditions of unforgiving heat and cold, human hands responding to the driving force and blusterous commands of the irascible Van Doke once cleared this wilderness for the growth of cotton; but vast spreads of virgin timber were still untouched by the blade. To get here from Nashville you followed winding wagon roads through tall dense timbers for well over a hundred miles southwest to the Big Hatchie River.

Jim and Lucy had promised George that as soon as they returned to Nashville and Jim freed himself of the affairs of court they'd drive down to the plantation and see about things, making certain of writing him of their findings with no time escaping. So one morning, the sky clear, the sun not yet lifting over the eastern rim, they left Nashville for the plantation, Brister at the reins and Prunelle sitting beside him, while Jim and Lucy occupied the seats in the rear. Jim had ordered their adaptation to a reclining angle so as to administer more comfort to the passengers and this was now the posture enjoyed by he and his wife. Bubbling over with animation Brister and Prunelle inundated one another with lively chit chat, much of it about the scenes of nature along the roadway and in the distance in front of them; and as regarded their friends on the plantation whom they hadn't seen in too long awhile. Without let up they moved and bounced about and pointed to whatever compelled them, and not infrequently broke out with laughter. Jim and Lucy were seeing a show, and filled with happiness over the excitement of their dear old house servants glanced with amused faces at one another. Driving all day, almost until sundown, they spent the night at an inn that accommodated wealthy travelers. They'd hoped to reach Jackson for the overnight's stay but that proved out of reach, even though Brister had kept the team at better than usual speed and at a steady pace. Brister and Prunelle were assigned to cottages in the rear which were a part of the establishment. After supper and a restful night's sleep and breakfast the next morning they left early in hopes of finishing their journey by mid afternoon. This time of year was the best of all, Lucy thought dreamily, to drive through this vast wilderness where once the Chickasaws roamed and hunted, where now as always the birds and heavier game darted from one side of the road to the other. She wished aloud that she could catch sight of a flock of wild turkeys which she'd seen previously when only she and Jim made the trip; and she kept on with her narrations while Jim and Brister remained by and large quiet, saying she'd once seen the sky literally blackened with a covey of quail flushed from the bush by the noise of their carriage wheels. She spoke more directly to Prunelle than to anyone else about the wonder of the beautiful flowers of many colors, Prunelle answering that yes, they sure were beautiful and that her eyes were kept more than busy just looking from one to the other. Finally Brister said "I sho wish I had my gun. I could have us a mess uv birds in no time. But what would I do with them? No place to cook um out here."

"No harm in wishing Brister," inserted Jim, "but if you really had them you could take them on with us and cook them when you arrived at the plantation."

"Ha, ha, ha. Youse right Moss Jim. You sho is right."

The sun was still high up, the hour at or near three o'clock, a long interval before nightfall at that time of year. Aware that they were nearing their destination Brister was prompted to rap the horses on their rumps to escalate the pace. Seeing the next winding road which he knew was there, he'd walked it many a time, told him that the plantation was just around the bend, and his face lit up when he heard the hunting dogs turn loose as a choral. He'd hunted them all, for coons, for foxes, and for swamp bucks in the breaks of the Big Hatchie River bottom. Letting go with a cacophony of yelps and moilings when the travelers had come within a half mile they made such an impact on Brister that he stood, his hand cupped to his ear, his eyes gleeful, and said to Jim that he for sure could make out each by the tone of the animal's voice. One by one he singled them out.

"You hear that high whine doncha Moss Jim. That's old Lija. He's sho a good one. Nothing he cain't track."

"He's the finest."

"Maybe wese could go down on the Big Hatchie and hunt one day Moss Jim. Be good for you."

"We might just do that one day Brister. We just might."

"Do that honey," Lucy urged. "You need the relaxation."

Once they reached the turn off to the main driveway to the mansion the white people scrambled to meet them, together with a sizeable group of servants. The driveway was a bit winding, as was custom in that day, made of aggregate pebbles dredged from the river, which reflected a carousel of pretty colors, and standing on each side was a line of stately oaks, very tall, towering, quite old by now, which followed the curvature until nearly reaching the frontage. When the carriage wheels cut into the aggregate there arose a peculiarity of sound in the semblance of a log tied to the back axle and dragged behind, slowly ground and grated to pieces. But the driveway was much smoother than the dirt road they had left. In the lead to meet them was Joseph Nomehart and his wife Angeline, Joseph the first cousin to the late Mrs. Van Doke, mother of Andre, George, and Jim. Joseph and his wife had made their home in the mansion with George since the death of the matriarch. Joseph attended to the affairs of the internals of the mansion, the superintending of the servants, the schedules, the cleaning, the arrangements for guests and the like. The servants went by the names of Cynthia, Hallie, Fannie, and Sol, faithfuls for a generation or more, now aging, the added weight at the midriff and the graying hair proving it, but able still to perform their obligations well and were thankful to be a part of the crown jewel of any job among any and all servants, which was to have a coveted place in the mansion. There were generous heartfelt hugs and laughter between Jim and Lucy and Joseph and

Angeline, and the same could be said of Brister and Prunelle and the mansion's servants, all moved and greatly excited to be among one another once more. The servants had begun to unload the carriage while Joseph, Angeline, Jim, and Lucy continued to stay as they were, their exchanges of elatedness not yet entirely cooled but beginning to subside. Leaving the rest of the unloading to the others Sol and Brister began leading the horses to the stables where they'd feed and rub them down.

"Well, let's go in," said Mrs. Nomehart momentarily. "Supper is nearly ready. In no time they'll have it on the table."

Chapter 3

THERE WAS an aura of cleanliness, of well keptness, as one passed through the doorway and once into the great hallway the eyes enveloped a string of freshly lighted candles variously mounted on richly painted walls. The oaken floors glimmered from recent polishing.

To the rear, but within easy hearing, there was a pounding, "wham, wham," which made its way to the inside, mauls in use by the servants to prepare the huge batches of dough which a kitchen worker was beating into an even finer substance on the dough blocks. With little delay the dough was rolled and cut into biscuits then slid into a preheated brick oven which contained exactly the desired temperature for baking.

Cynthia, busily going about setting the table stole over momentarily to her masters, her curiosity peaked about the wedding. They now sat in the vestibule, which was furnished with heavy imported furniture where flowers and paintings abounded throughout. Among the paintings there was one of Jordan Van Doke, stern, unsmiling, and without personality hanging from one of the walls and on another there was the portrait of someone that everyone recognized, Andrew Jackson, stoic and commanding, who Mr. Van Doke had copiously admired.

Cynthia began to ask Lucy of the wedding. "Oh I just knows it was divine."

"Oh it was Cynthia. I'll tell you all about it later. Tomorrow, I promise."

"We sho is glad to see you and Moss Jim, Miss Lucy. We sho is. Was yo trip down here good?"

Lucy smiled kindly and returned that it was and that the flowers were enticingly beautiful on the roadside and that everyone had talked their tongues off during the journey, except perhaps Jim who likely had unresolved court business on his mind. "He was somewhat quiet but he generally is."

"I knows Miss Lucy," she said, looking over at Jim with a twinkle. But then looked back at Lucy. "Is you all tired from yo ride and all?" she inquired.

Smiling buoyantly, Lucy said they were some but not greatly. Cynthia then put in that everyone had badly missed Moss George, "awfully,"and asked when he was coming home to the plantation with his new bride. Lucy said within less than a year to which Cynthia burst forth, "Mercy, they'll forget all about us in that time." Lucy replied cheerily that they couldn't possibly. Mrs. Nomehart seemed a slight nettled with her head servant as if she were intruding and out of place in talking as much as she was with her guests, upon which she spoke to Cynthia that she should be about her duties with readying the supper table. Jim frowned. "She's all right Angeline. Why dampen the little pleasure that she has? I find her curiosity amusing and I like it." But before Angeline could reply, Cynthia, understanding the rebuff, had suddenly turned and moved out of hearing. Seeing instantly that he disapproved of the way she had handled Cynthia, Angeline felt awkward and sorry about how she'd behaved and blushed scarlet. Jim quickly sought to relieve her of her embarrassment, assuring her that everything was all right. "I meant no offense Angeline. You did what you deemed best. It's just that these folks are seldom given a chance to join in on something like this. I was just expressing an inner feeling. I truly felt it would have been good to have allowed her a little more latitude. That's all."

"I feel that way too Jim. I was out of place. I just didn't think. I know how you feel toward Cynthia. She helped your momma raise you." This was a friendly exchange. Angeline had long been a part of the family and she and Jim on occasion bantered with one another and without sensitivity. Angeline was another of Jim's favorites and he usually found time to spend a while strolling with her alone when he and Lucy were on visit from Nashville, entering into a varied agenda of talks with her about his mother and past good times.

Meanwhile, Hallie, Fannie, and Prunelle had come to help with setting the table together with the transfer of the food to the dining room and moved about lightly while also setting out the glasses, plates, and silverware. The biscuits in unregimented heapings were transported to the inside on flat metal platters and then transferred into deep gorgeous bowls pottered in another age that Jim said were passed on to his mother from her mother. Cynthia worried constantly that she might break one. Shortly she called out that supper was ready. Jim and Lucy rose to wash, then came back directly and took their seats, Jim at the head and Lucy at his right. The spread of food was extravagant, much overdone thought Jim, until it occurred to him that after they'd finished the servants turn would come and that they would easily devour a greater portion of the surplus. Slices of tasty ham were plentifully cut and laid out on very large white plates fringed with a gold rim, and there was also veal. Jim leaned over to

Joseph and laughed and whispered that he'd always heard that indigestion is charged by God with enforcing morality on the stomach but on this evening he'd have to run the risk and hope his stomach remained unaffected. Heaped to the brim, a goodly serving of steamy vegetables were set out here and there in bowls of different shapes and sizes, butter beans, squash, sweet potatoes, corn on the cob, cabbage, and turnips. Cynthia had baked an array of cakes for the occasion. "Seldom does anyone count cakes around here, so we don't have a tally of how many she's prepared," said Mr. Nomehart. "But among the number, you can depend on a few made of bananas and coconuts. Her specialties." For drinks, there was iced tea, lemonade, and a flask of sparkling red wine distilled from grapes that were grown and gathered from the plantation orchard.

After supper Mr. Nomehart excused himself with the explanation that he needed to step over to the slave quarters to see that all were fed and that no one was left hungry. The slaves took their meals in a large mess hall constructed of heavy wooden slab measured and cut at one of the nearby saw mills. Jim offered to lend a hand but Mr. Nomehart dismissed the gesture as unnecessary, and said he'd see them shortly. When the white folks had finished with dinner and gone out on the portico, Cynthia and the rest entered and cleared away the food and tableware, then took everything to a second dining table in the rear where they too ate. Brister whispered to Prunelle before they had sat down that he almost starved while waiting, that his stomach started growling an hour before. She rolled her eyes in a manner that what he said would be thought impolite if someone over heard him. "Youse hold yo tader young man. Keep that to yoself."

That night as Jim and Lucy lay in bed both dwelt on the day past and how good it was to have the companionship of Prunelle and Brister. "They're the same as kindred, almost they are," said Jim.

"I was thinking that very thing darling," Lucy wove in. "You know, we all ate together out on the ground coming down here, reaching and taking chicken from the same basket, then separated for supper. It was a bit strange. There's something not right about that."

"Yeah. But that's the way things are and will be for a long time to come."

"Yes. That's true. They will be."

The next morning after breakfast Jim and Joseph toured the slave quarters and after this threw saddles on the horses with plans to ride over the plantation, including a trek on the banks of the Big Hatchie. The rain had fallen the night before. They'd hoped to have a look at the slaves working in the cotton fields in the river bottom but the soil was too soppy, the cotton too wet for picking. So they settled for riding along the shoreline while viewing the crashing turbulence which hurled the logs and driftwood about as if they were leaves in a storm. "Cotton mouth water moccasins are plenty thick as you are well aware Jim. Let's watch out. No need for a horse to get snake bit, or spooked and throw one of us off."

"Umh humh. How right you are."

Lucy and Angeline began the morning talking of the wedding, which did not extend to any appreciable length, for soon Lucy said she'd like to see in on the loom house where literally yards and yards of raw cotton material were continually processed and woven into clothing. With none of the workers seemingly aware of their presence they stood watching for a length. But the whirl of the loom house was uncommonly noisy which compelled Lucy to cover her ears with her fingers but in no way had she appeared to lessen her interest.

"This is fascinating. It surely is. It's like a veritable bee hive."

"I echo what you say. It certainly is. Well, shall we go on?"

"By all means. I've seen it all before, including this. Many times. You know I have. But I'm anxious to see everything again, just as always."

And then they crossed over to the cobbler shop where shoes were made for the people to wear as well as leather harness for the plough mules, and after this Lucy insisted on their looking in on the slave quarters, especially where the mothers were bathing and greasing their babies with hog lard. They went from cabin to cabin, the mothers eager to talk about their off spring, explaining that the grease was extra good for their skin. Angeline said she never failed to notice the babies full round faces and how they appeared happy. One mother spoke up and said, "It's dat good sweet milk we keeps pourin in dere bellies dat keeps dem so cheery and all."

Lucy was aware that it was practice for the older Negro women to help with the nurturing of the babies, bathing and changing their clothes and caring for them while their mothers were in the cotton fields. She'd noticed as well that it was the young strong Negro women who built the fires around the huge black wash kettles and pitched in and stirred the clothing and rinsed and hung it out to dry. There was a hum of washing activity on this morning; the fires burned high around the kettles.

"How many babies are there now on the plantation Angeline?"

"Dear me. Do you mean right this minute? Well," said Angeline, "I think we have ten or fifteen new ones right now. Babies here are born all the time. Seems like in droves. We're very proud of them cause they're so healthy and are such fine babies and they're the future of the plantation. Yes they are. Their strong backs and muscles will be needed one day. The mothers take good care of them and they are hardly ever sick."

"But they do get sick Angeline and it can be really bad, I mean the diphtheria, chicken pox, and the flu. So far there haven't been too many epidemics. Sasha, Andre, and the doctors from Memphis and Baltimore have held sickness pretty reasonably in check, among the babies and the middle aged and old folks too. You must miss them. We all do."

"You mean Andre and Sasha."

"Yes."

"Ah yes. Badly. George doesn't say much about it but he slips and lets it out every once in a while that they are really valuable. Of course he himself doesn't have a clue about doctoring to begin with."

"Well," said Lucy, seeing no need to further engage the present subject, "what do you say we pay a visit to the old log church? Jim reminds me now and then that Mr. Van Doke, our patriarch, or was, built it, or had it built, when he was a young man, as we both know, when Jim wasn't even born, and he was faithful about keeping it in good repair, removing rotting logs and replacing them with new ones, and keeping the roof patched.

I used to go there on Sunday mornings when Jim and I happened to be here. There was no minister. Mr. Van Doke was the minister. He didn't trust anyone else. He was afraid that preachers other than him might contaminate the slaves with some misleading ideas. They had a slave uprising not too long ago in Mississippi as you remember, on the Waverly plantation. He'd read the Bible and pray, and had the people sing and pray with him. Sol could really pray, deep down. He basked in the attention they showered on him for his moving prayer making. Once there was a white lady who attended church at Mr. Van Doke's invitation who sat by me a little ways back from the front row. I had to laugh after the service at what she said.

'It was about as near Heaven as I ever expect to be just hearing them sing Roll Jordan Roll.'

I said I understood. I loved hearing Roll Jordan Roll. I really did. It really touched your soul. But there was another whose name escapes me now that was done as a solo by an old Negro who partly sang it in a deep sad voice. In a kind of moan. The words went like this: 'Old Moster is coming on a cloud from the Heavens to take all his chillun home.'"

Angeline could wait no longer to join in. "Ha! That wasn't me standing by you when they sang Roll Jordan Roll. I'm confident I didn't say that."

"No Angeline, it wasn't you."

"But everything you've said I've seen and heard. And we've a good many times been there together."

Jordan Van Doke wore two cloaks, one in which there was a generous kindness, but in the other a violent temper, a carryover trait of his father, that sometimes leapt out of control, which sometimes found the man ordering some poor soul to the whipping post, his own hand doling out the licks. Lucy greatly loathed her father-in-law's disposition, at intermissions addressing the practice of the beatings with Jim, which she'd only heard of but not seen, who answered that he too vehemently disapproved, often revealing as much to his mother, who also said she too greatly resented her husband's demeanor.

"What you do is wrong Jordan, deeply wrong. It's against the scriptures."

"No it's not. It has to be. They'd get out of line if I didn't."

She pled with Jordan Van Doke to stop the practice, suggesting that kindness might yield better results, and for awhile he succumbed, abiding as his wife asked, but back slid, ending up at the whipping post again. He found it impossible to ever change. Before his death Lucy had begun to harbor a poignant disdain in her heart for him, or rather for what she considered the terrible wrong he imposed on his people and spent nights lying in bed wondering how the man could read the scriptures to his congregation and pray such reverent prayers then indifferently end up laying the lash to their backs. On the surface the slaves seemed to love Mr. Van Doke; they said they did in gracious endearing tones, but in time, when they had come to trust her completely, Lucy had learned from Brister and Prunelle that it was much to the contrary.

Chapter 4

"IS GEORGE now reading the Bible to them on Sunday the way his father did?" asked Lucy. "I mean was he before he and Elizabeth married and left for Europe?"

"Oh yes. He did. Joseph takes his place now and reads a chapter or part of one, starting without fail with John 3:16, and they sing and pray. Joseph doesn't much like praying or reading the Bible. He's not good at it. He'd rather someone else do that. But with George away he has no choice. I'm with him usually. When George and Elizabeth return I'm sure she'll really enjoy going to church with him, seeing him carry on with the worship." Lucy paused before saying anything, carefully gauging her thoughts.

"Do you suppose Angeline that Elizabeth will fit in here? She's a city girl and I'm wondering how all this will appeal to her, that is, I mean, everything about plantation life. The difference could be devastating."

"Well," said Angeline, "she made visits here while the old people were living and she acted like she was delighted with everything. Yet, to live here may change the picture. You can never tell. But she may like it. There are signs that she could and will. I very well remember once when she slipped off to the slave quarters and came wagging back one of the young babies to the mansion, coo cooing and talking baby talk and all, and when seeing this sight Mrs. Van Doke almost flew into splinters. 'Honey, Elizabeth, take that baby back to its mother. It's much too young to be out here.' One thing that Mrs. Van Doke didn't allow was meddling with the young. She never allowed anyone to meddle with the young people on the plantation, babies and children. But I'd see Elizabeth anyway talking to the ones up in age, say seven or eight, when she glimpsed a chance, despite Mrs. Van Doke's strictures. I do believe Elizabeth loved the babies and the children. She never seemed to tire of watching them play games in the dirt yard in front of the slave quarters and was much amused and laughed at the mothers greasing their young and just dearly loved to hear them sing to them. I think maybe that's why George loved her like he did, seeing she was an uncommonly understanding woman. Well, anyway, we'll see how she fares when she's back from Europe and settles down here into the routines."

☙ ❧

Angeline and Lucy were now standing on the portico and had come into the presence of Cynthia, who, like they, had caught Jim and Joseph in her gaze as they were riding up. "Here they come. They knows it's time for dinner."

"I heard you ring the dinner bell Cynthia a while ago. Everything is ready isn't it?" The slave people were seen a half hour before thickly congregating in the vicinity of the mess hall, anxious to eat.

"Yes Ma'am Old Miss, and we sho have a good dinner today cause Moss Joseph had two big hogs killed and do we have good eats."

Even in the hot summer, the Van Dokes laid fresh meat on the tables each day, and in that there were ponderous numbers of slaves to feed, and often a stream of company, two or three hogs at a time had to be slaughtered and dressed for consumption.

Dinner was served, whereon Lucy and Angeline started to inquire about what Jim and Joseph had seen around the plantation, the answers resulting that fall crops were fine, cotton everywhere looking mighty bountiful, and all work up to schedule. "Jim must write George," said Lucy, "as soon as we're back home. We promised we'd visit down here and tell him how everything was."

"That's mighty nice of you," Angeline spoke up. "Joseph and I have all we can do and we don't necessarily like to write. George knows that. But I'll do the best I can to drop you some lines when I can and let you in on things around here. Then you can send messages to George in whatever way you decide."

"I'll sure appreciate your doing that Angeline," returned Jim.

Someone said that time flies and that before any of them realized it George and Elizabeth would return, but went on to explain that another harvest was to evolve and pass before that happened as well as another spring and summer. Jim and Lucy spent a few more days on the plantation, among them, paying a visit to their dear friend Adelaide Sherette who lived close by. Jim went hunting one late afternoon with Brister on the banks of the Big Hatchie, and Lucy made another tour of the slave quarters. Time had run out. When Wednesday morning rolled around they drowsily lifted themselves out of bed, the hour hand on four o'clock, ready to leave for Nashville, and with very little time lapsing sat down to the best of Cynthia's breakfast preparations, who was trying to out do herself, which consisted of fried chicken, fried apples, flap jacks, fried corn cakes, biscuits, ham and eggs, hot coffee, fresh cold milk from the cellar, fresh fruits, which did not include strawberries because the season had passed and there were none; but there were overloaded bowls of delicious fresh peaches filling in as a replacement. And there was the fruit cocktail not heretofore mentioned.

"What a breakfast," said Lucy. "That fruit cocktail almost filled me to the brim. It was delicious beyond compare and I liked the way it was spiked with that good seasoned whiskey. It was a life saver considering the hour we got up." Jim reflected a countenance that echoed her sentiments and said that anyone who'd spent some years on the plantation was well informed of course that the cocktails were made from the old whiskey they kept in abundant supply in the cellar. Mrs. Nomehart uttered that oh yes she figured that it was almost a hundred years old, and that their patriarch Jordan Van Doke bought it on a voyage once to Europe when his wife was with him and had it shipped to his plantation, and that he had reliable sources tell him then that it was well over a hundred years old or at least a hundred years old. "We can't verify this exactly," said Joseph. "But it's old."

Angeline said it was certainly mellow and really made the fruit juice delicious.

"Jim, you and Lucy must carry back a jug with you."

Giving Jim no time to answer Mr. Nomehart declared with some uncertainty that they all might be mixed up about the age of the whiskey, and about which whiskey they were speaking of, that he thought he could verify that some of Mr. Van Doke's slaves made whiskey and made the best whiskey he ever tasted.

Raising his hands slightly upward and outward Jim said it was all the same with him, offering his appreciation in advance to Angeline for a jug of the liquor for one of his friends in Nashville, tacking on the quip that it was perhaps a mistake because the man would never end his quest for more after tasting one dram of the spirit.

Waving goodbye to Joseph and Angeline and the house servants bunched together on the lawn, Jim, Lucy, Brister, and Prunelle drove down the driveway and then on to the dirt road with sights set on Nashville. Brister rapped the horses lightly with the reins, anxious to hurry their pace. The sun was barely lifting from its perch in the east. Lucy was the talkative one of the foursome, taking up with Prunelle how it delighted her to see the birds and squirrels at play. From his driver's seat Brister spun around and said he feared that rain might fall owing to the liveliness of the squirrels. Jim said he hoped he was wrong but didn't suppose he was because he was usually right about predicting the weather from the way animals behaved. They'd stop for lunch Jim said, but not before one o'clock, feeling that somehow their moving as far as they could before taking lunch afforded some advantage. Brister knew what he was thinking. He often felt that way himself when he was trying to reach somewhere by a certain hour or day; but his reasoning was that if you stretched the morning you'd shorten your afternoon. He smiled and nudged the horses with the reins once more, then figured he ought to say something in response to what Jim had just said.

"Youse tells me when you want me to stop Moss Jim and we'll sho do it."

Jim fell to talking about the visit they'd had, bemoaning that it was too brief, and that it was a very good visit and that in his letter to George he'd have plenty to tell and that he was more than thankful that good news could be reported. "We'll make another trip down before the winter sets in, before the late fall rains, because then the traveling can amount to a quagmire, the muddy roads and all."

"George is mighty lucky that Joseph and Angeline are there to look after things," said Lucy.

"Yes he is, but Joseph has a good many people to help him."

"He does."

"Yes, the overseers."

"How many are there?"

"Ten."

"They're white aren't they?"

"All but one."

"I didn't know that."

"Who is he?"

"Coon. A colossus of a man. A fine man too."

"Is he a slave?"

"Hardly. He once was. Now he has rights that don't apply to the slaves. He has a pretty good house and a family. It's about a mile from the mansion."

"I never did hear of that Jim. Somehow it just slipped by me."

"You'll have to meet him sometime. He's our best overseer. He's a magician at handling the men workers. They're forever pranking with him, tempting him into a wrestling match. Finally he gives in and takes the playful dawdling on, then right easily flipping him on his belly and rubbing his nose in the dirt. 'Dere little man. Didn't ise tell you not to try things youse can't handle. Ha, ha, ha.'"

"Does he have a wife? And children?"

"Both."

"How many children?"

"Four. Three to ten years old."

"Will his children become slaves?"

"I think not. I don't want them to. I spoke to George that I'd strongly offer opposition to their going under the yoke. He's not about to try that."

"Did you see Coon while we were there? Did you talk with him?"

"No. I'm sorry that I missed him. He was away at Corinth to buy and pick up a wagon."

"Oh. I see. But darling, are the overseers free to do as they please with slaves, to discipline them as they see fit?"

"I guess you mean whip them like my father did. That's a peculiar thing really. In a sense it's rather ironical. Father used to say that good overseers create good slaves, that the thing that counts most is how you treat them and the way you care for them. I've heard him say many times that he'd hate to be a horse or an ox and belong to some people he knew. No, I don't think he allowed the overseers to touch one of them, not ever. He did that himself and believed apparently he was justified. Aside from the whippings which sometimes came on from a burst of temper he treated his slaves very well. Perhaps above the ordinary. That's the side that was good about him. The other was bad and in my heart unacceptable. But I was in no position to do anything about it. Now back to your question. No, the overseers don't whip them. And George doesn't either. I've had some serious talks with him about that. George has some questionable ways but he's not mean spirited."

ଓ ଓ

The fall rains fell, the snow came, and deep winter set in, which meant they'd not travel to the plantation until the spring as everyone regretted; and Jim wrote George letters giving the status of the affairs of things, some of these resulting from Angeline's letters which reported the various happenings as she and Joseph saw and experienced them from time to time. George and Elizabeth wrote letters to Jim and Lucy as well; and sporadically Jim and Lucy received letters from the Edoms of Chicago which let them know that from time to time they were hearing from George and Elizabeth, and that their letters contained accounts of things and places in England, France, Germany and the rest of Europe. "They make it all sound wonderful and grand," said Lucy. Winter began to fade and spring surged into life, and on June seven George and Elizabeth landed in New York, where after resting for two days they headed for Chicago, there staying a week with the Edom's before traveling on to the plantation. George had written Jim a last minute letter before their departure from Europe which revealed the date or approximate date of their return to America.

Dear Jim,

We're practically on our way, catching the boat in three days. Surely this letter will beat Elizabeth and me home.

You mentioned in one of your correspondences that you'd try to make it down pretty soon after we arrive at the mansion. I'll let you hear from me when we show up or not long afterward. Don't be in a rush to come, dear brother, for we'll need leeway for a little while to settle in, then there's the fact that you are yourself unquestionably faced with a draining schedule and demanding work load. You'll need to bide your time.

My very best,

George

After laying the letter down Jim reached to pick up the deposition which occupied his concentration just prior to opening it, but stopped short, then picked up the letter and read it again, this time more slowly. When he finished, he ran his hands through his nice head of hair and leaned back and sighed and looked with a melancholy stare for a minute or two out his office window. He did nothing for awhile, simply sitting and looking, looking, looking, at something that was not even there, then finally arousing himself said silently not of the lines his brother had written but of those he had not, "I'd hoped he'd ask if I'd heard from Andre."

I would be amiss if not here pausing to narrate a comparison of these two brothers. Therefore, I shall. They were in age approximately two years apart, Jim the oldest. In their portraits and artistic sketches one saw an inescapable resemblance, yet there was a difference in their countenances, one calm and ordered in his succession of process, and the other irregular in his behavior, irascible and unpredictable in the manner of his father. So between these two young men of wealthy parenthood and upbringing—though there was a strong general likeness in their common love of fortitude, in their eloquence and in their wit of mind, and in their attendance of public affairs—a gaping variation showed itself. Jim, in his form and expression of aspect, and in his gesture of motion, was gentle and composed; whereas, George was aggressive and vehement and roughly passionate. In their public speeches one spoke in a quiet orderly manner, standing throughout on the same spot; the other walking about on the stage or platform, and in the heat of his orations not infrequently tugging at his coat, and even at times abruptly throwing it off.

Chapter 5

WHO WAS Sasha? What was her family name, who were her parents, what was her blood strain, where was she when she was born, what curious circumstances lay behind her crossing an entire ocean to come unseemly to this region of the deep South, and where were the stations of her sanctuary during her long arduous journey?

Strange it may be, but to trace the footsteps of her life and to uncloak answers to these and other inquiries necessitates a glance at the most unsuspecting beginning, which was the San Antonio de Bexar, a presidio (a fort) lying in the territory of Texas long before the advent of the nineteenth century, and manned by soldiers of the Spanish Crown. The fort became in time the city of San Antonio, as it is presently known. A Pro Consul from Spain, Brigadier Pedro de Rivera on assignment in the territory inspected San Antonio in 1727, finding the presidio under good management and the company manning it so effective at responding to Apache attacks that he recommended diminishing the garrison by ten soldiers. Rivera's other recommendation also received serious attention and study, both in Mexico City and Madrid. Resultingly, in 1731, after almost two years of travel, fifty four Canary Islander men, women, and children arrived in the community, the first and last participants in an expensive and flawed experiment to populate a hostile Indian frontier with slim numbers of Old World peasants. The Canary Islands lie off shore from Africa by but a brief distance, midway between Morocco and the Western Sahara. Unprepared as these newcomers were to face the challenges and harshness of these open borderlands, they nevertheless gained privileges and favorable treatment from the Crown, which contributed to decades of animosity with other elements of the settlement but granted them mythical status in San Antonio history.

The Islanders (Islenos in Spanish) fought with everyone about everything. Inasmuch as they were granted by the Spanish Crown sole vecindad (citizenship) in the Villa San Fernando de Bexar, adjacent to the presidio, they occupied the complete run of municipal offices. Despite the fact that many presidio settlers—soldiers, retired soldiers, and their families—had more than a decade's residence in the settlement, the Islenos at first denied them citizenship and attending land and water rights. They argued with the missionaries over access to water from the San Antonio River, use of Indian labor, and the right to be the primary agricultural suppliers to the province's presidio. By the early nineteenth century, San Antonio's population stood at over two thousand souls, made up mostly of people of mixed blood, although scores of families who traced their ancestry back to the Islenos contended that they were pure Spanish. Gradually the forces of integration prompted a better unity among the people of the settlement. As small in number as the Islenos were on the beginning those reaching marriage age eventually had to find partners among the military settlers. A handful of Islander men even crossed over the line and abandoned their civilian status for enlistment at the province's presidios. Consequently, non Islenos, many of them of mixed Spanish-Indian-African ancestry, became successful petitioners for land and prominent members of the community in the latter decades of the eighteenth century. The unionization of the population segments is evident in the sacramental registers of the town missions, not only in the notation of marriages between members of the different groupings, but in the creation of ritual kinship bonds among them.

☙ ❧

Once Adelaide Sherette and her brother Lawrence lived on a tract of land near the plantation of Jordan Van Doke which was of ponderous size, requiring substantial effort and a few hours for a man to walk around it, and where their father quite successfully grew cotton in mass, not with the use of slave hands, but with hard labor which he bought by paying day wages, albeit such pay was meager. When they had barely attained to adulthood both the children were sent to England to enter preparatory school, the idea in their father's plan that they'd decide after this to attend one of the splendid universities of the country. But his dream did not materialize entirely, for his son upon completing his studies at the lower echelon, abandoned the aspirations he'd once had of attending a university, caught a boat for San Antonio of the Texas territory where after a convincing presentation of himself and his purposes, he was engaged as an associate at the mission known as the San Fernando Cathedral, founded in 1731. To become a Priest had been a cherished dream of his for a lengthy duration. "All my life," he contended in his presentation.

"Then you shall be my son. In due time."

Adelaide stayed on however and successfully completed her college work in England. With this behind her she rejoined her father to see what she could accomplish in the venture of growing cotton, succeeding very well by all accounts because she rapidly became the one person on whom he chose to depend entirely, and when he fell ill she suddenly found herself with the full weight of the enterprise upon her shoulders. Eventually he died. The doctors confirmed that it was from Malaria which he had contracted in India while in service with the English military. His wife lasted another two years, thus leaving Adelaide alone to face an enormous responsibility, but she possessed grit and intelligence, both in remarkable quantities, and did not shrink from asking Jordan Van Doke to let her learn as much as she desired and could by observing and studying the methods of growing cotton on his plantation, the size of which was some larger than her own. In actuality she did not need to observe or study. Already she was a prime grower in her own right. But she took the attitude that it wouldn't hurt. Jordan Van Doke welcomed her with arms wide open and said that after all he and her father were the best of friends over no telling the years and that he accepted him as a valuable neighbor and did her too. Adelaide was of the Catholic faith, as was her father and mother, and in that the city of Jackson, a straggling outpost then, was the nearest place, city or town, where they could worship in a Catholic Church, or in any event in a congregational setting with others of their denomination, Mrs. Van Doke and Adelaide began to travel there together by way of surrey for worship on as many Sunday mornings as were practical. It was not on every Sunday morning they could make the trip; the distance was quite far and on some day's inclement weather rendered travel prohibitive. Jordan Van Doke seldom went with them.

ᘓ ᘐ

While at the mission, Lawrence Sherette met up with Alfred Duval, a French citizen who'd also come to San Antonio, but not to try his hand as a Priest or function as an associate to one occupying that office. He was Catholic and had journeyed to the territory to carry out missionary work, and that only, on assignment by his church from his native country. The young men established fast friendships and enjoyed dining with one another, rehashing almost daily their lives back in the old countries, expounding upon the San Antonio culture, so new to them and different, and trading comments with one another on the nature of their work. In time Alfred told Lawrence that over the past several months he'd taken up with a beautiful Negro girl who'd ventured to San Antonio from the Canary Islands, where she'd lived for awhile, and was there employed. Her name was Izu. She had come to the Islands from Morocco. She was said to be pure African, although a discovery was made of some notes in a trunk when Sasha was older which evinced that Izu was mixed, a Nubian Egyptian.[1]

Why the girl left the Islands for San Antonio was never truly corroborated. Lawrence once explained that she left because a fellow assemblage planning to sail for America convinced her that there she'd find a land of milk and honey waiting for her and for them all. But he also told that they were perhaps a small band of missionaries with whom she had attached herself and that her cause for coming was to pursue the cause of missionaries in that domain. I cannot speak here that his remarks were solidly true. One day Alfred informed Lawrence with some semblance of joy on his youthful face that he and the girl were marrying and would make their home in the San Antonio community. Lawrence did not show surprise and asked of her name.

"Her name is Izu Lolano."

"Ha. A pretty name. Perhaps I may meet her."

"Yes. Certainly. At the earliest opportunity."

"Of what religion is she, if I may ask?"

"I don't know."

At this Lawrence appeared quite baffled and Alfred seeing as much felt persuaded to give a more complete explanation.

"Sorry. I should have said she has one and that it is Christian. It was formerly African, but she was converted by missionaries. It's African protestant. Though I simply cannot explain it to you because she has difficulty explaining it to me. Whatever her religion it will become the same as mine I presume."

"You presume?"

"Yes. She said so. She is well read of the Catholic faith."

"I see."

"Will you attend the wedding Lawrence? That would be most pleasing to me. And to her."

"Where is it to be?"

"At one of the missions."

"Gladly. Provide me the date."

---

[1] The Nubian-Egyptian relations are infinitely difficult to trace and understand. While warring against one another over the centuries the two peoples nevertheless showed peaceful exchange from time to time, mixed marriages notwithstanding.

The wedding was conducted but not in the mission of Alfred's apparent choice. After a few weeks he approached Lawrence with information that arrangements for the wedding weren't as easily effectuated as he expected, for the preliminary paper work was overwhelming as required by the office of the governor, and that he was unable to penetrate to the base of the trouble. So would Lawrence speak to Father Lumas of the San Fernando Cathedral to see if he might pave the way? Lawrence assented and did as requested. With loving demeanor Father Lumas took the matter in his own hands and conveyed that he was gladly consenting to marry them himself. Thus they were married, according to Catholic tenets, Lawrence attending, the girl dressed in white and looking quite happy and beautiful. The couple settled into the community, and time passed. Lawrence, a trifle puzzled, had it dawn on him one day that he was seeing his friend with decreasing frequency, only every once in awhile, and when their paths crossed there was hardly a word spoken of his marriage. Worried, he asked Albert if there was something wrong, meaning a discordance between he and his new wife, which Albert correctly interpreted, and assured him that all was well, then more fully explained that he worked throughout the day and felt indebted to reserve his evening and nightly hours for Izu. "He is right. That's exactly as he should do. I should have reminded myself that he is no longer a single man, as I am, and that that makes circumstances far different for us." Lawrence had hoped to see Izu more, adjudging it strange that he did not, and even suggested that the three of them should dine out some evening, enjoying food and some good wine at a nice night place where he and Albert had once spent countless fun filled hours. Albert returned that the idea crossed his mind often but it went unfilled. He once said that Izu was a private person in her ways, preferred spending time alone it seemed, and said she read books, many books, and that reading was good for her for it helped absorb her time. "Books are cold but they are sure friends Lawrence, and are steadfastly with you when you need them," he augmented with a phrase of wisdom, cocking his head with a display of jollity. She did not work, although she once had. Never did he intimate that there was a schism in their marriage, and indicated in every way to his friend that all was well with his missionary work, and therefore, with these two thoughts uppermost in mind Lawrence was stunned one day when Albert announced that he and Izu were setting sail to the Canary Islands. It was closer to his native France than America, far closer, to say the least, said he, and very close to Izu's native Morocco. Lawrence remembered him distinctly spelling out these reasons, and also that he was giving up the missionary field altogether. "I didn't argue against his decision. Yet I thought he might invite me on the day of their departure to wave and say goodbye to him and his wife. He didn't. I supposed he felt the choice might spare us both a little pain. I think it grieved him that we were parting." From all accounts Albert's hopes were high that he'd find opportunities in the sugar cane fields on the Islands, which he had heard were substantial, but it appeared that he did not fare well. At least after awhile he did not. Word came from a missionary source some few years later that a severe recession struck the Islands and it was deemed that Albert was caught up in the fray. The sugar cane industry had dried up.

Not many months following his departure he began to write letters now and then in an apparent effort to keep the lifeline open between himself and his friend far away in San Antonio. It appeared to Lawrence that he was exerting his best to rebuild a friendship that he felt was flagging in the few months prior to his sailing for the Islands, a matter which Lawrence dismissed without pause because in his thoughts there had never been a lessening of affection between them. "Alfred was a married man. What else was there to do but devote his hours to Izu? He knows that I know this. I will not dwell further on the subject." Though his lines were limited, which was his style, Alfred commenced to write more often. Once he wrote that he was stunned at how time had quickly vanished and asked Lawrence if he realized that it was nearing two years since he last laid eyes on him, and in the same letter revealed that Izu had given birth to a baby girl whose name was Sasha, which was, he explained, a Serbian name. His grandmother was Serbian, whose acquaintance he failed ever to make, for she died before that could happen. She died months after he himself was born. Serbia was too far away for his parents to travel there with him from France. His mother often talked to him of her. His father had perished in one of the Napoleonic wars not long after his grandmother had passed on. Lawrence increasingly looked forward to the receipt of Albert's letters, faithfully answering each without undue delay, striving hard to avoid writing the same ideas, not providing the same news over and over. Even so, he did not fail once ever in any of his mailings to convey a pinch of news pertaining to the San Fernando Cathedral.

Albert reported that he kept accounts for a sugar cane office, this being virtually all he said of the firm, giving no name of it, but made an effort to admit that he passionately disliked the job and that he hoped for something better. Lawrence wondered what had happened to his dream to become a capitalist in the sugar cane industry. Albert explained what had happened in a subsequent letter, perhaps thinking that Lawrence was curious and deserved an explanation. Albert had attempted to buy a piece of land for this purpose not many months after he arrived, even though meager in size, but his efforts failed to materialize, the bank doubting his credit worthiness, and therefore refusing the loan. He sought other backers which were to no avail. His vision was to start small, to at least get started, then acquire a large tract and grow sugar cane of somewhat aggressive proportions, and thereby realize very handsome profits. Small or large his designs faltered and died in their infantile steps. Embittered and beaten down he once lamented to his friend that he was misled by land promoters who had enticed him to leave San Antonio in favor of the Islands, but in the finale acknowledged that it was he who made the blunder, that the whole fault lay with himself, and that his hurt was worsened by the recurring haunt that Izu had not wished to return to the Islands to begin with. By now they were living more frugally than formerly, their savings seriously dwindling. He was still keeping accounts with the sugar cane firm. Albert stayed in touch with the local Catholic mission, seeking fragments of work for extra pay, which proved a useless effort, for the mission's answer, honestly given, each time was disappointingly the same.

Chapter 6

AS SHE grew older, both Albert and Izu taught Sasha, he mainly in literature and the scriptures and Izu in both literature and science, and Izu could draw and paint; she excelled in these spheres, and passed her talents on to her young daughter. She taught her to sew as well when she was old enough to learn. Sasha gorged herself on literature and science. She was fascinated by these fields of study, which was called to the attention of the family doctor one day, an Englishman, who was so profoundly impressed that he left with the young girl a montage of medical drawings of the internals of the human body. She appended the drawings to her bedroom wall which allowed her to handily study them at any time of her choosing. There was no public school for her to attend, therefore she was bereft of the interplay with other children from which she otherwise could have enjoyed and profited. She was acutely influenced by the English and French writers, their endless prolific creations whirling words and images into her young progressing mind as she thirstily turned the pages. Once Albert contrived an arrangement with the English Captain of a deep sea vessel to scrub decks as payment for the transport of himself, Izu, and Sasha to and the return from the two countries. On his way back the Captain altered the course of the return to include an excursion to Sorrento, a town in southern Italy. There was a trip to Morocco also, only one. It happened later. Morocco was close by the Canaries and Albert, as he had done when they sailed to Europe and back, craftily invented a way—scrubbing decks—to cross the waters for a brevity in Izu's homeland, where now she had no kindred left, their having perished from war, disease, starvation, and the ravages of old age, but nonetheless Izu wanted Sasha to lay eyes upon the land of her birth inasmuch as someday she'd walk upon it with her own and tell that her mother once lived there.

Sasha was eleven or twelve, I do not know specifically which, in any event barely past the age when she could count her years on this earth by the numbers of her fingers and thumbs. She would grippingly remember that year and in future times think of it with incessant repetition and sorrow. The small pox had come stealthily to the Islands the English doctor first concluded, with no known cause, although reversed his opinion when it dawned on him that a ship of Portuguese sailors had docked off shore, some coming inland for a few days to gad about, a costly furlough, for in the doctor's estimation the sailors had carried the virus that spread the epidemic, from which people died in scary numbers, not by the hundreds but many. The disease was serious and contagious, the victims marked by delirium, diarrhea, and high fever, among other symptoms. A vaccine against small pox was widely know of by doctors in that period and therefore no outbreak should have occurred, unless for whatever the reason people had failed to be inoculated, including Sasha and her parents.

Izu took sick first, then Albert, though not as badly, who tried everything within his limited capability to help his wife. Terrible sores broke onto her skin. The English doctor came, Doctor Carlos Enoch, and looked with worry and hopelessness at the patient, and then unbelievingly at Sasha whom he expected to be succumbing to the disease as well, yet there were no symptoms. None in the slightest. "How strange? Beyond a doubt she is protected by some unexplainable immunity. We'll see." His examination of Izu told him that she was gravely ill and was swiftly losing strength, with no will to fight for her life. Suffering immense pain and weakened beyond going on she died within two days. Sasha was devastated, Albert exerting his best to hold and comfort her, though too sick to attempt much else. Summoning forth the last ounces within him he stood with his daughter at grave site while the Priest uttered the appropriate words of burial in Latin. Some of the mission folks brought food to their home. Sasha ate but Albert was no longer able to ingest the least morsel and when the doctor came he asked Sasha to go outside and play while he talked with him. She did as he asked but was gripped with apprehension. He saw it. Albert silently wept for his daughter, who was so young to be a part of the awful scenes around her. He was at least glad and thankful that no sores had started to emerge on his skin. She could look at him without horror, as she had had to look at her mother.

"I am very ill doctor?"

"I will not misguide you. You are quite ill."

"Seriously ill."

"I meant that."

"Yes. Well, you need not explain further. I understand. What am I to do about Sasha? She is immune to this epidemic, is she not?"

"I think she is. Well, no thinking. She has to be. I am at a loss to explain why. She has not been vaccinated you tell me."

"No she has not. And you?"

"I am immune. I was exposed when but a lad. The disease only attacked me mildly."

"That is good. God has blessed you."

"Spared me."

"Either way. Well, I know that my time is limited, so will you please ask the Priest to see me as fast as he can?"

"As fast as he can. I will ask Father Kestner to be with you quickly."

Later in the day Albert called Sasha to his bedside and told her that he would not live and that before he died he was making sure to the best of his ability that she would be cared for by a friend. There was a feeling of horror and sadness that surged through her, which through sheer will she held undisclosed for her father's sake, and looked bravely into his pale and weakened eyes. Young though she was she had prepared for the inevitable. "You have heard me speak of him, Lawrence Sherette of San Antonio."

"I have heard you speak of him father. Is he a Priest?"

"I cannot vouch for that. It was his dream to fill that office when I was with him. He may have attained to it by this date."

"I will hope that he has."

Albert did not answer. Other thoughts were shoving this one aside. "Listen my darling, the Priest will see me this afternoon, and I will make arrangements for your passage to America. There is no one else to whom I can entrust you. The people here are of no blood relatedness to us and many I fear are sick, hard pressed to help themselves. My relatives in France are deceased, largely, all except my dear mother and your grandmother, infirm to the point that she is in the residence of a care home in Nantes, completely unable to care for herself. And there are none of Izu's relatives left in Morocco. So you see." Sasha's sad and bewildered face evinced that she grasped the implications. "There is only one soul that I can turn to. I must depend on my friend in San Antonio to see after your welfare for the time being; for how long I am unsure. Do you understand darling?"

"Yes father." She had concealed her feelings until she was no longer able and laying her head upon the dying man's breast began to weep uncontrollably.

"Now, now," was all his strength allowed.

When the Priest came, Sasha went outside and Albert in low strained whispers began to converse with him. The Priest moved closer, cupping his ear.

"You have heard me bring up the name Lawrence Sherette of the San Fernando Cathedral, haven't you Father?"

"I have heard you speak of him. Yes. He is your good friend."

"He is Father." Then he proceeded immediately on. "As you know, I am dying. I will leave this world in hours I am sure. There is not much time left for me to put everything in order for my daughter. With God's help and yours I will succeed. Now, here is what I am asking you to promise."

"What is that?"

"See that Sasha is transported to America into the hands of Lawrence Sherette at the San Fernando Cathedral of the district of San Antonio. In anticipation of this possibility I one week ago picked up pin and pad and drafted a letter to my friend entreating him to receive and care for her if she should in the near future knock on his door. I plead with you Father. Will you give this your best?"

The Priest, with his kindly face acknowledged that he would without having to utter it aloud, though reasoned silently that sending her to a convent in Europe, in Spain or France, might prove the wisest of all courses open to consideration. He did not share this idea with his patron, for he was not convinced that he was correct, surmising that the Master might be placing the fate of the girl under His wing personally for a purpose that completely transcended his earthly mind. To him, as it was with the doctor, a higher force was keeping her protected from the deadly epidemic.

"I will do as you ask my son. Boats are departing the islands on schedule every two weeks for America, some transporting goods, some a sizeable tally of passengers. I will ask one of the ladies who is to join the party sailing on the next passenger vessel to stay close to your little girl. She is journeying there to join her son. We will all do our best for your daughter."

Albert attempted to raise himself. "Is there a cost, I—."

"Shhhhh. The church will not stand for that. It will be paid for. The Captain will generously assent, and I will ask him to attend her as if she were his very own. He is one of the lambs of my flock and has children himself."

"Thank you Father. Now will you pray for my soul," he pled as he looked up weakly into the saintly face. Kneeling, then leaning against the bedside, the Priest laid his hand gently on the forehead of the sick man and fulfilled his wish.

> Almighty and Everlasting God, preserver of Souls, and dost correct those whom Thou dost love, and for their betterment dost tenderly chastise those whom Thou dost receive, we call upon Thee, O Lord, to grant Thy healing, that the Soul of Thy servant, at the hour of its departure from the body, may by the hands of Thy holy Angels be presented without spot unto Thee. Amen.

That next morning, an hour before dawn, with the Priest and his daughter holding his hands, Albert slipped into a coma and died.

When he had laid Albert to rest the Priest wept, not because he feared the man's soul was unclean, nor because he knew that he would likely bury masses of others in the weeks to follow and that this would be most pitiable, nor because of the terrible suffering undergone by Sasha's father and mother in the days just passed, that was over, so it was none of these; he wept for the young girl, and her pitiable plight, dreading and seeing and knowing of the countless travails that awaited her; she was so young, a child, he thought, now without parents, now lost, lonely, empty, bewildered, without kindred, facing a trip across a wide far reaching ocean for a new vista which she'd never seen, only heard briefly about from her father, a place called San Antonio, where she was to meet a stranger whose name was Lawrence Sherette, perhaps a Priest, perhaps not, and where would she reside when she got to her destination, and who would sustain her, providing her daily supplements, lodging, and care of health, for she was so young he kept telling himself, and how might she be protected in a wild frontier settlement as she went about, and by whom. "I shall impress upon Lawrence Sherette with my best letter that God is expecting the application of his hands to provide the fullest of care for her. He is the only one who can help her now. And I shall also send a copy to Father Lumas."

The following day he called to him Captain Eric Johansen, a citizen of Norway, a man of renowned sea skills, in his forties, and Mrs. Edweena Laster, a subject of Great Britain who had spent the last two years on the Islands as an employee of the British government. She was exquisitely proficient in the office of foreign trade. Her father served as an officer of high rank under Wellington in his victorious battle against Napoleon at Waterloo. Riding on his reputation she was admitted to the elite schools of pedagogy in England and trained and finished by some of the country's finest scholars. Early on it was noticed by the educationist and by anyone equipped with the faculties to distinguish such qualities that her very bearing showed her to be a person of dignity and of a mind no less elevated. She was now approaching her forty fourth birthday.

The Priest addressed them separately, beginning with the Captain.

"I need your help Captain Johansen, I badly do. There is a young girl who will be aboard your vessel to America at your next sailing. She is eleven years of age. Or twelve. Both of her parents died most recently from the epidemic." The Priest delayed a moment before proceeding. The Captain's eyes glinted and narrowed into an attitude of veritable seriousness. "She is alone in this world, certainly alone on this trip unless both you and Mrs. Edweena Laster in your own way consent to attend her. You know Mrs. Laster of course and that she is sailing on your ship.

"I know Mrs. Laster Father. We have both been members of your congregation. She will be good for the young girl."

The Priest went on. "I have such compassion and sorrow in my heart for the girl that I would accompany her on the voyage myself but I cannot. Unfortunately I cannot be everywhere at once"

"I understand Father," the Captain said, timidly lowering his head, feeling it awful that the Priest had to contend with these worries. "What can I do? Anything you ask. As you say to us constantly in your Sunday services, 'The highest duty is to think of others.'"

Pleased to hear that the Captain had been listening to his Sabbath messages closer than he had perceived, he coached a tender smile to his face and urged him with the highest charge, "See after her as if you were her own father."

The Captain, a man of deed and slight of words was brief. "Aye! I will Father. My eyes will never leave her."

"Bless you. I will pray to Him for your kindness." The Captain smiled and bowed after crossing himself.

"And when will you sail Captain?"

"Next week Father, on the tenth of October. We hoist anchor at dawn. I myself will be there on the hour or before."

"Good. I shall mark the date on my calendar."

Next the Priest met with Mrs. Laster. They talked while sitting on the front row of the mission sanctuary. He briefed her in full on the matter of Sasha, going over every word he had spoken to the Captain and then at last said, "And now Mrs. Laster. Your quarters are reserved on the ship already you have told me. I badly need your help as much as I need the Captain's."

"You shall have it Father. Please instruct me"

"The girl is tender, fragile, in other words quite young and needs a seasoned person in the manner of yourself to help guide her. To stay close, to offer comfort. She will be a lonely little girl, I assure you. And the voyage is lengthy. You must become her surrogate mother, until the trip has ended to say the least."

"I will Father. Instruct me further. Please."

"I am moving to that. After you have met her, there is the matter of pulling together her clothes ware, such as it is, and adding to it whatever we can. The good ladies of the mission will assume the lead in that regard. They may even pattern and sew some dresses together for her. If not, then they will find something stored back which is usable."

"When shall I meet with her and the good ladies you have mentioned?"

"Come see me tomorrow at the mission here. We will finalize everything."

Chapter 7

THE NEXT day arrived, finding Mrs. Laster knocking on the door of the mission, a kindly old lady opening it with an angelic smile of reserve on her face which asked in and of itself how she could help her without asking, Mrs. Laster beating her to it, "Could I see Father Kestner, he is expecting me." At that instant the Priest in his robe emerged from his office with Sasha at his side. He extended a cheery good morning to Mrs. Laster, thanked her for coming, and then introduced her to Sasha. Mrs. Laster, uncertain of what she should do simply smiled and uttered to Sasha that she would be close at her side on the ocean voyage to America, and then drew her into her arms and kissed her brow. At this the Priest smiled. Sasha smiled a little. She looked into Mrs. Laster's eyes as if she were examining her inner nature, judging whether the long voyage with her would go well.

Over the interim, until October ten, Sasha stayed partly with Mrs. Laster in her apartment, where she was inundated with books and newspapers, the newspapers reporting chiefly about the events of London, a slight old, a month at the minimum, and served hot or warm tea, whichever her choice, in beautifully colored China cups. The remainder of her time was spent at the mission, where there were certain ladies who took on over her with the most infinite tenderness while painstakingly gathering clothing for her trip abroad, most of the clothing dresses, yet there was a heavy red winter coat with a black furry collar someone had dug out that would be added to her wardrobe, which she'd badly need, especially on the open deck, for the winds were cutting on the Atlantic on certain days when the weather adopted a stormy mood. Next to the day of her departure, Sasha asked the Priest to take one parting walk with her through the home where she'd lived for her entire life, he of course consenting, letting her assume the lead when they arrived, he saying nothing. Slowly, she looked around with sad remorseful eyes, seemingly at everything, remembering everything, seeing memorabilia she'd seen a thousand times before, every morning when she arose from her sleep, now knowing that soon they'd be gone forever. What could have cut deeper and been more melancholy? Going over at the very last she gazed out the window at a swing set her father had built for her when she was but a child. She cried as she turned away. She had packed her trunk a day or two before, a huge gold and brown receptacle which either her mother or father had gotten from their parents—she didn't know which she'd told Father Kestner—which she mostly filled with books she had learned to love, together with every painting of her father and mother she could find. Being a painter, her mother had done a number of sketches of Sasha, Albert, and herself, in one instance a very large one of Sasha. Sasha had packed the trunk with no one else helping. To her that was an infinitely private matter. The Priest had told everyone to let her do it alone.

True to his word, the Captain stood on deck on the morning of the tenth issuing directions to his crew, a certain number of them standing close by talking in short snappy language to one another, ready to lunge into their routines. When the Captain gestured with his hand they ceased talking and mechanically began to lift anchor. All eyes of every member of the crew stayed fixed on the Captain, awaiting instructions, whether on deck or in the crows nest high above. Every man knew his task and began to carry it out with an exactness of punctuality once receiving the command, which was either a spoken word or gesture. At precisely dawn the fog horn blared across the way, the passengers already on board by a good half hour, Sasha and Mrs. Laster among them. The Priest had come with a handful of men that the Captain had designated to portage Sasha's few belongings, part of which was a carrier of clothes, which they stored in the cabin where she and Mrs. Laster were to reside during the voyage. As the ship commenced to edge slowly away, the Priest, a solitary figure in the mist, stood ashore waving, his hands shifting lethargically from side to side. Sasha waved back. Her eyes were wide and thoughtful, her face without expression. One can only wonder of the feelings and memories running through her, but that seems easy to guess. She clutched the two envelopes which the Priest had handed her just before he hugged her and said goodbye, and waved back at him one last time.

"Here Sasha," he had said, "give these two envelopes to the respective parties."

On their surface were the inscriptions of Father Sisco de Endera Lumas and Lawrence Sherette.

Rather than taking to her cabin Sasha chose to stay on deck, looking into the hovering fog. Captain Johansen had crept up along side her. She wasn't aware that he was there. His voice was warm and cordial.

"This will clear away with the coming of the sunrise. The sun will soon burn it off, then things will look pretty, the sky as blue as blue can be and the color of the ocean a majestic light tint of green. And the sea gulls all around us. You'll love the scenery. Have you ever traveled on the open sea in a boat?"

"Yes Captain," she replied with her girlish voice. "I once took a trip to England and France with my father and mother. And to Italy."

"Which you greatly enjoyed I'm betting."

"Oh very much."

"Good. You will this one too. Uh, are you warm enough?"

"I'm warm. My coat is quite heavy."

"Yes it is. And it's a pretty coat. Keep it snug around you. It's still very chilly. After awhile the air will warm and you'll find it much more congenial."

"I'm all right. I'm not cold."

When a patient is sick and ill and is suffering from shock, as was the case of Sasha, three things need to happen, which is, first, the patient must begin to try to heal herself, second, the doctor needs to apply his skills to the undertaking and third, time must be allowed to work its wonders. Sasha would not quickly recover from the recent ordeal through which she had passed. She would begin to try. In her own way she would. The Captain and Mrs. Laster would lend themselves to helping her. By infinitely small tidbits Sasha started to lift herself, though on the outset there was but little improvement that could be discerned.

They were nearing the end of their first week of voyage. Much to the surprise of the Captain the weather had held, the sun shone with luminescent beauty from daylight until dusk, and there was no wind that amounted to much, only enough at intervals to churn the waves above their usual crest. The Captain knew the weather would not hold as it was.

Sasha had begun the trip by sleeping well into the morning. She did not fall easily to sleep, tossing and turning, so she had to catch up. But all this abruptly took a new and different turn. She began to make it ritual to climb to top side and explore the sea each morning soon after breakfast, quite early, looking as far out as her eyes were capable, at first sitting in a deck chair for awhile, then crossing over and leaning against the railing for a better view, there staying for the longest, until someone called to her that lunch was served. Just gazing at the ocean waters, calm for the past few days, and viewing the sea gulls sweeping downward when they were near a splotch of deserted islands, gave her some semblance of joy. If nothing more it helped to fill the labyrinths of her mind with pleasant configurations, thereby blunting the awful mutations of the past. The Captain and Mrs.

Laster felt as if they saw an improvement of mood, though small, and talked of this and smiled.

The Captain wished to himself that Sasha were more talkative but understood. "She is as quiet as the lifeless moon, hush and dim and still. What eats away at her soul? Ha, I should not ask this silly question, for I know. She has lost everything. The better question is what can I do to help her overcome the torment of her memories? My answer is nothing. She is quiet and unresponsive to the extreme that I am uncomfortable to approach her. But I can keep trying. And there must be something I can do. Ah yes! There is. And past experience tells me what it is. Just give her time. That is all. She will find a way out of it."

In the meantime Mrs. Laster was making better headway. Sasha had begun to keep a diary, sitting in the cabin at evening time scribbling entry's, something very private Mrs. Laster gathered, and was careful not to show that she had even the meagerest of interest. Once Sasha stopped writing, and asked Mrs. Laster to tell her about the culture of London, about its people and the like. "It's a very great city," the answer came. She read something everyday in the magazines that Mrs. Laster had let her have, but seldom said anything of what she had uncovered. She preferred to question and listen. In particular she was fascinated with nightlife at the opera houses of the great city, but was even more attracted to hearing Mrs. Laster tell of the city of San Antonio and that the Spanish Crown once governed it for several hundred years, then Mexico, and finally Texas. Her father had told her of these things but it nonetheless intrigued her to hear them again. "It was the Southerners who helped Texas a great amount in gaining their independence."

"The Southerners? I've read of them. They were called Anglos."

The Captain was proud of his fine ship, and with good reason, for it was an imposing vessel, measuring 40 feet tall from the top deck to the tip of the mast and 98 feet from stem to stern, grand indeed for its day. One of its rare features was its speed. The owners required the posting of a bulletin from a London newspaper in the hallway with printed word that the ship had traveled from Liverpool to New York two years earlier in less than sixteen days, with Captain Johansen at the helm, and upon reading the print Sasha hastened to the cabin where she and Mrs. Laster were housed excitedly revealing what she had learned. Sparked by her finding she began to wander around seeking an opportunity to pick the Captain's brain; suddenly he was a celebrity. She had watched for some time the small man in the crow's nest, even his rather swift climb up, his legs churning in the manner of pistons, and nothing would do her but to learn every purpose of his job and wasn't it terribly dangerous and how far could he see and did he ever see passing ships that escaped the eyes of the rest of the crew, since he was up so high, and when the storms hit did he dismount from his perch? And the Captain did his best to answer every single inquiry. And that was only the beginning. An avalanche of others were working their way to the surface. The ship's mast and sails were monstrously imposing, and had been a target of her eyes from the first. Now she was ready for that too.

And consequently it happened that he sat down with her in his cabin one morning, pulling out a stack of large sheets with drawings of all sorts of masts and sails, some of the grandest of stature, and patiently began to guide her through them, she with unvarying scrutiny following every movement of his pointer as he emphasized a particular segment of the blueprint of the sailing vessel under examination.

"See that. See what I mean?"

"I see."

Amazed at her tenacity to explore and learn and her aptitude to instantly grasp the Captain was persuaded to express to himself, "What? A female and a young one at that drawn captivatingly by these unexciting if not dull technicals. That is not a common occurrence." But her persistence would mount. There was no doubt in his reasoning that it would not.

The mast of a sailing ship he explained to Sasha the next day was the tall vertical or near vertical arrangement of spars, in other words poles, which supported the sails, adding as well that large ships were equipped with a good many masts, with the size and configuration depending on the imagination and preplanning of the designer.

"This ship has several masts, does it not Captain Johansen, and therefore is a very large ship."

"It is one of the largest afloat in these times," he said proudly.

With this exchange over, the Captain proceeded with a plethora of other explanations, one of which was that originally ships masts were formed from a single piece of timber, typically from the trunks of fir trees. As time went by, he was careful to disclose, ships were built of a size requiring masts taller and thicker than could be made from single tree trunks.

"Ah," she let out. "Like this one."

"Yes my dear. Like this one. Let us step out on the deck where you can perhaps see more clearly what I am saying." The Captain guided Sasha to the door and opened it and they exited onto the deck where he once again took up the business of detailing what he felt she should know. "To achieve the desired height of masts for this vessel, the masts were built from up to four sections, known in order of rising height about the decks as the lower, top, top gallant, and royal masts. To give the lower sections sufficient thickness meant they had to build them from separate pieces of wood. "Look up there. Can you see these sections with your own eyes?"

"I can Captain. You are a very good teacher. I understood everything you pointed out." She stopped here, scanning with incisive scrutiny the various parts that he had mentioned and discussed, then turned her eyes upward to the small man in the crows nest, and was on the verge of taking up the subject as it regarded his duties, yet decided at the last she wouldn't.

"Well, I must leave off for now, for I'm afraid I have over taxed you. But if you will tolerate me more I shall return for additional lessons."

"But of different subjects."

"Perhaps."

"You are welcome back. Ha, ha, ha. And you do not over tax me. I am thrilled at your preoccupation with the ship. We will probe into whatever you wish as soon as you are inclined, be it the ship or something else."

She had started toward her cabin to join Mrs. Laster, but as if something had dawned upon her that she'd inadvertently left out she spun around and said curiously, "Oh Captain, this has slipped me. Sorry. We have been at sea for about ten days. If you will, can you tell me approximately the number of days our voyage still has to run?"

"Certainly. With good weather something in the proximity of what you have just said, ten days; if it is of a foul disposition then let me say twelve. I am unable to speak unwaveringly. A ship is unlike a wagon that a driver guides over a smooth and predictable roadway. A ship is faced with many sailing hindrances."

"But so far we have covered half way the distance. Is my math correct?"

"It is my dear. I agree with your calculation."

"I wish I could see on the map where we are."

"See me in the navigation room tomorrow and I will show you. Exactly. That is where we store our chartings."

"Where is it?"

"Next to my cabin."

She was there at the agreed upon hour. The Captain tugged at a drawer which was stubborn to open, keeping at it until he pulled it out. It was a huge receptacle and had to be to house the sprawling maps that he kept in it. "Ah. This is the one I wanted. See. We are looking at the Atlantic Ocean, and I can determine where we are by intersecting lines that are called longitude and latitude. That is rather fascinating isn't it?" Her smile and her eyes looking into his told him she felt it was.

"Will you show me?"

"Gladly. But let me simplify it. The process is much more complicated than you might think. We are here. See where I have set my mark. Observe now that the Canaries are over here by Africa, a circle around them which I myself drew, where we lifted anchor ten days ago, and over here to the southwest, but almost true west, is San Antonio, situated at the top of the Gulf of Mexico. San Antonio is where you are destined. You are right. We are approximately half way. We hope we don't plough into stormy weather, or that it doesn't plough into us."

"But Captain Johansen," she broke in, without regarding the weather, "I see on the charting map that San Antonio is not exactly resting on the water. It's some distance further inland, and since that is the case, where will you dock your ship?"

"Ha. We have omitted an essential ingredient of completing our journey, haven't we? No, San Antonio is not on the water, yet Corpus Christi is, the place where we will dock and where you and Mrs. Laster will start your journey by stage to San Antonio."

"Oh yes. We will. Mrs. Laster has said that. It's trying for me to think of it."

"How is that?"

"We will feel lost. I know I will. With you not around. Who will I talk to?"

"You'll have Mrs. Laster, a superbly nice lady."

"She is and has been the finest company as a roommate; still I am saddened about losing you."

"Ah, but you will still have Mrs. Laster as I have said, and then there is Mr. Sherette who is waiting for you in San Antonio."

Chapter 8

AS SASHA lay down in her bed that night she felt she'd drop directly off to sleep, for she'd grown tired toward the end of the day, she was quite tired, and Mrs. Laster had dropped off to sleep already. She could tell by the way she breathed, deep, and laboring a slight more than usual, and there was an occasional snore. A lady like snore she thought. For awhile Sasha began to toss and turn, and then think, and then toss and turn some more, and kept leaping back and forth between the two until at length she forsook sleep altogether. "Ah, my father's friend, his bosom friend, whom I do not know. I wish I could determine his looks. Certainly he is young, about my father's age I'd say, or some older. Likely he is a Priest, if the words of my father are correct. I hope he has read my father's letter. Oh there are so many things that beset me. What shelter will he have prepared for me, or will the Priest at the San Fernando Cathedral see to that? What is his name? Lumas. That is his name. Father Lumas. An older person I am sure. He married my father and mother. I am to hand him a letter from Father Kestner, and one to Mr. Sherette. Judging from the descriptions I hear, especially from Mrs. Laster, I feel a trifle uneasy about San Antonio. But Captain Johansen says I will find everything settled enough, and Father Kestner said it too. Oh, but if I could be sure, certain about everything. Well, anyway, I will breathe a sigh of relief when I reach San Antonio. I am certain I will. In the meantime, we are far at sea, sailing toward the Florida Keys, making good forward time to our destination of Corpus Christi, where we will board the stage, which I've never ridden before. Let me see. We are now approximately ten days away. I will ask Captain Johansen to let me see the plotting each day, for I am most anxious to keep up with where we are, and we most definitely have made good progress. No storms have hindered us. There may be no storms at all. The Captain would be quite in favor of that. I shall say a prayer that we won't."

The Captain could use her prayer sooner than she might have intended. Time had ticked off and they were nearing the Keys. That morning he was on deck earlier than usual, standing at the railing looking out to sea as far as his eyes would let him, there appearing something on the horizon that was of great attraction, then he looked up into the sky at the clouds that were beginning to mass, and then took measure of the wind that was beginning to accelerate, yet still a relatively light wind, all this while Sasha sat in her deck chair keenly observing, trying to figure what was so unusual in the Captain's behavior, because he seemed less calm than ordinarily. Not by much but by at least a tad. With her curiosity finally overcoming her self restraint she rose and approached him.

"Good morning Captain Johansen. You are up early."

"And you too dear. Did you not sleep well?"

"I slept well enough, thank you. Is there something you are watching that escapes me Captain Johansen?"

"Perhaps. Perhaps not. I am judging the weather. I believe a storm is brewing."

"Can you tell?" she asked, holding her hand up in a position near her face, wincing, as if that might shield it from the bright rays of the sun.

"Not exactly."

"The sun is rising in the east and a beautiful day is on its way. It seems a perfect day for sailing. The wind is up a little I notice but I see no signs of a storm."

"Ha, ha, ha. Sasha you have the makings of a good sailor. You are equipped with a great aptitude of sense. The wind I noticed too. And a beautiful day is launching. Just look at the radiant sun. But that is a slight misguiding. You see, there is an oft used phrase that a good pilot is apprehensive of a storm when the sea is most smiling. I am afraid the expression fits me precisely. But we shall know without a great deal of delay."

As the sun made its descent near the end of the day the Captain and a concourse of his crew stood with eyes fixed on the growing waves, only babies at present, but they would feed on the wind which was increasing steadily in intensity. After awhile the crew dispersed and set about to batten down any and all accessories that likely would be blown over board and lost for good unless tightly secured. Soon after this the Captain announced that all should take their meal and then wait out the certain tumult.

That night the wind began to howl and the ship began to sway. Sasha and Mrs. Laster felt it in their cabin. It was early; say the hour of ten, but by midnight there arose a repeated sound of tremulous rumblings, the storm escalating, and in true force blasting into the forward hull. By now, the Captain had taken over the helm, beholding that to his way of thinking this could be a rough one, but he judged that it was endowed of limitations and that within a few hours would dissipate and peel off to the northeast. Yet, this was a wild sea nonetheless, likened to an ill tempered bucking horse fresh from the chute, the wind and waves smashing at one another, which set the Captain off, "Ha, you devil. Have I not learned your disposition well? When I have surmounted one of your foamy crests I discover that you've another right behind ready to do me in. But you shall not have your way this night." Sasha had ventured close to the deck, but stood far back where she was safe, and could see men all over, carefully holding to whatever was solid, training their eyes into the darkness with an attempt to gain a fix on the waves that swept toward them, which was futile. The night was as dark as jet. The glow from the sizeable quantity of lanterns, perhaps fifty, hanging about the deck did not help them. The men had lived through many a savage storm but they looked afraid thought Sasha because their faces were ashen. So perhaps they were afraid. The Captain steered the great ship with steadiness, his expression remaining the same as it was the day before when the weather was serene and still. He was the epitome of strength. Personifying the ultimate of braveness, he at all times when an excited member of the crew hastened to him for instructions softly replied, thereby imposing calm upon the man. When told of Sasha's whereabouts he sent word to her that her Captain was fully in control, for her not to worry, and that the fury of the storm would soon tire itself out and start to move away. He was correct. Near the end of the night it began to lessen and by dawn had started slowly to wander off northeasterly. The Captain, still steering, smiled. "As I figured, we were only confronted by a corner of it."

Sometime during the late hour of morning Sasha intercepted the Captain on deck.

"Good morning Captain Johansen. It is much calmer out here than last night."

"Aye. I must concur."

"That indeed was quite a blow. The rolling of the ship was a frightful thing. I felt she might tip. But I knew she wouldn't."

"No," he answered, his voice carrying a laugh, "she wasn't about to tilt. That was not a very wicked storm. I've seen many that were far worse, and they lasted for days."

"I can't imagine. But I know this: I shall remember it for the rest of my life. I am so glad that it went by quickly."

"Indeed. And I too Sasha."

It was shortly after this that an incident popped up which the Captain had expected to occur many times before. But this was the first. Oddly enough. When it happened he was by a slight caught off guard, but lost no time erecting himself, knowing what measures he must take. He had prepared himself for this moment. It was on the eighteenth day of their voyage that a sailor came swiftly to him with a report that a strange vessel was sailing within a half mile of their ship and after having a look the Captain wheeled around to ascertain the whereabouts of Sasha, for he, as was his crew, was determined to shield her from what he saw and recognized, a slave ship, carrying Negroes, among other valuable cargo, from one port to another. The vessel was huge, a retired frigate from the Spanish navy, in its zenith a splendid thing upon the sea, but with admirable efficiency still rode the same warm currents that ranged from the upper Atlantic to the Caribbean. Summoning one of his most trusted aides he sent instructions to Mrs. Laster and Sasha, as well as to all other passengers, to stay in their quarters until otherwise notified, that there was a mishap on deck, a spillage of some sort, and that the crew must have an hour to rectify the accident. The slave ship soon passed and vanished. Of the true facts not one passenger aboard was ever able to decipher.

The days passed one by one, each day bringing them closer to their destination, Sasha viewing the plotting of their whereabouts without fail that Captain Johansen had marked on the map for her. And so one day she said, "Oh, Corpus Christi is very close, a mere quarter of an inch on the map." Time was running out, and soon their voyage would be over, sad for the both of them to think about. She had become a youthful joy to the Captain and he delighted her with his various and sundry conversations and stories of the sea, trying to fill up her time and block away the terrible specter which most recently had barged into her life. That her father and mother oft ran through her mind he was sure, but saw no visible sign of it. He had seen it only once, only on the beginning. She was disturbingly quiet and removed, he recalled, when the voyage had gotten underway. But the specter was still there and would always be. What the Priest had charged him with had daily loomed large in his thoughts, "See after her as if you were her own father," and now, with the voyage approaching an end, he could honestly and proudly answer, "I have done my best, I have done my best. I will pray to Him up there to escort her for the rest of the way, whatever that may be."

When they anchored night had fallen and lanterns and dock workers were all about. There was a stage transport waiting for passengers scheduled for San Antonio, which Sasha and Mrs. Laster boarded, but before this the Captain hugged them both, Sasha especially tight, and wished her God speed and success. "Write me my dear in care of Father Kestner and I promise to write you as well. I want to keep up with you. You've been a perfect joy. You will stay always in my heart."

With teary eyes, she replied, "You have been a joy too Captain Johansen and I will write, and I will pray that our paths will cross again. Goodbye."

The trip from Corpus to San Antonio was somewhat less than a two day ride. Something like twenty hours without overnight lodging. The stage would run straight through with the exception of necessary stoppages. Mrs. Laster and Sasha were the sole passengers and slept with minimal breaks until the dawn, both then awakening.

Sasha had read of this stretch of the West in books her father had supplied as well as one that Mrs. Laster had recently turned over to her and set her eyes to looking about with increasing curiosity. The land was flat to undulating, cattle country, and at intervals one could see for far reaching distances. Sasha thought in many respects the lay of the land resembled that of the ocean when it was calm, flat, quite flat, though in time the resemblance became vastly different, hills and Spanish moss trees dotting the scene, and the roadway winding and bumpy, and laden with rocks, often the culprits for seriously damaging the wheels, and despite the soft cushioned seats the ladies were jostled uncomfortably about. At some point in the vicinity of mid morning the stage drew to a stop at a way station to allow the passengers to breakfast and attend to other needs. When the driver was ready to leave two male passengers dressed in nice Eastern suits climbed aboard and sat down across from Mrs. Laster and Sasha. They doffed their hats. They caught the stage often. At first they smiled at Mrs. Laster and Sasha, and Mrs. Laster smiled warmly enough back but Sasha kept her eyes buried in a book. After a time Mrs. Laster began a limited exchange with the gentlemen, her dialect giving her native origin away, and of this they were particularly fascinated, pursuing her to go into not a few aspects of the old country. In turn they revealed that they were on a land purchase venture, representing a syndicate headquartered in New York and London who recognized the growing need for beeves on a world wide scale and intended to capitalize on the trend. But for the most part Mrs. Laster fingered through the supply of magazines she had brought along and napped.

Enduring the bumpy road with the pretense that all was well, Mrs. Laster took the aggravation in stride, smiling faintly into Sasha's lovely dark eyes when she once stopped her reading and looked over at her older friend. She knew that Sasha guessed why she was smiling. Sasha was equally uncomfortable. This was the first for either at riding a stage, which rambled onward, mile after mile, stopping here and there for a switch to fresh animals, and once when they came to a halt the driver said there was good hot stew inside. With the escort of the two gentlemen Mrs. Laster and Sasha climbed down and went in. It was an unpretentious and crude place but the stew was as the driver said. Good. They were hungry, all were hungry. Within a half hour they were on their way once more, the stage traveling at a faster pace in that the horses were rested and fresh. Thinking that it might be helpful to the female occupants one of the gentlemen spoke that in another two hours they'd reach the city of San Antonio. Sasha, shuffling the items around in her hand satchel, finally found the two letters she was to deliver. She sighed with anxious relief, exclaiming in a whisper to Mrs. Laster, who was looking on, that she was greatly relieved she'd found them. For a moment, she said, she had feared they were lost. "These are the letters that I am to hand to Father Lumas and Mr. Sherette; they are from Father Kestner. I will find them both at the San Fernando Cathedral, Father Kestner instructed me. I am wondering however, if I may, whether the stage driver will let me off at the Cathedral, then do the same for you at the Stage Post where you say your son will meet you. I had hoped you'd accompany me to meet both Father Lumas and Mr. Sherette."

"Oh. Let you off first at the Cathedral?"

"Yes."

"The driver will gladly do as you advise," said one of the gentlemen. His voice was friendly and of a tone to be helpful. He had overheard.

"That will be nice of him," said Mrs. Laster, acknowledging the gentleman's remarks with a smile then turning back to Sasha. "Do not worry dear. I'll go with you to meet Father Lumas and Mr. Sherette. But let's do it this way. After my son has met us I will ask him to carry us to them. Will that meet with your approval?"

"Yes. Thank you." The gentleman who had tried to be helpful smiled over at Mrs. Laster which told that he was relieved that the matter was settled.

When eventually the stage entered the city and drew to a stop at the Stage Post the two gentlemen rose politely, tendering their hands without pause to handle the baggage, carrying two loads to the carriage that Mrs. Laster's son had leased and made ready for the occasion of intercepting his mother. The carriage was exquisitely finished, endowed of a black shiny coach with lengthy red spokes ringing the interior of the wheels. Sasha commented to Mrs. Laster that its designers must have sought to make it in the manner of a toy. The gentlemen, who were yet standing around, looked at her and smiled. When Sasha had wandered out of their range of hearing one remarked that she had sailed in on the *Ignatius*, which originated from Europe, and that she must be French. The other answered surely so and spoke of her pretty white skin and compelling dark eyes and that in no time she was to become a beauty. One of the men within moments made the judgment to Mrs. Laster that she had a very pretty daughter, but was told she was not, only a young close friend and traveling companion.

Upon completion of loading, and after Mrs. Laster and her son had hugged and taken on over finally reuniting, she thanked the gentlemen for their thoughtful and kind assistance and they walked away, then she turned to her son whose eyes had fallen on Sasha. "Bryon, this is Sasha." Bryon's eyes brightened as Sasha's eyes shyly met his and thought silently that she was very beautiful and was destined to become increasingly that way as she aged. He judged her to be undoubtedly of European stock. She was again clad in her red coat, the time late afternoon, when the air had become chilly. Sasha only half smiled, making the slightest movement with her head that she acknowledged his acquaintance. Bryon was a tall young man of twenty six years with thick dark hair and a strong likeness to his mother. He was unmarried. She finally extended her hand to grasp his. When he had helped her and his mother up into the carriage, the custom being that women were to ride in back on occasions such as this, he clucked to the horses and they rolled away toward the San Fernando Cathedral. There was a nice even smoothness about the movement of the carriage as the horses easily pulled it along on the cobblestone street. Bryon had brought a parasol and mentioned to his mother that she might like to hold it over herself and her young friend, thus shielding them from the bright afternoon sun. Thanking him for his thoughtfulness she acted in accordance with his suggestion. Sasha stayed curiously busy looking at the unfolding scenery, poignantly studying the business frontages which were mostly of Spanish vintage, as she expected, for Mrs. Laster had described them before hand and she had formed an image of their likeness from earlier readings. The distance was only a half mile; it was but a fraction that they were there. Bryon had helped them down and now all at once they stood in awe of the magnificent façade, Sasha declaring silently that she knew she was seeing an edifice that had been created by artists and craftsman of extraordinary talents. “It’s gorgeous,” she said to Mrs. Laster, “as large and grand as anything I saw in England when my father took me there.” Bryon opened one of the two massive doors which led into the foyer, which connected to the sanctuary. When she had made her way into the interior and grasped the splendor of it all Sasha was as near overcome as she had been by the sight of the frontage. The décor was old Spanish. The spacing was of immense length and breadth and the vaulting of a height that caused one to wonder at the difficulty of a painter when setting up scaffolding to support his footing while performing his work. Someone in clerical garb had appeared, the Protodeacon, who inquired with a nice resonant voice of pastoral timbre if they were there to see someone in particular. “Yes,” the answer came, the voice of Mrs. Laster. “We are here to see Father Lumas.”

“I will tell him that he has visitors. Will you take a seat?” He pointed to a row of leather covered chairs with a curved backing which were aligned against the wall.

Chapter 9

WITHIN MOMENTS, an older man dressed in full Priest's regalia slowly approached, the angelic smile on his face exposing the kindness and goodness in his soul. Mrs. Laster introduced herself and Sasha to him and explained her affiliation with the young girl, exacting that Father Kestner had matched them together for their voyage across the sea. The Priest's eyes had quickly settled on Sasha as if studying some aspect of her, as if trying to equate her with his expectations.

"I see. I understand," he answered to Mrs. Laster," then proceeded to devote his attention back to Sasha, who now held him tightly in her scrutiny, and thought there was a favor in his face and eyes reminding her of Father Kestner.

"Sasha, you are here to meet up with Mr. Sherette."

"Yes Father."

"Well," and then he hesitated as if he should cautiously select the next few words, "Mr. Sherette is not here."

"Not here!" Sasha said with an exclamation, a shadow of concern sweeping onto her face. She began to cry. Revolving in her head was the long tiring voyage just ended, and now to meet with this disheartening news was upsetting far beyond the ordinary. Father Lumas was visibly moved, seeing her discomfort and her tears, which she was wiping away with her handkerchief.

"Now, now, my child. Do not be overly wrought. I will explain."

But Sasha, understandably bewildered and shaken, nonetheless could not resist posing a most natural question. "Where is he Father?"

"In New Orleans. But do not be concerned. He is there on appointment."

"But Father. Did he not know of my coming? My father had written him a letter more than a week before I left the Canaries. Father Kestner assured me he had."

"He wrote the letter my child. And I opened it after Mr. Sherette had gone. Mr. Sherette had urged me to open any of his mail that was routed to the Cathedral and act accordingly. And as you have just heard I did as he prescribed. The letter spoke of your arrival, or of your likely arrival I should say. I am saddened to have heard of your father's illness. What was his condition when you left?"

She did not answer, and with a sadness that Father Lumas found hard to bear, she with but limited movement of her hand deftly handed over the letter that Father Kestner had asked her to transport into his possession. When his eyes fell upon the lines that revealed Albert Duval's demise, he touched his fingers to his brow and uttered lowly, "Ah, I am deeply saddened. Did Father Kestner officiate the funeral?"

"Yes Father. And my mother's."

"Ah! You poor child" he said in words that were hardly audible, coming over and gathering her in his arms, saying a prayer in Latin which neither she nor Mrs. Laster understood. There was a gap in the conversation all at once where no one said anything, but finally Father Lumas broke the silence. "Well, I have made preparations for you my dear, so let me explain. Upon reading the letter from your father to Mr. Sherette I set about to send by courier to him that your father was likely to die or had died by the date the letter was received and that he in haste should board a stage to San Antonio. My serious belief was that you would appear shortly and wished to lay plans for you that were completely suitable to your liking. I am certain that he will arrive in three to four days, and in the meantime you are to stay at the Rectory. Please do not be concerned, for you are among the kindest and gentlest of friends who will see to your every need."

Sasha, in a manner that was more curious than anxious suddenly asked, "May I see the Rectory Father?" And glanced simultaneously at Mrs. Laster with a wish that she might see it with her. She imagined the interior to be of a strange and mysterious specter, and had no notion of what she'd make of it, but then in the same breath was ashamed she was having reservations about a Holy place. In any event she felt she needed Mrs. Laster to see the inside and help her judge whether she'd feel comfortable about sleeping and staying there. She'd find a second of privacy in which to discuss her findings with her, she envisioned, once Father Lumas had escorted them through. Then she added sheepishly, "Can Mrs. Laster go too?" Mrs. Laster smiled; she had read the reservation of Sasha's face prior to her last request and was prepared to accompany them.

Father Lumas had noticed Mrs. Laster smile and joined her with one of his own. Both understood the young girl's qualms. "By all means. Come, I will show it to the both of you."

"Wait a second Father. Please. I must instruct my son not to wait longer. I'm sure he is anxious to start unloading."

Mrs. Laster went to Bryon who waited at street side, voicing that he should proceed to his living quarters and store her belongings, that she'd be awhile longer with Sasha who needed her. Would he come back within an hour? She returned to the Priest and Sasha forthwith, and all three left the sanctuary through a side doorway, very quickly advancing to the Rectory. In that it was made of large blocks of stone, green vines of ivy had easily climbed high up onto its exterior. The tentacles had rooted to the jaggedness of the extrusions; and there were places where the vegetation was of such rankness that it was impossible to be certain of the material from which the walls were constructed. There too was a heavy wooden door coated of a hue of vibrant red with pieces of cut iron running along the edges and across the frontage in the shaping of a cross. If one had observed with only a modicum of astuteness the armorial bearings affixed above the entrance would have seemed to belong once to a Conquistador family long extinct. This door they passed through. As they entered and stepped onto the hardened floor, there was a hush so much in effect that a mere breath produced an echo; and the aura of the surroundings was of such vibrant freshness that Sasha and Mrs. Laster found themselves succumbing now and then to deep exhilarating inhalations. The flowers setting about were the aspect of all things tender and lovely, and as they glanced through the sizeable window from the sitting room they did not miss the gorgeous shrubs in the garden outside thirstily drinking from the streams of a marble fountain that rained downward on their branches and boughs. Both Sasha and Mrs. Laster commenced to smile at all that which seemed perfected for the eyes to see.

"And now Sasha, this is as good a time as any to let you hear of the staffing for this good home, which is not mine, no indeed, but the property of the great Catholic Church, which Mr. Sherette has seen times innumerable, and perhaps even your father set eyes on it from time to time, other than when he was here for his marriage to your mother. But about that I seem to have no certain and clear memory."

"The staffing Father?"

"Oh yes. A place in the manner of this one must have staffing. Guests coming and going you realize."

"But who are they? What are their assignments?"

"All right. There is the cook, then there is the butler, then there is the maid. You will love her. And the others too. But Chenelle, the maid, is as cheery as the sunrise. You are likely to meet her first because she lodges here. She starts at seven, and the cook and butler arrive shortly afterwards. They generally begin their duties at near the same hour. But I must retreat. There are two that I have thus far left out. One is the gardner who cares for the magnificent shrubs that you can see through the large window there." He pointed. "And of course there is a gentleman who is held accountable for maintaining the structure, I mean both the Cathedral as well as the Rectory."

"Ah! So many. I shall look forward to meeting them. Especially Chenelle. How old is she Father? I gather that she is young."

"She is twenty five."

From there he showed them the bedroom for guests, substantially spacious, equipped with a bed also of sizeable bulk which was styled and carved from the makings of the Italian Renaissance. An ottoman rested beside it which was less for décor than assisting persons of short height to mount the bed without undue struggle. "I would get lost in the night in something of this size" said Sasha. "It would swallow me up." The Priest smiled and Mrs. Laster laughed slightly aloud. Next he guided them to the dining room and kitchen, each conveniently linked together, he especially explained, thereby allowing the cook to transport food to the butler and then the food by the butler to the dining table, all this with a minimum of effort. The more than usual sized dining table was made from oaken timbers, covered from end to end by a white clothe with embroidered scenes of cherubs and graceful birds flying near a sea coast, and decorated with fresh pink roses arranged in a crystal vase with a long slender stem.

"We dine at six. It is now five. This is where we dine Sasha."

Sasha gave no response. Here again she was tentative, feeling the need to depend on the resources of someone else, those of Mrs. Laster, who by now had grown much into her being and Mrs. Laster could say the same of her.

"Alone with Father Lumas," she thought. "Ah, I am facing too much. His wisdom is immense and the supper will run awkwardly long, since obviously the words I need will not be handily available and I will become stiff and sit as silently as a statue. This evening especially," she continued, "I badly need Mrs. Laster at my side at supper and I will need her equally as much to keep me company throughout the night. The bedroom is gigantically large. It is more splendid than any I've ever seen but it is also strange. Ah, what am I to do, and how shall I bring up these things without offending our blessed Priest"

She did not need to bring them up, nor fret over offending the kindly Priest were she to make her worries known to him, in that the Priest was keenly wise in the understanding of humanity and saw into her soul as purely as a clairvoyant, and read her torment, deciding at once what he should do, which was to invite Mrs. Laster to take supper with them, as well as her son and Chenelle also if she were not detained. Mrs. Laster, relishing the idea of supping with Father Lumas at his table, readily accepted, and said that her son was returning right away and that she'd see if he might join them. When Bryon had gotten back she conveyed to him that he was invited as a supper guest at the Rectory and how it came about, to which he winced and lamented that he severely regretted missing the opportunity. He was called on an emergency. Employed as an engineer by the Germans who had contracts to erect a nearby bridge on one of the branches of the San Antonio River which necessitated his presence, there was no reasonable way that he could accept. The Germans had successfully contracted work over the years first with the Spaniards, then the Mexicans, and lastly the Texans.

"Bryon dear, I understand. There will be another invitation, I feel certain. Do not fret. You do as you must."

She as well went on to explain the recent eruptions in young Sasha's life and that she felt a great and pressing need to be with her as much as was practical, especially for a few days in this a new and strange environ.

"I do understand mother. She does look alarmingly young for all those things to have happened to her."

"Alarming for anyone dear."

"Of course."

"But there is more than the supper Bryon. Sasha is apprehensive of sleeping in the colossal bedroom to which she is assigned. You should see it. It's immense."

"What is wrong with it?"

"Oh nothing. It's splendid," she answered pertly. "But nonetheless Sasha is afraid. I can tell she is."

"To sleep in it alone?" He frowned.

"Yes."

"Then you should stay close with her."

"I know. Until at least she becomes used to her surroundings."

"That is surely the right thing. And you must attend her in every way you can. In a day or so, when our situation at the bridge is resolved perhaps I can help too. The three of us might take a stroll about the city. I might even lease a surrey and we can ride all over." He brightened at the prospect.

"Yes, yes. That sounds nice. And very sweet of you. Now one thing more dear. It will cost you another trip and for that I am sorry."

"And what is that?"

"Please return to your apartment and bring me my brown clothes case. My sleeping gown is in it and my robe."

"Ha, ha, ha. Sorry for what my dearest? I am your son you know. I'll return with it before you can snap your finger." There was great love in his heart for his mother.

At the hour of six they sat down to supper with Father Lumas, Chenelle there too, spending more than a whole hour talking and eating, Sasha riding on every word spoken by the Priest, her focus extraordinarily whetted when he began to tell of his youthful upbringing in Spain, during which he was seized by a yen to be infused into the Catholic order, and that eventually he was guided to America, specifically to San Antonio where he was promoted to his current position and where ever since he had lived and propagated the dictates of the scriptures and bore with his flock as they suffered their earthly debilities. He had returned to his mother country but once during all the years.

Sasha drew a breath. "That is not enough Father. Are you sometimes homesick?"

"I do not think of that my child. God's children are here even as they are in the old country. This is where He has led me, where He is beside me every day guiding me, where I have stayed busy fulfilling His will. This is where I am supposed to be. No I am not homesick, nor have I ever been. I do not think of going back. This is my home."

Chenelle was of a sunny disposition, as the Priest had said, prone freely to breaking into laughter if someone said something she deemed funny; and she kept looking admiringly at Sasha, talking quickly. Once she leaned over and whispered to her that she would quite well love the stores and streets of the city and that she'd gladly go with her for such an excursion when she had the inclination.

"I would like that very much," said Sasha. Though not vibrant she smiled gratefully. You could tell that they were warming to one another which was heartening to Father Lumas, for his hopes were high their acquaintance might take this turn.

When supper was at an end the Priest rose and expressed his elatedness at having such splendid guests dine with him at his table, then asked Chenelle if the master bedroom was in order, to which she gave assurance.

"Ah, you will sleep like a baby, both of you." And then leveled a quizzical glance at Mrs. Laster. "You are staying the night at the Rectory, aren't you Mrs. Laster?"

"Yes I am Father. I am very much looking forward to it, as is Sasha."

"Yes Father, I am," said Sasha, now glowing, for what she had hoped might happen had happened. She moved as rapidly as she felt proper to hug her dear friend, who was surprised to receive such spontaneous affection, and warmly pleased. She normally gave the first hug.

Father Lumas had premised correctly, that Sasha was strongly apprehensive about sleeping alone in a room which to her was strangely foreign and desperately wanted Mrs. Laster, to whom she was now very emotionally attached, to be close at her side on this her first evening as the Rectory's guest, but could not bear to ask his approval; and further, he surmised, if he hadn't initiated the suggestion, then Mrs. Laster would have done so.

Chapter 10

THAT NIGHT Sasha retired to bed early and lay and scanned piece by piece its various adornments and the whole room while Mrs. Laster sat crocheting some material she had had in her brown clothes carrier that Bryon brought her. Sasha's eyes had first fallen on the imposing headboard which towered above her, accentuated with splendidly carved lattice work and looping scrolls, and next took account of the heavy shiny posts that upheld the bed and there paused and asked Mrs. Laster to have a look at the head board in particular and to venture her opinion as to whether the designer of the splendid crafting was Italian or of some other ethnicity, whereon Mrs. Laster looked up from her work and smiled and said that it was a good probability the designer was Italian.

"But why Italian?"

"I am merely speculating, yet on the grounds that the work favors the Italian artistry of the century past. Truthfully, I cannot attest that I am sure. Father Lumas likely could tell us with exactness about the designer."

She was lured to the portraits hanging here and there on the walls more enticingly than to other furnishings, one of an old man pushing a cart loaded of firewood and another pruning a fruit tree, and since they were attired in similar clothing and of about the same age Sasha supposed they were brothers. As common and plain as these portraits were there was also a sort of newness about them, as if they had some perennial spirit and undying vitality, and Sasha sensed this to be the reason Father Lumas had hung them for display. After awhile, after studying everything that peaked her fascination, she slid out of bed and picked up a book from a nearby table and crawled back in. She pulled the covers partially up over her and heaped an extra pillow against the headboard and lay back and sighed and again looked around, then commenced to finger through the pages. Without awareness of it, she had vaguely begun to admire and love this room, even if quickly, which was no longer intimidating, but warm and secure and inviting and found herself unconsciously wishing that this was where she could stay and live when Mr. Sherette returned. The hour arrived when Mrs. Laster usually called it a day. Seeing that Sasha had laid her book down she ceased her crocheting and made her way to bedside, there lifting back the covers, and sliding in. She had no children other than Bryon, with whom she used to sleep when he was a tot. She had raised him alone. His father died when he was a baby. The remembrances and present associations took her fast into backward flight, where suddenly she was in the tender arms of her mother who kissed her and snuggled her close and began to tell her a little girl's story. She smiled, and the melancholy upon her face spoke the feelings of her heart: she wished she could recapture that scene again, if but for just one fleeting moment. Adjusting her position, turning slightly toward Sasha, leaning the side of her face against her hand which was supported by her elbow, she began a retreat to the events of the day now vanished.

"We have had a good day Sasha. Even if it has been long."

"Umh humh," she murmured. "We have."

"And what is the highlight, the best moment of all? As you know there is always something during the course of one's day that stands above anything else."

"Humh. I need to think. The stage ride, I suppose, but wait. Let me think. Perhaps not the stage. The carriage ride I liked very much. But not that either I suppose. Seeing the Cathedral at the end of our carriage ride strikes me quite sharply. Possibly that is it. Yes, I think that is what sways me most."

"Ha. I agree. It is towering, isn't it? Anyway, it heads my list. Or perhaps meeting Father Lumas merits equal weight. He is profoundly interesting. Don't you think?"

"Ha. You are confused just as I. Yes, Father Lumas is very interesting. He reminds me greatly of Father Kestner and I love them both."

They had lain there at length, an hour at the minimum, and with considerable zest had gone over a rash of things, and as always happens, each once in awhile had broken off to reflect on some aspect of the exchanges, Mrs. Laster once silently thinking that during their entire voyage they had not gotten remotely close to enjoying one another as much as now they did and this made her very happy. Once when amused at something said, Sasha laughed aloud with joyous abandon, as was not her custom and Mrs. Laster returned it. "This is like mother and daughter," she mused, "and I never had a daughter." She remembered the words of the Priest and hoped she was living up to the charge he'd asked her to fulfill. "You must become her surrogate mother, until the trip has ended to say the least."

"Yes Father, I remember, and I think the trip is not yet over."

Once Mrs. Laster reached and took her hand and patted it lovingly and did in like manner to her face also, looking over with unmistakable affection and wondered what was revolving behind those dark expressionless eyes and beautiful facade. Sasha lay silent, and looked back at her and smiled wanly. She did not speak it but in her heart was thankful for the dear friend beside her, and even though she lay silent and was without words she was not silent with her thoughts.

"My darling, what are you thinking, if you don't mind?"

"What am I thinking?

"Yes, if you are willing to share it with me."

"I was thinking of my father and the message that he taught me from the scriptures when I was a little girl, that God is love, and that His love is endless, and is everywhere, and will come to you if you but reach out for it. You love me Mrs. Laster, and have from the start, I know you truly do, and so does Father Lumas, and Father Kestner, and Captain Johansen. How fortunate for me that He has guided you all swiftly into my life at such a critical time. It seems that you have been purposefully set in place to help me through my dreadful loneliness which is painfully hard to bear."

"I believe that dear. With all my being I do." Eventually, after many words had been said Sasha evinced that she was on the verge of falling off to sleep, yawning then yawning quickly once again, upon which Mrs. Laster slid from their bed and blew out the kerosene lamp and slid back in. Much to Mrs. Laster's surprise however Sasha did not fall suddenly into misty slumber, lying there for a while longer, too quiet and too still to be asleep, a sign of continuing to turn something round and round in her head. Finally. "Sasha was there anything else you needed to mention?"

"No. Well, yes there is." Here she hesitated.

"Do go on darling."

"Only a remark if it's all right."

"Certainly. What is it?"

"Would you mind putting your arms around me like my mother used to until I drop off to sleep?"

"Oh you sweet little dear. I will. Very gladly I will."

So Mrs. Laster drew her into her arms and there held her tenderly for the length of the night, and would have held her longer but the dawn had broken, the period of morning to which she habitually awakened and arose.

In another day they were expecting Mr. Sherette's arrival, so said Father Lumas to Sasha. "I'm virtually certain; yes he should arrive tomorrow." Seeing Lawrence Sherette was an occasion to which she looked eagerly forward but with no extra thought to prepare for it other than to consult with Mrs. Laster with respect to the attire she should wear. Mrs. Laster offered a recommendation after picking through her clothing inventory which to her surprise was of exceptional quality and diversification. She advised that there was plenty of time yet remaining for making a selection.

To be sure, Mr. Sherette was on his way and would arrive by stage, though would have caught a sailing vessel to Corpus Christi, and from there traveled over land to San Antonio, but finding no boats available on the desired date of his departure, and not of temperament to wait longer, he had boarded a stage pulled by four handsome sorrels whose charted course was along the Louisiana and Texas coastlines.

On the second evening Mrs. Laster and Sasha dined again with Father Lumas, after which, they retired to the living room with the spacious window that looked out into the garden and sat and gazed at the rich interior of the walls and vaulting and at the ancient amphora pottery placed around the periphery of the room, this done without Father Lumas who had gone to his study and was at work; and after this, which was at the least an hour in duration, they made their way to the ponderous bedroom and eventually turned in. They did not at once fall into sleep, which in part was due to Sasha's preoccupation with the pastoral portraits to which she had paid too limited attention the night before. Moreover, Chenelle had brought in a complement of fresh colorful flowers to enliven the surroundings and upon seeing them they commenced to talk of how stunningly gorgeous they were and how thoughtful of Chenelle to have extended this nice gesture.

Then appeared the third evening, without Lawrence Sherette having shown himself. Father Lumas assured Sasha that he was almost certain to arrive forthwith, on that very evening, for he had himself in times past caught the stage from San Antonio to New Orleans and was able to calculate the days and hours of travel with reasonable accuracy. On that evening Mrs. Laster could not avail herself to dine with them, notifying Sasha well in advance of her decision when they were strolling about the streets at the noon hour, to which Sasha replied that she would fare very well on her own, for now she had gotten better acquainted with Father Lumas and was at ease around him and felt she could in a limited way stand on her own at making conversational exchanges. "But I will wait on him to take the lead. And I might even surprise myself at how well I do."

"Ha, ha, ha. I am sure you will dear. You are very conversant when you choose to be."

Sasha felt pressed to inquire of the reason that Mrs. Laster could not be present at the evening meal with her and Father Lumas, but held back. She did not wait long. Mrs. Laster explained that she had consented to be with Bryon at a dinner function which the Germans were staging for some of the city dignitaries and that he hoped that she could attend. What she did not disclose, because she hadn't heard him speak of it yet, was that Bryon thought it a superb idea to show off his charming mother from England to the Germans. Sasha assured Mrs. Laster that she'd do just fine without her and that there was absolutely no need for her to be concerned. Mrs. Laster felt greatly relieved. "She will do very well on her own. I am sure. If I didn't think that I would plead with Bryon to excuse me. But that is not necessary. She is much more open than she was on the afternoon of our arrival, and Father Lumas has observed this change to be for the better he tells me."

They sat down to supper, these two, far apart in age and demeanor, Father Lumas near the end of life and Sasha just beginning. No matter. There was more commonality between them than met the eye. He had been much likened to her when he was young and amusedly pondered over it. "Yes, I remember. I was much similar to her when I was her age." She, well read, greatly she was, possessed an understanding of books far beyond the youth of her age, and perhaps most adults, sometimes citing a passage from this source or that, and although it had not yet surfaced to Father Lumas's eyes there hidden inside was a fierce will to endure and overcome that which beset her, which later in life was to serve her to great advantage. Likely Captain Johansen saw something of these aspects in her during their short while together on the voyage from the Canaries. Father Lumas smiled comfortingly. At the beginning she was shy and discovered it not easy to talk. "Sasha," he said in observation of her hesitancy, "we are faced this evening with meager supplements but I can bear it if you can."

"I am fine Father. We have plenty; cheese cuts and chicken and also there is cabbage, one of my favorite garden varieties which my father taught me to set out and cultivate."

"It's nice to learn that about you. I would have liked to see you in your garden chores, which is rather easy for me to imagine, for my mother taught me much about growing vegetables."

"Oh. Not your father."

"No. It was my mother. My father was too busy with his professional vocation."

"What was that Father?"

"Clock making." And went on from there that he was greatly proud of his father, and that he was a well known clock maker throughout Grenada. "Well, the food is before us," he said, "so let us pray then serve ourselves." She bowed her head. God in Heaven must have beamed amusedly down on these very different two, a young girl and an old Priest about to partake of His supplements—what could have been more touching to His sight—and declared that the scene He witnessed was most unordinary and therefore gave it His especial blessing.

Sasha sparingly served her plate with the portions she had named to him earlier, and a piece of thickly sliced bread which she had not mentioned, nor had she said anything of the pitcher of milk which rested near the edge of the table. She stood and filled her glass then tilted the vessel and also filled his. He did not issue a thank you, but instead clasped his hands and gestured his face forward in barely discernable motions, in the semblance of a prayer of but few lines, then sat erect, again letting his eyes settle on the food.

"The butler will bring us a cut of pumpkin pie when we finish."

Sasha acknowledged the pie with a smile and remarked that she had plenty for now. She doodled with her food for a brevity then began to eat, but with deliberate slowness. She was clad in a full white dress with ruffles at the elbows. In retrospect, there was perhaps a shade of cream in the color of the dress and to say that it was entirely white is possibly in error. In any event, Mrs. Laster had tastefully chosen the dress for her and Father Lumas thought she might have made the selection. He told himself that the young girl at his supper table looked very appropriate and was conducting herself most satisfactorily. And she thought of herself in that manner too, no longer dreading the occasion and thinking it rare for someone such as she, so very young, to be dining with a renowned Priest, and that some day she'd look back on this scene and tell of it to her children. But for the moment she was restrained in expression, letting Father Lumas seek the initiative.

"Let me tell you Sasha some things about the San Fernando Cathedral. If you've heard them before will you not hesitate to stop me?"

"No, no Father. I know hardly anything at all."

"All right. Let's try it. The San Fernando Cathedral was founded in 1731, and I am assuming that is a piece of history with which you are familiar. Is that correct?"

"Yes Father. I knew that."

He released a chuckle, then his face grew somber and he continued. "For many years the church served as the worship place for all denominations of San Antonio. And do you know why?"

"No Father I cannot say."

"The Catholic Church was the only recognized religion of the Spanish and Mexican governments prior to Texas gaining its independence which was not many years ago."

"Not long ago," she added. "Only a very few years ago. My father had me read an article about it. The article was printed in a London newspaper. It said that the Cathedral played a role in the Battle of the Alamo when General Antonio Lopez de Santa Anna hoisted a flag of no quarter from the church's tower."

"Ha, ha. You learned well and retained well too. Your father would proudly acclaim you. Of course he wasn't happy, I am sure, with the church getting dragged into the middle of a raging battle. None of us can be."

"No we can't but that is a piece of history Father, and I am well served to learn of it."

"Of course you are. Oh let me see. There was something else. Now I have not yet said that construction of the Cathedral was not begun until 1749. And that is correct. But I have said that it was established in 1731. And by whom? Will it surprise you to hear that it was by the Canary Spanish Islanders who needed a place to worship?"

"Ah. I did not know that Father. I am a bit astonished. I am more kindred to this old church than I could have ever dreamed."

"Yes you are dear."

"Please go on Father."

"All right. Well, I remember Sasha when your father was leaving for the Canaries. I wished that he might decide to stay in San Antonio, but his mind was made up. I'd grown fond of him. You see, I am sure you are aware of this; I married him and your mother Izu. Right over there in the sanctuary of this very church. They were a beautiful couple, tenderly young and vibrant. You did know that I married them didn't you?"

"I did Father. I've seen your name in our family Bible over and over, each time I opened it I think."

"Ah. Our Lord acts in strange ways, doesn't he? They left me for the Canaries, and never came back. But I was recompensed, for He sent me you as a replacement. Yes, it may seem strange, but on the other hand, that is the way it was meant. And I am euphoric that you have come."

Chapter 11

AFTER THEY had continued a while longer, the Priest lifted himself from his chair and announced that he was to sit with a troubled family in the sanctuary and pray, regretting to Sasha that he couldn't extend the supper hour. He said he'd immensely delighted in their chat and looked forward to when they could resume. Sasha echoed the same. The Priest quietly left and Sasha went to her bedroom and began to read. Some time previously, near the beginning of their supper hour, the weather had turned foul, the rain beginning to fall and as she lay and listened she could hear that it was increasing in strength, evinced by the roar of the down pour and the wind beating against the outside walls. The hour was far too early for Mrs. Laster to return, but nonetheless she wondered about it and hoped she was having a good time wherever she was.

At the hour of nine there was a barely audible peck on the door, made from the hand of Mrs. Laster, who opened it and came in, all the while grappling with her parasol, which, wet from the rain stubbornly refused to fold; whereon, Sasha, rising from her bed went quickly over, there taking it from her and helping her remove her coat. She then took the coat and hung it in the closet. "Thank you Sasha." Sasha asked about the weather and if she had been much bothered by it, whereas Mrs. Laster let out in a tone of exasperation that she thought she'd be blown away, and then after Sasha said she was glad to see her safely back she inquired of the function she'd just attended, anxious to learn everything there was to know about the pinnacle events of the evening. Mrs. Laster praised the cordial niceties of the hosts as well as the display of the sizeable varieties of foods that were served, declaring there were many dishes she failed to recognize, since they were fashioned from the recipes of the old country which she had never seen nor heard of. "The German women are as crafty at concocting good and exotic foods as are their men folks at erecting bridges. I am fortunate that I was invited."

"All because of your son."

"Indeed. He is exceedingly blessed that he was hired as an engineer to work with them. The Germans are amazing people, resourceful in all they do."

Unknown to Sasha, Lawrence Sherette arrived that evening, the hour near eleven. The stage that waited for him to unload still lingered while he set his belongings on the portico of the Rectory, the heaviest and most cumbersome of which was a sizeable trunk which forced a grunt when he picked it up. The stage was splotched with mud from end to end and side to side, even the driver's seat, and the ordinarily nice red spokes of the wheels, an emblem of pride of the stage company, were especially covered with the messy glob. The rain was still falling, the driver's face unhappy and contorted as he glared from under the soppy rim of his hat, as if urging Lawrence Sherette to return in haste to check for any article that he might have overlooked. In seconds Lawrence was back and did his checking, then upon spotting nothing raised his hand, and the driver, adjusting the night lantern, yapped at the horses, the stage surging forward into the gummy mist headed for the livery stable a half mile down the street.

On hearing the commotion outside the Priest, sometimes reading into the wee hours, as Lawrence Sherette knew, was yet quite awake, and cracked the door and on seeing his young associate opened it widely and stepped out to greet him.

"Mr. Sherette, my boy, it's you, and you are wringing wet."

"Not altogether Father. Give me a second while I remove this slicker and these boots. Just look at them. Aren't they a sight to behold? Mud all over."

Removing the slicker he easily managed but the wet boots posed some degree of trouble. He grunted as he tugged, finally slipping them off. The Priest had offered to help but Lawrence Sherette thanked him and said he could handle the task himself. "You would only soil your clothes Father."

"Dear me, you have roughed through it. What a time for travel."

"I quite agree Father."

"Do come on in my boy. I'll make hot tea, something to warm your insides. Have you eaten? If not, I'll ask Chenelle to set food out for you."

"I am not really hungry Father. But a pinch of cheese I will relish. We stopped at an inn twenty miles back. I ate well. But I'll welcome a hot cup of tea or two and I will take a small slice of cheese as I said."

"I'll be quick. But please sit down and while the tea is brewing you can tell me of your journey."

"I will, I will. But before that let me explain why I decided to drop by the Rectory at this hour rather than choose the shelter of my flat. Did she arrive? Is she here?"

"Ah, I anticipated your asking as much. Indeed she is here. A lovely girl, and has been on pins and needles to meet you."

"And I her. I would have made better time but the blustery weather worked its will against me."

"No matter. You are here. And I am glad you proceeded to the Rectory instead of to your residence. You must spend the night."

"No need for that Father. I can—."

"You must. Besides. The weather. You'd only end up with another soaking. Staying here is solidly the best choice. We'll dine in the morning together, all of us at breakfast, and in addition I want to run through some matters with you before we eat, if you can coach yourself to make it out of bed without undue struggle. You've had yourself a trying trip Lawrence and look a trifle worn."

"I can make it up Father. Oh, I see the tea is boiling. As soon as I have a sip I'll recount my journey for you. But I will need to wash, as you can plainly see, then slip on my robe."

"Fine, fine. Your tea will be waiting, hot and steamy."

The two sat down, Lawrence Sherette picking up his cup and beginning to sip, the Priest's eyes curiously training themselves into his weary face.

"There is something else Father that I can hardly wait to verify, the subject that I would have gotten to before any other but of course the matter of the weather took command, as well as my condition of messiness, and then Sasha. I was distracted."

"And what was that?"

"Is Albert Duval yet living as far as you know? I judge he is not or else the girl wouldn't have come. And you did not say for certain in your courier message."

"You are correct. I did not say. No, he is not living. Father Kestner officiated his funeral and his wife's whose death preceded his own, and most thoroughly made arrangements to transport Sasha here to San Antonio."

Lawrence Sherette uttered a silent prayer then drew an invisible cross upon his breast.

"I see. I am more than saddened."

"Yes. You were close to him when he lived here."

Lawrence Sherette decided not to elaborate further. What was done was done. He pushed it aside.

"Well, the girl did not beat me here by more than a narrow stretch."

"No. Shall we say three days?"

"As I said, I would have covered the distance sooner Father, but for the weather. The whole coast line was over run with murky discharge, the air clammy and dense and difficult to see through. The stage company was reluctant to send out drivers but finally recanted. Passengers were few and there was only one the last one hundred miles, which was I. Fresh horses and new drivers were substituted each twenty to thirty miles."

"Ah. I can picture that."

Lawrence Sherette took a sip of tea then with a grating cleared his throat. "We steered away from the coast line by a good fifty to seventy miles, taking a detour route which was greatly time consuming. Word had gotten about before we left that the sea was flooding the low lands to the west. The bulk of the turbulence struck however when we had long crossed out of Louisiana into Texas, the last hundred miles I judge, when only I and the driver were aboard, no one else. Most times I sat beside him, enduring the wind and the pummeling rain, thinking I might help him better see. The storm was inconsistent Father, thank goodness, sometimes lessening and stopping altogether, but not delaying for long until recoiling and starting its unruly blast all over. Worst of all was the ordeal for the horses—my heart bled for them—the poor animals having practically to mash their way through the thick muddy slosh, floundering and stumbling, and once when we faced the crest of a hill I thought they were on the verge of balking, the leader violently shaking his head and snorting, protesting that he'd had enough. 'Wo ho. Wo ho.' The driver wisely drew back on the reins and gave them the signal to rest, smoky mist blowing out of their nostrils like puffing billows and their sides moving swiftly in and out as they labored for air. When we recommenced I concluded that I should walk, a wise option, perhaps the only option, for every ounce that we could relieve from the animals was imperative."

"And how long did you stay on the ground my boy?"

"For a mile at a time roughly speaking. I alternated. I rode when we were on generally level terrain, which was the usual posture of the land. It wasn't the walking that sapped me Father, it was the mud. I feared it might suck me under, if you will allow an exaggeration."

"You poor boy. You've told me enough. You can't feel like continuing. Your energy is near spent, I know, so finish your cheese and tea, and then I shall see you off to bed. Oh, one thing more. As you start to retire there is a letter for you on the side table leading to your bedroom, from your sister Adelaide. I left it off earlier." Sasha was to deliver Father Kestner's letter directly to Lawrence Sherette, she reasoned, and would wait until she met him face to face, handing the correspondence to him then. Father Lumas therefore did not know of the existence of Father Kestner's letter addressed to Lawrence Sherette, nor should he have known.

☙ ❧

He'd changed his mind. There was one subject he wouldn't address to Lawrence Sherette previous to the breakfast. Rising early, an hour before waking his associate, Father Lumas prepared coffee and sat and pondered the life of Sasha Duval, as much as he possessed of it. He had read a letter a day or so before from Father Otto Conrad Kestner of the Canary Islands which he had received by way of the afternoon stage mail, reading it repeatedly in the hours since, and had read it again soon after rising from his bed. He held it in his hands and scanned the lines once more.

My Dear Father Lumas,

I shall hope that this letter reaches you in time to be most serviceable, and ask you, realizing that you will understand, to treat it with the utmost of trust and confidence.

At the time of her departure I prepared a correspondence that Sasha Duval was to hand to you personally, which I am certain by this date she has dispatched. Given the nature of the lines which I now inscribe, I deem it best that they reach you by separate conveyance. I shall attempt to be at once brief and thorough.

Unless you had been previously informed you could not have realized when you looked upon the beautiful young girl in your midst that she was of mixed blood. Her father, Albert Duval, was a French subject and her mother, Izu Lolano, a former Morocco citizen of West Africa, such pieces of information about them not at all unfamiliar to you in that you married them, and since you effected the marriage, it is my humble opinion that your thoughts were when you first set eyes upon the off spring child of the Duval's that she should have naturally reflected some measure of darkened pigmentation. That was never to be; she was born as she now appears to you: I know, for I was present at the onset of her birth, at the doctor's side who delivered her, and have kept up with her ever since.

The tendency is strong for one to consider that she is a case of adoption. That is a mistaken view. As He was my witness I can assure you that I saw her delivered into this world.

She is a precious child to me Father, as she is already to you I am certain, and that is the spirit out of which this letter is penned. I have great passion and hope for her, daily praying to our Good Lord that He, as well as our humble selves, will stay close beside her and guide and protect her as she makes her way on the pathway of life.

My very best,

Father Otto Conrad Kestner

She is of mixed blood, he told himself, the daughter of Albert Duval, a Frenchman, and Izu Lolano, a Moroccan citizen some time ago; "and this," he said, "Lawrence Sherette knows well, but I do not feel that he is aware that Sasha's skin is pure white. I somehow feel he isn't, or otherwise one of the many letters from Albert Duval over time would have revealed the fact. I cannot believe that God in Heaven will condone my making a preliminary comment on one of his children to another of his children, and therefore my discussion with Lawrence Sherette prior to breakfast shall fall on something else, which is in the sphere of my business at this Holy church, more or less. We will have to wait and observe Mr. Sherette's countenance when he sees Sasha in the flesh.

When Father Lumas finally awakened his associate the both of them sat down at the table in an ante room a step off the kitchen and began to sip coffee. The subject of weather arose once more, Lawrence Sherette ridiculing himself for not waiting to catch a vessel sailing to Corpus Christi and there boarding a stage to San Antonio. The trip would have proved much less of an obstacle, said he, except for the over land distance from Corpus Christi to San Antonio, which was inundated by downpours and struck by forceful winds equal to those elements besieging the route way during the last several miles of his journey. Father Lumas added that one choice or the other was debatable, yet said in hindsight that traveling for the most part by boat might have turned out better. "On the other hand," he contended with a mirthful chuckle, "the ship might have succumbed to the storm and sank to the bottom. So there."

Lawrence had a laugh at the analogy and sipped his coffee. He complimented the Priest on the excellence of his process of brewing, and then embarked on the letter from Adelaide, his sister, who had written that she was hopeful of his relocating in New Orleans, for it was many miles closer to home, and that since the Catholic hierarchy was aggressively contemplating the erection of at least a few churches in Memphis good fortune might pave the way and guide him there.

"Is that so much idle talk Father?"

"No it is not just idle talk. The Catholic movement has begun to escalate toward Memphis and would have progressed faster," he speculated, "were it not for the battle between the British and the Americans at New Orleans and a rash of influenza and yellow fever epidemics."

"My sister informs me in one of her letters of late that Memphis is expanding. They're incorporated now and that should help push forward a broad front of enterprises."

"And the building of Catholic churches should fit in quite well with things. We shall see. In the meantime Lawrence, your settling into the New Orleans brotherhood portends good promises for you and them. They could use you. I think you are nearing a position of Priesthood there; there is a really good chance of it happening. But you have recently spent a while, though brief, with the Archdiocese leaders in that city, so how do you feel?"

"The Bishop was plain in speaking of my probabilities. Within a short while a Proto-deacon's seat will open up and I am likely to attain to it he says, if I want it. I'm debating the matter Father. I've been with you for years and—."

"You can't let that deter you. I am getting old, it's true, and you might replace me in time. Or at any time. Yet there are powers above me who will determine."

"Of that I am aware."

"On the other hand Lawrence, the Memphis churches will rise into existence faster than you can imagine. Our fellow brethren all around mention this to me. Just the other day I ran across someone in this city from the Saint Louis Archdiocese who offers cogent reasoning that we'll soon witness groundbreaking there, that it's on its way. You may want to keep your eyes peeled on this one."

"I heard this convincingly said in New Orleans Father while I was there. I will watch things attentively."

The table was set already by Chenelle and the Butler who tip toed about while Father Lumas and Lawrence Sherette talked, the time eventually approaching when Father Lumas stood and motioned for Chenelle to knock on the bedroom door of his guests. She went directly and did as she was asked, Mrs. Laster answering that they were about ready. Sasha had bathed and sat in a chair of elevated height before a large mirror in the bathroom while Mrs. Laster groomed and shaped her hair, leaving it hanging about her shoulders. She had chosen for Sasha a pretty blue dress with white thin lines running from top to bottom and ruffles bunched at her wrists; and there was a light pink frock that draped over her shoulders, which in the manner of her dress also fell to her ankles. "You look fine dear. Everyone will certainly see that. Let us be off to our breakfast and meet Mr. Sherette."

Chapter 12

WHEN MRS. Laster and Sasha entered the dining room Father Lumas and Mr. Sherette were sitting at the table but at once stood as the ladies made their way forward, all the while Father Lumas studying the confused and questioning countenance of Lawrence Sherette's face. The scene was something that Lawrence Sherette could not have expected even in his wildest. Puzzled and thrown off balance he began to ponder. A drove of questions swarmed upon him. "Who is this girl? Who is this lady with her, obviously well educated and of high breeding? Is this really Sasha, the Sasha that sprang from the sperm of Albert Duval and from the fount of Izu Lalano's womb? In his lifetime as a father Albert Duval wrote me reams of lines and never once mentioned this. She is lily white, and most beautiful. What do I see in Father Lumas's face? Nothing. It is as calm and still as a windless day. Has he failed to tell me something? Has he been misled?" But his incisive intellect quickened his way to unmasking the truth. "Oh, I see now. What is wrong with me? No. He has not kept anything from me, nor has he been misled. He knew all along the answer and presumed that I should know it too, or in seconds would. But I have almost misled myself. I have seen this before and many times have happened across it in my readings. She is the product of a genetic formation which did not function in accord with the usual biological code. She is white; she may be invisibly part Negress, but she is white; and this is the young girl you have inherited to care for Lawrence Sherette, the daughter of Albert Duval, once your bosom friend."

When Mrs. Laster and Sasha had reached the dining table and were about to take their seats Father Lumas began the introductions, "Mr. Sherette, this is Sasha Duval on my left and on my right is Mrs. Edweena Laster of the British Isles. Sasha, Mrs. Laster, Mr. Sherette is my associate. His full name is Lawrence Sherette."

In accord with a motion from his hand they sat down to breakfast, Sasha sitting by Lawrence Sherette and Mrs. Laster taking a seat by Father Lumas. Chenelle was sitting on Sasha's right, Sasha's smile revealing a gladness that she was there. Sasha had intended to hand Lawrence Sherette the letter addressed to him from Father Kestner but over looked it and left it in her room in the apparent excitement of meeting him that morning. She would give it to him a little later when breakfast was finished.

The table settings consisted of the usual expectations, eggs, sausage, biscuits, jams, and milk, and good coffee made by the Butler to Father Lumas's liking, and there was a lovely white tapestry spread across the table with a design of red roses embroidered on its surface here and there.

After delivering the prayer, Father Lumas picked up his cup and began to sip, looking over at Lawrence Sherette with eyes that said, "You go ahead, you lead the conversation while I savor my coffee; you are aware that this is the habit I have developed before eating," and discerning the cue Lawrence Sherette reached and tenderly laid his hand on Sasha's, saying that his heart was happy she was there with them and that he'd very badly wanted to at last meet her.

"I am glad that I'm here," she replied, but Lawrence Sherette revolved in his mind that if she examined what she had just said she would quite naturally conclude that it was only because of a previous terrible event in her life that she was there, and not by choice or gladness. "You poor dear," he said to himself, "you've lost your parents, both of them, and you suddenly are without a country to which you were accustomed for your entire life. How hard this surely is to bear. But unfortunately this is how things were bound to happen."

And then spoke aloud, "I knew your father well dear. We were the best of friends."

"I've heard. I'm so glad." Lawrence Sherette had hoped her response might be more cheery; it was neither cheery nor sad but there was a sadness inside her soul he sensed and felt, which only time could overcome, and vowed then and there with all his being to help her in her struggle.

"When we have more time together I'd like to tell you about some of the things he and I did together."

Her face lit up. "I'd love that."

They had gone on conversing for a slight, Lawrence Sherette mostly the one speaking, but trying to draw Sasha in more and more, and was about to inquire of her boat voyage across the sea. Father Lumas was heartened to see them starting into conversation, and so quickly, and waited with anticipation of their saying more, yet words from their lips did not directly come, for Lawrence Sherette had stopped; he was thinking of what in particular he'd ask her about her journey, while taking a bite of food, and here Father Lumas decided to fill the void.

He cleared his throat. "Ummmh. Forgive my omission Mr. Sherette. In the short time since your arrival I overlooked mentioning Mrs. Laster's background to you. I would have gotten around to that. But now is as good as any. She is from England, as I said, receiving her education there, leaving that quadrant to join the international office of trade in London which in time sent her to the Canary Islands, where she became a member of Father Otto Conrad Kestner's church."

"Oh. Father Kestner. I don't know him personally Mrs. Laster but have heard much of him."

"He is a splendid man."

"I feel that he is. And Sasha was in his church with you?"

Mrs. Laster glanced at Sasha as if seeking approval to answer for her, and then proceeded. "No she wasn't. She with her family lived several miles away and attended one of the outreach churches. Father Kestner often conducted mass at her church, and counseled and supervised the Protodeacon who as a rule officiated the services, but under his sway. I met her only recently. Father Kestner, who was close to her father and mother, and her too, arranged for me to be with her on the voyage from the Canaries to America."

"I am grateful she had your company."

"And I was grateful for the opportunity to share it with her. I can tell you Mr. Sherette, she is a perfect joy."

With this, Father Lumas decided he needed to insert a parcel of information that he had left out and wished to wedge it into the exchange.

"Excuse me. Permit me if you will Mr. Sherette to clarify a thing or two. It is this. I might have inferred that Mrs. Laster advanced directly from her academic training into the field of international trade with the British government. She may feel a need to set me straight. My too few minutes with her on the second day of her arrival, which was yesterday, may have imposed a handicap on our exploring the subject in depth; consequently, it is likely that I failed to glean her remarks as thoroughly as I should have."

"I can speak to that Father, if you like," said Mrs. Laster.

"Please."

"I did directly join the government, assigned to the field of trade, but within a short while I married and became pregnant with child, in time giving birth to my precious Bryon. My husband died when Bryon was a baby and therefore I raised him alone. I was not destitute. My husband had left funds and I had some of my own. Naturally I took leave from my post, but as Bryon grew older I returned to my previous work and helped finance his university studies. When he finished, he was hired by a German engineering firm in London, and approximately two and one half years ago, he was transferred to San Antonio. At the same time, whether lady luck smiled on me or not, I was offered an attractive position in the Canary Islands with the British office and dreading the thought of Bryon living an ocean away with me left in England, I opted to temporarily accept the offer, and stayed with the government in the Canaries until recently. It was then that I resolved to join my son in San Antonio, and so here I am."

"And here both of you are, you and Sasha," Mr. Sherette brightly said. "Isn't it odd that you caught the same sailing vessel on the same date?"

"One might say that. But be that as it may. It was due to the timing of the vessel's schedule that I met her, and for that I am thankful. I couldn't love this darling girl more. She is as my daughter, which I never had." And then with beaming face reached across and affectionately squeezed Sasha's hand.

Father Lumas broke into a smile, seeing how this fine middle aged woman and young girl were bound to one another, and that it mattered none that the bonding had risen to such intimacy in so little awhile. "Ah. How they have grown close. Their hearts are attached and that is wonderful, and receives my greatest blessing, though I fear there is a day approaching when Lawrence Sherette will gain a position with the Catholic establishment in New Orleans, thereby severing them apart. I can feel it hovering over us. The very thought of it is already in Mr. Sherette's soul gnawing away. He is strongly leaning toward New Orleans with a view that it is a stop gap pointing to Memphis, and I cannot blame him for that. If he stays here his chances of landing in that city are greatly less than if he were positioned in New Orleans. We are too far away here in San Antonio to help him very substantially. But that is not the thing that worries me. If it were only him I could bid him adieu with relative ease. After all he's a man that has to pursue his destiny to higher callings and I am indebted to offer him my blessings and will. It's Sasha that worries me. She doesn't think of it now, but she'll feel driven to follow him when the time to depart is here. She'll remember the wish and instructions of her father. The tug of his words in his daughter's ears ring powerfully, and upon that occasion will resound even more provokingly; and while in my opinion she will hurt deeply when faced with leaving San Antonio she nonetheless will. I must address the implication of this with Mr. Sherette. We should talk of it most thoroughly, leaving no stone unturned. For now, however, we should finish our breakfast and revel in our camaraderie."

What was to be done about Sasha Duval should Lawrence Sherette accept a position with the Archdiocese of New Orleans and make that city his residence? Was it best for her to remain in San Antonio or follow him? Lawrence Sherette would soon begin to toil over these perplexities as had Father Lumas, for he saw in his vision the same final outcome that had transpired in the reckoning of the Priest. As yet, these considerations had not descended on Mrs. Laster, or if they had she'd not revealed them, but they would in due time and she would find herself seriously sitting with the Priest and Lawrence Sherette in attempting a resolve.

As the breakfast ended, Lawrence Sherette committed to touring Sasha and Mrs. Laster throughout the city from time to time, with questionable sites circumvented, and pledged to start the day after next, the weather permitting, to which Mrs. Laster passed on that Bryon had said he'd also drive them around and could pick up where Mr. Sherette left off. She especially was preoccupied with the quaint and shiny German communities which lay on the outskirts, for that was the sector where Bryon leased a home owned by a German family with membership in the San Fernando Cathedral Church.

As they began to depart Sasha asked Lawrence Sherette to wait for her as she went to retrieve the letter that she was to hand him on behalf of Father Kestner. When this was cared for he opened the letter as if he could not wait, reading lines from the Priest that he hoped he would pour his soul into seeing after this very young girl whose father had entrusted her to him. That principally was the extent of the Priest's lines, nothing more. Lawrence Sherette smiled fawnly and answered underneath. "I have committed to that already Father. With my heart and my soul I have." In those days San Antonio was a melting pot of ethnicities, greatly struggling for social and economic survival and law and order. A major cause of the troubles that beset the city stemmed from the population mix, which in the end could well have given rise to its strength. Years later Sasha pulled from her papers a publication of the 1850 census which was taken after she had left the city, which one has to suspect omits a sizeable mass that went uncounted, and amusedly shared the data with Andre. Of the total of 3, 488 persons, there were 1,167 Native Texans, which surely were the Anglos, 678 from other states, 572 from Mexico, 455 from Germany and Prussia, 128 from Ireland, 92 from France, 48 from England and Scotland, 41 from other countries, 45 residents unknown, and 262 Negro slaves. Of these, the Mexicans and Germans are here drawn out because their life styles were glaringly distinct from the other cultures, the Mexicans most singularly, for it is they on whom the writers seemed to dwell so prolifically with their narrations, particularly a one Frederick Law Olmstead, who penned that the houses of the San Antonio peons (of that day) were built of adobe, one story high and thatched, and swarmed with mixed denizens, white, black, and copper colored: and added that their free and easy life style, which was characteristic of the lower order of Mexicans, was sure to take a stranger aback who was unaccustomed to this mode of informality. Then furthered that children of both sexes from two to six years of age were seen strolling about in the economically and closely fitting costume bestowed upon them by nature; and that women, short and dumpy, with forms of artificial fixtures, and in the single article of attire denominated a petticoat, brief at both ends, were observed in doors and out, manifesting not the slightest regard for the curious glances of the passers by. Parties of men and women and children, he explained, bathed in the San Antonio River, just outside the corporate limits, without the annoyance of dresses. The scenes of this custom were selectively avoided by Lawrence Sherette and Bryon Laster when Sasha and Mrs. Laster were in their company on tour.

A visitor was as likely to hear German as English or Spanish spoken on the city streets. The Germans had ushered in old fashioned industry along with their lager beer and their neat cottages and vegetables for sale dotted the suburbs. Some had established cute little cafes just off the side walks of the community, which with their abundance of charm were irresistible attractions to Sasha and Mrs. Laster. Each time they embarked on a tour they were ever alert to persuade Lawrence Sherette or Bryon to travel this routing, invariably stopping for lunch. Upon studying the menu Sasha once said she just loved German food. Mr. Sherette laughed and asked which of it did she have in mind. She answered, "All of it."

The Germans' ability to build was paramount. That was their trademark. With superior engineering skills they could build virtually any form or design, roadways, dams, bridges, levies, gristmills, street ways, any category of commercial structure. And along with this, during the period in which Sasha was in the city, they had also begun to erect residential houses on the higher elevations which were stylish and grand. As one might assume, only the rich Germans lived in them.

The Germans were the elite but were not alone at the top of the social and economic plateau. The Ricos occupied a seat alongside them and should be spoken of in the same breath. A small wealthy landholding populace, they were the merchants and traders who comprised the more controlling class, folks who lived in well built houses, with rooms of comfortable and occasional elegant furnishings opening onto interior patios; and manners and customs reminiscent of the Conquistadores. The Ricos had been around eons longer than the Germans, it's true, but the latter advanced swiftly when they once settled, melded well into the community fabric, and at this stage their numbers were proportionately large.

The fandango was the staple pastime of the nightlife people of the city, the rough and rowdy, frequented by the many sorts, the muleteer, fresh from the coast or the Pass, with gay clothes and a dozen silver dollars; the United States soldiers just from the barracks, abounding in oaths and tobacco; the herdsman, with his blanket and long knife; the disbanded ranger, rough, bearded and armed with his huge holster pistol and long bowie knife, dancing, swearing, eating, drinking and carousing; and there were the women, of virtually of all colors, ranging from ages fifteen to forty, the Creole, the Poblana, the Mexican, a part of the obscenity, but rarely, if ever, did a German so much as peep through the doorway. The fandango was unvaryingly consistent in its occurrence, that is, it was not a lively rowdy shenanigan which flared up once or twice weekly but every single night. The site of it was a large hall or square room, crudely built, lighted by a few lamps from the walls or lanterns suspended from the ceiling where a quartet of Negroes fiddled and 30 or 40 couples danced to the bolero. Somewhere in the room there were refreshment tables under the charge of a tough skinned woman of gall and grit, where coffee, fijoles, tortillas, and boiled rice, and other eatables could be bought, and judging from the brawls and free fights which often erupted liquor was made and sold without setting a limit on the quantity of drink a man could reasonably handle.

The life which abounded inside the fandango dance hall each night was a scene that Sasha never knew existed, her eyes and ears exposed only to the beautiful things which Lawrence Sherette and Bryon Laster arranged for her and Mrs. Laster.

Each day the two of them attended Father Lumas's mass, there at six in the morning then again at six for vespers. At this time of the year the Texas sun rose almost directly east of the Alamo which Sasha waited to see from her bedroom window, finding, if she checked later, that it had slowly climbed to the top of the taller edifices, making its way skyward. The days were mostly free of uncooperative elements, no rain to speak of, so they went unhindered all over in an open surrey. Before they'd leave on an outing Lawrence Sherette or Bryon generally asked the ladies if there was a preference of something they'd like to see or do, with both often choosing the old Spanish Governors Palace as the first stop because it was close by and then too immensely intriguing. A keystone above the entrance was marked with a coat of arms of Spanish King Ferdinand the Sixth. Sasha copied down the date. It was 1749. Going by the La Villita without letting the women get down to browse through the boutiques was not given the slightest consideration. They had to stop. The La Villita was a delightfully thriving neighborhood near the Alamo featuring an assemblage of small serried shops stocked with Spanish wares. Iced tea and sweet cakes were served at one of the boutiques but most generally Sasha and Mrs. Laster held back in favor of one of the small German side walk cafes situated along their path of travel.

The San Antonio River, its fertile banks growing and sustaining a conglomeration of semi tropical plants, crawled rather than flowed through the city and was one of their most intriguing sights.

Not in this vicinity but in another, as aforesaid, we know the Germans built astonishingly beautiful homes and Sasha and Mrs. Laster loved seeing these gracious structures as they rode by, even though their sights were limited to the exterior, including the grand array of beautiful flowers and shrubbery. Lawrence Sherette and Bryon tried with all they had to please them both, Sasha fore mostly, mainly done to help her better cope with the death of her parents and her sudden uprooting from the Canaries, her homeland, and felt they made a profound difference.

Chapter 13

SO FAR every scene that unfolded before Sasha's eyes was serene and beautiful. She had begun to wonder if anything within the borders of the city was to the contrary, until Bryon altered his routing one day and in a moment of thoughtlessness explained when Sasha inquired about it that the rather unattractive two storied stucco they were passing was the Council House, where the city fathers conducted affairs of government and that it was a pretty famous place. She asked why was that, to which he answered that a short time before, about five years previous he estimated, a band of Comanche chiefs showed up to negotiate with the white officials a claim to the Comancheria, a vast stretch of land to the west which the chiefs insisted lay in the domain of the Comanche tribe and rightfully belonged to them. Formerly taken captive there was a white girl of age sixteen who was brought along, a promise made to release her provided all went well. Bryon proceeded to say that there was a flare up in the talks which resulted in an outbreak of shootings and knifings in which sizeable numbers were killed on both sides.

"Heavens! How awful," Sasha cried out.

"Oh! Forgive me Sasha. I shouldn't have told that to you."

"There is nothing to forgive Bryon," she put in soothingly, attempting to make him feel better; "I am nearly grown up and have read in countless books about the savagery of the West." But she did not ask for further elaboration.

Bryon would not select this course of travel again. But the touring continued, sometimes daily, sometimes every other or third day, Lawrence Sherette one day driving the horses and Bryon the next, altering the routes from time to time, and everyday they seemed to see or do something new. Once, maybe twice, Sasha and Mrs. Laster attended an evening opera that was held in one of the splendid German homes, with virtuoso singers and violinists performing amidst glittering lights that hung from the ceilings and walls, whereon Mrs. Laster looked over at Sasha and declared that she was reminded of the magnificent operas she'd attended in London.

Near the end of her first month of stay Lawrence Sherette and Sasha visited one of the mercantile stores where he bought her a sizeable stock of fine clothes. Soon afterwards Mrs. Laster did like wise. Sasha might have suspected that these benevolences were exacted just to lessen her grief from her past misfortune. If she did she did not show it. Lawrence Sherette had begun to seriously trade letters with the Archdiocese in New Orleans to consider whether or not he'd accept an administrative post, and if they truly wanted him, and was leaning toward taking it; he was almost certain he would accept, he said to Father Lumas, for the correspondence from the Archbishop had mentioned his securing a Priesthood in Memphis within a year. Sometimes there was a look in his face as if he were lost in deliberation, perplexed no doubt over his impending decision. If she could have read his mind Sasha would have seen that it was all about her. Also unknown to her, of course, were the conclaves between Lawrence Sherette and Father Lumas who had endlessly subjected the matter to scrutiny, realizing that she was comfortably settled by then and of the opinion that if she had to pack up and move to a new and strange city the undertaking could become profoundly disrupting. Lawrence Sherette tottered on indecision, putting Sasha before himself.

"I am swinging back and forth Father. Sasha's situation is of major concern."

"And I too swing back and forth. That forever happens when you are attempting a decision on something whose outcome is of great bearing. I empathize with your dilemma, which I think is to accept the offer or forego it in favor of letting Sasha continue to reside here in San Antonio. Am I correct?"

"That is the question. Absolutely. "

"And you are thinking, as I am myself, that Sasha is now reasonably well settled, and that to uproot her again will be a bit if not a lot disturbing."

"Exactly. I think it would be."

"Which?"

"A lot."

"I have seen her Lawrence day by day, becoming happier, starting to beam, responding to the kindness you and Bryon have heaped upon her. It has warmed my heart to see her disposition soar. Still, you cannot think of her altogether. You must think of yourself too. Your career."

"I am Father. But I am distressed as to what action to pursue. To say the truth, I am trying to think of both of us. We can manage in New Orleans. I can help her acclimate. True. Time will be necessary, but—."

"Yes, yes. Time can heal all wounds they say and often does. And in that regard I do agree with you. But I also vacillate. I must confess my boy that I am fearful of opening a new wound while an old one is healing. One has to assess the consequences of suddenly breaking her away from what she is beginning to become accustomed. Still, as I said, I vacillate. In the end I am opined that you must give first priority to the position you seek."

"I know."

"And besides. What you do with your career may prove to work greatly in her favor. Your gain could be hers over the long haul. Within a few years she will have grown up and you will likely figure in whatever is her occupation. You will then occupy a Priest's office, and likely will wield substantial influence."

"Such a thought has occurred to me Father."

"She could stay here in San Antonio my boy, without you. That is an option. You could visit her now and then."

"But that—."

"Now, now. Hear me out. I'm only examining the other side of the coin. Not agreeing with it. Mrs. Laster would love to adopt her, to have her live with her and her son in the German settlement. Of that I am sure."

"She would be secure there Father, and happy, and I could not entrust her to anyone more caring than Mrs. Laster, who loves her dearly."

"I agree. But I find a serious gap in what I have intimated."

"What is that Father?"

"The wish of Albert Duval, which was that you serve as the guardian of her life, that she entrust her security and comfort completely to you and to no one else. That was a wish made on his deathbed, and it cannot be responsibly ignored."

"Nor will I ignore it Father. I only hope that I can accomplish two goals at the same time. That is what I am hoping. And if I can, that will satisfy my great friend's wish for his daughter, as well as the one for myself."

"And they are?"

"That I can obtain the position I believe they have offered me in New Orleans and gain Sasha's consent to go with me."

"Ah! The first is easy, the latter delicate in the extreme. I hate to imagine the look on her face when she suddenly perceives the gravity of your proposition, yet she is strong, and might fool me. A decision of that nature would not be the hardest of her young life. Let us bide our time and may I suggest that we invite Mrs. Laster to join us quite soon to assist us in the thrashing through of this stressful complexity. After all, she is a woman and therefore is likely to see things through a prism which is much different from our own."

Though Father Lumas was intent on their sitting with Mrs. Laster at the soonest he chose to let a few more days expire before addressing the subject of interest with her. He needed more time to think, he told himself, to examine and reexamine the matter, and when he was sure of his decision, as much as he could be—in his mind he yet wavered but kept it secret—he shortly thereafter asked Mrs. Laster if she might sit with him to engage in a matter that he had been bantering about and that he was certain she could aid him immensely in discovering a resolve. He added that Lawrence Sherette would join them.

"Certainly Father. When did you wish to meet with me? As you know, I am completely free of obligations."

He expected a curiosity to move swiftly upon her face, perhaps asking if this regarded Sasha in any way, but she showed no sign of the sort. Her attitude was of cheerfulness.

"Shall we say tomorrow morning at ten o'clock in my office? Will that suit you? It won't take long."

At ten the next morning the party of three sat down in Father Lumas's office and took up the subject of Sasha Duval.

"Mrs. Laster, we are ahead of you," the good Father said. "Lawrence and I have already talked, having pondered a matter that weighs upon us heavily, but without reaching a definite conclusion. And I am not sure there is one. But maybe you can help. It concerns Sasha."

"I see." There was not the least of alteration in her expression and her voice was calm.

"Yes. As you might suppose," the Priest said slowly, careful to choose the exact right words, "Lawrence is on the threshold of accepting an administrative post with the New Orleans Archdiocese. Yet, he is somewhat bewildered about making a decision to accept or forego the acceptance." Mrs. Laster's eyes swept over Lawrence Sherette and then back to Father Lumas. "The reason is Sasha."

"Sasha?"

"Yes. You are close to her, and love her with all your heart, which she senses and knows, and are like a mother to her."

"I am all of what you say Father. I love her dearly, as if she were my very own."

"Indeed she is as a daughter to you. It's as transparent as a serene and clear day. And that is chiefly why I have asked for your presence. You see, Lawrence feels duty bound to carry Sasha with him to New Orleans. He sees no other way."

"Duty bound?" Mrs. Laster repeated. She was oblivious to her fingers springing to her face. "You mean because of the wish of her father as he lay dying for Sasha to relocate to San Antonio and be cared for by him."

"You of course were aware of this."

"Yes Father. It was conveyed to me by Father Kestner. It was clear to me from the start that she was coming here for that reason."

"I have felt that you had to know. But let us take a step further. And may I be frank?"

"Please."

"Then let me examine with you an alternative: I feel relatively certain that you would agree to take her in and let her live with you and nurture and educate her until she is grown and independently capable of progressing through this difficult world."

She smiled lightly. "I say what you well know Father. I would not hesitate a second. I pray often this will come to pass. Already I have considered this possibility with Bryon, who would be delighted with a little sister in the household. But I also must be frank, although it breaks my heart. I am of the belief that the wish of Sasha's father will prevail over whatever I want to happen however fervently I might hope for it. As you say, Sasha and I are close and I can read her heart. When the time arrives Lawrence, she will be at your side. Do you perhaps differ?"

"I do not differ. The bonds of her father grip her tightly. They will control."

"As they should," Father Lumas entered in.

"Dear me," said Mrs. Laster, touching her fingers to her brow, "this is a hard moment." She wiped her moistened eyes with a handkerchief. "When we were sailing across the ocean for this place I envisioned it as her home, where she'd grow up, never dreaming something like this might crash down upon her, and upon us all. But such is life. And we'll have to deal with it."

"Ah, you are right my dear. And I am sorry that we have to. As is yours my heart is deeply saddened at the prospect of losing her. Deeply saddened." With this he hesitated, as if sorting through what else he should add, then, "Let me see. Now, let me ask you Lawrence. Does the Archbishop extend any clarity to you of when you might start with your new position?"

"Sometime in January. The middle part of. I am thinking that a good time to depart is after the Winter Solstice has left us. The extension of daylight hours offers much advantage whether traveling on land or sea."

"Umh. humh. Well, that allows us a while, and I am especially glad that it does because it means that Sasha will celebrate Christmas and New Years with us."

Father Lumas's tired face showed that he'd decided enough was said. It was his intention to call everyone back together at a later date to recommence where they'd left off. Everyone seemed to be running through something, toying with a solution. For now, there was little doubt that Lawrence Sherette would be leaving for New Orleans when January had expended half its life and that what had to be done was to create a softened way of telling Sasha of his impending departure and that he likely wouldn't make the transition unless she gave her consent to go with him. The dread of approaching her was enough to make them all take pause. Father Lumas was exploring whether he might deal with the delicate unpleasantry, but grew tentative, for a moment switching to the notion that Lawrence Sherette was more appropriate to carry it out. He would revisit these thoughts.

"I will talk with her Father if you want me to," said Mrs. Laster in helpful appeal. "Hopefully I can break the news gently, a small dose at a time, shall we say? But I'm afraid however that one slight hint of Lawrence's departure will suddenly give rise to the whole sky falling in. She is incisively intelligent. All at once she will see the complete picture."

"I fear so," said Lawrence Sherette. "And besides, the duty seems more mine than anyone else's. It's too much to ask of you."

"All right. But I'll do whatever I can. May I continue to think about this?" she asked, looking over.

"Oh sure. Let's all do."

"Of course," the good Father kindly added, beginning to rise from his chair, offering thanks for their joining him.

While they were seemingly stumped as a group on the tricky question of who would sit down with Sasha, Lawrence Sherette was definite of mind about another matter that had been gnawing at him. "It must be done without further delay," he told himself. "I have crossed the Rubicon."

Dear Adelaide,

In my last two letters I spoke to you of my impending position in New Orleans. Now I am virtually certain that I will be going, with the exception of Sasha who might hold me back, yet I don't think she will when I explain the importance of my making the transition. So far I haven't sat down with her but will shortly.

You will recall that I asked you to consider staying with us for awhile, nothing extended, to help keep her company and daily see after her welfare. I expect to establish residence in New Orleans in January and have earlier asked a contact at the Archdiocese to be on watch for a nice house that we can occupy; or you may prefer to advance ahead of me and make the selection yourself. We can afford it; the plantation is doing well, thanks to you, and this will mean much to the young girl, whom you will dearly love. Please reply soon.

All my love,

Lawrence

Life went on in the San Fernando Cathedral and in the city of San Antonio. The young men continued to alternate at touring the ladies, one day Lawrence Sherette stopping off at a Rico's ranch where he helped Sasha onto a horse and gave her a lesson on riding. By now, Mrs. Laster and Sasha spent only some of their nights and days at the Rectory. A fair amount of time was consumed at Bryon's home, where Mrs. Laster and Sasha leafed through magazines and read books and talked of many things and partook of hot tea at mid afternoon that Mrs. Laster prepared; and if not usurped by these pleasures Sasha did diagrams of the anatomical parts of the human body while Mrs. Laster crotched. Sometimes when all was quiet and Sasha was completely preoccupied with her work, oblivious to all else, Mrs. Laster would look sadly over with the realization that one day her sweet youthful companion would not be there.

"In what way will I miss her most? Oh they are limitless. Too many from which to choose. I guess it's at mass when we kneel before the altar. She prays with an angelic innocence. I think she is most endearing to me then than in all other moments."

Chapter 14

FATHER LUMAS and Lawrence Sherette conferred about various and sundry things from time to time, but whatever the subjects, the two that loomed large to the good Father was Lawrence Sherette's transfer to New Orleans, and whether he had yet arranged a session with Sasha, which he knew he had not.

"No I haven't Father. But will right away. I am a procrastinator I admit but will put this to rest very soon. I must. I am on the verge of sending my letter of acceptance to the Archbishop. I have also made tentative arrangements with Adelaide to join us for a while in New Orleans. To be with Sasha you know. Sasha will love Adelaide and Adelaide will love her. My sister is young and spirited and those qualities will endear Sasha to her."

"Yes she is young and spirited. As you will recall I met her twice before when she visited you here."

"That is right Father."

"She is endowed with many of your traits Lawrence, kind, thoughtful of others, sympathetic, forgiving, and always ready to help her fellow man, charitable, I mean to say. By all means charitable. "

"Oh yes Father. I've heard you refer to it how many the times. Let's see. What is it you say? 'Is it not when the fall is lowest that charity should rise to its highest?' Your pet line. Thank you for wasting one breath to associate me with that word. I don't deserve it."

"But you do. And also your sister."

"Thank you again."

"And Adelaide will blend well with Sasha."

"As I've meant to infer."

"Ah, but there is an additional scene poking up its head. Seemingly just a suggestion at this stage but it's real enough. Are you prepared for it?"

"Ha. What is that Father?"

"Mrs. Laster has conferred with her son about her going to stay with Sasha for awhile in New Orleans. Until she becomes accustomed to her new and strange surroundings."

"She spoke to you of this?"

"She did. And most seriously. She presented it as merely an idea. But she was serious. I could tell that she was. She of course awaits your talk with Sasha."

"So, then Sasha will have both her and Adelaide to keep her company. What a boon. That is certainly something to which I look forward."

"I can tell you that you should."

Lawrence Sherette patiently waited for his opportunity and when it availed itself he moved upon it with a design of succeeding in the fullest but going about it delicately. The day was sunny and brilliant when he picked Sasha up, his course aimed at venturing outside the city for a short distance, seeing that the soldiers were heavily patrolling the roadways and thinking that Sasha would delight at the rural scenery. She was clad in a nice pretty chemise of yellow and white overlaid with a cape of the lightest texture. Her hair hung to her shoulders, trembling daintily in the breeze.

"What a beautiful woman when she finishes growing up," said Lawrence Sherette as he glanced at her sitting close beside him. "I can see it easily. Perhaps I will be the one to marry her off someday to some lucky fellow. I just might. I am distressed that her father and mother won't be around to share that high moment."

It was indeed one of those glorious mornings, the weather moderately warm, and the animals and birds out in droves. Sasha viewed everything, animatedly turning and twisting about in her seat, sometimes looking backward at something she wanted her eyes to embrace once more, then explaining to Lawrence Sherette in detail the scenes that appealed to her fancy. He listened and smiled and kept his eyes trained on the horses and the roadway ahead. She had recently begun to talk to him more and more and of this he was warmly heartened. After awhile she asked if they could take the route that ran adjacent to the San Antonio River on the west side of the city, in that she was especially drawn to the semi tropical plants and trees that flourished on the banks of the stream.

"Did you know that the pretty Bella Donna plant is poisonous to the human system but also contains medicinal properties?"

"I didn't. But it's very interesting. Where did you learn that?"

"I read it in a medical journal that our doctor on the Canaries lent me. It was published in England."

The hour was closing on eleven, and deciding they'd driven around long enough, Lawrence Sherette proposed that they stop in at a small unpretentious café in the proximity of the German community, although the café wasn't German. It was Mexican.

"Oh, I like this one. It's caught my eyes before when we drove by."

Lawrence Sherette stopped the horses and hitched them to the hitching post, then he and Sasha went in. The waiter recognized him with an ebullient greeting and seated them at an out of the way corner table, which he knew to be Lawrence Sherette's accustomed dining niche. He had called Lawrence Sherette by his first name and Sasha took this to mean that he was a favorite here.

"He knows you."

"Yes. We've been friends for the longest."

"That is why he called you by your first name."

"Yes. I feel it is."

"And do you address him by his?"

"Come to think of it I don't. He goes by a name all right but I've never believed that it was his first name. It's El Tegre. That's what I call him."

"That's it?"

"El Tegre, yes."

"His only one?"

"Yes. His only one in so for as I know."

"And you've been friends for a good while. That is nice."

"A good while, yes, and it is nice and that reminds me of something I must tell you."

"Tell me?" she asked with breathless attention."

"Your father and I used to frequent this very little dinge and sat at this very table."

She drew in a breath. "Oh, I can't believe it! In this very room at this very table!"

"It's true. We did. Sometimes we sat here for hours, until the clock hand struck two."

"What did you do?"

"We drank coffee, and sometimes had a glass of wine. And laughed profusely at times."

"That sounds so nice. And what did you talk about? I'll wager you did a good bit of that."

"Hmmmm. Christianity, history, philosophy, politics, people, war and peace, longevity, the hard knocks of living, succeeding."

"And my father sat right here? And you talked of these things with him?"

"I did. I thought you'd like to hear of it."

"Oh, very much."

"And do you know something else? El Tegre, our waiter, still remembers him. Hold on. I'll call him over."

Lawrence Sherette raised his hand and motioned to El Tegre to join them, who moved to their presence instantly, but did not sit down.

"El Tegre, may I introduce you to someone."

"Si. Who is it?" he asked, fixedly looking down at Sasha.

"You remember Albert Duval, don't you?"

"Of course. Your young friend. I've not seen him in a while."

"No you haven't. But this is his daughter."

"Oh, his daughter. She is so pretty."

"Her name is Sasha."

"Oh, her name is pretty too. I did know your father Senorita Sasha, and I knew your mother too. Before they moved away they came together every once in a while to have food and drink. They were here only at night. They were like peas in a pod. Very close. Laughing and going on. I always lit a candle for them."

Sasha looked up into his eyes and smiled. Though beautiful, her face was not happy. Lawrence Sherette knew the inner workings of her soul and started to shift the subject without revealing the passing of Sasha's parents. El Tegre remembered they had moved away and that was all he knew.

"Well, let me see. While you're here," he said to El Tegre, "we'll give you our order. What do you prefer Sasha?"

"The frijoles are fine. And some good hot tea. Oh, the bread. That very thick bread we have at the Rectory at supper. Am I lucky enough that you have it here?"

"You are Senorita Sasha," El Tegre broke in, "I know exactly what you mean. It won't take long. In the meantime enjoy yourselves."

As he said he would do El Tegre briefly returned with their food and drink, lighting a candle after he had set the servings down, and held Sasha in his gaze as carefully and as long as he felt he could without overly arousing her sensibilities.

Lawrence Sherette kept nudging himself to get on with opening up his talk with her about the New Orleans imperative. One moment he would start to bring it up but the next he found his courage melting away. But now he paused no longer.

"Sasha, let me ask you something my dear." Then he hesitated.

"Yes." Her eyes leveled fixedly on his.

"It is this. What would you think of my accepting a Priest's position were it offered to me?"

Her face remained emotionless, and she did not answer without considering the question more than once.

"That is what you have wanted, isn't it? My father always said you did. I think you should accept it. Are you planning to?"

"I am seriously thinking about it, but there may be extenuating circumstances."

"And what are they that you cannot accept an offer to occupy such an important post?"

"It will mean that I can no longer stay in San Antonio."

"Oh dear."

Lawrence Sherette's heart fell. He expected her to come close to tears but she held her poise. "But I haven't accepted it yet, and do not have to."

"You must. Think of it. It's your dream."

"Dreams do not always have to be honored."

"Sometimes I think they should. What does Father Lumas think about this?"

"Of course he leaves it up to me. He will give his blessing."

"Where is it that you will take up your new position?"

"New Orleans."

"That is where you were when I arrived at the San Fernando Cathedral."

She stayed quiet for a moment or two, revolving it in depth, contemplating another unknown future, the troubles encountered with relocations, and adapting to new people all over; and suddenly there was a touch of anxiety that ran through her. She caught herself pressing her lips together but quickly stopped. Lawrence Sherette guessed at her thoughts.

"I would dread leaving here, truthfully I would. I am situated and it is heartbreaking to think of departing from Father Lumas and Mrs. Laster, and I will cry in my bedroom tonight, but so be it, I will not for a minute say to you to refuse your opportunity. I am young but I know better than that. If I should I could not bear the guilt. I know what you are thinking, which is, will I go with you. Please brush that aside, because I will. I am under your care and you are a very kind and good man. As my father would want me to, I will follow you to wherever you lead."

"I am amazed at what I hear my dear Sasha. How generous and unselfish your heart. But again, I do not have to make this transition. We can—."

"You must see this through and I will help you with it when we get there. It may be hard settling in a new and unfamiliar city but we together can work that out."

"But there is more than I have yet said."

"Oh."

"There is. I have not thus far revealed all. But must and must do it now. The situation, the position in New Orleans is an administrative one, which is a stepping stone to a Priesthood in another city. In Memphis sometime later on. Perhaps a few months. Perhaps a year. I cannot say at this time. But that is the plan of the Catholic hierarchy."

"Then your stay in New Orleans is for a temporary length."

"Only that. Will that matter?"

"I don't suppose. Could we ever come back here to visit Father Lumas? And Mrs. Laster?" Memphis is of a far distance you know. And Father Lumas is growing old."

"We could. I plan to. And you will be with me. It is not but a short run on the steamer from Memphis to New Orleans. And the boat ride from New Orleans to Corpus Christi is but three days or thereabouts. We will return and spend an entire month."

Breaking into a smile she reached and squeezed his hand. "That will be wonderfully nice. I can't bear never seeing them again. "

"But let me ask you. Has Mrs. Laster mentioned the likelihood of my relocation?"

"Only hinted. She said your name was under review for your assumption of an important office, maybe a Priesthood."

"Ummh. Well, let me ask you this also. Suppose she'd agree to spending awhile in New Orleans with us. Not long, but awhile. Would you like that?"

At this there was an apparent joy that rose to her face and she gave out the strongest sigh that her lungs could evoke, her response pouring forth in the manner of a rapid stream of girlish exclamations which attracted El Tegre's curiosity from across the room. "Do you mean that? Does she know for certain that you might be accepting the position? Do you know for sure she would go with us? Have you talked to her?"

Lawrence Sherette laughed aloud at the intensity of her suddenly born enthusiasm, which he hadn't seen before in such flurries.

"No I haven't spoken to her, though Father Lumas has. She knows I'm on the verge of accepting."

"And what did she say to Father Lumas?"

"That she'd go with us and stay for awhile. He said it was a suggestion in disguise more or less, but at the very bottom she was quite serious."

"Am I free to make mention of this to her?"

"Ha, ha, ha. You'd burst if you didn't. Certainly. Why not? You are the main person in this regard. I urge you to."

"Then I will. This very day. As soon as I can see her."

Chapter 15

IT WAS not an easy thing, a young girl beginning to heal from a searing tragedy in her life, now on her way to another uprooting, facing an unknown future in a strange and unfamiliar city, which would bring with it other upheavals. But Sasha was strong and mature beyond her years and decreed to herself that she must make the best of things, that she had someone hand picked by her father to guide and care for her, and that she was not leaving San Antonio and the San Fernando Cathedral once and for all. "I'll return ever so often; Lawrence Sherette promised, and we'll stay a whole month. All will turn out well. You just wait and see."

Father Lumas and Mrs. Laster were ecstatic to learn that Lawrence Sherette and Sasha had talked and that Sasha took the news better than expected. She had cried that night as she and Mrs. Laster went over her inevitable departure, Mrs. Laster holding her in her arms as she said soothing comforting words, yet both were swept away that Mrs. Laster was going with her and Lawrence Sherette to stay awhile. Both Bryon and Lawrence Sherette kept touring the ladies about the city, hoping to lift the sadness from Sasha's heart, to replace it with things light and uplifting. Father Lumas, though attempting not to show it, was as saddened as all the rest, but he knew that he must thrust this aside and concentrate on the celebration of Christmas, which was closely forthcoming, an event of great importance at the Cathedral, and this year even more important than ever because of Sasha.

"It will be her first and maybe her last Christmas with us at San Fernando," he silently lamented.

Lawrence Sherette had begun to think and plan for his upcoming duties at the St. Louis Cathedral in New Orleans, the place of his appointment by the Archbishop, though he was advised that he should only expect to remain for an abbreviated interval, there being a church in Memphis soon to need a Priest. Each time he received a communication from the Archbishop he sat down with Sasha and shared it with her, the purpose of which was to make her feel a part of whatever was transpiring in his life. He had not spoken to her of the existence of Adelaide, though had kept this necessity at the peak of his agenda, and one day when Adelaide's latest letter arrived he asked Sasha to read it.

"Adelaide. She is your sister?"

"She is. My only sister."

"I have not heard of her before."

"I was getting around to telling you."

"And she is arranging for a home that we are to live in. She must be a wonderful sister to do this for you."

"For us."

"Yes us. And Mrs. Laster too, for as long as she stays."

"And Mrs. Laster. Naturally."

"How old is Adelaide?" asked Sasha, holding her fingers to her chin, wondering if she were older or younger than he.

"Two years younger than I."

"Oh. What does she look like?"

"Very pretty. Her hair is dark, much like yours, though not as dark as yours, and she is as happy natured as the birds in the trees on a sunny day."

She began to take on a glow. "I am suddenly anxious to meet her."

"You will love Adelaide darling. And she will love you."

"The letter says she will arrive January 1, New Year's Day to begin remodeling and painting."

"Unless I tell her otherwise. And I won't. I have sent a return note for her to proceed with haste if she will, that we will be there the middle of the month. She has close friends in New Orleans who are consenting to help her. Mostly running errands I think. She will hire workers for the remodeling."

It seemed to Lawrence Sherette that from there on he opened a letter every other day from his sister. She was thrilled to death she said in anticipation of a vacation in New Orleans for a few months, explaining also that already she was making preparations to catch a steamer from Memphis down the mighty Mississippi to New Orleans, where with the aid of her friends of several years she would proceed to search for a house in which the three of them could live, herself, her brother, and Sasha. No mention arose of Mrs. Laster; at this interim she hadn't heard of Mrs. Laster. As he thought about various contingencies relative to their departure it struck him that he should go into a bit of detail about Sasha with Adelaide. He now recalled the shock of seeing her for the first time upon his return from New Orleans to San Antonio. He did not want his sister to be jolted with such a surprise, he felt, not that it would make all that much difference, for he could manage to catch Adelaide in a moment's privacy and explain. Years before, when they were substantially younger, he had told Adelaide that his close friend, a French Caucasian was marrying a Moroccan Negro girl, which made not even one ripple in her demeanor and thought. But as he saw things the matter should be now reintroduced, since Adelaide had to be of mind set that Sasha bore some measure of coloration, if not a great deal. It was somehow awkward to him however to pick up pen and paper and write lines that cautioned her that the young girl she presently envisioned depicted no exterior of darkened pigmentation in the slightest but was endowed of skin that was lily white. "I wish to goodness that I could see her face to face and explain this but I can't. She is there and I am here." He would wait. He would not write an explanation in advance. "After all it will be rather intriguing to see Adelaide's face light up."

Mrs. Laster plunged into sewing together three, four, five ensembles of dresses for Sasha—she kept no tally; she simply proceeded to work until deciding to quit—and bought additional clothes for her at one of the German owned mercantile shops situated on the corner of an intersection, though not knowledgeable of the climate nor the fashion in vogue in the city where destiny was to lead them. Once when answering one of Adelaide's letters Lawrence Sherette brought up Mrs. Laster's name, explaining that she was to accompany them, was a splendid woman to whom Sasha was affectionately attached and was busy assembling a wardrobe for the young girl. Adelaide wrote back her admiration of the lady, and near the end revealed that she too was actively spinning the same thing in her head—the idea of putting together some clothes for the young girl—though choosing to wait and see Sasha first, because then she could more accurately take down the tapings. The days marched on one by one, subtly sending a message to everyone that the date of departure was drawing near. There was more than one letter that Lawrence Sherette received besides that which Adelaide was constantly dispatching. About this time he opened an envelope which was alien to his customary sight, there removing the letter which he saw was signed Yours Very Sincerely, Otto Conrad Kestner. "Oh! Father Kestner. My goodness." He crossed himself. Of the several lines set down by unsteady pen Lawrence Sherette ran across a few that poignantly forced his concentration, those where the good Priest said that he knew that Sasha was by now safely in his hands, as he had prayed and hoped, and that he was praying additionally that she would have a joyful Holy season at the

Cathedral. He had heard, he said, what a splendid Christmas celebration Father Lumas annually made available, with the help of the Lord, to the poor and needy of the community. He ended with reference to Sasha's surely becoming much better accustomed to San Antonio by this intermission and that he was grateful to him for helping make this happen. Lawrence Sherette swallowed. "How will I answer?" he asked with troubled brow. "What sort of view will he have of the man on whom such dependence has been placed, who is now uprooting this lovely young girl when she has not much more than set her feet down on San Antonio soil? But I shall answer; I must."

Whether the city of New Orleans was better suited than San Antonio for the security and suitability of a young girl was debatable, and was prominent in everyone's thoughts, given that New Orleans was thickly entwined with people from a torrent of races and origins, a melting pot, French, Creole, Negro, Mexican, and every chiseler imaginable who prowled the streets night and day seeking to strip someone of his monies. Father Lumas overly and continually worried, fearful that New Orleans was a dangerous environ, for anyone, and especially Sasha; "But here we have the Comanches, and the Mexican banditos, and the rough and rowdy Anglos, so I don't know. Who was it that once said, 'Fate is to all appearance more unavoidable than unexpected?' Whatever. No place is without hazards. I hope and pray that all will go well for my dear sweet girl."

There was also the slave question. San Antonio was not without slaves, but there were many times over the number in New Orleans than in San Antonio, and slaves were everywhere throughout the State of Louisiana, a fertile belt of earth which grew cotton proportionate to the output of Mississippi or Alabama or Georgia. Near that same time Adelaide had devoted a line in one of her letters asking her brother whether Sasha had knowledge of slavery or had ever heard of the practice, wherein he, who was uninformed if she had or had not, casually broached the question with Bryon, who said that indeed she had heard of slavery, having read about it in a miscellany of books and newspapers belonging to his mother, and that also one day he overheard Sasha and his mother talking about its various aspects. When asked why he'd brought up these concerns Lawrence Sherette answered that he was afraid that if the institution of slave holding and its terrible defilement suddenly and for the first time ever landed on Sasha's young ears she might be severely affected.

"I see. Well, she knows. It surfaced once I can attest when my mother and Sasha were browsing through a stack of paintings and portraits that Sasha had packed in her trunk. There was a portrait which she especially pulled out. It was of a beautiful young Negro woman. Sasha said it was her mother and adoringly and lovingly looked at her for a spell without once removing her eyes. 'She's beautiful isn't she?' My mother quite quickly agreed and took the portrait, and as had Sasha, looked admiringly at it for some time while Sasha smiled; then after that they somehow took up the matter of slavery, one or the other declaring that it was a bad and inhumane thing that one race imposed on another. 'Man's inhumanity to man,' I heard my mother say. Don't worry. Sasha is well apprised and is quite mature for her age."

"My sister superintends the acreage that our father left to us in Tennessee, Bryon, a sizeable piece, requiring a good many field hands, not slaves mind you, to carry out the many things necessary, planting, cultivating, and harvesting, yet I am quick to stress that we do not work or use indentured servants. We hire them. That's what we do. We pay them. It was my father's strictest policy to stay free of slavery in any form, a principle that Adelaide and I resolutely obey."

"I'm sure of that. And I admire your morality. It's the same with the Germans for whom I am employed. Unless a man is unencumbered he cannot raise an ax with us or sink a shovel into the earth. He's selling his body to us by the day, absolutely he is, but he's paid for his toil and is free to proceed upon whatever the path that pleases him when the work day is over. Sometimes a man can't speak what's in his heart, but around you I can, even though you are of the South. I know where you stand; inside, you are the same as I, opposing with a vehemence the rigid hierarchy of the southern slave society, a vicious ugly specter which cannot last if history is a determinant, and one day we will read where historians have alluded to it as a failed system with a once glorious past."

❧ ❧

The Nativity season was upon them; it was ten days away from Christmas. At this time of year Father Lumas was in pressing need of help to prepare for his Holy celebration, the most crucial of which was finding a Christmas tree and workers for raising it upright, and in this regard consistently asked favor of the city sheriff, who, though dealing with every brand of rackety, often using quite physical means, the butt of a gun or his fist—was in his soul a Christian he said, and gladdened to help at anything the good Priest asked of him.

"We'll find the tree Father. I know just where to fetch it, free of charge. The same size as last year?"

"Yes, that is fine. We very much appreciate your favor at the church."

"You don't need to say that Father. I am too unworthy. Just tell me when you want this job done."

"No fewer than five days from this date. Sooner if you can. I'm sorry to have waited this long before calling on you."

"No Father. Please. Do not say that. I should have offered my services long before. How lax I am. But now we know what you need. And will take care of it. You can depend on my word. You will see your tree standing tall and proud and ready for Christmas in three days. That I promise."

There was a man named Billiard who spent much of his time confined to the cells of the Sheriff's jailhouse, not a bad sort, not a criminal, but as did other detainees drank excessively and forever ended up in the midst of brawls. It was this man on whom the Sheriff had decided to pay visit. He had climbed the stairs to the second floor, the site of the jail blocks, cells of living space which were uncomfortably cramping to the occupants.

"Billiard, I have something in my thoughts that I am asking you to lend your hand to. You are scheduled to spend nine days in this deplorable garret, nine days, but I'll tell you what."

"Hmmmm. And."

"I need you to take the lead in erecting the Christmas tree at the church for Father Lumas. You know of him, don't you?"

"Aye, I do. A fine Christian man. Far better than me."

"I dare say that's true. But let me finish. If you set up the tree for the good Father it will mean you'll have to serve five days instead of nine in here. And I'll toss in a bonus." Billiard eyed him warily. "I'll let you off for three days at Christmas time."

"Hmmmm. That means I'll only have two days left to serve. That right?"

"No. That is not right."

"But three days from five days leaves two."

"That's not what I mean. I'm simply letting you off three days for Christmas. Sort of like a furlough. An act of good will on my part. The three days in the least do not reduce your confinement time."

Billiard hesitated, waited, feigning a sulk, weighing the terms.

"Make up your mind. If not you, then I'll find someone else."

"I'll do it. Gladly. For the Father and the children."

"But one thing more. You and your friends will do your work inside a Holy place, around good Holy people, maybe women and children. I tell you straight. Don't forget where you are and let your mouth slip. If that happens, I will in the worst of mood land on you."

"No, no, no, Sheriff. I give my word. We won't forget, and to utter an obscenity in Father Lumas's place of worship! May the good Lord strike me over at once if I should! No Sheriff, I give you my word."

At the appointed date and hour, and using the inmates that Billiard had personally selected, the tree was brought in from a side entrance, the sheriff staying close by to assure that all behaved flawlessly. Work was about to begin.

Chapter 16

THE MORNING chilly, Sasha was attired in her red coat which was complemented with shiny black boots, and stood with wide eyed curiosity watching the workers move into their predetermined tasks. When they began to attach the ropes and cables to the tree trunk and upper extremities she became so concerned that they might break the pretty branches and boughs she forgot herself and called out in the most effeminate voice, "Please be careful that you don't hurt the tree."

Billiard looked around to see from whom the caution had sprung. Then he saw, and in his graveled coarseness tried his best to speak as softly as a young girl might, replying in a tone to which he was most unaccustomed, "Yes ma'am, Miss, Miss—." Her name had escaped him. He had heard someone call it out earlier but had forgotten it. His face reddened.

"Sasha, my name is Sasha."

Father Lumas and Bryon looked on amusedly.

"Sasha. Yes ma'am Miss Sasha. We won't hurt the tree."

"Thank you Mr. Billiard. Merry Christmas." He smiled from ear to ear and glanced timidly at the Priest.

Sasha then moved over to Bryon and asked when was the star to be appended to the peak, since in her conception there was not a practical method for affixing it after the tree was raised.

"Right before they start to lift it."

Shortly, someone handed the ornament to a worker who took it and set about to do what she wanted to see.

☙ ❧

Two days later the great church was now adorned with a tree that reached for the vaulting, the base of it encircled with gifts destined for children who'd come gleefully to take part in the festivity, but taking part meant more than receiving gifts; they'd be there to participate in the whole panorama, to marvel and shriek at the sparkling glitter of the Christmas tree lights, to mix and mingle, and stare at a tree of immense height, and sing Christmas carols with hundreds of others. Father Lumas had made a singular effort to invite Sasha to help with laying out the gifts, as well as assisting with hanging the bulbs and tassels from the branches and boughs. She stood on a ladder, as did several women, and spread tensile as far as she could reach. At that height the men took over. Children from throughout the city and the outlying areas, most of them from families of limited if not poor means, would be there, the majority of them Mexicans, but there were a sprinkling of Comanche's who'd settled into the community; then there were a good many German children who never missed a single celebration, but distinctly were set apart because they looked excessively clean and neat in comparison, clothes freshly starched and ironed, hair immaculately groomed, and shoes aglitter. If the rest were used as a standard bearer the German children looked clearly out of place.

Suddenly, the time was there. The celebration began with a litany of prayers which Father Lumas delivered in Latin, alternating at times with Lawrence Sherette, then sacrament followed, and then there was a Christmas pageant featuring the birth of Christ Jesus. The stable, the Epiphany, (the visit by the wise men) and Mary with child were the perennial scenes, which had been told of throughout the centuries, and reasonably well grasped by children of an age when the story begins to take on serious meaning. The sanctuary bulged with children and parents, especially mothers. When this phase of the evening was over the children were asked to gather around the tree and pick up a gift, any gift, for they were all alike, even though the wrapping was of varying colors. Sasha beamed at helping some of the smaller children, kneeling down and putting her arm around them.

"Here. Would you like this one? Good," she said, as the child reached and took it.

The mother was nearby, smiling. Very few of the Mexican mothers had seen Sasha before; they were the ones who did not attend mass regularly. They wondered at the presence of the white girl and some would say to her in Spanish that they hadn't seen her before, and introduced themselves, and when Sasha returned in their native tongue that she was Sasha Duval who but recently became a guest of Father Lumas they opened their mouths in aghast and covered it with their hands and rolled their eyes. Father Lumas saw that the Mexican women and children lovingly took to Sasha. "She has a distinct affinity for these good people; they sense it, they feed upon it, and she relays back to them the feelings in her heart that they have created. Her color does not matter to them. It's like they don't see it, and certainly theirs doesn't matter to her."

Sasha had been noticed at early morning mass from time to time by one of the German girls who though intending to make her acquaintance had not as yet approached her, but decided that now the opportunity was ideal. She was taller than Sasha, but not by a great amount; and two years older. She was pretty, with hair of auburn, and her persona was of a disposition that enticed people to like her at first blush. Father Lumas had persistently encouraged her to develop a closeness with Sasha and Sasha at the very first was swayed by the girl.

"Sasha, I am Paula Ness. I've started to speak to you before but just didn't. Now I have."

"I'm glad you did. I'm glad that somebody knows my name," she said, cleverly adding the last phrase as filler.

"Oh, we do. Lots of us. You are hard to miss. I love your beautiful hair."

"Thank you."

"Father Lumas tells me you are leaving for New Orleans right away. I'd hoped you might start attending school with us. We've started to talk about it; we've been enthused that you might join us. It's just too bad that you are leaving."

The Germans collectively hired their teachers and owned their own building where the children were educated.

"Yes, that is too bad. I would have liked your school I'm sure."

How unfortunate it was, she thought, that she could not be a part of this fine grouping of pretty bright girls, for she had never intertwined with those of her own age, except in books that she'd read.

Shortly following Christmas Bryon had asked Sasha if there was anything at all she'd like to see or do before they left for New Orleans. Pausing briefly, showing in her face the contemplation of a list, she answered yes, if he didn't mind, that she'd like to ride down by the San Antonio River and walk along the pathways and see the pretty flowers, and then visit the little German café, the one they generally went to, for a bowl of fine spicy soup which was always ready for serving. After this, she added another, the Rico ranch where either Bryon or Lawrence Sherette had taken her for a ride on horseback now and then. All of these wishes Bryon fulfilled.

From there on the details of leaving had to be worked into place, though some already were, the packing of clothes a leading chore, which called for an encasement for Sasha's swollen wardrobe. Someone said that contingency was previously cared for. At the suggestion of his mother Bryon had personally bought the item and presented it to her as a

Christmas gift. Nothing would do her but to retrieve it one evening after mass and proudly show it off to some friends of Lawrence Sherette and Father Lumas.

It was but shortly thereafter that Lawrence Sherette received from his sister a letter which he took to be crucial, the substance regarding the house in which they were to live.

"Sasha come quickly, you'll want to see this," he called out, for she was close by.

Excited, she hurried over. "What is it, what is it?"

"Here. Read it."

"Shall I read only the lines that count the most?"

"Fine. Please do."

"She says," 'I have leased the house and I have this day most energetically begun to start some minor remodeling, with my friends helping. A small construction crew is leading the way. Lots of room, more than adequate. And two stories with a view from the second floor of the Mississippi where you can see the boats of every conceivable shape and size rounding the curve. Oh yes! The address is 1004 St. Charles Street. Very famous. Please write it down. A carriage taxi can bring you there with absolutely no hitch.'"

"I'm more than relieved," uttered Lawrence Sherette. "I'm overwhelmed."

"Isn't that wonderful. She's adorable. Don't you think?"

"I always have."

They were to leave early on January the second, first taking in the fireworks on New Years Eve which were set off on a high place of the city, yet in sight of the church, where Sasha stood with the rest watching the swoosh of the rockets zoom skyward. The evening was cold, unusual temperatures for San Antonio, a north wind having made an appearance, with everyone snuggling in heavy coats and blowing gray mist from their mouths. Paula was there as an observer with a party of other German girls and stood by Sasha. The display was truly a panorama and kept the girls squealing and acting spellbound at each explosion. Sasha told Paula she was glad she had come over to stand beside her and Paula said to her that she was overwrought to see her depart, giving Sasha her address to which she could send letters and said she'd be watching for the first one. The fireworks over, Paula hugged her and turned and started home with her parents, Sasha's eyes sadly following her from the doorway.

On the morning of their departure they all had breakfast together at the Rectory, on which Father Lumas insisted, then went to the church sanctuary for a limited mass. When Sasha had finished with the wafer the acolyte had placed on her tongue and sipped from the chalice, Father Lumas moved over and held her while uttering a prayer in Latin, her countenance betraying her hope that he thought she might understand the words.

Knowing she didn't he merely gave her a kindly smile. Chenelle was also there, sitting on Sasha's left with a box of colorful wrapping at her feet, in which there was a several tiered cake that she with tedious care had baked for her friend as a going away gift. She waited until they'd started to break up from mass, then lifted up the box.

"Sasha. I have something for you." Sasha's eyes sparkled.

"What is it?"

"It's a secret for now. And you must promise not to open it until you have traveled for five hours. Do you?"

There was a vagueness of play that broke onto Sasha's face and she laughed. "I promise. And whatever it is I dearly thank you."

With that, Chenelle told her how much she loved her and that she had from the beginning and hoped with all her heart they'd meet again. Sasha then handed her a letter and asked her to mail it to Father Kestner.

My Dear Father Kestner,

I trust and pray that you are well. I should have written you before now. Forgive me. My stay in San Antonio with Father Lumas and Lawrence Sherette has been more rewarding than ever I could have expected. Mrs. Laster is as kind as an angel and Captain Johansen I found to be a most blessed and good man on our voyage across the ocean.

I regret to tell you that we are leaving this city for New Orleans, where Lawrence Sherette will assume a position with the Archdiocese. His sister who lives near Memphis is leasing a house in New Orleans for us and will come stay there for a while herself. I am uncertain of the duration. I am much uplifted that Mrs. Laster is journeying to New Orleans with us and will stay for three months, her son Bryon, who is like a brother to me, giving his consent.

We will leave right away on stage for Corpus Christi, then take a ship to New Orleans. Father Lumas is sad; I know he is. We all are.

The image of my father and mother are constantly with me and I often cry when in privacy. But I am strong and learning day by day to better deal with my painful loss.

I wish I could see you; I miss you dearly. Please tell Doctor Enoch that I miss him too. He did all within his power to lessen the struggle and pain of my parents as they were moving closer to death.

I will say bye for now. Please write when you can.

Love, Sasha

The carriage was loaded with personal belongings, Sasha's, Mrs. Laster's and Lawrence Sherette's, such that two carriage trips were necessary, the first to transfer the clothes and other adjunctive items to the stage post, the second to transport Sasha, Mrs. Laster, Bryon, the driver, Lawrence Sherette, and Father Lumas.

As if in the attempt of one last desperate grasp to hold on Father Lumas had decided to trail the stage for awhile when it left the city, and asked Bryon to drive the carriage, and in response to his further wish Mrs. Laster sat by him in the rear while Sasha sat by Bryon in the front. Lawrence Sherette would ride beside the stage driver. Father Lumas struggled with the thought of seeing Sasha go, but she was only part of the total equation. Lawrence Sherette was leaving too after all the years they'd been together. It was quite hard on the dear old man. But nonetheless the stage pulled away. The day was not what was hoped for. It was overcast and cool, the sun which was attempting to climb the ridge in the east hidden by the cloudiness, the winds blowing cool upon their faces from the southwest, which were a far cry however from the cold norther which had ventured into South Texas on New Years Eve, making it harder for folks to indulge in the festivities. Not entirely unexpected Father Lumas and Mrs. Laster talked but little, Bryon and Sasha doing a bit better. When they had traveled a distance of two miles from the city or thereabouts Father Lumas tugged at Bryon's coat to indicate that he was ready to stop, his voice sounding of sadness.

"It's time to turn around Bryon and let the others move freely on with their journey."

"Yes Father." Bryon tugged at the reins and the horses drew to a halt.

Sasha and Bryon jumped down, Bryon directly making his way to his mother, practically lifting her from the carriage. Lawrence Sherette was already there to assist her at boarding the stage. She could not help shedding a tear, and this moved Bryon to tell her that she was only to be away for three months, which was no time at all, and besides, he said, he was journeying to New Orleans to bring her back and that one day she'd look up and there he'd be. Sasha fell into Father Lumas's arms, unable to abate the sadness in her eyes, and he squeezed her as for dear life. Finally he let go.

"Goodbye," she murmured weakly.

Bryon, now climbing back up into the carriage, looked into Father Lumas's aging face and felt a lump in his throat.

"I know how badly he hates to see them off. He has to be thinking he'll never see either of them again. And that's likely true."

When Sasha and Mrs. Laster were comfortably seated the driver clucked to the horses. The stage moved forward with a snappy spurt and began to draw further away, while Father

Lumas and Bryon watched, and kept on watching until it had topped the hill and dropped out of sight.

Bryon promptly turned the horses around toward the city. As they neared the Cathedral he reached and clasped Father Lumas's arm just below the elbow, thus precipitating from the good Father these words; "Lawrence is gone Bryon. You must drop in on me often."

Two people were occupying the interior of the stage when Sasha and Mrs. Laster climbed aboard, an older man and woman, husband and wife, Douglass Wilkins and his wife Roberto, who introduced themselves, Mrs. Laster responding likewise. Shortly they revealed that they grew cotton on the broad low lands near Harlingen, which was their home. They were transplants from the East, as evinced by their quick choppy dialect. Mrs. Laster attempted to silently guess why they had at their age packed up and bought a home and land in the Wild West. She wanted to ask them but thought it best to decline. In time they began to trade varied thoughts and ideas with her. But Sasha remained quiet, choosing to avoid the conversation, yet her lovely dark and attentive eyes lent proof that she soaked in every word.

When the first phase of the journey was complete, which was within the realm of twenty five miles, the driver pulled into the way station to switch horses, an attendant waiting alertly to unhook the ones that had towed them over the distance from San Antonio. Sweating profusely, breathing hard, and issuing loud repeated snorts the animals unquestionably needed relief. He had nudged them onward as steadily as was wise, he judged, without exceeding their natural limits. Before they started to leave on the second run Sasha grasped Lawrence Sherette's arm and asked if she might ride atop. The sun had popped through and the clouds had largely disappeared.

"Why not? But you'll have to sit between us."

"That's all right."

"You'll need to snug up tight in your coat. When the stage starts rolling the wind is colder than you might think."

"I will."

Chapter 17

THE DRIVER was a young man, in his very early twenties, decked in a ponderous round hat with a rim that stayed stiff and unyielding until reaching the front, then drooped over by a slight, almost covering his eyes. He had to peep from under it to see. Handsomely patterned, he in a snap usually caught the eye of the opposite gender. But Sasha seemed not to notice. The young man however kept looking at her on every chance. Lawrence Sherette detected as much and smiled internally, keeping a poker face. Sasha was not in a talkative mood it appeared, electing to look here and there, never at the young man, admiring the broad and gorgeous landscape as she had when she and Mrs. Laster traveled this route on their way to San Antonio. But after a length her coolness lessened and she began to make comments to the driver of certain aspects of the trip.

"Do you drive this run all the time?"

"Every two days. I'll retrace this same road day after tomorrow."

"You're making good time today. When will we arrive?" She was knowledgeable of a close approximation because of her previous experience over the same course but asked nonetheless.

"Tomorrow morning about two, could be a short while after. But it all depends on whether we have good luck with us."

Hmmmm. Two in the morning?

"Yep."

"You sometimes gallop the horses I see. Is it good for them?"

"Yep. I do. But I don't ask them to do more than they naturally can. I know when they're starting to feel too much strain."

After an interval she said she'd like to return to the inside, the cold wind having worked its way into her skin, although the sun was now more radiant, whereupon the young driver stopped the horses and jumped down and then helped her down and then helped her into the stage. She took a seat by Mrs. Laster, and clinging to her arm let her eyes glance now and then upon the older couple.

"Cold out there," Mrs. Wilkins said with an emphasis as if she had been riding on the outside herself.

"Yes ma'am."

While Sasha was aloft the older lady had bragged exorbitantly on Mrs. Laster's beautiful daughter, and drew upright and sounded with disappointment when told that the young girl was someone she more or less was chaperoning.

"I would have sworn that she was your daughter; she is endowed with a great abundance of your charm Mrs. Laster, appearing well educated and the like."

"Thank you. I regret enormously that she isn't mine."

There sprang a wonder upon the lady's face; she did not understand, unable to reach into the depth of what was said.

When dusk had made its way the driver stopped and lit the lanterns that hung from the side of the stage, which were used to throw light on the sides of the roadway and straight ahead. The horses needed no light; they were born with eyes and a mechanism of sense that man did not possess. It was not long afterwards, the time necessary to cover ten miles one might have estimated, when in the distance the driver began to detect a glow of peculiar lights, moving, rapidly moving. Lawrence Sherette beheld them too. These were horsemen, with lanterns tied to their saddles but not securely fixed, bouncing, glittering, vibrating, undulating, jostling, an eerie sight, a mass of something in motion which at first they could not easily make out.

"Who are they? What do they want?" asked the young driver.

Tugging at the reins he stopped, and waited. The riders drew closer and halted a few feet away. There was a hard faced man wearing a tall hat that dismounted and strode over in confident long strides. In the shadows of lantern glow the collection of men who had stayed back cast a rough and scary visage, but the young driver did his best to stay calm. The leader of the troupe who was about to speak sensed his shakiness and sought to steady him.

"We're on the watch for banditos son, that's all. A rancher was shot up pretty bad by a band of the bastards early this morning south of here. Senseless. They didn't take anything. Not even his horse."

"Ah, I'm bothered to hear that."

"Mind if I see inside your coach," he said coarsely, as if not one of the driver's words had come through.

"No. Help yourself."

Stepping over to the window he held up his lantern which reflected a glow upon Sasha's face poking out, who with absorbing eyes had curiously taken in the commotion.

"Uh, uh," he let out, "sorry Miss. I didn't mean to scare you."

"You didn't scare me."

Then he started backing away to his cohorts, silently uttering, "Well I'll be doggone. What an answer. That youngster is made of some tough brass."

Crawling into his saddle he and his men spurred their horses and galloped away in the direction of San Antonio.

The stage rolled on, stopping, starting, stopping, switching from horses well worn to those rested, sometimes the driver pulling into a way station to let the passengers rest. They had traveled into the night, perhaps until ten o'clock, when he drew the horses into a way station where the passengers could buy coffee and something to eat. Sasha awakened rubbing her eyes. She had slept for awhile, a few hours, Mrs. Laster and the Wilkins couple too. The meal soon over and fresh horses now employed they took to the road once more. Sasha again elected to take a seat between Lawrence Sherette and the young driver and rode in this manner for a little while. It was brief. The cold got the best of her again, such that she switched to the inside and cuddled against Mrs. Laster, there falling off to sleep once more. The next she knew they had reached the outskirts of Corpus Christi, near two in the morning. The driver circled round for a time, zig zagging from one street to another, taking a short cut Lawrence Sherette deduced, then all at once pulled up in front of the hotel where they were to stay for the night, which was prearranged by the company that owned the stage. With a spirit of industry the driver began to help Sasha and Mrs. Laster with their considerable belongings, telling the older pair to sit where they were, that he'd attend to their needs right away. But Lawrence Sherette stepped forward and commenced to do this for him, which freed the young man to resume his attentions to Sasha and Mrs. Laster. Refusing to let either of them lift a hand he then bundled up all he could carry and started for the lobby, stressing that he'd return promptly for the things left over. Lawrence Sherette had finished with the older couple and had come back to lend a hand, the young man soon returning as well. The two of them together gathered up the remainder, wagging these inside to the clerk's desk where they set them down. With this concluded the driver doffed his hat to Sasha and left, but had said they'd see him there the next morning to transport them to the docking area where they were to board the vessel setting sail for New Orleans. They were to depart late.

"What is the name of our ship?" Sasha asked.

"The *Surety,"* replied Lawrence Sherette.

"That's a novel idea for naming a boat, don't you think?"

"I guess." Attempting not to be drawn away, he had kept at his paper work with the desk clerk, having only vaguely listened; but she in her usual good humor ignored the slighting and merely turned to Mrs. Laster and smiled.

That night, or the remainder which was left, they slept soundly, dead to the world, for the trip had been draining. But at nine o'clock, the hour that had been set for everyone to rise, Sasha and Mrs. Laster, after a stretch of groaning and taking on rolled out and began to bathe and dress for another day's journey.

"That was a grueling trip yesterday," said Sasha, "but no complaints. I liked it."

"Good. I'm glad you did, and I did too. But you do not misrepresent. It was grueling."

They sat down to breakfast, a good breakfast they all thought and said, orange juice, eggs, ham and biscuits, and the several jams that seemed even in that era to be on every table in Texas at breakfast time. The older couple was expected to show up but was nowhere seen, Mrs. Laster expressing regret at missing them, saying she exchanged addresses with Mrs. Wilkins and that she had promised to write to her at her son's San Antonio address.

"We'd better start moving," said Lawrence Sherette as soon as he was sure they'd finished. As he'd promised, the young man came and loaded their belongings into the carriage; and these together with his passengers he transported to where their ship was moored. A storage crew would take over from there. Sasha cautioned the dock foreman to watch out for her red and blue package, that it was a cherished gift from a dear friend.

Few passengers were aboard for the voyage but those that were had for the most part climbed the steps and were in place; Lawrence Sherette suggested that they too should do likewise. The *Surety* was a sleek looking vessel, modern in every aspect, among the first of the sea going steamers. They all thanked the young stage driver for his generous service—though he was paid by his company to provide it—and again he doffed his hat to Sasha. Impressed by his decorum Lawrence Sherette asked for his name. It was Bernie Shively. He and his father grazed cattle on the open range not many miles from Corpus Christi.

The ship stole stealthily away, the same as had the *Ignatius* when it left the Canaries with Captain Johansen at its helm, thought Sasha, and then she hurried up the steps to top side and crossed over to the railing where she commanded an open unhindered view of the shoreline, there seeing a small gathering waving energetically to her or to someone else or to several. But looking around she saw no one at all in her midst. It was she to whom they waved. Thus, she kept waving and they kept waving too; and this was continued while inch by inch the ship crept further and further away. The people on shore had become infinitely blurry, and at this point her waving ended. But not more than seconds afterwards she decided to explore the opposite side of the vessel, where the waters were visible in full expanse, and made her way hastily across, there for a while captivated by the sea gulls swooping and rising, and the waves swelling and crashing. Then looking upward at the bright blue sky and the radiant orange sun, she smiled.

"I wonder where Captain Johansen is this morning. Out to sea somewhere I'm sure. That's his life. I'll never forget him. I do hope I'll hear from him sometime. I love him."

But her mood would change. She had begun to reflect elsewhere. She looked even further out into the expanse, becoming still and motionless, her smile having left, her thoughts drifting back, standing and looking, looking, looking, for the longest while, until at length Mrs. Laster called out her name.

"Oh Sasha, there you are darling." Out of sight Mrs. Laster had stood observing her stillness, as if she were mesmerized by the immensity of the sea or its beauty. "What could you possibly see? What are you thinking?" There was a thread of concern in her tone. She hugged her.

"About several things I suppose."

"I'll bet I could guess."

"Likely. But I'll tell you; you don't need to guess."

"And."

I'm remembering Father Kestner. Standing on the shore waving pitifully when we were leaving the Canaries. That's what I've been thinking of. He was so sad. And Father Lumas was of that same sadness yesterday when we left him. I didn't want to look back at him. It would have just reminded me of Father Kestner."

"Umh humh. Anything else?"

"My mother and father. I am reminded of them too this morning. But I'm reminded of them every morning. They're with me eternally, all the time. But more today than usually. I am suddenly back to when I had to leave them for San Antonio, you know, buried there on the Canaries, and now I'm leaving San Antonio, the place where they spent such beautiful times together. They were so young then. They were young when they died. I'll never forget them."

She began to sob. Mrs. Laster pulled her into her arms.

"Of course you won't. You're not suppose to darling. You never will."

But Sasha couldn't help herself. She kept on sobbing.

"Now, now. Have your cry. These things are sad but there's a silver lining waiting somewhere behind the clouds. There always is. You'll see. Things will turn for the better."

Upon seeing them, Mrs. Laster's arms around Sasha, Lawrence Sherette sensed that Sasha had been crying and figured he knew why. "Ah, I understand; this is a particularly trying time for her. She is reflecting on many things at once, most singularly her deceased parents whom she must miss terribly. In my heart I truly understand."

Making his way over he wrapped his arms around both Mrs. Laster and Sasha, the three of them standing there for the longest, until Sasha had started to regain herself, which was just before the porter, a Mr. Sternweiss Crutcher, happened to approach.

"Ah! There you are. I've turned the bottom deck all over for you. If I may I'd like to show you your cabins. That is what my business is about. I am your porter Mr. Stirnweiss Crutcher" he said happily, extending his hand to all three as he talked.

"Yes of course Mr. Crutcher," answered Lawrence Sherette. "Give us another minute."

"I'm ready now," spoke Sasha. "No need to delay."

"All right dear. Mr. Crutcher we'll follow you."

The porter walked ahead at a pace of more than ordinary briskness, bouncing down the steps to the lower strata of the ship, and kept going, streaking by one cabin after another until reaching a certain whereabouts, then stopped. Very shortly his party caught up.

"This one is yours ladies, and sir, the one next door is yours. Let's see. I need to arrange the names straight in my head. You are Sasha Duval and you are Mrs. Edweena Laster," he said, looking at one then the other, each nodding accordingly. "And you sir are Lawrence Sherette without doubt."

"Without doubt," returned Lawrence Sherrette with a chuckle.

"I will bring your equipage forthwith. I've checked the tagging already and it is marked according to your names. I shan't take long."

He made an about face and began to walk away.

"Oh, Mr. Crutcher!" Chenelle's wrapping had suddenly shot into Sasha's thoughts which she hadn't yet opened. "My gift. I have a gift among my things. It's covered in pretty red and blue paper. Will you handle it with extra care?"

"Indeed I shall Miss Duval."

Lawrence Sherette looked on with a grin, heartened that Sasha's mood was lifting, and that she seemed for the moment to have pushed her sorrows aside.

That noon, the hour hand at nearer one o'clock than twelve, the passengers, who were earlier invited, made their way to take lunch with Captain Andrew Dolby, the head of the vessel, who, once they were assembled, announced his elation at their presence, and regretted to them the lateness of the hour for lunch. At his side was the ship's young doctor, a Robert Charlatan, who had but recently completed his internship in Paris, although he was British. No one knew his nationality at the time because the Captain hadn't introduced him; the Captain had not even told them of his own nationality but he'd discover an opportunity for extending such courtesy. The doctor was in the realm of age thirty, perhaps a slight older, and displayed a very nice handsome face, his eyes quite dark and piercing. Slight of build his clothes lay admirably on his person. Sasha kept observing his leather medicine case as if there were articles in it of invaluable use to him in his practice which she'd like to see. She had hoped to sit next to the doctor for the purpose of quizzing him on certain aspects of his profession, principally anything that had to do with evolving medical theories or practices deriving from London and Paris.

The dining space was limited and somewhat cramped but the invitees did not complain. Captain Dolby was a citizen of the British Isles, he reported, unexpected news to Mrs. Laster who spun quickly in her head, "My goodness. A Brit here. But Edweena, what would he think about you? I'll have to tell Bryon of this." He was, he said, an employee of a frigate line owned by an English corporation which operated passenger and freight service between New Orleans and Matamoros, Mexico.

"All of you are welcome, very welcome. Glad to have you, each and every one. I am honored, believe me. We are just too happy to serve you, and this comes not only from me, but fore mostly from the gracious owners of this good vessel. Now, our food is excellent, I do think you will find, as is our hospitality, but not better than the food, because the food is superb. Let us say that they are equal." He let go with an uproarious laugh as if his last remark had been fun to make. The food was promptly set out by a cadre of waiters moving snappily about, carrying huge trays of food on their skilful arms and shoulders, and depicting a smile that stretched from corner to corner. The food was served quickly and the guests began to eat and drink and talk to one another.

"Very good, excellent. Don't you think?" This was Lawrence Sherette speaking to Sasha, who had begun to sip her tea but as yet had not taken her first bite.

"I am yet to begin," she answered, "but every dish looks temptingly good and they are tremendously abundant. I am especially attracted to the chicken and dumplings and sweet potato pie. After that I'll just have to see."

As Captain Dolby had boasted, the food was superb; it consisted of dishes of a good many varieties, as Sasha pointed out, and was liberally provided. "I am overcome," said she to Lawrence Sherette as her eyes wandered over the meats and vegetables ranging from one end of the huge dining table to the other. Silently she alluded to each by name—let me see, "spinach, asparagus, mashed potatoes, lettuce, cabbage, lima beans, corn, beef steak, chicken, fish, cocoanut pie, sweet potato pie; oh, too much." She would start with a helping of chicken and dumplings, and asparagus, and mashed potatoes, and after laying her napkin lightly in her lap, as her mother had taught her, she with all the proclivity of etiquette softly asked Lawrence Sherette would he mind moving these servings within her reach.

When lunch was over and a trickle of the patrons had started to disperse, Captain Dolby, who had not infrequently caught Sasha in his glances came over and spoke, bringing the young doctor with him.

"And your name young lady is," he asked in playful friendliness. He had singled her out the moment she entered the room and had watched for an opportunity to make her acquaintance.

"Sasha Duval."

"A very pretty name. It sounds French to me. Is it?"

"Partly. Or possibly Serbian."

"Ah, Doctor Charlatan here knows something of the French. He is recently with me from his medical training in Paris, where they have the finest of schools. But he is a British citizen," he added.

The doctor and Sasha caught one another with their glances and smiled. They did not speak. Thereafter he not infrequently would pass her on the deck on his way to attend to someone in need of his services and skills, but always spoke and let out a nice pleasant smile, and sometimes stopped to chat about a subject that was totally inconsequential. As he made his way she would observe that he lethargically swung his medicine case with his arm rather than letting it bob up and down.

"And you are with?"

"Mr. Lawrence Sherette sir, on my right and Mrs. Edweena Laster who is on my left."

"So glad to make your acquaintance"

A man of serious temperament as a rule, the Captain was this day spilling over with frivolity and out of his way friendly to Sasha, perhaps because of her age, the rest due to her attractiveness. He wondered of the role that Lawrence Sherette and Mrs. Laster played in her life but made no inquiry. "Must be relatives." He then asked if the service and accommodations of the *Surety* were to their complete satisfaction, the answer yes returning, even better than advertised.

"We're not as luxurious as some boats," he said, "but we tax ourselves to please. You see of course that your reports to us are invaluable."

"Everything is fine," Mrs. Laster enjoined.

"Oh yes Sasha. We want to do something for you for the rest of your voyage. A simple minor courtesy mind you but you will relish it. Guaranteed. We are bestowing a gift on you, a set of binoculars for viewing into the great waters out there. You may be surprised at what you see. Dolphins are plentiful and will chase us the full distance to New Orleans."

"I would like that. Thank you."

"Good. I have none with me presently but I'll send the porter by with them. He's a very nice fellow. His name is Crutcher, Sternweiss Crutcher."

"Yes sir. I know. He serviced us this morning."

"Ah yes. I should have known. How thoughtless of me. Well, in any event he'll drop by in a while. He won't forget."

Sasha had entertained the notion of asking him of Captain Eric Johansen and would have had he not excused himself just then, turning to join other guests still seated or arising and about to depart.

Chapter 18

FOLLOWING LUNCH Sasha and Mrs. Laster dawned upon the idea of retiring for a nap, the time past two o'clock, still needing recovery from the long tiresome ride of the day before. Mrs. Laster fought valiantly to hold back a powerful tendency to yawn at lunch and won, but Sasha wasn't as successful. Increasingly, she held her hand to her mouth, hoping to conceal her slippage of etiquette, but Lawrence Sherette saw it and smiled and looking sideways out of his eyes good naturedly punched her ribs. Placing her hand on his she leaned over a little and whispered that she tried but for the life of her couldn't help it.

Side by side sleeping beds were provided in the cabins, not a significant amount larger than cots, but comfortable. Sasha pulled back her covers and slid in, falling quickly into sound sleep without effort. Mrs. Laster, who would experience far more trouble than Sasha at duplicating the same, tuned her ear and listened to her beautiful young friend's effortless breathing, her bosom rising and falling with flawless rhythm. And then Mrs. Laster also lay down. After a lapse and with constant yawning she too sank into slumber, helped by the gentle rolling of the vessel and the distant cry of the sea gulls. In time, Sasha sat up, looked over and smiled at her sleeping friend and then started to dress, choosing to equip herself with a top coat because of the winter winds, which were still cold upon the body even though the sun shone down with a radiance. Deftly pushing upon the door she stole outside, then two at a time dashed up the steps to the deck. For awhile she merely traipsed around, exchanging one side of the vessel for the other, finding the views virtually the same in either case. Yet not exactly. The clouds were heavier and hung lower on one side than on the other, the formations intimating that there was a storm brewing, soon to overtake the *Surety*. But the clouds were content to stay where they were. If they moved she did not see them. With repeated gaze she explored the towering mast and sails, these more than anything else, which flaunted their lordly height over all below, in no short intervals studying the separate parts in detail, recalling the lessons that Captain Johansen had taught her; and bemusedly followed the playful dolphins as they gave persistent chase. Suddenly she heard a familiar voice.

"How was your nap?"

"Oh!" It was Lawrence Sherette. She hurried over and slid her arm through the inside of his. "It was wonderful, thoroughly reviving. The boat rocks you like a cradle."

"Ha, ha. That's a nice thought. How is Mrs. Laster? I mean, is she sleeping?"

"I left her like that. I'm sure her nap is incomplete as yet."

"Good. She could use the rest. And what have you done with yourself out here on deck in the meanwhile?"

"I've browsed. Trying to spot something in the sea that I haven't already. Watching the dolphins at play. Look over there." She pointed.

"Yes. A whole colony."

"I wish I had the binoculars that Captain Dolby said Mr. Crutcher is to deliver."

"He'll bring them. And the Captain is right. You'll see things that are amazing. But why should I attempt to tell you as much. With your experience, I really couldn't tell you anything." At this, he asked Sasha to recount her adventure in coming from the Canaries to Corpus Christi with Captain Johansen and she delighted in reliving the most poignant aspects for a solid hour. With excited eyes she dramatically told him of the storm that swept upon their ship and spoke fondly of her living as closely as two peas in a pod with Mrs. Laster during the several days afloat.

"It was there that I really began to love her. Her beautiful soul drew me in. It shone. She became my mother; my real mother would have loved her just as I do and blessed her for promising the good Priest to care for me."

Lawrence Sherette listened with unwavering intent, configuring in his mind that which he had heard, but without responding decided to let the subject pass, substituting for another that he felt might further set her off. But was returned more than he bargained for.

"Did you spot a whale on your excursion? You almost had to."

"No I didn't. Not even one."

"I'm distressed that you didn't."

"Me too. The whale is a remarkable creature." Much to his pleasure, but struck somewhat with surprise, Lawrence Sherette had lucked onto one of her major pursuits of study.

"Have you ever thought about it? The whale is the king of his domain the same as the lion is his, the jungle that is. They're the bosses over their own natural territories. But back to the whale."

"What about him?"

"Many things."

"For instance?"

"Well, in some cases his longevity greatly exceeds that of man, though he's many times heavier and larger. His circulatory system is fairly identical to man's, both species having veins and arteries, and a single heart—unless there's a deformity. I'm unsure about the rate of his heart beat or his suspirations. But I'll see into this. And two or three characteristics more are worthy of mention. He can stay under water several hours without breathing. Though eventually he has to surface for air. Oh yes. He lives in a stable environment. Doesn't seem to rush things. No stress. That's why he lives as long as he does. Or is one of the reasons."

"My goodness. You're a walking medical journal. What else? Anything?"

"Disease and parasites. These aggravations are bad for the poor whale. Tape worms and flukes and such. And according to some writings he suffers or may suffer from bacterial and fungal infections. He may even develop stomach ulcers, skin diseases, and tumors. Scientists even suspect that the whale suffers from diseases of the coronary arteries, the same as humans."

"Ha, ha, ha. You are phenomenal. Where did you learn all this stuff?"

"Books and more books. Particularly those publications specific to a disease or ailments otherwise. Our family doctor back on the Canaries continually fed me with scientific papers of numerous sorts which were released and shipped from England. Sometimes reading from these sources was about all I had to do. So I learned to love it. It fascinated me."

With an impression that she had spoken long enough of the ills of the whale she at once asked Lawrence Sherette to walk around the decking with her, and this they did, meeting and greeting other passengers, but eventually dropped into a nice small tea shop where people were sitting and sipping and chatting happily. Deciding to have tea they went over and took chairs, a waiter not long in approaching, to whom Lawrence Sherette gave their order. The waiter asked if they desired something else besides tea and after looking over at Sasha, her countenance telling him that she did not, the answer was that tea would do. Only shortly after they'd begun to sip Sasha lowered her cup and called across to someone she recognized. His table was next theirs.

"Mr. Crutcher! You are having your tea. I am much surprised to see you."

"Good afternoon Miss Sasha," he offered, exhibiting a bow of politeness as he rose from his chair. "You should not feel surprise. Taking tea at this hour is my everyday ritual. I'm addicted to it you might assume."

"Please join us if you will Mr. Crutcher, or we will sit with you there if it is to your liking."

"Yes please join us," added Lawrence Sherette.

"I will join you, thank you."

"You said you were addicted. I haven't supposed there is an addiction to tea. But on second thought, I am now supposing otherwise, but not as is alcohol or its substitutes," said Sasha.

"Ah but tea addiction is real enough," Mr. Crutcher answered. "Especially if you're a native of England."

"England! The same as Captain Dolby and Mrs. Laster. And Doctor Charlatan. We are covered over with English folks."

"Where in England?" Lawrence Sherette intervened.

"Liverpool. It's a sailor's beehive. It's where I started my career, when I was a straggling sixteen years of age. It was there that I took up with Captain Andrew Dolby."

"You met him there? Was he from that city too?"

"Neither of us were. We had simply drifted there. But he first by a stretch. He was already up the ranks before I arrived, already having attained to Captain of a ship. As an earlier lad Captain Dolby served in the Queen's navy, and with distinction in battle."

"Hmmmm. That catches at me," Lawrence Sherette put in. "How did you gain your employment with him?"

"I went to him and applied in person, he requiring no other application. He hired me after a very quick interview exchange. My first assignment was as a cook's assistant." In an attitude of gratefulness he said that a lad had to expect to begin at this level of apprenticeship, and should be glad in his heart that he was fortunate to receive it.

They had not engaged much longer when Mr. Crutcher reported to Sasha that he had brought her binoculars to her cabin, finding though she wasn't there, but that Mrs. Laster was and feeling that it was perfectly suitable handed them to her.

" Sorry I awakened her from sleep with my knock."

"She did not mind."

"And I delivered at the same time your nice package wrapped in bright red and blue paper."

"Oh indeed. I'm grateful that you did. It's from a very dear friend and I have delayed too long in opening it. I shall very soon."

They continued to sip their tea and busily made talk back and forth, Sasha all the while itchy to try out her binoculars as well as opening her gift from Chenelle, and when deeming it opportune eased from her chair, though imagining she did hastier than the rules of politeness approved, and excused herself, leaving Lawrence Sherette and Mr. Crutcher buried in a miscellany of topics.

When Sasha entered the doorway, Mrs. Laster, seeing there was something jubilant about her, ventured to suppose what it was about and glanced in something of a suggestion at the binoculars and gift package lying on her bed.

"Mr. Crutcher told you didn't he?"

Sasha let out a laugh. "He did, not long ago in the tea shop. I couldn't wait to see them."

Opening the package, she saw the beautiful cake, all four tiers that Chenelle had baked and trimmed for her, which literally oozed with juices. It was cocoanut, one of her favorites.

"Should I slice it now?"

"Why not?"

"But Lawrence Sherette should be here for the occasion too. Don't you think? I'm sure Chenelle would want it that way."

"If you say so sweetheart. Whatever you want to do is fine. It's your cake."

"It will take only a minute. I know exactly where he is. Both he and Mr. Crutcher."

"Mr. Crutcher too?"

"Yes. They're talking, or were when I left them."

"All right. See if they are still there."

She left and was back in the snap of a finger, both gentlemen with her, curiously glancing about for the cake. Mrs. Laster had set it on a side table and laid out napkins. Chenelle had conveniently dropped a knife into the package, thinking they'd open it while on the stage, which Mrs. Laster had found when Sasha was gone. Elevated by the happy atmosphere Sasha began to slice the cake into four rather large pieces, "too large for me," said Mrs. Laster, but the men set no limitation on theirs, and neither did Sasha, although she ate it slowly. When they had finished, Sasha asked if anyone wanted more, receiving the answer that they did not, then she began to rewrap the sizeable amount that was left, commenting that certainly Captain Dolby must by all means have a piece, but would wait until later, perhaps until supper time, before delivering a serving to him.

She sat for the several hours remaining in the afternoon on the deck fixing her binoculars on the seagulls sweeping across her lenses. Though infrequently exposing itself, the stingray was the leading attraction of any sea life at all. But she had seen only two. Now she was stirring around from end to end and side to side of the vessel in quest of spotting another. "These are dangerous creatures," she advised herself, "but are beautifully intriguing as they fly over the water." She carried a piece of her cake to the Captain near the hour of supper though finding that he wasn't to be seen. He was below checking on a piece of equipment, reported the first mate. "Nothing wrong. He's merely doing an inspection. Something routine." Deciding she'd deliver the Captain a piece of her cake the next day, she gave the one she had to the man with a wish for him to enjoy it, "but please tell the Captain I was by and don't forget to explain for what purpose."

"You can be certain that I will Miss."

She promptly left and on returning to her cabin she and Mrs. Laster began to make their way to the passenger's dining room, not the Captain's, where they joined Lawrence Sherette. "Your binoculars, how did they work?"

"Splendid. I love them. I saw a stingray. No, two stingrays. Dangerous fellows if you get in their way."

"I'll agree to that. So you saw only two?"

"Two. But hopefully more tomorrow."

That night as they had settled in for reading and conversing there was a sound of rain starting to fall, the clouds that Sasha had spotted to the south earlier that morning having crept toward the ship and caught up, which was an unwelcome occurrence in that she was determined to climb to the upper deck that evening and view the stars, but that was not to happen. They retired to bed early.

The air was free of clouds the next morning when Sasha awakened and tip toed out which brought a smile to her face. Sitting in one of the gargantuan lounge chairs the previous afternoon she had basked in the rays of the radiant sun and on this day supposed she might take up one of the chairs again directly after breakfast. But the clouds popped up once more, sweeping surprisingly in, which forced her begrudgingly to retire to her room. Nevertheless, at ten o'clock she and Mrs. Laster and Lawrence Sherette decided to brave the rain with the aid of their umbrellas, and promptly went and took seats in the tea shop. No sooner had they gotten settled when Sasha excitedly let out, "Oh, how fortunate. There is Captain Dolby."

"Where?" Mrs. Laster responded. "Where is he?"

"In the corner over there. Someone has his ear. But I'm pretending not to see him."

"I hope he sees you, then you can offer him some of your cake."

"I'd have to run get it, but he wouldn't mind waiting I'm sure. But I am not going to him. He must come here."

"And he will too," ventured Mrs. Laster.

In no time at all Captain Dolby arose from his chair and made his way over. He'd seen them as they entered. The Captain was very good at that. Always on the alert for people, especially those he had recently met.

"Please have a seat with us Captain Dolby," said Mrs. Laster. Lawrence Sherette had moved a chair for him.

"That I will do gladly. Thank you."

Chapter 19

WHEN HE was comfortably seated Sasha thanked him for the binoculars, telling him about the fun she was having with them, and lest she forget it, she said, which would have never happened, she was saving him a piece of cake which she had previously shared with his Mr. Crutcher, hoping that Mr. Crutcher hadn't told him of it before she.

He laughed and informed that Mr. Crutcher had beaten her to him, who had elevated the quality of the cake with very lofty praises.

"Oh dear. Well, if it's all the same Captain Dolby I'll run this minute and bring you a serving."

While she was away Mrs. Laster asked for the day and hour of arrival in New Orleans.

"Tomorrow at near the hour of five. Are there relatives of yours to intercept the *Surety* at the dock?"

"My sister," replied Lawrence Sherette.

As anticipated Sasha was quick to return with the cake and promptly opened the box, then slicing off an uncommonly large piece she placed it on a napkin and handed it to the Captain, but asked him to delay until she secured forks enough for everyone. She did not need to proceed. The waiter, mindful of the presence of his boss, watching with vigilance from his station, hastily moved forward with the utensils and gave them to Sasha who passed them on to Captain Dolby and the rest.

"Thank you Sasha," the Captain said with appreciation.

"Now it is your turn Mrs. Laster and Mr. Sherette; tell me what size."

"Thin, very thin," both replied.

"Ah, but this leaves much untouched."

"May I offer a suggestion?" Mrs. Laster whispered.

"Please."

"There are only five patrons sitting at the table over there, only five. Why not treat them with what is left, which is sizeable?"

"I will. Why did I not think of that myself?"

Upon hearing this, the waiter hastened over with five additional forks, and handed them to Sasha. Taking the utensils she rose and crossed over to the five patrons, all men, who had viewed her serving the Captain and her associates, likely their mouths salivating in wont—it appeared so—and parceled out a cutting for each. She was given their thanks of appreciation as expected, and grinned most fun lovingly when they let go with an applause as she made her way back to her table. The Captain rose and caught her in his arms.

"Well done Sasha. Well done."

She tried to stifle her giggle. Then took to her chair. After a brevity of exchanges among the group Mrs. Laster made mention to Sasha that "Captain Dolby here says we are to arrive at the Port of New Orleans tomorrow afternoon at five."

"Oh! That is outstanding news. Yet, I am mixed. The trip has been most fulfilling and in quite a major way I hate to see it end."

"I too Sasha," said the Captain. But I am always like that. I am on the move constantly, and meet many new faces, which I hate to give up."

"Oh. It suddenly comes to me. May I ask you sir? If you don't mind."

"Not at all."

"Did you ever happen to meet or hear of a Captain Eric Johansen? He was the Captain of the *Ignatius* that brought Mrs. Laster and me to Corpus Christi from the Canary Islands."

He paused and wrinkled his brow. "Captain Johansen I have heard of but have not met. The *Ignatius* is a commonly known name. It is a sailing vessel, soon, I hear, to be replaced by one that is steam powered. Captain Johansen will be thrilled. Is it polite for me to ask why you are making your inquiry?"

"Captain Johansen was asked by a Priest to transport me to Corpus Christi; it was Father Conrad Kestner, a beloved Christian man. At his urging Mrs. Laster agreed to see after me on the voyage. When we landed at Corpus Christi we caught a stage to San Antonio where I met, as preplanned, this dear person here, Lawrence Sherette, who was expecting me. He is my guardian." She declined to tell him that her parents had recently died, determining that there was no significance in transmitting the occurrence to him at that moment.

"I see. You are a lovely girl and I don't know who is the more fortunate for having come across one another, you or them. Equal I shall I say. But let me say this in furtherance of Captain Johansen. I shall watch for him and will tell him that I had an inquiry on his behalf from Sasha Duval. I am assuming strongly that he will receive the news gladly."

"He will. And please relay my best for his good health and happiness."

That afternoon Sasha alternated between her room and the lounging area of the deck, the major fraction of her time spent putting her binoculars to busy use. When supper was over she went to the deck area again, this time to study the stars in the Heavens, and the moon, and the lights of passing ships. You could see so many different things at night time she thought. Lawrence Sherette and Mrs. Laster had come to sit down next to her, and within minutes Mr. Crutcher dropped by and availed himself of a chair. Sasha moved hers close to the railing, choosing this vantage to better see the silver pathway that the moon had cast upon the waters, dancing and rippling, finally dissolving as it swept full against the vessel's siding. She did not then join with the others in their various parleying, preferring to stay silent, wandering back over the hours since leaving San Antonio, speculating of those things in which Father Lumas and Bryon might be immersed at that moment. But soon she brushed these thoughts aside and looked again into the waters, to the north of the vessel where there was a clear visible outline of the land across the distance, the *Surety* never sailing far from shore. There, she detected a colony of lights trickling in the mist, a semblance it struck her, of the ghostly horsemen riding hard toward them when they were on the road traveling toward Corpus Christi. Forgetting about these things too she moved her chair back closer to the others shortly thereafter who were bantering back and forth a score of topics and after listening for a little while yawned and said she was now unfortunately a victim of sleepiness and rose and excused herself. Very soon Mrs.Laster bade goodnight and went to join her.

In early morning, near the hour of four, when Sasha and Mrs. Laster were yet fast asleep, the *Surety* lay anchored not far from the shoreline where a grouping of slaves were transferring a tally of several hundred drums of molasses onto the vessel for distribution in New Orleans. They moved in single file, each pushing a contraption that resembled a wagon of sorts which was used for transporting the valuable cargo. Lawrence Sherette, unable to sleep, had joined Captain Dolby who stood on the lower section supervising the regimen of loading as it pertained to his ship, with Mr. Crutcher helping. The procession of to and fro took place in the glow of lantern light, the slaves sometimes sounding a low rhythmic chant as they advanced at snails pace across the walk board, which was to Lawrence Sherette a scene he had observed times innumerable on Van Doke's La Belle.

"Bondage is bondage, ugly and evil, and is everywhere the same, no matter where you see it," he uttered silently.

"The slaves work on a plantation near here," said the Captain. "There's no port over there off land, therefore the plantation owner brings his commodity in a smaller boat to the *Surety.* They'll wrap up the business of loading in less than an hour, then we'll hoist anchor and start on our way."

Daybreak crept through, yet Sasha and Mrs. Laster slept past breakfast and much beyond. Sasha, upon waking, and in realization that this was their last day of the voyage, jumped out of bed and soon was on deck scanning the freshness of the sea, at once with her binoculars seeing a ship passing between the *Surety* and the shoreline. "A dangerous thing. They could run aground."

Yet the ship was staying well within the range of safety as concluded by the depth markers. Equipped with binoculars themselves, certain of the crew saw Sasha looking their way through hers and began to wave. She burst out laughing and with unrestrained enthusiasm waved back. Seeing her, young Doctor Charlatan, who was on his usual rounds, took it upon himself to drop over. She was about to be on her way back to her cabin she explained. He decided to accompany her, explaining that he was checking on everyone as the Captain had ordered, for there seemed to be a mild outbreak of upset stomachs, some vomiting occurring. As it happened there were only three such illnesses and these persons were confined to their room. It was later discovered that they had eaten sandwiches of their own making which were excessively held over. When they got to the cabin where Sasha and Mrs. Laster were staying Sasha opened the door and they went in, the doctor briefly going into why he was there with Mrs. Laster. Shortly he half concluded and half surmised.

"No trouble here, I presume."

"None doctor," replied Mrs. Laster.

"Is it a bacteria? asked Sasha, "or perhaps a case of seasickness that is only now taking hold?"

"Don't think its seasickness because the people who are ill are all together in the same suite. If their proximity to one another was not clear, then I'd be theorizing what you're intimating. But a bacteria is at the root of it all and thank goodness its effect is mild."

"We'll keep our fingers crossed that we don't fall victim ourselves," Mrs. Laster remarked.

"I'm with you there. I'm keeping my fingers crossed for myself. I always do. But I think I'm immune, or at least somewhat."

"Dr. Charlatan," Sasha intervened, starting with an inquiry which had been revolving at the moment he entered the doorway, "may I have a word with you that extends beyond our present subject, but in a way is relevant to it?"

"I'm your guest. I'm pleased to accommodate."

"Suppose sir, in the case of a severe disease, let us say smallpox, that the parents take ill, but their offspring, a young person of about my age is left unaffected. Why would she escape the sickness?"

"She was exposed. Is that correct?"

"Yes."

"I think I see where you're aiming, which is, was the young girl born with an immunity?"

"That is my question precisely."

"I see. But I cannot say. She could have acquired an immunity through an earlier mild case of the disease, but that seems unlikely since she did not know about it. I'm assuming she did not. I'll have to read into the journals where I hope to discover an explanation, but I think I'll emerge mostly with theory. By the way, why did you happen to ask about this dreadful complexity?"

"I am not long from the Canary Islands Dr. Charlatan where my mother and father perished from smallpox without the faintest of the illness showing up in my system. I am greatly curious that it did not."

"Naturally. But I cannot even hint of the answer, though I'll give you the orthodox explanation. You, like a precious few others, surely have a strong constitution for withstanding illness. Perhaps of the many forms and classes. Your body may elaborate its own immunity. But if it does we do not yet understand the mechanics of the process."

They once more ate at the Captain's table, the invitees not as many as the first time, some simply uninvited, while others declined because they were resting or still others preparing their belongings for unloading when arriving at the port of disembarkation. Seeing Sasha sitting by an empty chair when he entered, Doctor Charlatan proceeded directly to it and promptly sat down.

"Ah, pot luck Sasha. You are the person that I'd rather be sitting by than anyone else in this whole room, and so now I am."

Sasha, a little embarrassed by his flattery, exuded a nice laugh. Lawrence Sherette laughed too, for he felt profoundly happy when someone said something to her that was uplifting, and was especially glad when they began to converse on the topic of medicine of which Doctor Charlatan seemed vastly informed and in which she was vastly entwined.

"France," the young doctor proclaimed, "is the most prominent center on the continent for medical instruction of life science investigation. There, an understanding of human anatomy is well developed."

"Is such information published? I've not run across it in print. But my doctor on the Canaries said something of it once or twice. Please go on."

"Well, to further my thoughts allow me to report that Parisian hospitals have for some time been affecting a revolution in medicine; for instance, combining careful post mortem reexaminations of diseased patients with the clinical descriptions of their disease during life."

"Doctors are getting to be very specific that tells me."

"I'd say. And it's not accepted with open arms among general practitioners, who feel they'll lose patients to the specialists."

"And they will."

"Yes. But that's for the better. After all, they exist for the good of their patients, not for themselves."

"That is the way you see it."

"Absolutely. Even though I am a general practitioner myself. But I intend to pursue specialty studies in hopes of becoming a surgeon."

"Where will you study? Will you return to France or to England?"

"One of the two, yet in the meanwhile I will sit in on all the lectures that I can stuff myself with. As a matter of fact I will attend one in New Orleans. We plan to stay over there for three days."

"And who is the lecturer?"

"A noted man whose last name is Bonveniuve. I've forgotten his first, but I have it in my files."

"And what is his specialty?"

"Surgery. He's one of the leaders in the field today in Europe."

"I wish I could be there," she remarked wishfully, and upon hearing this, Lawrence Sherette spoke up that he didn't see why she couldn't.

"Could she tag along Doctor Charlatan? We will transport her to wherever it is the doctor is to appear."

"Certainly. The lectures are open to the public, although doctors are generally the only ones present. Tell you what. We're staying at the Hotel St. Charles where the talks are given, plus some anatomical displays by professionals of a lesser standing. But Doctor Bonveniuve will comment on these too. The lecture will commence day after tomorrow at thirty minutes of two."

When the St. Charles Hotel was opened in 1837 it quickly became the scene of endless business and social functions, a mecca of luxury, to say the least, and during the years that followed, it was the favorite place for balls and banquets and the meeting and lodging center for planters, and politicians, and medical professionals of many genres, including those from foreign soils.

The afternoon flew by, the voyage nearly over. They were approaching the bay, Sasha, Mrs. Laster and Lawrence Sherette standing together on deck vigilantly absorbing the spectacle. With dusk closing in Captain Dolby had relieved his first mate at the helm and had begun to steer the ship toward portside. The air was rank and thick, the fog having settled in, and seeing was now harder. Lantern lights were everywhere. The crews of the guide boats who had helped navigate them into the bay were now more careful than ever, edging the heavy vessel inch by inch to dockside. Suddenly the movement ceased, then there was an outbreak of busy chatter among the dock workers and the steersmen of the guide boats, a cacophony of various tongues, but despite their discordant speech they were a team knitted together whose job was to complete the entirety of the tasks (the tying down of the ship, letting down the walk board, the transporting of baggage, assisting passengers, unloading freight, other things innumerable) which called for precise and unfailing back and forth communications.

"Where is Adelaide?" Sasha cried out, peering down at the crowd.

"She's around. As soon as we descend the walk board and touch our feet to the docking platform she'll spot us and yell out. Right now she's watching with eyes wide open."

There was a porter working the dock area that was about to begin portaging their clothes and other belongings, but in response to the instructions issued from Captain Dolby, Mr. Crutcher had joined in to help and supervise. Meanwhile, Lawrence Sherette was staying close to Captain Dolby to whom he spoke with more than common zeal that he simply must meet Adelaide. Captain Dolby said that the crowd must clear first, but that afterwards he would be delighted to meet his sister.

"Will she have a carriage parked around close for transporting you and your group, that is to say, Sasha and Mrs. Laster?"

"Ah, to be sure."

The docking platform was heavily enshrouded in fog and this obstruction in combination with the lantern glow forced a blurring of any and all objects in view, whether moving or motionless. Adding to the erratic chatter erupting from the dock crews, a sizeable many of African Haitian and Creole descent, there was suddenly a piercing blast of a fog horn rising from a ship anchored a little further down, to which Sasha responded by pulling her tam over her ears, her dark eyes looking up at Lawrence Sherette, wincing and smiling simultaneously. The commotion of everything thrown together made for a strange and unsettling atmosphere.

The chatter of the dock crews was worst, sounding of a language completely foreign to Sasha and Mrs. Laster.

"Who are these people?" Mrs. Laster asked of Captain Dolby who had moved close to her.

"They're Haitians; formerly they were Africans. The French transported these people to Haiti for growing sugar cane. The white French plantation owners had offspring by the African women, maybe marrying them, I don't know, who became known as Mulattoes. What you hear is a language known as Creole, the result of this intermixing. Or likely many other mixes. Creole is a hodgepodge."

"It's a very strange language. I don't see how anyone could understand it."

"Their bosses do."

Chapter 20

ADELAIDE STOOD close to where the people were stepping off the walk board. Wearing a nice shiny black coat, because the weather was cool, she tapped her companion on his arm, asking him to stay alert to single out a tall handsome man most likely toting an encasement, as well as wearing a coat heavy enough to keep himself sufficiently warm in the coolness of the evening.

"And oh yes, two women will be with him, a young girl and a lady of about forty."

"I understand. I'll watch. It's good you have the taxi carriage waiting close by."

"Yes it is."

With Captain Dolby on his right and Sasha and Mrs. Laster on his heels Lawrence Sherette had slowly made his way down the walk board and landed, there stepping out into the open. Adelaide saw him.

"There they are."

"Where?"

"Over there," she answered, at the same time beginning to hasten toward her brother, and he seeing her clearing from the crowd also ran to her, picking her up in his arms and kissing her cheeks all over. Sasha watched with fascination.

"His sister, his sister. That's Adelaide."

"You made it," said Adelaide, "you made it, and almost on schedule. It's fantastic to see you."

"Same here sweetheart."

All had gathered around them at this juncture, Captain Dolby, Mr. Crutcher, Dr. Charlatan, Mrs. Laster, and Sasha, and upon taking notice Adelaide almost let out a whoop, "My, I don't know these people. They must be a part of your entourage Lawrence."

"Indeed they are, and introductions are in order. Since I have more with me than you, I'll take the lead. That okay?"

"You bet."

"All right. Adelaide this is Captain Dolby, who guided us safely here, and this is Dr. Charlatan who kept us well and healthy, and this is Mr. Crutcher, who made certain that we stayed on schedule while we were aboard, and didn't let our things get scattered."

The Captain laughed aloud. "That was quite a splashy introduction, but very good. We appreciate it."

"But I haven't finished. Mrs. Laster and Sasha are standing in wait."

"So you haven't. Why did I not catch myself? Shame on me. I am embarrassed. Please finish."

"No need for embarrassment Captain Dolby. In my profession I err every time I turn around it seems. Well, any way, this is Mrs. Edweena Laster, Adelaide, and lastly here in front of me is Sasha Duval."

"I am tremendously glad to meet each of you."

Sasha, in the lantern glow looked beguilingly beautiful. Despite herself, trying with all her being to stay concentrated on the introductions, Adelaide had drawn a bead on her as soon as her brother brought her into view. The revolutions of Adelaide's brain were beginning swiftly to spin.

"My Good Lord in Heaven, she is a thing of enchantment and as charming as a lily flower. I am certain this is the Sasha I've heard about, that I'm not dreaming, but I am bowled over. She is of the purest of whiteness. Why did Lawrence not write me of this? But naturally, that did not matter, nor does it matter to me now, although I am just slightly evading shock. I will ask him of this at the first chance but for the time being I am to demonstrate a calm and placid impression."

There had been a trace in Adelaide's countenance of what she was sifting through, and Lawrence Sherette, watching and anticipating, caught every tiny spec, with Adelaide realizing he had. The group started lightly into conversation, and kept at it until at length Adelaide taking control said she hated to disrupt a fine and lively gathering but that she figured everyone was anxious to settle in for the evening.

"Remember Sasha," spoke Doctor Charlatan with a reminder, "we are staying at the Hotel St. Charles. Don't forget the lecture series."

"I will not forget. Believe me. Thank you for mentioning it."

This said, the respective groups, Adelaide's and Captain Dolby's, bade goodnight and began separating, with Adelaide explaining to her brother that her friend had driven his own rig, which was to haul their clothes and other appurtenances, and that she figured the taxi carriage could accommodate her, the driver, and the two other women. "You will ride with my friend Lawrence."

"That's quite suitable. But what is your friend's name? And where is he?"

"His name is Harry Lancaster. We omitted him from the original introductions, but please, let's everyone consider that done now." She motioned to Harry to step forward, who had appropriately stood aside while the introductions were taking place, but within earshot. She pointed to Harry and then to the others. Captain Dolby and his associates had already walked away.

"Just one thing more Adelaide," said Lawrence Sherette. "I need to double check the address of our house. We might lose ourselves from you."

"Ha. You joke. Imagine Harry not knowing where it is. He's been there every day for two straight weeks. But you should have the address anyway. It's 1004 St. Charles Street, on out for some distance, quite removed from the downtown hustle and bustle."

Climbing into the carriages they were off. The house that Adelaide had leased lay ten blocks east up St. Charles Street, which at that time was somewhat away from downtown, for which Adelaide was thankful because the core of the city featured more than a lively behavior as the curtain of nighttime fell. She guardedly refrained from saying as much in Sasha's midst, but in private, in the company of Mrs. Laster, alluded to New Orleans as a "veritable city of bawdiness," yet added that perhaps it was the nation's best for entertainment and fine cuisine. When the horses had drawn them over the course of a full ten blocks, each block seeming to reflect bigger and finer homes, the drivers pulled them to a halt, Harry Lancaster calling out, "This is it." Sasha at once looked around, discovering they were now in a neighborhood of unmistakable opulence. "Is this where we'll live?"

"Yes darling. This is our house," answered Adelaide.

The house they were about to enter belonged to a prominent cotton planter with whom both Alelaide and Harry were acquainted, most especially Harry, for the gentlemen had to route his cotton sales through him, an attorney and an international cotton broker. Harry was actually the one that found and contracted for the house on behalf of Adelaide. The cotton planter owned and managed a slave plantation upstate from the city on the delta soils, starting ten miles east of the banks of the Mississippi River then going westward until reaching the great river's shoreline. The gentleman was on tour of the East Coast with his wife, of New York City in particular, the Ole Mammy keeping the children, which she customarily did irrespective of the whereabouts of the parents. Adelaide, through Harry, had negotiated legal use of the residence for three and one half months, subject to an extension, but not guaranteed. The house reached two stories high, which decidedly caught Sasha's fancy and forced a sigh, with a preponderance of windows staring out at the viewer from all four sides, the upstairs inclusive. Its styling was French, with an admixture of old Southern charm woven into the fringes. The influence of the French appeared prominently in the richly painted murals of the interior. Adelaide took extra pains to point out their very bright and varied colors, determined not to let such features go unnoticed. But she had to explain the presence of a few illustrated scenes of Italy, which seemed a bit out of character to Harry.

"Adelaide," he emphasized, "why Italy? New Orleans is French through and through."

"I agree Harry. The choice is unexpected, though to obtain an explanation that survives the test of scrutiny, you should consult the owner of this dwelling, or his interior decorator. It's my best however that it's because he's Italian."

Family portraits sprang plentifully forth to enliven the room, and most all other spaces throughout. There was a portrait of the first governor of Mississippi hanging from the wall of the drawing room and when they made their way to the much larger and grander space of the living room the young lady in the evening dress, the wealthy cotton planter's oldest daughter, a vision of beauty, inspired them to utter the most exalting compliments. The hallway was square in configuration, the wall paper delineating several scenes of the South, with a female slave in one of them carrying a naked baby in one arm while skillfully balancing a water jar on her head. Lawrence Sherette conjectured that she was an import from the West Indies. In one room that lead to the side portico there was the counterfeit face of an ancestor of some years ago about whom Harry offered the witticism that she had to have the emotions of a box of hammers when she was alive, to which Sasha and Lawrence Sherette virtually cackled. Adelaide and Mrs. Laster were only slightly less subdued. The monstrously large dining table would have dwarfed the room that housed it were the room of common dimensions but it was not. It too was monstrous. This was where they were to dine that evening; Adelaide had planned on it, and had prepared a range of casseroles, hoping that among them Sasha might find one, if not a few, arousing and pleasurable to her taste. The following evening they were to eat out at Antoine's, a fairly new establishment to the scene, but becoming already renowned. As it happened a full week was to pass before they crossed through its doors. As usual, Sasha was a tad reserved, but paid high compliments to the food, as did all others, all helping their plates with servings sufficient in diversity and amounts to support their praising and after awhile moved to the living room where Harry began to take up the history of the city. Born in New Orleans, but springing from Irish immigrants, was something of an irony since there was not one sign of an Irish accent in his speech. He aimed a great deal of his commentaries at Sasha, thinking that she, young and unschooled of the city, would in particular like the intrigue of its history.

"Sasha, New Orleans was founded in 1718 by the French. It was called Nouvelle Orleans. The city was named in honor of the Regent of France, Phillip II, Duke of Orleans."

"Nouvelle Orleans certainly is a romantic name. I'm sure that Phillip II was pleased that someone had graced him with the honor."

"Hmmm. I wonder. I doubt that he ever saw this place but if he did, the honor in his eyes was surely quite suddenly diminished."

"Why is that sir?"

"Well, I'm in an attitude of merriment here tonight, but perhaps not far from the truth about things on which I reflect. This place was largely claimed by swampy marshes when the French inhabited it. One of the Priests early on the scene described it as 'a hundred wretched hovels in a malarious wet thicket of willows and dwarf palmettos, infested by serpents and alligators.'"

"My Good Lord! That sounds terrible! But New Orleans has greatly changed since that time."

"Very much Sasha. Maybe it was because the Priest went on to predict for Nouvelle Orleans an imperial future. After all, it is now spoken of by many as a magnificent city. And to me it is. Naturally I'm biased. I was born here."

"But your parents weren't, I presume," Lawrence Sherette followed.

"No, they weren't. They were immigrants. Irish folks. Hard workers. The Irish still flock to these shores in droves. You saw them on the dock tonight, although I'm afraid that among the frenzied wild chatter, the unintelligible Creole jibber jabber going on, you couldn't sort them out, but they were there. They're workers, those Irish. They'll do anything to earn a dollar, a sizeable number beginning to replace the slave hands, on the docks quite plainly, and especially on the levees where danger is poised at every step."

"The slaves are afraid to work out there. Is that it?"

"No, not really. A slave is too valuable for the owner to run the risk. If his property is suddenly killed, swept down the river let us envision, his loss is huge. He could have sold him for a pretty fancy amount. Better to have had him on the plantation in the cotton fields. If the Irishman is suddenly wiped out his loss means nothing. He was simply a day worker. No one had an investment in him."

With his continuance of the old city until half past ten, along with not a few other stories, some of them yore, Harry stood and spoke warmly of having been among such good company, then Adelaide accompanied him to the door and bade goodnight.

"He's a nice fellow and a lively interesting talker, well versed on the city apparently and its varied background," said Lawrence Sherette.

"I'd say," agreed his sister. He's a trusted friend and has helped me tremendously in the cotton trade. If a speculator is shorting me Harry will see it and be quick to straighten the man out."

The hour was pressing toward eleven, the yawns beginning to show. They'd had a full day. Adelaide remarked that it was bedtime and began to assign rooms, telling Mrs. Laster and Sasha that there was one upstairs they could share or that there were others for separate use in the house elsewhere. Looking at Mrs. Laster, her inner thoughts riding to the surface, Sasha smiled and said that they'd prefer to share the room upstairs. Mrs. Laster echoed the same, then Adelaide led them up the stairway to the second floor, the steps of which were of Southern pine timber that shone as if freshly polished. The bed fashioned a high back head board, the carvings exquisitely flawless, hand made by a master craftsman. There was a lovely golden coverlet which was partially rolled back. Adelaide was at the root of this, and had set out a vase of flowers which rested on a side table nearby. Sasha smiled at the painting of a little girl of three or four clad in an expensive white dress with ruffles at the shoulders, wearing on her tiny feet a set of shiny black slippers. She cradled a large doll in her arms which obviously was why her eyes sparkled. Sasha pulled back the window tapestries, there looking out into the night at the flickering lights creeping around the bend of the mighty Mississippi. These were steamers, traveling both north and south, loaded with raw cargo and people.

"Are you tired dear?" asked Mrs. Laster. "I'm sure you are."

"Some. But I've loved everything. I can't believe what all we've seen and done today."

Lying down, they began to retrace the evening, Sasha lavishing heaps on Adelaide, who she said was the sweetest and gentlest thing; she too liked Harry, she said, a thoroughly entertaining man to be around. "I wonder if they are serious about one another."

"I think they're only good friends."

Minutes passed and then a half hour without Sasha blinking an eye, which wasn't like her. And neither had Mrs. Laster. But Mrs. Laster was given to requiring an extended period before falling of to sleep.

"Are you thinking of something that's keeping you awake? You don't seem to be drifting off very easily."

"I'm thinking."

"What are you thinking?"

"That I must write a letter to my dear ones, Father Kestner and Father Lumas. I don't know who first. But I think it should be Father Kestner. It has been longer since I saw him."

"Yes, that's a good idea."

"But I think I'll wait and learn more of New Orleans before writing either because then I can add to what I say."

"I agree dear. I think that's a good idea too. Now, let's try to go to sleep," Mrs. Laster hugged her and said goodnight.

ଓ ଛ

Lawrence Sherette and his sister were the last to turn in, but before that however they sat down for a last minute retracing of the day passed, she on the sofa and he in a high back close to her. As far as she was concerned there was but a singular topic to explore, the clarification regarding Sasha. She looked at her brother and smiled a smile as if to speak, "Now come clean. Why did you not tell me by letter that she was lily white?" But Lawrence read her smile and led off.

"My beloved. I saw your face when you first set eyes on her. You were stunned just as I when she appeared before me at Father Lumas's Rectory breakfast table. He'd told me nothing in advance and to this day he hasn't, nor have I asked him, because I knew how he saw her, God's child, born as she was for a purpose, which no human mortal, and certainly not I, could begin to understand."

"I see dear brother, and it would be terribly wrong if I had a view about her one way or the other, and I don't. As you say, she is God's child, but she is a lovely thing, no matter how it happened. I loved her immediately when my eyes fell upon her. She in addition to her beauty is endowed of a bearing which is obviously rare and that also affected me."

"You see it at first glance, don't you?"

"Yes you do, something of a sublimity of character, let me add, which is exceedingly hard to describe but you recognize it. It's there. I suppose the easy thing to do is to ascribe such prominence to the genes of her parents and let it go at that. You knew them well didn't you?"

"I was Albert Duval's friend for a long while, several years, but was acquainted with his wife Izu only briefly. I seldom saw her after their marriage. When I did she was quiet and reserved, and showed manners and mien of, of, well, of a kind of nobility, I guess I should put it. But how did I know, and I never did, for Albert made no mention of her lineage that suggested she was of lofty strain, and certainly she did not mention anything of the kind herself during the few times I was around her. As I've said, she was quiet of nature, or was in my presence."

"I can't help it Lawrence, so please forgive me, but why did Albert not write you about his daughter?"

"Well, he didn't. And I shall suppose that his decision not to was because he was of a bent that coincided with Father Lumas's. To say it another way, it didn't matter."

"And I agree. It doesn't matter, not an iota."

"But my dear sister, you are likened to me. You wonder, as I wondered, how the genetic process machinated in such a way as to yield a person with at least some degree of Negro strain but with the whitest of pigmentation. The answer is that I am insufficiently prepared to offer a treatise on the causations. I can only report that I have seen it before."

"Ah yes. And so have I."

"And one thing more, my dear, and what I have to express applies to the both of us."

'And what is that?" she asked with a searching countenance.

"You say she is lovely, and she is. She is stunningly lovely. And she is God's child, which we say as well. But if she were ugly, would we love her as much then, if at all? I am bothered by what I think is the answer."

"Do not be Lawrence, for she is here, just as she is. That's how it was meant. No need to think about anything else. I wouldn't change her for anything even if I could. I am only thankful that God has sent her to us."

Chapter 21

"BETTER GET up. It's ten o'clock," called out Adelaide as she poked her head through the doorway into Sasha's and Mrs. Laster's room, then went to Sasha's bedside and playfully mashed her beautiful head into her pillow, arousing a giggle. "A culinary breakfast tradition is coming up. It's virtually ready."

They arose without hesitation, dressing as fast as their nimble fingers could proceed. The sun was trying to pour through the window and as Sasha opened the curtains it swept suddenly onto her face, to which she responded by raising her hand to cover her eyes. When she had composed herself her thoughts suddenly broke away to the lecture at one thirty, and asked, "Who all is going? When should we leave?"

"We three, and we'll need to leave at one o'clock." answered Adelaide, who had sat waiting in one of the high backs. "Lawrence Sherette would attend the lecture too but he has to spend his day at the St. Louis Cathedral; he's intimated that he'd like for our driver to drop him off as we pass it by. The Cathedral is situated along the street that leads to the Hotel St. Charles." Lawrence Sherette would take a carriage back to their residence after his work, but expected to arrive late because much was on his agenda. Additionally, he indicated that he was soon to start staying at the Cathedral quarters at night part of the time. The Archbishop was making arrangements.

The breakfast was a hodgepodge, or so deduced Sasha and Mrs. Laster when Adelaide enumerated the ingredients which was an acute departure from the sausage and eggs and toast to which they'd become accustomed while on the ship. Creole cuisine was the featured dish, said Adelaide, possessing an incomparable succulent taste, a concoction enjoyed in the homes of well to do aristocrats, or those who imitated their lifestyle. It had evolved on the country plantation estates so beloved by the pre Civil War Creoles. Adelaide had partially learned to prepare the dish in Paris while taking a whole two months off from her studies in England. But she needed supplemental tutoring; consequently, Harry as of late had brought to her an Ole Mammy who was regarded as the best in the circumference of New Orleans at cooking the delicacy. Adelaide was determined to become expert and finally felt she had almost succeeded. Yet had not become as proficient at the art as the Ole Mammy whose skill she realized she would never equal.

"Mind you, despite its aristocratic roots," she said, "Creole cuisine does not include Garde Manger or other extremely lavish styles of the classical Paris cuisines."

Sasha had waited patiently but finally lost her resistance at holding back. "What are the ingredients?"

"Oh yes. We are at that very place. Among a host of others, hot peppers, rice, beans, tomatoes, pasta, cheese, onions, citrus juice marinades, fresh sliced pork—but the finesse of meshing all this together and bringing everything to a precise temperature at the right time, even stirring and turning it at the right time, I cannot reveal, my sweet dear, but before long I'll let you watch me; and if that doesn't do, then I'll ask the Ole Mammy herself to come over and give you her personal teaching lesson."

"And with so many ingredients compressed into one, one, oh what is it you say, one dish," Mrs. Laster spoke up, "would you contend that your creation is alone likened to no other?"

"Heavens no. It is a potpourri, a blend of many cultures, I'm the first to admit. Let me say that Louisiana Creole cuisine is a style of cooking that originated in Louisiana to be sure, with New Orleans as the center, where in an unintended way many recipes kind of wax together in tiny unrecognized fragments. Why? Well, they just do. In fine, New Orleans is the melting pot that blends French, Spanish, Canarian, Caribbean, Mediterranean, Deep Southern American, Indian, and African influences. That is what is generally said around this domain. And I think there is a touch of all these influences here on this delightful platter that awaits you. So get ready to thoroughly entertain yourselves."

The portico completely surrounded the house, a grand design with massive columns that upheld it, a place where people could sit and watch the traffic busily moving up and down the street. Near the noon hour Sasha left for the outside and began to wander around. She was dressed already for their departure to the lecture. Shortly, Adelaide and Mrs. Laster went outside too, taking a seat in one of the many rockers that the plantation owner kept in use for his family and guests, there engaging in chit chat until one o'clock. They had decided to leave at that hour in allowance of sufficient time for sight seeing. Unable to sit still for long, Sasha every once in awhile got up and walked around the portico, sometimes skipping, sometimes stopping to reach around one of the portico columns, there clasping her fingers together, and in an air of gaiety letting herself lean backward a slight, her beautiful hair falling loosely downward. Seeing this, Adelaide laughed amusedly and reckoned her as a charming budding Southern Belle, but further reasoned that it was an unseemly transition indeed for someone from the far away Spanish Canaries.

The carriage arrived late, but by only a fraction; there was a mix up in schedule, the driver reported, who had proceeded to the portico steps, with Adelaide relaying to him that there was no need for apology, then they rose from their chairs and climbed in. Adelaide instructed the man to tour them around for awhile, with her guiding him as to the streets and sights that she adjudged enticing to her party, and to drop them off at the hotel when she informed him the tour was finished. From there, he was to transport Lawrence Sherette to the St. Louis Cathedral.

Sasha zealously copied notes of everything along the way and as she looked them over that night in her bedroom she would recount that they had visited Orleans Street, then Jackson Square, then Camp and Chartres Streets, then Antoine's and had also ridden down Canal Street to the levee.

Doctor Charlatan met them in the hotel lobby and hurriedly escorted them to the lecture hall where Doctor Bonveniue was just beginning to start his address. The doctor had an array of charts and drawings on the lectern before him to support his presentation but hardly alluded to them, depending largely on his own words and memory to explain and emphasize. It should be said that a full account cannot be provided of his every topic, which would amount to a prodigious length; thus what is here given is an abbreviation, trusting that a nibble of the whole will suffice. The doctor would be specious in the time allotted to each topic, avoiding anything of great detail he fore cautioned, yet this proved not the case because his lecture range extended to the hour of five, with but twenty minutes for recess woven in.

Taking up the subject of appendectomies first, he predicted near the finish that a long while was to pass, years in fact, before researchers and doctors could release positive findings with respect to a surgical cure or alleviation of this illness, that it was dangerously risky, stating as well that more studies of the anatomy of patients who live and die was seriously underway, and needed, and that hopefully more progress might result significantly beyond his current outlook.

Next he turned to broken and smashed extremities resulting from obviously dangerous work jobs, which he stressed were often avoidable with the proper vigilance, and injuries incurred on the battlefield which were hardly avoidable at all. He concentrated on resetting the bones, where broken, and cleaning and disinfecting damaged tissue and sewing it neatly back to its original shape as much as could be. "Now, the chief worry with seriously injured bodily parts is infections, but the worst of the infections I should say, is gangrene. Let us delve into the definition, symptoms, and treatment of this ominous intruder, turning to the causes of it as we proceed further. Gangrene is the death of body tissue due to the loss of blood supply to that tissue, sometimes permitting bacteria to invade it and accelerate its decay. There are three major types of gangrene: dry, moist, and gas.

Dry gangrene is a condition that results when one or more arteries become obstructed. In this type of gangrene, the tissue slowly dies, due to receiving little or no blood supply, but does not become infected. The damaged area becomes cold and black, begins to dry out and wither, and eventually drops off over a period of weeks or months. Dry gangrene is most common in persons with advanced blockages of arteries.

Moist gangrene may occur in the toes, feet, or legs after a crushing injury or as a result of some other factor that causes blood flow to the area to suddenly stop. When blood flow ceases, bacteria begin to invade the muscle and thrive, multiplying quickly without interference from the body's immune system.

Gas gangrene is a type of gangrene that is commonly caused by bacterial infection with Clostridium welchii, or other species that are capable of thriving under conditions where there is little oxygen. Once present in tissue, these bacteria produce gasses and poisonous toxins as they grow. Normally inhabiting the gastrointestinal, respiratory, and female genital tract, they often tend to infect high amputation wounds, especially those individuals who have lost control of their bowel functions."

Upon completing a topic the doctor made it practice to pause for an interval, looking around over the audience, his glasses hanging half down on his nose, but not inviting questions, then sipped from a glass of water and moved on. During these interludes Sasha found herself highly desirous of making inquiries of the man, for his commentaries had captured her imagination, yet she held back, keeping the question alive until she might pursue it with Doctor Charlatan.

"Now I shall deal with disorders of head injuries which are the most difficult to understand of any part of the body, because they involve the brain, and are the most dangerous to the patient because of the delicacy of the brain itself. So here I shall have to stay most limited and acknowledge that we have just begun to pioneer. 'Hippocrates pointed out that injuries to the head could cause sensory and motor disorders and Galen included head injuries among the major causes of mental disorders.' The question becomes centered on whether surgery can be performed in such a case to effectively correct the damage and restore the patient to good health. In the era of Hippocrates and Galen, which was a long while ago, experimental surgery was attempted to make these corrections but in my opinion with little success. The patient usually ended up dying. But there is an instance that is far more modern which fits these disorders, with the outcome astonishing, and perhaps successful. In any event, let me share it with you. An accident occurring in one of the Napoleonic battles involved a canon blast that threw a rod of some sort through the face and head of a soldier. A large section of the skull was entirely torn away and later replaced and in time there appeared a deposit of new bone partially closing it over. The surgery was, it seems, a success but I cannot speak of the state of the patient's mental stability afterwards, for no affirmation is supplied in the journals.

I can see that we have visitors with us today, mothers among them I am sure. And my next remarks regard you, greatly so, for I am touching on the subject of boils and the lancing of these festerings, which you can do at home, and often must, although that worries me because of the danger of infection. But you can minimize infection by keeping the area around the boil clean. Please use lots of soap and warm water. Constantly laying a steamy cloth over the boil will help it come to a head faster. A boil generally takes four to seven days to form a head. Once this happens, you can lance it. But first, clean, clean, clean. This applies to the needle also, which you should sterilize by application to a flame or by dropping it in a cauldron of water that has been elevated to a very high temperature. Brace yourself because lancing a boil hurts. Now, you are ready. Carefully insert the tip of the needle into the center of the pus in the head of the boil. You shouldn't have to penetrate very deeply. Now, gently squeeze the boil to force out the pus. You're done. But the opening might continue to ooze for a day or two."

The lecture ended thirty minutes afterwards, with little time left for Adelaide and others to fraternize other than to find a side nook close by and briefly indulge in refreshments. They opted to a restaurant less than medium size just off the lobby, a busy place, and crowded, but cozy, that served food of many varieties, but no one was in wont of food. They'd settle for refreshments. Doctor Charlatan helped the ladies with their chairs. Sasha sat next to him, quickly bringing up a question that she'd held in since the middle of the lecture that afternoon. It was when was one to tell when an amputation was necessary due to a gangrenous condition, a dilemma that Doctor Bonveniue did not address. If he did it did not come across clearly, she surmised, and when she finally asked it of Doctor Charlatan he returned that becoming familiar with the symptoms as laid out by Doctor Bonveniue was the best a doctor could do, though contending that some doctors were better at making good and accurate diagnoses than others.

The waiter approached and took their orders. While he was away Mrs. Laster asked when Captain Dolby's ship was leaving port, the answer arising from Doctor Charlatan that the Captain had informed him they'd leave at ten the following morning, then Adelaide spoke that they'd be there to say good bye. The dock workers and travelers would be scurrying about she knew, making it difficult to spot the Captain and his entourage, but that they'd single them out.

"This is a busy restaurant I must say," commented the doctor, changing the subject as he looked around. "All of New Orleans is. I've heard that the population here doubled in the 1830's and that by 1840 this was the wealthiest and third most populous city in the nation. Makes me think I ought to set up office on this very street and start practicing."

"That would be nice," Adelaide followed, "but you'd become vibrantly busy with patients and making money, to the extent that we'd never be able to sit down with you just as we are now."

"No I wouldn't. I wouldn't let myself get that busy. But I'll bet that sounds like doctor's talk doesn't it?"

"Ha, ha, ha." Adelaide couldn't resist. "A tad."

Leaving the hotel, Adelaide, with Sasha and Mrs. Laster at her side, summoned a carriage driver close by, one among many, but he was nearest and she thought she knew him. Within a second she was sure she did. Harry had brought her to the larger restaurant, the restaurant elite at the hotel only nights before, and had taken his carriage. Then, as currently, a low soft felt hat was arrayed atop his head with the crown shaped into a narrow pointed crease.

"Chickery."

"Ah, Madame Adelaide, it's you," he exclaimed with a cheery air, lifting his hat. "Can I transport you and your party somewhere?"

"Yes you may. We'll be delighted to ride in your carriage."

With his help, they promptly climbed in, Adelaide giving directions to the man to crossover to Chartres Street and pass by Woodlief's, a leading store in the vicinity, also promising Sasha and Mrs. Laster they'd shop there at some convenient hour within the week. Chickery was a freed slave astutely in command of the French language. He was curious if they by chance were on their way to visit Bourbon Street that evening, Adelaide replying that no they weren't, that her guests were of a kind that would never pay call on that quadrant of downtown after dark unless fully and properly chaperoned.

"I understand Madame."

"As you well know Chickery, Bourbon Street has earned a reputation. I haven't told my guests about the favorite motto of the bourbonites yet, but it's very fitting."

"And what is that Madame Adelaide?"

"*Laissez les bon temps rouler.*"[2]

"Oh! Ha, ha, ha, ha, ha, ha. How correct you are. I am most familiar with it."

Sasha, also versed in the language of the French began to laugh with them.

Requiring little time in which to accomplish the distance Chickery drove past Woodlief's, which obviously was an enterprise of much heralded prominence and one had to conclude that its principal patrons were those of substantial wealth. This finished, he opted to Canal Street before angling over to St. Charles and then to their residence.

"Can I be of assistance in helping you ladies up the steps?"

"No thank you Chickery. But we appreciate your kindness anyway."

"Thank you Madame and goodnight to you all."

Harry was fond of Chickery. He had known him for a long while, even before he was freed, and considered him as his trusted friend, and told Adelaide how on his own, with some minor tutoring, he quickly became well educated. Despite its dealing with the slave trade, New Orleans in the proximity of this period had the largest and most prosperous community of free persons in the nation, who were often educated and middle class owners of property and businesses. Chickery, a man of craft and subtlety, quick on his feet, but with goodness and honesty in his heart, was one of these. Aside from his taxi business he and his brother operated a flower shop.

"He's the one who drives the elite around town," Harry had once said to Adelaide. "They like him because he is a man of impeccable etiquette, which endears them to him, and he fluently speaks both English and French and that draws them to him even more. They always ask for Chickery at the hotel desk."

[2] Let the good times roll.

Chapter 22

THEY HAD supper at home, not at Antoine's as Adelaide had counted on, because Harry had sent a note at mid afternoon which was appended to the front door regretting that he was tied up for the evening. "We will soon" he wrote. The early hours after supper were spent on the portico, the night air cool and pleasant, the breeze blowing soothingly on their faces, while Adelaide kept busy answering questions from Sasha and Mrs. Laster about the plantation on which she lived, explaining, among other things, that it belonged jointly to her and Lawrence Sherette and that the pay she received for her services as manager of the enterprise was subtracted from the cotton sales, which were considerable. As the evening wore on they opted for the inside and for awhile Adelaide sat at the piano in the living room playing a litany of waltzes. Only waltzes. She played beautifully, thought Sasha, and she did play beautifully, having been taught and trained as a youngster and ever since keeping her skills honed. Sasha watched her, studiously, to say it more definitively; she followed or tried to follow the least and finest of movements of her busy fingers as they flashed across the key board. She was tantalized. And when Adelaide had ceased and left for another room with Mrs. Laster to admire the colorful murals, Sasha stayed behind and began to peck out notes that were still fresh in her ears. And only quit when she began to yawn and decided that it was bedtime. It was late. But before she retired Adelaide entered her bedroom and sat beside her and made comments of those things which she had earlier set down while on the brief tour before attending the lecture, with Mrs. Laster listening in.

They were at the docking area at ten, intercepting Captain Dolby and party without trouble, who were standing away from the impatient passengers and the Creole, and Irish, and African workers with eyes fixed on the jumbled mass of steamboats and flatboats and seagoing vessels populating the riverfront. When spotting one another, the Captain and his entourage and Adelaide and hers hastened to join together and hugged and took on, the Captain seeming to wrap his arms around Sasha with more than moderate affection. The small consort, even though having known one another but a little while, had grown close. Even Captain Dolby was touched at their parting. He explained that they were leaving New Orleans for Mobile and there would turn around and set sail for Matamoros, Mexico without stopping off at New Orleans on their way back, which he said he sorely regretted. They'd return to New Orleans within three weeks, in the interim allowing time off for shore leave for the crew. Unable to hide it, Mrs. Laster gave off a somber face, thinking that within too brief awhile Bryon would arrive at this very port for her and that it would be most grievous to tear away from Sasha; she didn't know how she could stand it, she thought, and seeing her sadness, guessing what it was about, Adelaide reached her arms around her with an assurance that they'd meet her in New Orleans each six months so that she and Sasha could again be with one another. Time was escaping, even then; Adelaide began to set about devising an itinerary to keep Sasha and Mrs. Laster busy sight seeing the city in the time left. She even contemplated the notion of catching a steamer with them northward up the Mississippi to Baton Rouge, but Baton Rouge was situated too far away, thus she brushed aside the temptation.

The one event above all others to which Adelaide looked forward was a ritual which they repeated once or twice weekly for as long as Mrs. Laster was with them. And this was shopping at Woodleaf's and Barriere's. It was here that she indulged in scores of outings with friends, particularly female friends, but there were occasions when Harry was with her, for part of it at least, especially that part which had to do with dining out. Woodleaf's was a prominent oft frequented store on Chartres Street—and there was Barriere's on Royal—which one gifted user of the written word vividly described but perhaps overdid the embellishments: "Lavish displays were flaunted of every conceivable French Nouveautes of the day, beautiful barges, Marcelines and chine silks, organdies stamped in gorgeous designs, to be made up with wreathed and bouquet flounces, but above and beyond all else for utility and beauty." There was a large hotel called Lake End consisting of spacious verandas bordering indeed on a lake which ran parallel with Old Shell Road, where party people partook of a fine fish dinner and relished the light breezes that blew from the nearby salty marshlands, and this was where Adelaide entertained her guests when finishing with Woodleaf's and Barriere's. But a dinner at Lake End was an occasion, not a climax to a shopping venture. While waiting for dinner one could be served lemonade or orange flower syrup, which they often ordered and carried out on the veranda. The length of Old Shell Road amounted to a very long ride but an adventurous one, with Bayou St. John on one side, swamps on the other, and deep green rushes and palmetto strewn along its shoulders.

Not to be overlooked was the Old French Opera House. "What would the French do without their opera's?" Adelaide exclaimed with a chipper. It was grand, on the inside and out, and renowned singers from France with splendid voices entranced the gaping crowds that attended. No single seats were provided for ladies, only four seated boxes, but this was not a negative but a bonus, for no extra charge was assessed and it afforded more space. The treat was exquisitely lovely and Sasha uttered hopefully on most every occasion when they were leaving that she'd return every night if it were practical. Adelaide, who had attended operas in this grand old facility times innumerable gave out abbreviated bits of commentaries of small unknown or unnoticed features. "We had Robert le Diable and La Dame Blanche here last fall, and do you see the pit down there. Well, it's for elderly bald gentlemen only. Ha, ha, ha. Of course you know I'm jesting. But they do seem to congregate there in bunches. It's because of their wealth. They pay plenty for the recognition of sitting there."

There was one venue in the city to which Adelaide absolutely did not dare take her friends, the selling of slaves on the block, the barbaric practice of selling people to other people. An old freedman, a Solomon Northrup, described this pitiable scene of man's inhumanity to man in his publication of 1841.

> The very amiable, pious hearted Mr. Theophelus Freeman, part owner of the business, bustled about in a very industrious manner, getting his property ready for the sales room, intending, no doubt, to do a rousing business.
>
> We were required to wash thoroughly, and those with beards, to shave. We were then furnished with a new suit each, cheap, but clean. The men had hat, coat, shirt, pants and shoes; the women frocks of calico, and handkerchiefs to bind about their head. We were now conducted into a large room in the front part of the building to which the auction yard was attached, in order to be properly trained, before the admission of customers.
>
> The men were arranged on one side of the room, the women on the other. The tallest was placed at the head of the row, then the next tallest and so on in the order of their respective heights. Emily was at the foot of the line of the women. Freeman charged us to remember our places and exhorted us to appear lively, persistently exercising us in the art of looking smart.
>
> Next day many customers called to examine his "new lot." He was very loquacious, dwelling at much length on our several good points and qualities. He would make us hold up our heads, walk briskly back and forth, while customers felt of our

> hands, and arms and bodies, turning us about, and asking us what we could do and made us open our mouths and show our teeth, precisely as a jockey examines a horse which he is about to barter for or purchase. Sometimes a man or woman was taken back to the small house in the yard, stripped, and inspected more minutely. Scars upon a slave's back were considered evidence of a rebellious or unruly spirit.

It arose one day from the lips of Adelaide to Mrs. Laster that she was privy to seeing one slave auction in her life, just one, and it was in New Orleans, only a few streets away from where they sat comfortably rocking on the portico, and swore she'd never see another. She said it made her sick. "Slave auctions are not conducted on the Van Doke Plantation, never, not to my knowledge they aren't. He raises his slaves; by and large he does, and sells none. He loses them only because they die, or else he turns them loose, setting them free, if they want to be. Over the years one has run off now and then I understand."

"Did he pursue them?"

"No, he didn't I'm told. It wasn't worth the trouble he said, that he wouldn't miss them all that much anyway. He figured he had too many as it was."

☙ ❧

Day by day Sasha played the piano under the tutoring eye and exhortation of Adelaide, becoming better and better; she genuinely loved the instrument, eager at any moment to sit down and begin even though her last session was less than an hour past.

"You should rest Sasha," implored Adelaide, "or else your vigor and enthusiasm will suffer and you might not then want to continue."

"Oh, that won't happen."

So she kept on, her practice in no way slowing, her nimble fingers racing across the keyboards, unaware that some day she would attain to a peak of exquisiteness.

"My, how she has caught on," said Adelaide to Mrs. Laster who sat admiringly in observance. "Her progress has leapt."

"You are a superb teacher Adelaide. She thrives on your every word."

No letter had arrived from Bryon, Mrs. Laster having expected one with every drop off of by the postman. Her anticipation only energized her dread of the day that she would lose her precious girl. And while she did not show it as plainly, Sasha nurtured a gnawing inside of the same feeling. Each thought at night when they were lying close in bed of bringing up the unwelcome occasion but were unable to force it into discussion.

"Ah, why torment yourself with this Edweena?" thought Mrs. Laster, "for you were aware that there would come an end to this lovely dream just as there was a beginning. That is how life is. But you will declare that the few months with her outweigh by far not being with her at all. Ask yourself this a thousand fold and your answer will emerge the same."

With Adelaide leading them they continued as much as time permitted to ponder anything worthy of exploration. But taking mass was not one of these. It was predetermined. Not once did they miss. Near dusk each day they were found at the St. Louis Cathedral kneeling beside one another, Adelaide bunched in close, but never in between. Lawrence Sherette sometimes officiated the service. When the service ended Sasha and Mrs. Laster crossed themselves and it had become their habit to kiss one another's forehead and face. Eventually, they began to kiss Adelaide's brow and face also. One day when mass was over and they were leaving for home, Adelaide exclaimed that they hadn't gone to Antoine's as frequently as she had hoped; consequently, she promptly arranged a party of twelve, herself, Harry, Sasha, and Mrs. Laster among this number, Lawrence Sherette omitted due to unalterable obligations at the Cathedral. Her guests were lively and talkative, Sasha drinking in every word and admiring, if not amused, by the provocatively stylish attire worn by the women. Sitting between Adelaide and Mrs. Laster she was relieved in that this kept at a minimum Adelaide's party guests from prodding her into excessive conversation, too often bereft of substance, or inquiring of her past which she preferred not to divulge, most naturally not to strangers. The leader of topical matter around the table was Harry, whom Sasha liked and admired, having concluded that he was an extraordinarily intelligent man. He cut up and went on all through the evening, seemingly to steer the party away from things he felt might not be good for introduction to Sasha, but slipped once, suggesting that at the next scheduled Quadroon Ball they, this very grouping, should attend the function, revealing that he and the master of ceremonies for the ball were friendly to one another and that this person could seat them in an advantageous sector of the room. Adelaide cut her eyes toward his and then at Sasha, and he, catching sight of her reproach, proposed that they order, there motioning with his fingers to the waiter.

Appetizers were waived. The entrees were baffling, a preponderance from which to choose—Trout Meuniere, fried fillet of speckled trout with hot butter; Roasted Duck Breast, with a pepper sauce served with curry pecan; Crayfish Etoufee, a rich and spicy f'Fesh tomato based roux with fresh garlic, bell peppers, celery, and onions together with crayfish. Dessert consisted of Peach Melba, candied peach slices and vanilla ice cream on a vanilla pound cake with raspberry sauce, with chopped toasted almonds, or Mousse Au Chocolat, chocolate mousse with whipped cream, or Bread Pudding, a cinnamon and raisin bread pudding topped with warm rum sauce.

Everyone drew in a breath, asking the waiter to check with them a little later, finally making a choice from the overwhelming exotic names and descriptions that they had scanned up and down with busy eyes. After consulting with Adelaide for interpretations, Sasha arrived at a selection, saying she would like to try Roasted Duck Breast, for it somehow appealed to her taste. She'd have Peach Melba for dessert, the rich thin peach slices catching her eye, the singular determinant in guiding her to a final decision.

It was a fun filled evening for Adelaide's guests, and the rest of the party, all staying until the hour of eleven, and would have stayed longer, for there was no lessening of the frivolity, but Adelaide, judging it time to leave, gave an excuse of having to go downtown early next morning on an errand—in actuality turning over plans that she, Sasha, and Mrs. Laster would take a carriage up to the Lake End Hotel—and called a halt to the festivities.

Chapter 23

JANUARY, FEBRUARY, March, and deep into April had evolved and slipped by, too swiftly, and each day Adelaide had something aligned for them to do, some things repeated, the opera no less, some things they'd experienced before but had begun to revisit with refreshened zeal. Jackson Square was one such enticement. Sasha read from a brochure that early New Orleans was originally arranged around what was then called Place d' Armes (Spanish Plaza d' Armas). But after the Battle of New Orleans, in 1814, the Place d' Armes was renamed Jackson Square, where in the center of the park there stood an equestrian statue of the former president mounted on a steed rearing on his haunches. Few days were missed going to the downtown docking vicinity where there was a clear view of the armada of steam boats chugging up and down the Mississippi, and when it rained heavily in the heartland of the nation far to the north, pouring into the tributaries and then into the mighty river itself—forcing it to overflow levels—they stood and watched from the high ground overlooking the levees, the Creoles and Irishmen there laboring desperately at stacking sand bags, sweating, aching, cursing, their bodies drained of vitality by the time the sun had set, when a new crew with lanterns in hand descended on the scene with relief.

The letter at last arrived from Bryon, which announced his presence in New Orleans the first week in May. Mrs. Laster had hoped he'd say that he was sailing on Captain Dolby's ship. But that was not said. When Adelaide got the news it rang in her head that she must hasten, that time was running out. "Take them everywhere you can." As coincidence would have it, Lawrence Sherette mentioned to Adelaide close afterwards that the Archbishop was pleased to announce to him his new assignment, that of a Priesthood seat in the city of Memphis. They were arranging a church for him, a facility to be leased until a new one was built, the construction of the latter underway. Looking ahead Lawrence Sherette asked his sister what they might do about Sasha, explaining that living quarters was not a matter that had been worked out, and that he doubted there would be little more than suitable living space even for him when completed.

"My dear brother. I've longed for this day, with thoughts and plans for Sasha settled in my head some time ago. She will go with me; she will stay at Aurora where I will daily nurture and teach and care for her. You of course will miss her dearly, but we will see you often, journeying to Memphis for mass every weekend, or if not every weekend then every other weekend, I seriously hope. And besides, you will join us at home on every chance."

"You are splendid. What would I do without you? Now, one more thing my dearest, if I may. Will you talk this through with Sasha? I feel that you are far the better for handling this delicacy."

"I will. Gladly. I would have had to eventually anyway."

"She will love the plantation."

"She will. Yes. And I am thrilled. I am overwhelmed right this minute of the vision of her growing up there."

☙ ❧

Adelaide had spoken to Mrs. Laster of her brother's new appointment to Memphis, but not as yet to Sasha, as they sat talking that late afternoon on the portico. She asked Mrs. Laster to refrain from mentioning any of this to Sasha until she had talked with her. The news had set off a wave of unpleasant ideations in the both of them, but Mrs. Laster was more affected. Her tone was sorrowful.

"Leaving her will tear at my heart Adelaide. You can't imagine how close we've grown."

"Yes I can. I see it every day. I saw it in the both of you the moment you stepped onto the docking from Captain Dolby's ship."

"It showed I'm sure."

"Its funny, isn't it, how you can become so attached to someone in as short a while."

"Yes, and how strong and deep the bonds. In my case, stronger and deeper than usual I am sure, because you see my only child is Bryon. There was no daughter, no other child."

"But you have one now, a daughter I mean. She is your daughter, and you love her greatly, and she loves you just as much."

"Yes, yes. And that is what makes the thought of our separation deeply painful." She burst into tears, looking around as if she sought a handkerchief for daubing her eyes.

This sad impression very much prevailed upon Adelaide, who rose and went to her, using her own handkerchief for wiping the tears. "There, there. Don't allow yourself to hurt this way. Let's try to look at the bright side. There always is one you know."

"How is that," she asked, sniffling? "It is very hard for me to see."

"You will only be away from her for a little while," said Adelaide. "I promise that. The steamers run fast from Corpus Christi to New Orleans, as well as from Memphis to New Orleans, the latter distance requiring even less time. We'll meet you for a whole month here in this city where I have first met both of you. We'll do that often."

Mrs. Laster smiled and hugged her, concluding that Adelaide was a profoundly strong person, but foresaw her too, over time, growing as attached to Sasha as she, and some day finding it a hard painful thing to be stripped from her. They left the portico for the inside, there joining Sasha, who upon seeing them smiled and laid down a book that she a moment before had been reading.

☙ ❧

Came the day when Bryon got off the ship at port side. It was not Captain Dolby's. The party waiting would have recognized it. Mrs. Laster had watched anxiously for her son. Sasha was on pins and needles; finally, "There he is," she let out, running to him. "Bryon, Bryon," she called out to make certain he saw her and when she had run up to him he picked her up in his arms and whirled her around in mid air as if she were a feather then slowly checked the revolutions and let her down.

"It's so good to see you. I've missed you so," she said, kissing his face.

"And I you. What have you been doing for yourself? he asked, looking at her loveliness. "Everything I gather. This city is replete with culture I am told."

"It is. It is. And I've kept busy on the go. Adelaide has seen to that, touring us somewhere just about every day. I've been gorged with things to see and do."

"Whoa, who is this?" Bryon's voice had risen above the rumble and chatter resulting from the dock hands, seeing his mother moving hastily toward him, quickening his steps to meet her, Sasha still clinging to his arm. When he and Mrs. Laster reached one another he lifted her up as he had Sasha, spinning her once around, but not more.

"You'll drop me Bryon," she said to her son, laughing, then kissing his cheeks and hugging him again and again after he had let her down. She had a little cry and Sasha shed a tear as well. Adelaide then moved forward to them, taking Bryon's hand and shaking it lively, he returning the same. There was no need for an introduction. Who they were was well understood by each.

"I'm sure you've thoroughly entertained my mother and Sasha. I'm delighted at last to meet you. I'm very happy to."

"Same here Bryon. I have heard many good things of you, from both Sasha and your mother. Sasha told me she'd wager that you drove her better than a thousand miles over the streets of San Antonio in a stylish carriage, when all the while you couldn't spare the time but did."

"I did spare it, and it was great fun."

Bryon would stay three days and three nights before he and his mother set sail for Corpus Christi, acquiescing to Adelaide's insistence on his lodging with them on St. Charles Street, the first night, all of them, Harry there also, congregating out on the portico in quiet but lively exchange. Sasha sat by Bryon and held his hand.

"I do swear Sasha," said he, "you have grown an inch since you left San Antonio."

"Ha, ha. No I haven't."

"Yes you have."

"No I haven't," she returned, playfully landing a slap on his shoulder, to which he burst out laughing and squeezed her tightly.

Mrs. Laster, who'd sat taking in their camaraderie, broke in to ask Bryon of Father Lumas since their departure.

"Well enough I think. He's doing better now. For awhile he was less than eager to talk much and seemed awfully morose, let down I'm attempting to say. But I've been over to see him pretty often, even breakfasting once with him at the Rectory, and I believe my presence afforded a trifle of cheer."

"I sincerely hope so."

Adelaide informed Bryon of Sasha's experience in attending the lecture by Doctor Bonveniue, and that she'd been to three others since which were given by doctors of a lesser stature, one of these delivered at the Medical College of Louisiana, established in 1834, a mere fledgling in terms of time.

"Who went with you to these functions?" he asked, realizing that Adelaide was the dispatcher of the arrangements.

"Adelaide and Mrs. Laster went with me. They even took notes. Our friend Chickery drove us in his carriage, and retrieved us at the appointed hour."

Choosing an opportunity, Adelaide suggested to Sasha the next day in the early afternoon that the two of them take a walk down St. Charles for a short piece, being mindful that there was a tiny park relatively free of inhabitants where they might sit and chat without interruption. She felt the need to explain to Sasha her brother's appointment to

Memphis without further delay and that they together had decided the best thing all the way around was for Sasha to come and live with her on their plantation. When they had gotten as far as the park Adelaide sidled over to a bench with an accompanying table and sat down, Sasha joining her. The day was perfect, the sun resplendent, and they merely sat for awhile in the brilliance reflecting on things of recent happening, but eventually, Adelaide, driven by the invisible urge to open the principal matter of substance, commenced to speak.

"I have news to report sweetheart. It concerns Lawrence Sherette." Sasha's countenance hardly changed, none in the eyes of Adelaide. She calmly seemed to wonder at what Adelaide was about to say, but likely had guessed. "His appointment to Memphis is official. He will have a church there."

Sasha merely smiled. "That is what he wanted. I am more than glad for him. The journey toward his goal has been long."

"It has dear, very long. And you have been a part of it."

"I have. For a short while I have. And no one could have wished for his success more than I. I have prayed for him."

"I know you have, and so have I."

"When will he begin to occupy his office in Memphis?"

"I think he said the first of June."

"Not far away. It will be demanding on him to make the transition. So much to do."

"Time is short. Not much time for him to get ready. We'll have to help him."

"How can we? I will do all I can."

"Well, there's one way in particular. It's about living quarters. He has covered this with me and it worries him. He will speak to you next about it."

"What did he say? I hope that it is not excessively troubling."

"The quarters for him are not yet finalized. People are working that out. But he's afraid that when they finish the living space will be insufficient, and he also doubts that they'll have everything complete by June, thus forcing him to rent a hotel room."

"Is that his way of saying perhaps that he would be unable to care for me as much as he'd like, me being a girl?"

"Something like that, perhaps. But I told him to rest easy, that I'd see after you. And I will darling. Oh how I'd see after you. I'd love for you to come live with me on the plantation. It would make me the happiest woman on earth if you did."

Sasha could only smile, for she knew this had been trying for Adelaide, but more than anything, what Adelaide had said set off an avalanche of imaginations in her head. All at once she was deliriously happy. Although not letting it surface, she had incessantly contemplated what life would be like for her when they left New Orleans. She fell into Adelaide's arms and began to sob. "I have wished with all my heart that you might ask me. Now you have. He up there has answered."

"Ah my dearest, of course He has and has answered me also." She paused and then pressed her hands around Sasha's pretty cheeks and kissed her brow. "You will love it there with me sweetheart. We will lose ourselves in each other, with so many things to do each day. You just wait and see."

"How often will we see Lawrence Sherette once he is settled in Memphis?"

"Each weekend. Or every other week end. We will attend mass there."

"Oh. How far away is your home from Memphis?"

"Less than sixty miles. Less than a half day's drive if the horses are changed for fresh ones on the way."

"And how will we travel? By carriage?"

"By carriage, yes. Someone will drive us. It's the only way, unless we ride horseback or by wagon."

"No boats?"

"No boats."

"This is so sudden isn't it? A thousand questions swarm upon me."

"Which one compels you the most?"

"Let me see, oh yes. It strikes me again. When will you and I be leaving for your home?"

"By mid May I hope. I say I hope, for there is much to do. We must soon busy ourselves with planning and packing. But first before that we must train our thoughts on seeing Bryon and Mrs. Laster off. And I know that is not an easy thing for you and for her."

"No, it makes me tremble a bit. She is a mother to me, and we have grown as close as twins."

"I know dear. And I am glad of that. You needed a mother."

"Seeing her leave will be nearly intolerable. And seeing me waving goodbye will be the same for her. We will suffer alike."

"I understand. I will do all I can to help you both through it."

"I know you will." She cried once more, laying her cheeks against Adelaide's shoulder.

When Sasha and Adelaide returned home, Chickery was waiting out front in his carriage, acting on instructions to be there at the appointed hour of four so that Adelaide could accompany him to pick up and bring back two Creole women to prepare the evening meal. Harry and Lawrence Sherette promised on their honor to be there; Adelaide had told them she was giving it her best to keep moods uplifted and therefore expected them to match her efforts. When Adelaide had left, Sasha and Mrs. Laster sat down in the divan on the portico, at first rocking lazily, saying nothing it seemed—they'd talk when they went to bed; that's when they always talked—aimlessly looking at the street traffic passing by, thinking, perhaps dreading, fighting off time, a sort of silent last gasp to hang on to each other.

Chapter 24

THE CREOLE women came and began the meal, apologizing to Adelaide that they needed well over an hour to prepare it and set it out on the table, and asked if that was all right with her. She replied in her usual friendly voice which summoned smiles to their faces that what they had said was quite agreeable, then she remarked to Sasha and Mrs. Laster that Chickery was to transport them to the Cathedral for mass, promising to pick them up at twenty minutes of six. Mass commenced at six precisely. Lawrence Sherette conducted the ceremony that evening. When mass was over, Sasha, Mrs. Laster and Adelaide knelt at the altar, readying themselves to say their prayers, but just then Lawrence Sherette moved into their midst, placing his hand on their heads one at a time and uttered a prayer in silence. So they did not hear the words. When he had finished with Sasha, he lifted his hand but then lowered it again, looking down into her face. He smiled. It was a faint smile, with love and blessedness flowing from it. She smiled affectionately back and reached and squeezed his arm.

The meal was splendid, tasty Creole cuisine with Antoine's famous flat cakes that Adelaide had bought for the occasion, and red or white wine. A chocolate cake with a raspberry base was chosen for dessert, the only dessert, but she figured that one was enough. Leaving the dining table they moved to the portico where Harry soon mentioned that cotton planting time was almost upon them, that the ground was beginning to warm, whereas Adelaide said yes, it was, and that she'd been thinking the same. She guessed that Sam Feathers back home, her foreman, was daily in the fields estimating when the temperature would be precisely ready for dropping the seed into the soil. To her way of thinking the turning and the cutting and the smoothing of the soil was completed ten days previously. The procedure she pictured incisively in her head. For many a time she and Sam Feathers had walked the fields examining the soil, contemplating the best moment to start planting. Harry continued that he hoped that there would be a good price for cotton that year and ventured that the planters could depend on as much unless there arose some unexpected calamity. Bryon asked what that meant.

"Well, anything, I suppose. These days you never can tell what will spring out of the blue. I even hear the fellows around the office talking of the country breaking out into civil war if the Yankees don't stop meddling. Said something about Calhoun being at it again."

"Who is he? I haven't heard of him."

"The South Carolinian, the fiery intellectual Southern politician in Washington who's threatening to secede from the union."

"Does anyone believe him?"

"Yes. And seriously Bryon, I think it's possible."

"Gracious no, that cannot be," murmured Adelaide.

She couldn't fathom it entirely just then. She was too young. But Sasha looked on and heard, her beautiful dark eyes emitting a frown as if she sensed that there was a brewing specter about to erupt upon the nation. Seeing as much, Bryon shifted the subject to a completely different mood.

"We need to decide where we're off to tomorrow Sasha. I'm about to run out of time and haven't much more than started."

"Maybe we can ride up to Lake Inn tomorrow for lunch. The scenery is terrific on the way. Could we Adelaide?"

"Absolutely. And what about the French Quarter and Bourbon Street tomorrow night? What about it Harry?"

"Fine, that's fine. We'll start at seven and browse around for a couple of hours. The rowdy stuff won't start until after nine."

"You'll have to come back Bryon, if you hope to see it all," said Adelaide.

"We will. We will. You can rely on that."

Chickery was parked at street side waiting the next morning. It was nine o'clock. He'd been sitting there fifteen minutes. Seeing him as she peeped out the window Adelaide called to the others that the carriage had arrived. "He's here. Rush along everybody. Please." Not long afterwards they climbed in, Harry and Lawrence Sherette not among the number; they were at work. Adelaide directed Chickery to drive by the levee, then take the route that wandered by Lake Pontchartrain, about which, when he saw it, Bryon excitedly commented that it appeared to be higher than the road itself, higher than much of the city. Adelaide nodded in the affirmative, then went on to explain that the lake was not a true lake, that it was an estuary, connected to the Gulf of Mexico by Rigolets Strait, and was fed fresh water by five small rivers plus two bayous. Zigzaging around the rim of the city, they eventually took up Old Shell Road to Lake End, the ride requiring more time than usual because the women stopped Chickery often to observe and inspect the least minute thing, animal or plant. Flowers of countless specimens were in bloom on the banks of the marshes, flaming azaleas and lordly magnolias in particular, the latter throwing off an intoxicating scent that liberally perfumed the nostrils; and there were giant white blooms nestled amongst dark green leaves of unnamed carnivores which blanketed the undergrowth that took residence further out where the marshes converged with the swamp. On further, as they drew closer to the hotel, a growth of Carolina jasmine and wisteria were pointed out by Adelaide, the latter, known as a climber, wreathing its snaky tendrils up the street posts and along the wrought iron fences. Sasha asked Bryon whether the scenery here competed with that found on the banks of the San Antonio River, to which he laughed and teased her that she was trying to trap him into making a judgment with which someone might not agree, namely her, and asked how she compared the two. She laughed herself, and said she'd think about it. The lunch at Lake End was fabulous they all said. For awhile they sat out on the front porch looking at the flowers on the edge of the marshes and in the yards of the hotel. Checking her watch, Adelaide left to find Chickery, remembering that Sasha and Bryon wanted him to drive them around the streets of the city while she and Mrs. Laster shopped at Woodleaf's. "We'll need to head back soon if we spend any length doing the other things we've allowed for." She quickly found Chickery and shortly they were off. When they had returned to the heart of the city Chickery let Adelaide and Mrs. Laster off in front of Woodleaf's, then took Sasha and Bryon on their way.

Chickery kept the horses at a slow gate, Sasha taking the lead with the conversation, busily calling Bryon's attention to the plentiful things he had not seen and she had.

"Ah! You're an expert Sasha about everything but after all you've beaten me here by a few months."

"Unh hunh. I have."

Seeing her happiness Bryon was moved, his heart gladdened. There was a glow in her face and a particular satisfaction of something in her manner. He had to feel it just as she felt it; she did not speak it but he had become her brother, from that first moment it was so, a brother she'd never had, nor was there a sister with whom she grew up, nor any siblings at all in her family, and no children her age outside the house she lived in with whom she could establish camaraderie. All these experiences she had missed, but now, hers was a life drastically altered; time lost was getting made up. She now was surrounded by a thriving mix of people that had become her family. There was fun loving bright and educated Adelaide, artist as well as entrepreneur par excellence, and Harry, with a practically unmatchable repository of stories and facts, and Lawrence Sherette, bearing the promise to her father, who by his presence gave her courage and strength and conviction, and Mrs. Laster, her angel, her surrogate mother; and Bryon, who had won her heart the first day when he came to the Stage Post and helped her and his mother into his carriage.

"Do something for me Bryon when you're back in San Antonio," she said pensively.

"Anything."

"Tell Father Lumas I miss him very much and yearn to see him and for him to pray for me."

"I will. You can depend on it. What else?"

"Chenelle. Thank her for that wonderful cake."

"What cake?"

"The one she baked for me. I carried it along in a box when we were leaving San Antonio."

"I didn't know she baked you a cake."

Neither did I until we were aboard the *Surety* by a day. Not until I opened the package."

"Ha, ha, ha. What a story! What else? Is there anything else?"

"Yes. One thing more. There was a nice German girl, a Paula Ness, that I met at Father Lumas's Christmas celebration. I especially liked her. Please give her my most tender and loving regards and that I will be writing."

"I'm acquainted with the family. I'll pass your message along."

"Bryon."

"Unh hunh."

"Ummh. I guess it's nothing."

"You're sad sweetheart. And I wish it could be different but it can't."

"No. It can't."

"What were you about to say when you said it was nothing?"

"It was about your nice pretty home in San Antonio and how I loved it and hope that I can be going there again with not too many months passing."

"And you will. It will happen. Adelaide and I have already talked about it."

☙ ❧

They arrived at the French Quarter that evening at seven o'clock. Adelaide had hired Chickery to drive. He owned a six passenger carriage, this number including the driver, and it was needed. Lawrence Sherette was not with them. He was detained at the cathedral. He would meet them at Adelaide's when their tour was over. Chickery was familiar with every inch of this landmark; it was famous even then. Most of the buildings, he said, dated before New Orleans became a part of the United States. And then Harry added reinforcement. "The French Quarter architecture was designed and erected during the Spanish rule over the city."

The French Quarter ran far more than a mere block or two; it stretched a considerable length and Chickery did his best to cover every parcel, driving along the Mississippi River from Canal Street to Espalande Avenue, then turning inland to North Rampart Street. Once he pulled the horses to a stop, feeling that what he was about to say had particular historical importance and could be best said without having to concentrate on driving. "The French Quarter is also known as Vieux Carre; it's the oldest and most famous neighborhood in the city of New Orleans. And look if you will at the Spanish balconies with their shiny iron railings hanging out over the street. I should have said Bourbon Street because that's exactly where we are." Either he or Harry, or both intermittently, explained that Bourbon Street was a very famous passage teeming with human bustle that spanned the length of the French Quarter, and that it was named in honor of the House of Bourbon, the ruling Royal Family at the time of the city's founding.

Chickery, having started driving again, tugged at the reins, "Whoa," and let them off seconds later because Adelaide had told him that this was where they wanted to begin browsing around. Shortly they faded into the swelling noisy crowd.

"This is the street with the reputation," said Sasha, not asking, sidling over to Adelaide with a twinkle in her eyes. "That's what you said to Chickery."

"It is darling. But the rowdiness begins later than this." Bryon overheard and laughed and Sasha looked up at him and laughed too.

But even at this early hour the reputation was moving into feverish life, the bars open and bustling, jazz music cranking up, restaurants jammed, gentlemen's clubs (strip clubs) filled with a goodly supply of customers even at this hour, all of which melded together with other enticements to give it the distiction as the best known party street in the whole of New Orleans. The little group kept walking and looking until coming to a boutique where Sasha said she badly needed to buy a souvenir to send to Father Lumas by Bryon. The merchant was aggressively promoting the sale of wax statues of General Andrew Jackson, but both Sasha and Adelaide decided that since the General's past was publicly checkered such a gift was therefore inappropriate, thus finally, they settled on a handbook for Father Lumas's work desk with an embroidered Spanish design on its cover.

After a time, when their sightseeing had run its course, Adelaide glanced at her watch and suggested that they sit down in a nice sidewalk café and order coffee, but that they'd have to limit their stay. "Soon we'll have head for home." She did not mention that Mrs. Laster and Bryon were to be at dock side at nine the next morning to board their ship. But it was playing almost to the point of distraction on her awareness.

When they reached home all took seats on the portico, and there, contrary to what was expected, lapsed into relative quietness, the squeaking rocking chairs and the discordant noise coming from the crickets and katydids in the front yard momentarily taking center stage. Spring was about to burst through. Adelaide offered to serve cake and coffee and iced tea. No one refused. When he finished his refreshments Harry politely got up, and stretching, said he'd see everyone the next morning, but not mentioning where or the time, which would have amounted to nothing more than verbal filler, since the whereabouts and time were previously well discussed and rehearsed. It landed on him however that Mrs. Laster and Bryon were missing a chance to attend the most talked about extravaganza in New Orleans, the upcoming Quadroon Ball, but that he would have to look for a more seasonable opportunity to invite them. "That will have to happen sometime when they are on a return trip to the city, when Sasha is older." Chickery had been waiting in the kitchen to taxi him home. Soon Lawrence Sherette said he'd retire to bed. Adelaide had asked him to stay the night. Before departing for the inside he went over and hugged Mrs. Laster and Sasha and tapped Bryon's shoulder.

They were up early. Everyone. The smell of frying sausage pervaded the kitchen and dining area, the aroma of coffee as well, and the Creole women who'd availed themselves to prepare the meal were on the verge of scrambling the eggs, and had already set out the jams. "This is an old fashion Texas breakfast," thought Lawrence Sherette. Harry was there too as were Chickery and a second driver. Harry had intended to meet them at the docking area but had changed his mind and showed up to have breakfast. Sasha and Mrs. Laster picked at their food, mostly sipping coffee. No one ate as much as ordinarily. Harry and Lawrence Sherette helped Chickery and the second driver and Bryon set out and load the traveling parcels, the clothes encasements, the suit cases—a jumble of attire and toiletry that Mrs. Laster had packed and brought with her from San Antonio. A few of the items belonged to Bryon but they were limited in comparison to his mother's. The sun was pretty and bright in the east when they reached the dock but there was a pall of mist that hovered over them, though beginning to lift and cleared away altogether by the time the ship departed. Sasha and Mrs. Laster sat on a bench snuggled against one another, saying little, and did their best to smile, which was futile. Chickery had gone to the ship's dispatcher and was returning with word that passengers should move in place to ascend the stairway to the first level and accordingly they all began to amble toward the vessel, Mrs. Laster and Sasha clinging to one another, the rest looking sorrowfully on. Three powerful blasts erupted from the fog horn, the signal for passengers to start aboard. Mrs. Laster pressed Sasha to her once again. "Goodbye sweetheart; I love you," hugging her as if she would cling to her forever, and then upon kissing her one last time gave way to Bryon's tug, who knew he had to step in and do what he must.

"It's time mother. We have to get aboard."

So he took her arm and they walked away, Adelaide and Lawrence Sherette bunching around Sasha to offer comfort, trying with all they had to offer consolation. "Now, now, sweetheart. Don't cry. You'll be back with her in no time," said Adelaide encouragingly, but presuming her words uselessly spoken.

It required time. Thirty minutes or more. Then the fog horn coughed out another bellow and the great ship began its stealthy withdrawal, Mrs. Laster standing on the second tier by now, watching and waving, Bryon beside her. Sasha with both hands waved gallantly back." I love you." But Mrs. Laster could not hear her. No one could. It was uttered too lowly. Adelaide once again daubed her tears.

Chapter 25

NOT AT once did Sasha return to her normal self. She played the piano but cut it short, they traveled to Lake End for lunch but she was without good appetite and when they took to the banks of the great river to look at the boats chugging north and south she only but little got into the fray. Adelaide understood, patiently waiting and offering support. Sleeping alone the first night without Mrs. Laster she tossed and turned. On the second, when the hour was late, she with tip toe quietness went to Adelaide's bedside. "Adelaide," she said timidly, "will you mind if I sleep with you tonight?" Adelaide's smile practically beamed in the dark as she reached and drew Sasha into her arms. Soon she sighed and fell into misty slumber.

Eventually her mood began to lift, the first sign of it appearing when they went shopping at Woodleaf's, and the second happening when one day Adelaide took her to the plantation north of New Orleans, which belonged to her landlord, where the two of them rode horses for a fun filled afternoon. "Bryon has taught her to ride well," thought Adelaide.

Not long thereafter they began to plan for the transition to Memphis and to Aurora, Sasha's new home. Adelaide had brought far more than a few items to New Orleans, many more than she had remembered, Sasha's wardrobe and accessories, her family trunk not withstanding, appreciably exceeding Adelaide's packings in both quantity and weight. While lying in bed one night Sasha began aloud to check off the things she needed to do besides the completion of her packing, foremostly, the writing of a letter to her beloved Father Lumas. She knew that Bryon had conveyed her love to the good Father in keeping with her request. But she would not write just then, she told Adelaide; she would wait and write once they were settled at the plantation.

At three in the afternoon on a Monday they boarded the steamer at dockside and left for Memphis, leaving Lawrence Sherette and Harry waving after them, a little sad it seemed, but they kept on waving, just as Sasha and Adelaide continued to do, until the great boat had gone beyond the river's bend, then they were out of sight. "People are always leaving Adelaide, aren't they, and it's always sad."

"It is dear. But let's not think of that now. There are so many things to see on this old river, and along its shoreline. This is the Deep South you know and I don't think there is one single thing that influences its culture more than this ponderous waterway."

The vessel that carried them screeched and crackled, yet moved with steady precision; and the foghorn blasted loud and clear when the Captain called upon it. Sasha stood on deck looking every which way, upstream, downstream, and from side to side, making keen differentiations between this boat and the great ships on which she had traveled in the waters of the Atlantic and in the Gulf of Mexico. They sat up late that night reading in their cabin, so modern in appearance Adelaide had quickly observed when coming aboard, commendably furnished, and well kept. Sometimes they quit their reading or their conversations if that were the case and hastened to the deck to view a steamer some distance from them journeying southward to New Orleans. There was once a vessel which was equipped with such illustrious lighting that it glittered from stem to stern, resembling to some as a never seen before creature slithering through the night. The Captain pulled the rope to the foghorn and in answer, Sasha's and Adelaide's Captain performed likewise.

In time they grew sleepy, tired from a long day and took to their bed, thereby missing the city of Baton Rouge, but barely, and wide awake when creeping by Natchez later in the day. Sasha observed that the city was situated high upon a bluff and wrote this into her diary. Vicksburg was not far and she too set something down about it as they were passing by. Onward they chugged toward Memphis. By mid afternoon, some of the passengers catching sight of a sprinkling of Negroes fishing from the shore began to wave, the Negroes in happy spirit returning the gesture.

On Wednesday, near nightfall, in the proximity of six o'clock, the rain falling, but not heavily, their steamer edged along the wharf on the Memphis waterfront, the Negroes scrambling for the ropes to tie and secure it, while others were poised to load the ponderous stacks of hold over cotton bales from the season past. The cargo was destined for New Orleans, there transferred to deep sea ships headed for Europe. And still others had begun to unload massive compartments of clothing materials shipped to Memphis from England and France and New York City. Sam Feathers was there. He had parked his carriage nearby, which was equipped with a fringe on top to protect the ladies and himself from the weather. He was hurrying over to make certain they saw him.

"Miss Adelaide, here I am."

"Ah Sam. I knew you'd be here."

"Yes ma'am. I'll pull the carriage closer."

"Good. Sam this is Sasha Duval. She's coming to live with me."

Sam looked with absorbing scrutiny at the beautiful child standing by Adelaide. She smiled at him and reached to shake his hand. He took it warmly. "Welcome Miss Sasha, you're gonna love living at Aurora." You could tell that she at once liked him.

On helping each of them into a slicker he'd brought just in case of rain, Sasha's loose and excessively large, he spun and trotted back to the carriage, in no time guiding the horses to where their belongings were set off by the dock hands and started loading. The rain was peppering down, as said, not forcefully, but steadily enough to have gotten Adelaide and Sasha a mite wet before Sam Feathers made his way to them with the slickers. They had unfolded their umbrellas, which were not entirely sufficient given that the wind was blowing the rain against their legs. Sasha could hardly see in the darkness and mist despite the lanterns that were thickly around, hanging from platform posts and held by the hands of Negroes and docking foremen. The chatter rose and fell. There was a sound of wildness about it. To Sasha the surroundings and the darkness of night were understandably strange and somewhat unnerving. Sam looked gigantic to her in the mist. He was white she saw and spoke with a heavy coarse voice, but had a gentle bearing, and wore a huge felt hat whose brim he had purposely bent down in front to shed the water. The horses were of the handsomest stature, their hides of a sorrel hue, and they were outfitted in slick black harness which was accentuated with shiny brass rivets that especially sparkled in the lantern glow. Adelaide had told Sasha they were to stay at Tahitia Lillian's, a Negro woman of half white blood, a large woman, with magnificent form in her younger days, who was a lifetime friend of Adelaide's father until he died. Tahitia was once the mistress of a white cotton broker, who together with Adelaide's father, had bought a house for her in the heart of Memphis and established a sizeable interest bearing fund for living expense, figuring she would outlive them both and wanted to secure her while they could. It was a two story structure, serried among a regimen of others of like character, very brightly painted; but looked ghostly in the night as they approached it. Lantern lights, blinking prettily in the freshness of nightfall, were affixed to the columns that ran completely around the portico just as they did at the rental home in New Orleans. Tahitia stood waiting, and had since late afternoon, not knowing when they'd arrive, though Adelaide had mailed a letter two weeks beforehand telling her their steamer was to roll in at a late afternoon hour, likely near dusk. Sam let them out near the front porch then drove the team to the back of the house where a helper led them to a shed for stabling and feeding. After that, Sam set Adelaide's and Sasha's belongings on the back porch, figuring they'd need something from among them shortly.

"Lawdy, lawdy. You better git in out of that rain Miss Adelaide," said Tahitia. "You'll take a death of it."

"No I won't Tahitia. You worry too much."

"It's wonderful to see you my child. Just wonderful." They rushed to one another and Tahitia wrapped her large arms around Adelaide. "Ummmmph." And then, taking notice of Sasha, "Oh, good lawdy, lawdy. What do you have here? What kind of angel is this?"

Sasha, expressionless, wanting to look down but resisting the tendency, evinced a frown. Tahitia pretended not to see her shyness.

"This is Sasha. She's coming to live with me. I am so lucky."

"She's a beautiful thing. Yes she is. You don't see them often like this. I sho do wish we'll see you a lot Miss Sasha."

"You will Tahitia," said Adelaide. "We'll see you so much when we visit Memphis you'll get sick and tired of us."

"No I won't. Don't dare say that. You remember how your daddy used to drop you off for me to see after while he was on business downtown. Why Miss Adelaide, I just about raised you."

"You did. And I can't forget it. I'm eternally grateful. And I love you for it dear Tahitia. I greatly do."

"I know you won't forget it. I know your heart."

And after she was grown Adelaide had continued the ritual, often spending the night when she was on visit to Memphis.

Finally Tahitia brought up supper. "I'll bet I know some people who long about now are really hungry. I have supper ready. Good hot soup, and ham and biscuits. And lots of other cookings too. Are you hungry Miss Sasha?"

"Yes ma'am. A little." Tahitia rolled her eyes at Adelaide as if to say "Miss Adelaide, I wish you'd hear that, a beautiful white girl saying yes ma'am to an old Negro Mammy like me. That beats all."

"Ha, ha, ha. I hope you are. I sho do. And Mr. Sam Feathers here is just about soaked I see and I know he's as hungry as a bear. And he's just about as big as one." Sam had just entered through the back door with his suitcase in hand, thinking he needed to make a change of clothes without much delay, for the ones he wore now were wet and chilly.

"Ah, Tahitia," Sam spoke up, "you'll scare this doll of a girl to death. Don't pay any attention to her Miss Sasha. I'm as gentle as a lamb and she knows it." Sasha smiled amusedly at the bantering between them.

Tahitia pointed in the direction of Adelaide's and Sasha's bedroom, with mention that as soon as they could shed their uncomfortably damp clothes for dry ones, which was said to mean Sam Feathers also, they'd sit down and eat. At this, Sam went with Adelaide and Sasha to the back porch for their encasements that he would transport inside, making more than a single trip to deliver them all, in fact several trips. Sam was to sleep in the more than ordinarily large annex to the principal quarters of the house which Tahitia seldom opened up, keeping the door closed and locked to completely separate the sexes. It had its own private bathroom. They ate, but as soon as they had finished Sam bade everyone goodnight then left for bed. Adelaide and Sasha did their best to describe to Tahitia the experiences they'd had in New Orleans during the few months past, Sasha once asking Tahitia if she had ever been there. "Heavens no my child, but I sho am one of these days, if Miss Adelaide will take me."

"You know I will my dear," said Adelaide, tenderly laying her hand on Tahitia's arm.

Sasha stayed on for awhile then excused herself and left for her bedroom. She said she needed to sort through some of her clothing to see if they should be rearranged. She liked the room, that is, the taste with which Tahitia had decorated it, the paintings, the rugs, the nice window tapestries, but the eye catcher was the attraction of the bed, an especially crafted piece of work, which was composed of heavy oaken wood, with a width wide enough to sleep three much less two. It occurred to her that in terms of size the one in the Rectory at the San Fernando Cathedral was similar. But the architecture was purely American, she thought, not a great deal about it favoring the sleek European crafting. Tahitia had laid out two pillows each for her guests, fat and puffy, the slips bearing pretty blue flowers knitted into the fabric. Sasha crawled in, tired from a long day, but did not fall off to sleep, deliberately holding back, for it was her nightly custom to cross her heart and clasp her hands and pray for herself and for her parents, and for all the rest of her loved ones—and she would wait for Adelaide to join her and talk. When Adelaide finally left Tahitia she went to her bedroom and laid down, Sasha telling her that she'd already said her prayers, upon which Adelaide suggested that she say them again, and that she would say hers, then they removed themselves to the carpeting and kneeled down. After their prayers were said they kissed one another's brow and crawled back into bed. It was then that Adelaide noticed the poppy colored mole on the front of Sasha's shoulder, a tiny dot, such that one had to strain to see it. Her gown had dropped barely enough for the eyes to catch a glimpse. "Just another of her beauty marks. As if He hadn't given her enough already."

Sasha said she liked Tahitia very much and was inquisitive of circumstances that led to her father's acquaintance and friendship with her, to which Adelaide answered that she really did not have knowledge of how their pathways crossed. But she was aware that Tahitia was mistress to his cotton broker white friend. It would be some years before she revealed as much to Sasha.

"I liked Tahitia on first glance. She is joyful to be around. Will we stay with her when we come to Memphis?"

"We will. She would feel hurt if we didn't. Tahitia and I are very close."

"I can tell."

Adelaide explained that Tahitia enjoyed the good fortune resulting from a man who was her friend and together with her father had purchased for her this very home in which they'd sleep that night, and in nights to come. Sasha did not comment or pursue; she merely lay on her back staring at a fixed place in the ceiling, seeming to thoughtfully revolve the story she had just heard. They lay there for a little longer then Sasha began to reflect on the whirl of her experiences over the several months past.

"They're likened to a dream Adelaide. Sometimes I think they can't be real. Much has happened and I've been so busy moving about. Think of it. It was not a long while ago at all that I sailed from the Canaries to San Antonio, then from there went to New Orleans, and now I am this evening in still a different city, and tomorrow will set foot on the plantation, which I am bursting to see.

The rain fell with slow persistence the whole night through; they slept as a baby sleeps, awakening to bacon frying and coffee brewing. Tahitia would soon call out that breakfast was ready. But Adelaide and Sasha had now left their bedroom and sat down at the kitchen table, making that unnecessary. As Tahitia went about the kitchen, Sasha saw in her a favor to the Creole women that cooked breakfast on that morning they bade goodbye to Mrs. Laster at dockside. She so reminded her of them, and there was no debating in her mind that there was a strong resemblance to the bloodline.

Chapter 26

THE SUN was shining brightly and the day perfect for traveling. Sam Feathers was up much earlier, seeing after the horses and loading the equipage that belonged to the women. His, he had loaded when he rose from his bed. Adelaide the night before instructed him as to which things he could load before they were up the next morning, knowing he would rise more than an hour earlier, asking him to hold back the remainder until they ate and were preparing to leave. Sam had entered the back door and was waiting for breakfast, sitting silently at the opposite end of the table from Adelaide and Sasha. Adelaide asked if he'd loaded most everything into the carriage. "Yes ma'am. All but the rest of the things in your room." Asking everyone to bow their heads she then offered a prayer to the Lord for blessing them with the food they were about to enjoy. Then they ate. When he had finished his last bite and sipped his last sip Sam excused himself, and left for the carriage and horses, calling back to Adelaide as he passed through the doorway that he'd load their belongings whenever she was ready. Adelaide and Sasha left presently for their room to pull everything together. Tahitia had begun to wash the dishes.

That which happened next is not contended as an incident of rareness, for it was a simple minor thing, but it was, as one looks back, a sort of portent, a glimpse into the gateway that was opening to young Sasha Duval as she moved imperceptibly toward the medical genre of her life, for which she seemed irretrievably destined.

Suddenly there was a gasp from Tahitia, and a cry. She had cut an ugly gash into her finger by submerging her hand into the dish water, where unknowingly to her, a piece of broken glassware lay hidden. Hearing the commotion Adelaide and Sasha flew to her. Sasha quickly inspected the fissure, which was bleeding but not profusely, and finding no fragments in or about it asked if there was whiskey in the house.

"Yes, somewhere. Look in the cupboard Miss Adelaide," replied Tahitia with a grimace. "You'll find it there."

Adelaide was gone but seconds, returning with word she'd found it, and handed it to Sasha who had begun to submerge Tahitia's hand into a large bowl she had filled with warm water and suds in which she was cleansing and sanitizing the wound.

"Now, Miss Tahitia, let me lift up your hand and rinse it off, then I'll douse your finger into this small bowl that I have half filled with whiskey. It won't hurt, certainly no more than you're hurting now. Do you have linens?" she continued. "I must tear off strips for wrapping your injury. Germs you know. Soon the bleeding will stop entirely."

"Miss Adelaide," said Tahitia, "you know where they are, don't you?"

"I do dear. I'll have them in a jiffy."

Adelaide went briskly and found the linens, then upon receiving them Sasha tore off strips for bandaging she judged to be of suitable length and width, and then tore off a few more very narrow pieces which she twisted into the fashion of spirals, thus forming the tying cords, and asked Adelaide to mash the fissure together while she wrapped the bandages around it, at the same time tying the bandages as tightly as she determined was fitting.

"There. It's finished. I've wrapped your finger with extra cloth, so I think the bleeding will not pose further trouble. Now, please stay still. You'll be just fine."

Looking on, Adelaide had marveled at the proceeding. "How quickly and efficiently she has acted. How exactingly she has gone about it, as if she has prepared and rehearsed it all in advance."

Sasha was now wiping Tahitia's brow with a damp cloth, her face having broken out with sweat, which was also observable on her neck and arms. But she had begun to return to an air of calm, and was amazed, as had been Adelaide, at the decisiveness with which Sasha had proceeded to attend her.

"Where my child did you learn how to do this? Ah, you are better than my own doctor. He is not nearly as quick. About two months ago, Ezra," her Negro helper, "cut his hand real bad and Doctor Lundy took care of him. But he was awfully slow. Well, he looked slow to me. But maybe not. Anyway, he's a good doctor for us to have around. He's a middle aged man, and friendly. We like him. He sees after the Van Doke people. You know, the La Belle folks near where you and Miss Adelaide are going."

"Yes, and he cares for my people too," Adelaide threw in.

"I'd like to meet him," said Sasha.

Their departure was regrettably interrupted, but understood; the clock hand would move to the hour of eleven thirty before they could be on their way, Ezra having left a slight after ten to find Doctor Lundy, who as yet was not to be seen. Adelaide was determined to stay until he arrived. "We'll wait him out." When the hour was barely past eleven there he was in his carriage, calmly guiding his horses up the street, Ezra beside him. The doctor appeared to be in no hurry. Ezra had reported the mishap to him, naturally with an explanation of Sasha seeing that the wound was properly disinfected and wrapped. When the doctor made his way inside and over to Tahitia who was sitting on the living room divan he lifted her hand, looked at the wrapping, and turned and smiled at Sasha, and winked. She blushed. "A very nice job Sasha. Neat and clean. I can call you Sasha can't I?" He hadn't waited for her to respond. "Ezra here says that is your name." In actuality he had been aware of her name for some time because Adelaide in her letter or letters to him from New Orleans had made mention of her, not withstanding the fact also that she would be coming to live at the plantation.

"By all means. Call me Sasha. That's what everyone else calls me. I wouldn't know how to answer to any other."

"Ha, ha. Naturally not. But if I may, it's a beautiful name. Is it Russian? Perhaps?"

"No. It's Serbian my parents always told me."

"Hmmmmm. Well that's close enough. Not much difference between Russians and Serbians."

Sasha kept silent, unsure of the wisdom of drumming up an answer; she assumed he was probably correct, but her curiosity would in no little time force her to trace her lineage to make sure.

Doctor Lundy took another glance at Tahitia and felt her pulse. "You're fine Tahitia. You didn't need me. But it's good to see you, and you too Adelaide; and especially Sasha I am glad at last to have your acquaintance. Adelaide has written me many fine words about you. I'm totally delighted. So you're to live with her? She's a splendid thing. She truly is. You'll love it there."

"Yes. I will. I already do in my thoughts."

"Tahitia," he then spoke up," it's my understanding that these good folks need to be on their way; let's not hold them up any longer. Huh?"

"No Doctor Lundy. No need for that. I'm sorry Adelaide that you couldn't leave on time. Ezra, run tell Sam Feathers to finish loading the things for these dear ladies and to pull the carriage around front."

The road had not dried yet, still soft from the rain to the extent that the rims of the steel wheels cut easily into the soft earth and collected wads and strings of drying gummy mud. The weather was a picture of serenity, the air flushed and cleansed the night before by the precipitation that fell with undisturbed regularity. The animal life was excitedly astir, the birds in swarms flying in and out of the woods that crowded both shoulders of the roadway at this juncture of travel. Sam sat in front guiding the horses, while Adelaide and Sasha rode relaxingly in back, their seats inclined toward the rear of the carriage. Leaning further back Sasha looked for a while at the blue sky and the graceful trees that swayed across its endless expanse. Adelaide glanced over and wondered what was in her thoughts. "What a beautiful day," she said and Sasha's smile replied yes. After they'd gone on for some distance Adelaide asked Sam to stop the horses and moved beside him in the front seat so that the two of them could talk of the planting season, which was drawing near she knew.

"The ground is turned pretty well by now Miss Adelaide. We've been at that for the last two weeks. I never fail to love this time of year, the smell of newly plowed earth and all. You know what I mean. To me, there's nothing like it. Of course I've said that a thousand times. "

"Ah yes Sam. I understand. I've said it a thousand times too. I'm like you. There's something invigorating about it. It has its own special scent. I wish I could describe it, but I can't. You just have to experience it, don't you; I mean feel and smell it?"

"Yes ma'am. That's the way it is."

"When will you start planting?" She meant the cotton seed.

"Time's just about here. I'd like to see the ground warm up a bit more, then we'll start puttin them seed down."

"The garden's are in I'm supposing."

"A good many things are. Onions and cabbage we set out three weeks ago and we ought to put the tomato plants in the ground pretty soon too."

Sam gave something of a report that he and the workers had stayed constantly busy while she was away, mainly patching barn tops and sheds, and putting the machinery in condition—the cutting disks, the cultivators, the middle busters, the hay rakes, the mowing machines, the wagons, and the heavy wooden pull trailers which were used to haul the three tiered stacks of cotton bales to the river docking wharfs in Memphis at harvest time. Adelaide asked about his two children who attended school at the one room schoolhouse that she and Martha Van Doke jointly owned and equally paid the teacher's salary for supervising and teaching the children who went there. It wasn't easy for Sam to carry on a social conversation with Adelaide or anyone of an educated level, given that he was without an exposure to the sophistication of books and formal teaching and seldom thought about anything other than running the plantation and planting and harvesting, but for a moment his thoughts fell upon Tahitia, whereon he forced a remark that she looked to be in good health and was her usual friendly self. Adelaide agreed with a nod, then proceeded to say that Tahitia certainly appreciated him, and liked him, and eagerly looked forward to his trips to Memphis in late spring and summer because she knew he'd deliver her a basket full of fresh vegetables without fail.

At a midway point, at what was called an exchange or way station, they stopped for fresh horses. The exchange station was a two hundred acre plot owned by Adelaide and Jordan Van Doke tended by a hired farmer who mostly grew corn and hay on the soil and stayed alert to have ready fresh animals for carriage or wagon use when needed. There was a house situated close to the roadway and barns further back sufficient in number to quarter the horses and store the hay and corn crops. When they left, Adelaide was again in the back portion of the carriage with Sasha who began to pepper her with a swell of curiosities that she'd been thinking of, such dealing with what number of people lived on her plantation, and in what kind of shelters did they reside, and what did they eat, and what did they do for pastime, and so on until the one came to surface which in Sasha's vision intrigued her by far the most. "What does the plantation home look like Adelaide? I have been trying to fix it in my mind but can't. I keep altering my vision of it."

"Ha, ha, ha. I'll try."

And then Adelaide gave her best at telling that it was a two storied colonial with very large white columns on the front and extra large windows appended to both sides of the double front doors that led to the inside, and that the home was nestled on the periphery of a pretty woods that was vastly cut back and that a bed of crushed river rocks wound their way through the towering cedars that flanked the driveway, coming to rest at the front porch doorsteps. She could have explained that it was by every measure as grand and sizeable as the Van Doke La Belle but that was unlike Adelaide and so she did not. But did proceed to tell Sasha that she'd see when they arrived a nesting of small houses swept away from the plantation home by a good quarter mile, staged in something of a semi circle, plain, some painted, some not, but inside decently livable, excepting that the space was too often crowded. In these dwellings the preponderance of Adelaide's field workers lived their lives and raised their families, the parental mates lying by one another at night after they'd gone to bed talking of the struggles of eking out an existence. They were mostly Negroes.

"When they take sick who sees after them?"

"Doctor Lundy, and a fairly young doctor in the summer who comes down from Baltimore. He takes care of the Van Doke people too, just as does Doctor Lundy. They mingle their efforts and talents."

They were approaching the Big Hatchie, and when they crossed over the wooden bridge, which generated a rumble of low thunder as the carriage wheels struck the uneven planking, they were but a limited distance from the plantation home, "three miles" Sam answered when Sasha asked, and soon would be catching the Aurora in their sights. When they had traveled another half mile the land suddenly leveled and the trees opened up and there it was jutting skyward, the Aurora. Closer and closer they came, until at length the carriage wheels crunched into the river rocks of the driveway and began to follow the curvature of the cedars. Sasha's eyes fell excitedly upon the white columns of the portico, in fact upon the whole posture of the grand edifice, and looked speechless over at Adelaide and sighed and smiled a little.

"Whoa," Sam called to the horses, jumping abruptly down, beginning to unload the equipage, immediately bolstered by a cadre of helpers who hurried to assist, excitedly welcoming Adelaide home and picking up an item or items as Sam accordingly instructed.

"Just see that our things are set on the front porch Sam. I'll have someone carry them inside later and store them where they belong."

"Yes ma'am."

As they neared the entrance, a tall taciturn woman appeared, but remained inside, hesitant to step out onto the front porch. One had the immediate impression that it was her nature to stay quietly back from the whirl of things. A clearer observation of the woman would have revealed that Choctaw and Negro blood ran together through her veins, as evidenced by the darkened color of her skin, her high natural cheekbones, and eyes of keenness—but they were soft eyes and depicted a friendly bearing. Those eyes at once leveled on Sasha, struck by her youth and beauty. When they moved even closer, stepping on to the portico flooring, one of the double doors opened wider and the woman came out. Adelaide spoke.

"Good to be home Mary Tonka. I have missed you." This last expression seemed to ignite a feeling of warmness inside the person she had addressed, for the smile that was trying to break through now no longer was faint and reserved but full and freely offered. It seemed to stretch across her entire face.

"And I have missed you too. Badly."

Then the two women hugged, an affectionate embrace that told Sasha there was a depth of caring between them of long duration.

At this, Mary Tonka turned to Sasha, waiting for an introduction. Up until now she had not attempted to speak to the beautiful young white girl, but Adelaide read her countenance and saw that already she was favorably swayed. It was now Adelaide's obligation to bring them together.

"Mary Tonka, this is Sasha; Sasha this is Mary Tonka. Sasha, Mary Tonka is the head housekeeper. I don't know what I'd do without her."

It was but shortly that supper was served in the immaculate dining room where Mary Tonka had set the table and spread a lavish array of meats, vegetables, and desserts. Adelaide and Sasha were hungry. They ate well. When they had finished Mary Tonka began to clear the dishes. Adelaide had taken Sasha to the drawing room to show her the many magazines to which she subscribed, suggesting that she sit down and pilfer through them or some of them while she helped Mary Tonka with the rest of her chores. "We don't need you to help us dear. Just sit there and enjoy yourself." When Adelaide returned to the kitchen area Mary Tonka moved close and inquired quietly of that which was beginning to run curiously through her.

"In which room is Sasha to sleep?"

"In my room Mary Tonka. In my bed, with me. She's accustomed to sleeping with me. I'm her substitute mother."

"Her mother?" Mary Tonka let out with a tone that intimated she was not less than vastly confused.

"Yes, her mother. You of course do not understand, so I shall tell you. I would have in due time. She is a child or young girl, whichever you take her to be, whose sorrows run deep. They are great and they are fresh, lingering hard and fast in her mind. It is not yet a year ago when her mother and father died of small pox on the Canary Islands where they lived and where Sasha had lived all her life. When they had perished, the Priest, a Father Kestner arranged to have her sent to San Antonio to join Lawrence, my brother, and of whom you are very fond."

"Lawrence! My word!"

"Lawrence."

"How? Why him?"

"Lawrence was her father's friend in San Antonio when they were younger. His wife had just died, and he knew also that he was soon to pass, so thinking over the whole of the matter he concluded that Lawrence Sherette was the only friend in this world on whom he could truly depend to be guardian of his beloved daughter, and therefore set about to persuade the good Father to guide her to him. Keeping his promise, the Priest worked a plan for her to sail to Texas to be with Lawrence but at the same time called upon a seasoned and good lady to stay close to her while on voyage, who graciously consented. Her name was Edweena Laster, who was on her way to San Antonio to join her son. Sasha was so lonely, you understand, leaving her parents behind, who lay beneath the soil of her native country, which was crushing to her heart. Imagine it. She must have cried a river of tears. She told me the Priest cried too when she left. Being so moved at her plight I'm sure. Nighttime was the worst and sharing a cabin with her on the vessel Mrs. Laster saw and felt how she suffered. Mrs. Laster told me she did. It was during this voyage, on the first night I think, or was it later when they slept in the Priest's Rectory in San Antonio, I'm not exactly sure which, that Sasha asked her if she would let her come to her bed and hold her in her arms like her mother used to. That is how it started. I think Mrs. Laster held her until she fell off to sleep. They became mother and daughter. They were so bonded that Mrs. Laster decided to go and stay awhile in New Orleans with her and Lawrence when they left San Antonio. When Mrs. Laster left New Orleans with her son to return to Texas it was to Sasha almost like losing her mother all over. It became my lot to fill in. That is the end of my story."

"Hmmmm. Will I need to add covers?"

"No dear. Just keep things as usual. But on second thought I think she'd like those pillow slips with the embroidered pink flowers on them. Don't you?"

"I know she would."

Chapter 27

THERE WAS an extended uninterrupted sleep that followed upon their retiring to Adelaide's huge bed that she had slept in since she was a tot. It once belonged to her grandmother. The sun was faintly making its ascent in the east when the light knock sounded at the bedroom door, a barely audible murmur announcing that breakfast was soon to be on the table. In response, the two sleepy persons rolled quickly out and as hastily as reasonable washed their faces and groomed themselves and made their way to the dining room. This was an early hour for Sasha who had fallen into a habit of sleeping far later. But from here on she'd rise early, determined never to be late for Mary Tonka's exquisitely prepared breakfast, careful as well never to miss issuing an appropriately timed compliment, which drew a smile that seemed nonetheless to struggle to break through. Sasha, however had earlier pieced together that this was Mary Tonka's ordinary bearing, and though limited in warmth as compared to Adelaide's effusive persona her smile genuinely flowed from her heart.

A few weeks passed and Adelaide and Sasha were seen riding daily into the fields, where Adelaide explained to her the undertakings of planting and growing the crops, when certain crops were started with the injection of seed into the ground and then with the passage of time, when the seed had burst open and turned into a plant and the plant had begun to grow, the field hands appeared with chopping hoes to chop away the grass and plows to loosen and aerate the soil. Sometimes Sasha rode alone. Unbeknownst to her, Adelaide and Sam Feathers and Mary Tonka had spread word to the field hands working in any realm to watch for her and take care that she did not stray off course, thus ending up lost or worse. She would need to learn the lay of the land, where it was safe to go and where it was not. Sasha was intercepted by everyone's quickened glances as she made her way about, this being mostly the men folks at first, before the seed were in the ground, whose job was largely disking and harrowing the land, which were the last two tasks before planting. She did not altogether ride, rather, electing to take brief walks along the roadway through the sun dappled woods of elm and oak and silver maple and blooming red buds which grew on the roadside leading into the bottom lands that adjoined the Big Hatchie. But if hiking, she seldom ventured more than a stretch from Aurora. There was a creek fed lake within a half mile that invariably tugged at her fancy, an idyllic pretty thing, practically clear, and here she always stopped for awhile to sit, usually, if patient, glancing the flopping of a catfish which in search of a bug or a fly had broken the surface of the placid water, or train her sights on an alluring glade of lily pads growing wildly in the breaks and shallows. Once there were two Negro children fishing in this small inlet who looked up and saw her and waved, unafraid completely of this stranger, this beautiful white girl, but curious. They had heard of her.

The name Sasha had spread around the Van Doke and Sherette plantations with sudden swiftness. The beautiful white girl they said was smart and quick with her thoughts, some saying they'd heard that she was inclined toward medicine and that surely that was why Miss Adelaide had brought her there, and they all said at one time or another they'd seen her riding at Miss Adelaide's side in the fields or along the roadway, and someone spoke that she was seen riding in the wagon with Sam Feathers to the freshly mowed clover fields to watch the work crews bale hay. Sam explained to her that the hay baler was a vital contraption to the plantation because they had to feed so many livestock. She seemed allured by the mechanical but disliked the grating and clanking that it produced, which in fact was horrendously noisy. Adelaide drove them one day in the carriage to the Van Doke slave quarters, though was disinclined to stop or introduce Sasha to anyone, yet waved at some of the people she recognized and Sasha waved too. They knew Adelaide at a glance and smiled, but looked curiously at her companion. Adelaide hoped to catch Cynthia or Hallie or Fannie or even Sol about the grounds. None of them were around however. She had hoped to pay them visit. Mrs. Van Doke was not there either, and if she had been she would have come forward with warm greetings and insisted that they join her inside for tea.

"This is La Belle, where the Van Doke family lives Sasha. You're in the heart of the Van Doke plantation." She did not allude to the people as slaves, forever keeping the term excluded from her vocabulary.

"The houses are so small; they're more like shanties. Much smaller than those where your people live."

"Yes, I know. They are small. As you say, they are much smaller than ours. I see you call them shanties which is an apt name; my father used to make reference to them as ramshackles. Either way, they're the same."

In time Adelaide would have her talks with Sasha in explanation of the differences by which the two plantations were managed and directed, most singularly that aspect which dealt with the people, where on the one hand there was compassion and kindness, and on the other an attitude that by and large a slave had to be dealt with as a slave. But Sasha, in a brief while, would begin to make these distinctions on her own.

They passed quickly on, Sasha twisting around as they moved further away to reexamine certain visages that had attracted her: the mothers, it was the mothers, still there, with their naked babies in their arms standing in grassless dirt yards staring vacantly after them. Whatever lured her she did not address it to Adelaide aloud. But did offer a commendation of the Van Doke mansion.

"It's grand Adelaide. Much like yours, stately and imposing. But it's closer to the living quarters of the people than I had supposed."

"It is close. That's how it's been ever since I first remember."

"I'm attempting an estimation. How far away to your home from here?"

"Two miles. The homes are two miles apart."

When they had neared the end of their trip that afternoon Adelaide guided the horses into the winding driveway and upon reaching the front of the Aurora she drew them to a stop, where without instructions a field hand standing ready took hold of the reins. After Adelaide and Sasha had gotten down he led the animals to a shed where he stored the carriage, then further led them to the barn which was swept back from the mansion by a substantial distance and out of sight, and watered and fed them. When Adelaide and Sasha made their entry Mary Tonka met them with a large package in her arms.

"Sam Feathers drove to Brownsville for the mail. He brought this."

It was from Lawrence Sherette, which Adelaide and Sasha eagerly opened, finding books, a sizeable many books, sent to Sasha with the package marked in care of Adelaide Sherette. Dr. Carlos Enoch of the Canaries was relaying them to her through Father Lumas who was relaying them on to Lawerence Sherette, such books consisting of scientific subjects in general, but freshly published, and replete with descriptions and drawings of an admixture of medical procedures. There were a few Russian and French literature works among them though quite limited. The more scientific sources were designed to appeal to practicing technicians who had chosen by and large to treat human injuries of a common sort.

"Oh, wonderful," Sasha exclaimed after she had thumbed hastily through the pages of one of the publications, "I'll add them to the library Adelaide."

"Yes, do."

The note from Lawrence Sherette was brief. "Will be there soon," he scribbled. "They say that church construction is progressing markedly well. Miss both of you terribly."

And after this, with Adelaide's eyes glued fixedly upon the lines, Sasha read with voracious excitement the note from Dr. Enoch. "Sasha, it seems so long. I miss my little associate. I have no one now to tote my black bag around and keep my medicine straight and help me sew up cut hands and arms and set many broken fingers. You must write. I am anxious to hear from you."

"Did you do that, all those things?"

"Just about. I was an onlooker attendant, but I was careful not to get in his way. He was teaching me. Never did I sew up a fissure or set broken bones on a human being, but I could have."

"Did he ever give you a chance to try?"

"Yes, a few times. On a puppy and larger animals. I did it with him looking carefully on."

"How did you do?"

"Ha, ha, ha. Very well he said. And I really think I did."

What grand and fascinating ideations started to journey through Adelaide's fertile brain. People of the plantation met with similar hazards very constantly, she reasoned, and on the Van Doke plantation too, without proper care, if any at all, for Dr. Lundy was at such an excessive distance from them that it was outlandishly impractical to hope that he'd arrive in less than two days when sent for, and the old doctor at Brownsville, chubby and awkward in his movements, and getting old, took longer ordinarily than Dr. Lundy traveling from Memphis to diagnose and treat the afflicted. Her thoughts refreshingly gravitated to Sasha. "She is learning about medicine and medical practices with leaps and bounds. In no time look where she will be? While a tot she was exposed perpetually to the ills and treatments of the sick and injured, watching every move of her dear Dr. Enoch who for some reason had taken to her and with divine assistance, I conjecture, saw great promise in the young girl at his side. She could do much to help treat and heal the people here, certainly she could I do fervently believe, if Dr. Lundy will lend his support and guidance, and I do think he will. I'll speak to him. I will at his next calling."

She shifted away from her suddenly borne vision regarding medicine and Sasha, recalling the note that Lawrence Sherette had written. "I shall be so happy to see him. I had begun to wonder when he would send us a line or two, and of course he did. But the delivery of a landslide of scholarly compositions to Sasha pleases me more." She stopped and sighed and seemed to let her thoughts slip back to what else of significance Lawrence Sherette had set down in his note. "Ah yes. The church. It's progressing well, he says. When he comes to Memphis, Sasha and I will soon go see him. He will stay at Tahitia's, as we will also."

Sasha the next day stored her new collections in the library, a very roomy space built next to the drawing room, with an entry door between the two, though exercised care not to mix the medical books—the texts and journals—with the rest. While this was underway, she had remarked to Adelaide that for the sake of convenience the more medical texts would serve a better cause should they be placed in the infirmary, such as it was. "The books would be handier for reference that way."

"You are right Sasha. Tomorrow let's look at our infirmary and discuss the changes that we should make to improve it."

Thus the improvisation of a modernized medical space was launched, the completion of which did not reach a terminus until the passage of several months. The current infirmary was an attachment to the rear portion of the mansion and was replete with inadequacies; consequently, it was dismantled and rebuilt. This time it was appreciably larger, with carefully given thought to the sectioning of the space for specific applications. Of particular note, the building was equipped with a high up cathedral vaulting, with walls therefore also high up, a great number of large windows installed for the admission of lighting, and there was a separate examination table in a room to itself, augmented with medical cabinets and shelves and linen storages and a multiplicity of medicines and disinfectants. During this interim, Doctor Lundy excitedly helped them in their analysis of what was to be placed where and why and doggedly emphasized that, among other things, they keep at all times certain essentials in a designated storage facility, these entailing a handy supply of whiskey and rock candy for combating the influenza, a supply of quinine for treating Malaria, a chlorinated lime solution for cleansing surgical instruments, a stock of carbolic acid for disinfecting open injuries to the flesh, an abundance of clean surgical and nursing gowns ready for use when the need arose, and adequate amounts of morphine. Morphine was the chief pain killer of the day and was virtually indispensable to the performance of serious surgical procedures on the human body. It was discovered as the first active alkaloid extracted from the opium poppy plant in December, 1804. The drug saw extensive use during the American Civil War and was greatly indispensable in the lessening of pain, but allegedly resulted in over 400,000 injured soldiers falling victim to morphine addiction, the effect known as "soldier's disease."

Mary Tonka was an imperative part of the small grouping, called in for good cause by Adelaide in that she was the midwife for the Sherette plantation, the only one. Doctor Lundy and Adelaide and Mary Tonka, all three, felt that although the occurrence was nominal, the deaths resulting among the women after childbirth was in another sense alarmingly unacceptable. But still, the number of these deaths was far under the number accounted for at the Van Doke plantation. Looking back, it is now know that such fatalities resulted from what was then called "childbed fever," an infection of the uterus. Poor sanitation practices were at fault, the use, for example, of unclean surgical instruments, failure of the midwives and doctors to wash their hands, and wearing unclean uniforms and gowns. Sasha had read where in 1795, Alexander Gordon Aberdeen of Scotland suggested that the fevers were infectious processes and that physicians were the carrier and that, "I myself was the means of carrying the infection to a great many women."

☙ ❧

Over the next few weeks the excitement had not lessened, but had grown throughout the plantations of the Sherette's and Van Doke's regarding the beautiful young white girl in their midst. Everyone seemed to speak of her on every breath. One did not need to stretch his intellect to determine how it had happened. It was because of the mysteriously quick and effective grapevine that extended throughout the two communities. Adelaide had suspected correctly that Mary Tonka had gotten word through some of the field hands to either Cynthia or Sol or both, for not many days thereafter, at mid morning, here they came in a black shiny Van Doke carriage in pretense of paying call on Mary Tonka, their old friend.

Never did they enter by way of the front, generally by the back door, but on this date through the kitchen and then out onto the back porch where they sat down in the swing by one another. Mary Tonka pulled up a cane made high back close to them.

"All is pretty and green, Mary Tonka," said Cynthia. "I can see way across the fields from here, all the way to the woods. I'll declare it sho is pretty. Umph, umph."

"Yes it is Cynthia. And it does me good that you and Sol are here this morning to share it with me."

Cynthia did not answer but had an inquisitive air about her. It very quickly surfaced. "Where is Miss Adelaide, Mary Tonka?"

"She rode into the fields with Sasha to check on something with Sam Feathers. I look for her back in no time."

They had sat talking back and forth with one another for what Cynthia judged to be a half hour or more, Sol remaining mostly quiet, honoring the stricture that Cynthia continually laid down. "Now Sol, when women are visiting, don't you butt in. It's not polite, and it ain't liked. It's yo place to stay back out of it."

"Okay, okay. Don't you fret yo self. I knows what to do."

The thirty minutes having passed, the ladies rode up, and Adelaide jumped off her horse and hurried over to the presence of Mary Tonka's guests, dashing up the steps and hugging them both.

"Why have you not come to see me Miss Adelaide? Oh, I know. I sho do. You've stayed awfully busy with the work in the fields and all helping Sam Feathers see after things."

"I've meant to get over Cynthia. I seriously have. And I did once. I swear. Sasha was with me. But we saw nothing of either of you, so we left."

Sasha had broken away from Adelaide as they turned the horses over to a field hand, and had bounded for the drawing room, entering the side door, but presently, still dressed in an adorable riding habit, came on to the portico, where Adelaide promptly officiated the introductions. Cynthia's eyes widened, and so did Sol's, both unaware they were staring in awe, and Sasha at an indecision as to whether to shake their hands or move forward and hug them. Adelaide saw her tentativeness and smiled and Sasha read it, taking it as a signal not to hold back. Within another second she had entered into Cynthia's over fleshed arms and would have hugged her in return except for the fact that Cynthia held her with such compression that she could not have successfully effected a wiggle even if she had so chosen.

"You sho is a beautiful thing Miss Sasha. Everything and more that I've heard. At last I'm gittin to know you and I'm so glad."

"And I'm glad to get to know you too," answered Sasha, making an effort to return the embrace, yet only partially able to reach her arms around Cynthia's expanded form.

Sasha looked at Sol and smiled at the vacancy in his puzzled face and concluded that she should hug him also, then went over and put her arms around him, the old Negro so dumbfounded that he made no effort to hug her back, merely letting out a chuckle, bobbing his head in something of a tremor.

"Miss Sasha," Cynthia broke in, who was hard put to conjure up something to say which she felt was appropriate to the young girl, "I've known Miss Adelaide for the longest, I mean for a long while, and Mr. Lawrence too. We are so glad youse is here as part of the family."

"And I'm glad too," Sasha replied timidly.

Mixed with the conversations, Sol and Cynthia continued to eye her admiringly, likely with a rash of questions revolving curiously in their heads. And Sasha, with a feeling of shyness showing itself, released carefully guarded glances at them too, surmising that with the passing of a slight of time she'd get to know and like them and that her shyness would be a thing of the past. Mary Tonka had drunk it all in with one of her infrequent smiles crowding through, wondering what Cynthia and Sol were thinking and pretty well knowing, for the time wasn't far removed that she too had met Sasha for the first time.

They stayed but a while longer, with all three, Adelaide, Mary Tonka and Sasha walking with them to their carriage, which was ready and waiting, a field hand holding the reins.

"She's a pretty thing Sol. The prettiest thing I ever did see," said Cynthia as they rolled along toward La Belle. "I tell you she sho is. I hear theys starting to fix up the medicine room. I sho would like to see it. I would have asked Miss Adelaide to let me see it today but felt ashamed to. I keep hearing Sasha's making a doctor. Can you imagine that? A woman! A doctor!"

"Well, Cynthia, we have midwives all over who bring babies into this world. All the time they do. What's so strange about that? If that ain't doctoring, then I don't know what is."

Chapter 28

THE DAYS marched by, one by one, fall starting to creep into the scenery, as evinced by the yellowing leaves clinging tenaciously to the branches that had sired them but soon was to give them up. Sam had returned from the post office at Brownsville with an envelope bearing the name of Adelaide Sherette. The sender was her brother. Sasha hovered closely as she opened it.

"My dears," he wrote, "will you meet me on the date of October 27 at Tahitia's. I am at last coming to Memphis to hone in on the ending phases of the construction of my church. As you did when you left New Orleans, I will travel by way of steamer to Memphis, and should arrive in late afternoon. In the event you are supposing that I have written Tahitia of my arrival, let me assure you that I have.

I am beside myself with visions of seeing you. There is no way that I can tell you of my love for you both, but it is very great."

Sasha was suddenly ecstatic, thrilled through and through, and tapped the earth a time or two with her slippers. Immediately, as if seized by celebration, they fell into one another's arms.

"We're going to Memphis Sasha; at last. We're on the threshold of seeing his church, which has taken eons to build, or in any case that's the way it seems to me."

Sam Feathers would drive them, pretty weather expected he ventured, but suggested that they each carry along a parasol. In play, Adelaide rolled her eyes at Sasha, which spoke that Sam was truly a good fellow, always trying to be protective of them, but as to the parasol, well, that was a mere minor thing to think of. Sam went on to emphasize that if it started to rain or storm, the parasols wouldn't be sufficient, nor even the carriage enclosure if the storm was too blustery, but if caught in a predicament of that extreme they could stop off at someone's house and stand or sit on the porch until the foul weather had cleared.

They wouldn't stay long in Memphis, two nights and one day. Sam was itchy about the time he was having to take off from the plantation because at this phase of the year the cotton harvest was at its peak, but he, fretting a mite, accepted that the trip was inevitable and prepared to leave the tumult of things in other good hands. For a month Sam and his haulers had stayed busy transporting cotton to the ports of Memphis. Fascinated, Sasha watched them leave at early morning as they passed nearby the mansion heading for the main road, the mist not yet lifted. She waved at Sam Feathers from the portico whose wagon occupied the front position. While the load the horses had to pull was heavy, it was not as burdensome as might have appeared, for there were six of them hitched in tandem, and the roads were dry and hard. They moved as a caravan, slowly trudging forward, the trailers and wagons heaped three tiers high with glossy white cotton bales fresh from the gin, which they'd unload on the shore embankments at Memphis before nightfall, or with the help of work slaves roll their cargo directly onto the steamers or barges. All this in its monotonous cycle had continued since the start of the harvest season and would not wane until fall was at an end. Not only did the Sherette plantation gin its own harvest but the harvest of many other producers, jointly owning a cotton gin with the Van Dokes, the only gin for miles around, avidly fed by prosperous West Tennessee farmers who owned deep rich soil that yielded a high grade commodity with a long and heavy fiber. The city of Memphis lent impetus to this bustling enterprise, claiming to be the biggest inland cotton market in the world and headquarters for the financial intermediaries of the whole Mid South region that provided planters with quick operating capital and a guaranteed market outlet.

When they arrived, Lawrence Sherette was sitting on the portico in the swing with Tahitia at his side raining words upon his ears with unchecked rapidity, who had taken time out now and then to return to the kitchen to fetch a glass of lemonade for him, and would have kept at it but he told her that if she didn't stop he might burst. Tahitia was in a whirl; she hadn't seen him in years. Sasha let herself down from the carriage even before Sam Feathers and Adelaide had made a quiver of effort, scampering up the steps to Lawrence Sherette, kissing him all over his face and squeezing him with every sinew of strength she possessed, both flooded with glad emotion.

"It's you. You're here," said Sasha with an outburst. "You are such a dear sight to see." She squeezed Lawrence Sherette again, then he took her into his arms.

"Whoa! What do I see here? This girl has grown as fast as a puppy since I last saw her," he let out, and died laughing.

"No I haven't. I haven't at all. It's just been a little while."

"You're right Sasha. It hasn't been long, but it seems like it has. I have missed you dearly. I really have."

It was then Adelaide's turn. "Lawrence, come here. I must embrace you, and my, you look vibrantly good. Who has fed you so well since we left?"

"I've eaten at the Rectory," he reported, looking down into her bright, intelligent face.

"You're kidding me."

"No, honest. That's where I've taken my meals. The archbishop insisted."

"Ah, that's good. I worried that no one would take care of you. I kept thinking of you when you were away in San Antonio for so many years, with no one seeing after you, and swearing I wasn't about to let that happen again. Ever."

As they looked over Tahitia came wiggling across the portico toward the commotion, coming from the kitchen to which she'd momentarily slipped off to check on the supper preparations as her company was driving up, gathering Sasha and Adelaide together into her heavy leanless arms. She kissed their cheeks and they kissed hers, Sasha releasing a miniature giggle.

"Let me see your finger Miss Tahitia." Tahitia held it proudly out. "Why, it's well. The scar is only slight."

"It's well Miss Sasha. Doctor Lundy was by a week ago and inspected it. He said the same as you, that he didn't see much of a scar. You sho made yoself a big impression on that man. It wouldn't do for me to tell how he bragged on you. You'd get the big head." Sasha smiled meekly and blushed.

They sat for a while and talked and told funny stories. Tahitia was a lively teller of stories, most of which she had lived through, and spoke of them in rapt detail, most happening when she was growing up. Lawrence Sherette and Adelaide began to take up things attendant to their recent short while in New Orleans, the subject of Harry Lancaster popping up first, Adelaide asking how Harry was presently faring and if Harry saw him off when he caught the steamer northward to Memphis. And lastly asked if the Archbishop hated to see him leave. Eventually, when they had lapsed into a more settled quietude the church's progress began to occupy center stage.

"You must take us for a look at it Lawrence, first thing tomorrow."

"You may be assured that I will," he answered, reaching and pinching her cheek.

Sasha smiled, and thought to herself that the gesture was a loving affectionate thing to do to his sister.

Tahitia called them to dinner. She had left for the inside to see if the house girls were finished with it, finding they had. Sam Feathers was already sitting at a side table in the dining room sipping a cup of coffee that one of the girls had set out for him. He had been occupied with stabling the horses in the shed to the rear and had fed them, and had set a basket of vegetables on the back porch by the door, a gathering of late cabbages, and tomatoes, and freshly pulled turnips. When Lawrence Sherette entered he whisked over to Sam, putting his arms around him, saying how good it was to again be with an old friend. "We'll need to find some time Sam to dig into a bunch of things and catch up."

"And we will too."

The food was served with great plenty, Tahitia knocking herself out to plan it all. She'd spent days thinking about it. When Lawrence Sherette finished the blessing they shuffled their chairs, moving an inch or two closer to the table, and with hungered appetite began to fill their plates. It was a splendid meal, capped off with coffee and a banana cake.

"Its what I used to bake for your daddy when he would drop by," said Tahitia to Lawrence Sherette, patting his shoulder and hugging his neck with her fat arms, he laughing aloud, reaching his hand up to her face to let her know that he felt the love she had for him in her heart and knew that it had always been there, ever since he was a small boy.

"We're to dine you out tomorrow Tahitia," he said, "to compensate for all you've done, and that includes that underground night place over by the government districts where you've taken us before." Tahitia very well knew that prior to leaving the next day, or near that hour, Adelaide would slip her from one to two hundred dollars, without disclosing that such moneys were to offset her troubles for lodging and feeding them.

"To that night place in Orange City. Randolph's."

"That's the one."

"I think they're at a loss over there as to why I've not brought you to see them for a few years."

"Well, that's all the more reason we should drop in."

Then Adelaide cut in with a suggestion that had to do with their itinerary the next day. "We'll start out with breakfast here in the morning folks, if that's all right, with the view that we'll stay out for most of the day, so that means we'll have to plan for lunch. But I think we'll need to count on returning here at some time during the afternoon to freshen up before leaving for dinner at Orange City."

"All right. If you say so Miss Adelaide," said Tahitia in concurrence. "And will you be thinking about what I should wear tomorrow? Going to the church, I mean. I'll need to look proper. Who will we see there?"

"Not anyone we know," spoke up Lawrence Sherette. "The head builder and his workers, that's all."

They slept well that night and rose early for breakfast, if eight o'clock was early, and left for the church construction site at nine, Sam driving them in the carriage.

When they arrived the crew was well engrossed in their work, starting at seven, but the superintendent divested himself from them to show his visitors around as soon as he learned the identity of Lawrence Sherette, the new Priest.

As they could see, the man explained that the exterior of the church was made of huge blocks of gothic stone and that although the doors to the frontage were not set in place they soon would be. They would be painted red, he furthered. Lawrence had previously asked the architect if the doors could be hinged in heavy cut steel, designed to reflect a medieval vintage, and asked the superintendent if this was still the plan. The answer was in the affirmative. Lawrence Sherette was a bit doubtful. He'd talk with the architect. The superintendent went on. "Notice too that we've set the spire and the steeple atop the church already. I'm sure you spotted them when you first drove up. They really add a special reverence to a church. I've always thought that but I didn't know why they were there and still don't. I love the stained glass windows. So many of them, really tall and narrow, and they're in all kinds of colors with all sorts of cherubs and other spiritual scenes put on them. I don't know what they mean either but they're beautiful."

"How much longer before the church is finished sir?" asked Lawrence Sherette?

"Two months, or maybe just a short time beyond. I think two months is a good guess. We're working hard. It's my thinking we'll finish on schedule."

At this, the superintendent bade them good day and cautioned that they take care not to trip over any unnoticed obstacles scattered about, lumber or tools, and to help themselves to the inside of the sanctuary, which was virtually complete.

It was not a tall edifice, and it followed that the vaulting of course wasn't tall either, but it was nice in appearance, painted very reverentially, which depicted worshipers in prayer on their knees, and some with eyes raised upward as if praying to their Lord.

"The altar is noticeably striking," said Adelaide. "They've already laid a scarlet tapestry across it. And just look at the choir seating, will you. You'll have a crowd of singers if they fill up the space. I love your church Lawrence, I really do, so refreshingly bright and new, and the years you've waited for it are now justified, aren't they?"

"Yes they are sweetheart and you've every day been a part of them. I don't think I could have succeeded without your strength behind me."

"And the Good Lord's."

"And the Good Lord's"

They all wandered around for a while, venturing outside and then coming back in and kept repeating themselves. Once Lawrence Sherette went to the beautifully finished chair in the pulpit vicinity and sat down, trying it out more or less, predetermining how he might feel sitting in it on the Sunday he'd conduct his first mass. The pews were finished of fine oaken wood that literally shone, which Sasha had detected at first blush, and now she had sat down on the very front with Tahitia joining her. Then they turned their faces upward toward the vaulting, studying the scenes of artistry which were painted in magnificent varying hues. Sasha thought that even though the vaulting was impressively high it still wasn't as grand and high up as the one in the San Fernando Cathedral in San Antonio. But it ran through her that she should not lay bare her observation, lest it be taken in the wrong light and prove hurtful to Lawrence Sherette, whom she loved with all her heart.

Next they left the church and began to usurp the time by driving around through the city, Sam choosing the routing, sometimes the others chipping in, once stopping at a plaque which read that Memphis was named after the ancient Capitol of Egypt on the Nile River. Court Square was another attractant that earned their pause, a small park in the center of the city with pretty trees, nicely finished wooden benches scattered about, and gurgling fountains whose origin was borne from the mouths of a multiplicity of Grecian statues, which marked the distinction of the little square more than any other enhancement. It was here that a private discussion rose between Lawrence Sherette and Adelaide as to where lunch should be taken, considering that white restaurateurs disallowed the commingling of blacks and whites inside their walls. Shortly Tahitia moved over to join them and offered a solution.

"Why not pick up barbeque and iced tea and whatever else and find a nice cool shady place down on the river banks and have a picnic. That would be fun. We could look at the cotton workers and at the boats oozing around the bend."

"Indeed yes," Adelaide said with a chipper. "Let's do that."

And that is what they did. Sam, after the picnic was nearly over, pointed toward the endless layers of cotton bales stacked on the shoreline, saying they were lying in wait of the work slaves who'd soon be around to roll them aboard the steamers or lesser boats. The rest munched their sandwiches and drank iced tea while he kept divulging his knowledge of the surroundings. Sam was greatly acquainted with life on this shoreline and the handling of cotton that went on there. He even knew some of the slaves and non slaves by first name. Talking on the subject for the rest of the afternoon would have been no test. What he did not speak of, because he did not dwell much on such context, was that the cotton economy of the antebellum South depended on the forced labor of large numbers of African American slaves, and that Memphis had become a major slave market.

It should also be inclusively said that prior to the civil war, which was in the proximity of a decade from this date, one quarter of the city's population were slaves. A good many had sweated for years on these very banks serving their master. Sasha made no mention of the workers hustling two and fro, pushing or pulling the loaded cotton rollers, though without doubt understood that the majority were slaves while some were freed Negroes working for wages. Once she asked what happened to the heaps of cotton bales lying on the ground when the rain started to fall.

"We try not to be caught like that Miss Sasha. If we know it's coming, and we do, we just bring in more and more men to climb up on top and cover it up."

"Ah, I see. But let me ask you Sam Feathers. Does the city ever flood, I mean over where downtown is situated?"

"Some. But it's built on a bluff, much of it is, and as you might figure that makes it impossible for flooding to happen. The banks do have their low places on down below here, a mile or more. Down there the water kinda creeps and crawls over the banks and cuts around and spreads where nobody wants it to. But no flooding here. See that hotel sticking up high on the bluffs. It's the Gayoso House. It was built not too long ago. Say about ten years. It was built there cause it would be high up, out of danger. You ought to see from up there how it looks down here on the river." Recognized as a singular land mark of the day, this fine accommodation would sometimes be visited for lunch by Adelaide and Sasha when they were in the city.

The remainder of the afternoon was spent sitting on Tahitia's front porch sipping lemonade while she went over old times with Adelaide and Lawrence Sherette, Sasha honing in on every word and syllable. Not once did Tahitia remotely mention her former white lover, nor how it happened that she met him. One would not have expected her to. What mattered most to Adelaide and Lawrence Sherette however was that both Tahitia and her lover were inseparable friends with their father and that she cared for them whenever their father brought them to Memphis, which was often. At the hour of seven they left for dinner at the Negro establishment in Orange City, which was named after its owner whose family name was Randolph, by which he chose to be addressed. Sam did not drive them, staying behind at Tahitia's because he did not like eating out in public diners, and sighed gladly when Tahitia said Ezra was available for filling in for him, who would stay outside waiting in the carriage for the length of the dinner as she would ask him to do. "He'd be totally out of place among the crowd we'll meet Adelaide. You understand I'm sure."

"I do dear."

Chapter 29

RANDOLPH WAS everyone's friend, cordial and a gentleman, whose laugh often burst across the spacious room. He was well liked by the white folks, who frequently took dinner at his place, and was revered by his native race. He was looked up to by the neighborhood. A handsome man of age sixty he stood as an imposing figure at the doorway where he consistently greeted the visiting patrons. On this evening he purposely left his station to accompany Tahitia and her party to their table. "It's a while since I've seen you darling," he said, giving her a lavish hug after pulling back a chair, then holding onto her as she took her seat.

"Ýes it has Randolph, but I'll see to it that I do better."

"You will. And I'll help you. I'll come to your home and remind you if I have to. Ah, I remember Lawrence and Adelaide, your young friends and I also remember your daddy," he said, looking them over carefully, bringing his recall sharper into focus, then fondly hugging them both. Smiling broadly, their faces proved that they were delighted to be once again at his dinner table. Though so far pretending unawareness of her, Randolph at last turned his attention to Sasha, poignantly, penetrating, absorbingly, as if he were taken over by this young girl in their midst. "And Tahitia, who is this lovely flower? May I touch her?" Before Tahitia answered he hugged Sasha with one arm around her shoulders.

"She is Sasha. She makes her home with Adelaide on the Sherette plantation."

"I am on a cloud that she is part of you all. Now that you have brought her here Lawrence I am certain you will bring her again. You will come back won't you Sasha?"

"Gladly," she quietly answered, looking into his face with dazzling eyes, so affecting the man, apparently, that he could think of nothing else to say, and excused himself, returning to the doorway to greet more incoming guests.

Ribs and hams were cooking over an open pit fire, easily visible from where they were sitting, smoke lifting to the ceiling where there was an unseen outlet to draft it through to the open air. The room was lowly illumined, the space consisting of a fusion of misty haze evolving from the smoke, and a tint of purple which also was born from the same source. It could not be said that the crowd was rowdy and loud, as one might expect; their talk was low and subdued, in the semblance of a murmur. Sometimes, but in the manner of good taste, the members of a table joined in convivial laughter at what had been said. Perhaps a joke was told. Sometimes, the patrons of this table or another glanced inquisitively across at Tahitia and her party, inordinately respectful in their countenance and obviously pleased to see her and her guests. Many had known her since they were of a young age, now grown up, her name revered among them. They had seen Adelaide and Lawrence Sherette before, but of some years past, for Tahitia had brought them with her, and a few, as they trickled over to speak courtesies to her conveyed to Adelaide and Lawrence Sherette that they had kind remembrances of them as well. But the beautiful young white girl they had not seen, and were curious about her, why she was among Tahitia and her friends and where it was that she had come from. But this they did not speak of aloud, merely wondering about such things and later talking lowly of them among themselves.

With Randolph standing at the doorway exerting efforts beyond the ordinary to thank them for having graced his business, Tahitia and others left, Tahitia wagging a box of food that Randolph had ordered at her request for Ezra who waited patiently and humbly for their return. He would delay eating until they were home.

When Adelaide and Sasha retired to bed Sasha said to Adelaide that she liked Randolph and would like to revisit his restaurant sometime, the answer returned that of course they would. Tahitia came into their bedroom and put her arms around them each at a time and asked if getting up by six thirty was agreeable. Adelaide said yes, that the hour was fine. When Tahitia left, Adelaide rose and snuffed out the reading lamp setting on the side table then crawled back in bed. Almost, but only almost, they forgot to say their prayers. They agreed they'd say them in bed, that it was too troublesome to get up. When their prayers ended and they had pulled up the covers Adelaide called over, "Goodnight sweetheart. The day was a full one, wasn't it?"

"Very. I loved the church, didn't you, but everything else too."

Adelaide laughed amusedly. "I'm glad."

Before they slid out of bed the next morning Sasha mentioned to Adelaide that she hoped Doctor Lundy might show up for breakfast, recalling that Tahitia had told her she'd invited him. They were to leave at eight. Sure enough at seven he was there with an exaggerated announcement that his hunger was ravenous. When the prayer was said they sat down, Sasha slipping into a chair beside him. In his thoughts, which he had shared in a private moment with Adelaide soon after his arrival, Sasha was destined to go a very long way in the field of medicine, perhaps rarely, because, "She is already astonishingly into medical research, and really, really, really is leaps and bounds ahead of me Adelaide. Her work will catch many an eye. She reads everything and reads all the time." He had some books to give her on the subject of appendectomies but cautioned, as would the books, that the invasion of microorganisms was a possibility when opening up the human body. "Cleanliness is the answer so far," he said, "but we need something additionally to combat those bad little monsters before they get started, to kill them before they take hold and kill us." That would partially happen when carbolic acid (phenol) was modified and advocated by Doctor Joseph Lister for use in the engagement of surgical methods.

They left just after breakfast, Adelaide and Sasha repeatedly exchanging embraces with Lawrence Sherette and Tahitia and Doctor Lundy too and saying good byes. Doctor Lundy promised to visit the plantation in the neighborhood of Christmas in that he wasn't married and his father and mother and the rest of the family lived in far away Louisville, Kentucky.

"You'll enjoy a wonderful Christmas with us Doctor Lundy," said Adelaide, "and while you're there you can inspect the progress of our infirmary."

"Indeed. When I was at your place a few weeks ago you were doing very well with it. I'm looking forward to seeing how far you've progressed."

"And Lawrence and Tahitia will be there too," she added, without acknowledging his last remarks.

"Indeed."

Likely Doctor Lundy would pay call on the plantation much in advance of Christmas to see about patients who suffered from various ailments that he knew needed his care, and while there would also visit La Belle to observe and treat the sick or injured.

On their return, just east of the way station, they met the Van Doke caravan transporting a load of cotton to Memphis, George Van Doke, the middle son of the family, in charge of the procession, but had temporarily moved to the tail end on a handsome bay that he now was coaching into a prance. George was attired in dark riding breeches, and a shirt to match, and also a hat of the same hue styled with a ponderous broad brim which gave it a distinction of western culture. Sitting proudly erect on the handsome animal he gave one the impression that he was trained to ride in the posture of the military. When the last wagon had passed he sidled his horse over to the carriage, Sam drawing the team to a stoppage.

"Adelaide."

"How are you George?" she asked in not the most convivial tone, but on the other hand was not coarse and unfriendly.

"Fine. Thank you. You folks been to Memphis I'd say."

"Yes we have George."

"Well, who is this?" he said, condescendingly looking down at Sasha whose name had begun to sound in his ears ever so frequently over the last several weeks. "Ah, I know. Don't tell me. It's Sasha." Sasha merely curtsied her head with the slightest of movement, and said nothing. Neither did she smile. To put it succinctly, she mildly frowned. At this, which was completely unexpected, George was suddenly caught with a loss as to what to say or do next, and unable to contrive another option, he doffed his hat and wheeled his horse around, spurring the steed into a gallop as he headed away. She had ruffled him, as he had her. It had appeared that he was of the attitude that she would bubble with youthful excitement to meet him. Since he had not made her acquaintance before this occasion he had no way of knowing her inner strength and of the rigid pride that ran through her. Had he, he might well have behaved more earthly and less lordly. Adelaide was ready with not the kindest allusions to the man.

"Ostentatious," she murmured. She knew his mind.

"What did you say?"

"Ostentatious. He's an uppity. Arrogant. I could say that he got that way in the military as a younger man, but he's always been inclined to aloofness, much like his father. Sorry Sasha. But you would have heard it from me sooner or later."

This was the beginning of George Van Doke's and Sasha Duval's acquaintance, not at all auspicious, and would carry forward for years to come. She in an instant did not like him, the first person ever, she said to herself, that she did not welcome on the outset as a potential friend. It was an uncomfortable feeling.

On their return Adelaide commenced planning for Thanksgiving, to which she would invite the workers of the plantation and their families. And it ran through her too that she would be helping Sam Feathers with various decisions pursuant to the finishing of the cotton harvest and the planting season of the next year. "The spring will be upon us Sam before we know it," she said one day not long afterwards. "The seasons are like a circle, round they go and back they come. And they go by so fast. As soon as one is gone another is here to take its place."

"Yes ma'am, they pass quickly."

Sasha had begun to busy herself with this thing or that, playing the piano, bent fervently on conquering Mozart's compositions, reading the medical journals, riding everywhere around the plantation with Adelaide, sometimes visiting Sam Feathers in the fields, kindly offering to help, which was declined. Sam would reply as politely as he knew how that every job was covered. And not the least of importance among her busy pursuits—perhaps it was the most important—was the joining of Mary Tonka in the delivery of babies, where soon in her place she began to lift out the infant and sever the umbilical cord and wash off the reddish excess. In her every action the cautions of Dr. Lundy echoed an alarm that cleanliness was imperative, and that the chlorinated lime solution, which Mary Tonka called "lime" should be plentifully applied in washing the fount of the birth channel and surroundings. In no time they meshed into an agreeable and effective twosome and Mary Tonka began to depend heavily on Sasha to be close at her side on every birthing, and when Doctor Lundy once visited, this happening before the Christmas days set in, she spoke to him of her young friend's astonishing efficiency and stone like courage and said she hardly knew how during all the years she'd gotten by without her.

"Ah, that's good to hear. Very good. I will encourage her to help you even more. You could use it couldn't you?"

"Very much Doctor Lundy."

The days were not many in passing when an accident occurred in the fields with a worker whose hand had become entangled in the jaws of a hay bailer, badly mangled with cuts and bruises all about and two broken fingers. He was brought as quickly as could be to the infirmary. Sam Feathers had driven him there in a wagon at a gallop. Adelaide looked out the window as they approached, the clamor having attracted her, the high creaking of the wheels, the clanging of the trace chains, the pounding of the horses hooves, and the rickety transport itself throwing off a hundred different squeaks and gratings.

"Whoaaa," the voice of Sam Feathers rose high in a tone of apprehension and excitement. Quickly he lifted the man down, who was holding his injured hand, grimacing in pain. "In here. Come with me in here," Sam said excitedly, tugging the man along as he neared the infirmary doorway.

"Sasha," Adelaide almost yelled. "Come quickly. Someone is hurt."

Both Sasha and Adelaide met them at the infirmary door, one or the other holding it open, Sasha directing Sam Feathers to seat the injured. Adelaide had already set water on to boil and now was fetching clean padding from the storage cabinets. Sasha began to hold the padding to the bleeding hand, within a brevity stopping the blood loss and began to soap and wash it in cold water and after that submerged it in the chlorinated lime solution which Adelaide had poured into a receptacle.

"It hurts, I know," said Sasha. "But be patient if you can. I won't be long in caring for you." It was obvious that the man's thumb and its nearest finger companion were badly broken, both warped and disfigured.

"I'll have to reset them Adelaide. Will you bring me the splints?"

"Yes, of course," she replied, and was quickly back with the thin but hard and strong pieces of wooden carving Sasha had asked her to retrieve.

"This will hurt you sir. I could give you whiskey to lessen the pain, but really I don't think you need it."

"Unh, unh. I don't."

"Good." Then she bent the thumb back into place, carefully affixed the disinfected splint, and then tightly bound the injured extremity, repeating essentially the same for the finger, and bandaged as much of the whole hand as she determined necessary.

"There." The man looked relieved, but was clearly still in pain. His face showed it. "Sir, you'll need to stay here for a while to allow us to watch after you. You may need to spend the night. We'll see about that. You're a strong person. I can tell. I believe you'll do just fine. If you think you need it, I'll let you have some whiskey, but I'd rather not."

"No need ma'am. I can hold out."

ꟃ ꟃ

Thanksgiving came and went, a festivity that drew every plantation family and child to the south lawn of the mansion where it was held, Sasha going among them with Adelaide and Mary Tonka passing out plates of food and drink. Cynthia had come from the Van Doke mansion to help. The children found it joyfully tempting to reach and touch the young white girl among them, who returned their adoration by laughing at their excitement and gathering them into her arms. Their mothers had attired them in nice little cotton dresses and did their best to polish and shine their footwear.

The days wore on. Sol and Cynthia could not stay away, returning ever so often to say hello, they said, bringing with them Hallie and Fannie, hoping Sasha was there, and if she wasn't, she likely was riding across the fields, explained Adelaide, and expected her to return in short length. Once when they were on visit Sasha showed them the infirmary, Cynthia commenting that it was a beautiful medicine room, and took on profusely over it, and Sol, cutting his eyes to ascertain that no one saw him, sniffed and wiggled his nose at the odors.

One late afternoon Sam Feathers handed Sasha a letter from Mrs. Laster, which she anxiously opened. They had written one another over the months past but the correspondence was largely abbreviated, mere notes more or less. But this was a long one by comparison. Adelaide stayed back, afraid that what was said might tend to make Sasha cry and that she preferred not to let her emotions be seen. It was a beautiful letter, overflowing with affection and at the same time rather sad. Mrs. Laster felt that something precious had been taken from her life, which was enunciated in the opening lines.

My dear beloved,

I miss you so. From the depth of my soul I do. I think of you at every sundown, or every time I kneel in prayer, or when on some crowded street I hear a lovely voice that reminds me of yours. I am so lonely without you, and I am more so with the coming of the Christmas holidays, which are close upon us and which I shall celebrate at the San Fernando Cathedral.

You know that Father Lumas will put together a grand occasion for us all, especially the children that you hugged and played with during our last one nearly a year ago. Their mothers still ask about you. Bryon and I are sending you a gift, but separate from this letter. I will not tell you what it is, but I think you will like it. I trust that you will. My fingers are crossed that it gets there before the Holy date arrives.

In your notes you have told me very little of your life on the plantation, but you have revealed the most important thing, and that is that Adelaide loves you to death. I knew she would. I read this to Bryon and he laughed and said, 'now she has two mothers, not one but two.' Oh yes, I almost forgot. But Bryon wouldn't let me. You and Adelaide ride horses together, I hear, a long way too, with you on a splendid red sorrel. You must look adorable in your riding habit. I am so glad for you.

Adelaide says in some of her scribbling to me that you are performing marvelously well on the piano, even better than she—I swear she said that—and said that Mary Tonka said she could sit and listen to your music for hours if she but had the time. I wish I could hear it too. She also reports that you are reading every medical piece of research in sight and predicts wondrous things from you. Keep at it. We'll read about you some day.

Before I sign off my darling let us not forget our promise to each other that we'd meet again in no time in New Orleans. Remember. So much to see and do there, and the city is close to half way between Memphis and San Antonio. Bryon says he will come with me. Will you remind Adelaide of this? She said she would bring you. I do look muchly forward to it.

Please write soon. I love you.

Edweena

When she finished with her reading, and handed the letter to Adelaide, she exclaimed most emphatically, "I shall write her this very day"—but she actually would delay a week or more, during which Mrs. Van Doke paid call, unable to resist any longer seeing the young charming girl that tantalized everyone in her midst. Even George, who felt she had shunned him, reported with unbiased honesty to his mother that she was a thing of culture and beauty.

Chapter 30

AT THREE or later in the afternoon Martha Van Doke guided the team of splendid horses to a halt that pulled her carriage. She looked about while waiting for the attendant to relieve her, admiring the décor immaculately in place which surrounded Adelaide's home. She had driven herself. She was a stubbornly independent woman, often resisting others helping her, no matter the task, but if the truth were known she on this occasion sought to go overboard a bit, showing that she was completely self reliant, as she knew Adelaide was also, and had heard that Sasha was of the same temperament. But she had not been known to drive as far away from her home as she just had unless someone was at her side. The attendant took the horses by their bridles and led them to the pavilion where carriages of guests were emplaced until returned to later use. She had dismounted from the carriage unaccompanied, waving the attendant off, who tried to help, and was on her way up the portico steps when Adelaide saw her. Wasting no time Adelaide laid down her work and went to the doorway, and from there met her neighbor and dear friend mid way.

"I do declare. An unexpected guest and one badly missed. How are you Martha?"

"I am fine Adelaide. And I can tell that you are. The rosy pink of your pretty face says it all. You are at the peak of your verdure."

"Thank you. We are all grateful for health, every second of it that He gives to us. But do come in. I shall start tea immediately. We'll sit in the drawing room if you like."

"Very good. I love that room. I have always. So selectively endowed of exotic paintings from Europe where you were schooled, and books. Many, many books of all sorts devised by the hands and intellect of the most illustrious authors."

"Yes, it is a nice room and I thoroughly love it. But before I start to digress excuse me while I begin our tea."

As her visitor looked around her eyes of incisive detail settled upon the windows, wide and lengthy with a splendid view to the west, adorned with costly silk curtains and rich Toulouse and Turkestan tapestries. The books of innumerable subjects and classifications which were neatly ordered in the shelves running the full length of the walls for a moment held her—but what she searched for mostly was the painting of a young girl. Adelaide would have been quick to set it out on display. Martha was not long in spotting it. There it was on the side table slightly behind a Persian lamp of green and gold, having gotten pushed from full view for some reason or other. She was seven or eight, her admirer adjudged, dressed in white, hair hanging over her shoulders, trying to smile but not quite making it. "You could see she was a comer even then," thought Martha Van Doke, "primed to bud and bloom. She must be astounding now. Well, I shall see."

Soon she would have the answer, for within a brevity Sasha suddenly made her entry, with Adelaide yet in the kitchen. She had spent the past half hour servicing the knee of a young girl who'd punctured it when she inadvertently bumped into a nail protruding through a board in one of the barns. She had swabbed the puncture with disinfectant, probing to the bottom of the injury, thankful that it wasn't deep, but she feared the invasion of the potentially deadly bacteria Clostridium tetani, thus producing lockjaw. No antitoxin drugs at that stage of medical history were available for use, and would not be developed until the 1880's. The mother and child had left by way of the back entrance.

Thoroughly unordinary for her, Sasha's hair was pulled up on her head which was bedecked in a stylish green cap. It was then that she removed her white coat, in which she had attired herself while in the infirmary, thus exposing plainly her pretty white blouse, ruffled and full. Her skirt of pale green dropped well below her knees. It was from a material of chiffon.

"Oh," let out Martha Van Doke, "no doubt about your identity. You are lovely, as they say, and at last I get to meet you." She went briskly to Sasha, who hardly knew how to take the woman, and enfolded her in her arms. "How lovely her eyes up close," she thought. Sasha then embraced her in return, but only lightly. "I am Sasha Duval and you are Mrs. Van Doke." Sasha wished that Adelaide had returned from the kitchen a minute or so earlier. She felt uncomfortable in the introduction of herself to the aging woman, wife of the Ethnarch of the Van Doke plantation.

"Yes I am dear, and I am so glad to make your acquaintance."

"So you two have met, or shall I say are meeting," Adelaide's voice rippled forth. "I didn't even get to introduce you." She laughed a laugh that said 'you didn't need me, did you, and I am delighted that Sasha did it on her own.'"

"We have, and are, as you say," answered Martha Van Doke.

"Let us be seated," Adelaide suggested. "I mean be seated again," she clarified, coquettishly making play with her guest.

Sasha chose the gargantuan sofa for her sitting, already lowering herself onto the thick plush cushions, and now removed her archer's cap, whereupon, down plunged her plentiful beautiful strands, floundering as they cascaded onto her shoulders, now drawing an absorbing glance from Martha Van Doke, together with a low sigh. She then enfolded her hands and sat erect in silent pose in anticipation of the older women taking the lead in conversation. But the conversation stayed narrowly on her.

"While sitting in wait of Adelaide, Sasha, my eyes caught sight of your portrait. That's the one right over there on the side table." She pointed. "You were younger then. I am glad that Adelaide has thoughtfully set it out for people to see."

"You are correct. I was younger, seven or eight. Forgive me. I cannot be exact. My mother called in a British artist for the sketching when I lived on the Canary Islands. I remember him well. I kept altering my position, my face, I should explain. I think he was nettled. But we finally struggled through it."

"It's adorable. But do you have one more recently done?"

"No ma'am. Not yet."

"But we'll see to that Martha," said Adelaide. "She is at an age that is passing swiftly and every day counts. Today she is no longer who she was yesterday. It has dawned on me for a while to take her to Memphis just after Christmas and employ one of the more prominent artists there to do the sketching."

"Fine, fine. And may I place my request here and now for a posing of your selection, for I must have it, and will pay dearly for the adornment."

As the conversation moved further, and shifted from topic to topic, Mrs. Van Doke finally inquired of the infirmary, the new infirmary she'd heard so much about from Cynthia.

"Your new infirmary. I am dying to see it," she exclaimed, glancing back and forth at Adelaide and Sasha, taking it that Sasha was the key element of importance in the superintendence of the facility. Mary Tonka incessantly told Cynthia of Sasha's help to her in the delivery of the plantation babies and of the ailments of many sorts she was beginning to attend on her own, and Cynthia passed all this on to Mrs. Van Doke.

"Surely you may. We'd be delighted," answered Adelaide, rising from her seat, as did Sasha.

Mrs. Van Doke had long felt disappointment with the facilities for treating the sick at the Van Doke plantation, the doctors left with no choice but to enter the cramped space and jumbled carnage of the slave shacks and there carry on with their practice. Privacy for the patient during or after the treatment was non existent, no quarter available for isolation from other members of the family, whose only recourse was to pray that their loved one would soon heal and in the meanwhile themselves endure the moans and cries and the tossing and tumbling throughout the night. Mrs. Van Doke had heard also from Cynthia of the nice conveniences of Adelaide's and Sasha's infirmary, how equipped it was with a private bed and a private toilet, and a vaulted ceiling with wide angled windows for the admittance of lighting, and this she saw in a second as they entered, as well as the paintings of quiet rural scenes populating the walls.

Martha Van Doke drew back, letting out a breath. "I am lacking for words. Amazing things have happened here. I've heard you were making changes, Adelaide, but did not dream you were starting from scratch at erecting a new complex."

"It was time Martha. We decided on an all out effort."

"My, my. You certainly did. I am sick with envy. We have nothing at our place. Nothing. The people's houses are the infirmary. And that is a terribly unsuitable situation. How long have you been at this?"

"Several months. We are still working at it."

"Goodness. Fast. Who did you employ for the work?"

"Sam Feathers arranged for a contractor and architect from Memphis. They moved swiftly with the more general aspects, the cruder things which obviously had to be done, and with the finer things less fast. Once this was behind us Sasha and I, with many suggestions from Doctor Lundy, dove into the layout schemes. Where everything was to be placed. See over there. That's where the medicines are stored, and over there the surgical instruments."

"And this is the examination table, is it not?" asked Martha Van Doke, lowering her hand on it.

"Yes it is. And there is a room in the back with a bed and toilet for the recovering patient."

"This is fantastic. We must copy it. I must tell Andre of it when he's here over the holidays."

Sasha seemed to ponder this last remark, unable to fit the name into the scheme of things, and observing her perplexity Mrs. Van Doke explained.

"Andre is my youngest son, dear, very wound up in medicine. He's making a doctor."

"Where is he now?" asked Sasha, to this date wholly unaware that there was an Andre. It swept through her that he was perhaps likened to his brother George and this was not an agreeable evolvement.

"He's in Baltimore, learning as much as he can by tagging along with the doctors at one of the hospitals. He studies hard all the time, as I hear you do. Reads, reads, reads, all the time. He's under the supervision of Doctor Shane Givens, who comes down each summer to care for the sick at the Van Doke plantation, excepting he couldn't make it this summer past. Andre works with him as an intern."

"I didn't know," said Sasha, the very slight contraction of her brow telling that she had learned something which seemed quite intriguing in her imagination.

Adelaide had not before brought up the name of Andre, for she knew very little of his association with Doctor Givens in that when the doctor came to the Sherette plantation to look after the sick Andre was not with him.

"You must meet Andre, Sasha," said Martha Van Doke. "You two seem to have goals in mind that are very much similar."

"Yes we seem to. It would be nice to talk with him."

The lady had stayed longer than she intended, and stayed still longer, such that Sasha had to excuse herself to accompany her friend to look in on a woman on the verge of child birth. Mary Tonka had stuck her head in the doorway twice before, appearing anxious to leave. So Sasha explained to their guest that she must bid good day, but with regrets, and found Mary Tonka waiting on the portico, the two of them climbing into the carriage and driving away in the direction of the woman's home more than a half mile in the distance. Martha Van Doke and Adelaide watched them through the window until the bend of the road took them behind a grove of trees and out of sight.

"She's a lovely girl Adelaide, so quick with her intellect, and a careful conversationalist. You'd think she was twenty five."

"I agree. She's all of that, and more. She'll become an exceptional physician one day. I am certain she will. She loves the medical field, as does your Andre. I think you'll be seeing her at your place with Doctor Lundy when he's there looking after the sick. He's getting fast attached to her and sees where with her knowledge and background she can be of invaluable benefit to him."

"I think so. I certainly do. Already she's helping Mary Tonka with childbirths. That's what Cynthia tells me."

"She is. They're molding into a fine team."

"Ah, that is so interesting, and I'll look forward to seeing her when she comes with the good doctor. To do whatever. But let me say this Adelaide, before it slips me. Actually I'm thinking of two things in one. May I?"

"Whatever you wish dear. Go right ahead."

"The first is concerned with erecting a new infirmary at the Van Doke plantation, identical to yours. The possibility has sent me whirling. I keep dwelling on it. I can't let it go. I'll want to share this with Andre. Will you mind supplying me with the name of the architect and the builder from Memphis?"

"Not at all. I'll hand it to you before you leave."

"Good."

"And the second item?"

"I'm thinking of the Christmas holidays. I'm aware of the celebration that you have for your people on Christmas day, the tree, the food, the gifts, and that is wonderful. Do you think you and Sasha might come to dinner at my home on a date that doesn't conflict with your plans?" This was an affair of superlative recognition to which she alluded, people of opulence attending from as far away as fifty miles out, men dressed in suits and women clad in expensive raiment, their children with them, dressed expensively as well. The Van Dokes also provided for their slave people on Christmas day much in the manner that Adelaide took care of hers, the tree, the food, the gifts, but she did not open that up for elaboration.

"I don't see why not Martha. I'll speak to Sasha about it. We'll see you in a couple of days to settle on the exact date."

"I do hope she'll come. She would so light up everything."

"I'm glad you like her."

"I do. But more than that. I'm fascinated with her."

Shortly, Adelaide helped Martha into her carriage, handing her the name of the architect she'd promised, and Martha, taking hold of the reins, drove away toward the La Belle. On the way she had an after thought or two, which she started to bring up during her visit but let them slip; besides, she felt it improper to address the subject in the presence of Sasha. She had meant to ask Adelaide why Sasha came to live with her, and why was it that she had lived once on the Canary Islands, but these ruminations lingered only temporarily. She soon dismissed them as inconsequential, swayed more by far by the intellect and charm of the young girl which was yet fresh and vivid upon her and it was these images that occupied her for rest of the mileage.

Adelaide had suspected that Mrs. Van Doke was on the threshold of raising these inquiries. She wasn't a mental telepathist but felt throughout her visit that her friend and neighbor was on the edge of curiosity, especially weighing why Sasha was there to live with her. "People will by small tiny increments seek the answers. Their inborn tendencies will make certain of that. They will want to know everything there is to know. But they will not succeed. They will never see the letter that I have seen. They will never know the real truth unless some day Sasha cares to divulge it."

She had spoken of "….the letter that I have seen." What she had reference to was the recent letter she had received from her brother in response to Father Lumas's letter to him. The lines most poignant to her were fairly brief and there was no doubt what they said.

> Before he passes on Father Lumas deems it best to ascertain that I know beyond the thinnest of ambiguity that Sasha Duval was born by Izu Duval, her mother, a young Negro woman, in the presence of Father Otto Conrad Kestner, and Doctor Carlos Enoch, the attending physician. This was never before revealed to me. 'In the presence of' is apparently the key phrase here. It is to verify in other words. The good Father proceeded to emphasize that in future years and perhaps sooner than I might expect the knowledge of this event could prove vital to my decision making and care of Sasha, who is now under my protection and guidance and likely will remain so for some time to come. It might even have legal implications, he said, inheritance and such. Even marriage.

Father Lumas had apologized to Lawrence Sherette that this transmission of fact was excessively late, that he should have acted sooner, though felt it unnecessary. But had changed his mind.

Adelaide sighed when she had read the letter, reflecting impassively. "Now I know. There is not one figment of doubt that Sasha sprang from a Negro mother and a white father. But what difference does it make?"

Chapter 31

SASHA HAD met George Van Doke already, and Martha Van Doke, the mother, and now was about to meet another of the family, the youngest son, Andre. Christmas was a week away. Adelaide had previously let Mrs. Van Doke know they would attend the dinner to which she'd invited them. Sasha that morning was out riding about and tromping in the fields with Sam Feathers, returning by noon to have lunch, and after that retiring to the drawing room where she began to read a miscellany of articles from the several journals at her disposal and was still reading at the mid afternoon hour or past when a light knock sounded at the front door. Adelaide went and answered.

"Andre, I am pleasantly surprised. Please come in."

"Thank you Miss Adelaide," he returned, moving through the doorway, starting to look around. She motioned her hand for him to take a seat.

"Thank you. I'll sit for a slight. But cannot stay long. I simply wanted to say hello." Adelaide had long thought that Andre was a fine young gentleman. And today he was no different. He was astutely courteous.

"You're home for the holidays."

"Yes ma'am. I'll be around for about two weeks. It's good to be home. Baltimore is a far piece."

"Doctor Givens didn't come with you."

"No. He's with his family. He only spends time on the plantation during the summer months."

"So what will you be doing while you're here?"

"We have the Christmas gatherings, as you know. So I'll be into those things, and then if Doctor Lundy is here, I'll stay as close to him as possible. You know, to help him and to learn."

"Your studies and work in Baltimore, at the hospital I should say; are they going well?"

"Oh, very. It's hard work but I love it."

He kept lowering his hands on his knees off and on then raising them. "Youthful nervousness," she thought. Adelaide grasped too that he busily trained his eyes back and forth toward the doorways that led to various rooms close by, as if anticipating something, the emergence of a person. It was clear to her that Mrs. Van Doke had told her son an earful of Sasha Duval, and deemed that that was the reason he came calling. She felt an obligation to raise her name with no additional passage of time.

"You have heard of Sasha Duval, have you not? My Sasha, who stays with me."

"I have Miss Adelaide. My mother has reported of her to me. Says she is much taken to medicine."

"She is. This is her home now. She is in the drawing room studying."

"But I don't want to disturb her, I—."

"Not at all Andre. Just sit still."

Adelaide left and opened the door to the drawing room, whispering lowly to Sasha that they had a guest and felt sure she would like to meet him.

"Who is it? asked Sasha, her eyebrows lifting, her face lightening.

"Andre. Andre Van Doke, Martha's youngest son. You heard her mention him. He's in the living room. He stopped off to say hello. He's home for the holidays."

"Oh. All right. I'll come this minute."

Sasha left her chair, felt of her hair, which was as usual, lapping over her shoulders, and then brushed off her clothing with a stroke or two, though there really wasn't anything to brush away. She was acting from habit. It was a lovely garment of pale yellow, let us emphasize, the upper bodice adorned with plentiful ruffles that ran down to her mid portion; the skirt clung loosely and flowed to her ankles, and there was a collar of deep jet black that encircled her pretty white neck. The cuffs, themselves liberally ruffled, were enlivened with spangles, which as she moved her arms and hands discharged an array of tiny fragments of glitter. Adelaide was especially fond of this attire, for she had patterned and stitched the pieces together; her soul was in it. Sasha often wore it while in study. Adelaide did not know before the present that Sasha had chosen to slip it on for her reading but spilled over with delight and broke into a broad grin when she saw it again upon her. "It becomes her, quite becomes her," she said silently.

Stunned by her remarkable beauty of person, entirely over and above that which his mother had conveyed, Andre gave every evidence that he was frozen into a dilemma, neither able to speak outright nor could he remain quiet. That first acquaintance he described to his wife years later when reflecting upon the scene with steadier calm, obviously delighting in going back over it.

> On seeing you for the first time I declare I swallowed. I remember it still. I thought I wouldn't be able to speak, to greet you with even one word. I hoped Adelaide would hurry up and introduce us. You were a dream sweetheart, far surpassing what my mother had said of you, which was a plenty, all of it casting a wonderful sweet image; and though you were three years or more behind me in age, I fell in love with you at first sight. I swear I did. And my brain swam with fantasies. Even though you were somewhat younger I would bide my time, I said. Adelaide must have seen in my countenance how you had gotten to me, but I steadied myself and finally managed to shake your hand. How awkward! Shaking the hand of a beautiful young thing like you! Why in the world did I do that? But we did say hello too, and things went very well after that.

When finally they had clasped hands and said hello, Andre was by and large recovered from his jitters, and they began to converse with only a trace of inhibition. In contrast to her usual character, which was to be a bit reserved with strangers, she was now outward, taking an even part in any topic that cropped up. It was she that unleashed the opening remark. Adelaide was relieved when she assumed the initiative.

"You're here from Baltimore for the holidays."

"I am. For two weeks."

"That's nice."

"Yeah, it is. I look forward to it."

"When did you get here?"

"Today, at noon."

"They were glad to see you I'm sure."

"Indeed. My mother especially. You know how mothers are. She took on for the longest. I've been with her all afternoon, bringing her up to date. Until I decided to drop by here and say hello to Miss Adelaide and Sam Feathers. Does he happen to be here?" Adelaide couldn't resist a hidden laugh.

"No, he's in the fields," answered Sasha.

"Still there?"

"I think so. They're working late. Until night fall. They're trying to store several loads of freshly cut wheat in the barns. I was out there with them this morning."

"You go into the fields, I mean, do you go out there a lot?"

"All the time. I love it."

My mother tells me you're pursuing medicine. What a discovery. What attracts you to it? I mean to say, what branch, what particular area draws you?"

"Ha, ha. Everything. But seriously, surgery appeals to me most. I'd like to become a surgeon."

"Hmmmmh. Wow. So much to be learned there, so many unknowns. That's what Doctor Givens says, my supervisor at the Baltimore hospital."

"He certainly is right I'm sure. The more I read and study, the more I find what he says is so."

"Andre, did you hear yet of our new infirmary?" asked Adelaide, concluding that it was time to invite him to see it, that it was part of the reason he came.

"Oh, yes ma'am. I have. I'd love to see it," he answered, while rising from his chair, Sasha's eyes running up and down the attire in which he was dressed: trousers of plain khaki, a simple light sweater of blue upon his upper portion, a pair of newly purchased field shoes on his feet. They were tan. There was as well a thick shock of hair on his head, dark in the manner of Sasha's and carefully combed. But what swayed her most impressively was his persona, his friendliness and joyfulness, his openness and humility, his boyish manner. And his handsomeness. She liked him. She did at first blush.

Though greatly elated over this fine facility, Adelaide chose a background stance, which left Sasha to take the lead. And as she often did with visitors of an educated level she began to point out things in detail. He marveled at the surgical instruments stored in the cabinet marked "surgery," and the natural lighting pouring in through the ponderous windows, and the rows of medicines in the cabinets marked "medicines," such medicines ranging from whiskey to morphine to sodium chloride and them some.

"My," young Andre exuded, "this has required work and thoughtfulness. Much, much thoughtfulness. I am on the brink of losing my composure. We must undertake something like this at our place. Doctor Givens and Doctor Lundy would be pleased to no end."

"And your mother," Adelaide put in.

"Yes. She said as much."

After further and various exchanges, his eyes fell upon the voluminous display of medical journals lining the shelves, Sasha proudly explaining why they were stored there, and tacked on that a Doctor Charlatan whom she'd met while making her way to New Orleans from San Antonio had recently mailed to her a bulky volume of medical sources. Yet here the subject of medicine was beginning to wane and so she began to explore with their guest the titles to the great many books of literature positioned attractively upright in the shelves of the drawing room, this too however eventually running its course. Andre had prefaced to

Adelaide that he was there for a brief visit when he first came but the stay had lapsed into more than an hour and he showed no signs of departing. By then they had moved to the portico, Adelaide and Sasha taking a seat in the swing and Andre choosing one of the high back rockers.

"I was going down to the Big Hatchie when I stopped off," he said, "just riding around. I trust you didn't mind my tying my horse to the tree over there Miss Adelaide." Adelaide had on the first conveniently seen the animal through the front windows.

"Not at all. He's a handsome sort."

"I hear that you ride too Sasha. That you're a very good rider. Anything to that?" He felt the need to smile and did a little.

"I ride. How well, I'm afraid to say."

"She's superb Andre. I know. I'm out with her several times a week."

He saw no reason to respond to Adelaide's evaluation, but began to struggle with an idea that he knew he had to resolve. So he came out with it, though somewhat awkwardly.

"Er uh. Would you like to ride with me down to the Big Hatchie," he asked bashfully, looking into Sasha's eyes, then turning his face downward, and then back to Sasha. "I was on my way there."

"Well, I—."

"Oh that would be splendid," Adelaide lost no time wedging in. "Sure. Go Sasha. It's a lovely part of the day, the sun still high enough in the sky, and the mist will not have covered the bottom lands."

"All right. I'll go. Let me change."

When they stepped off the portico, heading to a nearby stable for her horse, the sorrel, Andre's eyes settled for a moment on the pretty riding habit that Adelaide had recently bought for her. As riding habits will, this one very aptly showed the contour of her splendid form, and one would have to logically assume that while already under the influence of her great beauty and charm, this drew him even further into her sphere. Sasha saddled her horse, Andre attempting to help, but opted to step aside, since she was minutely acquainted with the assortments—the strapping, the buckles, where this fit with that, and was well on her way to skillfully and quickly meshing everything together. Suddenly, she finished, and sprang atop her mount, then he on his, both simultaneously coaxing their steeds into an easy prance toward the curve in the road where they would disappear from view behind the trees.

The sun was yet above tree level, still bright, the temperature pleasantly cool, the mist not to settle in for some time, when the sun was beginning to drop out of sight. With but limited words between them they rode on, already past the orchards, now approaching the vast cotton fields, with rows that seemed to extend forever. The cotton was gone, only fragments of it left, clinging pitiably to the brownish dead bolls that the pickers had stripped of substance. They kept their horses at a trot, sometimes prompting them into a gallop. At every opportunity Andre cut his eyes over at Sasha, but done swiftly, hoping she didn't see him. But she did. She thought she might smile, and more than once almost let one break through. Yet held it back. In time, they would reach the corn fields, planted further west, nearer the river, and lastly the hayfields that bordered the river, which from time to time jumped its banks and flooded the lower landscape, though the damage to the hay crop was much less in terms of dollars and cents than might have been to the cotton or corn. When the water receded the grass recovered and a large amount was salvaged. In the month of December the river seldom flooded, so there was no present worry over it jumping its banks. Not far in the distance they saw Sam Feathers and his crew of twenty or thirty working feverishly to load and haul to the storage warehouses the browning wheat that was cut three days past. It was the second crop. Sasha waved and he waved back, holding his hand up to his forehead, with eyes narrowed, trying to recognize the stranger beside her. Then it came to him. "That's Andre. I see him clearly now. His horse. I'd know that animal anywhere, and Andre too because of the way he holds himself up in his saddle." He then waved his arms and hands wildly. When they reached the banks of the Big Hatchie the water was muddy, the rains having fallen several miles up stream the day before, but it wasn't enough to dissuade the Negro fishermen who had strung their lines and baited their hooks. They were just beginning to light a fire, which they'd keep feeding with drift wood until the dawn.

"What will they catch?" asked Sasha.

"Catfish, carp, brim. But the catfish they'll keep. The rest they'll throw back."

"You've fished the Big Hatchie?"

"Many times when I was a boy. Sam Feathers took me. We'd spend the night here. All night. We fished in the back waters. In the sloughs. The Negroes are going to do some of that too. Sam is the best at catching catfish." In the meanwhile they had tied their horses to a bush, electing to walk along the river banks, looking at the thrashing turbulence.

"It's so muddy. I can't understand how fish could live in it."

"They can. The muddier the better."

"Look at the logs and debris. It's ugly Andre. I mean the logs and the water and everything." But Andre gave no answer. He simply agreed by means of an ineffable nod.

They began to walk further along the shoreline, the overhanging branches rank and prickly obstructing their pathway, tearing at their clothing, and there were logs and pieces of driftwood scattered here and there that Andre moved aside before they went on.

"I agree Sasha. It's not a pretty sight, and it's dangerous out here."

"You mean the high water?"

"Well that too, but that's not what I had in mind. Cottonmouths. Their bite can be deadly. They're thick in these waters. And on the banks too. Careful that you watch out for them."

"Oh. I will. But they aren't around this time of year, are they?"

"That's right. Only in the warm season. I should have said that."

The sun had dropped below the horizon and the mist had begun to dim the landscape. Suddenly it was later than their senses had recognized. Shadows were falling. Andre said they'd better go, though the old owl secluded by the craggy boughs of a tree somewhere, up or down stream—they couldn't tell which—seemed determined to entice them to stay on, if but the slenderest of time longer. They sat down on a log and listened.

"Did you hear that?" he asked, "the old guy is hooting at us. There he goes again."

"Hooting at us?"

"Well, not really. I guess it's his way of talking with his companions. Or about to. Pretty soon you'll hear an echo from one of them."

Very soon there evolved a consonance of hoots, all synchronized in some semblance of a purposely timed cadence, Andre and Sasha listening with growing amusement.

"That's so intriguing. I don't think I've ever heard an owl hoot before. But all this reminds me of something I read about once. It came from a book that my father gave me. Shall I tell it to you?"

"I can't resist. Please do."

"The Romans, in their period of glory, seemed to have a premonition about dark birds, crows and owls and such. Mainly these two I think. On the day of Caesar's assassination a crow kept following him around, lighting on a high stone wall once along the great man's pathway where the bird knocked off some loose fittings that fell near his feet, an omen, they later said; and there were other strange happenings caused by this bird on that same day. As to the owl, well, the Romans called him bubo. Why, I do not know but it is said they did. And there's a story about him too, even more dramatic. But supposedly true."

"Bubo."

"Ha, ha. Yes, bubo."

"So tell me."

"I will. There was a principal man once of the nation of Judea who was placed in bondage by the Roman Emperor Tiberius Caesar, and saw no hope for release. Tiberius was a very evil emperor who apparently meant to let the man in bondage die in chains. This man's name was Agrippa, who is not likely to be unfamiliar to you. On a particular day this man Agrippa, a relatively young man, stood in his bonds before the royal palace, leaning against a certain tree in grievance of his ill fortune, with many others, who were in bonds adjacent to him. It happened as well that a certain bird, bubo, sat upon a limb of the tree against which Agrippa was leaning, at which time, strange as it may sound, one of those that were bound also, a man of Germanic descent, spoke to him in his native tongue, 'My dear young fellow do not grieve so, for it cannot be that thou shouldst long continue in these bonds, and will soon be delivered from them, and will be promoted to the highest dignity and power. But, do remember as well that when thou seest this bird again, that thou will live but five days longer.'"

"Oooooh! Was he freed? Was he promoted to great power?"

"He was freed and made Tetrarch of many vast provinces by the new emperor of Rome. Tiberius had unexpectedly died."

"When did Agrippa die?"

"Years and years later."

"You are an enthralling story teller Sasha, which is evidence that you must surely and continually wander deeply into the pages of the most eminent creators of ideas and adventures. I saw this afternoon many of those names with my own eyes, and the stories you have this minute relayed to me are grounded in ancient cultures. You are far ahead of me. I do not apply myself that broadly. In this regard you remind me of my mother."

With this said they again looked at the dusk that had closed upon them, the sorcery of night about to follow, Andre again cautioning that they'd better go, for even though the horses knew the road home without human steering, there was the danger of an obstacle lying unseen by either horse or human.

"We can gallop for a piece Sasha, then we'd best slow to a trot."

"I'm with you Andre. Gallop then trot."

When reaching the mansion, an attendant stood outside waiting, taking the bridles in his hands as the riders dismounted and strode with better than a usual gait across the portico. Adelaide was sitting with her knitting kit, stitching a garment together she'd set aside months ago, now taking it up again.

"Hello," Sasha's voice came floating to her hearing.

"In here sweetheart, in the sewing room."

First Sasha entered, then Andre, Sasha going over and planting a kiss on Adelaide's brow. Adelaide kissed her in return. This was a good sign to Andre who suspected without good cause that Adelaide was fretted over his keeping her Sasha out until after nightfall.

"We erred Miss Adelaide. My apologies for keeping her. We got to listening to the hoot owls."

"Oh goodness Andre. You should not give that a second thought. No, no, no. Not a second thought."

"Thank you." He smiled, feeling relieved. "Well, I must get on," he said, edging toward the door. "Mother will worry. You know how mothers are."

"I know."

"Goodnight, and thank you Sasha for keeping me company."

"The same Andre. It was fun."

Chapter 32

WHEN HE had left the portico Sasha dashed to the bathroom, there beginning to draw her bath water and at the same time pushing back the clothes in the closet for her robe. She did not have to look long. Adelaide had hung it on the near rack for her when she'd finished bathing. She smiled at the note appended to it. "Now aren't you glad you went? Don't you agree he's the nicest young man on earth?"

Once in her robe she hurried to the sewing room where she had left off, finding that Adelaide was no longer there, having gone to the kitchen where she was ironing a few clothes to relieve Mary Tonka, who had had a long day. She sometimes did this. She touched a finger to her tongue and then to the iron, showing by the slightest waver of her head that it was still hot enough for use and went back to work. In no time Sasha found her, approaching from behind, there reaching her arms around her and squeezing, pressing her face to her shoulder. Adelaide heard the cute girlish giggle. It said everything. It was what she was hoping to hear. She, herself, broke into a happy joyful laugh, pleased to no end that Sasha was ecstatic, immeasurably gladdened that she had discovered a playmate of an age close to her own. A tad older, he was, but not by far.

"Did you have a good time sweetheart?"

"I had a wonderful time Adelaide. I really did. Andre is a very sweet person."

The interval yet remaining before Christmas was dwindling down, in which Adelaide and Mary Tonka busily set about to put the mansion in order, the hired help performing the cleaning of floors and curtains and washing the windows, and baking, Sasha helping in some way or the other. But sometimes she was interrupted by Andre who had dropped by to ask if she cared to ride with him, which Adelaide preferred that she do above anything else. Adelaide swelled with gladness when she saw him riding up. "Sasha, Andre is here. See what he wants."

Tahitia had been brought from Memphis two days before, now diving into the whirl as much as Adelaide would let her. "You don't need to bother yourself with all this Tahitia dear. You're my guest. Rest yourself. Take a seat on the portico and look at the scenery." Sam Feathers called in the field hands to help set up the tables on the south lawn, very long and ponderous tables, made of rough river bottom oak, later covered with white sparkling linens, where the field hands and their families were to be treated to the best Christmas that Adelaide and her helpers could devise. The Christmas tree glittered with decorations. At the Van Doke plantation the events were unfolding in a similar fashion, though the Christmas tree was erected in the middle of the slave quarters, in one of the largest dirt yards, not on a pretty grassy lawn. But food would be available in great supply and gifts handed out. It was a happy time of year for the slave folks.

In all this, the preparations in other words, Sasha still found time after she and Adelaide had knelt one night to say their prayers to sit down at the side table within reach of their bed and there take quill in hand and draft what she considered an overdue letter to Mrs. Laster.

My dearest,

I am too long in writing. Forgive me. To begin with I wish you were here in my presence. I would hug you twenty score times. And should Bryon be around also I would extend to him the same. Please give my dear brother all my love. And Father Lumas.

I miss you awfully. I think of you every waking hour. I wish with my very soul that I could return to those sweet tender times. Just once. I am often lonely thinking of when we were together but it lessens when I busy myself with something.

So much is happening here. A short while ago Adelaide and I took a trip to Memphis to see for ourselves the construction progress of Lawrence Sherette's church, which is almost complete. Soon we will start attending mass there every other weekend.

We have built an infirmary at Adelaide's home, and have stocked it with surgical instruments of the many kinds, and with other medical necessities too, gowns and wiping cloths and medicines. It also has an examination table. I have added many of my own journals to its shelves and Adelaide has added numerous others that she owned or which someone has recently sent her. She subscribes to Kings College Hospital of London for their latest publications, even though there is a fee.

You have not heard of La Belle, the mansion on the Van Doke plantation, a slave plantation that is next to us, where people are kept against their will and work and are treated badly. These are Negro people and I will likely be helping to see after them when they are sick. They are often sick. There is a Doctor Lundy of the city of Memphis who tends to the people on Adelaide's plantation and on the Van Doke plantation as well. He has become my friend. I will aid him in this work to the extent of my ability. He has asked me to. He is a friend of Adelaide and Lawrence Sherette of long standing.

I have met the mistress of La Belle, Mrs. Martha Van Doke. She came to see us one day not long ago. She appears to have goodness in her heart and yet it is trying for me to understand how she can be good and still have something to do with the governance of slaves. But I do like her and I think she likes me. She seems to like me very much. In this same breath let me say that I very much like her son. I met him recently. This was after Mrs. Van Doke's visit. He just dropped in. I think she persuaded him. He said he was going riding down along the Big Hatchie. That's a river running through Adelaide's land. With some difficulty he after a while asked if I would like to join him, and at the urging of Adelaide, who gave her approval, I decided I would. He was such a nice young gentleman. I could tell that Adelaide wanted me pretty badly to accept the invitation and know that she wants me to join him on other outings when the opportunity arises. Maybe it's because he is so near my age and that she feels I should be around people like that a little more.

We are planning an enormous Christmas here. It's much different from Father Lumas's. It's mainly for the field hands that work for Adelaide. Already she has bought no telling the number of gifts for both parents and children. I marvel at her goodness. We will have tons of food. Forgive me. I am overstating, but truly I am astounded at the poundage of chickens and hogs they say they will be barbecuing over a fire in a pit. I haven't seen this done before. The custom is strange to me.

Lastly, I refer to New Orleans. We must do that. We must. I have not yet taken this up with Adelaide. But will. I'll let you know.

Will write you again soon.

I love you,

Sasha

Christmas Eve finally arrived, and Adelaide and Sasha, having stayed up late wrapping gifts, began to talk with one another, Adelaide opening a subject which was surprisingly unexpected to Sasha. She'd always tried to be strong in her presence but tonight she weakened.

"I think of my mother at Christmas Sasha, more than at any other time. It's a hard time, the hardest of times. It's the little things we did together that play upon me. We were just getting to know one another when she left me for Heaven. Oh, it broke my heart. She was dear to me you can't imagine how much."

Tears welled up in her eyes and Sasha, with tears in her eyes too, never aware of Adelaide's hurt before now, leaned over to her.

"Oh Adelaide, you have never said any of this to me before. I didn't know."

They were sitting on the rug floor and had put their arms around one another.

"No, I don't think I have. After all, I was of some age then, when she went, and that made a difference. You were so young when your mother left you, and your father, and the sky must have fallen on you much harder."

"It was bad. But yours was too. It's bad no matter what the age."

"Well, we both understand sweetheart what it is to lose someone so tied to us, so embedded in our hearts. The hole they leave is enormous and is never to be filled."

They knelt and said their prayers as usual, Sasha leading, whereas the next night Adelaide said it first. After the "Amen" Adelaide turned to the thought of her brother which she often did when she dipped into loneliness. His kind and friendly image uplifted her.

"Lawrence will arrive tomorrow morning early. Ezra will drive him. I hope he will stay awhile."

"Let's encourage him all we can. Both of us. But of course he has many things on his shoulders. I guess we'll have to see. I can hardly stand still until he's here."

"The same for me sweetheart."

The next morning at nine o'clock Lawrence Sherette was there, he and Ezra having been on the road since four. Lawrence admitted that his dear reliable friend had born the greatest burden by a sizeable amount, for it was he who had to guide the horses and remain alert. Sasha had run to meet them when the carriage pulled up. She climbed up on the wheels and then into the carriage to hug Lawrence Sherette.

"Hey, who is this?" Lawrence called out exuberantly. "My, my, you are enthusiastic. Careful that you don't fall and hurt yourself."

"I won't. I'm used to it."

She then kissed and hugged him, and after all three had let themselves down Sasha insisted on taking Lawrence Sherette's clothes encasement, though was refused.

"A man's job sweetheart. Ha, ha."

He then looked and saw the pretty red rose affixed to her hair, and complimented it. The sun was out with a brilliance that morning and the rays against her nice white skin accentuated the adornment even more. She merely smiled that he'd noticed. He accused her of wearing it just to cheer his day. She laughed and said such a nice idea had occurred to her but didn't actually admit that was the reason.

As they entered Sasha's youthful voice carried with raised elevation across the room. "Mary Tonka, I have someone with me who is dying to see you."

Mary Tonka looked up and stopped in her tracks, as if suddenly frozen. If something had been in her hands she surely would have let it fall.

"Lawrence, Lawrence," she called his name to the top of her lungs. "Come to me my boy. I thought you'd forgotten me altogether." She hurried over to him and began to sob. He took her in his arms, and kissed her face. Touched, and yet rejoicing at the same time, everybody watched. She began drying her tears, Lawrence Sherette helping with his broad white handkerchief, then she began to apologize for her emotional display.

"No, no. I won't let you. Cry all you want dear. It's good for you. And us too. It reminds me of when Adelaide and I were tots and that you would always come to us and let us lean on you when things went wrong. True, I've stayed away too long darling but it won't be like that anymore."

"I know. You're in Memphis now.

"Yes. I'm there. I'll see you often. I promise."

"But today. Christmas Eve. You're here and that is special. Very special. I'd so hoped you'd make it. I remember my Christmases with your father and mother and with you and Adelaide when you were only tykes."

"And I remember them too. At least a good many of them."

Mary Tonka was picked from the Choctaws by Adelaide's and Lawrence's mother to come and live at the plantation and work for her, the church paving the way in helping find the young girl a home. Lawrence Sherette and Adelaide were then mere yearlings, clinging, wherever she went, to Mary Tonka's coat tail as a calf would to its mother cow, habituated to her every word and movement, even tagging after her on blackberry pickings on the edge of the woods in the peripheral thickets. They loved her as she loved them. Mary Tonka often claimed that Adelaide was much like her mother, the prominent reminder seen in her tender ways toward others.

The breakfast table, though ponderously large, must have groaned under the weight of the food that Mary Tonka had stacked on it.

"There's enough on this table to feed a hungry Catholic congregation of Priests" said Lawrence Sherette, who had released her—ham and sausages and biscuits and blackberry jams, which I'd heavily counted on. I knew you'd set them out Mary Tonka. And the smell of that coffee. Oooooh! What an aroma." He then went over to her again and kissed her brow.

Before they sat down, and before he delivered the blessing, Lawrence Sherette had conveyed a funny remark to Tahitia and she to him.

"Ha! Tahitia. You beat me here."

"Yes, my dear. I had a faster driver," and then she wrapped her big arms around the small frame of Ezra, and chuckled, as if making up for her slippage, "but you are the best driver ever my dear, the best." Doctor Lundy had gotten there in mid afternoon of the day before but did not indulge in the tease. He merely looked on and laughed. His personal driver drove him who had returned to Memphis to spend the holidays with his family. Lawrence Sherette delivered the prayer and they sat down to breakfast, and then began to eat.

That evening at four o'clock the crowd began to gather. The feast was commencing. The precisely cooked chickens and pigs were lifted from the pits by the skilled and tried artisans of barbecuing and laid out on the massive tables running the full length of the south lawn, evoking from Adelaide that she'd never seen so much food spread out on one table, though realizing she had, dating back to when her father and mother were alive, then in charge of these giant feeds.

People had flocked from every household, in endless numbers it seemed, dragging in one at a time or in lots of several. None of the workers nor their family members would serve the food. This was their day for enjoyment, and to do the serving Adelaide had engaged the likes of, in addition to herself, her brother, Sasha, Mary Tonka, Doctor Lundy, Tahitia, Sam Feathers and his wife and Cynthia and Sol from the Van Doke plantation. Of those that would be coming Sasha had in advance arranged in her mind in terms of personality and age the manner in which she would relate to each.

The small children, some scampering about, she picked up from time to time and hugged and loved and made babyish sounds to, just as she had a year ago at Father Lumas's Christmas gathering. There, they were Mexican children that she lifted into her arms; today, the majority were of Negro heritage, and next there were the parents, most of whom she knew or knew about, in their strong years of child rearing age, between twenty and forty, to whom she extended her hand, smiling with friendly face, which was proportionately returned, and next there were the old men and women, long past their best days, wandering in late, dim eyed, toothless, bald, bloated, and gaunt and wrinkled. For the most part they sat quietly in their places, staying silent, or if they walked about and talked, they attached themselves to someone younger. When she found the time she went over to pour them a lemonade before the meal, receiving strange glassy looks from some, who could not fathom the beautiful young white girl in their midst. They'd never seen her before, only heard of her in whispers from their children with whom they lived, grasping but a smidgen of who it was they spoke of, but understood Sasha's intent of kindness, acknowledging with an expression of grateful acceptance the refreshment she set before them.

Then there were the girls, those of her own age whom she had gotten to know on her visits into the fields, many by first name, her friends, she liked to think of them, who like any girl at that age had wants and needs and aspirations and desires and fantasies and a yen to travel to far away places, no matter how menial their heritage. Why was it meant by the Good Lord, she asked, for all his children to spring from the same earth but with some allotted substances of life that were glaringly superior to those received by others. The girls smiled and spoke and so did Sasha, but she would not leave it at that. She couldn't. As it had for weeks, a voice deep down kept resounding over and over: "You have everything, they have nothing, you have everything, they have nothing." So one day near sundown in the weeks ahead, when she judged the opportunity suitable, she would sit down by Mary Tonka in the swing on the portico and draw her into counsel.

When dark fell, a celebratory bonfire was lighted that threw an immense glow across the grounds onto the Christmas tree where an array of gifts lay for the children and their parents. Taking time about, Adelaide and others called out the names of the recipients who approached for their gifts, receiving them with spontaneous joy and laughter, many choosing to open their endearment then and there.

Though late, in the vicinity of nine o'clock—the crowd had been slow to break up and go home—there was a gathering in the great living room by Lawrence Sherette, Adelaide, Doctor Lundy, Mary Tonka, and Tahitia to listen to Sasha play the piano, her nimble fingers and mind sweeping across a host of chamber, operatic, and choral instrumentations that Adelaide had taught her, compositions that sprang from the brilliance of Wolfgang Amadeus Mozart who lived and created his masterpieces in the century past. Adelaide had marveled at her prodigious ability from the start, so quick to perceive and understand, and even lightly thought of suggesting that she might ought to pursue music as a career rather than medicine, but pulled back. "What a tragedy that might be. What a loss of care and help to those in pain and suffering." As Sasha played, Tahitia and Doctor Lundy, who were stunned at what they were seeing and hearing, smiled approval at one another. She saw and felt their excitement, which inspired her to try even harder to attain to her best. When the hall clock gonged at the hour of ten it told that she'd been at the keyboards sufficiently long—this was exacting hard work—then she smiled demurely over at Adelaide, which asked, "Have I done enough?" Adelaide arose and announced that the entertainment was over, then they all gathered around Sasha to congratulate and embrace her. When Sasha looked up into Lawrence Sherette's beaming eyes, her face lit up. It was his approval she sought most. Little by little the congratulatory session dissolved and eventually they all retired to bed. Before Sasha fell asleep Adelaide said with playful accolades that even Mozart would have been proud of her. An amused girlish laugh and a thank you sounded gratefully back in the dark.

The next morning at breakfast Lawrence Sherette mentioned that he planned to walk about the fields for awhile, given that some years had slipped away since he had, the words of which Sasha overheard as she entered the dining room. She spoke cheerily to all, apologized for being late and promptly sat down beside him and took a sip of coffee.

"You're planning a walk in the fields? Is that what you said?"

"I did. And guess what? I would feel honored if you were a part of it."

"Oh good. I was hoping to hear that. What shall I wear Adelaide?"

"You're not riding, you're walking. Which is the first consideration. I think putting on a pair of your riding pants is advisable, the dark ones, which will better help ward off the cockle burrs, and briar stickers, and whatever else. The going can be a mite challenging as you know."

"Yes I know."

"It's nippy this early in the day. That's another consideration. I'm suggesting that you cover yourself with a cloak and a sweater underneath."

Lawrence Sherette would wear a pair of field clothes and heavy work shoes. On his head he would place a broad brim. As soon as breakfast was over, Sasha left for her bedroom where she changed into the attire Adelaide had recommended, but adding to this a heavy pair of shoes for her feet and a cockney cap for her head. They left straightaway from the portico in the direction of the orchards, Sasha in heightened mood, talking as fast as Lawrence Sherette had ever heard her.

Adelaide had been right. The air was nippy and there was a breeze; the frost had fallen thickly the night before. Lawrence Sherette pulled his coat tighter around his frame and looked up at the sky, and Sasha looked up at it with him, each seeing the fleecy clouds floating across the Heavens, occasionally veiling the sun.

"It's a great day, isn't it darling?"

"Christmas is always a great day," she answered.

They kept walking, she keeping pace with his widely spaced strides, soon coming to the first of the hay fields, the ones that Adelaide alluded to as the minor hay fields, where once green rye and oats appeared but appeared now as unsightly brittle, awaiting the plowman whom Sam Feathers would send in late January to turn under.

Sasha was happy. "Oh, what shall I talk to him about? I am so glad to be with him. What was he like when he was a boy? He grew up here, in these very fields, walking and going about, covering this very ground where we now trod. Did he work? Did he work at all, just as the people of this plantation work? No, no. Not that Sasha. He helped his father. He was learning to be an overseer. His father was training him. He did work like that. Funny, isn't it? Adelaide wasn't trained, not like him, and yet she ended up running things here." In these ruminations she was silent and Lawrence Sherette wondered curiously about the things she had spinning on the inside.

"Look Sasha," he suddenly let out, "the peach orchard, then over there the apple trees. All dead and lifeless. They're long past their ability to bear fruit until the next season"

"I see. So vast. They run everywhere, with no end."

"Ha. They have an end. But they are large orchards. And let me tell you a little story if you will. When I was a boy, these were my chief assignments. And Adelaide's too. And Mary Tonka's. When the bearing season was at its peak we were on the ladder shaking the limbs, while Mary Tonka steadied it with her support, then when we'd shaken enough fruit to the ground we'd fill our baskets. Many baskets. Someone came along sooner or later and hauled them to the shed where they were canned in fruit jars or sliced and dried for the folks of the plantation here. The surplus was hauled to Memphis to the broker or else there sold on the street."

"I can't image it. You did all that as a little boy."

"I did. We were busy in those days of growing up. My father wisely taught us both to work, Adelaide and me. That was his legacy to us." All this she drank in with consummate fascination and appeared to delight in every word.

"She's happy here," he told himself, "despite the dull formalities of farm life. She's got to be. She couldn't possibly pretend it." He decided he'd ask. "Do you like it here sweetheart, or is it terribly boring?"

"I'm quite happy, so much to do. Every day is fresh and new and Adelaide and I are perpetually on the go. The plantation boundaries reach forever. It's completely unlike the big cities where people live out their lives in bits and pieces and are hopelessly crowded against one another." As she retraced what she had said she felt that her descriptions of city folks may have sounded as a replica of his life style in Memphis or his existence in San Antonio or New Orleans. "But it must not have fazed him. He's not commenting."

Suddenly, Lawrence Sherette was distracted by the early morning "coo" of a dove across the way, stopping and cupping his ears. "Hear that? Isn't that serene? So innocent, so harmless, so soothing. It comes from God's chosen creature, I do believe."

"I've learned to listen for them," said Sasha. "Mainly at noontime. Do you suppose they're celebrating Christmas?" She chuckled. "It's not too inconceivable that they celebrate Christmas too, is it?"

Letting out a laugh that caused her to laugh too, Lawrence Sherette in good fun proffered that truly since the dove was a favorite bird of nature, and of the Lord's, he would not feel surprised if she was correct.

It was two hours since they had left the mansion, at this time approaching the cotton fields, which were nothing more than a mass of dried stalks standing shoulder high, they too dead like in the manner of the peach and apple trees and the brittle left in the hayfields. As he gazed across the unending rows he suddenly was reminded of his sister.

"Adelaide is incredible Sasha. She manages all this, she and Sam Feathers, but she's the one with the grit. She's the leader. My admiration of her is immense. I don't know how she does it. My father had meant for me to succeed him and manage the affairs of this plantation, but it wasn't to be."

"You were destined to become a Priest," she returned with proudness.

"I was destined toward that end. I fully believe it."

"And I am eternally gratefully. Think of it. If you hadn't been, what would I have done? I would have no father."

"But you have. And I couldn't love you more my darling. I couldn't love you more. I thank God that you happened along. And Adelaide does too. You will always be ours."

Sasha was ready to cry. But she forced herself to hold back. Then Lawrence Sherette brought up something else that he'd hoped to mention ever since they left the mansion that morning. He had kept reminding himself not to forget it.

"Adelaide says you are making great strides with your medical studies, that you are progressing with leaps and bounds, and Doctor Lundy is more than impressed."

"I'm pleased."

"Good. And do you talk about medicine with Andre now and then?"

"I do. We talk some. We ride together. I like him."

A glow of happiness suffused his face. "He's the finest. I'm glad he's your friend. I see an opportunity for the both of you to work side by side someday, practicing, or learning shall I say, on the Sherette and Van Doke plantations, where you're badly needed."

"Adelaide has mentioned that idea to me. I will strive with all I have to see that it happens."

"When is Andre due back in Baltimore?"

"Within a few days. Not long after the dinner."

"The dinner. Oh yes. At the Van Dokes. Too bad I can't attend."

"Oh! You're not going?"

"Sorry. I have to return to Memphis."

"I'm so disappointed. I wish so that you could."

"You'll enjoy it anyway Sasha, and they'll all love you."

She declined to comment but continued with her regret.

"I wish you didn't have to return to Memphis. I'd bet you'd love the dinner, and besides, there's so much here to do."

"I agree to that. But I have to. I'll be returning soon however. And incidentally. You and Adelaide will soon start to attend mass every other Sunday at the church."

"Yes we will. We've talked about it often. We look forward to it."

Altering their course home they cut northward to the dirt road despite knowing of its continuous wagon ruts, which split sharply into the woods a short piece further, or kept going on a straightaway course through the lower fields, then eventually to the Big Hatchie. Sasha told him of her trip to the Big Hatchie with Andre. He smiled, for Andre was his favorite, and he knew also Adelaide's. He hoped silently that Sasha would see a lot of him in the time to come.

Chapter 33

SHE HAD quite numerously ridden deep into the fields when she knew Sam Feathers and his crew were nearby working, each time passing by the trail that led into the woods. It was an idyllic pathway, where on a clear day the sunrays dappled prettily through the density of leaves, a haven for countless birds that were so alive and flitting busily about, but she had never taken it. She had only heard about it from Adelaide, and wouldn't chance upon it unless she went with Andre or Adelaide, she thought, irrespective of the strength of the temptation. But this she did not share with Lawrence Sherette. It was simply something that shot momentarily into her consciousness then vanished.

The clock showing that it was nearing dinnertime, Adelaide began to look westerly for their return. But they were not to be seen. She had erred by not turning her eyes northward, then she would have discovered their approach, and not too far off, moving as fast as when they left, already passed the shacks of the workers where in the back yard a skein of things, shirts, pants, sheets, quilts, were hanging from a wire drying in the air.

"Are you tired dear?" asked Lawrence Sherette. "We've been out a while." She wondered the same of him.

"I'm fine. Adelaide and I walk often. I'm used to it."

"We could have ridden the horses."

"Did you ride often when you were a boy?"

"All the time. And if I had more time on this trip we'd saddle them up."

"I'd like that. The next time you're here, maybe?"

"You have my word."

There was one more question he had to address before reaching the mansion.

"Do you hear from Mrs. Laster often?"

"I do. I did within the last few weeks. She said she missed me."

"Yes. And I understand why. She is a dear caring soul. You are the world to her."

"A dear, dear, soul. Yes, that's what she is. And I love her tremendously. With every beat of my heart."

"Did you write her back?"

"I did. With little delay. I recopied the letter I sent. You must read it."

"Do you want me to? Really?"

"Yes, of course."

They slipped into the kitchen door rather than through the front one. Mary Tonka was preparing dinner.

"Ummmm. Turnip greens," Lawrence Sherette blurted out. "You know exactly what I like Mary Tonka, and you're cooking them in that same cast iron pot. I mean since I was a boy."

"The same one Lawrence. And still dropping in a slice of fatback to give the taste a lift. Just like always."

"Aw, yeah, you wouldn't forget that. And I'm for some reason persuaded to assume that you're baking some of that mouth melting crusty cornbread to go with it. Aren't you?"

This amused her. She had to laugh. "How did you know that?"

He meant further to say something funny, but Adelaide had entered by way of the door adjoining the living room, speaking before he had a chance.

"So there you are. I kept expecting you two to return by way of the fields. You fooled me."

"We turned north dear and took the wagon road on our return. It was a mite rough, the ruts that is, but better than the other way."

"I'm sure. Did you get tired Sasha?"

"I didn't. I enjoyed it. I'd like to do it again."

"I'll bet you would. Well, the food is almost ready, with fried chicken, in addition to the turnip greens Lawrence. And more. Well, by the time you have your baths and change into some other clothing it'll be ready. So shoo for now."

Soon after lunch they all settled on the portico, because the temperature had elevated and the rocking chairs were tempting. The first remarks originated from Adelaide who reflected on how nice and rewarding Christmas had been.

"Yes, and the nicest part of all was being here with you Lawrence," said Tahitia with a peal of happiness.

Lawrence Sherette was the center of everything in everybody's heart. Everyone went out of their way to see to his happiness. It was a long time past since he had been home and the general intent was to help him make up for what he had missed. Tahitia and Mary Tonka were the major characters in the effort. They could reach far back into the distance of years and bring up memories that he fondly liked to hear about. It fell hard on them all when after awhile he relayed to Ezra that they'd leave for Memphis the next morning at four o' clock and that the horses and carriage should be ready at that hour.

"Theys will Master Lawrence. Youse can count on it."

Ezra had joined them on the portico and had sat quietly rocking in his rocking chair without uttering a word. No one hardly knew he was around. By his nature he was quiet, but was greatly dependable, the reason that Tahitia needed and hired him to help with the maintenance and management of her home.

No one said to Lawrence Sherette, "Oh must you leave? I wish you'd stay longer." Knowing his mind was set such would have been a waste of words. Sasha had said nothing either, merely looking at him regrettably with dark melancholy eyes.

Lawrence Sherette hadn't had a tour to his liking of the new infirmary, and at his request, both Sasha and Adelaide leapt at the opportunity to show it off, spending at least an hour going though it with painstaking thoroughness. Lawrence unleashed a stream of questions, profusely curious. It so happened that while this was underway there was a knock on the side door by a parent whose child of six years had cut her hand on a shattered glass. Someone summoned Dr. Lundy who was in the front yard looking at the carriage with Ezra; he came at once, though when entering the infirmary found Sasha already cleansing and disinfecting the injury, and resultingly he merely watched and smiled. She wrapped the child's hand and told her she'd been a good patient and that she was a brave girl, and then saw them to the door. She told the mother as they were leaving that she'd need to have a look at the hand the next day.

"She's a wonder," Dr. Lundy later said to Lawrence Sherette, both of whom had stood and observed. "She's as quick and nimble as a cat. I can't wait to see her when she reaches her zenith and I pray that I live to see that happen. Someday she'll fly with the eagles."

Sam Feathers pulled up in front of the mansion that afternoon in his wagon, coming to fulfill an agreement with Lawrence Sherette that he'd ride him around the plantation for awhile, meaning only to certain areas. There were changes underway that he and Adelaide had planned which he'd like to discuss with him on site. That was part of his reason for coming; the other was that that he simply wished to be with Lawrence Sherette for a while to reflect on old times, just to quietly be around him so they could talk.

"I'm ready Sam. Let me get my hat. How long will we stay out?" he called back as he started inside.

"As long as you say."

Sam knew that Sasha was hoping to come too, and had made allowances. "She won't be a bother," he put in, throwing a heavy padding across the double wide seat in the rear before he left his home which obviously was to make for an improvement in comfort. She was sitting in the portico swing looking hopefully at him when he called out to see if she'd like to join them, the answer coming with a touch of thrill, "I wouldn't miss it. Wait. I'll be right there." She was already dressed for the ride, and sprang up lively.

"Okay. Come on. I'll help you climb in."

They had not gotten into the excursion by more than twenty minutes when looking up they saw a rider galloping hard to catch them, whereon Sam called out to his team.

"Whoa. Ha. It's Andre. Is everything all right?" he asked as Andre drew abreast.

"All's fine. I dropped by the mansion just now and Miss Adelaide told me you were headed out to look at things. I thought I'd tag along if it's all right. Such a pretty day you know."

"Sure, sure. But you can do better than that. Tie your horse to the wagon gate and crawl up beside Sasha and ride. That's easier than getting bumped about in that saddle till your insides git shook loose. That all right with you Sasha?"

"Sure."

Andre then tethered his horse and climbed aboard and sat down by Sasha who had been pointing to the seating with her hand on which he was making an effort to lower himself, which was to say, "Sit right here."

Riding by Sam Feathers in the wagon high up on the crude front seat suddenly took Lawrence Sherette back to that day on the stage coach when Sasha sat between him and the young driver on their way to Corpus Christi. "I've completely forgotten his name. Oh well. She didn't last too long up there. The chill saw to that. But she was game for a while. I just wonder if she's remembering that scene long about now. But I won't ask her."

Then he took up Andre. "Andre," he said in a voice of discovery, "you've changed." Leaning over, he wrapped him with affection on his shoulder and would have hugged him except he was a little too far away. "Haven't seen you in a while. So glad you caught up with us. So good to see you again."

"No sir, you haven't seen me in awhile," he answered as if to confirm it, "and it's really good to see you too."

Lawrence looked over at Sasha's smile, and smiled too. "She likes Andre," he mused, "and that's very good, because Andre is a fine young man. And he surely must like her, or else he wouldn't have busted a gut riding that horse like thunder to catch up with us."

As they had left the mansion Sam indicated that they were planning to erect a new warehouse not far away, a mile or thereabouts. When they arrived at the exact spot he stopped and pointed it out. The boundaries had been tentatively marked off.

"How big is the warehouse to be?" asked Lawrence Sherette.

"Forty thousand square feet. Close anyway. A whopper. We'll use it for storing cotton when the weather's bad. We'll keep it there until we haul it to Memphis."

"What'll happen after that?"

"You mean what'll we do with the empty space?"

"Yes, that's what I mean."

"We'll store grain in it, and if any space is left over we'll lease it to some of our neighbors."

"You and Adelaide sure look ahead."

Sam said nothing with regard to what he just heard, but his countenance showed that he liked the compliment.

After a piece further, he drew the team to a halt, reaching his hand as if engrossed by something in the near distance.

"We'll not plant cotton again in that big field over yonder next year. The thinking is to sow it in wheat or rye, maybe lespedeza—you know, let it rest from cotton. Or plant it in corn. Adelaide didn't decide just yet. She will when she wants to. But she'll do it. Said it's best to spread crops around, putting one here this year, then somewhere else the next."

"Crop rotation."

"Unh hunh."

Sometimes moving, sometimes stopping to talk about the crops they'd begin to plant in the spring, sometimes circling and sometimes traveling in a straight line, they eventually returned to the mansion, the time in the vicinity of five thirty. At six, Mary Tonka would have dinner on the table. Lawrence Sherette warmly declared that he was greatly refreshed by the events of the afternoon, and so did Sasha and Andre. They bade Sam Feathers goodbye as soon as Andre disconnected his horse. Andre said he'd best be going too. Sasha invited him in for supper, though he declined, thinking it wasn't proper to accept on such short notice. Therefore he begged off with grateful apology and mounted up, starting to ride away.

"Andre!" Stopping, he turned and went back to where she stood. "Lawrence Sherette is leaving in the morning for Memphis. Really early. I'm thinking of following them on my horse as far as the Big Hatchie bridge and say goodbye there. Will you go with me?" Adelaide was to ride with her if Andre said he couldn't.

"Sure. Gladly I will. When do you want me here?"

"They leave at four."

He answered without flinch or pause.

"Count me in. See you at four."

Entering the dining room they found that Mary Tonka had set supper on the table. She then asked Lawrence Sherette if he'd deliver the blessing.

"Bow your heads please," he asked. He would pray a prayer of exceeding brevity, he said, which he usually did when praying in the presence of the family. To utter one long and drawn out seemed to him out of place. But despite its length this one was special.

> "We are sinners, Dear Lord; we were born so. Forgive us, and help us do better. We pray fervently and earnestly that You will bless us each and every one, this family here assembled on this Holy day, which I have longed to be with again. We are mindful Dear Lord, also, that You have this season used Your divine hand to increase our number by one, and she is here, our beloved and Your beloved Sasha. For this, and in His name we reverently thank You. Amen."

Her day had been perfect. Sasha had spent the largest part of it with Lawrence Sherette, some of it with Andre, a small portion, but it was joyful, and had sat down to supper with these people who not long past were strangers, but now profoundly dear to her; and then to have Lawrence Sherette utter a prayer thanking the Good Lord for the wonderful thing He had done for her was almost too much. She couldn't help herself. Big lovable teardrops rolled down her cheeks which Lawrence Sherette, alertly whiffing out his over sized handkerchief, wiped away. The other women in their compassion silently said as they looked on, "now, now." He held her to him until she was more composed.

"How about it sweetheart. Want to eat now?"

"Yes, yes. Let's do. But before I take my first bite I just want to let all of you know that I'm the luckiest girl in the world," then she started to cry once again.

"And so are we, and so are we," said Adelaide with a gush of emotion. "Aren't we Tahitia, aren't we Mary Tonka?"

They couldn't answer because they were daubing their own tears with the napkin that lay by their plate.

"Well," said Adelaide, "let's do eat. The food will cool off before you know it and that wouldn't be fair to Mary Tonka."

Mary Tonka had prepared ham and eggs which she emphasized was the main course, with butter beans, cabbage soup, potatoes, hot biscuits, jams and peach pie which she said in a tone of jest she threw in at the last moment as a supplement. Feigning a frown, as if he didn't understand, Lawrence Sherette relayed to Mary Tonka that he didn't know which to actually say was the main course, the ham and eggs or all the other. She answered that it didn't matter as long as he ate well. When the dishes were put away they left for the portico in that Adelaide had said that it was very peaceful in the rocking chairs watching the sun dip below the red and orange horizon. On this evening, there was less orange than usual which was replaced here and there with fragments of purple, the sign that a storm was possibly brewing, one or the other speculated. Lawrence Sherette shrugged and muttered that he hoped not, then in a burst of reflection proceeded to tell of his ordeal in the rain and wind when it took him several days to return by way of stage coach to San Antonio from New Orleans.

"I was coming to you darling. Yes I was. You didn't think I'd make it, did you?"

"I didn't know. I hoped desperately that you would. But through it all I had faith."

"That's good sweetheart," he said, carrying on a bit, "and I'm glad you did because once or twice when the storm swept upon us with an unmerciful fierceness I pretty well lost mine."

That night at the mansion and across the plantation there was a tomb of quietness, excepting there was a dog bark off in the distance, and the only lights showing, aside from the lamps of the Aurora, were those twinkling through the tiny windows of the house shacks where the day laborers lived.

They sat scanning the Heavens for the stars that Adelaide said she always watched when darkness came on thickly. Tahitia wasn't able to distinguish clearly the big dipper, Sasha taking pains to configure it for her, then leading her into the yard to show her the Eastern star. On seeing it she began to take on over its brightness. In a vein of fun Lawrence Sherette said that it must have taken eons of patience for an artist to paint all those stars on the backdrop up there. Someone exclaimed that they'd in times past made out the shape of an animal on the full moon, a goat or a cow, or a human form and someone else said they'd seen that too and figured that the tale had been told and retold ever since the dawn of man. Finally, as if concluding the evening, for he was soon to take to his bed, Lawrence Sherette offered a recitation from Genesis.

> And God said, let there be lights in the expanse of the sky to separate the day from the night, and let them serve as signs to mark seasons and days and years and let there be lights in the expanse of the sky to give light to the earth.

"How remarkable, how amazing the moon, the sun, and the stars which we take for granted to serve us. And they do. Think of it. We couldn't exist without them. Not one grain of corn would grow on these very lands, and neither would a single tree, nor a head of cabbage, nor a blade of grass."

Lawrence Sherette yawned after a time and the rest began to rise and shuffle about. "I have to turn in. Morning will be here before Ezra and I know it." He had intended to retire much earlier. Adelaide set the clock, as she did customarily, on this occasion especially taking no chances she'd fail to awaken to join Mary Tonka in the preparation of their breakfast. During the afternoon Sasha had gone into Lawrence Sherette's bedroom and slipped a copy of the letter under his pillow that she had written to Mrs. Laster. She hoped that he would find and read it.

Chapter 34

THE ROOSTER had not yet crowed when the lamps were lighted, with Mary Tonka beginning to start breakfast, and Lawrence Sherette having awakened to Adelaide's knock was up dressing. So was Sasha. Ezra had risen even earlier and had the horses and carriage ready and waiting. He had packed the major portion of Lawrence Sherette's belongings that night after he had gone to sleep. The weather was cold. Ezra had warned in late afternoon of the day before that snow might fall. Andre rode over early, hitched his horse and rapped lightly on the door. Adelaide let him in and invited him to breakfast. He said he wasn't hungry at that hour. She told him that he could eat when he and Sasha returned, for Sasha had said she wasn't hungry either. Lawrence Sherette and Ezra were already eating. Sasha had chosen her heavy black coat and riding boots for wear, together with a pull over hood that she might or might not use. Given the temperature outside she said she'd likely keep it over her head. At the hour of four Lawrence Sherette hugged and said good bye to Adelaide and Tahitia and Mary Tonka who were gathered on the portico, and climbed aboard the carriage, whereon Ezra clucked to the horses. They pulled away, Sasha and Andre closely following on their mounts. It was yet dark. There were two lanterns affixed to the framing of the carriage directly in front of the driver and passenger which furnished enough glow to allow Ezra adequate visibility for seeing the roadway a short distance ahead. There were also two lanterns mounted on back which were of much help to Sasha and Andre trailing behind. Adelaide, and Tahitia, and Mary Tonka stood shivering in the cold watching the carriage leave the driveway, staring after it until it had gone at least a half mile. Ezra nudged the horses to pick up the pace to a trot, showing anxiousness to get back to Memphis. Lawrence Sherette swiveled his head to see if Sasha and Andre were trailing and seeing them he waved, then pulled his ponderous coat up tighter around his body, lifting the collar up as well to shield his neck. The horses snorted as Ezra clucked at them to move a bit faster, their nostrils exuding a cloudy moisture that appeared as smoke when they breathed out. It was inconceivable to any of them on that early morning that in a few short years Lawrence Sherette would not be riding a carriage on a crude dirt road to return to Memphis; rather, instead, would be traveling by way of a comfortable passenger car of an iron train speeding along on two steel tracks laid a few feet apart. But neither could they fathom the tragedy of the great civil war that would soon burst into existence some few years later.

Pretty soon, they had reached the bridge, the white washed banisters illumined in the lantern glow. Ezra stopped the horses and looked over at Lawrence Sherette, waiting for Sasha who had jumped down from her horse and was climbing up to let him hug her.

"Take care of yourself sweetheart. I'll look for you and Adelaide in two weeks."

"We'll look forward to it too. Goodbye. And take care of yourself."

She then jumped down and climbed back on her horse, with Andre handing her one of the two lanterns he lifted from the back of the carriage, keeping the other for himself. She looked back once or twice at the blur of dim lights which were moving further and further away. Suddenly, with the carriage having vanished just below the rise, they seemed so alone, and with only a menial glow thrown off by their lanterns the surroundings were thick and spooky. Unaware of it perhaps, Sasha reined her horse over a little closer to Andre. "Strange is the dark," thought she, as they traveled along, "shadows on every side that seem to be something they are not, yet in one's imagination they are as real as life itself, where truly a bush is supposed a bear." She recalled reading a poem or play to this effect. She would take it up with Andre some time but not now. It was too early for such a treatise. But made an inquiry that was kindred.

"Andre do robberies ever take place out here on these roads?"

"I don't know of any. But a thing like that could happen. Why do you ask?"

"I was thinking of Lawrence Sherette and Ezra and if it's safe for them to travel at this hour of night."

Darkness is the black enormity of nature, and darkness makes the mind giddy, and whoever plunges into the opposite of day feels his heart chilled and when the eye sees blackness the mind sees trouble. Man is born of this inclination. Even the strongest and bravest are anxious when it comes upon them. Andre gave every impression of courage, saying to himself that he must, by all means in the presence of Sasha, and since his appearance was calm and steadfast the contagion helped her feel more secure.

It was but a stretch until the nighttime began to bid adieu, the shadows disappearing, and though barely, the riders began to pick out the clumps of birches that ran adjacent to the roadway, which, smitten with due, would glisten as jewels on fire when the sun came on and struck their pretty white cloaking. Their thirsty roots fed from the ever present moist banks of the creek that ran collaterally with the roadway, which with creeping slowness eventually drained into the Big Hatchie. The birch was a tree of celebrity, used in the main by nearby wealthy planters for enhancing their plantation yards, looking healthy and decorative the year round.

The lights from the Aurora suddenly whisked into view as they rounded the curve. They saw them at the same time.

"Mary Tonka will have breakfast," said Sasha, "and you're to eat with us, Adelaide said to tell you. You will won't you?"

"Sure. I'm hungry. Are you?"

"Very."

When they had ridden further, substantially closer now, Adelaide sighed. She had stood watching.

"I see them Mary Tonka. You have everything ready don't you? Being out in the cold at this hour is bound to have given them a voracious appetite."

଼ ଼

The Van Doke dinner to which they were zealously encouraged to attend by Mrs. Van Doke, both of them agreeing, would happen three days hence. Adelaide explained to Sasha that Jim and Lucy Van Doke were counting on attending, she was sure, for they never missed one, and that she herself had been present at many. "Jim is the oldest son, and Lucy is his wife. She's a darling, I love her, and Jim is exceptional too, a gentlemen, a person of cardinal principle, much in the manner of his younger brother Andre."

"Who else is to be there?"

"No one dear that you know. Well, Doctor Lundy will be. And Andre and Mrs. Van Doke. It's a shame that Lawrence couldn't come."

"Mr. Van Doke, the father and husband. He will be there no doubt. Oh I shouldn't even ask such a question. I know he will."

"He will be. He'll preside."

"I see. Well, what will I wear Adelaide? Have you thought about that?"

"I haven't actually, have you?"

"I love the emerald green dress you made me in the fall. I haven't worn it yet. Do you think it's appropriate for the Christmas season?"

"Oh I do. It's ideal. Is that for sure what you'd like to wear?"

"I'm sure. It's lovely, and will go well with my dark cloak, which will be just the right weight for the mild temperatures we are having."

"Good. That's such a becoming garment also."

The dinner affair would be splendid, the opulent of the surrounding domain proudly attending, sitting at immaculately dressed tables lighted with the popular Argand lamps not long before imported from Sweden. Few people could secure them, but Jordan Van Doke had his connections. The lamps may seem as a crude form of lighting as one looks back to that mid century, but they were magnificent in their beauty and lure, exquisitely devised of thick blown glass, and complemented by a blue green globe. When fixed at an exact level the wick emanated a bewitching glow that compelled something of a seductive dazzle in the eyes of the women, and at the same time provoking a sparkle from their jewelry. A sizeable many folks could be seated at a table, for the tables were large in their capacity, and handsomely overspread with white expensive linens of fine embroidery gathered in patches at the center. The Argands were not alone in the supply of a romantic aura; this too was effected by the Victorian lamps adorning the walls, which were held upright and in place by the gold plated sconces, though fewer in number than the Argands. The Victorian was indeed an elegant fixture, shiny, frivolous, and made even more elegant by ornate shades of thin material that circled round it and a raft of tassels dangling from its framing.

"Is there an expectation of exchanging gifts, Sasha had asked Adelaide a day or two before the event?"

"No exchanges of gifts. That has been the convention ever since I can remember. None from the Van Dokes and none from the guests. It's understood. We're only together to fraternize."

To Sasha, the hour for their departure to the Van Dokes had arrived far too slowly but finally was there. Doctor Lundy had earlier reported to Adelaide that he must pay call on a sick Negro woman on the Van Doke plantation and would meet them later at the dinner, hopefully on time, and for them to save him a seat, he added in jest. Then he left with one of the field hands who drove him.

Adelaide looked upon Sasha with a sigh, absorbed in her youthful beauty. "Pull your stole around your neck and shoulders sweetheart. Bad luck it certainly would be if the only physician of the house fell sick. Ha, ha." Sasha in a mood of courtier gaiety glided lightly over to one of the portico columns, keeping her steps close together as she moved, then spun around and stood with her back to it, kind of smiling at Adelaide, kind of playing, kind of posing, putting on, grinning beautifully, as if to say, "Do you like my pretty dress Adelaide?" Adelaide loved it and the cuteness of her capers too.

Sam Feathers, dressed in a suit for the occasion, was to drive them, though successfully pleading with Adelaide to excuse him from the dinner, which he stoutly preferred to miss, but would return at the appointed hour and wait for them in the reserve designated for securing the carriages. Adelaide and Sasha were the only ones going from the mansion. Who else was there? There were Mary Tonka and Tahitia, whom Adelaide wished badly could attend but social and racial taboos weren't about to let that come to pass. Both understood, blessing and hugging them as they left the portico for the carriage, their beautiful silk dresses rustling and crackling, which they carefully lifted up to their knees when climbing aboard.

As they drew closer to the Van Doke's, Sam turned the carriage into the entrance of the driveway, where a young man was seen in the gathering mist standing in wait, alert and watching. The young man was Andre Van Doke, who else, who was determined to exercise the very best of chivalry at helping the ladies from their carriage. His mother had urged him to. Sam Feathers pulled to a stoppage when they rolled abreast with the frontage, whereon Andre stepped forward with a nimble bounce and said, "I'm so glad you all could come."

"And so are we Andre," Adelaide courteously returned.

He helped Adelaide down first, then Sasha, whose perfume of the evening rose sweetly into his nostrils, and this, coupled with the face and eyes that smiled with indescribable loveliness, triggered a feeling that made his heart melt. Moving to the middle, Sasha on one side and Adelaide on the other, he proudly offered his arms for escorting them to the door, where Mr. and Mrs. Van Doke were greeting the guests.

"Goodness, there you are," Mrs. Van Doke said vibrantly. "I am terribly delighted. How are you Adelaide?"

"I am fine Martha. Thank you."

"And Sasha. You lovely thing. I am beside myself with happiness that you have come too," she said, with a rising but cultured tone, her eyes twinkling as they shot across to her son who was drinking it all in.

"Thank you very much. I am equally delighted Mrs. Van Doke."

Jordan Van Doke had stood back but only for a second, anxious to say something to the two guests, most singularly to Sasha, whose charm had rocked him. "So this is who they've raved about. What gorgeous eyes, so much of depth, a beauty like I've never seen before. Whoa! There's a tint of European in her features I dare contend. A touch of French I think. No one else has seen it. But I have." They had seen it but he surmised that he was the only one.

He spoke first to Adelaide, both exchanging greetings, but after this turned to her young friend.

"Good evening Sasha. I am Jordan Van Doke. I feel like I've met you even before now. You're on everyone's agenda. I join my wife in expressing gladness that you have decided to be with us."

With an eloquence that surprised even Adelaide, Mrs. Van Doke affected the same, she answered with a display of courtly protocol.

"And good evening to you sir. I thank both you and Mrs. Van Doke for inviting me. Adelaide has told me what a fine occasion this is and I would not have missed it for anything."

"What a nice sonorous voice, she has," said Adelaide silently. "She is changing. Have I not just heard the vibration of some new notes that are quite akin to those of a woman?" While Sasha had not attained to womanhood, she in her voice was nearly there, the inexorable change especially beginning to be noticed by those close around her when in the company of persons of high dignity to whom she spoke slower and more selectively.

Almost at once, Jordan Van Doke, impressed if not jarred by how well this young person before him apparently had been thoroughly schooled by someone over the course of several years, commenced to try to resolve something of which he wished he were apprised, but wasn't. No one was, except Adelaide Sherette. "Where," he asked himself, "has this beautiful thing come from? Who is she? Why is she staying with Adelaide? Who knows the answers, apart from Adelaide, and under no circumstances will I pry into her business. No sir. I am not about to ask Adelaide Sherette about this."

The conversation seemed to abruptly break off, Mr. Van Doke discovering no additional topic that he felt might appeal further to Sasha's repository of interests or to Adelaide's for that matter. Sensing as much Mrs. Van Doke touched his arm and he perceiving what was meant—that they had held up Adelaide and Sasha sufficiently long, and should be departing themselves to the inside. Others were stepping forward to say hello but this soon ended, or they had to end it, for the time to announce dinner would soon be upon them. Andre, who had finished guiding his two lady companions to their table had by then returned and would take up the greetings of latecomers on behalf of his father and mother.

Jim and Lucy sat with the Van Doke heads and George was there too, sitting on the opposite side of Lucy, whom she did not like but neither did she dislike him. She simply tolerated him, often mentally comparing him with his two brothers. George had escorted no one to the affair, a young lady in Virginia not yet having arrived in his life. Looking around at the well dressed guests populating the room, animatedly interchanging conversation, amiably lost in one another, the women especially, his eyes fell on Sasha, then left her then wandered back, remembering his self initiated introduction the day he met her and Adelaide and Sam Feathers returning from Memphis. He recalled that their first meeting went less than well. When Mrs. Van Doke leaned over a slight to speak to Lucy, George eagerly listened in, perhaps anticipating that Sasha was in the central sphere of the remarks, and that his mother desired to share it with her daughter in law.

"She is a charming thing, isn't she, sitting so serenely dignified by Adelaide. She's the ornament of the evening."

"She is charming," answered Lucy, "I've watched her ever since she came in. What gentleness and nobility there is in her features."

"I was with her the other day," said Mrs. Van Doke, "up close, as close as you and I this minute, and saw more than beauty, mind you. She aptly holds her own in conversation, as much as an adult. "

"I'll bet she does, judging simply from her demeanor that I gather from here. I speak of the way she is so stately composed as she sits. One cannot easily miss these attributes, you know. I must seek acquaintance with her after dinner. And Jim too."

Adelaide and Sasha were situated close to where the Van Dokes sat, though both parties were out of hearing range of what was said by the occupants of either table. Where Adelaide and Sasha sat there were, in addition to themselves, a Mr. J. Otis Presly and wife Estelle, a Mr. Prudence Autry and wife Arlene, a Mr. Benjamin Donovan, a railroad executive by profession, who sat with no wife at his side. Dr. Lundy was to join them, yet thus far not showing up. Sasha kept glancing around to see if she might spot him, breathing a happy sigh of relief when he entered the room and hastened over and slid in beside her.

"I got here as fast as I could."

"I know."

J. Otis Presly was a large scale cotton grower, perhaps on a slightly smaller scale than the sprawls of the Van Doke and Sherette enterprises, his land and home lying some five miles away from theirs, a parcel of it touching the Big Hatchie River. In a sense he was their neighbor. Prudence Autry had introduced himself as a banker in the City of Louisville, Kentucky and in his double breasted brown suit unequivocally looked the part. He was a quiet man, with narrowing eyes that took measured bead of the person with whomever he was conversing. He delighted in his wife, an outgoing gregarious lady, who took the lead from him in all settings that were social, such as was the circle of the present dinner table guests. One was struck with the impression that she reveled in the art and thrill of social exchange. Benjamin Donovan was a railroad man, endowed of a tall slender frame, and sported a shiny gold watch affixed to the under part of his vest, which he sometimes removed and began to swing from side to side. Doing this seemed to afford the man a certain bit of therapy. Not surprisingly, Mr. Autry, the banker, and Benjamin Donovan, were somehow associated with one another. The Autry's and Mr. Donovan were staying as guests with the Van Dokes for a limited while, three days at the most.

All those at this table would have some remarks to make and some ideas to pursue throughout the course of the dinner, some contributing much more than others. The people represented a well balanced cross section of views. Mrs. Van Doke surmised as much when she imprinted their names on the seating tabs, or else she would not have bunched them together. Adelaide alone could have kept the commerce among them charged and moving, yet there was Mrs. Autry whose nature veered far away from Adelaide's, with no flair for business whatsoever one would have surmised, but who was capable of taking over at group gatherings and with an acceptable disposition.

No sooner had they all sat down when Mrs. Presly began to take scrutiny of Sasha, obviously because of her charming looks. The lady sat two seats up from her across the table. Now and then she turned to her husband, speaking a word with him, but soon again glancing back and forth at the beautiful young girl. At times Sasha pretended not to be aware of her, taking up idle talk with Dr. Lundy, figuring that this might divert the woman's focus and that she would commence to feast her obsession on someone else.

"You have the prettiest eyes," the lady all at once said, leaning across her husband, attempting to move closer, which resulted in a blush to Sasha's face. Dr. Lundy smiled. Sasha said a thank you to the lady, who continued to lean across her husband.

"You live with Miss Adelaide I hear. That makes you my neighbor. We only live five miles from her." Adelaide was occupied with Arlene just then and did not hear Mrs. Presly's remarks.

"In which direction?"

"North."

"And you grow cotton, just as Adelaide and Mr. and Mrs. Van Doke and their sons," said Sasha, with the belief that this was an aptly chosen topic, for it was one the lady understood and about which she could easily converse.

"Yes, that's what we do."

"That must keep you busy."

"It does. Awfully busy. Keeps my husband on the run from daylight to dark," she said, looking sympathetically over at Mr. Presly. "He has to get up to see that the workers are in the fields and that they stay there till quittin time." Sasha wasn't sure whether she meant freed people or slaves. "But that's about to change. Our son is twenty two years old and he's taking hold really good. Some day he'll run things. Anyway that's our dream."

"I do hope it turns out well," said Sasha, wanting to be agreeable, but with an intent of feigning that what the lady said about her son truly engrossed her, or at the very least was of ordinary fancy.

"He'd be here tonight except he had some things to do, working on a barn, I think, and that kept him."

"I'm sorry about that," remarked Sasha, "he's missing a really fine dinner."

But just then Doctor Lundy cut in, apparently feeling Sasha might welcome a stint of relief.

"Er uh, excuse me folks, but before I forget it, I was in your home a year or so ago Mrs. Presly, when one of your relatives had the flu." In fact, he knew that it was five years since he had been there.

"My, my. Doctor Lundy. It's you. I failed to recognize you. Honey this is Doctor Lundy, you remember him" she said to her husband, as if he should feel of equal excitement, who grinning, let out an affable hello and that he hadn't seen him in a while. "Yes Doctor Lundy," she continued, echoing her husband's remark, "we haven't seen you in a while."

"No you haven't. Is that because you're taking such good care of everyone that they don't need my services?" he asked in a vein of humor, which, a little late she recognized as a kind of pun. She tried to laugh to denote that she'd caught on, and she had, but was gapingly delayed. She liked the doctor; there was evidence of that, and cheerfully answered.

"No Doctor Lundy. But one never knows. We might need you as soon as tomorrow. Although Memphis is quite a long way from here. It's hard to get you out to see about us country people."

"It is. I admit. But I'll do better. I'll have to recruit some of the young medical folks to help me."

Chapter 35

MRS. PRESLY was a genial person and throughout the evening brought up a good many subjects she apparently deemed to be exciting and stimulating. She tried hard, but was lacking the inborn or learned traits of a luring conversationalist; she was boring, and both Sasha and Doctor Lundy were glad when she retired into her normal seating posture and for awhile into relative quietness. The lady sitting diagonally across from them took up the slack, starting to expound on a fashion show she'd attended two weeks past at the Galt House in Louisville, Kentucky. This was Arlene Autry, a tall attractive woman with a mass of plaited hair and much exposed white shoulders and neck, the latter around which she wore a triple string of pearls. Sasha involuntarily gazed at the lady in admiration and curiosity. It was illogical to her why a woman of such charisma and charm was there, but reasoned that she could have asked why anyone was.

Once Arlene launched into her spiel everyone became convinced that she was endowed with expert knowledge of the world of female clothes ware and that on a recent evening she had been privy to a splendid showing of lovely models in Louisville, Kentucky, who spun and paraded and pirouetted, thereby prompting every woman in the audience to drool over the fashionable Victorian and Edwardian dresses they exhibited. "Their skirts full and colorful literally touched the shiny floor," she declared, these last impressions lending additional vividness to the scene she'd witnessed which was now in the minds of the listeners a grand panorama. But in that she was a teacher of theater and a connoisseur of history as it pertained to womens' style of clothing she left the report of the immediate subject, taking up another but not greatly dissimilar, to which she alluded as the romantic era of fashions, which as long as it lasted kept Sasha and Adelaide and Mrs. Presly irremovably captivated. The men listened but were less attentive.

Arlene chose to refer to that narrow period between 1825 and 1840 as the romantic era of fashion, saying it was then that women loved to wear ribbons and bows, together with other light adornments, and were highly feminine and that she liked the style, sorry to see it gone, if indeed it had, lamenting that women's clothes again had become conforming and that some styles were injurious to health. "Corsets" she contended, "restrict the development and functioning of internal organs and prohibit deep breathing, and the placement and structure of the sleeves bar badly needed arm movements;" and went on to further emphasize that "....the weight of the numerous petticoats discourage much needed exercise. It's too hard to get about in them." When she stressed that she'd heard someone proclaim that needle work and dressmaking were now of the devil's doings, designed to keep women from study and professional advancement, she burst out laughing, Adelaide laughing with her and simultaneously nudging Sasha. Adelaide's countenance suggested that she was about to applaud.

Dinner was well on its way, Cynthia and Hallie and Fannie buzzing around faster than their usual pace, bringing heaping plates of food on which there was a bulky serving of chicken and dressing and an assortment of vegetables, including imported melon and fruit; and as an extra, layers of tasty country ham were offered on a side platter. There were two desserts, cherry and pumpkin pies. Pretty red wine imported from France was served in finger glasses. When it seemed appropriate, the guests quietly settling down in response to a spoken request, Jim stood and asked the blessing, his father having asked him to. Though Christmas had passed, Jim cited that the feeling was still joyfully alive among them and thanked the Lord Jesus for the food upon the tables. Within seconds of the Amen the people, who had been standing, pulled back their chairs and sat down and began to eat and drink, a low humdrum of chatter starting to spread throughout the room. Sasha glanced subtly around at the crowd, at the men in their blue or brown suits, at the women in their costly silk dresses with excessive necklaces and bracelets on their necks and arms, touching a finger to her lips, and for a reason that only unfolded slowly retreated to an age when she was seven or eight. She had attended a similar event once, but larger and more grandiose, and was making an effort to amplify it more distinctly. It was a dinner at the Spanish Embassy on the Canneries to which her father and mother were invited, including her as their child, where the guests bore rather distinct differences from the rural Southern folks gathered in the great Van Doke dining room this evening. Now she strained with more determined intensity, finally drawing the scene into sharper focus, and at last could surmise about it. "Their clothes were finer, that's it, that's what I saw." she recalled, "old European finery, their mannerisms more graced of education and etiquette, and they had the complexion of old European wealth. That is understandable, for the Europeans had honed their culture and compiled their wealth for centuries; the Southerners have for only decades." She had hoped that at a later date they'd attend again, asking her father if that was likely, who answered that the personages they saw at the function were of court royalty, and that he and his family were only invitees through the graces and connections of Father Kestner. "No, we won't attend another my dear," he extended with a tinge of regret. "We are not of that esteem."

"I mean no discredit to these good people here tonight," thought Sasha, "for they are my people, I love them. I am blessed to be here. I am now one of them even if I am of foreign heritage, and there is weighty chance that I will live here for the rest of my life." Suddenly she was awakened from her reverie by Doctor Lundy's nudge, who began to heap praises on the tastiness of the pomegranates and pineapples that were set out on a shiny platter with Latin etchings on the rim.

On the whole everyone talked less while eating. When the meal was largely over there was a corresponding increase of enlivened buzzing among the guests. Arlene was about to start up again and would have had her husband not nudged her in his bid to move closer to Adelaide with whom he and Mr. Donovan wished to confer. Adelaide understood what they wanted. She and Jordan Van Doke had sat down a few months earlier to discuss it, both agreeing at the time that it would be good to invite the gentlemen to the dinner. The men shifted their chairs, nudging closer to Adelaide, and Doctor Lundy and Sasha moved their chairs over a bit to allow more room for all three. The meeting wasn't private, or else it would have been declared to the contrary; consequently everyone was welcome to listen to what was to be said. Aroused, Mr. Presly moved his chair forward, nearer to Adelaide. The men said they figured that Adelaide had previously gained knowledge that there was a plan afoot to build a railroad running the long distance from Memphis to Charleston, South Carolina. She answered that she'd heard whispers of it for months, keeping her fingers crossed that this grand venture was more than an unverifiable rumor. She felt that it was real now. Like Autry and Donovan she was elated.

"It's an exciting prospect Mr. Autry. It opens up many dreams."

"I'll say it does. Think of it. Passengers boarding a train and riding all across the South to the east coast. It boggles the mind."

"Cargo. Don't forget that," said Mr. Donovan. "Logs and cotton and corn and mining commodities. All that stuff has to be hauled."

"Hmmmm. Logs. Have to be hauled," Adelaide mused, at once catching hold of the implications and opening them up for self scrutiny.

Stands of tall oaks and ash crowded the western reaches of the Sherette plantation near the Big Hatchie. It resounded in her head that these bottom lands were rife with timber, trees crowding other trees out, more trees than she'd ever know what to do with, and that through the use of the rail system, when it was fully born, she could ship endless supplies of board footage to the big cities.

She hadn't forgotten cotton and the long arduous trips to Memphis, the ponderous loads drawn by wagons and pull trailers that wore the animals down, recognizing in a snap that railroads would put an end to all this. "Sam would welcome the railroads." She was without proof at the time but suspected that Prudence Autry and Benjamin Donovan were astutely aware that the greater bite of the rail system was charted to cross her land, substantially more than on Jordan Van Doke, and that she would have to deal with imminent domain. They knew as well that the switching tracks would be set and a depot built on her property. The engineers and surveyors had worked this out in the preliminary studies. Autry and Donovan just hadn't told her yet, but soon decided to reveal it, inclusive of the fact that the rail corporation was on the verge of tendering a lucrative sum for a certain measure of her acreage on the north side.

The presence of railroads in this sector of the state and throughout the South Adelaide had long hoped for, reading that by 1840 railroad tracks in the United States had reached almost three thousand miles and that at present they stretched for more than nine thousand miles. Ten railroad companies were chartered in 1846, she'd read, and seven had emplaced the bedding and laid the rails.

"When will you start to build?" she asked.

"Not long from now. We must be on with it soon. There's a completion date set for 1857. That'll get here in a blink."

"I am enraptured at the drama of it all," Adelaide said to the gentlemen. I'm addicted to travel. Things will change vastly won't they?"

"I don't think we can imagine how vast," one or the other replied.

About then their exchanges were necessarily halted, for Jordan Van Doke had stood up from his chair, greeting everyone the second time, the first at the frontage as they arrived. "I'm deeply happy you all could come;" then after a limitation of additional glad expressions he began to deliver something of a progress report, something of a synopsis, starting with the lucrative cotton results for the planters over the year past and voicing a positive view for the season upcoming. On the negative side he complained that the Northern politicians were imposing tariffs on the goods the South was buying from England and that this practice was severely restrictive and damaging. "We need to put an end to that. We absolutely do. We must. We will." To this there was a rising applause. He proudly revealed that on his land they were clearing away one hundred acres of timber, thus allowing for a weighty increase in cotton production and said that he felt they'd be done with this by the middle of the year. With much hope for the reduction of human suffering he welcomed the new infirmary at the Van Doke plantation which he said was underway, fashioned after the modern facility that now was nearly completed at the Sherette plantation. He referenced the good work of Doctor Lundy and Doctor Shane Givens at both plantations, confirming that Doctor Givens was to return at the beginning of the season of summer, taking two or three months leave from the Baltimore hospital. "We regret that he wasn't with us this past summer. But he'll be here this time." Being a man of few words, ordinarily, unless someone set him off, or if he were preaching to his slave congregation, he thanked the guests again for their presence and sat down by his wife to a glass of tea. His wife was glad that his oration was brief; he was not famed for his ability as an elocutionist.

Lucy had sat still long enough. She vacated her chair, gave an excuse to Mrs. Van Doke, and with few steps had moved to where Adelaide and Sasha sat, hugging Adelaide before she slipped into the only chair free by the young girl who looked curiously over at her with dark wondering eyes. "Sasha, I'm Lucy. I just had to come over without any more waste of time. I've heard many fine things about you, even in far away Nashville."

Sasha had heard Adelaide speak with praises of Lucy, and as Lucy felt she already knew Sasha, Sasha felt the same of her. There was a look on her face of admiration of this newly met woman. To all who met her, Lucy was adorable. Sasha hardly knew what words to choose. She chose these.

"And I you. And Nashville too. It's a hundred miles from here. Is that right?"

"Very close. Slightly more."

"Andre told me about it. He tells me he's been there to visit you and your husband and that it's a really nice city."

There was an affinity between them which happened as quickly as one might snap his fingers together. Sometimes that is how it goes between two people. When Lucy squeezed her arm her touch was velvety gentle. Sasha liked her. The warmness of her youthful smile confirmed it.

Jim had also moved to his wife's side, there momentarily standing, his eyes glancing about for unfilled chairs.

"Jim, this is Sasha. You recognize her I'm sure. You know, seeing her from our table. Everyone has said so much of you dear that they feel they already know you," she said, looking tenderly at Sasha.

"Certainly I do," said Jim. "It's my pleasure Sasha. I've wanted all evening to drop over and meet you. Both of us have."

He smiled down at her and she returned it.

"Thank you. That's kind of you to say. Please sit down with us. Andre, help me pull up some spare chairs," she said, rising animatedly, beginning to look around, turning her face here and there. Andre had come over seconds before and was standing by her.

"Absolutely, I'll borrow the extras from our table," he suggested, starting on his way.

Jim took Sasha by her arm to hold her back. "No Sasha dear. You shouldn't. I'll help Andre."

For the rest of their visit Lucy and Jim showered her with silent admiration, they couldn't help it, drawn by her charm, knowing that all they had been told was true, especially when Andre had excitedly talked of it and now again spoke it presently. "Didn't I tell you how gorgeous she is Lucy, didn't I?" he said, not asking for Sasha's confirmation, expressing his words in an attitude as if to suggest 'anyone could see it.'"

In her countenance, Sasha was pleading "Oh Andre, you embarrass me. Please don't."

But Andre did not hear. And besides, both Lucy and Jim spontaneously agreed.

"When will you leave for Nashville, Lucy," Adelaide joined in from across the table?

"In another three days. Could be two." Turning to Jim she asked for his confirmation. "Is that right honey?"

"Hopefully three days. I've promised Brister that I'd go hunting with him in the bottom lands."

"Good. Then you can visit us over at my home Lucy. There's much to talk about." That Jim and Brister would be off on a hunting trip afforded an opportunity for them to be together with few around, with Lucy spending as much time as she liked. "After all," Adelaide deduced, "Jim wouldn't relish sitting around listening to us women gab anyway."

Lucy, with delight in her eyes, agreed to pay call on Adelaide, perhaps the next day, but before they had all finished with dinner, George decided it was his obligation to greet Adelaide and Sasha, and the rest at their table, which he had so far delayed. It was getting late. He must do it presently. First, in a voice of reasonable cordiality he spoke to Adelaide, which she accepted and nodded a courtesy, speaking also something likened to "How are you this evening George?" There was no effort on the part of either to extend their remarks. George then delivered a friendly gesture to the rest around the table, especially to Doctor

Lundy, but excepting Sasha, then coming to her, or should it be put, that he looked at her and issued a friendly smile. Adelaide was watching out of the corner of her eye. Sasha glanced at him with her deep radiant look, then nodded in return and released a smile that was decidedly weak. At best, it was less than a half smile, which was quickly turned off. Years were to pass before Sasha would warm up to him. "There's something of a moral barrier that seems to exist between George and me," she once explained to Adelaide.

About George, we shall undertake a limited overview, particularly covering those personal inclinations associated with him at that stage of his life. As with every soul, he was imbued with desirable and undesirable qualities—the tree of knowledge consists of both good and evil, we are told—though one might well conclude that he was far more comprised of the latter than the former. Some of these qualities of undesirability we have substantially unearthed and exposed in an earlier comparison with his older brother. What is mostly brought to surface now is the good side of the man, yet singling out one mode of character that is to the opposite, which evidently touched his mother with unrequited embarrassment and anger, for she felt that such carousing would eventually land him upon ruin.

One could not reasonably assert that he was given to wild dissipation, as the wealthy segment of the community sometimes thought, quietly alleging that he was; he wasn't, nor was he a drinker, and neither was he vain, caring little if anything at all of what people thought of him. Nor was he mean. And he did not refuse anyone who asked of him. What he seemed to care largely about was grinding out profits for his father's plantation, and therefore for himself, but one cannot wrong him for his tendency to greediness. Greed is not necessarily an ethical or moral failure. It was said that George indulged freely in the gaiety of women, some questionable, finding nothing dishonorable in these tastes, and incapable of considering what the gratification of his tastes entailed for others, so complained several young women from time to time who were upstanding of reputation but made the faulty judgment of seeing too much of him in secluded places. These complaints he completely ignored, and laughed about, honestly thinking himself irreproachable, and with a tranquil conscience carried his head high.

When he had met Sam Feathers and Adelaide and Sasha returning that day from Memphis, he gathered that his air was offensive to Sasha—she refused to speak, she barely smiled, if at all—and later he relayed this to his mother. Evidently it bothered him and bothered her also. "The young girl may be telling you something George. You might have struck her the wrong way, committing some caprice of which you are unaware. I suggest that you think about this. And my dear," she said, as a loving mother might express a regret in jest, "I sincerely hope that she didn't demolish your self esteem beyond recovery." On this evening, he may have acted on his mother's advice, or in any event satisfied an impulse to go over and speak with the others, waiting to speak to Sasha last, hoping that she might be inclined to show a brighter side this time. If he had this as his guise he was fooled. She did little better than on the first occasion he met her. He couldn't figure it out.

"She dislikes me. She does intensely. And yet she is most charming, smiling and carrying on with everyone. Well, not with everyone. She is a bit reserved toward some. But she profoundly enjoys Doctor Lundy. I see that clearly enough."

As by now, one must surely adjudge that Adelaide Sherette, a savvy person, was endowed of a propensity for seizing upon a business opportunity when it availed itself. It was inborn or else copied from her father's style of management, or both. She likely felt little surprise when on that same evening, just as the social was drawing to a close, Prudence Autry, the banker, invited her aside to submit an offer to join him in equal partnership in a state of the art saw mill venture. He too was quick to grasp an opportunity, particularly one that was monetary. He had mulled it over all evening and one could well reason that he had begun to thoroughly revolve the potential of a joint contractual affiliation before they had first entered into negotiation. What he proposed was that they install a modern saw mill on the periphery of the property, her property, through which the railroad was to pass. The saw mill industry, he explained, was undergoing radical change, from a one to two man operation to large industrial enterprises employing from twenty to one hundred men. Up to date modernized rotating steel saws, machinery, and the steam engine that generated the power was leading the way.

"Think of it Adelaide," said Mr. Autry, hardly able to blunt his excitement, "we'll have the mill right here on your land, right by the railroad, where thousands of board feet are hauled in each day by the timber cutters and readied for shipping to the large cities. They'll haul in the logs to us from miles around. It's a natural."

Adelaide saw it all as clearly as he and extended a handshake. The deal was done, merely awaiting her lawyer and his to finish off the legalities.

The movement of the sawmill industry was led by the railroads—timber and sawmills simply followed—which were beginning to connect areas of timber surplus with those of high timber demand, wholesale centers mushrooming all over as swivel points between forest products and markets. Sawmill operators had eager buyers at their fingertips and this was to intensify, for shortly the governments, the Union and the Confederate, found themselves needing wagons and barracks and temporary hospitals; and after the war, the burgeoning cities of the North and to some extent the South, hungrily usurped the supply for building houses and ports, extending the railroad empire, and erecting business enterprises of various designs and purposes.

It was somewhere in the realm of this period that Adelaide sold off huge timber tracts to the railroad corporation, receiving a handsome sum for the timber as well as for the land, whereas the corporation would use the timber for crossties, the construction of bridges, and hundreds of shipping depots strewn up and down the train tracks reaching across the nation. From this same cutting, she, on the advice of Harry, built two edifices of monstrous size for use as warehouses, thus gaining the advantage of holding back cotton sales until the price was more favorable.

"Do it Adelaide. Believe me. It will pay very nice dividends."

Chapter 36

NOT AT that same time, but neither a long while later, Adelaide bought a parcel of no small acreage from a neighboring planter who had grown too old to tend it, who now was wifeless and bereft of heirs; and somewhere in this same period deeded 300 acres to Sasha's name, Mrs. Eastbrook's records confirm, and a like quantity to Sam Feathers. She had done likewise for Mary Tonka some several years previous.

On the day following the Van Doke dinner a shiny black carriage pulled by two imposingly fine horses rolled up the driveway that led to Aurora. The afternoon was mild but cloudy, bringing a threat of rain. But so far only a threat. The well dressed lady who sat to the right of the driver held an umbrella in her hand which she had not unfolded. This was Lucy Van Doke, the driver her husband Jim Van Doke. Lucy had gotten together with Adelaide at the dinner the night before concluding that she'd come to see her the next day at mid afternoon. Jim let himself down from the carriage then reached for his wife. Adelaide had made her way out to meet them, surprised that Jim was visiting also, for he had mentioned at the dinner that he and Brister might embark on a quail hunt. He'd changed his mind, hearing from Lucy of the lovely finesses of Sasha at the piano and that she was promised by Adelaide that Sasha would consent to play for her. Sasha had not greeted them at their carriage, remaining inside as she and Adelaide had agreed was best, for the dress in which she was clad was of Victorian fashion, full blown and dropping to the floor, thus posing a potential hazard that she might trip as she left the portico.

"Just wait inside dear. Greet them there when they enter," said Adelaide.

Upon seeing Sasha, Lucy moved to her, both exchanging embraces. Lucy chuckled, saying something to the effect that it was exceedingly good to see her again even though it was so soon, and Jim did essentially the same. Jim and Lucy were outstandingly good people, endowed of grace and civility and hearts of warmth and kindness. Adelaide had attended their marriage.

They were first seated in the great living room where Lucy in good taste glanced admiringly at the adornments here and there, the splendid paintings catching her eyes more so, none of which was familiar to her, and since this was the case she decided to remain quiet about any of them. She would dwell on something else. Mary Tonka had entered the room and both rose to embrace her. She was like family to Jim of long standing. She sat down by him, he taking her hand. For a minute or two he made light talk with her, a dear woman with whom he and Lawrence Sherette, both of the approximate same age, had many a time gone hunting for blackberries and polk leaves that grew wild on the edge of the woods. "We followed similar pathways, Lawrence and I, he forever seeking the ministry, which his mother raptly encouraged, and you too Mary Tonka, and I the legal profession, which my mother persistently guided me to pursue. We both seemed to get what we wanted."

"Your home is fabulous Adelaide," Lucy broke in, "inside and out, as I've told you many times. I saw your pyracanthas just before coming in. They're adorable. You certainly have a touch with plants and shrubbery."

"Thank you," the reply came, "they're among my best choices."

"I grow them in my backyard in Nashville. The tendrils climb up the brick wall as if they're running a race with one another. I love them but I have to keep them cut back, or else they'll get away from me. That's why I noticed yours. I'm not sure when to prune them or how much. That's troublesome. It surely is. Perhaps you could give me a tip."

Adelaide was on the verge of calling Lucy's attention to the eglantines that occupied a plot in front of the pyracanthas, the former of which in the spring were thickly populated with fragrant and numerous small pink flowers. She changed her mind. The pretty pink flowers were not yet there for Lucy's eyes to see. By the heart of winter the plants that bore them had retreated to a cast of unsightly gray and brown, with thin brittle branches and prickly stems, and would wait until the new season surged into life before they reemerged.

"I'll do my best. As you know, the pyracanthas bloom in spring and produce green fruit that turns red in the fall. Then they are truly a sight to see. The plants often hold on to the berries in winter; sometimes I elect to do the bulk of pruning in this period, even if it means removing the berries that are lingering, which hurts me awfully, I admit. Here's a caution with regard to timing. If you prune just before spring, you'll diminish blooms, which, of course, diminishes your berry count. So watch out."

Sasha looked on with the politest of attentiveness and smiled, while Lucy switched back and forth in admiration of her and the beautiful dress she wore, while attempting not to miss a word from Adelaide.

Lucy again reflected on the paintings, fastening her eyes on one especially, the creation of artist Franciso de Goya, entitled *Young Majas (the love letter).*

"Ah, what's this?" she let out, as if surprised, in a manner that indicated she hadn't noticed when first entering and likely had not. Adelaide commenced to explain and interpret the work. Majas in the era of the painting, she pointed out, was a term that applied to the lower female classes of society, especially in Madrid, who distinguished themselves by their elaborate outfits and sense of style in dress and manners. They flourished from the late 18th to the early 19th century and to some extent later.

There in the frame were two pretty young girls, one clothed in a dress of chocolate brown that reached to her ankles, adjusting an umbrella, while the other, with a scarf over her head and a white ruffled blouse on her torso, was clad in a dark black skirt. The latter was preoccupied with a letter, her eyes poignantly drawn to the lines of endearment. A small white puppy had reared up and placed his tiny paws on her dress, pleading for recognition, yet she did not appear to see that he was there. The letter from her lover or admirer consumed her.

"I bought the painting as a girl in my late teens when I was in college in England," Adelaide further elaborated. "Somehow it tugged at me. I have seen many of the great painter's works, the themes transitioning from merry festivals in his early years to scenes of war, dark and macabre, as he grew old. Clearly this one you see hanging in front of you embraces a theme of love and that is why I chose it."

Jim was anxious to make an inspection of the infirmary, and with no waste, Adelaide rose and beckoned that they follow her and Sasha. As they entered, Jim's eyes were suddenly filled with curious wonder, one of his first inquiries centering on Andre.

"This is a veritable clinic," said he. "I assume Andre has seen it."

"He has," Sasha returned proudly.

"I can't fit it in my head," Jim exclaimed, "you two as our doctors of the future getting your training right here together. Well, at least part of it."

Jim looked at Lucy and Lucy looked at Jim, both swept away at what they were seeing.

"According to what my father said at dinner last evening, this is the replica they pretty much are copying for designing the Van Doke infirmary, and apparently, as short handed as we are for medical help Sasha, you'll render a good bit of service in both places. You and Adelaide are to be highly complimented for what you've done here."

"Thank you Jim, you're nice to say as much," returned Adelaide. "But before we spend too much time here, even though this is a very important place, let us turn to one of the leading reasons you came, which was to entice Sasha to play for you. You can tell by her attire that she's already consented." At this instant Tahitia slipped in and took a seat, then looking over twiddled her fingers at Lucy and Jim in the semblance of a greeting. She smiled vibrantly. Lucy and Jim smiled back and Lucy spoke silently with her lips that they'd talk later. Jim had enjoyed Tahitia's acquaintance for almost as long as he had Mary Tonka's, and it was of much significance to him that she was always close to Adelaide's and Lawrence Sherette's father.

When Sasha was beginning too sit down to play she reached and held up her dress to make certain that it would fit agreeably over the seat upon which she was to arrange herself. From the moment they had arrived Lucy had admired it, and now that she saw it from the angle of a side view she admired it even more and told this to Adelaide. It was essentially a dinner dress of embroidered muslin, endowed of three stylish flounces, below which there was a plating of green ribbon. The sleeves and cape were trimmed to correspond with the skirt and a sash of green and white, and a headdress of green and white loops. Her hair was done up in a lovely chignon and not to be left out were the tiny rosettes on her slippers. Lucy started to ask Adelaide about additional specifics that pertained to the attire but just then Sasha touched the beginning note of her concert.

She did not confine herself to only Mozart, as Adelaide had expected, for secretively, when Adelaide wasn't around, she had dug into the compositions of Beethoven, and would now play pieces from each of the great men. Beginning with *Fur Elise,* Beethoven, and finishing with this work, she then crossed over to *Sonata,* (k330), Mozart, and then to *Rondo Alla Tunka,* (k331), Part 1, Mozart, and then *Rondo Alla Tunka,* (k331), Part 3, Mozart, all of which were lengthy even though she had cut them short by playing an abbreviated version. Returning to Beethoven she selected *Moonlight Son*ata *and Pathetique,* which she also abbreviated. Adelaide rejoiced. "Such a show," she thought, as Sasha, when the music called for it, bent to the keyboards and crashed upon them much as Mozart and Beethoven would have had their mighty orchestras do, and then softly retreated—delicately, subtlety, lowly, tenderly. Jim and Lucy sat in spellbound admiration.

"I can't fathom it all," Jim leaned over and said to Adelaide, having lost a nip of his usual steady composure. "How has she learned to play music of such complexity, and certainly, may I add, in such an infinitely short while."

"Inborn, Jim. As soon as she hears it she can play it. Or read the notes and play it. There are those, you know, who can do that. She is one of them. Little did I imagine in my wildest when I set out to teach her what she had inside musically and where it would lead. I am thrilled, I am overcome that I had a hand in it all."

There were other pieces from the great men's work that she performed that afternoon, the beauty and excellence of which Jim and Lucy embarked upon for the entirety of their trip back to Nashville. The holidays had run their course. Tahitia had gone home to Memphis, taken there by a man and his wife who worked on the plantation, who, at the direction of Adelaide, had done this many times in years past. Andre stayed on and rode over once or twice more to see Sasha, sitting with her one evening in the swing on Adelaide's portico anticipating his departure the next day with mixed feelings. He hated to leave, he would miss her; he hadn't realized until now just how very much, yet also looked forward to his return to Baltimore.

"If it were summer time Andre, we'd hear the crickets and tree frogs, I mean really hear them. They truly are noisy."

"I know. I've heard them all my life."

"Yes you have. I keep forgetting. You see, where I came from, I don't think we had your night creatures. Not the same kind."

"And that was where?" He knew. He was merely filling in.

"The Canaries."

"Oh yes."

Suddenly she lifted herself and went over to the edge of the portico, clasping one of the great white columns with her arms, looking into the Heavens. She sighed. "Just look up there Andre; the sky is as full as I have ever seen it. There must be a gillion stars out tonight. Oh, there it is. Sirius, the brightest star in the sky. See it?"

Andre had followed and stood gazing at that vast mystery of the cosmos with her, agreeing in something of a murmur that he saw the star, and that she was right, that there must be a gillion stars up there. But there was a distraction to the young man, his eyes having fallen on another star, to him this one brighter than any. With the upward slant of her face, her hair had fallen over her shoulders. It was a beautiful enchanting picture and he meant to observe it longer and would have had she not caught him; that is, she suddenly turned and there he was, not watching the stars at all. He blushed. She merely smiled. What was there for her to say? One has to suppose that she knew she was the object of fascination and enjoyed it. What woman, young or older than young, would have not?

"Let's sit back down, shall we," she suggested.

Andre felt it was his turn. "Did you know that Sam Feathers is driving me to Paducah to catch the boat tomorrow?" he said, deliberately inventing the line because his embarrassment continued over Sasha catching him staring at her in the moonlight.

"I didn't know that Andre. So soon?"

"Yeah. I have to go. I've overstayed as it is. I just wanted to come over tonight to tell you, to say goodbye and tell you what a good time I've had riding around with you everywhere."

"I've had a good time too. But we'll get busy and forget all about that. You'll have your hands full with Doctor Givens and the hospital, and I'll have mine full here."

"Yeah, but we'll write won't we. You know, letting one another hear how we're doing. We could do that."

"Yes we could. I'll write, I promise I will. Will you give me your address?"

"I've already written it out," he said with a spirit of mirth, grinning, handing her a white piece of paper which he had folded to envelope size.

Shifting from topic to topic they continued on, none of it dealing with medicine or music, which she chose to avoid, preferring something lighter. Sometimes she brought up the most unsuspected subject, the one this time for which Andre was exceptionally thankful because it was helpful at keeping the conversation going and would last for awhile.

"Do you know what Andre?" she once let out with delight in her voice.

"What? In no way can I guess."

"During the summer past we had ice cream freezings out here on the portico and I got to turn the crank. It was great fun. Sam Feathers usually came over with his family and helped. I asked Adelaide once where the ice was gotten for the freezing and all. Do you know what she said? I'll bet you do."

"Sure I know. I've helped do it. It was cut out of the ponds when they froze over, or someone hauled it in from points north when we didn't have any freezes down here, say from the Ohio River."

"Ah! You're right. And I've seen how it's kept in the cellar below all covered with big piles of sawdust. I've gone down with Adelaide now and then to get a chunk and had to shovel the sawdust away."

"And did she explain where the ice comes from for making iced tea?"

"She did."

"And how was that?"

"Clean water is drawn from the well and poured into tubs or wooden receptacles and let freeze when the weather turns cold. It's then taken to the cellar and covered with sawdust, piles of it, just like the ice made from pond or river water. But kept separate."

"And if the weather doesn't turn cold enough. What then?"

"A man hauls the ice in from some where."

Andre stayed on another hour, pushing the floor with his foot to give the swing thrust, sometimes Sasha pushing it with hers. Both ran out of words and ideas every now and then. Sometimes she went for a minute or two without speaking anything, just caught up in the lull of the silence. It was at such a moment that he wondered what was revolving in that beautiful head. "I wonder at her thoughts, if they are in the remotest of me. I like her, I like her very much. I wonder if she does me. I mean, in the same way I do her. But I'm not brave enough to ask, not now anyway. Besides, she's too young for things of that kind."

Finally, he said he'd have to leave, yet not before bidding goodbye to Adelaide and Mary Tonka, and then stood up, Sasha rising with him, both going inside where he uttered a few words regarding the splendid time he'd had over the holidays, being back home and all, and then bade them all goodbye and left.

Adelaide knew Sasha was sad. She had learned to detect her slightest shift in mood. She was without remedy for uplifting her but she'd at least try something. "Your bath water is drawn dear; don't let it cool down too much."

☙ ❧

There were days in her life for the rest of the winter and spring that crept and crawled, while others sped and vanished, though in any event they were all the same in one major respect: she had an abundance of things to keep her occupied; one was that she and Adelaide rode practically every day.

In other realms she stayed busy responding to calls from the workers of the plantation, or members of their families, who suffered from minor ailments to which she gave attendance. There were instances when the ailment was far more serious, an attack of appendicitis, for example, which Sasha could do nothing about; few doctors could in that era and by and large when they were successful this was accomplished in the great hospitals. Sasha hoped that eventually she would have the knowledge and skill to perform these surgeries but for now, she was not ready, so sorrowfully she stood helplessly by and watched patients die of gangrene.

But she and Mary Tonka spent many an hour successfully delivering babies for the people of the Sherette plantation. Being astute to Sasha's competency, Mrs. Van Doke asked her, and Mary Tonka, to help with the delivery of babies on her plantation, somehow concluding that whatever Sasha's method it lowered the incidence of child bed fever. Seeing that Sasha subscribed to the usage of chlorinated lime solution to promote cleanliness and the application of carbolic acid for disinfecting the open flesh would have told her of the reason. Where deliveries were effected for Mrs. Van Doke's slave people it increasingly took place in her new infirmary, which was not yet complete but almost and well stocked. When Doctor Lundy came to visit he studied a report from Sasha on the patients she'd seen during his absence, the nature of the ailment, and in what manner she had administered treatment. Knowing he would make this inquiry Sasha prepared in advance an annotation of these occurrences in order to more precisely discuss them with her friend and tutor. Sometimes when he was there he witnessed her in the delivery of a baby, either for one of Mrs. Van Doke's people or Adelaide's, pulling it out, severing the umbilical cord, and washing it off. This was of great sport to Doctor Lundy, who watched and winced and applauded with twists of his face at her every skillful procedure she exacted, wishing that Andre could have been there to take part.

Wholly unexpected to her Doctor Lundy one day asked Sasha to ride five miles away with him to the J. Otis Presly plantation where Mr. Presly's son while stringing wire next to a thorn tree inadvertently hooked a thorn into the fat of his hand which according to the letter that Doctor Lundy received looked odd. The incident had happened a month previous.

"I'd better have a look. Can you join me Sasha? Sam Feathers says he'll drive us."

"Gladly. When shall we leave?"

"Tomorrow morning at seven."

The patient Sasha could not have expected to meet under any circumstances, but now she had. He lay on his bed resting, flat of his back with two bulging pillows under his head. The young man smiled at Doctor Lundy and at her, trying to appear brave and unconcerned. He was feverish, though slight, a condition that nevertheless brought a wrinkle to Doctor Lundy's brow. The swelling was more prominent than he expected, the thorn, which was poisonous to the human system ordinarily, having penetrated deeply on impact.

"Bathe it constantly in water as hot as he can stand it," said Doctor Lundy to Mr. and Mrs. Presly who looked anxiously on. "That's all that can be done. I wouldn't dare attempt removing it by surgical means. It'll take time but one day it'll all come to a head, then we'll lance it, and drain out the pus."

With these, together with a minimum of other instructions, Doctor Lundy said they'd be on their way, that it was a long road they'd have to travel, adding before they left the doorsteps that Sasha would drop in once a week to determine the patient's status and to see to what degree that pus was forming. As they were returning Sasha pumped him about the swelling and whether in his opinion the patient was in potential danger, to which Doctor Lundy answered, "possibly," and proceeded during the conversation to say that a whitish or yellow brown exudate would develop in time, which was what he generally expected to see during the course of an inflammatory bacterial infection, where the white blood cells were fighting to do their job. He laughed. He had for the fun of it overextended. As she knew, and as Doctor Lundy knew she knew, pus was a thick porous fluid elaborated by the body to fight infection—this was the simple way to put it—but his more technical version was appreciated, and too, the literature on the subject that he later donated to her for her medical library.

With Sam Feathers driving her she once a week paid call on the Presly boy and sent with no delay a letter by mail or courier of her observations to Doctor Lundy in Memphis.

Mrs. Van Doke dropped by on every chance, increasingly entreating Sasha to play some of the classics of Mozart, with Adelaide quite often sitting in to listen, as did Mary Tonka, but there were times when Mrs. Van Doke was the sole member of the audience; and Sasha believed she would have sat listening for hours had she kept playing. And why was this? Was it a kind of emptiness in the soul of the wealthy lady? Something missing? There were whispers for years that she fervently wanted a daughter in her family, a wish in vain, because she was never blessed with one.

Chapter 37

THE RAINS fell in torrents that spring, soaking the earth until it was soppy, forcing a lateness of planting, the planting finally happening however when the rains ceased and the temperatures elevated. All at once the soil was swollen and nature lunged into life, and the fields were turned under and harrowed, and the seeds were sowed and then sprouted, and grew into plants and the plants grew stronger and taller. The most beauteous of the flowers were those that blossomed first, thought Sasha, the yellow daffodils, which she fondly collected from the fields—they were everywhere—and made bouquets for Adelaide and Mary Tonka. One of her great joys was to mount up and go riding with Adelaide, almost every day, though sometimes she rode alone and stayed as long as mid afternoon, carrying lunch in a dinner pail that Adelaide had packed for her. And there she sat with infinite patience and attentiveness, with hands cupped to ears, listening to the coo of a dove across the way, or to the immutable deet-deet-deet-deet of a killdeer close by, not yet knowing its name, yet had seen it times innumerable, because it ranged the open fields and wasn't afraid of her. "It has a brown back and wings, a white belly, and a white breast with very black bands," she explained to Mary Tonka who assured her that there was no mistake, that she was talking about a killdeer.

Sometimes she lay flat of her back gazing up at the awesome azure obscurity, that endless ceiling of Heaven, wondering without answers what it was all about, and felt there were none for mortal humans. She wrote to Mrs. Laster, "I try to grasp this vast space and its attendant partner we call time, an effort wasted, for there is no science for understanding these twins of the universe which have no beginning and no end." She loved the openness, the green growing fields, the refreshing breeze at night time and the kindness and simplicity of the workers. Everywhere she looked, every sound she heard prompted a surge of happiness within her. "There could be no other place on earth like this. I knew when I first set eyes on it that something extraordinary had happened to me." She was reminded of Andre. She missed him, her newly made buddy, her friend. It hit her suddenly that she did. They could talk about such things and endless more if he were there.

She kept an unwavering vigil of the Presly boy, seeing in on him once each week, studying the swelling with incisive closeness, assessing that the pus was battling to form a head. But this is all she did. She would continue to watch.

☙ ❧

Lawrence Sherette's church was finally complete, and Adelaide and Sasha started attendance of mass there every second Sunday, seldom missing. Mrs. Van Doke did not attend the church, nor had Adelaide gone to mass with her in Jackson since Sasha had come to live at the plantation. It was a beautiful church, the altar overlaid with a rich gold and black tapestry, the altar cloth, and the vaulting imbibed with scenes of Christ presiding over the last supper. Of these things Adelaide and Sasha said the sweetest reverential words. Directly after the first service was over Sasha ran and hugged and kissed Lawrence Sherette; he chuckled aloud and hugged and kissed her back, and then it was Adelaide's turn. They stayed the night with Tahitia, or whatever the number of nights they were in the city, in as much as there was limited room in the Rectory, receiving unnecessary apologies from Lawrence Sherette together with an explanation that drawing board sketches were underway for the construction of two additional rooms. As a rule they took their meals with Tahitia, but sometimes when out in the city shopping they had their lunch at the Gayoso House in the sumptuous dining room where the food and service were incomparably the best, so said Adelaide. Clad in fine attire they were striking women, turning the heads of many a young and old cotton broker. It was Sasha's choice to sit by the massive glass window looking out at the lazy Mississippi rolling by. The Gayoso House diner was the foremost place to which cotton brokers repeatedly made their way to lunch. Their river front offices and warehouses were close by. A goodly number were always there. Intertwined with the general conversation were the undertones alluding to the continuing rift between the North and South, with a reference thrown in at times as to the bravery of the Southern boys who supposedly were superiorly trained in the art of military warfare, thus unquestionably giving the South the upper hand in the event that hostilities broke out.

When she reached home she planned to ask Sam Feathers to drive her the next morning to the Preslys. They left at seven. She frowned when she looked at the hand of the patient, seeing in his face anything but calm; to the contrary, it showed that there had been pain and restlessness over the last several days and nights. On an impulse she remarked to Mr. Presly that there was a need to lance the hand with little loss of time, that the pus appeared to be trying to implode.

"Sir, you will need to transfer him to the infirmary at my place. There, we are equipped with everything necessary. Can you leave with him right away?"

"Yes I can. We'll follow you and Sam Feathers if that's all right."

"Yes of course. I urge you."

At mid afternoon the Presly boy was washed and changed into a gown, and moved to a reclining chair that was standard equipment for the infirmary. It was adjustable to almost any angle. There was an arm rest affixed to it covered with thick smooth leather, quite wide in its width, thus permitting the patient's arm to lay upon it with full extension, with minimal chance of slipping off.

"I will only mildly sedate you, "she said to the young man. "The incision will hurt some but I'll be as easy with you as I can."

He looked anxiously up at her and weakly displayed an effort to smile. It was more of a quiver that she saw. The father and mother stood by as calmly as they could under the circumstances. Mrs. Presly gripped her husband's arm while Sasha proceeded with steely resolve to do what she must. She lifted young Presly's hand up and laid it flat on the arm rest, then removed the silver lancing knife from the small box that Adelaide handed her. The thought of Doctor Lundy ran through her once again, as it had a few minutes before. She reassured herself that this was the only thing to do. The pus had to come out and Doctor Lundy was many miles away. Looking into the young man's eyes once more she smiled, if but faintly, he trying his best to smile back, then she bent over and aimed the blade exactly at the spot where she'd enter her cut. In a flash the incision was made, pus billowing through with a gush, while Sasha pressed the flesh on both sides to force the surplus outward. She did not wince at the massiveness of the whitish yellow material that kept coming, oozing, but sometimes more than oozing. She kept squeezing, gently, as gently as could be done. It was then that the thing happened that she had calculated might; young Presly, unable to longer bear the pain, suddenly struggled to raise himself, for a little at least, then began to convulse, this followed by one last gripe and a rolling of his eyes that came to rest in locked fixation on the ceiling. He had lost consciousness. He had fainted.

"Good," said Sasha. "I wish he'd done that earlier. He's okay," she assured the mother and father. "He's on his way to healing. I'll clean him up while he's asleep. When he awakens Mr. Presly you can help me transfer him into the recovery room where there's a bed."

"Yes ma'am Sasha. When you're ready."

"It'll be awhile. I'm sure you and your wife would like to sit here and stay with him in the meantime. Just pull up those chairs over there."

The next morning Mr. Presly helped his son into the carriage and then their trip homeward began, with Mrs. Presly clutching a folder of instructions from Sasha as to how the patient should be cared for during his convalescence.

"See you in ten days," she reminded."

When they had reached the end of the driveway it dawned on her that there was an obligation she had to attend to, the preparation and mailing of a report to Doctor Lundy of the surgical proceeding that had taken place. He'd want to hear. As she turned, there were Adelaide and Mary Tonka, both sliding their arms around her. They'd walk with her to the inside.

ꙮ ꙮ

The girls' of Sasha's age who like everyone else came that past Christmas Eve to take part in the festivities and to receive their gift, wearing their pink and blue and white dresses and clad in the best pair of shoes they owned. Now, Spring was nearly at an end. Yet their faces refused to leave her. She felt for them a consummate sorrow. Over time her sadness had vacillated, sometimes increasing and sometimes waning, but today it was resurrected to its former height. It had worsened. She and Mary Tonka were alone, Adelaide away at Brownsville to pick up a box of fabrics from a friend with whom she was contemplating a quilting party. She had left word with both Mary Tonka and Sasha that she'd return near nightfall. The sun was dying in the west, with barely a few thin streaks of orange and red left when Sasha sat down by Mary Tonka in the portico swing.

"Can we sit and talk Mary Tonka?"

Her dear old friend looked over with an air of curiosity, for never before had Sasha asked if they could sit and talk. She usually kind of plopped down, leaning against her, and got busily into the subject, such being exceedingly pleasing to Mary Tonka, who felt honored, for it reinforced that Sasha had taken to her and esteemed her as a confidant.

"She is somber," it ran through Mary Tonka. "Where is her cheeriness? Where has it flown to? Is there something that troubles my sweet precious girl?"

"We can talk all you like, just as we always do," she answered, drawing Sasha snuggly against her, kissing her cheek with tender affection. "Now what is it? Tell me."

"The girls. The girls that work in the fields."

"What of them dear? There are so many. Do you have a few in mind or many?"

"One on the beginning, then all."

"I don't understand."

"I can explain. You see, this afternoon when you were taking your nap, Gila, one whose friendship I covet as much as any, or more, knocked on the door. She wanted to borrow a cup of sugar."

"That was no bother, surely."

"No it wasn't. Anyway, I let her have it and she said she'd return it as soon as they could buy some. It hurt me deeply to hear her say that. I would have given her a whole bag if I'd thought she would have taken it. I said as quickly as I could get the words to flow out of my mouth, 'Oh, Gila, don't think of that.' Nonetheless she pled that she'd return it. I further urged her not to think anymore about it, that we had plenty, more than plenty."

"She knew that Sasha. She knew that Adelaide insists that when a parcel of something is borrowed, it's not to be returned or paid for. They all understand that."

"Yes, that's right. But it set me to pondering. Just as it did at Christmas."

"Christmas! That was a while back."

"Yes, it was, but still I remember my conscience when they, the girls, came for the celebration. They were dressed as well as they could be, and they looked so good, they really did, wearing their pretty dresses with colorful flower formations sewed on some. They looked so nice, all of them. But even if they did it wasn't in me to shut out the vision of the lavish beautiful clothes patterned and stitched for me by you and Adelaide, not to mention the hosts of others that Adelaide had bought for me at the Memphis stores. I couldn't help but think of what was alive in their thoughts. 'Look where she lives, look at all the fine clothes she wears going here and there.' These things must have revolved in their heads, they must have. They must still. 'Look at her sitting by Miss Adelaide in that fine carriage and look at her on that handsome prancing horse.' It's true, Mary Tonka, they must see it. They must think about it, that I have everything and they nothing, no hope at all, none for rising above where they are, and hopes bleaker still for their children some day to be born. I cannot purge all this from within me, and don't think I ever shall, nor should I."

"Ah, my dear one. You have a heart of tenderness that is rare. Not only are you beautiful, you are morally beautiful, caring deeply for everyone in your reach. But accept it from one who has grown old and experienced numerous ups and downs of life. You must look at things differently. You cannot lift up every person's burden to your shoulders. Poverty is a good neighbor to misery, which I have uttered silently many times, but it is the truth that you oft times are helpless to do anything to relieve either, even though you wish with all your being you could. And besides, I offer that the girls hardly realize that they are poor or miserable. They do not see things as you see things. I can assure you. They are more content than you can imagine. They do not feel as you say they do. And they in truth look up to you. They do not in any way begrudge you. They love you. They tell me they do. So please. Forget your concerns for them. And do not forget who you are, my sweetheart; you are Sasha, whose destiny was carved out by Him before you were born. You will do great things; I see it, we all see it. Everyone from Father Kestner onward has seen and recognized it. If you happened to be situated in a formal school of studies no one can imagine you finishing in the middle, but unstoppably at the top. That is what they all contend when you are under comparison. You will become a great and renowned doctor in your time, or a great pianist. You are blessed, given talents by your Maker that are reachable only by a few. You must keep your sights tethered to them. The lot of most of us is to struggle slowly up hills of little grade; yours is to dash up mountains. So do not let your sorrow for the girls hinder you. It was not meant that they should wear fine clothes, nor understand the mystery of arcane medicine, nor play wondrously beautiful music. That is your crown to wear, not theirs. But you some day may save their child's life, or their own. These are the things you were brought into this world to do, and that is all I can tell you my darling; so please, no more. Put your concerns about the girls to rest." And following, there was a pause. They sat practically unmoving but moved a little, enough to force the chains that upheld the swing to yield a high edgy squeak when altering any part of their body to a different posture.

"She is infinitely wise," thought Sasha. "I grasped the depth of it when I first met her that day as I entered the front door, the vividness of it bleeding immediately through. She has lived a long while. She is without learning from books, but yet goes far beyond the limits of the written page. If I too am wise, I shall heed her; certainly, I will do my best."

With that, she leaned her cheek against Mary Tonka's shoulder and sighed. She did not thank her for her counsel; she only clasped her hand with hers, that's all, but as close in daily friendship as they were she considered this sufficient, and equal to expressing her gratitude aloud, and thus with this done she went on to something else that had drawn her.

"What is it you're reading from the Gospel Mary Tonka? I saw it by your side as I joined you." Mary Tonka made it practice to read scripture while sitting in the portico swing a while each afternoon when she had the natural light with her.

"I had intended to read a verse from Proverbs. I didn't. I'll read twice as much tomorrow to recover from my shortcomings. I became distracted by the splendor of the sunset. Just look at it; it's beautiful, but almost down, and then after that night will have come. I hope Adelaide will soon make her way home," she said anxiously, with a quickened narrowing of her eyes down the driveway and then outward toward the main road. "I don't like it when she's out after dark."

Chapter 38

SPRING WAS about to bid adieu and summer was seeking its rightful place among the seasons. Sasha and Adelaide daily rode their horses on the road that led deep into the yawning fields of corn and cotton, the pretty healthy greenery inciting a sparkle in Adelaide's eyes. They would further on come to a cluster of arbutus, rhododendrons, syringas and guelder roses that grew unattended as a thicket on the edge of the woods. When the road was rerouted these shrubs once well nurtured and weeds kept cut back were stranded as islands in a stream. Blooms of many variegated colors had broken out among them, the sweet odors of which reminded Sasha of Andre, who'd sent a letter of recency that he and Doctor Givens should be expected to arrive by the middle of June, hopefully earlier, but was doubtful.

Doctor Givens was one of the much lauded surgeons of the hospital, heir apparent to the surgeon in charge, a man in his sixties, who was reputed to be in consideration of retirement in the near term, say in another year the talk around the hospital had it. The news in Andre's letter implied that because of his prominence Doctor Givens was faced with a load of cases that he had to work off and put securely in place before leaving. Sasha wished that the doctor could be there earlier, for there was a patient, an aging worker on the Sherette plantation immobilized from a diabetic condition that doubtlessly necessitated surgery. His toes had to be amputated. Doctor Lundy did not think positively about undertaking the procedure himself, deciding to wait for the doctor from Baltimore, a bona fide surgeon, to perform the removal of the worker's extremities. He had examined the patient with increasing frequency over the past few months, with Sasha looking closely on, concluding each time that the aggravation was approaching a status of criticalness. He'd seen this type of thing before. He worried, yet was disinclined to take action. To have done it would have posed no trouble to him. He was a skilled and knowledgeable doctor, yet felt that Doctor Givens was the specialist for this case, for throughout the medical society he was without reproach and was lauded highly in the professional journals. They had worked together closely in times past on both plantations. In his mind he would be acting with the faultiest of judgment were he not to depend on the other doctor's expertise. Doctor Givens was only two weeks away, or thereabouts. He'd chance a wait. That night after Sasha had slept for awhile she awakened to the thought of the patient and the impending operation, the reality settling into her conscious that it would be carried out in the infirmary, theirs, the one not many feet away, and without disturbing Adelaide crawled out of bed to go check her supply of chloroform and morphine as well as the dates of purchase. "Will he opt to local or general anesthesia, I wonder," it ran through her.

Besides the letter she had last received Sasha had opened a good many others previously, twice a month in any event, with careful wording, careful in the sense that Andre's amorous feelings tempted him toward affectionate tones, yet he dared not. He wrote that he had spoken of her exceptional efficiency to Doctor Givens and that his superior was impressed, especially when he had relayed to him her experience with lancing the hand of Mr. Presley's son due to an infection resulting from the lodging of a poisonous green thorn, and he had told him of the succession of infant deliveries performed by her and Mary Tonka. "He was impressed; I could tell that he was. He listened with the keenest. He's anxious to meet you." Among the several other things he had relayed to the doctor was that she played piano with the proficiency of a virtuoso.

"She does that too? Ha, I will most certainly have to hear her."

Sasha generally wrote less frequently than Andre, and with much less to say. But in response to his last letter she answered with lines that covered more space than ordinarily, a good many more than ordinarily. Her enthusiasm soared. She had written that she and Adelaide had started to attend mass at Lawrence Sherette's church, that summer was approaching and that she looked forward to sitting on the portico watching the cute little fire flies turn their lights on and off, that the cotton and corn crops were swiftly growing in the fields and that she'd recently gone walking among them, sometimes Gila going with her, and that the corn stalks were already well above her head, that she couldn't wait to meet Doctor Givens, that Mrs. Van Doke dropped over now and then to listen to her play pieces from Mozart and Beethoven, and that Lawrence Sherette was being called to the New Orleans diocese in the late fall for an ecumenical consortium. She said she'd asked of the likelihood of her and Adelaide accompanying him and that he was delighted at the idea, and that he was already considering that they should join him and that he'd ask for an extension of stay—performing some function at the Saint Louis Cathedral—which if granted meant that they'd have more time for indulging in the life of the city.

"I'm so depending on this coming true. Going back a few days past I've written Mrs. Laster with hopes she and Bryon can meet us there, and stay awhile. She'll hardly know me. I'm sure I've changed. I've not yet heard from her. I will soon. I'm sure. Adelaide said if Lawrence Sherette can't stay as long as we like that we'll arrange to stay on anyway. I don't know where we'll lodge. Adelaide will work that out. Or Harry. Oh yes, Harry. He'll do that since he's there handy. You've heard of him, haven't you? He's Adelaide's invaluable friend. He's an attorney in New Orleans and an international cotton broker.

That is all for now. I have exhausted my supply of words and ideas. Please take care of yourself. Goodbye until I see thee."

☙ ❧

It seemed to Sasha that Andre and the doctor from Baltimore would never get there. Finally they arrived in a shiny black carriage at approximately four o'clock one afternoon, the two of them climbing nimbly down then began to stretch their limbs. A trim man, the doctor moved with as much youthful agility as Andre. Within a brevity he commenced to survey the exterior of the mansion, seeing that it was immaculately kept and surrounded by botanical growth just as it was when he was there last. Like Adelaide, Mrs. Van Doke was a stickler for pretty flowers and shrubs and he observed these adornments quicker than anything else. Did the doctor pretend that he did not to see the unsightly slave quarters close by, together with the straggling children playing in the dirt, as he glanced curiously but fleetingly about? Who would know? If he saw this it was done in the fraction of a glimpse. Andre was inclined to believe that he did, yet after revolving the matter for a second, felt he was in error. "But either way what does it matter? It doesn't, except I know how he feels about slavery, and I am without words to address it with him."

Mr. Van Doke was away. But Mrs. Van Doke was home and came out in haste. Making her way over to Andre she hugged him as if he were missed more than the true scriptural prodigal. Doctor Given's stood back looking on, warmed by the way she showed the love she had for her youngest son. "I'm so glad to see you my baby." This embarrassed Andre. When releasing him she then naturally crossed over and embraced the doctor, expressing the warmest words of welcome, with him relaying that he was pleased beyond description to be there. It was but a narrow interval that she began to lead him inside to a lovely spacious room with an array of large windows which was to be his accommodation. The servant had followed, carrying some of the doctor's lighter luggage and lowered it cautiously to the floor, leaving for the portico for additional equipage. It wasn't Sol. He and Cynthia were sent to Brownsville earlier that day to purchase and bring back an assortment of needed provisions for the mansion.

"All is virtually the same as summer before last."

"Yes. The same room. And a fine and inviting one."

"We hope you'll like it."

"Oh I will. I'm already drooling at the gorgeous paintings hanging here and there. But don't I detect a new one or two?"

She smiled at his discovery. "I felt you'd catch that. I hope you'll enjoy them all." There was but one new work that refreshingly spun the doctor's mind, a portrait of La Valliere, Duchess of Valliere and Vaujors, mistress of Louis XIV of France, 1661 to 1667, none of the history behind it known in his store of knowledge. It was the background colors that ensnared him, this with the three flounces on the dress and the pose of the irresistible face.

At this intermission the servant was heard struggling to wag an overload of baggage into the vestibule, forcing up a raucous grating because parts of it were dragging on the flooring. Andre excused himself and went to help the man. Mrs. Van Doke was momentarily distracted and when she resumed conversation with her guest she remarked no further of the paintings.

"We'll do our best to make you comfortable and well seen after. Your meals will be taken with us at the family dining table. But you know this. It's a waste for me to tell you. You are as family to us."

"Ah, thank you. You are more than kind as usual. I will enjoy my stay, I know that, and look forward to getting much done."

Andre was itchy to leave for the Sherette mansion almost from the moment he set foot on ground, and Sasha, aware that this was the date of their journey's end, was as restless as he, part of the reason being to see him again, and the other to finally meet Doctor Givens. She had mentioned to Adelaide some time during the day that she'd like to be there to meet them on arrival, but was dissuaded. She had no notion of when they would get there. Both Sasha and Andre would have to wait until the next day. Things would not happen that quickly, for Doctor Givens had to unpack his belongings and settle in, and when this was complete he admitted he just had to see the new infirmary Andre had told him much about. Mrs. Van Doke and Andre were riding on clouds when they walked him through.

The doctor bent his neck, turning his eyes upwards in study of the vaulting, looking around slowly.

"Ah, good lightning. Smart architectural planning by setting glass in the roof. It admits the sunlight in just the right angle. We need good lightning in our work, all we can have. I see your examination table. That's good too. Everything is good that I see. How could it not be? You've done commendable work in building this facility, which was long overdue."

Andre added that there were two rooms behind the closed doors to the side, one with a bed for recovering patients and the other used as an auxiliary.

"Ah yes," said the doctor, and walked over and opened the door to the accommodation that Andre had referred to as the recovery room, nodding his head in approval.

"And we have stored behind the glass there the surgical instruments we felt might be needed, or which Doctor Lundy felt we might need. The various medicines are stored across over there in the cabinets," he said, pointing. "They're all carefully labeled." Andre went over and opened the cabinet doors.

"Ah yes," said the doctor again, then put his fingers to his chin as if pondering. "You once said Andre that there is a replica of this one at Adelaide's, which was the prototype. Both not far from each other. What? Three miles?"

"Two," returned Andre.

"My, my. Two infirmaries, and two miles apart. You folks have been inspired. Who was the first to initiate the undertakings?"

"It was Sasha, Doctor Givens," said Mrs. Van Doke. "You've heard of her through Andre here. It was Sasha and Adelaide together. As a team. But this is a story of itself, and you're better to hear it from them than me."

"Needless to say, I am inspired by all I see and offer my congratulations. This was badly needed. It will help me boundlessly in my attendance of your people." His glances were at Mrs. Van Doke.

"We hope so. We pray that it will."

"Yes, rest assured that it will. And by the way, will you prepare for me a list of people I should examine on the outset. I'm counting on a good start, proceeding from there as systematically as possible."

"We will have it for you tomorrow morning," she answered.

Mrs. Van Doke marveled at the extraordinariness of his charm and politeness. She had since her first acquaintance with him. "He is nothing less than a rare gentleman. I cannot help but consider that in his previous youth he was socially conditioned by a foreign tutor," she declared to herself. No wonder she as a mother was thrilled through and through that her son was receiving his medical training under his care and direction.

Doctor Givens was a nice looking man, not handsome, but nice looking, with a distinguished air about him, and was for the most part melancholy and serious in manner, smiling rather than laughing if an antic amused him. On this day he was dressed in a pinstripe suit of brown, which was complemented by an expensive gray vest and a white shirt and red tie. Graying at the temples one might have guessed his age at forty five years, with a year or two allowance either way. No one had ever asked him of his age in the Van Doke family, but they did know he was the father of two boys, who had been motherless for a long while, his wife dying of typhoid fever when they were children. He had chosen not to remarry throughout the years since. He was of the Catholic faith and it was due to the urging of the Catholic Church that he had begun to offer his temporary services to the Van Doke and Sherette plantations. This was his third year to extend his generosity. Let alone this side of the man, people were endeared to him because of his mild demeanor and soft voice.

A segment of his medical training was acquired in Paris, France, his very earliest, his tenure there issuing to him the facility to speak the French language when he chose to employ it, and since Andre's first telling of Sasha's origin he'd begun to envision that he would sooner or later trade words in French with the young lady, if only a limited number from time to time.

They would delay until Mr. Van Doke was home to take dinner, Mrs. Van Doke feeling that the evening would be spoiled if her husband was not present at the table when they had a guest of eminence dining with them on his day of arrival. They sat for awhile, then Andre suggested that he walk the doctor about the grounds, but exercising care to lead him in a direction opposite the slave houses. The doctor was swayed by the elaborate trellis that held the mass of grapevines that ran to the back of the mansion and beyond, starting with the frontage, and he too was a bit fascinated by the allegory gargoyles, with atrocious bulging eyes, that spouted water from their mouths, which curved downward and fell with a gurgling into a pool of gold fish. The water originated from the diversion of an all weather creek that meandered close by. Andre would have kept on leading the doctor from one attraction to another, mostly to eat up time, but heard his father's voice, "Whoa," as he reined up in his carriage. A servant was standing by to take over the horses. Someone he had encountered on the plantation a good distance beforehand had told him that the doctor was there, and when he passed through the vestibule his wife informed him of this as well.

"I'll have a bath quickly and dress. These things I have on are a sweaty mess. It won't take long. Oh yes. Where is the good doctor now?"

"Andre has him outside showing him the grounds. They'll return shortly."

"Good, good. I'll not be long."

When Jordan Van Doke entered the living room he happily greeted the doctor. "I am beside myself to see you Doctor Givens, very happy indeed that you and my son arrived safely." He extended his hands and reached his arms partially around the doctor. Andre was standing close by, smiling, waiting his turn, whereon his father reached and pulled him inward and lightly patted his face. Mrs. Van Doke, anxious for dinner to begin, announced that as soon as they took their places in the dining room it would be served. Mr. Van Doke sat down at the head of the splendid shiny table, which could seat thirty people, with Doctor Givens sitting down from him on his right and Mrs. Van Doke sitting down from him on his left. Andre sat directly across from Doctor Givens.

The guest was clad in a white waist coat for dinner, a lush white garment that Mrs. Van Doke took to be fashioned after the French. It looked smartly becoming on him and the blue tie that he had on was an added complement. He sat erect. Mr. Van Doke asked the blessing, then Hallie and Fannie busied themselves with the servings. He instructed Hallie that he needed an abundance of iced tea, that he was extra thirsty. He talked as he ate, Doctor Givens quite little, mostly responding to what Jordan Van Doke was saying, if he felt as if a response was needed. On the beginning the host explained that he'd spent the goodly part of the day with the loggers, the crew of slaves, that he had put to hard task in quest of clearing the trees that were to make way for one hundred acres of new cotton land.

"He works too long, he works too hard," his wife reproached.

"True, true," her husband retorted, "but lazy hands make a man poor, I have heard," releasing a guttural laugh that rose from deep in his chest. Though unnoticed by anyone, her eyes flashed. She thought her husband's laugh crude and disagreeable, and his remark not in the least clever, of which she might have been more forgiving were they not in the presence of their refined guest. Unless quite familiar with their lives no one could have gleaned the antipathy they held for one another in that their charade was exquisitely camouflaged.

The doctor silently attempted quick calculations to determine the gain in proceeds that one hundred acres of cotton might bring on the market. But with no earthly notion of the realistic value of cotton per bale or per pound he brushed aside his curiosity. Judging that his revelation as regarded the clearing of the trees raised little interest to the doctor, if any at all, Jordan Van Doke next commented that he guessed he was a busy man at the hospital in Baltimore in his care of the sick.

"Yes, quite busy. Sometimes the day passes into evening and I find that I'm still on duty. There are no holidays for illness. But some days are easier than others."

"And what are the hardest?" asked Mrs. Van Doke, substituting for her husband who was detained from speaking because he now chewed vigorously a mouth full of roasted veal chops with mushrooms."

"Anything having to do with appendectomies. We are a long way from eliminating this aberration. We are making strides. And research and experimentation are leading the way." The doctor did not elaborate further. He chose to be brief on any inquiry or comment.

"I see." She didn't see, and neither did her husband, who out of desperation sought a topic about which they all might more readily converse. Anything was worth a try. He knew nothing of medicine himself and felt that soon he'd begin to bore the doctor with trivial inquiries and astound him with stupid speculations. Trains. The state of Maryland, the doctor's home base, was pouring money right and left into constructing locomotives and laying steel railways. He'd open that up and see what happened, choosing as his entry an allusion to the new mode of travel that was beginning to blaze its way across the Northeast.

"Doctor Givens. It's not much longer that you'll come to see us by boat or carriage. Another kind of travel is on its way."

"Ah yes. You're speaking of rail service. Trains. There's considerable rail activity in and out of our city as of this date."

"How is that sir?"

"Rail service connects from Baltimore to the tracks leading into Philadelphia, and to a good many other terminals. I catch the train to Philadelphia and Washington regularly. Special surgical situations dictate these trips."

"I see. Well you folks up there are ahead of us. But we're making progress. Maybe you've heard that serious plans are on the drawing board to lay rails all the way from Memphis to Charleston, South Carolina. Won't that be something?"

"Yes it will. Things are changing. Rail travel is certainly in vogue. Why, within the year past a most modern passenger and cargo facility was erected in my city. It's a remarkable engineering achievement. They call it the President Street Station. I'll predict that in the near future I'll intercept you and Mrs. Van Doke there when you're paying me a visit."

"Ha, I'll count on that. And while we're on the subject of visiting, let me tell you that I was in your city some few years ago and saw your fine seaport. Ships swarmed all over the harbor."

"Swarming is a good way to put it. I like your usage. And the harbor is one of the country's finest. Baltimore has grown like poppies. It's now well known for its sugar granaries that serve the colonies of the Caribbean."

"So many ships. Yep, I saw them. Coming and going no telling where to and from. Some from the Caribbean I'm sure. Trade. That's what it was all about. Good for Baltimore, good for the country."

"In most respects, yes. But sir, as a doctor I see it out of slightly different lenses."

"Ahh."

"Permit me."

"Please."

It might sound insignificant, even petty. It's simply this: the Caribbean's are heavily contaminated with diseases that don't plague this region of the world very seriously. Not yet. Quite frankly, that worries me. When a ship sails into port, say for example from Haiti, from Haiti in particular, you never know what's about to land on shore. You've heard of the terrible epidemic that struck the island in the first decade of this century."

"And that was?"

"The yellow fever. A dreaded feared disease. Thousands died, thousands of soldiers, that is, thousands of Napoleon's soldiers. But in comparison, hardly any natives at all. I can see the questioning on your face, so let me go ahead and explain."

"Please do."

"The West Indies was quite simply a death trap for whites without immunity to the disease, to yellow fever. The natives had developed an immunity. Shall we say they were substantially less affected. The French soldiers died at a rate of thirty to forty per day. As many as fifty thousand perished. The chief antagonist in this horror of nature, we suspect, but still can't corroborate it, was a mosquito."

"Why do you say this?"

"I say it because I've learned through the medical journals and the war annals that the small number of French soldiers taking refuge in the high mountains, leaving the steamy swampy marshes, fared much better; many surviving. Mosquitoes you see, do not thrive in high and relatively dry atmospheres."

"Ah, you have educated us good doctor. It's clear that you worry over this a great amount. Do you perhaps over worry?"

"Not a fraction. We all should worry. It will strike again, and Baltimore could be ripe for the picking; as well as your Memphis west of here on the Mississippi."

Mr. Van Doke glazed his chin, reflecting. "I'll swear. Amazing. What started out as just a casual allusion to the railroad industry has swollen into some fairly deep medical revelations."

Andre, who'd sat quietly listening to every word without releasing one himself, glanced at his watch, moved by the thought that they'd engaged the doctor long enough, and besides, there was more unpacking to attend to. "We've had a long day. There are still a few things to unpack, and now if we can be excused I'll lend a hand to help Doctor Givens in whatever manner he needs me." Mr. and Mrs. Van Doke graciously bade good evening and thanked the doctor for his taking the lead in an enriching exchange of ideas and knowledge. They'd all turn in not long thereafter, each mindful that the topic of the epidemic wasn't finished, that it was now primed and set in motion to emerge and reemerge for discourse throughout the long hot summer.

Chapter 39

THEY LEFT for the Sherette mansion the next morning at the hour of nine. Mary Tonka surveyed them at a distance and called out to Adelaide and Sasha that Andre and the doctor were turning into the driveway. When they had climbed down from the carriage a worker climbed up and started the horses toward the coach houses and stables. Adelaide and Sasha were waiting to greet them. Andre rushed over to Adelaide, throwing his arms around her, and then next, rather indecisively, embraced Sasha, a greeting of this nature which he'd never attempted before. Sasha, looking over at Adelaide with a countenance of surprise, hugged him also. She laughed a little. Adelaide exchanged hellos with the doctor and then introduced him to Sasha.

"Sasha. I am so glad to meet you at last. I've heard much of you." He raised and kissed her hand in the manner of olden social ways to which he was accustomed when meeting someone new. She curtsied.

"And I you sir. I dare say that I've received much more about you than you have about me. There isn't much about me, actually, that anyone could speak of." She smiled at Andre and then turned back to the doctor.

"That's not the way I gather it," he said. "I have a list in my head of your achievements, and I am impressed."

The doctor left it at that, glancing over at Adelaide to pick up from there.

"We have coffee and crumpets if you'll join us inside." She knew that Mary Tonka would have refreshments ready. They had talked of them beforehand. Andre beat everyone to the front door and let them in. They sat down in a small nook just off the great dining room, the sunlight streaming through the plentiful side windows, where Adelaide poured the coffee that Mary Tonka had set out while Sasha passed around a serving of crumpets to the guests.

Sasha was attired in a Carven Blue Serge, a French style of the late eighteen forties. Not to be left out were the adornments appended to her slippers, two tiny red rosettes. She looked radiant. Andre's eyes followed her at every movement and the doctor, while saying nothing then, to himself or aloud, later remarked to Adelaide: "What a beauty. She's as lovely as a Venus. Andre fell short in telling me of her."

The coffee is splendid thought the doctor, and the crumpets are equally tasty. It was then that Mary Tonka entered the room, at which time he stood and pulled out a chair for her.

"Mary Tonka. So glad to see you again. It's been a while."

"Yes it has. Quite a while."

"Mary Tonka," Adelaide spoke up, "I've told Doctor Givens that you prepared the coffee and crumpets for us this morning. He has spoken lofty appraisal of them."

"Yes I have Mary Tonka. I'll need to somehow steal away the recipes from you."

She laughed softly, as if mildly amused. "No need for that Doctor Givens. I'll see that you are delivered copies before you return to Baltimore."

The social amenities having run their course, Adelaide suggested that the doctor might enjoy seeing the infirmary, starting to move toward the doorway that opened into it, followed by the rest. It was a close replica of the one at the Van Dokes, the only variation of significance seen in the windows, there appearing a good many more in this one than in the Van Doke infirmary. And there was another variation which he had not seen. Not as yet. Sasha moved across to a door which was closed and opened it, and then there before his eyes was a shiny new laboratory.

"What's this?" he let out with surprise. "Why it's a laboratory, a chemical laboratory. Are you into such arcane things? I guess you are," he answered for her, "for don't I see all those Bunsen burners and flasks and test tubes, and a great many bottles of chemicals occupying the shelves?"

"I experiment, though in a limited sense. I have a very good supply of chemistry books and journals in my medical library."

"I noticed. And a microscope I see. Goodness. Where were you fortunate enough to happen upon it?"

"Doctor Enoch, my doctor on the Canaries gave it to me. Doctor Charlatan also gave me one. When I sailed from Corpus Christi to New Orleans he was the ship's physician. I remember Doctor Enoch telling me that the microscope was used in Italy as early as the

1660's and 70's. They seem to be now plentiful in Europe among the learned people of science."

"Yes, and so you have one. No two. This is stunningly unexpected. Microscopes have not long been in use in the hospitals of our big cities, I mean to say Boston, Philadelphia, New York, and Baltimore and they're mere fledglings compared to the great scientific Mecca's of Italy, Holland, France, and England. The Europeans have achieved much with the power of the lenses dating back to much earlier times. Let me think. Oh yes. It was Marcelo Malpighi of Italy who began the analysis of biological structures beginning with the lungs and Robert Hooke's *Micrographia* had a huge impact, largely because of his impressive illustrations. Perhaps the greatest contributions came from Antoni Van Leeuwenhoek who discovered red blood cells and spermatozoa and helped popularize microscopy as a technique—and on the ninth of October, 1676 he reported the discovery of micro organisms." Both Doctor Givens and Sasha had digested this same research. With a slight of playfulness in his tone the doctor said to Sasha that it was because of the noted scientist that "we now know how to look in on those pretty tiny bugs that can kill us."

Moving about he glanced at everything he saw in careful detail, stopping once to finger through a workbook that she apparently used for copiously setting down notes of her experiments and findings. On one page there was a scribbling that chlorine added to sodium produces table salt, on another that magnesium is a mineral found in the body and is essential for regulation of muscle function, whereas on yet another there was the complete periodic table of the chemical elements, symbol and name: H, Hydrogen, Li, Lithium, Na Sodium, K Potassium, Rb, Rubidium, Mg, Magnesium, Ra, Radium_______________.

"Are you certain of surgery? I see a biochemist about to bud."

"No, surgery is my dream. But understanding the properties of the numerous chemicals and how they act in association with one another is essential to good surgery. Would you agree Doctor Givens?"

"I do totally agree. But it is mind stretching to see that you are so venturesomely pursuing them, and on your own. I will not be in the least surprised to see one day something rare resulting from all this. When it does the world will welcome it. But as of this minute, let us talk of the patient who is facing surgery because of his diabetes."

"Yes sir. Where shall we begin?"

"You've examined the patient frequently with Doctor Lundy. Is amputation the only option?"

"Yes sir. Gangrene is approaching a dangerous level."

"Very well. When can I see him?"

"Will you want him brought here?"

"Here, if you can."

"We'll get him. I need an hour or less."

"Are you picking him up yourself? Who'll help you?"

"I'm going myself. He's less than a mile away. But on second thought Andre won't mind assisting me."

While Sasha and Andre were away Doctor Givens browsed the infirmary more absorbingly than he had already, this entailing a careful inventory of the supply of medicines and drugs.

"Hmmmm. Very good. Ether, morphine, chloroform, sodium chloride. Very good."

When they brought the old man into the infirmary and laid him down on the examining table, he seemed to be only foggily cognizant of the nature of his surroundings, blurry as to why he was there. As Doctor Givens began examining his toes, mashing on them one by one, asking if he felt pain, he was met by bewilderment and confusion.

Accustomed to her, the old man turned his eyes up to Sasha. "Does that hurt you?" she asked. The old man shook his head from right to left.

"Is surgery imminent?" she asked the doctor.

"As soon as we can prepare."

"This afternoon?"

"At three o'clock."

"I'll have everything in order. I'll go over the preparation check off list with you?"

He smiled at her grasp of the things that had to be put in order. "Very good."

By two thirty, Sasha, Andre, and Mary Tonka had washed the old man and swabbed him with a disinfectant. They'd dressed him in a gown and he lay unassumingly waiting, still and quiet. Sasha had set out the anesthetics, all of them, not knowing the one of the doctor's choice. She was clad in a cotton white coat and when Doctor Givens entered she helped him into his. The surgical instruments lay on display on a clothe that he was certain had undergone sterilization in the extreme.

"Everything is ready Doctor Givens."

"You've given him the opium sedative haven't you?"

"Thirty minutes ago as you instructed."

"Good. Now, hold his leg tightly, tight enough that he can't move it. I don't think he can, but I'm cautious."

"Yes sir."

The doctor proceeded to apply a local anesthetic, one toe at a time with a needle, then up the foot toward the leg. It was done quickly and skillfully. Within not more than fifteen minutes the amputation was underway, the doctor implanting an incision across every toe with one swipe, whereupon he turned to Sasha and asked for the powerful cutting instrument which she promptly lifted up and handed to him. With one stroke the bones were severed from the rest of the foot.

"Your turn Sasha."

She did not flinch or pause. With speedy response she daubed a compression of gauze against the area of flesh of which the toes were once a part and held it there until determining that the bleeding had stopped. In a while, the gauze was removed and the process of disinfection was begun once more, after which the doctor began to stitch the wound. When this was finished Sasha applied the bandages and with Andre and Mary Tonka helping her rolled the old man to the recovery room.

She then relaxed long enough to retire to the kitchen for a glass of iced tea which Mary Tonka had set out. Doctor Givens joined her. There was a smile in his eyes.

"You could have done the same thing, couldn't you Sasha?"

"Yes sir. I believe I could."

ꟷ ꟷ

Across the summer Andre and Sasha sat many an evening in the portico swing sipping tea or lemonade, which Mary Tonka habitually supplied together with sweet cakes spread on a silver tray. The swing was their gathering place. With the push of Andre's foot on the planking it shot abruptly backwards but soon slowed into laziness, picking up again when the next thrust came, while its occupants took up one thing after another; the growing crops of cotton and corn and hay, the impending trip to New Orleans, the city of Baltimore and its enticements of culture, the benefits of working shoulder to shoulder with Doctor Givens, Andre's departure in the fall, Lawrence Sherette and his church, the coming Christmas when Mrs. Van Doke said she was planning a ball of gala acclaim to which folks would attend from near and far, going to the Big Hatchie to set out lines and hooks for catching catfish, provided Sam Feathers went along to protect them from cottonmouths, and whether the pretty lightning bugs that flickered their magic glow in the moon lit night had social laws much in the manner of those invoked by human society.

They were friends. She did not wonder if he had designs of her that went further than this. What Andre hoped for was not what he read in her and as usual, not even as much as lightly touching her hand unless by mistake, counseled himself that she was too young for such seriousness and could not harbor the slightest of amorousness for him. She savored his company and placed great value upon it, yet was glued to her work with Doctor Givens, attempting to gain every ounce of knowledge from him while he was at her disposal.

Adelaide had become some time ago everything to Sasha, her surrogate mother. Yet more; her confidant, her intimate. Adelaide supplied substance that no other could, unless that was Mrs. Laster, who was far away. Still a young girl, she needed Adelaide and Adelaide did not fail her. At one time or another Sasha told her of everything she had said or of anything she had done, and not withstanding were the numerous things that she and Andre had explored during their chats in the portico swing.

"Andre likes you Sasha," said Adelaide when Sasha had once returned from the portico for the evening."

"I think he does."

"He's enamored with you. Would you say that?"

"I believe he is and he is wonderful. I cherish his closeness. But I am too young for anything more Adelaide, and besides, I have many other things to do. Sometimes, maybe, but not now."

"And I agree. You are wise. You are far too young. But it's good for you to have his companionship."

"Dearly, it is."

As Adelaide lay in bed that evening, Sasha already fast asleep, she returned to where they left off. "In time. In time. She'll fall in love with him some day. It will happen gradually, without her hardly knowing it, but it will happen."

❧ ❧

Knowing that Doctor Givens was caring for the ill on the plantations Doctor Lundy had begun to avail himself much less. He'd return to his usual schedule in the fall when his renowned friend left for Baltimore. Doctor Givens stretched himself to attend to as many patients as his schedule and endurance allowed, the purpose being, naturally, to fulfill the needs of the multitude, but as well to thoroughly expose Andre and Sasha to his experience. The string of illnesses were incessant, the infirmaries of both plantations resembling over crowded medical clinics. If not upset stomachs, then German measles, and if not this then the common cold, and if not the cold there was a cut to a child's foot that had to be medicated and stitched. These were the easy ones. There were other cases appreciably more serious. One lady had unsuspectingly swallowed arsenic, luckily an infinitely small amount, that necessitated a procedure for pumping out her stomach, whereas in another incident, a young man of age twenty five got his leg caught under a wagon heavily loaded with logs which required amputation. A section of the leg was virtually smashed. Bleeding was profuse. The doctor showed signs of anxiousness as he struggled to stop it. Finally he succeeded. "There is no choice but to amputate," he said, looking over at Sasha who had hovered over the patient with him. So they set about for surgery. He had taught her the technique of inducing sleep by anesthesia, thus, she became his anesthesiologist. The anesthetic was ether. Doctor Givens was thankful that Sasha was there to assist, when with a cutting saw he severed the leg equidistant between the ankle and knee.

"She's the epitome of a perfect stoic, completely aloof from emotion and anxiety. It's as if she's shut everything out, all except the undergoing procedure and the patient. She's remarkable. I'm happily astonished. What aptitudes she has. She belongs in the hospital in Baltimore with me where she can spread her wings. But unfortunately that can't happen here."

When he had concluded with the surgery and stitching he did not need to ask Sasha to disinfect the ugly stub of blood and flesh and to press it with gauze until the bleeding ceased. She seized upon it with not the least of pause, and with this finished, when the blood had sufficiently coagulated—she disinfected again and bound the leg with several rounds of wrapping.

The doctor had stood watching. "Good Sasha. Bacteria are our worst enemies in surgeries, in all surgeries I should add, but this one I predict will turn out well. Andre, give us a hand and we'll transport him to the recovery room."

That night Sasha slept in the space adjoining, with the door open, vigilant to every miniscule sound, even to the patient's breathing, sometimes visited by Mary Tonka who appeared more concerned for Sasha than the patient. She would come to Sasha's bed side and lean over and press her to her bosom.

"Are you all right dear? You are not sleeping I'm sure. Why don't you let me take over? You need to retire to your regular bed."

"I can't Mary Tonka. I have to stay here. You are more than kind to ask and I love you for it. But I'll have to stay here."

"Are you sure?"

"I'm sure," she returned sweetly.

Nearing the date when Doctor Givens and Andre were to set out on their journey back East, Adelaide had contrived a journey for them in addition.

"Time to get away for a while, a day or two in any event. We need a respite from everything. Everyone has been terribly busy, and moreover, Doctor Givens has never seen the city of Memphis."

Chapter 40

A BRILLANT sunny day lay ahead. Doctor Givens sat in the rear of the carriage with Adelaide, while Sasha sat up front with Andre, who drove. Daybreak was still unseen. They had earlier sat to a fine breakfast that Mary Tonka had prepared, and she had, in consultation with Adelaide, packed their lunch in a cane made basket designed and fabricated by a local artisan.

Doctor Givens was lofty of mood and as the sun broke through the eastern horizon he stretched his arms and looked at the massive blue sky, declaring that there was nothing more beautiful created by the Lord. The road was unpaved then, often requiring smoothing after the rains fell and when the rains fell the wagon wheels cut deep ugly ruts into the bedding. A crudely made grader of heavy coarse wood pulled by a team of four mules was used for working the surface back in shape. The road was largely straight, though winding and twisting at places, thereby avoiding the marshes of the low terrains and the undulations and hills, and nature in her insidious way unsparingly encroached here and there on both sides, the woods almost triumphing, the beeches and birches with white naked branches growing into and around one another, let alone the other species of indigenous stock, the elms, the oaks, that swayed with abandon as the wind picked up. At agreed upon stages the planters and woodsmen of the region combined efforts in cutting back the growth. Doctor Givens was taken aback by this rare savage beauty, not manifestly changed since the westward movement of the earliest pioneers, foreseeing that one day when the state was heavier populated the road would undergo widening and be constructed of a bedding of gravel and rocks.

It seldom happened but at one interval all grew quiet, all submerged in their own private fantasies. Adelaide smiled at the young people situated side by side in the front seat,

Doctor Givens wondered of Memphis, of what it was like, and Andre was telling himself that he was fortunate to be so warmly received by the Sherette plantation family. Sasha had her privacies as well and suddenly shared one, the language so unexpected that it caught the rest by surprise. "*Ce jour-la la parfaile. Je suis tellement rappele les Canaries.*"[3]

Doctor Givens understood, amused to the point of laughter. This was his first to hear her speak in French.

"What are the Canaries like Sasha?"

"Lots of islands. All close together and surrounded by beautiful emerald waters. My father used to take me boating from one to the other. And the breezes never stopped."

"Somewhat likened to the seaport of Baltimore I gather. Perhaps at least there's some likeness. You'll have to see it sometime."

They continued on toward Memphis, halting at the way station to change pulling teams, then at a grove of umbrella oaks stopping again to spread lunch, the ham and biscuit, the fried chicken, and deviled eggs diminishing quickly. A watermelon followed. Andre had lifted it from the storage compartment of the carriage. Adelaide insisted that Doctor Givens do the cutting, adding the pun, "since you're the surgeon." Reaching Memphis by mid afternoon they drove by Tahitia's before checking into the Gayoso House where Adelaide had seen to reservations.

"Lawdy, lawdy, lawdy, Adelaide. This is a surprise."

"It has to be dear," she answered.

The embraces were delivered and a tear or two shed, excepting Doctor Givens who smiled and shook hands with Tahitia, and was introduced to her. Tahitia did not realize the importance of the man until she and Adelaide were temporarily alone, where she learned he was an eminent surgeon from Baltimore, then she suddenly grew nervous. Adelaide said they'd need to be going in that everyone was tired from the trip and would welcome a rest at the hotel, if not a nap. She asked Tahitia if she'd accompany them to Orange City the next evening for dinner at Randolph's. Tahitia was glad to answer yes, adding that she'd been cooped up too long in the house, and besides, she hadn't seen Randolph in a while.

When they drove under the canopy of the hotel, Andre handed the reins to a livery worker, who led the horses to the stables and watered and fed them, having stored the carriage in the coach house. A porter had taken the baggage and delivered it to the respective rooms, a room each for the doctor and Andre. Adelaide and Sasha would share one. As

---

[3] This is the perfect serene day. I am reminded of the Canaries.

Adelaide had indicated to Tahitia that they would be, they were worn now, most everyone choosing to sleep, everyone except Doctor Givens who after a time left his bed and dressed and went outside, taking a seat on a wooden bench of sizeable measure with an inclined rounded backing. After studying the texture and the finish of the wood he surmised that it came into possession of the hotel through the graces of a local church. In any event, from the vantage he occupied there was discernable movement on the waterfront of the great river, the slaves and day workers rolling produce, tomatoes, cabbage, and early sweet corn, on to the steamers whose destination was New Orleans or Saint Louis. Looking further out, out into mid stream, his eyes fell curiously on other vessels moving north and south, the height of the water on the siding confirming there was a weighty load aboard. Apparently these vessels did not originate from the port of Memphis. When several years had passed, when the civil war was over, he looked back on this peaceful interlude and revived it to Adelaide. "That was one of the best days of my life Adelaide. Isn't it funny? I remember it transparently clear. I guess it's because I had absolutely nothing to do for a change except languish in the peace and quiet. But if I'd had a crystal ball and had put it to use, I would have seen the serenity of that day grotesquely shattered. The gun boats of the Union forces were destined to invade. How sad war. How tragic." But this was today, not the future, so he kept his view on the intrigue below, with hardly a variation other than with his eyes until Andre joined him.

"Do you sometimes help with the delivery of cotton here Andre?"

"No sir. I don't. I have in the past. I came along, I mean to say. My brother George and my father do the overseeing of the deliveries."

"I saw them leave with a load just the other day. Several loads if I'm not badly mistaken. That was cotton wasn't it."

"It was. It was held in storage since last fall in order to realize a better price. That's often their choice. That was George and his helpers hauling it. He's been overseeing the transporting for a while."

"I see. Well, this is quite interesting. I take it that the bulk of the cotton shipped from here is destined for New Orleans."

"A great amount is. Not all. A sizeable lot is sent to St. Louis. They have cotton mills up there and we trade off with them. They have supplies that we need, machinery and so forth, so we trade off."

As the sun began to set Andre and the doctor were returning from a walk along the bluffs that overlooked the river, hastening their pace back to the hotel because of the dark clouds swiftly closing. The doctor had wanted to wander down stream for a ways where there was a better view to the boat traffic as it rounded the curvature of the shore about a mile north of the city. Sasha saw them from the hotel frontage and waited, intimating with the motion of her hand that they should hurry on.

"Adelaide suggests that we take our dinner in the hotel. The tearoom is very nice. You'll like it."

"If you say so Sasha, we believe you. It sounds too good to refuse. Give us a trifle of latitude to tidy up, and we'll join you. Will thirty minutes do?"

"It very much will. I'll tell Adelaide."

Soon after they had begun to take their dinner the rain began to fall, striking the huge windows next to where they sat. It had blown in from the west, on the beginning not hard and pounding but quickly took that form, thrusting heavy sheets of water against the expansive plating. Sasha, who sat closest to the windows, became fascinated with the streamers wriggling downward in the manner of a worm, left then right, then left, repeating the same, until dropping away and out of sight. With this over, she turned back to everyone and burst into laughter. She knew they'd watched. The candles on the dining table with a shiny white cloth spread over it emitted a soft illumined glow that accentuated the largeness and darkness of her lovely eyes.

They sat chatting and sipping coffee while anticipating the soup to arrive, which was brought promptly, the Negro waiter, standing particularly erect, asking with dignified politeness if they had sufficiently considered which of the meats was to their liking, a choice of two available to them from the three on the menu.

"Let's see. Veal cutlets, a cut of pork, and fish. Of these?"

Adelaide was the spokesperson. "Veal cutlets and a cut of pork. We have unanimously agreed. We're sure they're quite good."

They were a striking assemblage, these four, Adelaide dressed in a pretty white blouse with ruffles at the shoulders, and clad in a stylish dark skirt that spread nicely about her lower frame. There was a barrette affixed to her hair. Sasha was attired in a solid pink dress and had elected to let her hair dangle loosely about her shoulders. The men sported fashionable dress suits. The conversation covered an assortment of topics, lively pursued. There was one however that was off limits. Adelaide had suggested earlier in the day, shortly after departing the mansion for the city, that this was a trip where thoughts and worries were to be left behind, and everyone had cast agreement.

The rain refused to let up, continuing to sweep hard against the windows from time to time, Sasha settling in again on the streamers wriggling downward, crawling, wriggling, crawling, wriggling, until crashing on the sill below.

"Sasha and I have our sights on shopping in the morning," Adelaide mentioned. "Hopefully this rain will let up. I hope you and Andre will fare reasonably well."

"We'll make out Adelaide," said Doctor Givens. "Don't give us a single thought."

"Andre knows the city. May I suggest that he carry you for a tour, assuming the weather permits."

"Gladly," Andre spoke up.

"I'd like that Andre," said the doctor; "let's take Adelaide up on her suggestion."

"Ah! That's what we'll do."

"Good," continued Adelaide. "But let me suggest something else. There's a gentleman that lives in this city who migrated from Ireland. His name is Magevney. He built a house more than two decades ago on a street not far from this very hotel and later the first Catholic mass in Memphis was celebrated in it. Isn't that interesting? Lawrence and I have attended church there. Take Doctor Givens by to see it Andre while you're on your tour. You know where it is."

"I will. I'll make that a must."

The waiter very shortly brought out the veal cutlets and the pork with a crowded platter of southern vegetables. Garbed in a waist coat of white and a pair of brilliant black trousers he obviously was prepared and skilled in the etiquette of serving and pleasing the wealthy echelon. He had recognized Adelaide and Sasha as soon as they entered. Later, when he came to ask his guest if the meal was to their satisfaction Sasha uncloaked a question.

"May I trouble you a moment?" she asked.

"Please do."

"What is the name of that fine soup you served us? It was delicious."

"Ah! I'm glad you asked. It's call seafood ravioli."

Later, when deeming it appropriate, he returned to inquire of their choice of dessert.

"Now your dessert. We offer on the menu raisin pudding topped with wafers, strawberries on muffins, and another that is new. I will recommend it with your permission."

"Why not," Adelaide exclaimed with an inquiry that suggested he'd struck a chord of enticement. "What is it?"

"It's called alfajores. Do not let the name mislead you. It's a simple shortbread cookie with a sweet crème filling at the core. It's most delicious."

"Let's try it," said Adelaide, glancing at the others to receive their approval.

"Yes, let's try it," said Sasha, "I'm curious of its taste."

When they had sat for two hours at dinner or thereabouts the camaraderie was about to draw to a close. Sensing as much Doctor Givens proposed that he deliver a toast.

"Shall I?"

"Please," Adelaide entreated.

"Very well." Holding out his tea glass which the rest clinked with theirs he began. "Here's to the beautiful day just passed, that I know we all have enjoyed, and we do thank the Lord for it; and to Sasha and Andre, who if they are half as successful in the profession they are taking up, as I think they will be, they will do boundless good in this world and their names will become widely and variously known."

Adelaide and Andre clapped their hands, but softly so as not to disturb the patrons sitting close by, and Sasha, the glow of her visage conveying that she was stirringly moved by his confidence and belief in her and Andre, reached across the table and touched his arm.

Chapter 41

THEY SLEPT soundly. The rain still fell, a gentle rain in the latter hours, the peak of the storm blowing off to the east during the night. Breakfast was served late. They slept late, until after nine, and upon their last cup, Adelaide and Sasha climbed inside a hack driver's taxi and went on their way shopping. He'd drive them from place to place. Adelaide had contracted his services for the day.

Doctor Givens broke away to the lobby frontage where he began to look down at the docking area of the river in curious study of the activity there happening. There was none to speak of, only a scattering of workers, slaves mixed with day workers clad in slickers. The whole of the place was enshrouded in mist and vapors, a smoky colored substance in any event, which looked as smoke that rises from burning green brush that a farmer has set fire to that smokes more than burns. His next steps were to the lobby desk, there acquiring a newspaper, the *Inquirer,* for a nickel, and found an easy chair and began to digest the reporting of local and regional events, with Andre all this while en route to deliver a set of papers to a cotton broker for his father. These were contracts the man needed to sign. As did Adelaide, he also hired a hack driver to transport him about in the foul weather.

Adelaide told Tahitia the day before to ask Doctor Lundy, if she intercepted him, to come to the Gayoso House. Tahitia did better. She sent Ezra to find the doctor and tell him. She did not live a far piece from his office, and neither was the Gayoso House far from his address. Nothing in Memphis in that period was far from anything situated inside its limits.

"Ha. So glad to see you Doctor Givens."

"Same here my friend. It's an uncooperative day for you to make it out. Hope you're not excessively put upon to join me. Adelaide said you might show up."

"No indeed. I'm not put upon. Not at all. I've wanted to visit with you a great deal more than I have. Where are the others?" he asked, looking about.

"Andre just left a while ago on an errand for his father. Adelaide and Sasha are shopping."

"Ah, so they are."

"Yes they are. That's the nature of women. They like to shop."

"Ha. So they do. And speaking of women, how is our Sasha fairing with you?"

"She's a jewel. Far advanced beyond where I thought she might be before I met her. So quick of intellect. I'm astonished at her repository of knowledge. She's a rare one. Had there been no Sasha surely the Lord would have eventually invented her on the strength of public demand, if I may here loosely parody the words of Voltaire."

"I told you."

"I well know that. And you also told me of the two infirmaries. They're excellent, well laid out and equipped. They're clinics actually, the only thing lacking is the personnel in sufficient numbers to staff them."

"That will happen in time."

"With funding behind the facilities I believe it will. Certainly Adelaide and Mrs. Van Doke will do their part. I take it also that Mr. Van Doke's thoughts will coincide with his wife's."

"I hope. By the way, how have you found him during your stay? Sometimes he's a grouchy soul, sometimes downright belligerent."

"He's exhibited manners becoming a host I have to report. But he and his wife are radically different, he rather coarse and, and—.

"Uneducated and unfinished. Forgive me for completing your thoughts. Sometimes, I dare say, he's downright boorish and abrasive and puffed up and his head excessively heated. "

"Ha, ha, ha. Thank you. Yes, I have seen flashes that tend to validate that you have fairly sized him up. On the other hand, Mrs. Van Doke is utterly charming, a lady by every distinction, and her schooling of her early years is evident."

"She's English you know. Did her education there. When she was in her very early life her family moved to Virginia and that is where they met. I've heard that her father returned her to England for a while to pursue and finish her studies."

"Ah, I'll declare. So she received her schooling in England. I'm not the least surprised. She's deep into art as you are aware. It's profoundly evident in her many tasteful, if not quite uncommon collections. I can't determine if her husband joins her in these pursuits."

"He doesn't. I can vouch that he doesn't. But that is not the only place they diverge. They are eons apart on the issue of slavery. I don't see how they live together."

"Oh!"

"Quite simply, I should state, she's against it, and he's vehemently determined that it should exist and continue forever as an institution."

"She's hard abolitionist; he's hard pro slavery."

"That's it."

"The rest of her family, the boys: with whom do they take sides?"

"Jim and Andre are with their mother, George is clearly in his father's camp."

"I'll declare," Doctor Givens exclaimed. "Factions in the family. Think of it. This could get to be severely complicated, with thousands of families it could, especially if war erupts, and there is talk that a calamity of that magnitude might spread upon us, though I pray not."

"I've thought of this too dear friend. As you well know there's bitter argument on both sides, the abolitionists taking the stance that the institution of slavery should be destroyed, wiped off the face of the earth, much in the manner that the Romans scattered salt on the state of Carthage to assure that it could never rear it's head again; while the opposite view argues that slavery is an institution guaranteed by the constitution, and if deprived of cotton, the textile industry—and therefore the entire economy—of the North and England will collapse."

"These are serious arguments all right. The news sources are replete with them and others. A day before leaving for the Van Dokes I read in the *Baltimore Sun* an article regarding run away slaves. But this has been a most lively issue for some time."

"It has. But changing the subject, allow me to express that I'm concerned about Sasha almost as much as I am anything else, who hears all these things. I don't see how she can escape it."

"No. And she doesn't escape it. She's read about it no telling the times."

"I never hear Adelaide speak of it, and if anyone knows what Sasha reads and how she feels about something that has to be Adelaide."

Surely. Well, I'm supposing we're at a stopping place. But this is almost laughable isn't it, two doctors of all people exploring the depths of the most heated topic of the century. Yet in a way there's nothing exceptional about it. We should address the issue as quickly and thoroughly as anyone else."

"I agree. It's a threat that faces us all, and won't be easily resolved."

During Doctor Lundy's short stay further the men spoke casually of other topics of currency, then very soon Doctor Lundy regretted that he must be going and left.

When Andre returned he changed clothing, the pants he wore wet from the knees down to the ankles—then he and Doctor Givens set out on their tour, Andre having retained the cab driver he'd used for his errand to the cotton broker.

"Sorry Doctor Givens. I would have gotten back sooner but quite a few business folks were ahead of me. I couldn't have afforded to leave. The contracts absolutely had to be signed."

"That is positively all right. I had a nice visitor to keep me company."

"Ah. Who was that?"

"Doctor Lundy."

"I might have known."

The horses hooves struck the cobblestones loud and sharply, while the doctor poked his head through the open window to garner a less obstructed view of the towering sycamores, which added style and charm to the disproportionate presence of stately homes that ran parallel to the street one after another.

"There's wealth here Andre. Who are the people living in these fine homes?"

"Former landed gentry. They like the city better than the country, many do I should explain. So they've moved to town. Some are Germans. The Germans are good managers, astute business people. They like the city too. I don't think they'd do well in the country." The Chickasaw bluffs Andre also thought informative to speak of, and said that they were ideal for settling Memphis. "The bluffs are too high up for flooding. You saw that yesterday afternoon when we were looking down at the river on our walk." Then he recited one of the business feats of Andrew Jackson which he deemed would be appealing, the purchase of a tract of land in the high up area on which he and some associates founded the city, lore having it that it was fashioned after the ancient capitol of Egypt.

"This place is undergoing swift transition Doctor Givens; the city is a busy stage coach terminus, home to a fleet of Butterfield overland mail coaches. And I'm taking it that you've heard of the six miles of railroad track that run eastwardly from here. People are whooping it up that the railroad corporations will waste no time laying the tracks on out further."

"I'm confident that will happen. But let us back up a minute. The houses we passed back there. The two story structures, quite grand in comparison."

"In comparison?"

"To these we're passing now. Small, common, weathering, in wont of paint. Who lives here? Not wealthy citizens it's plain to see."

"No sir. People of wealth sure don't live here. It's the Irish. And they don't for the most part own the houses. They rent. They set foot in Memphis first, then the Germans found their way here. The Irish are no match for the Germans at managing and merchandising and amassing property. Coming from the old country with no marketable skills the Irish drew the short end of the straw, settling for the sweaty reek of cutting roads and erecting buildings and constructing levees and digging and cleaning out canals."

"You're very well on top of things Andre. You'd make a splendid teacher. I must compliment you. How did you happen to learn all this?"

"I've been tagging along with my father to Memphis ever since I was a small boy. Just picked up bits and pieces a little at a time as I moved up in years."

During the tour Andre asked the taxi driver to swing by the Magevney house, nothing more than an unpretentious small wood board dwelling that Mr. Magevney used for his home and for offering mass. Its days were numbered, its worshipers starting to take mass at Lawrence Sherette's beautiful church of Gothic architecture.

At three they had made their way back to the hotel. Adelaide and Sasha weren't there. They'd left a note. It said they were at Tahitia's, and planned to return in the late afternoon in time enough to dress for going out that evening to have dinner at Randolph's. Doctor Givens seemed as content to rummage about the hotel as much as touring. Little wonder. The Gayoso House showcased a stunning façade of Greek Revival which easily ensnared the eye of steamboat travelers, and this, coupled with wrought iron balconies that added a summary adornment to the frontage, brought irresistible distinction to the city. The hotel was a Memphis landmark, an oasis of modern luxury frequented by travelers passing through the city by river, road, and later by rail; and with its own water works, bakeries, wine cellars, sewer system, and indoor plumbing which featured marble tubs and silver faucets and flushing toilets, it offered amenities far beyond those available to the usual citizen of Memphis. The doctor sat down in the lobby in the same easy chair he'd occupied that morning. Andre was gadding about down street.

"Hmmmm. I was ten. We moved from New Hampshire to Maryland. That makes me part Yankee, part Southern, I'm supposing. Something like that. I've never given it much thought. I grew up hearing both views. I could argue either way. I say I could. But I doubt it. The human sentiment in me would win out. I'm against slavery. How could I not be? How could anyone not be? Think of it. One man owning another as chattel, as if he were a mule or a wagon or a tree.

I worry about Memphis. It's a charming town, but it's a burgeoning slave trading block. I'm afraid the practice will reduce it to ruin sooner or later. And I worry about something else too, something worse than slavery. Possibly worse. Malaria, yellow fever. Memphis is ripe for these outbreaks. Just look at the influx, the Irish, the Germans, the Jews, and the

Africans—the latter by the hordes that grow exponentially. They're piling up on one another. Throw all this with the lowness and wetness of the terrain, the marshes, the sloughs, and the drainage channels that do no better than sluggishly creep and crawl, then you have the perfect formula for a disastrous outbreak. I suspect the mosquito, I very seriously do. Some of my colleagues don't. Someday I think they'll agree with me.

But enough of these things. I should turn to something else now. The Magevney house. It's sad to see it start down hill. So Adelaide and her brother attended church there. Lawrence presently has his own church. That's good. I'm glad Andre walked me through it. What a splendid sanctuary."

☙ ❧

Upon approaching the frontage of Randolph's night place Adelaide and the rest found him waiting at the doorway.

"My friends, my friends. Please come in." As Sasha was passing he bowed. "And how are you this evening Miss Sasha?"

"I'm fine, and you?"

"Very well, thank you."

Randolph seated them directly in front of the gargantuan fireplace a short ways back where the meats of multiple sorts were prepared over an open bed of coals. The aroma pervaded the dining space throughout, the heat felt as far back as the center of the room, yet it was not greatly bothersome. From where they sat the Negro cooks were seen in their white coats which dropped to their knees, while flipping the meats with a spatula, an instrument with a long wooden handle and a broad flat edge. They were intentionally showy, sometimes tossing two pieces into the air and catching both as they came back down, never erring. Randolph himself was showy, but with people, amazingly able to call anyone and everyone by first name before their dinner was over. Tahitia had responded to him earlier when he had hugged her and showered her with inflated compliments as to her beauty.

"Liar," she whispered. "But keep it up; I do like it despite its emptiness."

"No, no, no. I mean it from the bottom of my heart."

"What heart you rascal? But so much for that. Here, take this." She had handed him a note. "Something else begs for your attention. We have a prominent doctor with us. That's him sitting by Adelaide. I've written his name down for you. Coach yourself to pronounce it correctly." Randolph made his way over as soon as he deemed it tactful.

"Ah, Doctor Givens. We're so graced by your presence. You are with us all the way from Baltimore."

The doctor did not show surprise, having suspected that Tahitia had tipped him off.

"Thank you. Thank you very much. I'm delighted to take dinner with my friends at your restaurant. Many good things they've said about it, especially Sasha," he said, airily looking over at her. She danced a smile with her lovely eyes, warmed that she was a part of the merriment.

"And is Adelaide taking good care of you doctor?"

"As much as I can," Adelaide answered before the doctor did, "but he's staying at the Van Dokes."

"Ah yes. Forgive me. I'm slipping badly. Ah yes, at the Van Dokes."

"You remember Andre, don't you?"

"I do. How are you Andre? Forgive me if you will. You have not visited here in some time. You used to with your father."

"I did. At every chance."

"I remember you. But you have a great advantage over me."

"I do?"

"Yes, you have grown, now a very handsome young man, while I, I. Well, I've stayed much the same, but have added a few pounds every year."

After Randolph had left, the waiter was quickly present to take the orders. The barbecued roast beef was their choice and it was not but a fraction that a platter was set before them with the succulent meat stacked in many pieces one upon the other. When they had gotten largely through dinner someone drew a curtain back in the mid space of the room and a band began to play and four singers began to sing. Randolph pulled up a chair beside Doctor Givens. The musicians played on the loud side but Randolph acted with no effort to curtail them.

"They're Creoles doctor. I guess you can tell by the banjo picker and the fiddlers."

"Creoles you said? I wouldn't have known. Louisiana, I take it? But where are they from exactly?"

"New Orleans."

"We're going to New Orleans this coming fall," Sasha scrouged in, suddenly uplifted. "We are, aren't we Adelaide?"

"We wouldn't miss it for the world." Sasha put her fingers to her lips and smiled with happiness.

"Ah! So Sasha you're going to New Orleans," said Randolph. I've spent many an hour in that lively city. Adelaide, don't forget to take her to the Quadroon Ball if it's happening when you're there. It's a must for her to see."

"I don't know," said Sasha, displaying a tinge of doubt of Adelaide's approval, though very much feeling that she'd love to attend such an event. She'd read about Quadroon Balls during her former stay in that city, grasping that they were a slight risqué.

"You'll take her, won't you Adelaide?" said Randolph, feeling sure that she would.

"We'll place the affair high on our itinerary. We'll see."

"Please do take her."

The band played on for awhile. To be polite Adelaide withheld that they were anxious to leave, so they stayed on. When she'd made up her mind to tell Randolph they'd have to go she gave as a reason their departure for home at seven o'clock the next morning and that they needed to turn in early. As they left he stood at the doorway graciously bidding goodbyes, one person at a time, and invited them back. They drove Tahitia home then went to the Gayoso House and crawled in. The next morning they breakfasted at six and after Adelaide's several boxes of shopping purchases were loaded left for Aurora. The hour was seven.

For awhile Sasha leaned against Adelaide's shoulder and slept. She'd traded places with Doctor Givens, who now sat in front by Andre, looking curiously about. The day was fair and sunny. The sun, together with the rising temperature, promised to dry out the road, but it was yet soft and irksomely muddy in places, the wheels of the carriage sinking better than ankle deep if measured by a man's extremities, the ugly mud caking on the pretty red spokes, the wagon tongue, and on the bellies and legs of the horses.

"Messy," said Doctor Givens.

"Yes sir," replied Andre. "It forces the horses to pull extra hard."

"They sweat already."

"I know. We'll change at the way station. I think we'll add two more when we're there. We need a team of four considering the mire."

"You'll rest these two often until then."

"About every thirty minutes. We're in for a slow trip."

At mid morning Sasha awakened and sat up, and looked around, asking where they were and how far they'd come, to which Adelaide answered they were less than two hours from the way station yet were nearing a farm home a slight off the roadway where they'd stop to refresh and have coffee.

"At Mrs. Gish's?" said Sasha.

"Yes. We stopped there once before, remember?"

"Of course. She's a very nice lady."

Staying but briefly Adelaide gave Mrs. Gish some money and they returned to their journey, reaching the way station on the morning side of noon, the mistress of the house pleading with Adelaide and the rest to grace her table by having a bowl of soup and drink, which Adelaide had done countless times. But she politely declined.

"We lodged at the Gayoso House. I ordered a basket of food for spreading at some shady grove close by the road. We're looking forward to that quite soon. To accept your generous invitation is to spoil our appetite. Next time my dear."

With four horses hitched to the carriage they pulled back onto the high road, the load lighter now by one half; Andre felt the carriage moving easier. There was no jerkiness in its motion.

Adelaide had carefully kept her bearings on the spot which she had spoken of to the lady at the way station and when they had reached it she asked Andre to stop the team, that this was where they were to spread their food. Not tarrying for long, they ate and went on, coming eventually to one of the places where the leaves and branches bent lowly over the roadway, where the dappling of the sunbeams begrudgingly sprinkled through. By now the clouds had drifted away, the naked sun now in full view, bearing unrelentingly down on the carriage's occupants as if attempting to make up for lost time, forcing the heat to a level which noticeably exceeded the temperature in the earlier hours of the day, and as they traveled on for awhile Adelaide and Sasha opened their umbrellas. Sasha had exchanged places with Doctor Givens and sat by Andre in the front seat.

Adelaide was curious. "Did Memphis disappoint you Doctor Givens?"

"Not in the least. I found it charming, but in the same breath, let me augment, there's a raw ruggedness about it that you quickly see. New cities are like that. It faces growing pains."

"Memphis does have a way to go."

Sasha knew much about the Big Hatchie, for Sam Feathers had taught her well. She even knew with pointed accuracy about how high the water had risen before they reached the river. She had seen it with him when after a torrent of rain fell it appeared to be possessed of a rage, threatening to jump its banks, or when the waters were so low that they seemed to stand still, their width no wider than the length of a cottonwood sapling.

"Look Doctor Givens." They were then crossing the wooden bridge, the accumulation of logs and brush tossed and rolled savagely about by the frothy turbulence. The horses clomped heavily on the planking, the carriage wheels sounding a rumble akin to low continued thunder. Doctor Givens hadn't seen this behavior of the river three mornings ago when the party had left for Memphis. But then there had been no rain and darkness enshrouded the bridge.

"This is the Big Hatchie. It's the one you say you fish with Sam Feathers."

"It is. I'm quick to go whenever he consents to take me."

Doctor Givens did not let out that to him the river was horribly ugly but Sasha knew how he felt, the same way she felt when she first saw it.

"It's an ugly river Doctor Givens. I admit it, but it's full of catfish and they're easy to catch if you know what you're doing, and Sam Feathers does. Sam's the best."

They'd had their stay in Memphis. They were home now. The plantation was abuzz with the cultivation of the cotton plants, which was the harrowing of the rows on both sides and cutting away the grass with chopping hoes, the phase just before "laying by." The picking season was but weeks away, and when it commenced the cotton would be ginned and transported to the shipping docks that Doctor Givens had seen from the Gayoso House. He and Sasha and Andre resumed their care of the patients that needed them, and Adelaide was entrenched with Sam Feathers in the preparation of things for the crucial harvest ahead. Every grown person on the plantations sensed or knew that Doctor Givens and Andre were on the verge of leaving for Baltimore, and that the days were swiftly dwindling down.

"When they leave a big hole will open up," said Mary Tonka to Adelaide. "Sasha will be crushed."

"She'll have Doctor Lundy and you Mary Tonka. There's always someone to step in to fill the gap. And she's strong, don't forget that. People like that find a way to lean on themselves."

"Umh. Humh. She is strong."

Not long before the date of departure, Sasha and Andre climbed on their horses and rode toward the river, never making it that far because when they came to the pathway that broke off into the woods, which Sasha had never yet traveled, she reined over and Andre fell in behind. It was an idyllic narrow trail, clear and unobstructed of brush or thickets or fallen trees, covered by dense hanging foliage that, except for the faintest breaks, kept the sun largely unseen. Spurring the horses into a lope they came with little lapse upon the bridge that overspread the pretty creek trickling under it. Adelaide had told her of it times innumerable.

"It's beautiful," she said, climbing down. "I'm glad we came. Adelaide and I never once got this far, but intended too."

"You've not been here before?"

"No. Have you?"

"Often. Ever since I was a small boy I've been coming here."

"All by yourself?"

"Sure. What was there to be afraid of?"

"Nothing I guess."

"Tell you what," he said. "Let me crawl down and pick up some of the pebbles for you to throw out into the water like I used to."

"As a little boy?"

"As a little boy," he answered.

"Like you used to! Please. I'd like that."

Then Andre crawled down the embankment into the shallow clear stream, picked up as many pebbles as his two palms could hold and delivered them to Sasha.

"Here. See how large a ripple you can make."

"All right. Like you used to."

"Like I used to. Ha, ha, ha."

Sasha took the pebbles and began to throw them upstream as far as the strength of her arm would let her, reloading with a new handful when these were expended which Andre was happy to supply. Finally, having her fill, she suggested that they mount up and start back.

"I'll race you," she challenged, goading her horse into a sudden sprint, Andre giving chase. The horses flew. Sasha pierced the air with a shriek of delight, scaring the wildlife in all apparentness, for they had turned lifelessly still; and if not affrighted they were amused into an attitude of silence. Sasha leaned low against her steed as the wind shot over her, Andre in close pursuit, the trees seeming to fly by, the dappling playing games upon their faces, striking, vanishing, striking, vanishing, done faster than lightning. Beautiful horses with thin swift legs and shiny chestnut fleeces streaked as an arrow upon the pathway, two beautiful people on their backs, Sasha clad in her riding habit of black and a fox hunter's cap on her head; and Andre in common clothing, his capless hair buffeted wildly about by the wind. What a moment it was. What a carefree moment it was. There were no sick and suffering patients that weighed upon their thoughts, none in their past, none in the future to come, none in that brief interlude of youthful joy.

Mary Tonka saw them coming. "Ha! They've been racing."

"Seems so," confirmed Adelaide. "I think they're trying to forget."

"Forget?"

"That Andre's leaving right away."

When they reached the frontage, drawing to rest under the towering cedars, Sasha dismounted, a worker taking the reins. But Andre did not leave his horse. He'd hurry on. He bade goodbye and said he'd see her the next day.

Chapter 42

AS HE entered the Van Doke mansion he saw his mother sitting at a small rounded side table with a lamp on it reading a book. Ever gracious, he went over and kissed her cheek.

"You've stayed awhile."

"Um humh. Sasha and I were riding."

"She's a good rider, isn't she?"

"Very good."

"She's good at anything she does, don't you think?"

"I do. I admire her proficiencies. I very much do."

"I know."

It happened two days before Andre and Doctor Givens left for Baltimore. Sasha had agreed at the urging of the doctor to play the compositions of the great men for awhile. With the busy summer they'd had there wasn't time until now for him to hear her, or else they simply hadn't committed themselves to it. The playing was arranged for mid afternoon, Sasha and Adelaide surmising that the doctor will have had his fill after an hour. Sasha would begin at approximately three and cease at four. Not without knowledge of the event, Andre passed it on to his mother, who in turn asked him to ask Sasha if it was satisfactory for her to sit and listen also; and naturally Sasha urged him to welcome Mrs. Van Doke and to tell her that she was distressed that she'd neglected to convey the welcome in the first place. The concert, we shall call it, began at three, with Mrs. Van Doke, Doctor Givens, Andre, Adelaide, and Mary Tonka sitting in half circle. Sasha was clad in her blue polka dot that fell to her ankles, no jewelry on her person other than the braid gold chain about her neck and a barely visible spangle on the bosom region of her dress. She took her seat and paused, then turned and looked piquantly at her audience. A little smile subtly showed itself but left with a dart as she turned to face the piano, lightly touching the first note. She played for the full minutes of an hour, her fingers trickling across the keys, sometimes delicately, sometimes running the keyboard from top to bottom without a break, sometimes striking the notes with dashing vigor but at all times arrestingly. Sometimes she closed her eyes, as if floating vicariously away to some distant paradise. The doctor sat enchanted, once leaning over to Adelaide with words of praise, even venturing that when he attended the symphony in the late fall in the city of Baltimore, where he had season tickets, the remembrance of what he had seen here would command an uppermost place in his thoughts. What was it about the young beauty that so fascinated him, that fascinated everyone: her nice shapely arms as they swerved every which way across the keyboards? Or the magical flitting of her fingers? Or her lovely hair as it flounced upon her shoulders? It was none of these alone, but these and immeasurable others conjoining that were mesmerizing. Mrs. Van Doke smiled adoringly and quivered the ebony fan which she eloquently held with her finger and thumb as if applauding.

"She is a dream Adelaide," said Doctor Givens. "Are we amiss not to encourage her to enter that mystic realm we call music?"

Adelaide smiled and shook her head. "That can never be. She's set on the other."

"That is true. But the opposite is tempting."

Doctor Lundy arrived from Memphis a day before Andre and Doctor Givens were to leave, earlier than he intended, yet while on his way began to think of what must be done when he got there and that likely he had waited too long. What he needed to do, he thought, was to look over a list of the sick that he and Sasha were to attend after Doctor Givens was no longer around and review the recommendations of treatment for these persons that the doctor had prepared, and next, with Doctor Givens and Sasha, visit the patients who were in the greatest need of medical care. That is the manner in which events unfolded. Sasha had developed a list of these patients and they, all three, sat down and went over it then began their on site visits, this meaning in the patient's home.

Moving from house to house they were able to see a sizeable number that afternoon. Sometime during the next day Sasha and Doctor Lundy would continue. Sasha listened to the doctors' busily exchange talk and made copious notes in her head which she later transcribed to print. The afflictions of dominant occurrence fell upon the aged, many not expected to live for a significant length. A great many suffered from ailments of the heart, emphysema, arthritis, bone degeneration, failing eyesight, general debility, cancer of the skin, rashes, and conditions of pneumonia.

"They're old Sasha," said Doctor Givens. "Perhaps through the future discoveries of science and medicine we can do something for them. We could if they lived that long. For now, the focus has to be not on cure and restoration of health. It has to be on comforting, attempting to alleviate suffering."

It had long been in Sasha's thoughts that to think of rehabilitating the aged was futile but that every doctor must approach a patient as if that were possible. "The Hippocratic Oath demands it." Neither doctor mentioned that the use of opium was an alternative to blunting their discomfort and suffering, but sometimes prescribed it. But it was not limited to the aged exclusively. It was used for stopping diarrhea among all ages and the doctors administered it as if it were an essential medicine for this affliction. Sasha was well aware, as were the doctors, that the people secretively had possession of the drug and used it for social enjoyment without permission or recommendation.

Pregnancies, healing breakages, and non threatening infections and the like that pertained to younger patients were on Sasha's list but these persons were passed over for the time being. She and Doctor Lundy would look in on them in the following days. For this, she would compile the names of all patients into categories of serious, mildly serious, and non serious, laying the list on the work desk in the infirmary for Doctor Lundy should he need it in her absence, keeping a copy for her own files.

The hour was late when Doctor Givens left for the Van Doke plantation, saying that most of his belongings were packed and that it was on his itinerary to leave the next morning at eight. He said the key words that Sasha wanted to hear, that she'd been a joy to work with, that she'd been greatly helpful with the patients, and that he would miss her terribly. Adelaide asked if his thoughts were to return for another summer and he replied perhaps, unless extenuating circumstances at the hospital dictated that he couldn't. He told Sasha that he'd write and would be sending her a continuous flow of medical research and welcomed a report from time to time regarding her patients. Then he said that this all sounded as if he were saying goodbye at this very moment, but that he wasn't, that it was his intention for he and Andre to drive by on their way to Paducah the next morning. Sasha smiled and said she'd expect them. Earlier, Mrs. Van Doke had mentioned hopefully to Adelaide that she and Sasha might drive over to her home and see Doctor Givens and Andre off from there, which Adelaide was disposed against, but said nothing. It was a given that George would be on the scene seeing them off also, and she knew that his company she would not in the least enjoy and that Sasha would entertain like feelings.

The next morning Doctor Givens and Andre arrived, driven by a white employee that worked for the Van Dokes. The hour was ten, a later start on their journey than predetermined. Both climbed down and went over to the portico where Sasha, Adelaide, and Mary Tonka had stood looking for them.

"We're late," said Doctor Givens. His countenance was melancholy and Andre looked equally if not more downcast. "I'm sorry, but we'll have to be brief."

"Which we sorely regret, but if you must," answered Adelaide. He smiled and thanked her.

"It's been a splendid stay, and you've been one of the bright spots of the summer Sasha," he said, his eyes meeting hers. "Andre feels the same I'm sure."

"Altogether the same," Andre uttered. "I wish we had it to do all over."

"Me too," Sasha replied.

Adelaide explained that Doctor Lundy left early to see a patient some miles away, and that through her he conveyed his regrets for his absence.

"I understand," Doctor Givens warmly replied. The farewell talk had continued but a slight when the doctor spoke that they'd better go, moving simultaneously to each of the women with an embrace. Andre did the same, saving Sasha for last.

"Goodbye Sasha."

"Goodbye."

And then in an air of somberness the men walked to the carriage and climbed into their seats, the driver clucking to the horses. They began to move away. Sasha waved until they entered the main road.

"Goodbye" she said once more.

In the earlier part of the afternoon she left for a ride, inviting Adelaide to go with her, though Adelaide tactfully pretended she had some pressing things to do. She sensed that Sasha was saddened by the departure of her friends and that it was best for her to spend time alone. At first she rode into the fields of cotton, now a sea of white waiting for the workers to come with their sacks and baskets and mournful songs, then back tracked to a hay field recently cut, there happening upon her little friend the killdeer running just ahead, leading her away from her nesting chicks, then from there reining her horse toward the river until intercepting the pathway that she and Andre had recently taken to the bridge that crossed the narrow stream. She went the whole of the distance, even guiding her mount across the bridge and back when she got there, not stopping to climb off, merely looking around and into the clear trickling waters where she'd thrown the pebbles. She smiled at the remembrance. Then turned the sorrel for home. Adelaide and Mary Tonka heard her ride up, relieved that she had returned.

"Did the leaving of Doctor Givens and Andre get her down?" asked Mary Tonka.

"Some. But with her intestinal fortitude, not for long. Anyone is down now and then. As a matter of fact I've felt down myself this afternoon."

Quickly Sasha bathed and slipped into a pretty red robe, which she seldom wore but on this day decided in its favor, then proceeded to the piano and began to play;—sweet and lovely notes, springing from the heart, not from the compositions the great men had set down on paper, but of her own contrivance, low and lilting, like a melting rhapsody thought Adelaide from where she sat sewing—and played for a very long while, until suppertime, when at last Mary Tonka came softly to her.

"The table is set dear. Supper is ready."

"Thank you Mary Tonka, I'll be right there."

When they had eaten, Adelaide and Sasha elected to sit in the swing on the portico. The night was cool and lovely, the sky aglitter with the stars. The moon was in full glow, the crickets and fireflies busy at play.

"Look, there's Heaven's lamp" cried Sasha, her dark eyes sparkling with excitement. "Just look." It was the full moon to which she referred. She stood and wafted over to the portico's edge to acquire a better view. Adelaide was amused at her description. Mary Tonka joined them, taking a seat in the chair they alluded to as the huge high back.

"It's been a wonderful summer," said Adelaide, "busy but wonderful, and the fall promises that we'll be equally as busy, you and Doctor Lundy caring for the people, Sam and I seeing that the cotton is picked and ginned, and we'll have to set about with arrangements for the trip to New Orleans."

"When? When is it?"

"This afternoon Sam brought me a letter. Harry has found a place for us to stay, and has reserved it from October 20 throughout November should we need it that long. I sincerely hope that Lawrence can be with us. I'll ask him. You'll need to write Mrs. Laster right away."

"I will."

Upon attending mass at Lawrence Sherette's church on the next Sabbath, they learned that at almost any period he could accompany them on their sojourn to New Orleans, he and Adelaide deciding then and there on October 20 as the departure date. Steamers were coming and going daily, thereby assuring that the date on which they had concluded was workable. Adelaide and Sasha dropped by to visit briefly with Tahitia, and while there Adelaide invited her to join them on their trip. Tahitia begged off, giving as her reason that it was too long for her and that she didn't feel she could bear the strain. Adelaide reluctantly yielded and tried further persuasion.

"I promised to take you. That's why I'm here today."

"I know darling. Next time."

On the way home Sasha scribbled out a note to Mrs. Laster.

My dear one. We are leaving Memphis on the 20th of October for New Orleans. We should arrive on the waterfront at mid afternoon of the 21st. Can you and Bryon make it on that date? I know you can. You said in your last letter that anytime in October was fine. Please let me have confirmation. Oh. I am so excited. It will be like Heaven to see you.

With all my love and more,

Sasha

Within days Mrs. Laster wrote back that she and Bryon would be standing in the area of the docking port on the date as stated.

The leaves of fall had turned to gold and brown. The cotton gin hummed a steady rhythm and there was a consistent flow of cotton bales from the Sherette plantation to the port of Memphis. Doctor Lundy and Sasha stayed busy attending to the ailing. Doctor Lundy would miss Sasha. "A whole month you'll be gone? I guess I'll have to depend as much as I can on the chubby old doctor at Brownsville and the new one over at Jackson as my fill ins. But I don't like it." Sasha laughed and pampered him.

☙ ❧

The days of fall moved on step by step, then suddenly there was the 20th of October, which found Sasha, Adelaide and Lawrence Sherette dressed and packed for the trip, handing over their baggage to the boat porters for transfer to the cabins where they were to lodge. It was barely daylight. When the steamer pulled out into the river the air was cool and there was a breeze. When they had steamed southward by some distance the air became even cooler and the breeze stronger, but this did not deter Sasha from spending time on deck looking about and engaging in conversation with an assortment of people. She was clad in a stylish brown topcoat with a hat on her head that tilted a slight to the left, and on her feet she wore a pair of shiny black slippers. She looked a shade Frenchy in her attire said Adelaide, both laughing at the analogy.

"I'll bet you even dream in French Sasha."

Sasha burst into greater laughter, admitting in a flare of play that sometimes she did, but if she now looked Frenchy it was purely accidental.

The rains that fall were slack, the river water in consequence subsiding to an unseasonably low ebb and contrary to the trip when Sasha and Adelaide had earlier come to

Memphis from New Orleans few logs were seen afloat. At noon Adelaide opened the food basket that she had filled, and shared the packings with the two porters assigned to see after their needs. They ate on deck in the fullness of sunshine. That night they slept in cramped quarters, Lawrence Sherette more so, but the space was clean and tidy. Sasha knocked on Lawrence Sherette's cabin door before they all turned in, saying that she'd like to stroll awhile on deck and asked him if he would go with her. Gladly he would he answered. Adelaide was reading; she preferred to stay inside. "It's too chilly, and besides, I don't want to dress again." The tiny stars filled the Heavens, and since there were no clouds, they glittered with an intensity, but these were not the only sources of glitter on that clear evening; there were the lantern lights on the shorelines, which the Negroes necessarily used for checking their pole hooks and trotlines.

"Sam Feathers is the best at catching catfish," said Sasha, the lantern lights reminding her of the hours she had spent with him on the banks of the Big Hatchie.

"He says you're a pretty good fisherman yourself."

"I'm learning."

Sasha was thrilled as always to be close to Lawrence Sherette and recalled that morning on which she first saw him, which was at Father Lumas's breakfast table, a handsome strong figure of a man with very dark hair likened to hers. She would never forget that scene. She also recalled how afraid she was, suddenly among strangers in a new city, wary of what the next day was to bring, but Lawrence Sherette had spoken to her with such soft and comforting words that she knew then he was a good man and would be her father for the rest of his life. She hugged him as her thoughts ran backward. "I'm excited that you're on the trip with us. It wouldn't have been the same without you."

Next morning the Captain anchored his vessel at Natchez to pick up fresh fish. Lunch was served in the diner in two shifts. They took the last. There would be no fish; the fish were to be reserved for supper, and by then they will have set foot in New Orleans. But much to the satisfaction of each the servings at lunch consisted of steak and chicken with an assortment of vegetables, and this, they claimed, was better than the fish anyway. The morning had rolled into the afternoon; they were close. Another hour had vanished when the Captain eased his vessel into port and anchored. The Creoles and Irishmen were on the scene as Sasha had expected, darting about, toting baggage and pushing carts of luggage, gibbering in near unintelligible language. Mrs. Laster, Bryon, and Harry Lancaster were standing on the port frontage. Sasha saw them as she descended the gangplank.

"There they are," she said excitedly, and ran at her best speed until reaching the arms of Mrs. Laster. "Oh my goodness," she uttered. "At last."

"You are grown, you are grown," cried Mrs. Laster, "I hardly recognize you."

"I'm still me, still the same."

"No, you have grown so. You are grown."

It was a tearful, joyful reunion that Mrs. Laster had begun to believe was never to happen. A year and a half had gone by since they had last seen one another.

The rest watched with amusement and gladdened hearts as the two kept clinging to one another, and then it came Bryon's turn. "Come here you beautiful girl," he cried, reaching for her. She laughed with boundless joy.

"Bryon. You made it," she said, falling into his arms. "I'm so glad. I have many things to tell you and to ask you about. I have missed you terribly."

"And I have you Sasha. But as mother just said, you are grown. You've changed."

"Oh, don't say that. I'm still the same."

"Ha, ha, ha. No you're not. Believe me."

"And how is that? she asked, puckering her pretty lips.

"You're—you're, now how shall I say it?"

"Just say it. You're rousing my suspense."

"Well, you're more like woman than you were, but it's all for the better."

"Ha, ha, ha. All right my dear brother. In that case I'll accept your observation."

Everyone then collided with a maelstrom of embraces and warm affectionate words. When the emotions and tears and excitement at last subsided, calm again reigning, Adelaide stepped into her usual persona of consul in charge by asking Harry of the whereabouts of their lodging, who explained that it was on 535 Bourbon Street, near the heart of the city.

The carriages were more than sufficient for transporting the party to the residence that Harry had supplied. It was a two storied edifice, exaggerated with French trimmings on the inside and out, and having space enough to accommodate two hundred or more occupants. They could subtract one from the total; Lawrence Sherette would take lodging in the Rectory of the Saint Louis Cathedral. The doors to their quarters, inclusive of those of the entry way, were of French design and those to the bedrooms opened onto a small balcony fringed with an exotic maze of intricately shaped iron works. Between the spindles there was affixed a diminutive statue of a Napoleonic soldier. When she thought of it later Sasha asked Harry why the unseemly art piece, to which he replied that when Napoleon was exiled and power passed to the Bourbon Monarchy, a sizeable number of his faithfuls fled to New Orleans and that the statue to which she alluded was in remembrance of the Emperor.

There was a bedroom with a small round table covered with a luxurious blue cloth that especially appealed to Sasha's fancy. A red flower in a crystal vase was placed upon it. She hoped the room could be hers because there had been installed in the walls a set of twin windows, tall and spacious, thereby letting her look downward into the street at the incessant clamor, people walking about and others riding in modern expensive carriages, people of wealth, and from this angle, if she opened the windows and walked out onto the balcony, the towering Saint Louis Cathedral in its whitish stateliness was readily visible. The stairway was supported by a banister of polished teak that rose elegantly to the first landing, then there it turned and continued its upward flight to the second floor. A chandelier of ponderous span hung in the center of the huge living room which was furnished with colorful high backs and mammoth soft couches selectively arranged for accommodating social gatherings. The interior was light and airy. Adelaide said she loved every aspect of the residence and Sasha and Mrs. Laster said they did too.

While Sasha was enamored with the bedroom with the lovely blue cloth on the small round table she was suddenly beset with a dilemma.

"No, no need to think of that Sasha. Neither Adelaide nor Mrs. Laster expects you to sleep with them as you long have. It's time you were weaned. Bask in this lovely room for your own pleasure. They would want you to."

Before little time had elapsed she went to them and asked if she might have the bedroom on the second floor that each knew she was desirous of claiming. Their smiles of amusement telegraphed the answer before they gave it. "Of course you can darling." So Sasha had her bedroom unto herself. But did not sleep altogether in it; sometimes in the wee hours she would steal deftly to where Mrs. Laster or Adelaide lay and gently wake them.

"Can I visit for a while?"

"Oh indeed yes sweetheart," the reply came. "Here, (while rolling back the cover) crawl inside and visit as long as you like. I'm so glad you have come."

Sometimes she stayed for the rest of the night, sometimes for a lesser length, but whichever, they lay there snuggled together for a very long while with the quilt pulled up to their chins and talked of everything under the sun.

It was but an inkling into their stay when one night Sasha crept into Mrs. Laster's bedroom and lay down beside her. Of their many topics there was a remembrance of Mrs. Laster's of a conversation she'd had with Father Kestner shortly before they'd left the Canaries, in which he'd spoken of the afternoon when Sasha was born. He had declared that baby Sasha was the prettiest thing he'd ever seen, prettier than the stars, and that he'd seen many babies born. Doctor Enoch had proclaimed the same, he said, and went further, swearing that the new born looked him squarely in the eyes when he was cleansing her and was trying to say words to him. The Priest had laughed at the fabrication. "But she was a lively baby, kicking and carrying on" he confirmed. Mrs. Laster said she had written the good Priest a letter within the month and that he had answered.

"How is he getting along?" asked Sasha.

"Well enough, but he is old."

"And Father Lumas. How is he faring?"

"Like Father Kestner, he is old and does not move with agility. I take mass at the cathedral daily, the early morning session. I see him constantly. He grieves to see you. You do write him don't you?"

"I do. But should do better. I promise I will."

"Chenelle asks about you too. She's still with Father Lumas. You know of whom I speak. She's the one who baked a cake for you to take on your trip when you left San Antonio."

"Surely I do. Bless her. She was the sweetest thing. Please relay my love to her when you return. I will remember her in my bedside prayers."

"She will like hearing of that."

"And what of the German girl? Paula, Paula Ness. I wish I could have known her longer. We promised to write, but so far we haven't. Do you see her at mass?"

"I do. Most every day. She's very pretty, and tall."

"I remember. She was taller than I when I knew her."

"She will finish girls' school within another year. There's talk about her relocating up East for awhile to pursue an academic career. She'd like to teach, or become a nurse."

"I'll keep my fingers crossed. Tell her I wish her well."

"I will darling. But let me say something of you for a moment. I think of you many times throughout the day, many times, especially how you are filling your hours on that massive plantation that you and Adelaide tell me about in your letters."

"It's wonderful. Something to do all the time. I ride often, and do my best at Adelaide's shiny piano."

"I hear you do. Adelaide says you play marvelously."

"She is partial."

"She says she isn't."

"Ha, ha."

"What else at the plantation?"

"I love the patients. I pour my heart and soul into helping them. I have the kindest person in Doctor Lundy as a mentor, and this summer Doctor Givens from Baltimore let me work closely with him. He seemed particularly to invest a good amount of time and effort in me, all that he could spare. He's a specialist in surgery. I learned much and hope some day to join him in Baltimore and advance further under his guidance."

"You will too. Adelaide says you are progressing with leaps and bounds and that the man you just mentioned, Doctor Givens isn't it, proclaims you will rise to remarkable heights."

"I'd like to think he's right."

"Adelaide assures me that he is."

Lost in the past and immersed in the present and overflowing with speculations of the unpredictable imagined future, they lay there until well after two o'clock and then for another hour. When Sasha finally yawned Mrs. Laster knew that she was about to doze off, and when she had fallen fast asleep, tucked the covers close around her and tenderly planted a kiss upon her face. Nothing had changed. It was like always.

Chapter 43

WHEN ADELAIDE left Memphis she did not have in mind for certain the span of days they would spend in New Orleans. Two weeks were mentioned, she knew, then three, then a month, neither of which was a solid confirmation. What she knew as a fact was that Harry had written that he had negotiated an obligatory contract for a place of residence for a month or more. As it happened their visit was reduced to two weeks, for Bryon soon had to return to San Antonio, his experience and capability making his presence necessary for the erection of a bridge that his company had contracted to build, and Lawrence Sherette felt potently drawn to get back to his congregation. As it was with Bryon he could stay for two weeks only, saying however, that he hoped Sasha and Adelaide might stay longer. They considered the prospect. When they had thrashed it through both opted in favor of leaving when Lawrence Sherette left, Sasha offering the rationale that she missed her patients and felt in her heart that she should return to them. It was thus decided that plans would be devised for compressing as much into every available hour as could be envisioned.

The place of carefree togetherness was the great living room. Adelaide called it the situation room. It was here where they talked and told jokes and listened to the many stories Harry unraveled of the happenings in New Orleans since he had last seen them, and it was here that they decided which dinner place they would patronize on a given evening of their choice. Seldom did they take a meal at home. By and large they ate out together, but not without variation now and then. When they ate at home it was usually for late breakfast, whereon Adelaide called in the Creole cooks Harry had found and hired, who prepared and set out on the table large colorful spreads of oatmeal, ham and eggs, tenderloin, sausages, biscuits, strawberries, jams, melons, a dish of their own making which had no name, and hot coffee and milk. Though busy with obligations at the cathedral Lawrence Sherette skillfully revised his schedule so as to never miss this excellent feed, and while so, he found it not as easy to break away from the affairs of the cathedral to take part in the continuous carriage rides. But at Adelaide's and Sasha's persistence he did once or twice.

There were times when Sasha and Mrs. Laster and Adelaide went shopping at Woodleaf's; there were times when only Mrs. Laster and Adelaide went shopping at Woodleaf's; there were times when Sasha and Bryon and Adelaide and Mrs. Laster sat in a shiny black carriage and rode about the city sightseeing; and there were times when only Bryon and Sasha took a shiny black carriage and went sightseeing about the city.

Sasha never said it aloud but it was this excursion that she seemed to relish the most, when she had Bryon all to herself. It should be recalled that her closeness to him arose from her beginnings in San Antonio, when she was struggling to convalesce from the death of her parents and the impact of suddenly having transferred to a new and strange land. He had devoted every available hour to help restore her to emotional normalcy, part of which was to rent horse and carriage and transport her to every sight of noted attraction in the city. He later did the same when he came to New Orleans to accompany his mother back to San Antonio. Sasha had missed him badly and this was especially prominent when sometimes she lay flat of her back in the fields of the plantation looking up at the Heavens. He was there in her heart.

But this was now. She was back in New Orleans a second time and he was with her once more. In her memoirs years later she spoke of the frivolity and care freeness of gadding about with him during these precious two weeks. Bryon was of stupendous fun to Sasha, older than she, but they related, a camaraderie easy to understand, for after all it was people much older than herself with whom she had been intertwined for the entirety of her life. They went up and down and across every street in New Orleans, or so it seemed to Sasha, then when these pursuits lost novelty crossed over to the waterfront and sat on a rise watching the steamer traffic come and go, sometimes hitching the horses and going out on the docking where the Creoles and Irishmen were toiling and grunting. Now and then they'd let out a profanity and Sasha, holding her hand to her mouth would look over at Bryon and see him smiling. His bent for store shopping was less than exuberant but offered no resistance when Sasha set about to lure him in. The stores strewn along the streets, little boutiques, were as thick as bees and brimmed with trinkets. Sasha bought but a limited quantity of items, one or two for Mrs. Laster and Adelaide; mostly she looked about and sorted through the merchandise, ceaselessly turning it over from top to bottom to give it careful scrutiny, which the merchants seemed not to like but tolerated her without saying anything objectionable. Once Bryon bought her a shiny bracelet.

The days were relatively free of inclement weather, no rain to speak of, but the rains did fall sporadically. New Orleans is a bit balmy and semi tropical; it figures therefore that it has its rains. The rain was of minimum bother, for the top cover to the carriage could be erected if need be. Usually Sasha's very large parasol sufficed. When the sun burst through, bathing the earth in its radiance, she put on her oversized white hat with a pink rose pinned upon it. Bryon said it made her look exotic. She inquired of him what that meant exactly. He said she looked a little Gypsyish, then laughed. She gouged him in his ribs then his laugh became more vibrant, and then he told her she looked lovely as always, and that he wasn't kidding. She blushed at his compliment, and said she hoped she had blushed because she wasn't a vain person.

While sitting in the great living room one night they all decided to try their luck at fishing, all except Lawrence Sherette. The waters were calm in the Gulf next day, as Harry had bet they would be, having received assurance from a trickle of commercial fishermen, his daily friends, on whom he kept tabs. Harry rented a fishing boat which was manned by a Captain well known to him who went out of his way to assist his passengers. The Captain graciously helped Mrs. Laster bait her hooks and Harry replaced the Captain when he was needed elsewhere. Bryon helped Sasha. Adelaide needed no help. She and Harry had been on these waters innumerably and through this experience she had mastered the particulars. The day was a good one for fishing. The red snapper bit hungrily and continuously. Sasha loved it. Sometimes she stood by Bryon on one end of the vessel and then went to stand by Mrs. Laster, who shrieked from excitement as much as she when making a successful catch. They stayed until nearly dark, then the Captain headed the boat for shore. The next night the Creole women came and cooked the fish, a quantity much larger than could be eaten; and resultingly Adelaide gave the surplus to them to take home to their families, as well as the raw fish which had been salted and temporarily stored in the cellar. Close to the date of their departure for Memphis, Bryon and Sasha went out on the waters again, the same Captain commandeering the vessel. Sasha reported when they returned that the best of luck was not had but that the warm sun and moderate temperature more than compensated. "Though it was a tad choppy out there," she said. They thought of a third day's excursion but became sidetracked with other competing lurings.

Soon after they'd landed in New Orleans Bryon had noticed a small café on the fringe of the docking, there soon beginning to have breakfast in that those of the household generally slept late. Due to the nature of his job he had become habituated to eating early. He started inviting Sasha who thought six o'clock was quite too early to get up, she being accustomed to sleeping a good stretch beyond this hour. But she sighed and rolled out nevertheless. Not infrequently there was a thickly mist that rose up in the earlier hours, enshrouding the waterfront, making the streets and docking troublesome to see. It was still there when they arrived. But this only added to the mood, to the illusion that the dampness and the fogginess of the atmosphere produced an even better than usual taste to the coffee and breakfast. They'd sit and sip until seven thirty and then order. These were good hours for Sasha. She could have sat across from Bryon at the small table with a checkered cloth on it and talked without end. She loved it; and so did he. "Bryon understands me," she said silently, "and he's gentle like Lawrence Sherette and like Andre. He has a wonderful sense of humor" When Bryon was once explaining the particulars of the bridge his company had begun to build he used his finger as an imaginary pencil to write them on the table cloth, and Sasha playfully interrupted with a quip that he had forgotten to insert a needed punctuation. Pretending a scowl he reached and pinched her cheek. "Little devil." And burst out laughing, slapping his hand up and down against the table top up. The waiter and a triumvirate of patrons at a nearby table looked at them curiously. They talked of many and sundry things and seemed never to exhaust their supply. Once she asked him if he saw Paula Ness very much at mass, the answer given that he did. Sasha knew that Paula was appreciably younger than he yet fancied that they'd fall in love and marry someday. She didn't know why she did, unless she pictured them both as near perfect human beings and that in the eyes of the Lord they'd make ideal partners. As she requested of his mother she requested of him also to tell Paula hello for her. She wondered in the same breath about Adelaide and Harry, whether they were in love and whether they might sometimes marry. Sasha had never said anything to Adelaide about it and had no intention of the sort. She had seen them stealing off to the Hotel St. Charles a time or two for lunch, which prompted a smile of very pleasant ideations.

Three times the women folks, Sasha, Mrs. Laster and Adelaide attended the performances at the Old French Opera House, the men abstaining. It was comprised of a splendid interior and decorated with the most eloquent antebellum furnishings. They could have gone every night, even if the performance had been an identical repeat. In time the names of the vocalists faded away from Adelaide and Sasha; they wished they'd written them down as keepsakes. With Bryon driving they made their way up the Old Shell Road to the Lake End Hotel as frequently as time allowed, which hadn't changed an iota thought Sasha, the meals as rich and tasty as ever, and when they had finished they'd slide into the rockers on the veranda and talk and gaze about at the pretty green lawn and the stately geese ambling toward the marsh for their daily swim.

Nearing the last of their stay there came the peak of the year's extravaganzas as far as Sasha was concerned, the Quadroon Ball, for she had carried it for a year in her thoughts and now reality was on the verge, she hoped. "There's nothing like it," Sasha recalled Randolph's praises. They sat on the huge sofas in the great living room debating whether to go, Sasha keeping her fingers crossed that they would, but remaining quiet. Without revealing it to her, Mrs. Laster and Adelaide felt that she was too young and innocent for the event. They did not decide just then whether to attend or not. Harry spoke on Sasha's behalf. "Ah, let's take her. It'll be educational." Catching Adelaide alone Sasha asked what was decided and Adelaide smiled and said that Harry had arranged for reserve seating.

"I rejoiced silently," said Sasha, looking back. "I had wanted badly to see what it was about, but wouldn't let on until just then."

"Where is the ball held? Sasha asked Harry. He had in his repertoire a great wealth of knowledge of many aspects of the city and Sasha was ever alert to ask him about things she did not know.

"At the Orleans Theater. That's where they have them."

"Them?"

"I'll clarify. Several are held during the year. How many, I don't know. October is the month of the pinnacle affair, the really big ball; or it is sometimes held in December."

"And what is the ball about? Dancing?"

"Some of it is for sure. But we're invited guests. That's all. We don't dance. There is much more to it than dancing. It's done in the manner of a debutante affair where beautiful young women are shown off."

"And why is that?" she asked, wrinkling her brow.

"Let's start with the word itself. Quadroon. It means mixed blood. You see, by process of selective breeding, the French produced in Santo Domingo an exotically lovely woman. She was something. She is something. Straight lithe figure, small hands and feet, and an exquisitely chiseled face. Such women have come to be called 'Les Sirenes.' That's who you'll see at the ball. Les Sirenes. New Orleans is replete with these young women. You see, with the upshot of the slave uprising in Santo Domingo, Napoleon's fiasco, the planters, the rich plantation owners, fled to Louisiana, bringing their mistresses and children with them to the city. It was the daughters of these women and their daughters' daughters who came to be called Quadroons. The name is in error, since a Quadroon is a person made up of one fourth Negro and three fourths white blood. Many of the young women have only a small bit of Negro blood, the ones you'll see at the ball, and therefore are not truly Quadroons, yet everyone calls them Quadroons. They are not even Octoroons, who are only one eighth Negro. The young women you will see are much less Negro than the Octoroons."

"Oh, how utterly telling."

Harry skillfully diverted the conversation for the time being, realizing that Sasha would sooner or later come back to the question which he had not yet answered.

"She will learn quickly enough."

The next evening their carriages pulled up in front of the Orleans Theater, the *personne en charge* standing at the foot of the steps to greet them. He and Harry were friends, business friends and social friends as well. The man was quite handsome, a white Creole with smooth dark hair attired in a bright expensive tuxedo, his age in the proximity of thirty five years. His speech was of heavy French accent and he was well educated, having been sent to France for his schooling by his wealthy French father. He responded to the name Mouton. There is good reason to suppose that he was seen as a man about town, shrewd and quick, speculating in buying and selling real estate, owning rental property, operating grocery stores, buying and selling mortgages, and even owning and renting out slaves. Harry acted as his legal counsel, Mouton astute to the necessity of legally protecting himself by retaining an attorney.

"Monsieur Harry. I am more than glad you have come and have brought with you your guests. Your seats are reserved." He leveled his eyes temporarily on Sasha, then quickly took them away, motioning for Harry and his party to follow him through the doorway. Sasha and Adelaide wore beautiful fall dresses with a cloak over them. The night was cool. Sasha had selected her black chiffon and adorned her neck with a white pearl necklace. There were no other embellishments upon her person, no make up of any sort. She did not need them.

"She is a beautiful young lady," said Mouton in a whisper to Harry as Harry was beginning to take his seat.

"Yes she is. Thank you."

"She is part of the family?"

"Part of the family."

"I understand. Well, I am so glad you are here. It does me honor." Bowing to Sasha he took leave.

Sasha sat between Harry and Adelaide, Mrs. Laster between Lawrence Sherette and Bryon.

A low murmur rolled throughout the room, many now seated, others now coming in, beautiful glitzy young women, each escorted by a strong athletic looking man of forty or more and a woman who one would judge to be her mother. The woman trailed behind the young lady and her escort by a few paces. As the young ladies moved deftly toward their seating the eyes of handsome dark haired males from across the way looked on with devouring hunger. Each was the son of a rich French marquis and had much of his father's wealth at his disposal or had attained to prodigious sums of his own effort. Only wealthy men were invited to attend, for they were thought to be good protectors of their chosen lover in this system known as placage, the custom of placing a young woman with a young man. The young ladies were exhorbitantly gowned, their smiles appropriately coming and going as they spoke and one could not have missed that they were practiced in the use of subtly and coquettishness. They were captivating, beautiful to look upon.

The master of ceremonies, Mouton, the same gentleman who had greeted them and led them into the theater, rose from his chair which was near the orchestra and offered greetings, the crowd lapsing into a sudden hush. The gentleman was brief, emphasizing in the main that this was a grand occasion for the city, that he was delighted to see them out in such a throng and that a sweep of his eyes assured him that the loveliest young ladies in all of New Orleans were there to grace his ballroom. The orchestra struck up and a goodly number of the young ladies were approached by young white men, white Creoles, and they began to glide around the shiny floor. They had huddled together earlier in the evening, the mother giving her consent. Some of the lovelies were not yet approached.

"Why is that? asked Sasha. "I see a host of young men standing around looking their way. Why don't they cross over to those young women and take their hand?"

"Ah! You have hit upon it."

"Hit upon it?"

"Yes. The young ladies are here in search of a protector, not a husband but a protector. The young women are not to be legally recognized as wives, only as placees. The people of free color view these placements as *de la main gauche* or left handed marriages. The young men are madly in love with them and when they think the opportunity is right they will approach the young woman's mother and bargain for her."

"Bargain for her! I've never—."

"Bargain. If the mother feels that the young man is suitable and is sought by her daughter she will then take up the matter of finances that he is to supply, as well as a house in which her daughter will live and receive him from time to time or live in it continually with him."

"A mistress! That is who she becomes. Bought. Living with the man out of wedlock."

"As peculiar, if not astonishing, as it is to you Sasha, it nonetheless is the way of life here."

"It's so hard for me to fathom."

"And it was me too. I accepted it nonetheless and adjusted to it. It's part of the New Orleans Creole culture."

Hoping to lessen the impact of this sudden revelation on his young friend, Harry proceeded to explain that the Quadroons were not in any sense prostitutes; that they were courtesans, sweet and submissive, with most adorable manners, many as tenderly and carefully brought up as any white girl, and that until they secured a protector were just as virtuous.

They attended, according to the written records that have endured, the color annex of the Mount Carmel Convent School. If they did not learn much more than to sing a pretty song and sew and seam, neither did the white girls who were also schooled by the Ursulines, their Catholic teachers. While they never read much, they were accomplished in music, which they loved, and at embroidery, which they most disliked. The nuns also taught them painting and drawing.

Food was served, colorful full platters of food, the meat steamy hot and gilded with pomegranates and oranges and bananas, and lettuces. Sasha did not hunger much for it, eating but a small amount, her thoughts pondering what Harry had told her and that which she had seen by looking about.

"The life of a Creole Quadroon is romantic, I am supposing, and in some ways peculiarly pleasant. But it's appalling. May the Good Lord forgive and love and bless her."

The hour hand had struck eleven. Balls of this nature generally lasted until three. Catching a nod from Adelaide, Harry concluded they had had enough, and so rose, the rest emulating his movements, and when reaching the exit Mouton met them with an expression of buoyant gladness for their presence and bowed to Adelaide and Sasha.

On their way home, Adelaide, who rode in the carriage with Sasha and Harry, alluded to the ball as a grand affair indeed, yet lamented that when grasping the nature and purpose of it she deduced that the formality amounted to selling the girls into bondage. Sasha, in something of the same notion, asked Harry what would eventually happen to the girls.

"Let me answer like this Sasha. Quadroons never desert their protector or betray him. Sometimes, when their lovers leave them they commit suicide. Many remain widows and move to the country. Sometimes they marry colored men, but I doubt that any colored man ever gets to know a beautiful high class Quadroon until a white man is through with her. Sometimes, they make domestic connections, finding work as a dressmaker or as a nurse."

Sasha had left her own bed that night to lie down by Mrs. Laster, this, the last time to lie beside her great friend to trade back and forth things that were endearing to them. Sasha pled with her to come visit, bringing Bryon with her, stressing that ships were traveling faster than ever before and that reaching Memphis was a matter of short duration, and went on from there to commit that she'd find Adelaide and her standing by to greet them when they arrived. Mrs. Laster assured her that she would, that she was dying to, and that she and Bryon had discussed the subject continuously.

The next morning they rose early and had breakfast that the Creole cooks had prepared and then left for portside. The carriage drivers unloaded their luggage and were standing by to wag it aboard whenever the steamer's shrill whistle pierced the air which signaled to the passengers to ascend the gang plank. Adelaide, Lawrence Sherette, and Sasha were to leave first, Mrs. Laster and Bryon an hour later. In a short while the whistle sounded and tears were shed and goodbyes uttered. Sasha clasped Mrs. Laster to her once more.

"I'll never get used to goodbyes."

"Nor will I my sweet darling. Write me on every chance."

Sasha then turned to Bryon and hugged him dearly. "Take care of your mother and don't forget that small dinge where we had breakfast. That was great fun."

"Yeah. Me too. I look forward to doing it again sometime Sasha. You take care of yourself." Bryon was choking up.

Standing next to Harry, Adelaide thanked him for all he'd done to make arrangements for them during their stay and then they kissed, which was followed by his promise to see them at the plantation in not many months.

Chapter 44

ON THEIR way up the Mississippi, Sasha, Lawrence Sherette, and Adelaide spent a great amount of time on deck, their eyes tracing the waters and shorelines, while appreciating the nice clear weather. In that Adelaide had packed food before leaving New Orleans they ate lunch on top side while in transit, relishing the open air despite its coolness which was offset by the friendly sun rays that beamed against their clothing and faces. The fresh soft breeze unrelentingly played with Sasha's dangling strands, which were too often swept across her eyes and thereby kept her constantly busy at clearing them away. If thought was given to the Quadroon Ball it seemed to be minimal, yet once Sasha told Adelaide that Harry was right, that the affair was richly educational and that she'd remember it always.

Sasha had begun more and more to think of Mary Tonka and spoke of her in a vein of sadness.

"She was so lonely looking when we left her on the portico with the lantern in her hand. I can't wait to see her."

"She was lonely," Adelaide put in. "She tries not to show it. She's made of iron, but it has its soft spots."

Sam Feathers had driven the horses harder than usual to Memphis. Adelaide had asked him to meet them when they departed the boat. It was their second day since leaving New Orleans. The sun was setting in the west. Adelaide and Sasha would spend the night with Tahitia. Sam had met them and Lawrence Sherette at shoreline, dropping the women off at Tahitia's then taking Lawrence Sherette to the Rectory, and then returning to Tahitia's for the night. They left Memphis but a stretch after daylight. The hour was past one o'clock when Sam Feathers swung their carriage into the serpentine driveway, the towering cedars bemusedly eyeing their advance, and when Sasha looked to see if she was there, she was, Mary Tonka, standing beside one of the portico columns, waiting, silent and still, her eyes twinkling.

Scampering down from the carriage when it rolled to a halt Sasha ran to her, "Mary Tonka, Mary Tonka," each embracing the other with loving tenderness as they came together.

"I have missed you."

"I've missed you too my dear" returned Mary Tonka, her eyes filled with moistness. "You don't know how much."

Adelaide had stood back, joyfully watching, moved at how their love poured out to one another. When Adelaide hastened to her she was received by arms outstretched as had been Sasha, and welcomed home with words of endearment that sprang from her heart. Over the years Adelaide had returned from a journey many a time and always Mary Tonka's inquiry was of standard sameness.

"Was your trip a good one?"

"It was Mary Tonka. Over too fast but to get away for a short span was good for us, just the tonic we needed."

"I'm glad to hear that. But I worry when you're away. Things can happen when you travel."

"We were fine. You shouldn't have worried."

"But I do."

Sam Feathers and a worker unloaded the luggage onto the portico and Sam volunteered to set it inside, Adelaide replying that it was all right where it was and that she and Sasha would later carry it indoors and unpack when they were more settled. She thanked Sam for meeting them in Memphis. He then turned and left for his home. Mary Tonka reached her arms around Adelaide and Sasha and walked them through the double French doors that she had left open.

"I'll have late lunch ready for you in no time. I know the both of you are hungry."

Mary Tonka told Sasha soon after they had eaten that Doctor Lundy had been there and had left notes on the infirmary writing table for her to read. Sasha had already seen them. He was asking her to examine an elderly woman who he said was down with pneumonia.

"She has a respiratory condition in which there's inflammation of the lungs."

There was also another case that he brought up, which had to do with a young girl about to give birth that was bound to prove difficult.

"She needs a caesarean, a terribly risky procedure. You know the dangers, hemorrhaging and infection. Her skeletal structure is made too tightly. I don't see how this can be a normal delivery. We'll talk about it. In the meantime please check on her. I'm concerned."

Time ran swiftly, which she variously filled, the things she did now a matter of routine; walking in the open fields in the late afternoon, riding with Adelaide, sometimes as far as the Big Hatchie, sitting with Adelaide and Mary Tonka in the evening on the portico, traveling to Memphis with Adelaide each two weeks to attend mass in Lawrence Sherette's church, this including lunch at the Gayoso House, playing the music of Beethoven and Mozart, seeing after the patients with Doctor Lundy who alternated back and forth, and reading, reading, reading every medical publication she could lay her hands on. "She does not read books," once said Lawrence Sherette. "She devours them."

Though receiving them at staggered intervals she had recently opened three different letters, one from Mrs. Laster, one from Father Lumas, and another from Andre, who mentioned the upcoming Christmas ball at his parents home, adding at the finish that he missed her. "Misses me! Hmmm." Her eyes danced. She promptly penned her response.

"Indeed your agenda runneth over sweetheart," said Adelaide to her one day.

"I know. That is what I said to Bryon when he asked about my life on the plantation. 'Always something to do,' I answered. That is why I love it so I guess."

"I'm glad."

When there was a moment's lull she sat on the portico watching the caravan of wagons loaded with cotton pull upon the main road to Memphis, which she saw as vividly as she saw the back of her hand. She could summon to her mind the exact whereabouts of the rise where the mules had to labor hardest, or a certain small stream they were to cross, or the length of time required to reach the way station where Sam Feathers would hook up a fresh team. The wild geese had started to fly southward, the cotton season nearing an end, cues that another season was subtly approaching, and invariably, if their paths crossed, Sasha would ask Sam Feathers if there was much left in the fields to gather.

Within the coming weeks Doctor Lundy arrived and right away took up the most serious cases with her. She had written that he should come. The day after his arrival, in the vicinity of one o'clock in the afternoon, the young pregnant girl had begun to suffer from pains in the abdominal region, labor pains, which rapidly grew worse. She lived nearest the Van Doke mansion, therefore they took her there to the infirmary. Nothing was to be done but wait and watch and hope all went well. Sasha insisted that she stay with the girl, letting Doctor Lundy return to Aurora for some badly needed sleep. The hour was eight o'clock when he left. He'd been busy throughout the day running from one patient to another. It was Sasha's first time to stay the night in the Van Doke infirmary. She doubted she'd sleep. Adelaide drove over and urged strongly that she stay with her. In something of a subtle laugh Sasha answered no, that it was time she was weaned from her sleeping partner.

"Okay. If you insist. I'll go back home, but I'll worry. Doctor Lundy and I will return early to see how things are."

Sasha made no effort to object, saying nothing, but hugging her as she and the doctor started to leave. As the night progressed the girl's pains worsened and she periodically asked Sasha to press her hand to her back. Sasha knew the first pain was ordinarily the one of longest protraction. The girl had passed that stage. Sasha looked at her watch. The last pain had lasted for less length than the one before. The girl was perspiring heavily and murmured that she hoped this one went quickly. Sasha wondered why she said that. She'd never had a baby before. "Yes sweetheart, it will." The girl's voice was strained, as well as her face. Sasha lifted the sheet and saw the bleeding. She went to the door and looked into the night, the air feeling cool upon her face, and after inhaling a deep breath returned to the girl, seeing her writhing and straining. The girl looked tired and worn. She tried to be cheerful, but it vanished as quickly as it came.

"Oh, oh. It hurts. Oh how it hurts. Could you put a wet rag to my face?"

Sasha removed a cloth from one of the cabinets and wet it and laid it tenderly on her forehead. Her complete thoughts and energies were concentrated on what she might do to bring the girl relief. As she moved about, her shapely legs in blue stockings looked out from where her uniform reached up to near her knees. The collar was also blue, as well as the pockets which were attached below her waist. She sometimes wore this attire because it provided contrast, blue and white against each other. On this night she hadn't the least inkling of what she had on; if someone had asked her she would have had to glance to know. She was too caught up in the tumult.

"There one comes," the girl yelled out, cursing. "Oh God help me."

Sasha's watch validated that the interval lasted in the proximity of two minutes.

Dressed in a white uniform Mary Tonka opened the door and moved to Sasha's side, looking worriedly down on the girl. Sol and Cynthia had picked her up and brought her to the Van Dokes. Mary Tonka's face was grave.

"It's nine o'clock," uttered Sasha. "She's been at it since one." The girl heard nothing she had said. "She's worn out, but she'll have to keep at it." Truly, Sasha wondered if she could. That was her first time to doubt.

"Have you eaten Sasha? You haven't. I'll ask Cynthia to fix you something."

Sasha agreeably nodded. Cynthia soon brought the food and Sasha took the tray and left for the other room. Mary Tonka relieved her. Sasha ate a pinch of ham with biscuit and sipped at a glass of tea. She wasn't hungry. She leaned back in her chair. "And this is the price you pay for sleeping with someone. But we'll all do that sooner or later if we marry. Pity the young Quadroons, and pity the young girls we have here right under our noses, just like the one in there. She can't die. She mustn't. I pray that she won't. I'm worried. I can't deny it."

Doctor Lundy returned at eleven, Adelaide driving him.

"How are things with the patient?" he asked. Sasha was pulling the sheet partially up over the girl. With firm steeliness she explained that there was no movement toward the baby getting born.

"It's like its stuck Doctor Lundy, if I may put it that way. I think we have to force it or else perform a caesarean."

"Hmmmm. That bad? Let me have a look." He was not long in making his examination. He'd done many of them before. This one was an exception. "You are right Sasha. It's a toss of the coin. It's the caesarean or an ordinary delivery that's not at all ordinary. In other words, a high forceps delivery which can be very dangerous to the mother and the baby. Tearing is one of the main fears. But we're faced with one or the other. No choice. Unless that baby decides to slide out of there of its own accord. I'm joking. I shouldn't be at time like this. She's exhausted, a great amount of her strength drained out of her and every passing minute is crucial." Doctor Lundy had performed these surgeries before, many times before. He had received the best of training in medical college abroad when he was young and had stayed up to date with medicinal usage and surgical procedures in childbirth, though his surgeries were not of everyday occurrences as they were in the hospitals of the large cities.

The pain lasted longer now, sustained, continuous, the girl cursing and praying alternately. "She doesn't even hear herself," said Mary Tonka, looking at Sasha and shaking her head. After this episode the girl began to sob, Sasha and Mary Tonka looking pityingly on. Sasha pressed the wet cloth to her face and asked her to breathe hard. She raised the sheet and looked and Doctor Lundy looked with her, their faces somber as they drew back. Doctor Lundy said aloud that he wished the girl were at the Baltimore hospital where they were better equipped. "But they lose them too." Sasha remained emotionless. They got ready. Mary Tonka washed the girl and thoroughly disinfected her. They'd use morphine to control the pain. Together they decided to perform the caesarean. It was not a lengthy procedure but would seem long. Needing to work quickly when the surgery began they had rehearsed the routine in minute detail at least twice. Doctor Lundy would guide her through. This was her first. With catlike skill she swiftly made the incision and shortly pulled the baby out. Blood was everywhere, the baby covered with a mass of reddish excess as she handed him to Mary Tonka for washing and drying. Sasha began to look down at the girl, leaning over close to her face. It was deathly pale. She grimaced. Then she began to sew up the gaping incision, opened with exact preciseness by her steady true hand and fingers. "She'll grow out of the scar," said Sasha.

"Yes. She will."

The strain had been tortuous on Sasha and the doctor, but was nothing compared to what the girl had endured. She was informed that she had a fine little boy, really kicking and clawing with his arms. She hardly responded, only half rolling her sick eyes. The doctor left for the other room for a brief rest, Sasha staying by the girl, Mary Tonka sitting feet away in one of the soft cushioned chairs ready to do whatever Sasha asked. Sasha was not of the conviction that the girl would live. Her breathing was in gasps. She and Mary Tonka exchanged places, and momentarily Cynthia entered with hot coffee. Mary Tonka poured herself a cup, but Sasha asked Cynthia if she might bring her a glass of warm milk.

"I will Miss Sasha. You just rest. I'll be right back."

Time had been moving along. It was past two. The girl no longer screamed and cursed. The effect of the morphine still lingered or else her strength was so enormously sapped that she was virtually lifeless. She eventually fell into unconsciousness. It was nearing four o'clock. Sasha went and awakened Doctor Lundy.

"What is it?" he asked, startled from her touch.

"She's passing away. It's the bleeding. She's unconscious." Doctor Lundy sprang up.

"I'd better see." He went and looked, feeling her pulse and observing her breathing. He shook his head from side to side. His face said it all. Then he spoke aloud. "A matter of time Sasha. We did everything we could. Surgery as we know it today is a very inexact science. If Doctor Givens had been here the result would have been the same, mark my word. Someday when medicine is further advanced and doctors have evolved more sophisticated methods they'll save lives that we presently lose. That's the future. We live now. We have to deal with our own time and its limitations."

Despite her steely disposition there was nonetheless moistness in her lovely young eyes which turned into tender soft tears. Doctor Lundy reached his arm around her.

"These things will happen Sasha. This isn't the last. Life and death are not ever very far apart." Releasing her he went over to the dead girl and closed her eyes and pulled the sheet up over her, noticing that there at last was a peaceful look upon her still face. He sighed and crossed himself and uttered something. You couldn't hear it; you could only know it was happening by seeing the movement of his lips.

"You go on home Sasha," urged Mary Tonka. You need rest. Adelaide will drive you and Doctor Lundy. Sol will drive me over later."

"No I'd rather not. I'll clean her up. I personally owe her that."

Mary Tonka made no effort to pursue, knowing that the short while Sasha had attended the girl she had taken on a special feeling for her. So Sasha cleansed her and smoothed her hair while the rest waited, during which Cynthia had gone and pulled out a nice cotton dress to put on her. She helped Sasha slip it on. They left at daylight, all except Mary Tonka who'd see to the necessities remaining. On the way they had stayed silent, even Doctor Lundy, until it was broken by Sasha.

"Adelaide I want to pick out one of my best dresses for her to wear at the funeral."

"Sure sweetheart. That's so thoughtful."

When they drove up in front of the mansion Doctor Lundy stretched his arms and yawned and looked eastwardly at the blush of dawn.

"I wish you'd look at that glorious sun peeping through. It's going to be a beautiful day. Well Sasha, why don't we sleep until noon then start our calls on the patients. Adelaide, what's for breakfast?"

Not that night, nor the second night, but one not far removed Sasha and Adelaide lay talking. Sasha had read something of compelling interest; many things of interest were always compelling to her. She would share it. She hadn't lifted it from a medical journal but from a book or an article on philosophy or metaphysics, the latter concerned with what types of things there are in the world and what relations these things have to one another.

"It has to do Adelaide with the premise that life moves with an absolute continuity, and that all the forces of ingenuity that man can improvise can't turn it back. It said something like that"

"And what do you conclude?"

"This. If we could alter it, this absolute continuity, think of it: we could snuff out such things as the deadly plagues, such as yellow fever, that destroy us by the millions with one quick swath."

"You're thinking of her."

"The girl."

"Nothing could have saved her. It was her time."

"No. It couldn't have. In a later era. Perhaps. Doctors are ever hopeful that there is a medicine or method that can make a difference. They never stop thinking about that."

"I guess they don't. Hoping is a good thing."

"It's a very good thing and also the will and effort to improve at what we do."

"But in the meanwhile, while we're waiting for those wondrous discoveries we hope for, we have to accept this inexorable journey of ours as it is. One day with the snap of the finger we're gone from this earth. The journey is over. So be it. That's the way it was meant. The way of absolute continuity, as you put it. Yet, while we're here let's live life to the fullest, one hour, one day, one week, one month at a time, whatever is allotted to us."

"That's your philosophy?"

"Not all of it." Sasha had set her off. "I'm not a complicated creature sweetheart; to the contrary. I'm quite simple. If someone asked me why I was brought into this world I'd answer that it was to serve my Lord and then after that my fellow man for as long and as well as I can. That, I try to do."

"I like that. I'll try to emulate it."

"You already do darling. And more. Now, let's go to sleep."

Chapter 45

THE CALENDAR bespoke that Thanksgiving was startlingly near and that Christmas was close on its heels, the two inextricable holidays they say. Adelaide and Sasha had bought gifts while in New Orleans for Christmas though not nearly enough and Adelaide's need to purchase an extra number was monstrous in comparison to Sasha's; but both aspiring to buy more they set aside two days for a trip to Memphis to shop. Sam Feathers was swamped with work and couldn't drive them. Adelaide chose not to ask. She and Sasha drove, taking time about. Adelaide carried with her a loaded shotgun, a practice that she warily exercised when she and Sasha were traveling alone for any length or when she was by herself. She referred to the gun as a Napoleonic grapeshot distributor. As usual their choice of lodging was at the Gayoso House. "I'm tickled to my toes," said Sasha. "I love the Gayoso House. *Penser a leur menu rend mon eau a la bouche."*[4] Each day they spent a while with Tahitia and had mass with Lawrence Sherette at early morning. They carried Tahitia with them to Randolph's to take dinner on the evening prior to the next day's departure. As was his custom Randolph stood at the doorway, his hair a stylish pomade and there was a whiff of sweet perfume on his person. Dressed in a new suit of clothes he looked as smart as a military officer at arms. He did not lessen from his usual amiability.

"Sasha! Did you have your evening at the Quadroon Ball?"

"I did."

"And?"

---

[4] Thinking about their menu makes my mouth water.

"It was an experience; it really was an exceptional experience. The girls were so dressed up."

"Did they dance with the young male Creoles?"

"You know they did."

"Doubtless. She did like it, didn't she Adelaide?"

"Oh yes. All of us. We were enthralled. How might we have otherwise been?"

"You couldn't have. Well, I'm extra glad you got to go Sasha. Ya'll come on in. I have special seats for you."

For two days they had shopped, buying more gifts than the storage space in the carriage could hold, thus Adelaide wrote on her advisory pad to ask Sam Feathers to pick up the rest on his next business excursion to Memphis. She hired a porter at the Gayosa House to load the gifts they were to carry with them. On the way home Sasha regretted that Doctor Givens couldn't attend the Van Doke ball. Andre had mentioned in his letter that counting on the doctor to join them over the holidays was out of the question.

"Of course I knew he couldn't. I hope he'll return next summer. He simply must. Do you think he will?"

"I think he will. I have a confident feeling about it. You might write him to learn of his intention."

Thanksgiving had come once more to La Belle and Aurora, the formalities a repeat of those exacted in the years previous. Sam Feathers had some of the workers dig a barbeque pit where a substantial quantity of dressed hogs were cooked over an open bed of coals. No one had anticipated a sharp change of weather, but the temperature unexpectedly dropped below freezing, a cold spell as they called it. Sam said to Adelaide that cold weather resulted in pork sausage and tenderloin tasting better than normally and on thinking it though she asked him to kill an extra hog.

"I'd planned on a surplus from the barbequing Sam for distribution to the workers and their families. But I don't know about that. If they eat like I think they might, you know, because of a whetted appetite owing to the cold spell, there won't be anything left. To be on the safe side kill one extra. Maybe two."

Lawrence Sherette and Doctor Lundy weren't there for Thanksgiving and its spate of festivities, but showed up that weekend, whereupon Mary Tonka prepared fresh sausage and tenderloin and hot biscuits for breakfast.

"This is the best sausage and tenderloin I ever tasted," Doctor Lundy voiced with jovial but sincere praise. Mary Tonka accused him of being a big kidder.

That afternoon Sasha and Lawrence Sherette saddled up the horses and went riding, going helter skelter over the fields, virtually from corner to corner, deciding on the last to ride down to the Big Hatchie. It was late when they arrived.

"Listen to that! That's Bubo."

Then she explained the role that Bubo played in her life, that she and Andre had visited the banks of the Big Hatchie when she first met him, and there had encountered the mysterious bird. She then told Lawrence Sherette the same story that she had conveyed to Andre.

"Ah! Bubo. I haven't known him by the name Bubo but I've listened to him for years, since I was but a boy. If not him then one of his ancestors."

It was past nightfall when they reined up at the barns of the plantation. No one was there at that hour. Lawrence Sherette dismounted hurriedly and made an attempt to lift the saddle from Sasha's horse. She shooed him away.

"I'm used to this. I can manage it. I do it all the time. So does Adelaide."

He chuckled and smiled at her independence. "I enjoyed the ride darling."

In a flash Thanksgiving swept by and eyes and thoughts fell upon Christmas, which was but days away. Adelaide, who was occupied with various things at the time, asked Sasha to deliver the gifts she had bought for Sol and Cynthia to Mrs. Van Doke. As was so of the Sherette plantation it was the custom of the Van Doke plantation to convey gifts by setting them under the Christmas tree with each person's name affixed. Sasha drove the team to Mrs. Van Dokes by herself. She wore a lovely dress of white and a heavy cloak that fell to her ankles. Mrs. Van Doke offered commentary on the attire—but more about Sasha.

"You look so elegant in your dress and cloak Sasha. I don't think I've ever seen you wear those things before. Yes, you look so lovely in them, you surely do. But you look lovely in anything you wear."

"Thank you." Sasha was at a loss to reply to the compliment, and decided of a sudden to gamble that it was appropriate to shift to other subjects, which was easy, because she had two in her hands.

"I brought gifts for Cynthia and Sol. Adelaide wanted you to have them in plenty of time for placement under the tree."

"Isn't that just like her? She always does this for Cynthia and Sol. Please tell her how sweet I think she is."

"I will. She is very glad to do it. They are such nice people. They dropped by to visit with us at Thanksgiving and she gave them some fresh sausage and tenderloin. They were carried away with her generosity and kept thanking her over and over."

"Ah yes. That's how they are. I am more than fortunate to have them with me. I meant to visit with you and Adelaide myself during the holiday but had my hands full here."

"I understand. I'm sorry Andre was unable to come home and join us."

"I am too dear. We'll see him shortly. He's due right away."

Mrs. Van Doke was lifted by the conversation, and would have kept on for the longest, frowning regrettably when Sasha apologized for leaving. Sasha gave as the reason that she must check on the inventory of some medicines that Doctor Lundy had asked her to see about. She left and went into the infirmary, there finding Cynthia inside cleaning. Upon seeing Sasha, Cynthia broke into her broad smile and hurried over and gathered her into her arms.

"I'm so glad to see you darling. You always light me up. You sho do."

"Ha, ha, ha. Thank you Cynthia. You do the same for me."

Cynthia continually told Adelaide that she was crazy over Sasha and Adelaide replied that she didn't need to tell her because it showed in her face and in her many other ways. As Sasha was about to leave the infirmary Mrs. Van Doke met her. She had waited at the door, daring not to interrupt while she was busy.

"Sasha dear. I forgot something. I have bought a new piano. Perhaps you might like to see it."

Sasha knew that she'd have to take a look, that politeness had to rule, and besides, she was curious. She then followed Mrs. Van Doke into the spacious room where the piano was emplaced and indeed it was the finest specimen of a musical instrument, imported freshly from Switzerland.

"Would you like to play it? Your fingers would be the first. No one has as much as touched one key of this adorable thing, not even me."

In her mind Sasha gathered that she had been baited, that all along Mrs. Van Doke had invited her to see the new piano with the intention or hope of persuading her to play something for her on it; and Sasha did not disappoint. For nearly an hour she sat and played first Beethoven then Mozart, while Mrs. Van Doke leaned her head against the backing of the rocker in which she sat and closed her eyes, with a contented smile visiting her face. When Sasha deemed she'd played enough she pushed away by a little, and then Mrs. Van Doke rose and clapped with a gust of enthusiasm, following with a discharge of praising that might have more naturally sprung from a person of younger age. "The piano music was perrrrrrfect Sasha." She hoped thereafter, almost daily, that Sasha might find extra time on her visits to the infirmary to come by and play for her then, but there was little space in her schedule for honoring such wishes, which in Sasha's heart she sorely regretted because she sensed a loneliness in the lady that was born a long while ago, from which she could not extricate herself. When Sasha played one lovely refrain after another her loneliness seemed to go away and she became greatly uplifted. When did it happen? Was it when she first met this beautiful young girl in Adelaide's home or was it something that occurred bit by bit over time? In either event, Mrs. Van Doke had begun to love her as if she were her very own.

Preparations were vigorously underway for Christmas, also for the ball, which was alluded to as the Christmas ball, a misnomer, for the ball was scheduled to take place halfway between the Christian Holiday and the New Year; thus the more proper and accurate name was the Post Christmas ball. Adelaide and Sasha set their sights narrowly on the occasion, knowing that the affairs of Christmas at the Aurora were exacted with well established regimen and that they could let their thoughts fall somewhat on other things. Tahitia and Doctor Lundy joined them on Christmas Eve and Christmas Day, riding together, with Doctor Lundy driving the team, yet regretted they had to leave for Memphis after the holidays ended.

For the ball Adelaide suggested that Sasha wear a white merino, in actuality a gown, comprised largely of velvet, which was suspended by thin fine beads that rose from her back and traced over her shoulders to the front. Adelaide was undecided on something for herself, yet was considering the lovely emerald green she hadn't worn for awhile. They debated whether they would wear white elbow gloves; Adelaide finally was inclined to wear them but concluded that Sasha's nice pretty arms should stay sleeveless and exposed. Sasha liked the idea of wearing the white merino and keeping her arms free of coverage.

"Yes, I would like that. And oh! Who is to be there?" she asked, even almost before she finished her consensus of agreement.

"The rich, their sons and daughters with them. You won't believe it but the planters and their wives are surprisingly graceful at performing the various dances. But there are more people than this to come."

She meant a very wide variation of the populace, cotton brokers from Memphis, the owners of the LaGrange (a plantation south of Memphis), political figures, ministers, former military officials, merchants, bankers, the elite of the current society, some driving a distance of more than one hundred miles.

"It's the first ball of this excellence that they've had at the Van Dokes in some years, and Jordan intends to make the most of it. I pray that he doesn't implode from pride. They'll serve supper after the ball has been underway for awhile."

"My. I did not imagine. Naturally, Jim and Lucy will be on hand?"

"Naturally. They wouldn't miss it for all the gold, and they'll be here for the holidays beforehand. They're due to arrive from Nashville any time. Perhaps they'll drop over."

Adelaide had danced at many a ballroom function at the Van Dokes and at other plantations, some of them in Northern Mississippi and Western Kentucky, at Paducah and Hickman, and was well skilled in the finesse of the art. Sasha was without this repertoire but her intelligence together with the keenness of observations that her eyes had beheld over time augured in her favor. She recalled her father and mother once whirling around the magnificent ballroom of the Spanish Embassy on the Canaries and the sessions she'd had with her mother as a pseudo partner, who taught her about rhythms and movements and pirouettes, while a quartet of Spanish musicians fiddled waltzes in their living room as they went through practice after practice. And it was a matter afresh that she had sat and seen the pretty Quadroons and their lovers dancing in the splendor of Mouton's ballroom in the city of New Orleans.

Finally, "You will do more than well Sasha," remarked Adelaide in response to Sasha saying she hoped she would. "You are amazingly quick to grasp. I am anxious to see you on that shiny floor at the Van Dokes in your white merino."

"Does Andre dance well?"

"Very well. You two will look striking out there, set apart completely."

Sasha laughed a girlish laugh.

On the evening of the ball the governor arrived early, the crowd suddenly stirring and pressing forward then moving back, as he and Jordan Van Doke entered to the strains of lovely music. The two men were attired in clothing of the revolutionary period. All men had agreed to comply with Mrs. Van Doke's desire to have them dress in clothing of this decorum, the governor and Jordan Van Doke not withstanding. They walked rapidly, the governor bowing right and left, Jordan Van Doke talking as fast as he could move his lips, appearing to have something ponderously significant to say to the highest political figure of the state. Jordan Van Doke was bursting with pride. To have the governor at his side was a star of lofty essence in his crown as he saw it. The men made their way to the drawing room, then disappeared behind closed doors, then reappeared in a little while and took chairs in one of the corners of the vast expanse, where the ladies, married and non married, adorned in glitzy expensive gowns came up and curtsied, hopeful they'd be asked for a turn later on by either of the men but with the governor taking precedence. The ballroom was prominently of European eloquence, with huge chandeliers hanging from the vaulting by means of extended gold chains. Roman arches appeared at the extremities, an array of Grecian figures populating the columns that upheld them. The floor was of inlaid parquet, brilliantly shiny.

The crowd had gathered without uniformity adjacent to both walls, Sasha among them. Most of the ladies of this grouping had counted on dancing the first dance and had already gathered their partners to them, now preparing to take up their positions for the polonaise, which as Sasha knew was a slow dance of Polish origin done in three quarter time, something of a stately march—principally a promenade by couples. Sasha stood among them, not far from where Adelaide and Lawrence Sherette sat looking on, her glittering dark eyes showing at once a semblance of excitement and apprehension, for she was bent on participating in the first dance and Andre was not yet there. He had relieved his father and mother at the doorway entrance to greet the guests, some holding him up with prolonged conversation, making it not easy to break politely away. Sasha had stood with bated breath waiting for him to appear. At last, there he was, moving with long quickened strides from the opposite end of the ballroom toward her, attired in revolutionary clothing as required, including white stockings that terminated at his knees. Still, what he wore resembled a tuxedo. A long tail piece was attached. His dancing shoes were a shiny dark black as were his pants and top piece.

Sasha smiled over at Adelaide, which conveyed in its message, "He does look a slight different, but isn't he handsome."

Quickly Andre and Sasha took their positions, he sliding his hand around her waist and she placing her hand on his shoulder. There was an illumined sparkle in her eyes as she looked into his. The polonaise was not lengthy and when it was finished they with quickened pace, Sasha skipping once or twice, hastened over to the vestibule for a sip of lemonade, which was served by attendants dressed in tuxedos completely unlike the clothing worn by the rest of the men. They spoke with a trained French accent. Sasha said that one glass was to do her and Andre echoed the same.

Next came the cotillion, more thrilling to Sasha, and to many others for that matter, for it coincided with her idea of a dance more than the polonaise, though not any more spectacular. There were four couples as a group in this dance, she and Andre and three additional couples. Sasha knew they were to respond to a caller who called aloud the required formations, that is to say, the repeated figures that were to be interspersed with changes of figures to different music. The music commenced, Sasha smiling radiantly, looking up at Andre, then all at once they changed partners. She was glad to match up again with Andre when he came back around. Andre thought it strange to see Sasha in some other dancer's arms and was glad to see him release her. On and on they danced, Sasha's white merino spreading and flashing as her partner deftly turned her, a procedure repeated over and over. After a goodly length—this dance was substantially longer than the polonaise—something of an intermission occurred and Sasha and Andre left the floor for their table and sat down. At this point the governor excused himself and said goodnight to Mr. and Mrs. Van Doke, pleading that there was business elsewhere demanding of his time. As an astute politician will he waved his hands at the crowd as he exited the doorway.

Sasha and Andre sat at a table occupied by Lawrence Sherette and Adelaide and other men and women with whom they were acquainted and Andre was acquainted with them as well. But Sasha was not. Lawrence Sherette had gone for a glass of chilled red wine for them to sip and had it ready when they sat down. Andre squeezed his hand and thanked him. Lawrence Sherette removed his handkerchief and daubed Sasha's brow. Across the way by a short distance was the Van Doke table, where in good spirits, chatting and laughing and keeping an eye on the dancers, its occupants sat: Mr. and Mrs. Van Doke, Jim and Lucy, and George and his fiancé from Virginia, who had visited the Van Dokes twice between July and October and was back again for the extravaganza. She and George rose and went over and assumed their places for the next phase of the cotillion. Lawrence Sherette joined them with some lady who was sitting at their table. No man had yet sought to ask her to dance. She looked as if she were about to cry, but her mood was transformed into sudden ebullience when Lawrence Sherette extended his hand. Andre excused himself to Sasha, explaining that he needed to have a look at the frontage to see if late comers had arrived, determining when he got there they were locked out. He had closed the doors when the polonaise was about to begin, thinking that no one else was to seek entrance. But he wanted to check. Sasha then decided to go and sit by Adelaide who had not yet elected to dance with her partner.

"You were fabulous," said Adelaide.

"You mean I tried to be."

"No, you were. All you had to do was to let the magic of your little feet do its work and listen to the music with your ears, and you did."

"I loved it Adelaide. I greatly did. This was my first very real dance."

"I know. Which did you like the best, the polonaise or the cotillion?"

"The cotillion."

"I knew it. It's more fun. It's because of the social mixing I guess. You see, when the French originated it, they had in mind that the participants could introduce themselves and flirt with other dancers through the exchange of partners within the prescribed formation."

"I didn't flirt." She frowned. "I was more than glad when Andre came back to me."

"You didn't flirt with them, but they did with you. I saw."

"No."

"Oh yes."

"I take it back. They did flirt and looked down at me with nice engaging eyes. But Andre is my partner and I so hope they'll start the valse without much delay. It's the really fun dance and I can dance altogether with him."

In her thoughts Adelaide was saying," We'll see about that."

When the music lifted, something of a signal, the valse dancers began to move onto the floor. The valse, meaning a waltz in German, was first danced by the societies of Berlin, St. Petersburg, London, and Paris in the early 1800's, reaching its apex of popularity in the realm of the 1850's, and it was delightfully danced to at the Van Doke ball on this evening. Seeing the other dancers beginning to form Sasha showed a bit of anxiousness, hoping Andre soon would relieve himself of the dignitary who was eating up precious time bending his ear. The man sought favor from Jordan Van Doke through his son.

"Hrmmph. Excuse me," said Andre. "I must dance. Gladly will I take this up with you at a more opportune time. At a dance one must dance." The dignitary smiled politely and bowed and moved away.

Going to Sasha, who was patiently waiting, Andre apologized and placed his hand on her waist and she her hand on his shoulder. The strains of the valse lifted higher. Andre and Sasha were the second couple to enter the circle, but the couple already there deferred in their favor, stepping back to allow Andre and his beautiful partner to go first, the latter of whom everyone curiously inquired as they set eyes upon her during the evening. Such deference was displayed because Andre was the son of the hosts of the affair and this was the means of offering politeness and gratitude. The music commenced with an accent on the first beat and with this they moved away.

Chapter 46

ANDRE WAS one of the best dancers of the many there. But Sasha also danced exquisitely, swiftly and lightly moving her feet, turning, pirouetting, her dress flaring, her hair flitting and falling on her shoulders and upon her lovely back. The sounds of the violins were sweet and warm as they twice glided round the room, like swans moving serenely upon a lake, the analogy might be offered, then the other dancers joined them, beautiful dresses of many colors whirling with infinite togetherness, the music of the violins rising and falling: and as Andre embraced Sasha's supple figure, which stirred so close, her face smiling radiantly up into his, a feeling of rapture swarmed upon him. The wine of her charm had flowed to his head and he began to silently evolve the sweetest words, pretending to himself that he was talking directly her.

"You are such a beauty. Never have you been this close before, not like this. You overpower me. You are a dream. I wonder if you suspect that I am absolutely crazy over you. You have to think something like that. My feelings surely show it. I did not in my remotest think you could dance so splendidly. I could dance with you the whole night through and hope that it would never end."

It ended nonetheless. And they returned to their table and sat down. Lawrence Sherette had counted on taking her hand next and spoke to her for it but was in for a disappointment. Just then the aide de camp, a superb professional, the coordinator of the dances, came over and beat Lawrence Sherette to her, then they sailed away, her smile aglow as she looked up into his eyes, the same as she had with Andre. When passing under the chandeliers the radiant downpour of lighting seemed to enwrap them. "Aren't they a thing of majesty," some one near Adelade said, nudging her. At the appropriate beat of the ever quickening music the aide de camp exacted a turn and Sasha spun gracefully from his arms and instantly back into them, the beautiful white merino doing what it was supposed to do, spreading and flaring.

"Aren't they lovely," said the lady sitting by Lawrence Sherette.

"Yes they are. Quite lovely."

And then he thought silently. "I couldn't have possibly imagined this when she first came to me. She is a wonder. In many ways she is and this is one of them. I am glad with all my heart that I am with her tonight." He seemed lost in thought. The lady was curious of his silence.

"Were you thinking of saying something else sir?"

"No, nothing else. I was actually talking to myself. Merely remembering something. I'm sure you understand."

"I do. I've done that many times."

"Where did you learn to dance so well?" asked the aide de camp. "What you do is divine."

"Not at all sir. I do well to get by."

"You are too modest. You are an excellent dancer, a complete natural, and I am honored that you accepted me as a partner, even if it has been regrettably brief."

She curtsied as they parted, and then Jim rushed over to have the next dance, his arm extended.

"May I."

As they moved away she quickly glanced at Lawrence Sherette and feigned disappointment, as if to apologize. "I'm sorry. I just can't fend them off. I'm sorry my darling. Patience. I will get to you."

Adelaide had moved beside Lawrence Sherette for a minute, merely to drop a remark. "I'm so glad to see her happy. She is too much daily in the midst of seriousness, her books, her experiments, and the sick which seem never to slacken. "

"I quite agree. But it's those things that she was destined to pursue. It's like He stamped a mark on her at birth. On the other hand, she finds time for other outlets, mainly with you Adelaide, riding across the fields, the walks and so on. She loves the out of doors and I've heard her speak times innumerable of the joyful trips to Memphis she takes with you. And now, she's taking up with Andre, and I am greatly delighted that she is."

The Blue Danube began to play, the favorite of the evening, the master piece by Johann Strauss. They danced round and round how many the times. Jim was like all the rest, stunned at her charm, grateful to have her for a partner even though for a fleeting while. She felt Heavenly in his arms. To him, like unto the others, her laugh and smile were enchanting, destined to linger in his head for days. "She is such a natural beauty, and truly, doesn't even know it. Andre better watch out. Any number of young men here tonight are conjuring up this very minute how they might snatch her away."

Virtually no time had past when his point depicted some degree of merit, for a rash of young men began to trek over one after another for a turn, until finally, flushed and tired, and in need of respite, she broke away to her seat beside Andre, and consciously or unconsciously laid her hand on his arm. She sighed.

"Oooh! I need to catch my breath."

"I should say. At least a bit before you go again. Poor Lawrence Sherette," he said, casting an eye over at him. "He hasn't had a dance with you all evening."

"No. I'm so sorry for that. But there's plenty of time left."

"Plenty."

"What is next? More of the valse?"

"The cotillion is next, and after that the valse again."

The dance lasted a long while into the night, the cotillions and valses taken up one after the other and Sasha was engaged continuously with a flow of admirers asking for her hand. Andre would have loved to be with her each time the music struck up but understood that the social etiquette of the evening and the dance itself dictated that the dancers change partners. She did not dance with George and was grateful that he declined to ask. She did at last dance with Lawrence Sherette. It was inordinately moving to Adelaide to see them together. It had a particular meaning to her, one that only she and her brother and Sasha understood. With adoration in his eyes he looked down and told his young partner that she moved with the ease of a gazelle; she insisted that he was partial and pinched his cheek with feigned objection. He laughed and turned her, amazed at the swiftness with she had picked up the whole of everything, especially the timing, supposing that much of it resulted from her playing the piano, that when Adelaide was teaching her she had learned the technique in accord with the composers that wrote the music and through self initiated practice had become finely honed. Lawrence Sherette had observed all evening that Mrs. Van Doke had barely been called upon by any of the male dancers, other than her sons, and remarked to Sasha that he must do what he could about it, exclaiming also that he needed to pay like honor to Lucy. When he left Sasha off beside Andre, he proceeded without pause to Mrs. Van Doke and took her hand, his thoughtfulness bringing a glow to her face. Several times he guided her to the floor for the rest of the evening, and arranged a number of spins with Lucy. Gracious as he was, he congratulated Mrs. Van Doke on the magnificence of the decorations for the occasion and regretted to her that Jordan Van Doke was unable to join in the festivity because of the condition of his leg. He had injured it in a wagon accident. And furthered in the conversation that in his opinion the two young people, Sasha and Andre, were the sensations of the evening, which lit her up.

"Without a doubt. They're the sweetest things gliding around out there? So graceful. The waltz is what I like to see them do the best. It brings me almost to tears."

Somewhere in between the cotillions and the valses supper was served, a grand affair where the tables were inundated with displays of lavish colorful foods set out by hired professionals from Memphis. Cynthia, Hallie, Fannie, and Mary Tonka were asked to help and thus were in the midst of this beautiful evening and thrilled and thankful that Mrs. Van Doke had contrived to make them a part of it. Once when Cynthia came to where Sasha was sitting she leaned over and whispered that she was the most beautiful thing there.

Sasha sat between Lawrence Sherette and Andre. The Autry's from Louisville were sitting at the table adjacent to them. Arlene was in her usual talkative air, leaning over repeatedly to say something to Adelaide. She had danced at every opportunity, including a round or two with the Van Doke brothers, while her banker husband elected to sit it out. He had to. He had never learned the art of dance.

When midnight had knocked Sasha was seized by the idea of her and Andre going for a carriage ride. It had suddenly popped up. "It's the perfect way to finish the evening," she suggested to Andre. He lunged at the opportunity and asked Sol to obtain a helper and hitch up the horses and park the carriage in front of the mansion.

"Adelaide, Andre and I are going for a carriage ride. We think we've danced enough. He'll bring me home. We won't stay out long. We'll probably get there before you."

"Ah! That's a grand idea," she quipped with mirthful eyes. "It's the perfect night for it. The moon is high and the stars are aglitter."

"Oh Adelaide." She giggled.

Adelaide laughed with her but had further remarks. "Seriously sweetheart, have a splendid time and do keep your heavy coat pulled up really tight. It's cool out there. Sam Feathers says frost is due."

"I will."

"Is she in love?" asked Mrs. Autry who had table hopped over to sit beside Adelaide to indulge in a word or two. Sasha was then out of earshot.

"She's getting ready to be."

Mrs. Van Doke watched Andre and Sasha leave, moving closer to Lucy; they looked at one another and nodded their heads in agreement about whatever was said and smiled. Sol had the carriage at the frontage. Andre helped Sasha up to her seat, then dashed around the backside and crawled up himself. Sol had hung two lanterns on the front and two on the back.

"You be careful Mista Andre."

"I will Sol. We'll do just fine."

Sol thought about asking Coon to secretly follow them to make sure they were all right, that no one in hiding sprang out and accosted them, but he figured he'd better not.

"If Mista Andre found out he'd skin me alive."

Andre drove toward Brownsville with no intention of covering more than four miles at the most. Sasha pulled her huge fur up tightly and slipped on her gloves.

"Adelaide said that Sam Feathers predicted frost tonight."

"In the morning hours. That's what he meant."

"I'm sure."

The carriage rolled along quietly, the wheels burrowing into the soft moist earth with only a sound of muffled crunching, the clanking of the trace chains more pretty than noisy. The handsome black horses drew their load easily. Andre glanced over at Sasha, not saying anything, just glancing over, seeing the moonbeams trickling across her lovely face.

"Do you know what I'm thinking Andre?"

"No, what?"

"This reminds me of scenes I've seen in magazines."

"In what way?"

"Of when the snow falls, when people in furry clothing ride in sleighs drawn by handsome horses such as these. Did you ever go sleigh riding?"

"No. But I've seen many a snowfall in my time. I played in it as a boy. I still like to."

"I had hoped we'd have some this year. There was no snow at all last year. I was very disappointed. Mary Tonka kept telling me to keep my fingers crossed."

"Let's hope you're not disappointed this year. You just might see some. January is the most likely month for it."

"Hmmm. I hope so."

"Did it snow where you came from, you know, the Canaries?"

"I'm afraid not. The climate is to moderate there. My father for the longest intended to take me to the Pyrenees in Spain which were not far away, saying that in the higher elevations there were tons of snow. I really did want to go. But he never found time to do it."

"I wish he had. But as I said, you may have your wish pretty soon. I'm making you a bet it'll snow the middle of next month."

"I wish. But the pleasure will not happen without blemish."

"In what way is that?"

"You will have returned to Baltimore. You won't be here to see it."

"Ah yes. I regret that. People are forever going away aren't they? And of course you know more about that than me. From the Canaries to San Antonio then from there to New Orleans and then on to Adelaide's. Guess you figured you never would stop moving to some place else. You've traveled a lot and very far. The Canaries seem very far away to me."

"They are far away."

"Do you miss your homeland?"

"Of course I do. I miss my parents more than anything. I'll never get over them. They're with me every day. You know about them don't you?"

"I've heard. I'm sorry."

"Thank you." She paused for a second and appeared to be thinking of something, her father and mother and losing them Andre supposed, then continued. "And you've heard of Father Kestner. He was my family's Priest. If it hadn't been for him we wouldn't be here tonight on this wonderful carriage ride. Think about that."

"I am thinking about it. And I'm thanking Him up there that he did."

They drove on in silence, other than the sounds emanating from the crunching of the wheels and the clanking of the trace chains. Andre looked over at Sasha bundled in her heavy fur. Barely visible exhalations of mist escaped her lips and the moon now shown more brilliantly upon her face. The trees on the roadsides seemed suddenly thicker. Andre said that pretty soon they'd turn around, in case she wondered, that he expected to see a bridge anytime with white banisters, within the next quarter mile, and that that was where they'd start back the other way. Sasha said she wasn't wondering about that and that there was no need to turn around if he didn't want to. She said she wished they could ride all night, but knew they couldn't. Andre smiled. He asked her if she was cold. She said no. He felt she was at least chilled anyway. He'd give anything to put his arm around her, or at least hold her hand, but couldn't bring himself to that either. To Sasha, being out in the night with Andre was merely friendship at play, to Andre amour.

"You mentioned Father Kestner, your Priest. Do you write him? Does he write you?"

"We exchange letters. I think I owe him one. Thank you for reminding me Andre."

"Will you ever return to the Canaries, I mean to visit?"

"I hope. I wish so. Maybe I can some day. I could travel to Baltimore and there catch a ship. I'm sure Adelaide would accompany me. Of course she'd have to. Would you join us?"

"In a minute. I've never been abroad."

Suddenly he switched to something else. "Are your feet cold," he asked? He'd been thinking they were for awhile and was aware he'd asked her something like this once before.

"Some." Andre stopped the horses.

"I'll fix that. There's a blanket in the rear. We keep one in the carriage in winter, always, especially in mother's."

"This is her carriage? I feel honored."

"It is. She especially wanted me to take it."

Andre lifted out the blanket and slipped off Sasha's slippers. She giggled.

"Careful you don't tickle my feet."

"Ha, ha, ha. I won't. But I need to wrap them up. If you catch cold and take sick my mother won't easily forgive me."

So he wrapped her feet and drove on, having crossed the bridge some time back and turned around, then crossed it again and headed back toward the Van Doke mansion. When they passed it the crowd had hardly lessened, the lights glowing inside and out, and the strains of the violins sweetly wafting to the roadway. Andre looked fawningly over at Sasha, who had sighed and leaned back in her nice leather seat, her eyes lovely and wondrous.

"This is our first carriage ride," he thought, "and I am so in love with her."

They now were not far from the Sherette mansion. Sasha, who had said virtually nothing of the dance during their ride began to speak of it which for them had ended, exclaiming among other things, that she had hoped fervently that Doctor Givens could be there, that she would have tremendously liked dancing the valse with him, and ventured that he would have been a most smooth and proficient partner.

"He's superb. I saw him once in Baltimore at a dance much like the one tonight, and by the way, he sends you his regrets that he was kept away by uncontrollable circumstances and he also said for me to speak to you on his behalf about the girl."

"The one that died in childbirth?"

"Yes."

"What did he say?"

"That he was sorry for her and you and that in time your hurt would heal. I think he'd like to talk to you about it whenever he sees you next."

"That's sweet of him. Tell him I am recovering. I mean, well, I'm learning to live with it."

"You said something of your New Orleans journey in one of your letters and of your stay there. You must have enjoyed it, and Adelaide and Lawrence Sherette too."

"We did. Not enough time though. Lawrence Sherette had to get back to Memphis and Bryon had to return to his job in San Antonio."

"Bryon? Yes, I've heard you bring up his name. He's Mrs. Laster's son."

"He is. He's wonderful. He's the same as my brother. I think of him as if he is. I love Bryon. He took me carriage riding about every day, just as we're doing now, and we'd have breakfast at a small smoky dinge and drink coffee. Going there was well out of character for me. But I loved it. I told Adelaide about it and she just laughed. She loved Bryon for taking me under his wing."

"Anything else?"

"Too much to tell, really. One of the highlights was the Quadroon Ball, which was a spectacular something. It was grand, with lights and music and colors and every pretty Creole Quadroon in New Orleans must have been there."

"Who were the Quadroons?" Andre's face overflowed with curiosity.

"Creole girls. They attended the ball in wont of a rich young man to adopt and care for them."

"I'm not sure I grasp all you're saying."

"Neither did I. But I caught on. The girls are beautiful and groomed and taught by their mother for years to come to the ball some night and pick out a lover, not a husband but a lover. He has to be rich or else he can't claim the girl. Her mother won't accept him otherwise."

"She's to be his mistress in exchange for his up keeping her. That's the deal."

"Exactly. Can you imagine that Andre? How can the girl submit to something like that? How can the young man agree to such an arrangement?

"Oh no! No, no, no. I can't. Of course people like us don't have to give a second thought to something of that sort. We weren't born into that society. We're lucky, aren't we?"

Stopping the horses in the driveway, Andre jumped down to help Sasha from the carriage, who had held back for him to assist her. Mary Tonka stood on the portico. She had heard them approach. Sasha and Andre briefly covered the distance to the steps, where she hugged Mary Tonka, then all three went inside.

"You're already home Mary Tonka," said Sasha. "Did Sol bring you?"

"He kindly did. It was late for him and I regretted calling on him to convey me, but was tired out and needed to go to bed. He said he'd gladly do it. I'm sure Adelaide and Lawrence Sherette will be here shortly."

They sat and talked about the dance, though not for long. Mary Tonka said to Sasha that she was the most beautiful girl or woman there, and Andre enthusiastically reinforced her acclaim. Sasha blushed. They had sat only for a little while longer when Andre, looking at one and then the other, rose from his chair and said he'd better go, that the horses were left untied and standing alone and might of their own accord decide to wander off without him. Sasha accompanied him to the door and out onto the portico. Taking it that Andre was too shy to embrace her goodnight she reached her arms, and he caught on, wrapping his around her.

"Goodnight Andre, the evening was splendid. I'll forever remember it."

In his thoughts, so would he, for it was his first at hugging her goodnight. "It was wondrous." He could hardly contain himself and virtually skipped and bounced to his carriage. Sasha sort of giggled and stood and watched until he left the driveway, the lantern glow growing dimmer with each turn of the wheels, then she returned to the inside.

"You must take to your bed Sasha dear. You have to be worn thin. You must have danced a hundred miles."

Very soon Sasha scribbled a note to Adelaide and left it on the side table nearby.

"I couldn't hold out any longer. I said my prayer and crawled in. I'm fast asleep now. Sorry."

Adelaide read the note and leaned over and after lifting a portion of Sasha's locks that had fallen across her face tenderly kissed her brow.

Chapter 47

ANDRE LEFT for Baltimore two days thereafter, Sam Feathers driving him to Paducah to catch the steamer on the Ohio, yet Jim and Lucy stayed on past New Year. At midweek Lucy joined Adelaide and Sasha on an excursion to Brownsville. Cynthia went with them. Lucy was swept away that she got to spend an entire day in the presence of Sasha and started several times to bring up Andre, though catching herself, fearing that Sasha might take it that she was trying hard to play cupid. She'd had her private conversations with Adelaide about the two. Adelaide vouched that she knew Sasha liked Andre a great deal and that she hoped her fondness in time turned into something more serious. Lucy even put in that Sasha would make a splendid addition to the family, adding also that Mrs. Van Doke was enchanted by her and that so was she.

Adelaide had driven the full length to Brownsville. When they started their return home Sasha took the reins and guided the horses the whole way back, stopping at the Van Doke mansion to let Lucy off. Sasha was down first and helped Lucy from the carriage. It drew Lucy's laugh.

"You're a sweetheart dear," she said. "Thank you." She then kissed her.

For the rest of the winter and on into spring events unfolded as usual at Aurora, Doctor Lundy and Sasha attending to the sick, Sasha playing the piano for Mrs. Van Doke, devouring the pages of the medical journals in the manner of a puppy gobbling up a fresh piece of meat, and she and Adelaide failing but few times every other week end to travel to Memphis to have Holy Communion with Lawrence Sherette. Mrs. Laster wrote her letters and Sasha wrote Mrs. Laster letters. Sasha described to her the Van Doke ball and Mrs. Laster took on for the full course of two pages that it must have been a most splendid thing. Mrs. Laster had taken a position with the German firm where Bryon was employed, yet mentioned little of the particulars, only that she was keeping the accounts. Easter came and went, Lawrence Sherette conducting a special program for celebrating the hallowed occasion. It was his belief that Christians should celebrate the resurrection on Easter Sunday two days after Good Friday and three days after Maundy Thursday, which is the Christian feast or holy day falling on the Thursday before Easter that commemorates the last Supper of Jesus Christ with the Apostles.

The sun rose and the moon took flight and the sun set and the moon returned, one revolution after another, and no one made an accounting; but the calendar kept up with the turns, and let everyone know when June made its advent, when about the mid part of, Andre and Doctor Givens drove up in front of La Belle, and Sasha, who was notified of their arrival date by Mrs. Van Doke, ran to meet them, and fondly hugged them both.

"Je suis tellement contente de vous voir."[5]

Interspersed with the many of those of a lesser bearing there were three events in particular that loomed on the unforeseen horizon, destined to impact in various ways on Sasha and those close around her. As said, there were three, the latter two profoundly different from the first. There was the budding romance between Andre and Sasha which began to blossom and grow, and there was the horrible public hanging of two slaves in Nashville that struck Sasha unsettlingly, and then the revelation of her blood line to Andre. We shall pass to these in due order.

Soon after his arrival, Doctor Givens asked for a session involving himself, Sasha, and Doctor Lundy to survey the condition of the patients to be attended during his stay. Afterwards he and Sasha and Andre began their work. Sometimes Andre and Sasha drove as far as five miles away to see patients. Doctor Givens was seldom with them. Doctor Lundy had recused himself for the summer, planning not to join them unless to visit and socialize.

There was no appreciable travel for pleasure during the short period that Doctor Givens was there, for they were too busy for such travel, or else convinced themselves they were, but indeed the calls upon them had increased due to an outbreak of dysentery. Their furthest trip of a non business nature was once to Memphis.

Nearing the date of departure for his return to Baltimore Doctor Givens one day paid call on Adelaide. He needed to check the infirmary for the availability of a certain medicine. Only she and Mary Tonka were home. Sasha and Andre were attending a worker who

---

[5] I am so glad to see you.

was sick. The doctor had looked for an opportunity for some time to confer with Adelaide and had decided he'd better address the matter that revolved in his thoughts. It was about Sasha.

"I wanted a chance to speak to you about her Adelaide. Sasha is a brilliant person, with a marvelous future ahead. It will not sufficiently spring to life here, if you know what I respectfully mean, not like it will in Baltimore with a vast and complete medical facility behind her."

"I understand."

His countenance showing that he was happy with what seemed to be her concurrence, he continued. "She does things already that are a physician's envy. She can make an enormous difference in the world if she is appropriately cultivated and given the chance."

"I have thought of these things Doctor Givens. You are correct. You absolutely are. We will discuss this as time goes along, by letter if you like. Naturally it would devastate me to lose her. She is deep into my soul."

"I know. Yet no change is necessary now."

"Yes. I'll keep that in mind and for the time being will not pose it before her. We'll have to prepare her gently."

The romance so long in the making between Sasha and Andre was at last to spring into fruition during that hot enjoyable but busy summer, for which Sasha appeared to be too young; but yet, after all, in those years girls were married off a good while before reaching her age. Still, Sasha had no notions of becoming that serious, not anytime soon, likely several years, whereas Andre likely was. The spark that ignited the whole of it was not the yellow moon in the night sky hanging high overhead, nor a lovely ride in a gorgeous black carriage, not these enticements in the least, but an incident of the work place—the infirmary where day after day they went about in close proximity, often touching, their faces sometimes very close to one another, until at length it happened. But this story is best told by Sasha herself in her diary, that no one knew she was keeping, which she once relayed to her children; two girls and one son, who one might surmise had attained to their teens.

> We were in the infirmary putting away medicines and filing reports. The morning was in the early hour, of which I am in unmistakable remembrance, for one's eyes sparkle more brightly in this parcel of the day and Andre's sparkled as if he were a young fawn. They were beautiful. I remember that well. Our hands had touched many times before; they were always touching, a natural thing considering how closely we worked together and the intricate things we did. They now touched once again, or shall I say that our fingers clasped as I handed him a container of

medicine for storing, our faces so close, my eyes locked with his, which had happened before, many times before, and to speak the truth I had secretly wished he had kissed me then—the urge for him to do so forcefully surging up inside me—; but this time neither of us turned away, like we had previously, pretending nothing had happened, that there was no feeling whatsoever, or didn't dare go further. I cannot say who kissed who; I think we kissed at the same time. It was wondrous. For a moment nothing was said between us, nothing. We just kept looking into one another's eyes, my mouth partly open with wonder, until finally I drew a breath and heard myself saying that that was nice, meaning of course the kiss. No other words would come to me.

"I hope it doesn't displease you," said Andre shyly, as if he'd done something wrong.

"Oh no. It doesn't. Why haven't you done it before now?"

"I, I just haven't. But have always wanted to."

"You can from now on when you like."

"Was this your first kiss?" he asked.

"My first."

With these exchanges we simply withdrew, with the excuse we'd best get on with our work, and there was no additional amorousness that took place, not one kiss more, not then, but there were many that followed afterwards when we were sitting in the portico swing with the gorgeous moon beaming down on us. I once asked Andre about that first kiss, if it did to him what it did to me, his answer coming as an exaggeration that his heart beat so fiercely he thought it might leap from its boundaries, and asked me if I felt it jumping about. I said I didn't.

"Did you fall madly in love with him Momma, I mean that time when he first kissed you," my daughter asked?

"I had a ways to go, but soon began to love him with all my heart, my tenderness toward him redoubling, and knew I could not live without him. Even before this I realized your father was a splendid man my darling."

After this, the nights for Andre were never more filled with charm, the trees more lovely, the aroma of the roses more intoxicating; never did the doves of the fields coo with such serenity; never had his heart beat with such a feeling of love; never had he been as happy; never had he been more enamored, more in ecstasy. Such was the impact of Sasha's never before touched tender lips on the young man. For the rest of that summer things between them weren't the same, nor could one have expected them to be, for they had fallen in love, that is to say, Sasha had; Andre had fallen in love on the first day he saw that beautiful young girl emerge from the drawing room, when he had dropped in on Adelaide and her and finally worked up courage enough to ask if she would like to ride to the Big Hatchie with him.

ꝏ ꝏ

Approaching Doctor Givens with an imploring tone that he give his blessings for him to stay on longer, and forego a return to Baltimore until the turn of the year, Andre received it, for the doctor had happily viewed the growing affection between him and Sasha and felt it a desirous and good thing for them to be together for the period requested. Sasha was overjoyed, for now she would be near Andre for an interval much longer than she'd ever been, and moreover, in her thoughts he would greatly lessen the load that she and Doctor Lundy normally ministered to the people. Jim and Lucy returned that mid fall, Brister and Prunelle with them, the purpose of which was to see in on Mrs. Van Doke who had not felt well in recent weeks. She suffered from intermittent headaches and weakness. George Van Doke broke off relations with the young Virginia woman, taking up pursuit of another with whom he had maintained contact by letter for sometime, yet exercising care not to expose his covertness. He had begun to visit the city of Chicago for two weeks in duration to be with Elizabeth Edom, to whom he would soon forward a betrothal.

Mrs. Laster wrote her regret that she and Bryon must delay joining them at the Sherette plantation that fall, as promised, her job forcing an alternative, which was that she and Bryon had settled on seeing her and Adelaide in the spring. The nation subtly and gradually edged closer to the horrible war, fanned on by the inflammatory rhetoric of the Southern politicians and wealthy cotton growers, and the abstinence of the Northern politicians to attempt to lessen the approaching storm, choosing rather, to stir stronger the winds behind the sails that drove it. Jordan Van Doke was the leading voice for the cause of the wealthy landowners of the surrounding region, one hundred miles in any direction, who looked upon him as an indispensable apotheosis, with the resultant effect that he literally basked in the glory they showered upon him. When Jordan called a meeting of his constituents, George, his middle son, was generally amidst the company.

There was no issue to the contrary that George's manner of temperament was glaringly likened to that of his father's, yet not so of Andre and Jim, most especially not so of Andre, who remarkably was of gentle and tender trait, and who was as different from his father as is the abyss from the loftiest peak. It is here fitting to borrow lines of verse from the poet Blake: "Did He smile his work to see? Did He who made the lamb make thee?"

Splitting the national fabric further apart were the incidents of public hangings, horrid gruesome scenes where Negro slaves and non slaves alike were wrongly accused of breach-ing the code, social or legal, a fiery outcry rising that a Negro had laid hands on a white woman, or lesser still had let his eyes wander upon her person. Sasha and Adelaide had traveled to Memphis to intercept Harry Lancaster who at last was to be with them for two weeks at the plantation, and while there, at the Gayoso, Sasha, ever inquisitive, bought a news paper that reported a spectacle that forced a gasp to her lips, which registered no less on Adelaide when Sasha showed her the article. It was chronicled in the *Nashville Gazette.*

> Between eleven and twelve o'clock yesterday, Henry and Moses, two slaves accused of murder, were taken from the county jail, and conveyed, under strong escort, to the gallows, which had been erected about one mile from town, in the vicinity of the Murfreesboro Turnpike and Brown's Creek. About four or five thousand persons assembled on the ground, as we are informed by our reporter, among whom we regret to say, were a large number of females. A short time before the execution, the Rev. Mr. Brown, a Catholic Priest, ascended the scaffold, and addressed a few words to the crowd. He stated his firm conviction, as a minister of the Gospel, that the prisoners were both innocent of the crime for which they were about to suffer death. The reverend gentleman then went through the ceremony of prayer, after which the halters were adjusted on the necks of the criminals. Henry and Moses then each addressed a few words to the crowd, in which they persisted in declaring themselves innocent. Henry said: "gentlemen, I am innocent. I never did any murder, and when you take my blood, you take innocent blood." Moses said: "I have but one word to say: I never murdered any man; if I did, I don't know it. That's enough." After these declarations were made, the rope which supported the scaffold was cut by the sheriff, and the criminals were launched into eternity.

The journalist reporting the event went on to say that though greatly in the minority a corps of white men and women alike, wandering through the crowd with eyes flashing of hatred and in a spell of euphoria, uttered that the offenders got what was coming to them.

When they later took it up Jim and Lucy reacted with a feeling of disgust and loathing against the horrendous spectacle. Lucy, wasting no time to unleash the strength of her feelings said, "Jim, you must use every means of your power of the law to extinguish this manner of evil," and Harry on the day that Sasha had procured the paper which ran the article used such language as deplorable, dastardly, inhumane, and ventured that the news was certain to land with revulsion on the ears of Lawrence Sherette, if it had not already. Silently Adelaide had crossed herself: "My Good and Great Lord, all loving, all kind, all forgiving; unless you hover close to keep them straight, are men's souls empty of morality; are all horrors to them possible?"

That evening when it was nearly suppertime Lawrence Sherette stood in the lobby of the hotel waiting for the others to avail themselves; Adelaide and Harry appeared first, but Sasha was temporarily detained. She wasn't entirely satisfied with some minor quirk in her dress. She'd come along shortly. Meanwhile, the others found a seat and began to talk, quickly falling upon the spectacle in Nashville. Adelaide said she had spun it without let up throughout the day and was concerned about a certain aspect of it, that she was anxious as to how Sasha might be internalizing it all. "She is so young, so innocent," she remarked to the men.

"Not as much as you might think," answered Lawrence Sherette. "She is too intelligent for that and thoroughly read and informed. I remember Bryon telling me that sometimes Mrs. Laster and Sasha explored in detail the differences between the races of the South and that the Negroes were wrongfully lorded over by the whites. Let her work it out to her satisfaction. If she wants to talk about it you're the first she'll turn to, and Mary Tonka is a close second." When Sasha joined them they crossed into the dining room, Adelaide instructing the host to seat them near the window overlooking the Mississippi. Sasha smiled in such a way as to let Adelaide know that she felt the choice seating was arranged especially for her. The supper was splendid but the adults seemed to converse less than usual, perhaps feeling a slight of guilt for making Sasha the center of conversation in her absence.

In their bed two nights later, Sasha, who was propped up on her pillow softly laid down the book she had been reading and said to Adelaide, "I've thought of that tragic thing that happened in Nashville Adelaide. I believe you think I am worrying over it. I'm not. I hate it terribly, just like Mary Tonka, and Harry, and Lawrence Sherette, but I'm like all of you. I have to deal with it and I can."

"I know you can. And for that I'm thankful. Sleep tight."

"You too."

Chapter 48

SINCE THE time that Adelaide had first set eyes upon Sasha in New Orleans, neither she nor her brother had spoken of her heritage, resolving unto themselves that she was God's precious creation and that whatever her blood line, it was the great and omnipotent Maker's doing, and that it was unchristian and unfitting for them who loved her more than anything on earth to entertain it in their own individual thoughts, let alone opening it up for elaboration. When in years past Lawrence Sherette had written to Adelaide briefly alluding to Albert Duval, his bosom confidante, a young Frenchman, who was marrying a girl of African descent, she passed the remark on to Mrs. Van Doke, which was taken to be hardly more than a grain in terms of consequence. Ever since the days of her young womanhood Adelaide and Mrs. Van Doke were close, and in their hours together often shared the most unimportant things with one another—a mere reflection on something trivial, and when Adelaide had made the conveyance to her older friend it was casually stored in her subliminal extremes and never later retrieved, not until shortly to follow, when a most unexpected coincidence was to jog the memory of what was once said.

Adelaide was ironing clothes, helping Mary Tonka catch up following Thanksgiving, which was not far passed. Sasha was in the bedroom pilfering through letters she had received over time, studying patterns of clothing she had kept, looking at scenes in magazines, and fawning over a portrait which was brushed in recent years. It was that of a fairly young woman. She had laid out these articles on the huge Victorian because it amounted to a sprawling table that could accommodate them severally. Andre had begun to knock on the front door and since she was closest to it Adelaide answered and upon letting him in relayed him to Sasha's whereabouts.

"You go on in Andre. She's browsing through some old treasures."

As Andre entered, Sasha spoke as ordinarily and motioned him over.

"Come look at these things with me."

"What are they?"

"Oh, just things."

"Ha, ha, ha. Not too important then, being just things."

"I'm sorry. I should have answered you better. They're more than just things; they're relics of a special sentiment, and one is very special."

"And that is?"

"My mother. Let me show you. See." She pointed to Izu's portrait then picked it up and held it closer to him. "Isn't she beautiful?" Andre looked, and with searing quickness his mind became frozen, if but for a second, then began to dart from one thing to another, yet he was settled enough in his senses to caution himself not to betray that he felt shock. If he had felt it, Sasha gave no signs of detection.

"Am I seeing the truth before me?" thought he, "or is this something of a sudden madness on my part, or is it a prank? No. Not madness nor prank. Sasha is serious. Did you not hear her words, did you not see her face? She has presented this beautiful woman as her mother; so I must not inquire further whether she is mistaken or whether she is instituting a game. But no again. Neither is she mistaken nor is it a game she has devised. And I cannot be so bold as to ask. She is my beloved, the girl I love with all my heart and soul, the one that I intend to marry and live with the rest of my life, who will bear our children. I'll ask Adelaide about this, but that will not help me now. Surely what I have heard is correctly given, and if it is and I appear strained that could be the end of it for us, and I could not bear that."

Having regained his balance Andre replied, "I agree. She is most beautiful. And this is your mother who died in the Canaries?"

"This is she. My dearly beloved, who is with me every day. When I close my eyes at night Andre, before drifting off to sleep, she comes to me. I hurt for her. I miss her infinitely."

"I hear it in your voice. And if her other attributes were equal to her beauty, then she was astonishingly endowed."

"They were, they were," she cried. "She was versed in music, in literature of the most varied origins, and in art. And she taught me in these refinements."

Andre declined to pursue the matter further, surmising that this was a complexity that was beyond his grasp and that whatever the truth, whether this was her real mother or not, he could not allow it to be of consequence to him, for Sasha was Sasha, high born beauty of superior intellect who lived deep inside his heart, whose aptitude and achievements exceeded those of anyone he had ever known and that she would be loathe to an extreme to entertain questions regarding the person in the portrait. These things he thought, though also, why had Sasha never mentioned anything of her mother before, yet concluded that such was of no significance, for "after all why should she, no more than I should strip my previous life bare for her awareness? I will plunge each and every one of these issues into the deepest recesses of my brain. I will think of them no more."

Just then Adelaide poked her head through the doorway to inquire of Andre if he might welcome a glass of iced tea.

"Ah yes Miss Adelaide. The weather is warmer than usual today and it has elevated my thirst."

"I'll see that your thirst is shortly relieved."

But before turning to leave she paused to add, "Oh, I see that you have joined Sasha in browsing through her treasured collections."

"Yes he has," Sasha broke in, "I showed him the portrait of my mother."

As calm as Adelaide was about everything she did, she nonetheless heard Sasha's words race with phantom speed through her brain and knew she should come to grips with a response. "Whatever I do I must do it instantly," thought she. Unaware of it, she declined to glance at Andre, or Sasha either, in avoidance of giving herself away, while she wondered what must be revolving in his mind. "Sasha's mother is clearly of Negro origin. Is this to him of any concern? Was he thrown off balance upon first seeing her? Did he truly feel she is beautiful? She is a great beauty. He could not have missed it. He is so calm, so in control of himself, not one trace of affectedness, and it is at least a slight interval ago that he has seen the portrait. Whatever he had to deal with in his head he has brought it to a resolve and is evidently through with it." All this she had considered in the flash of a second. Ah! What marvelous speed lies within the capability of the human brain? "Well, I must get hold of myself."

"She's beautiful, isn't she Andre?" said Adelaide with maximum steadiness in her voice.

"Very."

"Well, come on in you two and I'll serve the iced tea. Mary Tonka brewed a fresh pitcher full an hour ago."

Did Sasha not see the woman in the portrait as others saw her? Was she insulated from how the portrait might strike others? Ah! What mindless questions? One would defy the rules of logic if determining that she felt otherwise, would he not; for after all, this was her mother, her flesh and blood mother. What can be assumed with conviction is that as high born and superior as was Sasha she never sank to critically pondering the variations of skin pigmentation of a people and therefore gave no hint of wonder or curiosity of the ideations that flew round in

Andre's head. She only beamed with happiness that he gave every semblance of joy upon seeing her mother for the first time. Yet there is still a line or two more of supplement that begs to be heard and is here set down. When as a child in the Canaries Sasha was at her mission, where she took mass, one of the little angels serving as an altar girl, mixing and mingling with the congregation, whose numbers were of large count and origins of broad diversity, Spaniards, Africans, Byzantines, Portuguese, French, Turks, Egyptians, English, whose lives each Sunday became immersed in hers and hers in theirs, all there with a singular purpose, to worship in the Lord's sanctuary, irrespective of who they were or from whence they came and it was in this milieu that Sasha was conditioned year after year, and this is who she was in some large part when brought to the plantation by Adelaide.

When Andre drove home that afternoon he betrayed his pledge. The thought ran through him once again of Sasha's mother. To blot out the image was a feat greater than his mind could perform, for no one can forget what has happened an hour ago. And the image of his own mother also came to him. "How can I keep this secret from her when it is gnawing savagely at my internals to let it out. Will she see through my disguise? Will I slip? No. I will not. It will stay down deep, never seeing the light of day." While Andre struggled hard to guard his commitment, he need not have, for it was to be discovered by quite another means. Two weeks had gone by, Christmas was astir, and Mrs. Van Doke had driven over unaided to wish Adelaide and Sasha happy holidays and as she took her seat in the drawing room, where Adelaide had led her, she was told that Sasha was not there, to which she emitted a particle of disappointment.

"She's riding Martha. I look for her to return within the hour."

Andre would have been at her side had he not by necessity journeyed to Brownsville with team and wagon to purchase and return with a load of barbed wire. He had wished to Sasha that the material was transportable by way of carriage and with that as fact she could go with him, but acknowledged that the wagon was excessively bumpy for her. She said that wasn't a good reason, not in the least the reason for her declining. It was because there was a sick person, an older woman, she must see about.

"Let us hope so. I haven't heard her play in some time." It was in fact just barely a week past.

"You make yourself comfortable while I prepare refreshments."

"You need not d….."

"Yes I must. I want to." Then Adelaide left the room.

In her absence Mrs. Van Doke feasted her eyes on the adornments populating the walls, paintings of pastoral scenes and portraits of renowned and unrenowned personages, one such fixture catching at her strangely, that of Izu, whose portrait Adelaide had hung on the wall with Sasha's help and approval within the week. She had said to Sasha in fun loving conversation that Izu had stayed long enough in the huge gold and brown trunk, which yet contained a good many articles never removed since Sasha's arrival. Izu was the only woman of dark complexion among the several of exhibit, and her singularity easily engaged the eyes of Mrs. Van Doke. She was at once curious. She had never seen the portrait before on her countless visits.

"Adelaide," she called out as Adelaide reentered with coffee and a platter of croissants. "I am suddenly gazing at one of your wall collections, which has totally escaped me in my previous visits. Is it a new hanging?"

"Which do you mean?"

"The Negro woman. Quite young in appearance."

"It's newly hung."

"It's extraordinary. I am at a loss as to its significance, and why you have chosen it for showing."

"That is easy Martha," responded Adelaide in an attitude of naturalness and calm. "She is Sasha's mother. Izu. She went by the name Izu."

That Mrs. Van Doke was struck with surprise is doubtless the milder way to explain her suddenness of change in disposition. The rigidness of her form together with the stuttering of the words that she spoke confirmed more than surprise. She had sat straight up in her chair, startled, with her fingers to her lips, stunned, unsure of that which she had heard.

"Did, did, I, I, hear you correctly Adelaide? What have you said? It, it, it. I can't finish." She might well have believed that Adelaide had concocted a joke.

"You did Martha. Believe me. You did. She is Sasha's mother. I can imagine how this must fall upon you. So suddenly sprung and unexpected."

"I search for words. I am somewhat unsteady. Give me a minute if you will."

"Take your time."

When Adelaide had determined that she had started to regain her composure she spoke again. "Do your best to restore yourself to normalcy. I will help you understand."

"But Adelaide, how can this be? This woman is of color. Sasha is as fair as any young girl in this land, and brilliant, far ahead of any of us. What you tell me is wholly outside my sphere of absorption. I cannot absorb it. My heart palpitates."

"As I say, I will help you understand. It may require time but you will."

"Forgive me. Is there a probability that this is not Sasha's mother, that somehow Sasha is the off spring of another woman, a white woman, handed over to this one by some dreadful mistake?"

"Ah! Wishful. But wrong. There is no such probability. You are reaching into the dark for an answer that doesn't exist. The things I say are certain and fully vouched for. There was a doctor Carlos Enoch, who delivered Sasha under the watchful eye of a Priest, Father Otto Conrad Kestner, a fact corroborated by him in a letter to Father Sisco de Endera Lumas of the San Fernando Cathedral of San Antonio, Texas. There is not the thinnest chance that what I have told you is in error."

"But why? Why was this not made known before now? Why did not Sasha make it known?"

"Why should she have? This is Sasha's flesh and blood," she uttered, with hand stretched toward the portrait, "her mother, her beloved, who taught her many of the fine things she knows, who raised her, nursed her, nurtured her night and day throughout her young life. Let us suppose that she might have come from the fount of a white woman's womb and is someone other than the darling we know. Perish the thought. Cleanse it from my lips. Sasha is Sasha; she is who she is because He made her that way and I thank Him every night on my knees for her. And I also will share with you this: when I beheld her for the first time I almost melted. She was more beautiful than a spring flower. I could not stop looking at her. When Lawrence Sherette revealed that her mother was Negro I was temporarily jolted, not shocked but in a sense I was, yet immediately asked, 'Who am I to meddle with His creation, for she is of His making and is one of His special angels, and said so to my brother, who said that was exactly what he had told himself and that he was ashamed he'd ever wondered an iota of her heritage and that he made a Christian vow never to think of it again and that is what I did too."

"You have known all along."

"I have. All along."

Mrs. Van Doke had puckered her face as if feeling remorse. "Forgive me Adelaide. I did not behave well. I am not of that sort. I will pray to our Lord that he does not see me in that light. You are right. Sasha owed no one a disclosure about her mother, nor did you. As you say, Sasha is Sasha. I cannot fathom her differently, nor would I ever want to. She is a dream as she is. I love her with my very soul, and Andre loves her with his too. He has several times told me. She makes his heart sing." And here she stopped and lapsed into pensiveness, then, "Who is to tell him of this? Is it I, or Sasha, or you?"

"No one. He already knows. And has for days. Sasha showed him the portrait when he came in one day while she was sorting through a mishmash of collections. I wasn't in the room with them except on the last, when they had practically finished talking about it. I said to him that Izu was beautiful and he replied 'very.' That was the end of it."

"Oh, the end of it. Yes. But I still don't know what I should do."

"Meaning"

"About taking this up with Andre. I will find it hard to live with it inside, me knowing that he already knows about it. I will practically burst."

"In time he will take it up with you. In the meanwhile I suggest you sit back and wait and stay as patient as you can. But on the other hand why not mention that you saw the lovely portrait in my drawing room and that you admired it, which is certain to invite a response."

Sasha stayed away much longer than Adelaide expected, failing to return until near sundown, Mrs. Van Doke having given up and leaving at some length before. When Sasha returned she explained to Adelaide the reason for her extended absence, hoping that she wasn't worried.

"While out Adelaide I dropped over to check on the elderly lady, Mrs. Murchison, who's suffering badly from a pneumonic condition. We're concerned about her."

"You mentioned you might call on her. Poor dear. I know you'll do your best. Your water is drawn. When you've finished bathing we'll have supper. Mary Tonka has prepared veal cutlets."

Mrs. Van Doke had continued to recall the image of the portrait the whole night through, tossing and turning, the enchanting beauty of the young woman in it refusing to leave her thoughts. Sometimes she saw features of Sasha, sometimes none at all. She had as well begun to retreat to an earlier phase of years past, struggling to recall something that Adelaide had once said to her, finally succeeding in pushing the fogginess away. She then remembered with translucent clarity. "I'd forgotten all about it, almost. Adelaide had mentioned but casually that Lawrence had taken up with a young Frenchman who had fallen in love with a girl missionary of African descent and was marrying her. This woman was to be Sasha's mother, whose daughter I adore with my complete being, destined, I hope and pray, to be my daughter in law." The next morning she asked Sol to hitch the team to her carriage and drive her to the Sherette plantation.

"I slept restlessly Adelaide. Something fell upon me that I must put before you." Then she reproduced the story she had recalled during the previous night.

"You have said it exactly Martha, the exact way it happened, or certainly very nearly the way it did. Lawrence was friend to both, and Albert insisted of course that Lawrence attend the wedding. I don't remember an awful lot of anything he said of it, other than to declare that Izu was quite beautiful."

"I don't find that troublesome to imagine. She is most beautiful. It is a point of wonder that Sasha has not hung her portrait before now."

"Only Sasha can answer that."

They had Christmas as usual at both plantations, with loved ones coming from relatively far distances to be there, Dr. Lundy, Tahitia, and Lawrence Sherette traveling together from Memphis, and Jim and Lucy from Nashville. George Van Doke's fiancée, Elizabeth Edom, joined the Van Dokes from Chicago. During the holidays she asked to meet Sasha, about whom she'd heard the most illustrious allusions, yet when Lucy once drove her over to the Aurora for an introduction they discovered that Sasha was away seeing patients, splitting the load with Doctor Lundy. The flu was astir. No other meetings were successfully arranged, therefore Miss Edom returned to her native city somewhat disappointed. Doctor Lundy, Tahitia, and Lawrence Sherette left for Memphis the following day and Jim and Lucy left two days thereafter for Nashville.

Since seeing Izu's portrait, Andre had kept silent, Mrs. Van Doke as well. The day before he was to return to Baltimore she was unable to longer keep her secret extinguished. She and Andre were dining together that evening, just the two of them, which was understandable, for George was occupied on a mission of business and couldn't be there, and Jordan Van Doke never dined with his wife unless guests were taking dinner with them. Starting soon after Andre was born they were estranged.

How was Mrs. Van Doke to begin with her son? She had pursued the question up and down. In her mind she was knowledgeable that he had viewed the portrait; in his mind he wasn't sure whether his mother had or had not.

"Andre, I had an interesting visit with Adelaide some few days ago. I'd like to share it with you. I feel very much in need to."

Andre reacted only mildly, for some time acquainted with Sasha's decision to hang the portrait in the drawing room at Adelaide's and guessing with good accuracy that his mother had set eyes upon it. "She had to," thought he. "She's visited Adelaide with more than usual frequency in recent days."

"I've seen the portrait of Sasha's mother. She's lovely."

He smiled with unfeigned subtly and laid his fork down. There was not even a quiver of arousal in his face. "I figured you had. Since you hadn't told me for sure I felt I'd let it go until you did. And I concur. She is a beautiful woman."

"What were your thoughts when you saw her? How did you feel?"

"To be frank, I was moved. No, I don't mean that exactly. Better for me to say that I wasn't expecting to see that Sasha's mother was colored. With incomprehensible swiftness my senses cautioned that I should not let on. Sasha was in my presence showing the portrait to me. I couldn't believe what I was seeing. It was too amazing to believe. But I had to believe it.

Sasha was telling it to me. Many things ran through my head as fast as a racing streak, many questions, and when that was finished I heard myself making a silent resolution."

"And what was that darling?"

"That whoever the woman, her real mother or someone else, it did not matter. Sasha was the same to me. Wonderful by every measure, living deep in my heart. And I hoped that someday she might take me as her husband, God willing. That is what I thought."

"Those are my feelings exactly. I too met with surprise. More so than you apparently. Stunned. I was stunned. But I recovered. Not as quickly as you. But I recovered. You and I passed through the same trial. I love Sasha Andre, with all my soul I do; she is a bright glowing light in my life, and like you, I cannot do without her. Let me say this also. Izu is Sasha's mother. Do not doubt that fact longer. Adelaide explained to me that she is, that a Priest witnessed Sasha's birth, and later communicated this happening to another Priest who passed it on to Lawrence Sherette."

Andre tepidly bobbed his head as if he understood and accepted what he heard as the truth, showing not the faintest of surprise, then paused in expectation that she was about to continue, and since she did not he moved to further enlarge upon that which he had previously expressed. "I wish Mother that I could have met Izu. I deeply do. I am thankful for her, that she at one time existed on this earth, because if she had not there would have been no Sasha. The day I saw the portrait I was not greatly affected. Except for a second or two. The impact sped from me quickly. But I would have remained crazy over Sasha no matter what I saw or what was said. Also, what you have unearthed here has no bearing either. The only thing that matters is Sasha. And with that said I think we can now put everything once and for all to rest."

"But it cannot altogether be that way my darling. There is still your father, and knowing him, I am afraid he will not take this well. I must tell him, you know. Better I to reveal it without lengthy delay than have him hear it second hand and then come irately to me."

"I see. There is no alternative. You must. I agree. What a pity I am to be away when you do. Already I feel the guilt. I should be here to help you. To perhaps tell him myself."

"No dear. That duty is to fall on my shoulders. Not yours. I will choose my time, as soon as I can, but not rushing. What I need is sufficient latitude to determine what to say and be prepared to counter his outbursts, if there are any."

"You've planned your strategy well. You know best. I desperately hope that it goes better than we are adjudging."

Chapter 49

THE COLD wind blew from the north that mid January, the woods now stripped of leaves which had been plentiful until winter set in and without the leaves their great branches looked splintery and shapeless. There was a lonely whistling that blew through them. The stubble in the fields left over from the fall cuttings wriggled and trembled and the blackberry brambles at the edge of the tree line twisted and shook. The landscape was sad, because Sasha was sad, Andre had gone, and to elevate herself she rode her handsome horse to the Big Hatchie, turning around however to head home once she was there. The cold was too bitter. The steed, who was of gentle stock and faithful always to heed her command, on this day appeared impatient and blew moisture from his nostrils and snorted and undulated his neck and head, anxious to return to the relative warmth of the barn, there escaping the unkind elements. Sasha drew her heavy coat in tightly and pulled her Russian fur down over her ears and leaned forward and let him run as fast as his great body and mind desired.

"Whew." She had shot into the great room where there was a warm blazing fire, her cheeks reddened from the wind. "It's punishing weather out there."

"Villainous," answered Adelaide. "I worried about you. Here, sit in this chair and I'll help you tug off your boots. Your toes need warming sweetheart."

That night the snow fell, the mass everywhere blanketing the landscape. At last it was there, the first for Sasha, which was forecast by Sam Feathers and Mary Tonka the previous day. There was no snow sled at the mansion. There were wagons, and Adelaide urged Sam Feathers to hitch up the team and take Sasha for a ride. The air was cold, though there was no biting wind as there was the day before. The heavy coat she wore and the Russian fur lowered over her ears and the cider jug of hot coffee that Mary Tonka sent along were enough to keep her warm. Likened to Sasha, Sam Feathers was wrapped from head to toe, a heavy hunting coat enveloping his frame and rough thick brogans on his feet. Something of a Cossack cap was fitted on his head, which Adelaide had bought years before during her travels to Poland while she was attending college in England. She called it an Astrakhan and had given it to Sam Feathers. He kept the garment pulled down snug around his ears. Sasha laughed to herself at the sight of him. His cheeks were of a rosy red, and the smoky moisture poured incessantly from his mouth, neither of which were bothersome, or even the minutest in his awareness, apparently, for he whistled a great amount of the time when she wasn't talking to him or he wasn't talking to her. It was something of a waltz she felt, tempted to suggest in jest that his efforts were terribly devoid of timing.

"Would you like some coffee Sam Feathers?"

"Thank you I would. Glad Mary Tonka set it in for us."

Sasha poured a coffee cup full and handed it over, volunteering to relieve him of the reins in order that he might better sip the beverage. He said he'd manage. She then sat back and began to enjoy her own as well, starting to look around again at things up close and things afar, everywhere the land covered by a full five inches.

"Isn't it a wonder Sam Feathers," she exclaimed. "Think of it. Not one plant is alive out here this morning but in no time the cotton and corn and tomatoes will be growing like poppies. Isn't nature a miracle?"

"I'd say. I've always thought that. Yep, that's a good way to put it Sasha. A miracle."

It was almost a scene unfathomable, these two sitting side by side, in such fun, in such complete accord, where on the one hand there sat Sam Feathers, limited and weighted with the common mind that the Lord had bequeathed to him, born to the rural, understanding little but the nature of the soil and what it took to force it to yield up its annual bounty; whereas, and on the other, there sat Sasha, brilliant, lucid, creative, curious of everything, who had read Revelations before she was ten, which to Sam Feathers was merely a name, no more than that, of which his preacher made mention fewer times than the fingers on one of his hands during the sermons of a whole year; and if she had tried to tell him of Paschal's lines they would have gotten no further than the outer layer of his skin: "The conduct of God, who disposes of all things kindly, is to put religion into the mind by reason, and into the heart by grace. But to put it into the mind and heart by force and threats is not to put religion there, but terror, *terrorem potius quam religionem*."

"He does not need to hear of these lines," thought she, "nor know of Paschal, nor understand Revelations. He has heard of the Lamb and that his blood was spilled for the salvation of mankind. Our Lord Jesus would vouch that that is quite enough."

Near the last she asked Sam Feathers to drive the team into the woods, down the narrow pretty pathway leading to the small bridge that ran over the gurgling stream. The woods were quiet, save for a scattering of birds tweeting and making many assorted noises, darting from limb to limb. Sam Feathers looked over at her.

"They're hungry Sasha. Scouting around for breakfast."

"I know."

She thought of Andre and how he once brought her there, and that they had dismounted, and that she threw pebbles into the stream and that they had raced each other home.

"I think he let me win. I really do. He does things like that to please me. He doesn't think I know it but I do. Andre's heart is gentle. I love him for that. I miss him. I wish he were here. He is my playmate."

Suddenly Sam Feather's voice interrupted her reverie. "Well Sasha, we'd better get along. It's already past dinner time."

Word of the intriguing portrait began to flow, spreading like wild fire from one to another once people caught hold of it. Who was the one to light the match? Not Andre, not Mrs. Van Doke, not Mary Tonka, but Adelaide, for to her the match was already struck, happening the moment that she and Sasha exposed Izu Duval for all to see by hanging her portrait on the oft frequented drawing room wall. Perhaps knowledge of it was picked up and disseminated by some wealthy land owner's wife who was on visit and had seen it, thus making an inquiry, with Adelaide unaffectedly explaining to her the identity. Or the first whisper might have begun with one of the female workers from time to time hired by Adelaide to come to the plantation to iron and clean and do a myriad of chores. Irrespective of where and how the seed was planted word had gotten about. All that heard responded much in the manner of Mrs. Van Doke when she had first set eyes upon the young Negro woman, some in slave talk, some in language of the relatively educated landed gentry but all thoughts identical in meaning, "There is some mistake, surely there is. Just look at Sasha. There has to be a mistake. She was adopted, that's what; Izu is nothing more than an adopting mother. That is the truth of it." Or, "There was a mix up at birth, where Sasha, the baby from a white woman's womb, was handed over to Izu." Or, "Izu was hired by Albert Duval as a house keeper to care for his white baby who came from Heaven knows where and they later married"

Speculations ran without end, but when the reverberations had settled the people were of all minds the same as Cynthia.

"I couldn't love her more. No I couldn't Sol. Whether there's Negro blood flowing in that child's veins or she's purely white, she is Sasha, and I was crazy over her from the start.

I would go to her this minute and gather that sweet baby in my arms and tell her how deeply and tenderly I love her. I would but she already knows that anyway." Cynthia paused to draw in a deep breath and sighed. "But even if the people love her just like me they'll keep on talking about it. They will for a little bit longer. And that's what worries me."

"Why so?"

"Sasha will hear about it."

Sasha was not long in hearing. Adelaide saw to that, surmising it best that she and Sasha should talk through the matter, and in the larger frame was apprehensive that Jordan Van Doke might already have gotten wind of it. Sasha was of her usual aplomb when she had sat down with Adelaide and answered to her opening remarks.

"Do not worry over me Adelaide. We knew when we jointly hung the portrait of my precious mother that the many passing through this home would in the midst of other friends begin to privately trade remarks of it. As you say, we are not naive."

"I am not concerned my beloved. I simply felt you should know that word is afloat, just as I know it, and that people, all those you have met, rich or poor, now love you even more. But either way, the consequence would have been the same to me. When you hurt, my darling, I hurt; when you rejoice, I rejoice."

"And it is the same with me. I pray thanks to Him nightly that I met you Adelaide. You have become my life."

"And you have become mine."

"I cannot help but wonder. What is Mrs. Van Doke saying to this? She must have heard."

"She has heard. I have talked with her. You have become her life as you have become mine. She dreams of you and Andre and the future that awaits you. She loves you with her very soul. She does now more than ever, and reports to me the most touching thing. Andre said to her he wished he could have known your mother, for it was she who brought you into this world and if she hadn't he would have had no life at all."

"Ah. Andre. His endearments are overwhelming. I feel as if I will cry." With that, Adelaide reached and wiped away the tender sweet tears from her cheeks.

"Andre is like that. Endearing and gentle. He always was. But quite shy. Much unlike his father."

Sasha had regained her composure, save for the sound of a little sniffling, and raised an issue that had not been addressed by either but had to be. "And what does his father have to say about everything? About the portrait?"

"Mrs. Van Doke is to take that up with him. We'll have to see."

ℭ ℵ

The winter was harsh and too long extended its stay, stubbornly hanging on, marked with unrelenting visits of sleet and snow, people sicker than ordinary and travel from place to place an ordeal. Not every time did Sasha ask the sick to be brought to the infirmary, judging the patient too ill and too old to endure leaving bed, then riding herself a short or lengthy distance in a rattling wagon driven by Sam Feathers to conduct examination and treatment—not in the nice infirmaries of the Aurora or La Belle—but in their houses, small cramped bedraggled shanties, where the family was several and on cold days huddled around a wood burning stove or in front of a fire place, often in the same room with the ailing.

Near the last of the month of February Sam Feathers drove her to see an elderly sick woman, a very old and feeble grandmother, bed ridden with flu. At first blush Sasha was moved by the old woman's emaciation, deciding that about all she could do was to encourage her to eat and drink, and asked her daughter if her mother had ingested anything for breakfast.

"No Miss Sasha. Not yet."

"Try hard to get her to."

"Yesum."

Feeling that she herself might induce the poor thing to take nourishment she leaned over and looked into her pale weak eyes and said soft words of comfort and encouragement. Mustering the best within her the old woman attempted a smile that failed soon after it started. Sasha understood and patted her cheeks. She sat for a while at bedside holding her hand, concluding that there was nothing else she could do other than hope that she might on her own make an effort to ask for a biscuit and bacon. While Sasha was there no one had left the room, this because the morning outside was grippingly cold, and also because they just wanted to keep looking at the beautiful girl in their midst, most never having seen her up close. No one stared directly, settling for quickened short glances, flashes, all except one, a young Negro of Sasha's age, who in something of a catatonic fix held her in his gaze. If Sasha saw it she pretended not; but the boy's mother noticed and with the motion of her hand summoned him outside to the front porch.

"Boy. Keep yo eyes off that doctor. She's white woman and tryin to help yo grandmother. What you doin will lead youse to trouble. Now mind my word and stay out heah til she leaves."

On their return she was silent for most of the trip, Sam Feathers a bit thrown at her quietness, yet was of mind that he shouldn't intrude to learn why. Sasha was in fact ruminating through the earlier mention by Adelaide that Mrs. Van Doke was to take up the subject of the portrait with her husband, surmising that apparently she had not, or else would have revealed it to Adelaide by this date. As it happened Mrs. Van Doke had delayed day after day in dread of coming to grips with what she must, yet finally decided to leave a note one late afternoon a slight before dusk on the foyer table that Jordan Van Doke intercepted before going to his private room or to his office. She was sitting in her favorite chair reading, though hardly concentrating on the substance of the lines in as much as she was aware that he had found the note and expected him briefly to come see what it was about.

"You have something you need to discuss."

"Take a chair Jordan. I do."

"All right." He laid hold of one that was nearest and dragged it even closer. His eyes darted and gave him away. He had attempted to figure what this was about since picking up her note.

"You have not heard of the portrait I presume."

"What portrait?"

"The one of Sasha's mother."

"Of course not. Why do you ask? I had no knowledge that there was one."

"There is. I've recently seen it. It was just the other day hung on Adelaide's drawing room wall."

"Surely you are leading me somewhere with this. Can you get to the point?"

"I can. Sasha's mother is Negro. She's a beautiful thing."

His eyes narrowed, his jaws dropped, yet he did not exhibit great surprise. His eyes were more analytical than awe struck. But the effect showed in his voice. He bellowed out quickly, "What did you say?"

"I said she is of Negro blood."

"Bah! What foolishness. What trickery is this that you bring?"

"No trickery. I tell you the truth, which you should know."

"Ah woman. I cannot believe what I hear."

"You must believe it. It is so. I've gone to some length to make certain of it, to gain proof."

"Ah gracious. I am hit suddenly. This is stunning. And lacking credibility. I presume you are not on drink. No, you never use it. And you appear well."

"I am well Jordan. And I have never bent to the use of alcohol."

Rising from his chair, which implied there was a tinge of irritation besieging his soul, he appeared as if he were walking away, yet did not and promptly sat back down, raking his fingers through his course gray hair which once was handsomely red. He searched his wife flittingly.

"Where is this so called portrait? I must see it. I must see it for myself. But no need to tell me. It's in Adelaide's home as you have said and she would never invite me to enter as much as a half foot through her doorway."

"No she would not. You'll have to take someone's word. Mine, if you will."

"Yours. Oh yes, yours. And would if this was not a hoax of a tale. Anyway, let me say this. Sasha is as fair as any I have ever seen, a beautiful young girl. If she has an equal I have never discovered that person. She could not have sprung from a Negress. Never, never. Something is amiss here."

"You are rash. You are hit broadside. As was I when I saw with my own eyes the portrait."

"An imposter. A hoax."

"No. Listen to me. It was freshly hung. I noticed it as soon as I was seated. The young woman was beautiful. I asked Adelaide about her. She explained that the young woman was Sasha's mother."

"Bah! That cannot be."

"It can and is Jordan. Believe it. Believe it now or learn the truth by slow begrudging increments. Whether it's one or the other you will come to believe it."

"What an unsteadying stroke. What a sudden rip. I need time to digest this. It is a strange piece that you have delivered. But wait! Here I am letting myself go. What is your attitude about all this?"

"Toward the portrait? Toward Sasha?"

"Both. My words are clear."

"The portrait portrays a beautiful woman. Now to Sasha. She is a jewel, deep into my heart. She has always been. She is still the same. How could she not be? Andre loves her as you surely know. With all his being he does."

"So he has heard. Has seen the portrait?"

"The first to see it besides Adelaide, who has long known of it."

"Adelaide. Long ago I'm sure. If it is a fact."

Jordan Van Doke rose again, and left by way of the side entrance, with a sense of having fallen into a maelstrom, refusing to believe the story his wife had transmitted, which if he ever came to believe it he will have sifted the things he had heard through his brain for hours and days before becoming convinced. Though he departed in surprising calm, he gave no explanation of where he was heading, nor did she ask. She opined that he was setting out on a long walk to cool down, to gain perspective, to try to make sense of things. Striving to clear his mind he in the coming days strolled the fields and worked with the slaves for hours at a time, his mood usually settled and calm, yet at times anger boiled to the surface, such that he was seen then to reach for a twig or piece of stubble and when grasping it snapped it into, violently throwing the fragments into the wind, or take hold of an idle shovel and heave it aimlessly with all his strength, the slaves growing nervous at the sight of his behavior, afraid he'd transfer his belligerency to them and that one might resultantly fall victim to a flogging. Several times he returned to his wife to pick up again where they'd left off, though to no advantage, for all had been said that could be, and then returned to the fields to be with the slaves, plunging into sweaty toil and talk. The more talk the better. It relieved him. But the portrait did not leave him, the talk of it anyway, nor did Sasha. She was riveted to his thoughts. When he grew tired he sat down on the hard ground and ate slave food that one of the women had packed in a straw basket and drank water from a cider jug; then invariably began to run through the scenario once more. She was too white to be part Negro, he over and over contended to himself. He even approached Sol when catching sight of him at the mansion, asking in kind tone if he was aware of the portrait, if he had seen it with his own eyes, the answer coming from Sol's lips, "No sah," but hesitantly done; and then he asked Sol if Cynthia had witnessed the portrait, the one hanging in Adelaide's home, and this time Sol uttered in something of a murmur, "Yes sah. She has." Jordan Van Doke then asked him if he believed it. Sol shook his head to denote the contrary. "No sah. I don't. That can't be Sasha's mother. Cynthia don't believe she is either. No slaves round heah do. A pretty white girl like her can't have no Negro blood in her. But we wouldn't care one way or the other if she did. We loves her like she is our own and she loves us too like we's her own."

Chapter 50

JORDAN VAN Doke swayed back and forth, grinding away at the perplexity that consumed him: was she altogether white or was she part Negress? One day she was white, the next Negress. "The possibility, the possibility," he kept exclaiming. It thudded in his brain. The possibility that there was Negro blood coursing through her had brought him nearly to the precipice. Weeks passed, and as his wife predicted he, by some feat of reasoning, convinced himself that Sasha was Negro, some Negro at any event, upon which there arose the consideration of his youngest son. His mind swept wildly. What was he to do about Andre, who he knew was smitten with Sasha, his soul lost in her, which he had known about for a good long while? Nothing, he supposed. It was all right as long as there was no marriage, nothing as fatuous as that, no children of mixed heritage to taint the Van Doke name. "A preposterous thing, disgraceful," even though he recalled having his nights with a slave woman, more than one, but this was not known by anyone except himself and the woman—at least he thought so—on whom he showered affections and expensive favors, who dared never tell. Never again was there to be a beautiful ball where Sasha whirled round and round with his son on the most splendid evening he had ever witnessed, nor any more fantastic dinners to which she was invited, for that would be too embarrassing. "After all, what would the people think?"

These were the ideations that played upon the communicants of his brain, which sprang back and forth between suspicion and reality, and in his anger and unsteadiness decided on the position he was taking toward Andre. His son could run free, could be with Sasha in whatever way he liked, as long as she was not a part of the social affairs of the Van Doke mansion. His wife received his words with bitter rejection and delivered scathing retaliation.

"Ah miserable! You snap my patience. You are vile. You are foolish, if not mad. You are whirling the whole family upon ruin. You are positioning yourself to be another Priam,"[6] she flared out. "You will lose all. You suffer from vanity and narrowness, Jordan Van Doke, unable to gather the loveliest rose ever in your arms, and love her, who is ten times better than any of us. You could do great good. But you won't. You'll cling to your evil enterprise. That's what you enjoy. Go ahead. Enjoy your slaves. But I shall tell you this. These slaves are yours in this hour but one day you will be hers."

"By Heavens! What are you saying woman?" His tone was scornful.

"One day you will lie sick or injured and she will hold the power to restore you, or let you die."

"Bah! Wild imagination."

"Bah you say. You repulse me. It will happen as I foretell, and you will moan for her skilful hands and incisive intellect to help you. Do you fail to recall the adage that any straw will do when one is sinking. How swiftly your imaginary honor will vanish."

Strong and clever, Martha Van Doke could best him in this mode of encounter if she wanted, and then and there was suddenly determined to muster the utmost of her capabilities to keep her husband from raining unhappiness on the two youth she loved more than her own self. Still, she had no choice but to grievously relay the results to Adelaide and Andre, and Andre would have to talk with Sasha.

He'd had enough. Angrily, he left. He'd return late to his quarters, to his office or bedroom, and rise early the next morning between five and six, Cynthia faithfully up a sizeable stretch before this to prepare and have ready his breakfast. Mrs. Van Doke emerged from her bedroom an hour or more after he had left, vigilant of his schedule, as he was hers, skillfully avoiding his presence. People are known to have for decades lived under the same roof without speaking, or at the most, speaking a word or two, and this had come to be the norm for the both of them. As one might expect, it brought worry to the brow of Mrs. Van Doke that their incompatible relations affected Andre and she tried to make sense of it to him in private talks, in which she received assurances with an ever ready embrace that he understood, though the mask of his calm hid the consummate sorrow he held in his heart for her.

Throughout the night she lay and reminisced, retreating to long ago yesteryears. She was young then, a girl in her teens, whose parents, Nathaniel and Mary Nomehart, had left

---

[6] In the siege of his Troy by the Spartans, King Priam refused to leave the city and one by one his family left him.

England for the shores of Norfolk, Virginia, the year of which there is no accounting, where Nathaniel was invested in the construction of seagoing sailing vessels of the most modern mold, which were lately designed and built, an enterprise which in time led to the steam engine ships supported and encouraged by Queen Victoria. She and her first cousin Joseph, whose folks had earlier died, lived with her parents in a two story white house on a relatively high hill with a cluster of gables and sharply pitched roofs, each indentured with a complex of dormers shaped in the attitude of the letter A, or better still and more vividly put, in the resemblance of a bird house amplified many times over. These dormers were fitted with very large windows through which she could gaze at the serene Atlantic when it was calm and peaceful.

In as much as her father was endowed with a penchant to enjoy the warmth of a wood fueled blaze while relaxing in the evening, he ordered the erection of a cluster of fireplaces and chimneys when he had the house built. There was as well another house that was built on this very spot in a distant time, oaks, willows, cedars, left untouched by saw and ax until it finally gave way to demolishment. The trees stood in near artistic symmetry, close on the border of the street which did not lie by any sizeable length from the porch of the old previous house. He knew this by inspection, and by determining from hearsay the exact whereabouts of the structure because the walkway that ran through the center of the yard came to a terminus where the front porch once was situated. And by this same walkway there stood a giant oak, around which it was diverted. Her father was strict to insist that this handsome specimen not fall victim to alteration, nor be cut down.

But let us return to the house that her father built. It is well to say that she recalled much more than the tangibles of the quaint exterior of that dear edifice, for there were many vicissitudes the inside walls had witnessed. The personages visiting in the evenings to sit with her father by the fire were too numerous to account for, their times present too many to have been made of record. They were of a unique brand, these fellow comrades, all endowed with some little artifice, clever, not false or insincere, that set them apart individually in her mind. She saw and heard them from the background in the spacious room where her father had told her she could sit and listen and learn provided she did not disturb. She recalled them one by one, and that once she had set down on a parchment a description of their personalities: Person A, mannerly; Person B, thoughtful of others, does not interrupt; Person C, too talkative; Person D, vain, quite vain, should have a look in the mirror; Person E, tells tall tales; Person F, dresses in nicely tailored suits, dapper indeed. "Different, very different," read the concluding footnote. But they were to the last man of common character when it centered on arguing an opinion, and this was done with unrequited aggressiveness, even by the mildest of the lot. They often took up the rash of hostilities with Spain, most holding to the position that war was inevitable. When the issues grew heated she sometimes from her distance wished she could jump in and deliver her own opinions and after the men had left for the evening relayed this urge to her father, who answered that he was glad to see his daughter of this spirit and that there would come a time and place when she could wisely speak her piece, but added that she should observe that thoughts are best delivered without emotion and hoped that throughout her life's journey she in every case exercised restraint. While she had many fine teachers during her emerging years her father was her favorite, who strove to the utmost to impress upon her the importance of self dependence, instilling in her also a complement of other qualities, an appreciation for art and travel and plays and operas and reading and politics, which she painfully missed when she and her husband moved away from Virginia. While living in the western sector of rural West Tennessee, far from Norfolk, she managed for awhile to return for abbreviated visits with her parents, and would have continued this invigorating reunion for no telling the length had not a savage fire ignited one night, destroying the house in which they lived and them with it. Joseph escaped unharmed. Martha invited her first cousin to move to Tennessee and stay with her, which she badly wanted, but Joseph chose to remain in Virginia, where he was kindly accepted and welcomed by friends of the deceased, there residing until his public schooling was complete.

She met Jordan Van Doke at church one Sunday morning, a man in his mid twenties, she still in her late teens. He took the liberty of introducing himself. He had ventured to Norfolk on business, traveling there from far away Brownsville in Tennessee where he had set his sights on a spread of land tracts of which he hoped to gain ownership and amass them into one giant unity. On the outset they seemed to have affections for one another and his commitment to attending church appealed to the values she held dear in a man, as did her parents. Less than handsome he off set this shortcoming with cavalier mannerisms and a dashing style of dress. It was a bit unorthodox, the congregation thought, but made no issue of it. Little by little they were drawn to one another. During his intervals in the city they strolled the coastline on Sunday afternoons from the vantage of a swollen area of the earth high above sea level and talked of the romance of seagoing vessels sailing away to exotic places. His speech was gentle and reassuring to the young girl and this quality was buttressed with a continuous flow of bouquets to her doorway, without signature, thus adding mystic appeal and amour to the man who obviously was opening serious inroads to her heart. It was not long thereafter that he asked her to marry him. She hesitated, remembering the dear love in England who had twice sailed across the ocean to see and be with her. They had grown up together since childhood. She would have gladly waited for him, she yearned to, for that was where her heart truly resided; but finally after his letters stopped, she resigned that their love was not destined to prevail. "It was so long since he had been with me, so long since I felt the caresses of his arms and the sweetness of his lips," she once shared with Adelaide. Thus she promised to marry Jordan Van Doke despite the ominous consciousness in her being advising against it. They were married in her church in Norfolk and for a while established residence near her parents. They appeared to be happy. Jordan Van Doke openly shared his future dreams with his new wife, revealing very early in their marriage his intentions to build an empire of cotton growing and described to her the plots of raw forest soils where it was to be achieved. But he needed money. At his persistent urging she reluctantly asked her father to invest in the budding enterprise of which he had told her. While her father listened with an open mind, feeling that he might provide support, he was far from turning money over to his son in law without carefully drawn up constraints, starting with a deed clearly showing that his daughter was an investor and owner proportionate to the amount paid for the property, including future developmental values accruing to her through martial rights granted by law. And further added teeth to these strictures by requiring that paper work—the deed, letter exchanges, receipts—be stored in a bank vault in Norfolk of his choosing and that an attorney in Norfolk, also of his choosing, superintend the legal work, not the lawyer in rural West Tennessee who Jordan Van Doke had hoped to retain.

She never breathed a word to her husband of the young man of her heart in England, with whom some years after her marriage she reestablished a connection through the liaison efforts of her trusted first cousin in Norfolk, beginning once more to exchange letters, keeping alive this surreptitious affair until after Jim was born, toying with the notion of joining the still relatively young Englishman; but the lure of feverish youth and moonlight nights had weakened, let alone the realization that she had a young child on her hands and that her fraction of the jointly owned property could not be easily sold without suffering a serious discount in value. She had told this story to Adelaide some several years past, after Jim and George were born. Adelaide breathed none of it to anyone, not even to Lawrence Sherette.

"You decided to stay."

"I had no choice. The boy. Jim was first. When it came to him I wasn't about to let myself count in the least miniscule way irrespective of how unhappy I was or would become."

ஐ ଓ

She awakened at eight the next morning, asked Sol to hitch the horses to her carriage, climbed up to her seat without pausing for assistance from the gracious old man and set out for the Sherette plantation. Sasha was away; that was good, for she could reveal to Adelaide the most recent encounter she had had with her husband, what he said and what she said, both Adelaide and her deciding then and there not to reveal a word of it to Sasha for the time being. This should wait. But Mrs. Van Doke would write a letter to Andre.

My dear son,

My talk with your Father is over. I must tell you that he did not accept it well. At first he was in denial of Sasha's true heritage, then after thrashing through everything for a time he concluded that the beautiful portrait in Adelaide's home was in fact Sasha's mother. Somehow he cannot stand the thought of it. He keeps seeing dark offspring in the family. He cannot have missed the deepness of your affections toward Sasha and surely has realized that some day she will become your wife, as I fervently hope.

I am advising that we string along with things as they are, given the fact that already I have gone over the matter with Adelaide, and likely she will take it up with Sasha, who will not be pleased with his attitude, but strong as she is will slough it off as if it is of trivial importance. You may want to write Sasha after Adelaide sits with her, or else she may choose to write you.

Do not let this news bear upon you worrisomely. You are faced with enough at your work. I will continue to keep you posted. I do so look forward to seeing you in the summer.

Your loving mother

Adelaide picked her time; it was one night not long after they had said their prayers, lying in bed immersed in idle talk. When she had spoken of what Mrs. Van Doke revealed to her, she found that Sasha was not in the narrowest trace ruffled, nor the least surprised. She had expected it.

"I shall utter a little prayer for him tonight. May Andre forgive me if he ever finds out, but I must say Adelaide, his father is a complete boor and aloof and overbearing. I have always seen him in that image. Oh, horrid. These are terribly demeaning words I have landed on the man." She crossed herself. "But in truth I must say further that it is a mystery to me that Mrs. Van Doke has withstood him all these years.

"She hasn't easily dear. I can attest to that. I claim knowledge of her feelings exactly."

Sasha would not fret, not for a minute she declared. "It's not worth a straw's worth of consideration." But she felt for Andre and had begun to worry that the recent events weighed heavily upon him.

"I will write him Adelaide, I feel that I badly need to. Better to address it now than to keep him in suspense for so long a while."

"If you think that's best."

"I'll take extra care not to offer a hint of my disenchantment with his father."

"I know you will. Although, Andre likely knows. He has a keen sense about what people are thinking and I can tell you now there are many things about his father with which he takes issue. He doesn't speak of them to anyone except his mother."

"He is greatly fond of her, greatly endearing. Are Jim and George equally inclined?"

"I think they are. In their own way they are. Except when schisms arise between her and Jordan. Then George seems to side with his father, Jim with his mother, and Andre vigorously with his mother."

Sasha wrote her letter to Andre. "It's not a critical thing Andre, so please do not let it divert you from your important work with Doctor Givens."

Andre, ecstatic that Sasha said she was not in the least perturbed, thanked her for the lines and confessed that he loved her more than ever, if that were attainable, wincing and smiling at the same time at his heartfelt confession. There was once in the near past when he wouldn't have mustered the slightest nerve to hint of it.

A little time stole by. Faces were happy when winter decided to move on, taking with it the nippy morning frosts and the continual threats of snow. The general mood was one of good riddance. This one had been severe, the worst that Sam Feathers could remember. The dogwood blooms of pink and white had not yet crowded through. But almost. Soon another seasonal miracle would appear. The dewy youth of spring was upon them. The field hands clucked to the horses, the monstrous turning ploughs moved forward with a surge, the blades of sharpened steel slicing the earth apart. Then the planting. Sasha had received word from Mrs. Laster that their plans were finalized, giving notice of their probable arrival in early fall, perhaps as early as September, by October without fail she underscored. The railroad construction gangs crept eastward, the bedding on which the rails would in time be laid visibly progressing each day, axes and saws and wagons and crude earth moving mechanicals perpetually in motion in the transfer of great heaps of dirt from one place to another. They had crossed the Big Hatchie. Sasha watched from a distance as she sat on her steed, fanaticizing that she and Adelaide one day would ride in a sleek passenger train to a distant city, maybe to the coast of Virginia or the Carolinas. Spring had died away in favor of summer, the atmosphere now charged with steamy thick mist, as soon as mid morning or before. Even at that early hour the men's work clothing clung to their bodies as a mass of soppy wetness.

What next happened was so unexpected that neither Adelaide nor Sasha could have envisioned it in their wildest, not that the incident was of astounding rareness. Adelaide was away at a worker's house to deliver food for the family, letting Sasha know beforehand that George Van Doke had made arrangements through her to meet with Sam Feathers on the frontage lawn of the mansion at three o'clock to negotiate a subject of business. They were clearing the land for the furthering of the railroad bed after it had crossed the Sherette plantation. George needed extra field hands; they were cutting up freshly fallen trees into lumber logs and his regular crew could not sufficiently complete the job on time without help. George was there in the vicinity of fifteen of three and seeing that Sam Feathers was not around knocked softly on the side facing of the front door, which had been left open. What breeze there was passing through it helped cool the inside. The afternoon was sweltering. Being engrossed in her work Sasha did not stop to even vaguely think that the knock she heard originated from the hand of George Van Doke, but that it was from one of the workers, perhaps one of the girls of her age who often came to visit.

"Come in." When she looked up there was George Van Doke, standing stiff like, as if he were unable to comprehend what he was next to do. Though it threw her off balance Sasha spoke with calm decorum. She thought quickly.

"Will you take a seat Mr. Van Doke? Sam Feathers is due any minute."

"Thank you." He reached for the nearest chair and sat down. She wished he had retreated to the outside and waited and that she had told him to do as much.

When Sasha had looked up to speak her head was thrown back and her lovely white neck was a thing of arresting lure. She instantly resumed her work, the patching of a shirt for one of the old people on the plantation. She worked with her head bent down; she said no words. She kept at her task. But was aware that there was perspiration above her mouth, on her neck, and on the upper portion of her bosom which was rising and falling with regularity and not at all scarcely defined. She and Adelaide often went about the mansion in lightly clad shirts with sleeves rolled up or wore soft cotton blouses that opened below the neckline. "Is he looking me over? Likely. How do I know? I dare not look up to see." If she had she would have caught George's absorbing eyes flitting upon her now and then and as quickly as lightning turning away lest he be seen. That she felt a glint of discomfort is a natural conclusion. Clearly she did; and contrived with little waste to extinguish her dilemma. Rising, she gave only a quick superfluous show of her face to the visitor and announced that she was to join Mary Tonka to assist her with what she was doing.

"Please make yourself comfortable. I'm sure Sam Feathers will be here right away."

Befuddled, but perceiving the hint, George stood and bowed, departing as soon as Sasha had exited the room and took a chair on the portico. While in her presence he was respectful by ever good measure, not snooty, not ostentatious, not puffed up, not a rake, but a gentleman and quite down to earth, which he had learned she demanded in his first encounter with her, and regretted that he had stumbled in upon her presence.

Sasha spun the matter for a fraction then brushed it aside. "Why didn't I answer the knock to begin with, then I could have told him to take a seat on the portico? I was never so embarrassed in my life. Getting caught like that in this garb. Now he sees how informal the women can be around Aurora when there's no company here. Mary Tonka and Adelaide will have their laugh about this." She returned to the sewing room and took up her work once again, anxious to finish. She had promised to deliver the shirt to its owner before supper.

The Negroes of the community as a whole were only vaguely aware of what went on about Sasha's mother, the talk and all, yet this commotion in no way applied to Sol and Cynthia, nor Brister and Prunelle, all of whom had access to family privacies. The truth was, nobody cared. They would have loved and adored Sasha whether she was Negro or white. Race would have been without influence. It was Sasha; she was the apotheosis, the brilliant one, the beautiful one, God's gift to them all, and all loved her passionately. After a while the gossip died away completely as if nothing had happened and in Sasha's mind nothing had. It was as if she stood high above such calumnies without consciousness in the slightest of their presence. She seemed to be occupied with that phase of summer more than anything else when Andre and Doctor Givens would be there, the latter planning to arrive some time later than Andre who in his letter to Sasha indicated that he could only stay for the abbreviated period of two weeks. She frowned as she read the words. "Only two weeks!" But after all the only reason he was coming was because of her, to be around her, or at least that is a good assumption. It was not to practice medicine. He was to consult at best. Likened to everyone else he was fascinated by her glowing youth and quickness of intellect. Sasha's most fervent thoughts were that he'd keep his promise and not fail to show up, for she was dying to have his company, but there was another reason of some substantial significance: there was a man that she had examined and diagnosed as having an ulcerated stomach. Neither she nor Doctor Lundy were sure. They would welcome another opinion.

Chapter 51

ANDRE ARRIVED. It was mid afternoon. His mother urged him to hasten to Sasha. When his carriage pulled to a halt she was standing on the edge of the portico, from which she dashed down the steps, Mary Tonka catching her breath that she'd fall, and ran to him, who had by then literally jumped from where he stood to the ground, and with one huge involuntary swoosh lifted her into his arms and kissed her lips and cheeks as if he'd never stop, and she his, while Mary Tonka and Adelaide grinned and looked at one another and nodded.

Mrs. Van Doke wasn't well, which was quite generally known. She seemed to have drifted downhill in recent weeks. Andre saw in a glimpse that she had lost weight. Who knew why? Little did they suspect leukemia, "a weakness of the system," they said, and blood samples that Sasha had subjected to the microscope revealed nothing. Despite her fatigue she had someone drive her over frequently to hear Sasha play. The driver was usually Sol. She would have attempted it alone but he protested. "Youse caint do that youself. No suh. I'se gonna take you."

A faintness of suppressed mirth issued from her lips. She was amused at his doggedness. "All right Sol, if you insist."

The playing kept her going, she once remarked. "I wouldn't miss it for the world. It renews me." She seemed to be possessed of a premonition that not a great while longer was she to endure, but was resigned to enjoy it while there was yet time. Not always did Sasha play for her. She sometimes read. In recent days Mrs. Van Doke had thumbed through the library shelves of the Sherette home and had happened upon a work of the medieval period that she had read as a young girl. She no longer read well, her eyesight failing, and asked Sasha if she would go over the lines for her, but not all of them just then. She had reference to a play which was penned by the hands of Jean Racine, a story of pity and terror and unrequited love, where Phaedra, the dominant character, was neither completely guilty nor completely innocent; yet nevertheless was plunged by her fate into an illegitimate passion about which she felt horror from the start. Making every attempt to overcome it, she found she could not. So Sasha for days but in short intervals read and read, the same tragedy over and over while Mrs. Van Doke sat in her rocker and rocked ever so slightly with her eyes closed. Did this story remind her of her own unsuccessful, oft regretted marriage, or did she yearn to hear it again without end because her father had suggested it to her in the freshness of her youth? Sasha wondered, but she would never know. Martha Van Doke was not a lustful woman as might have been just now inferred; she was chaste and a good mother. She was not a Phaedra. The only breach to her credit was the revival of her love for the youth of her childhood after she was married. With the least of perplexity she is here pardoned on the grounds that she was innocently enticed to choose an incorrigible as a mate.

One of the girls on the Sherette plantation announced to Sasha that she was marrying. It was Thea, one of Sasha's closest friends of her age. Sasha and others were invited, Adelaide, Mary Tonka, and Mrs. Van Doke and Andre. They would attend. The wedding was conducted on the portico steps of the plantation home, the bride attired in a lovely pink dress that Sasha had bought her for the ceremony, as well as a pair of solid white slippers for her feet, and had further bought a white pearl necklace which she proudly wore. Mary Tonka had done her hair. Sasha said to her in a whisper that she looked beautiful and Thea hugged her and smiled glowingly. The old minister of Thea's church presided, honored that the ceremony was arranged in this august setting. As he performed the rites Sasha stood on one side of Mrs. Van Doke, Andre on the other. At some point Andre fetched a chair for his mother, realizing that she was tiring. Every once in a while she looked up into Sasha's face and smiled and squeezed her hand as if silently sending hopes and wishes to her.

All through the night Sasha let her thoughts fall on Thea, of her happiness or unhappiness as she moved through the years, for certainly she had lived in poverty for her entire life and was now resuming the pattern, with the prospect that soon she would bear children, and that this too would add to her burden. These things continuing to bear upon her, she the next afternoon at dusk, when the hour was early and the air cool, sat down in the swing by Mary Tonka with a head full of ready questions, but those that mostly prevailed were, "Will she be happy, will she still live in poverty, will marriage and whatever comes with it simply add to her burden?"

And her wise old friend responded without effort, as if her answers had been freshly contemplated and practiced. "I can answer to none of these with sureness my sweet dear. I will reflect where I think I can with a clearness of vision. Poverty is something that is an old companion of mine, or was until I was brought here, and even now I see it all around. I have concluded that it is not poverty however that matters, it's love; if love abounds in a family, no matter the extent that they are lacking, they are happy, the chances are. It's love that overrides. I knew of a man when I was little, a father of a small daughter that he worshiped more than the sun in the sky. They were poor, and he drank some, which added to their burden. I say "their" because he had a wife, though no other children. When he came home at night, out all day looking for work, sometimes finding it, he crept softly to the bedside of his little daughter who was fast asleep and kneeled and woke her and kissed her cheek and scribed the sign of the cross. Going about in a tattered old topcoat, severely denying himself, he spent every spare dime on pretty nice dresses for this little loved one. Indeed, they were poor, but there was love under the roof of that bedraggled house, and God too. He was there. God and love; if these two things are present everything else will work out well. Thea will do all right Sasha; she's strong and was born of the right fabric. Together, she and her husband will break the yoke that binds them. She will see to that. Now, I'll let you guess who that proud father was that I spoke of just now."

"When did he die?"

"Before I was seven. Both my parents."

∞ ∞

When Sasha took up Thea's marriage with Andre some days later he replied that he'd be the best husband that ever was and father too, and she believed him. She had adjudged as much long ago.

They sometimes attended mass in Memphis, sometimes in Jackson, which was but a short distance in comparison; and sometimes Mary Tonka sat between them in the portico swing reading verses from Ecclesiastes, Isaiah, and Proverbs, seldom from the New Testament, but sometimes from John. Once they traveled alone to Jackson when on the way Andre got to thinking about Sasha's loveliness, and how he'd missed her, and when he no longer could stand it he stopped the horses and drew her into his arms and kissed her. She returned it but laughed. "What brought that on my dear Andre? It is so sudden." He answered that he was just thinking about all those days and nights when he was away at Baltimore and she so far away at the mansion, and asked her pleadingly when she would be ready to come start her work with Doctor Givens.

"In due time. He will have to decide that. There's plenty for me to do here in the meanwhile. But thank you for the kiss. It was nice. You'll have to do it again sometimes. Ha, ha, ha." He accused her of being a tease and kissed her again right then and there.

"Do you remember the night when I first sat with you in the swing?" he asked. "I trembled at your closeness. Your beauty frightened me. I was horrified. I wanted to kiss you so badly I didn't know what to do. But hadn't the nerve to try. I'm glad that's over."

"Me too. I enjoy you much more now."

He knew his words were futile but spoke them nonetheless. "And you will even more if you move to Baltimore where I can be with you every free moment. Please hurry and do that."

"In time Andre. There is no rush."

Doctor Givens finally arrived for his two weeks visit, examining the man with an ulcerated stomach—he confirmed the ailment, a peptic ulcer—prescribing a soft diet as a remedy, soft grains and skimmed milk and toasted bread and mirthfully but seriously at the same time suggesting that he refrain from ingesting fatback and leave off alcohol and tobacco. Realizing that treatment of an ulcer of this classification did not prove effective in every instance, and that in the future surgery therefore would become a part of the means of correction, he especially discussed his diagnosis and prospects of cure with Sasha. The patient reported continued weeks of pain followed suddenly by no pain whatsoever. "And awhile after I eats it starts up hurtin again." The final decision for treating the man is not known, that is, the medicine prescribed, if any, for the records are insufficient to bear it out, which is unfortunate, for we would have appreciated knowledge of the outcome, yet enough was said in the narrative and attendant notes on which our story is founded to undergird that much more was known of stomach ulcers in that period of history than is ordinarily vouched. The medical journals of the European hospitals offer the proof. They knew then as they know now that peptic ulcers are open sores that develop on the inside of the human stomach, upper small intestine or esophagus, and that the most common symptom of such an ulcer is abdominal pain: and that peptic ulcers can develop in the lower part of the esophagus of the stomach, the first part of the small intestine (the duodenum) and the second part of the small intestine (the jejunum). It wasn't too long ago that life style factors such as a love of spicy foods or stressful jobs were thought to be at the root of most peptic ulcers and likely Doctor Givens took this to be the fact. Now days doctors contend that a bacterial infection or some medications—not stress or diet—cause the majority of these ailments.

ꕤ ꕤ

She cried when Andre and Doctor Givens left. Time spent together had been splendid for each of them, however brief with Doctor Givens; she clung to them tightly before they climbed into the carriage as if she would never let go. "*Au revoir. Je vous aime beaucoup toutes les deux,"*[7] she called out as they pulled slowly away.

Fall was upon the Sherette plantation once more, the asters and golden rod, Sasha's favorites, proudly flaunting their sparkling beauty, now in their prime and everywhere running rampant, in the glens, in the wood paths, in the stretching expanse of the open fields. "They are likened to a smile on nature's face," she wrote in her diary, daily browsing among them to gather bouquets, bringing them back to Adelaide and Mary Tonka who profusely made fuss and with painstaking exactitude emplaced the lovely fragrances at the perfect conspicuous spot in this or that room, but saddened at the thought that each was soon to lose its luster. The last of October was drawing to a close and Mrs. Laster and Bryon were on the verge of arrival.

They'd stay for a month, they said, upon exiting the steamer onto the Memphis shoreline, joyousness erupting, while the dock workers stared, the bulk of them Negroes, the larger fraction of the lot slaves. Sam Feathers was exerting an effort to bunch together the belongings which he'd load into the carriage, anxious to get started. Sasha tugged Bryon over to where he was occupied and introduced them, whereon Bryon began to pitch in with helping Sam finish his work. Continuing to speculate about the dock workers, which started with his first glance when descending the gang plank, Bryon turned to his new acquaintance for enlightenment, which was brief.

"They're slaves. Are they not?"

"Most are."

"Just like in New Orleans."

"Could be. Never been there."

"Any of them Creole?"

"I doubt it but some might be."

The hour was early, the vessel having docked not a long while after daylight, when the fog was beginning to lift. Sasha sat between Sam Feathers and Bryon as a starter and would ride most of the distance in that position, with Mrs. Laster and Adelaide sitting in the rear seat. Mrs. Laster had pulled a blanket up around her. They stopped for breakfast on the edge of the

---

[7] I love you both very much.

city, a very short stop, and soon after resuming their original seating continued the journey. When traveling a piece more the sun had begun to uncloak its warming rays, and Bryon commenced to look busily about, swarming Sasha with a multitude of curiosities which included that he'd heard this region of the South was prone not at all to infrequent rainfalls. Sasha answered that was so, but that on the day ahead the weather looked fine for the entire trip. "I'm thankful for that," she added, clutching Bryon's arm and then giving him a little hug. They stopped at the way station for fresh horses, then proceeded to near the end of their trip to the Big Hatchie. Sasha offered no apology for its ugliness, explaining instead (as she had to Doctor Givens) that it looked awful to her when she first laid eyes on it, though had adapted to it more and more until at length the river had become a part of her, as if it were an old friend, and was friend to the many various wildlife depending on it for sustenance. "Good fishing there too Bryon. We'll try to go while you're here." Stopping the carriage after crossing the bridge, Sam Feathers said it might be a "good interesting thing" to the guests to look around; this took but a twinkle. Sasha decided she'd sit between Mrs. Laster and Adelaide for the rest of the way, beginning to feel that Mrs. Laster might be hurt if she didn't, and told herself that she ought to have initiated this change some several miles back.

"And your boat ride, how was it? I hope not too taxing on you."

"It wasn't my dear. It was a good trip. It reminded me a hundred times of our sailing together from Corpus Christi to New Orleans. Steamers had just been put onto the high seas as you know and were much faster than the old sailing vessels, especially faster than the one on which we crossed the Atlantic. I'm grateful that Queen Victoria threw her strength behind the modern replacements."

"So am I. We certainly could have used a faster one then. The trip was so long. And wearing. What would I have done without you to help me make it? And Captain Johansen." Mrs. Laster reached over and affectionately hugged her.

When they suddenly broke into view of the mansion, looming lordly through the cedars, Sasha pointed, explaining in the same breath that that was Aurora, and upon seeing it, Mrs. Laster gasped, "So this is where my darling girl has been living. Oh my! You didn't explain all this to me in your letters."

"Better that you see it with your own eyes than for me to explain it with the written word. And there is much to be seen and talked of when we are settled. I will serve as your personal guide."

For awhile, after Sam Feathers had unloaded their belongings, together with Bryon, they looked around throughout the mansion, traversing from room to room. Mrs. Laster broke into a softened smile when her eyes fell on Izu's portrait. Finally Sasha led them to the infirmary, excitedly probing into as much detail as time allowed, but not much was, for just then Mary Tonka whispered to Adelaide that she had set out the supper and asked if she'd return thanks unto the Lord. When all were seated, Adelaide, as was her custom asked that they bow their heads.

> Lord, you have delivered them to us; our loved ones are here, safe and sound. You have protected them while they traveled along their way; we thank you, and now that they are here at this table and we are about to enjoy your bounty, I know you will be pleased with a prayer that my mother passed on to me a long while ago, which I shall now utter: Bless us, oh Lord, for these thy gifts, which we are about to receive, and as we partake of this sustenance may we be mindful of the needs of those who have less. Amen.

"Amen," Mary Tonka added.

During the supper talk Bryon said he was especially attracted to the serpentine driveway and the aggregate pebbles overlaying its surface that led to the mansion, taking care not to leave out the graceful cedars that lined the periphery. "I loved those trees the first time I saw them," said Sasha with tender feeling. "On the very first night I sat out in the swing and listened to the wind blowing through the boughs and limbs. It was a kind of whisper, like the trees were talking to me. Just like they do now when I sit quietly at night listening. A cedar is a beautiful handsome thing Bryon. I agree. I can't think of a single other that matches its stature, but they do seem so lonely."

That night, the splendid bed with the high headboard, graced with the rounded scrolls that capped its foot posts, accommodated a new guest, Mrs. Edweena Laster, who Adelaide had asked to sleep with Sasha.

"Oh, I can't do that. You two continue as you have. She is accustomed to you now. It's just not right for me to break you apart. Any bed will suit me."

"Shhh." Adelaide lifted her finger against her lips. "That cannot be. She was your daughter first, and greatly in need of your arms and comfort. You two will have a lot of talking to do, a lot of catching up."

When they had settled in that evening, lying happily as mother and daughter by one another, Sasha turned to Father Lumas, although she had inquired of him while they were enroute from Memphis.

"How is our Father Lumas, the dear soul? Tell me everything you can."

"As well as to be expected. He is frail, as you surmise in your thoughts, creeping more than walking. While I am around him almost daily it seems he ages a whole month a day at a time. But he is lucid and very lively in his thoughts. Who knows how long he will go on living? Perhaps a long time."

"I am glad to receive your letters of him; I greatly am. I kiss you for them; and do you hear anything of Father Kestner, my other dear soul?"

"About as you do. He is well, or was the last I heard from him. He is ever quick to ask of you. I return an answer to his letters without delay. Your lines lift him up, he tells me; please continue them, and I know you will, and they keep me uplifted too my darling. I try to live and breath with you through your letters. I miss you terribly."

"Yes, and I you."

"When will you take up residence in Baltimore? Is there any hint from your Doctor Givens of when you will start your work there?"

"Next year I feel. The year after, I am fairly confident. He does not pin a time frame down."

"Do you play often for Mrs. Van Doke? Adelaide has spoken of her, says she has known her for a good while, practically for a lifetime. They are close; I sense that in Adelaide's letters to me. She mentions that you play for the dear lady as frequently as your busy schedule allows. You must play for me too, and you will of course. You have become an accomplished pianist, a rarity I think."

"I will play for you my dearest and gladly. I will feel honored and hope that you like what you hear."

"I will, I will, just as Mrs. Van Doke. Ah, when will I meet her?"

"Very soon. I will see to that."

"Oh yes, very soon. But do not go out of your way. You are busy enough as it is with the sick you have to attend. You had to leave from the supper table to see someone in your clinic, your infirmary. Was it serious? Are you pulled away often?"

"Nothing serious. A girl was to pick up medicine for a cough. It seldom happens that I'm pulled away."

"You are so marked, so destined? That is what Father Kestner never fails to stress, and Bryon says it too."

"I will try hard. We shall see. And speaking of Bryon, let me ask of your work with his firm."

"I love my work. I handle the accounts and oh, I haven't written you of this. I'm familiarizing myself with the German language again. The home office is in Berlin. I exchange memoranda with the office people there. They were writing me in English for awhile, until learning I'd studied German in college, and then they almost abruptly started writing everything in their native language. Isn't that hilarious?"

"It's fascinating."

"It is."

"Does Bryon speak German?"

"No. Not fluently. Says he doesn't have the time to learn."

"Or the desire."

"Ha, ha. That's more the truthful reason. I tell him that anyway. I must say that they like him, if salary raises mean anything. And they've rewarded him with two nice promotions."

"Oh."

"Yes. They're moving him increasingly into public relations. This past Christmas he was master of ceremonies at the annual event, at the dinner that is, and the remarks of him by the company officials were most complimentary. I was so proud."

"I'll bet you were. I wish I could have been there."

Time was running out, or so it was in the thoughts of Sasha, for she realized that a month would whiz by and all at once Bryon and Mrs. Laster will have gone. Conscious of this she avidly prepared an itinerary. With Sam Feathers driving, they some days climbed into a lumbering wagon, Adelaide and Mary Tonka with them, and rode and bounced across the fields. Sasha and Adelaide alternately poured out a litany of words describing the scenery, pointing to where they grew cotton and corn and vegetable crops. On other days they rode in the carriage to Brownsville where there was a dry goods store, usually a trip when only Sasha and Bryon and Mrs. Laster were the travelers. If she wasn't inundated with work or community obligations Adelaide accompanied them.

Often Sasha and Bryon strolled the plantation fields alone, staying out a full half day, returning when they were hungry. She had forever savored his companionship, but it seemed more now than ever before, sometimes evinced in her youthful spirited laughter at what perhaps was a funny remark he had relayed. Did she now look at Bryon a bit differently? She was older, was she not, attaining fast to womanhood. Young woman, we will agree. But a gorgeous young woman. Perhaps she was in love with Bryon without consciousness of it, no longer viewing him as big brother. Who can say about that? But lest one is here misled I should hastily clarify that this is merely my own thought and should not be treated even as speculation. She did adore him, and he her, one can be sure of that, and both remained close and affectionate for the rest of their long lives.

"I am thinking of something," he all of a sudden let out, when there was an infrequent tiny moment that exchanges between them had lapsed into silence.

"What? Tell me."

"I keep going back in my head to the day I dropped you and my mother off at the San Fernando Cathedral. You had come there under the guidance of Father Kestner, your dear friend the Priest, and were joining another Priest, Father Lumas and still another, or soon to be, your guardian Lawrence Sherette. Inundated by the Priesthood and its persuasive influences I am amazed that you did not join the nunnery. You could have easily ended up in a convent."

"Easily? Not really. That wasn't for me. My mother might have made a good nun, but not me."

"Why not you?"

"Several reasons. It's just not in me, and you can't be married or previously married. I want a husband and children in time, and truthfully I don't think I'd like to wear the standard clothing."

He had to laugh a little at this. "I can understand. I can't see you in a habit. But have you said it all? Do you have more?"

"Some. The process of advancement is rigorous, you know; you start as a novice, then proceed to a level they call Rassapore, and then to Stavapore. Simply steps up the ladder."

"So you never let it cross your mind to be a nun?"

"Nope."

"I'm glad of that. I like you just the way you are. We all do."

"Thank you. But let me say that I admire the Sisters, Bryon, I deeply do. It's just that being one is not for me. I'm a good Catholic, but don't think my Lord had in mind my being a nun."

"Ha, ha, ha. That's rich. I don't think He did either. He had a work agenda for you that involved tons of other assignments, like joining Doctor Givens in the field of medical surgery. By the way, when will you go to Baltimore?"

"In a year or so."

"That's good. It's a thrilling thing to think about. You'll do much for humanity."

"I do think about it. I often catch myself imagining what it will be like there in a great medical center."

"Will you hate to leave the plantation? And Adelaide?"

"Honestly?"

"Honestly. Of course."

"It'll break my heart. I cry even now thinking about it. I've learned to love this place."

"But you must proceed with your dream. It is your dream, is it not?"

"It is. And I won't really be leaving for good. Nothing like that. It's just the thought of leaving that weighs on me. I've been here for a good while. This is my nest. But I'll return during the summer to work with Doctor Lundy. I owe that to the people and to Adelaide. I try to think of going to Baltimore as an extended vacation, then returning for a stay back home."

Chapter 52

MRS. VAN DOKE could wait no longer to pay call. It was a week after Mrs. Laster and Bryon had arrived, and knowing that they were at Adelaide's she had grown quite anxious to have Sol drive her over to meet Mrs. Laster, whom she had heard much about through Sasha and Adelaide. Mrs. Laster had asked Adelaide what she could expect to see in the woman when she met her, taken by a very pleasant surprise when they came face to face, for despite Adelaide's descriptions she kept perceiving in her mind's eye that she was to meet a person of inborn haughtiness and self appointed loftiness, neither of these traits proving of fact. On the contrary; she found the lady to be of kind disposition and down to earth—but well finished, cultured, and well read—and could readily see why Sasha loved her. When they met, they comfortably began to speak of their native cities, Liverpool and London, how they were different and how they were alike and how they missed them, both cities substantially large, London awesomely large and laying claim to the most renowned theaters in the world. Both women had seen *Othello* and also *Oedipus Rex* on its stages of drama.

"When did you establish residence in America?" asked Mrs. Van Doke.

"Only recently. A few years ago. And you?"

"Too long ago to be exact. Honestly, I don't recall the year. I crossed the Atlantic on a sailing ship of some age and very slow of speed; I definitely recall that experience, whereas, I have word that you traveled by steamer."

"On this last trip from Corpus Christi I did, and the one before that from Corpus Christi to New Orleans. But previous to these two trips Sasha and I traveled on a sailing vessel."

"Oh yes. I think that's what I understood Adelaide to have said."

It was anticipated. As soon as she set foot in the room Mrs. Van Doke migrated straight to Sasha, kissed her on the cheek and slipped her arm around her waist, seemingly reluctant to let go. She had even held onto Sasha while she and Mrs. Laster were introduced and continued to hold on to her as they talked. Yet, after a lapse, withdrew. Sasha said she was about to play. She was attired in her light blue dress with white slippers on her feet and wore a shiny gold bracelet on her wrist. Nothing extravagant. But her attire was perfectly selected for the occasion of which Adelaide and Sasha never failed to make certain. She looked over and smiled at those sitting in wait, but at no one in particular, and as she sat down, the tips of her lovely dress crumpled against the floor. As was usually her custom she played from sheet music, though this time from the works of composers of less stature than Beethoven and Mozart. The new composers were from Baltimore, Doctor Givens having taken the liberty to suggest that they send Sasha a limited selection of their works. Mrs. Laster pressed her hands to her breast and rolled her eyes in exclamation at Adelaide and thought this: "She has awesomely improved, truly a virtuoso. What a beautiful rhapsody. Ah, just look at Mrs. Van Doke. Medicine is not half this good for her."

When she had played for an hour Sasha glanced at her watch and stood.

"Sorry. I must go and change. Doctor Lundy and I are scheduled to see some one that's ill. Is he here Adelaide?"

"He's here. He's in the drawing room. He listened from there. He peeked in on us while you were in session and saw that I had a chair reserved for him. All the same he chose not to disturb. He's ready when you are."

☙ ❧

Lawrence Sherette drove up from Memphis, mindful that Mrs. Laster and Bryon were to leave within two days, and while he intended to see them off when they boarded the steamer for home he nevertheless felt that he should be with them one more time at the plantation. Jim and Lucy had driven down from Nashville to check on Mrs. Van Doke, learning when they arrived that Adelaide was holding a farewell dinner for Mrs. Laster and Bryon that evening to which they were invited. "Adelaide insists on your presence." No seating was prearranged for the dinner, each taking a place helter shelter, which found Sasha sitting between Lawrence Sherette and Mrs. Laster. Lawrence Sherette in his rendering of thanks to the Lord chose a prayer, or a litany as it might be called, that was completely unexpected. It was the Litany of Loretto, which is summarily brief: "Lord, have mercy on us. Lord, have mercy on us. Christ, have mercy on us. Christ, have mercy on us. Lord, have mercy on us. Amen." Then extended the prayer to include blessings on the travelers who were about to embark on their sojourn to San Antonio, terminating with another Amen. When they had shifted to the great room Sol availed himself to feed one log after another to the lapping flames in the fireplace, particularly welcomed by the guests on this evening inasmuch as the weather had turned foul, the thermometer reading dropping by a good twenty degrees.

The talkers were mainly Sasha, Lawrence Sherette, Adelaide, Jim and Bryon, with Mrs. Laster, Mrs. Van Doke, Lucy, and Mary Tonka staying relatively quiet, certainly Mary Tonka, who seldom said anything at dinner or in the midst of guests. The topics were several and sundry, too many here to take up altogether. Lawrence Sherette started with an allusion to the year's harvest, stressing that it was plentifully bountiful and that nature had once again yielded up its kindness, to which in an attitude of joviality Bryon put in that nature was neutral, uncaring whether it yielded up or not, and that God took that stance as well, "for He has to, otherwise what does one say when droughts invade, the crops wither, and the people suffer. Is that God's fault? I don't think so. He's neutral." Lawrence Sherette bobbed his head good naturedly and smiled. From there they moved on to another sphere, to a book recently published and circulated across Europe that was sent to Adelaide by a friend in London, a work penned by the Russian Turgenev who had named it *Rudin.* Sasha co read it with Adelaide, watchful when Adelaide was elsewhere to pick it up and probe into the intriguing contents of the story.

"Did you like it?" asked Bryon.

"I did. I liked the author especially."

"Why is that?"

"His sereneness, his goodness, his style. He has no time for low corruptive plots, that is to say, people at their worst; he is decently restrained in erotic scenes, and steers clear of cruelty and brutal violence."

Lawrence Sherette brought up the probability of civil war breaking out—this was mentioned just once then abandoned—Jim answering that it simply must not be allowed to happen, exclaiming that the voices of the North and South must coalesce into a peaceful settlement of their differences. There seemed to be a mystical notion in the mind of the general public, he said, that if they did not address the subject, putting their heads in the sand so to speak, pretending it wasn't there, the growing storm would dissolve and go away. This was the mystical notion. In truth, their real and recurring notion was that the Great War was eventually to erupt more likely than not. Everyone far and wide had something to say of it, many ill informed. Even the old rustic men of the rural back districts drove into

Brownsville each Saturday to jawbone the issue while lying around on the seed bags in the rear of the general merchandise store.

Mrs. Van Doke and Adelaide had caught a moment when they were alone, managing to disappear into the library to retrieve Turgenev's book from the shelves, for Mrs. Van Doke said she simply must read it, yet they failed to secure it just then, due to a distraction by something else. It dealt with leaving, not the leaving of Mrs. Laster and Bryon, but the future departure of Sasha, which in recent weeks, ever since Andre and Doctor Givens had returned to Baltimore, had weighed heavily upon both women.

"I can feel it coming," said Adelaide with regretful tone. "I don't know when. It gets closer every day. And when it happens it will just about kill me."

"And me too. I can sympathize. But it will land on you the hardest. You two are like two peas in a pod."

"It's the little things I'll miss, the sound of her cheerful voice at early morning, or her kneeling with me in prayer at bedtime, or the sight of her galloping her sorrel across the fields. As the old saying goes, I'll miss her presence more than her absence." Martha Van Doke laughed softly. Then Adelaide paused for a moment, putting her fingers to her lips, pensively glancing across the lawn at the cedars and went on.

"Well, there's one good thing about it. Doctor Givens says she can return and do her work here for the people in the summers and Heaven knows I'll be thankful for that."

☙ ❧

When they gathered at the passenger's dock in Memphis two days later Sasha and Mrs. Laster clung tearfully to one another, both pouring out utterances of loving affection, with Sasha promising to visit her and Bryon in the not very far off future, yet not really seeing how she could break away to honor her commitment.

"You must darling. The steamers move slower than we'd like and the trip is long, but—."

"That won't matter. That won't matter. I must visit. Oh, I wish the trains would hurry and start to run. I mean everywhere, and then I could come to see you any time and be there in short length."

"Yes you could. And I hear that the trains are on the verge of starting up in Texas pretty soon. Won't that be nice, and you can be there often as you said."

They sent Mrs. Laster and Bryon on their way, though Sasha remembered that there was another farewell waiting to be affected within the next few days, that of Jim and Lucy, who were leaving for Nashville, and when that hour was upon them she was there to say goodbye, with Lucy gathering her in her arms and hugging her and kept on hugging her, finally letting go, then climbed into the carriage. Sasha looked on wistfully.

"We'll see you in the spring," Lucy tearfully said. "I love you."

"I love you back Lucy. And you too Jim."

They had said their goodbyes to Mrs. Van Doke a few minutes before, who elected to remain inside. Neither Mr. Van Doke nor George was in sight. She turned and went in to spend a while with the ailing lady but was not asked to play. She was too tired. Sasha then put her to bed, tucked her in, and kissed her brow.

The calendar foretold that Christmas was again upon them. But the people needed no calendar to tell when the holiday season was to occur, for that had become second nature to them; they could sense it, as surely as the human system senses and knows that spring or summer or fall or winter is just around the corner. But neither the people nor the calendar could portend the unfolding of other eventualities which were to take place in the near days and continue on into the summer. We shall take these up as they sequentially fell into play.

Christmas came and went, the same as the year before, and the year before that, the same as long before Sasha's presence on the plantation, the gifts delivered to the workers and family who had assembled on the north lawn, singing and spreading good cheer, with the men bantering in repartee, telling jokes and casting funny clever remarks back and forth, while the children squealed and dashed about. Andre had returned home earlier than expected, having gotten there a week before Christmas. Sasha had put him in the serving line beside Sol.

Sasha and Sol had gone on a quail hunt with him the day after his arrival in a brushy terrain on the breaks of the Big Hatchie bottom lands, carrying with them Sol's two pointers. Sasha had relayed to Andre that she was not a hunter of wildlife, that she couldn't bring herself to pull the trigger whose deadly intent was to snuff out a life forever, but pledged that she'd not interfere with him in his pursuit of the sport. She'd turn her head she said and plug her ears with her fingers.

"Life is too precious to kill, is that it," he returned, "even if it's one of the lower species?"

"A life is a life Andre. My job is to save a life, not take it."

"But there are exceptions. We have to butcher hogs and kill chickens. The meat sustains us."

"Agreed. But what I'm talking about is killing for the thrill of it. For sheer pleasure. Target practice. In that, I see wrong."

Andre hardly agreed, quail being one of his fondest delicacies, and knew that Sasha tremendously savored quail meet too. But his heart was tender to her inclinations. He reckoned that the small bird was such an infinitely pretty little thing that Sasha could not bear to see it destroyed. "Sol can steal off out here and hunt," he thought, "and drop off a mess to Adelaide cleaned and ready for the skillet."

It then was not surprising that he stood and watched a sizeable covey peacefully wander off without firing a shot, calling off Sol's two pedigree pointers who seemed confused, whining and moiling as if they had failed to discharge their proper duty, and motioned to Sol to unload his gun, who understood. He'd heard the conversation. Never again in his lifetime did Andre forage for wild game. He decided it then and there. "Sasha is right. We are doctors; we are supposed to save lives, not take them. And the truth is I do this more for sport than for need." But Sasha liked to fish and saw this as an acceptable substitute. Somehow she could reconcile this sport as long as the fish were plucked from the water for human consumption or thrown back if not used. When their children were young Andre particularly told to them the story of the bird hunt that never fully happened, how the attitude that Sasha took toward needlessly taking the life of an animal rightly affected him and that he hadn't since picked up a gun, hoping they were of like mind when they grew up."

"Is that true Momma?" one of the children asked. "Did he quit hunting for good?"

"It's true darling. I believe it's true. If he's broken his promise I don't know about it."

The winter night was cold, the sky serene, and the moon shone down with incandescent brightness. Despite the frigidity of the air they sat in the swing and laughed and talked, wrapped in bulky furry coats, a blanket covering their feet that Mary Tonka had supplied, and gladly accepted the hot cups of coffee she thoughtfully served. There was another night when the moon was full that they walked rather than take the carriage to a square dance to which Thea had invited them, held by the workers of the plantation, with Andre grasping the lantern as they sauntered along while she clung to his arm. The site where they were going was less than the distance of a mile. When they arrived, the musicians had been for awhile playing, a good half hour at the least, and people were circling round and round in happy abandon. A cacophony of laughter rippled across the terrain. The caller could be heard plainly above the banjo picking and fiddling, and the laughter, commandeering the "do se do."

"Let's find an opening and take part," said Andre.

The dance was mostly that of a square dance, but replaced at times with the contra dance and the polka and with other varied forms. The workers knew many dances. Andre and Sasha were amazed. The one in which Sasha delighted the most required partners to advance and pass right shoulders, where without turning each moved to the right and passed in back of the other whereon then they faced one another, then moved backwards and passed left shoulders, then returned to their starting positions. And so it went. Sasha found it natural to be among the Negroes, who were expert at the art. For Andre to be among them in this fashion was less natural, but if Sasha participated, so would he and never let on.

On and on they danced, the good people looking on, honored that two young doctors were a part of them, as if they were family, and each time Andre and Sasha arose from their respite, they were met with applauds, and yipes, and effusive clapping. When they were ready to leave an old man, an apparent spokesman for the community with weather worn face and aging posture slowly edged over and murmured "Thank you," meaning for their coming, seeming at once frantic and delighted in the same countenance when Sasha reached her arm around him. It was late, past one. But the yellow moon had only slid westward by a slight. On their way home they walked briskly, Andre holding the lantern higher at times to help them better follow the narrow pathway while Sasha stayed close at his side, sometimes slipping her arm around his waist. She talked incessantly; she was happy. She'd had a good time."

Chapter 53

DRAWING EVER nearer the climax finally had to boil to a head, the confrontation of father and son, shades of Theseus and Hippolytus, characters in the Greek tragedy where Theseus, the father, wrongfully forces exile on his son. Andre was to leave the next day for Baltimore. Apprehension had begun to run through him that the face off was soon to happen, yet hoped almost with desperation there was some way around the unpleasant episode. When Jordan Van Doke asked his son to sit with him in the living room at mid morning he was not the least uncivil but polite and fatherly. In his heart he greatly loved his young son, perhaps even more than his two oldest, and perhaps it was the sentiment of this love that had brought on his disturbance. Andre listened attentively as Jordan Van Doke was certain he would.

The father commenced with an allusion to blood mix, contending that it was a bad thing for the lineage of the family, his family, meaning the resulting off spring from Sasha and Andre, beseeching him to consider the troubles that derived from the fusion of genes of opposite color. "Things like that just can't be. They're ruinous to the family stature. Think of the social and political ties suddenly splitting away from us, let alone the potential of high positions for my sons in government. Besides, you'll grow tired of her eventually."

At this Andre flushed crimson, feeling an impulse to staunchly reject the words that had fallen on his hearing, insults to the purest and dearest person in his life, without whom he would have no life at all. But he did not just then retaliate, the iron will of his reserve counseling him to hold his composure.

Then Jordan Van Doke continued, intending to carry on for the longest while. He had decided to infer a threat. Not in words plainly spoken but in cleverly veiled innuendos he came close to letting his young son know that should he not heed his wishes the resultant effect might well be that he would take the necessary action to remove him from his will. It was clear to him that Andre had grasped the meaning and it was here that he was interrupted, would not be allowed to go on without contest, for his young son had stiffened, half rising from his chair, bristling with anger, and finally lifted himself up entirely and began to speak. Jordan Van Doke had seriously misjudged.

"You do not know her. She is incomparable, far above me, far above most, born of great intellect and character. Don't you see that she's a medical genius, far surpassing me? She's the one who will attain to prominence, not me. I love Sasha, I love her with all my being. I cannot live without her. The question is not will I have her but will she have me. I pray that she will. As to whether I'm part of the plantation in future years, that is of no consequence, for my sight is set on the practice of medicine, along side Sasha and Doctor Givens in Baltimore. Growing cotton is nowhere in my veins, not even a figment's worth. It never has been. Let those that deserve the land have it. Give it to the slaves."

Jordan Van Doke had not attempted to interrupt, although bitterly stunned and ready to snort, feeling at the last second however that the wiser course was to hold it in because the schism might worsen and escalate into a full scale eruption, and at once began to soften, to wish that he had employed a different tactic, yet was at a loss as to what that might have been. His son had stood up to him, had revolted, which he least expected, and now he, the father, had begun to feel regret. But the damage was inflicted, and so what could he do, he surmised, but back away, politely, softly, with remarks that they could take up the matter at a later time. With this he strode to the door and left.

Andre, still flushing, went to see about his mother who had heard.

"You did the right thing Andre. You had to declare yourself. Your honor was at stake. You had to defend Sasha. Settle down. All will turn out well. Sasha loves you, I am confident she does, and that is all that matters. I wish with all my heart that I live long enough to see the two of you happily married."

☙ ❧

It was a short time thereafter that in an air of excitement Sasha opened a letter from Mrs. Laster, having expected one any day.

> My dearest. I cannot tell you in adequate words of my ecstatic happiness of being with you for a whole month. You have changed a bit, yes you have, and you are more beautiful than ever. When I returned home I was suddenly lonely, terribly lonely, but recovered and presently I am writing you this letter.

It is yet strange to me. You started out on an island off the coast of Africa, and went from there to San Antonio and then to New Orleans and then from there to the Sherette plantation, a beautiful place that seems to be designed just for you. I think God follows you around to see that you are cared for. I thank Him every night for watching after my angel.

You and Andre are indeed a handsome pair. I haven't seen you together, you realize, but Adelaide says you are. She is very fond of Andre, and his mother. One day you will marry Andre. Mark my word. You mentioned when I was there, when we were lying in bed encompassing everything under the sun that you felt a touch of guilt in regard to Mr. Van Doke's disposition toward Izu's portrait, that it's like you are coming between him and his son. Pshaw. Wash that away. They are lucky that God brought you to them, and as for the old man, well, he needs a new head screwed on his shoulders.

And now that I have spewed out this last emboldened line, I shall go, but not before reminding you my darling that you are to come see me within the year. I love you more than I am able to express.

Edweena

Then there was another letter, not to Sasha but to Adelaide, a fairly lengthy one from Harry—their letters to one another were seldom less—in which he swept across the occurrences of New Orleans society in recent weeks and wove in his usual amorous affections, at last scripting a line in which he said he couldn't keep up with everything whirling about in Washington, because that was too far away, yet had a trickle of news that he said might prick her ears, quoting a snippet from the article that he had read. "The Democratic Party is the pawn of Slave Power and the Slave Power with its abundance of cheap labor intends to destroy the workers of the North." He went on to say himself, "It looks like the national congress has a divisive issue on its hands and I'm wondering about the eventual backlash of all this on the South. Lincoln is bound to win the election and Lincoln is Republican." Adelaide decided to let Sasha read Harry's letter—who'd been stretching to make out the wording while standing virtually against her—thinking that his commentaries and descriptions of societal happenings might produce that warm glowing smile she so much liked to see, for Sasha was ever consumed with the Crescent City, particularly anything having to do with the events of a social flavor. Sasha eagerly took it and read it twice while Adelaide amusedly studied the changing of her countenance; yet Sasha surprised her, mentioning only herself and Harry, nothing of the contents making up the rest.

"Ah, Adelaide," she exuded with a flush, "Harry is the sweetest kind of fellow. He loves you. I know he does. Someday I hope you will marry him."

"Ha, ha, ha. How imaginative. But maybe I will. We shall see."

☙ ❧

Spring revolved around once more, evincing that another season had passed, heralding that the cutting ploughs were soon to be pulled from the storage sheds to turn and condition the soil, and then the smoothing, the task of the harrow, and then next there was the planting machine, a contraption of four metal cylinders called hoppers that housed the seed and fed them into the furrows with an exactness of calibrated revolutions. The industrial age of Europe had advanced across the ocean to America, even to its vast back lands of agriculture. This was a time also when Adelaide, Mary Tonka, and sometimes Sasha were seen with hoes and rakes and instruments needed for pruning and tending and nurturing the hydrangeas, the daffodils, and azaleas, and no few number of varying species.

"Sasha won't join us today Mary Tonka," said Adelaide.

"Oh! Something happened. Somebody sick?" Mary Tonka had spent the night with someone herself, a sick worker, and had returned late that morning.

"Andre popped up unexpectedly to see in on his mother. No one knew he was to be here."

"Ah. When did he come?"

"Yesterday. Late in the afternoon. As you can guess he wasted no time zipping over to see Sasha when he arrived."

"I didn't see him."

"You were away looking in on a neighbor."

"That's right. I was. How long is he here?"

"A few days. A very few he says."

"Where are they now?"

"On the planting machine. They're planting early corn."

"Planting corn! I've never—."

"Well it's like this. Sasha started thinking she'd like to try her hand at planting. The contraption somehow fascinated her, you know how she is, so she talked Sam Feathers into letting her do it for a test."

"And Andre's with her?"

"Unh hunh. When he arrived she told him what she was going to do the next day and rather than spend time without her he pled with Sam Feathers to allow him to ride with her. Sam told me about that. 'Ain't that Sasha something,' he said and burst out laughing. I think she could talk him into anything in the world, don't you?"

"I do, and I agree, she is, she is, oh, indescribable. But if she likes it let's let her do it. I wish I could be out there seeing the two of them right now. What a sight that would be." Mary Tonka attempted to smother a giggle by holding her hand over her mouth as if embarrassed at her own antics.

"Yeah, I'd like to see them too," said Adelaide, but her thoughts were on something else. "Anyway, I'm glad Andre's home. Martha isn't well. Seeing him gives her a badly needed lift. He didn't say exactly how long he's to stay. Just for a few days is what he said. But I wish he would for quite a while."

When Andre had been home for two days Jim and Lucy arrived, more than a coincidental occurrence in that Andre had written Jim of his intention to visit their mother on a certain date to ascertain her condition and to provide comfort for a short while. Jim had decided he should be there as well and had specified his date of arrival in a letter that he had mailed to Andre. Prunelle and Brister were also a part of the trip. During their stay, Mrs. Van Doke asked Andre to pay call on the minister of a small white church in the back country which she had established in years past to determine the quantity of hymnals needed for the congregation and to make preparations for buying them. Andre said gladly that he would and would attend to it the next morning, instinctively thinking of taking Sasha with him, provided she could break away. As it happened Sasha said she'd be delighted; but there were those in addition who were desirous of going too, Lucy and Prunelle, for whatever the reason. In not too many years expired Lucy vividly recalled the events of their trip.

> The sun was shining brightly but the air was uncomfortably cool for that time of year. Downright chilly. It was late spring. Jim and I had decided to take a trip to the plantation to check on Mrs. Van Doke and give her all the moral support we could. Prunelle and Brister decided to join us. After we'd arrived by about a day Andre told me that he and Sasha were going to the little church to arrange for the hymnals. I wanted to go too and so did Prunelle when I said to her I was going along. I wanted to more than any other reason just to be around Sasha.
>
> We were riding in Mrs. Van Doke's carriage, Prunelle and I in the back and Sasha sitting by Andre. They were so beautiful, so young. They talked excitedly all the way, not paying me or Prunelle the least of attention. I didn't want them to. I only wished that what I witnessed could last forever. Sasha had met Andre, Prunelle and myself at the La Belle, where I climbed into the waiting carriage and sat down in front. Andre had helped me climb up. Sasha and Prunelle climbed up and took

seats in the back. When Andre had driven a distance well beyond the mansion, well out of sight, I'm guessing a mile or so, he stopped. "Whoa." No one should see what he was about to do. Certainly first and foremost Mr. Van Doke, my father in law who was ruffled with his son and had been ever since a heated exchange between them. Sasha and Andre preferred that Mr. Van Doke not see them together side by side in the carriage. They were doing all they could to avoid making things worse. Everything was sort of secretive. As the carriage drew to a halt Sasha rose and started climbing down, Andre hurrying around to reach his arm to steady her. Prunelle rolled her eyes at me. There was a mischievous smile on her face and I smiled back. I knew what Andre wanted. For Sasha to sit by him; that was the scheme, which Prunelle and I knew of well in advance, so I, with Andre's help, lowered myself to the ground and climbed in the back with Prunelle. Then he helped Sasha into her seat up front next to his. They were obviously not trying to restrain the excitement that shone in their faces. Prunelle rolled her eyes again. She loved those two young people and loved seeing them together and knew that I did too. Our thoughts always seemed to coincide. At times I think of her more as my friend or sister than I do as my servant. I felt then, as I do now, that besides my husband, Prunelle was my best and most trusted friend, and I have to speak the truth, at least with myself. There are things, tiny secluded secrets, which I share with her that I won't with anyone else. I love her.

Well, there they were, two beautiful young things side by side. They were so in love, that was plain, but I don't know when it started. Maybe when they first saw one another. Prunelle said there was talk of it among the slaves soon after Sasha arrived. I don't know how they knew. Sasha was a beautiful thing, a European looking girl with apparent French features, about sixteen years old at the time, enviably slender, straight up and down shoulders, and nice white effeminate skin, so nice and inviting that you wanted to touch it. Especially the males, Negro and white. But it soon got about that Andre had eyes for her and so the Negro males tried their best not to look at her if they felt some one might see them. She smiled wanly. That seems to stand out in my remembrance. She had smiled all the way. I liked that but actually didn't know whether she smiled a lot or not. I hadn't been around her all that much. But this I did know or found out. When Andre looked over at her, sometimes touching her arm, her smile became broader, much broader and ebullient and lovely. Her face literally lit up and her eyes danced and sparkled. Ah, she was so redundant of life. Her coat I must not pass over, especially the way it fit upon her. It was of a nice expensive texture, perhaps woolen, yes I think it was, very dark, pulled snugly around her slender figure and buttoned all the way up, from top to bottom, with extra large sized buttons. I think they were gold. They stopped at the collar which circled her neck and fanned outward at her throat. And there was something of a soldier's cap atop her head, dark black in the manner of her coat and there was a tiny spangle affixed to the side of it that glittered when she was in the sunlight. It was precious and I judged expensive, as was every piece on her person. I began to wonder where it all had come from but shouldn't have. She and Adelaide took many a trip to Memphis where they stayed the night then the next day spent hours in the biggest and best stores getting Sasha measured and outfitted.

We were going to a white Methodist church four miles north, way back in the country, to see about purchasing some hymnals for the congregations' use and to take up a number of other needs with the pastor. The pastor watched us drive up. He was expecting us. He knew Andre was there on behalf of his mother who helped him generously with his ministry. We stopped and Andre jumped down and hurried over to help Sasha from the carriage. Then he came to help us down, first me, then Prunelle, and then we three women walked ahead of Andre toward the church doorway, Sasha in front. The pastor invited us in, vibrantly assuring us that he was glad to see us. I think he truly was. He shook Andre's hand then did the same with the rest of us. He stole repeated glances at Sasha. They were quick but I noticed. I wondered if he had an inkling that he had come face to face with the beautiful girl of the plantation he'd heard so much about, or if this was someone else. He seemed puzzled. I could tell that he was moved and stunned by her beauty. She would have caught anyone's eye. Just as she did mine. Now and then he glanced at her black lace up boots with high rounded heels, high, but not very high. The leather leg covers rose above her ankles by eight inches I supposed. At first I wasn't exactly sure because her coat dropped down to practically ankle level and covered most of her footwear. But every once in a while she pulled her coat up a bit, and then I could see that I was about right with my supposition. Her boots were pretty and shiny and very stylish, as I recall. Something you'd see in a magazine from Paris. That's how they struck me. I had the impression that she and Adelaide conferred with each other quite thoroughly in regard to her clothes wear.

Andre said we'd need to get on with business, that pretty soon we'd have to start home. He didn't tell the pastor about it, but Sasha had said she'd like to stop on our way back to break branches from the wild bush that grew on the shoulders of the road which were loaded with pretty red berries. She'd hang a wreath of them on the walls in the infirmaries. We all sat down around a heavy oak table without a cloth on top. Andre mentioned the hymnals. The pastor said he needed twenty, or thirty if Mrs. Van Doke could spare him that many. "Gladly," answered Andre, then volunteered that Sasha and Adelaide probably could pick them up for him at one of the Memphis publishing houses. The pastor answered "By all means, if they'd be so kind." Andre brought up the accounting of records, mainly that Mrs. Van Doke liked efficient record keeping and was there anything that could be done about that while we were on visit. He answered he had a few items that he knew should be entered into the ledger. Andre looked at Sasha, who spoke up that if he had any to give them to her and she'd take time to post them. The pastor left for another room and promptly brought back a good many disheveled papers. Sasha took them, as well as the new ledger that Andre had brought, and went over to a side table. She was quick, looking at each sheet for only a fraction. Her nimble fingers had done the entries in minutes, then she returned the ledger to Andre. After a peek at the figures he said fine, that they looked good, and then said to the pastor that perhaps, if Sasha had the time, she might return every other month to attend to additional entries. He repeated that Mrs. Van Doke liked good records. Sasha said she'd do it and the pastor appeared delighted and grateful. I didn't know it at the time but one day afterwards Jim explained to me that Mrs. Van Doke owned the church, paid the pastor's salary, and paid all other expenses of the little recluse. She had even set off a section for cutting timber which when sold the proceeds went to the church. I'm sure that's why she was insistent on good record keeping.

Andre asked was there anything else, and the pastor, hesitatingly, shy like, said he needed extra seating. "How many pews?" Andre asked. The pastor said he didn't know, then Andre said that if he had a tape handy they'd measure the space and that he'd see into having the seats ordered. The pastor smiled gratefully and walked hastily to a back room and returned with a yardstick. The two of them measured off the section in need of the seats while Sasha copied down the figures. Just before we departed Sasha proposed that the church could use an icon or two of the Virgin Mary, and suggested that she might get them the next visit she made to Memphis. The pastor said he'd be grateful if she did. I don't think there was anything else. So we all got into the carriage, Andre giving us support, and went on our way.

I am now so reminded of that trip and how happy Andre and Sasha were. When we return to the plantation they won't be there. I'll miss them terribly. They're in Baltimore presently into their medical studies. Let's see, she's about nineteen or twenty or maybe eighteen. I really can't be sure. Andre's about twenty three. Maybe twenty four. They'll make wonderful doctors. I need badly to write Sasha a letter. I simply must.

ꕥ ꕥ

When Andre had left the mansion one morning his father had departed hours earlier, in an effort, apparently, to avoid coming face to face with his son, against whom his anger had grown. Little suspecting that his timing could not have been worse Andre left for Baltimore the next day, as planned, compelled to join Doctor Givens, feeling that he was badly needed to help with patient care. Bidding goodbye to Sasha, he crawled into the carriage with Sam Feathers and started eastward. He had meant to consult with his father, his own feelings having softened, hoping for a reconciliation, which was an accomplishment that fate had designated not to happen.

Jordan Van Doke had gone somewhere that morning, but where no one knew, unless it was Sol, who shared with Cynthia that he most likely was with the attractive slave woman who, because of the continual flow of gifts he showered upon her, welcomed his company or in any event tolerated his presence. On this occasion he stayed away two weeks or more which was corroborated by Sol, not by Mrs. Van Doke, who sought by every means to avoid intercepting her husband. Jordan Van Doke's health had recently worsened from the increased use of alcohol and it was noticed by George that his choice of decision as it pertained to business was often fraught with error. George took it that it was due to his father's irascibile nature, and that any ordinary thinking person might have adjudged in like manner, on later reflection however surmising that the oddity of his behavior was a signal of his impending demise. His illness was more severe than suspected. In time it worsened. They found him in an open field on a fall morning, face down, his life virtually over. He'd suffered a stroke. He was discovered by a field hand who went scurrying as fast as his legs were capable to Sol.

"Mas Jordan fell. Mas Jordan fell."

"Where? Where?" Sol's mind was wildly in flight.

"In de field."

"Git Master George."

George, who was nearby, went swiftly, running, panting, frantic, consumed by fear, upon arrival dropping to his knees close over his father, slightly lifting his head, hoping there was still a breath. A semblance of garbled murmurs issued from the lips of the dying man that George seemed to decipher, and then there were no more. Lowering his father's head tenderly to the moist earth he stood erect, motioning for Sol to take charge, who began to deliver instructions to the slaves gathered around to pick up the body and transport it directly to the infirmary, not to any other room, for that was contrary to Mrs. Van Doke's preference. The body would lie there until prepared and removed for burial.

Paying call on her friend Martha the next day to speak condolences Adelaide was intercepted by George on leaving the premises, who ventured to ask for help in the selection of a minister to preach the funeral, the name of Lawrence Sherette foremost in his mind, and was relieved when Adelaide answered with minimal contemplation that perhaps her brother was the most suitable and available person for performing the ritual. George at once agreed and thanked her, yet was not finished. There was the further necessity of choosing the funeral whereabouts, not a difficult recommendation for Adelaide to render, in that she knew it could not be conducted in the Van Doke mansion. As an alternative she suggested that a huge tent be raised at the family grave site, allowing for an overflow in attendance, particularly from the slave community. Again, George concurred.

In their early marriage years Jordan and Martha had selected a family cemetery plot near a wooded grove of cottonwoods, a well known fact to their three children, and to others, chief of which was Adelaide, Mary Tonka, Sam Feathers, and Cynthia and Sol. This decision had not been altered over the years, nor did Jim and George now seek to change it otherwise, for where else could their father have undergone burial.

Word did not reach Andre in time for him to be present, the matter receiving extensive discussion between Jim and George that they should delay the burial, yet realizing finally that to wait longer was impractical. Not surprisingly, only a trickle of slaves had congregated in the back of the huge tent for the service, silent, somber, old people who had been tied to Jordan Van Doke for much of their lives, and then there were the expected ones who sat at the very front, Jim and Lucy, George, Adelaide, Sasha, Mary Tonka and Sam Feathers. Doctor Lundy had also come and sat beside Adelaide.

Lawrence Sherette did his best. What could he say in good conscience about a man who in his mind had sinned against God and humanity. "He was a slave owner. What else can I say? Well, I won't say that. I'll speak of the positives, his family, his sons, that he migrated here in his youth, that he was a friend of my father, and that he did much to promote the affairs of the community," and after these acknowledgements were properly enunciated he uttered a very brief prayer.

> Oh God, Who has commanded us to honor our father and mother, have compassion in Thy mercy on the soul of this father and forgive him of his sins, as You would forgive all who have sinned, and may You grant that his children one day will meet him again in the joy of eternal brightness. Through Christ our Lord. Amen.

Chapter 54

THE FUNERAL over, the body was transferred to the burial plot amidst the cottonwoods where again Lawrence Sherette uttered the best words that he could derive which seemed to him appropriate. Sasha stood between Adelaide and Mary Tonka, her face still and emotionless, perhaps dwelling on Andre, and that in a sense she was standing in for him in his absence. She was attired in black, as were Adelaide and Mary Tonka and wore a hat upon her head to which a veil was attached that fell across her face. When the cool wind blew caressingly upon her the adornment seemed to quiver. Adelaide reached and took her hand. Lawrence Sherette uttered the closing remarks, an old Negro woman began to sing mournfully, and when she quit the last note Jordan Van Doke was lowered into his final resting place. The small crowd began to disassemble.

Andre was home shortly, Sasha doing what she could to offer consolation, staying close, particularly observing that he took his father's passing stoically, showing but a tinge of emotion, but she realized that there were undulating thoughts, conflicts he was sorting through, for after all, she reasoned, he had brawled with his father wherein on both sides feelings were injured, and the aftermath was that he felt some measure of guilt. Andre did his best by his mother, who he saw was not feeling well, offering comfort to her by his presence, which brought comfort to himself, yet declined to bring up his father, not at first in any event, asking her nothing of the funeral, aware that she had opted to stay home from the service, figuring she must be working through a preponderance of misgivings toward the man. He would remain home for some time, well into the spring, and then begrudgingly leave for Baltimore.

Jim and Lucy had elected to stay on for a while, seeing as how, the same as Andre, that Mrs. Van Doke was going down hill, although there was another reason: Jim needed to inspect the will, a new one he had learned of, shocked at what he found, for Jordan Van Doke had instructed his attorney to draft a radical amendment to the original, naming therein Jim and his middle son George as the beneficiaries. Andre's name was glaringly absent. "Great Holy Spirit, what have we here?" Jim voiced in silence. His mother had entitlement to the entirety of his father's holdings, money and property, and it would accrue to her under the law of the state, and to no one else, and besides—and Jim was cognizant of this—she had an investment right to the plantation that her father had concocted years previously when she married Jordan Van Doke, a document that Jim would inspect with tedious scrutiny. One way or another, in his judgment, she had rights entire to every penny of her husband's worth, and hers, as provided by the existing statutes. It was his immediate conclusion that the deed his father had recently directed an attorney to prepare was null and void and frowned at the attorney's decision to yield to his father's wishes. "Perhaps there was a reason that now eludes me. I shall see." He would withhold this knowledge from his mother for the time being, until he had subjected it sufficiently to incisive scrutiny, and thoroughly worked through it with George; and neither would he divulge it to Andre. "This must be handled with caution. I must set this matter right. I need time."

And time marched on. The holidays had made their advent and left, but the winter persisted, a very long and dreary winter, accompanied by snow and sleet, forcing the people of the community to stay inside far more than they liked, those of the Sherette plantation sitting by the fireplaces, Adelaide and Mary Tonka sewing and knitting, Sasha attending to the affairs of the infirmary and reading. Jim and Lucy had returned to Nashville some time previously. Lately it was Mrs. Van Doke's tendency to lie down for a midafternoon nap, in part because it helped her feel better, the other part due to the dreariness of the weather. She had awakened to find Andre sitting at a side table in thought, not reading, but pondering, and thus waved him over, reaching for his hand as he sat down on the bed beside her.

"I've put something off Andre. I need to address it." Her words and this unexpectedness landed on him with a jolt. But it wasn't what he feared. "It's about your father."

"You don't have to—."

"No, listen. I need to, I choose to. Hear me."

"Of course. Whatever your wish."

"He was not altogether a bad person; there were good qualities in him, as there are in every human. He loved his sons, often saying as much, and I think he loved you the most. And all in all he treated me fairly enough, especially at the beginning, but then he became unfaithful."

"I didn't know that."

"I spared you. Jim knew. I discussed it with him. I see he never revealed it to you. He said he wouldn't. Jim is such a good man."

"Jim's never said a word."

"I'm glad he didn't. But let us go on. When I married your father he was a nice looking young man, and a swashbuckler. Nevertheless, I had on the beginning some reason to believe we'd make a go of it; and I think we would have had he not started to pursue the use of slavery. On that we clashed, fiercely."

"I've heard. I've seen."

"I felt for awhile he'd back away, quit, and he promised to, though in time backslid. Increasingly it became harder to bear, sinful I thought, and it was sinful, and would have left him were it not for the three precious children that I was to raise and care for."

"I'm sorry mother."

"Don't be. Do not needlessly concern yourself with what might have been for me, or what was on me that was hard to endure, for there were many things in my span that were magnificently enjoyable, starting with my sons, and having Adelaide and Mary Tonka close by was another; and then the last and most recent, our beloved Sasha. I wish so badly that I had met her a long time ago, but on the other hand I suppose not, for she did not exist a long time ago. She does now and you sense what I am leading to." Andre grinned. "If God is willing, someday marry her, beg her if you must. She will make a precious wife and mate and a most splendid affectionate mother. There is no other like her."

"I echo that."

Then Martha Van Doke ceased to say anything else for the time being, appearing to rest, glancing with a face of melancholy through the massive window at the frigid snow and ice, and then inhaled deeply and let out a breath, after this closing her eyes as if she were sleeping. She wasn't, she was thinking.

"I have a feeling about Sasha that bother's me Andre. I wish I didn't but I do."

"What is it?"

"I wonder."

"Wonder what?"

"Whether she feels a bit of guilt over your clash with your father."

"What! For Heaven's sake. How could she?"

"Only by reasoning that if she'd never set foot on Sherette soil all would have remained well between father and son."

"Ah. I cannot believe that such thoughts are anywhere in her. She surely understands. Sooner or later a rift was bound to happen irrespective of the reason. My father was a volatile person."

"Precisely. And I hope that I am wrong, for she is the dearest thing and I would not see her hurt for the world."

☙ ❧

Wrapped in heavy furs and thickly insulated boots, Sasha and Andre took rides here and there in the carriage and one day covered the entire distance to Brownsville and back because supplies were needed, relieved to be outside in spite of the cold. The road was icy, slick and hardened, the condition proving to be a good thing in that the frozen surface lessened the effort on the horses because the wheels rolled easier than otherwise.

"Lucky horses Andre, don't you think?"

"Yeah. I do. Lucky in the respect that the road could be worse, you know, snowy and muddy.

"Is there a livery stable where we can leave them while we shop?"

"There's one. I've used it many times."

"Fine. And aside from buying the supplies, what else for us?"

"I'm hungry already. There's a feeding place, a café that serves all sorts of vittles and coffee."

"That sounds good. But Mary Tonka packed food for us and a cider jug of coffee." Sasha had served them coffee from it once while enroute, of which Andre had not since commented.

"Well maybe. Let's see how things pan out."

When they reached Brownsville and turned the horses over to the livery owner for feeding and watering Andre and Sasha went to the general store and bought the supplies, then next decided to look in on the small café that Andre had spoken of.

"Let's see about coffee," he suggested. "After that we can leave if you like."

The façade of the establishment was of rustic crudeness and of discouraging appearance in all other regards. Sasha had misgivings about going in. But she said nothing. Meeting them as they entered was the waitress, there was only one, with an apron tied to her waist, grossly overweight, depicting a rounded pinkish face, though a pleasant face and friendly. Sasha pictured in her mind how she might look and feel if she weighed fifty pounds less.

"What can I do for you? Did you want to eat?"

"Just coffee."

Sasha began to muse, studying the coarseness of the walls and windows and suddenly the plush restaurant just off the lobby of the Gayoso Hotel shot into view. She smiled at the difference. The coffee was served in heavy pottered cups of crude finish, except for the eagle embossed on the surface. The level of the liquid was poured to the brim and as Sasha took her first sip there was a savory appearance that showed in her smile.

"Good?" asked Andre.

"Good."

They stayed on but for a brevity however, for Sasha, though relishing the coffee, felt discomforted by the too many men in the limited space, folks of rugged rural culture, rough of dress and coarse of thought, who kept raking their eyes up and down her form even though she was sitting.

"Isn't it time we were on our way?" she asked, the vexed tone of her words indicating they were out of place and shouldn't have come.

Andre started to lift himself from his chair to abide by her wishes but before he followed through someone with quickened steps approached, the owner, happily exclaiming that he knew who she was, the young doctor at the Sherette and Van Doke plantations, and said this sufficiently loud for the ears of the patrons to hear, who glanced with raised brows at one another, their countenances manifesting shame and apology for what they regarded as a slippage of respect. She smiled at the man and then she and Andre shook his hand, promptly leaving for the general store where the livery owner had taken their carriage for loading. While on the way home Andre apologized for the embarrassment he had caused her.

"I shouldn't have taken you there Sasha. I'm sorry."

"You don't need to say that. You didn't know who was there. Blame it on the snow and cold. They couldn't work, so it's something of a place where they can coop up until the weather improves. We just happened to be there at the wrong time. I'm glad for them in a way. Besides, we might discover that one of them, if not several, is a patient of ours some day."

"You're so nice. Always looking on the better side."

Shortly Andre asked Sasha if it was time for lunch, for it was long past; she said yes, opening the box in which Mary Tonka had packed fried chicken and biscuits and they began to eat and sip coffee that she had poured from the cider jug, while he drove.

"We'll need to keep moving. Sundown is not of much length from this hour."

When having traveled further for a while a late afternoon wind picked up, the air turning even colder, such that it prompted Sasha to draw a blanket around her feet and up to her chin, at the same time looking over at Andre with a smile and then lapsing into quietness. She was sifting through something, so he concluded. He missed the delight of her chatter.

"You're without words all at once. What is it?"

"Mary Tonka. It's about her. When I leave for Baltimore, Andre, I'll miss her good cooking awfully. She has no equal."

"I'll support that."

"Speaking of Baltimore, will I find living accommodations without much bother?"

"Easily. Doctor Givens and I will comb through the listings before you're there and you can choose from among those that suit. The hospital keeps a file of such rentals as well."

She sighed and seemed content, pulling her blanket up tighter, and then began to look about at the ice and snow and the frozen tree limbs. She began silently to ruminate.

"I love all this. I deeply do. There was no snow in the Canaries, too mild, but I've read of things like this in great vast Russia, in the novels, and I don't remember a single one that failed to picture a snow scene." After a bit she shared these thoughts with Andre.

"Why does the writer do that?" he asked with a curious brow, then answered his own question. "It's because the snow lends itself to romanticism. All the Russian writers I know of are romantics."

She smiled wanly at the unexpected response and closed her eyes, declaring she must set down the various things she'd experienced on the trip in her diary that very night lest she forget. Pretty soon the sun popped out from behind the dark hovering clouds on the horizon, then Sasha stretched her arms above her head and yawned and fell off to sleep, the pale gold flecks of dying sunlight trickling across her face.

"Ah. She works too hard, going all the time. I've never seen such a use of energy. But she paces herself, like right now. What is it they say? A good soldier sleeps at every opportunity. I am forever overcome to be with her, to have her by me. Isn't she a lovely thing? I know I've proclaimed it time and again; I can't help it." And then there was a fraction of hesitation, something of a running back over what he had momentarily said. Shortly he resumed. "I am so thankful that she loves me, but in truth I love her, I think, much more than she does me, that's what I think, but in time she'll come to love me just as much as I love her. I'll see to that. I'll make the greatest husband ever. Sometimes she doesn't respond to my amour as warmly as I would like, but that's all right. There'll come a time, when we are married, when those lovely arms will twine about my neck, when those proud lips will eagerly seek my kisses, and when those intellectual eyes flow into mine with tenderness, yes, with tenderness," and then he came to himself, feeling a tinge of ridiculousness for his fantasy. "But why should I feel that it's ridiculous? She will be my beloved wife when these imaginings are born true, and does not a future husband have a right, a natural inclination, to think lovely things about his mate? Well, so much for that. Much water is to pass under the bridge before I tell her of these, my inner secrets; but when I do I can just hear her now. She'll pinch my nose, as she forever does, and then, 'Why Andre. It's so nice that you had such romantic designs of me. Tell me about them again,' and laugh that beautiful teasing laugh." With not more than a tender effort he tapped the horses on their rumps, sending them into a trot.

The winter seemed an omen, or so it did to Sasha as she looked back, for when spring had broken through and Andre had left to take up his duties and training with Doctor Givens, Sam Feathers fell ill with undulant fever, the cause of the disease unknown by medical scientists in that era; yet the symptoms were apparent, which were characterized by a wave of up and down fever episodes, together with bodily weakness. Some diagnostic headway was experienced by the late eighteen fifties as to the cause by European military doctors but with effective treatment lagging until near the end of the century, when it was discovered for certain that the bacterial germ Brucellosis was at the root of the illness. The disease was highly contagious, spawned by the ingestion of milk which lacked sterilization or meat from infected animals or close contact with their secretions, and it was learned that even transmission from human to human, through sexual intimacy, or from mother to child was possible yet rare. Sasha did what she could for Sam Feathers, prescribing rest and wholesome foods, and listening patiently to his daily groans that the constraints of lying in bed with nothing to do would surely kill him well ahead of the disease. Months would have to pass before his recovery. Sasha tried to avail herself to help Adelaide see after things in the fields, the scheduling, the planting, the directing of the workers in their various chores, but had her hands full with meeting other demands. Picking up pen she wrote Mrs. Laster that it was beyond her to come to San Antonio within the year as she'd promised. Perhaps next. The letter was timelier than she foresaw. Aside from Sam and the usual illnesses among the people a sudden outbreak of small pox struck. "What after this?" she wondered. When convinced that it was truly the dreaded infection she acted with wings of haste, imposing a quarantine on the small number infected, with candid and clear instructions that no one was to enter their residences, no one but herself, who alone occupied a house among theirs. She hoped that the disease was of the milder form and wouldn't spread further, but prepared for the worst, contriving arrangements whereby each day, before mealtime, either Adelaide or Mary Tonka delivered food and water and medicines to the base of an appointed tree where there she intercepted the provisions and dispensed them to her patients.

"She's too daring," uttered Mary Tonka. "I'm afraid for her. Small pox is a dangerous contagious disease." She had not read from that classical Grecian drama, nor ever heard of it, but her apprehension was the same as its words. "Oh, noblest in desire, thy mind, thy mind inflamed with others' good, will set thyself on fire."

"There is no cause for tremble Mary Tonka. You see, from what is given me, she is strangely immune. Her mother and father died of small pox but she was unscathed. I have often considered that strange. Even now, she is never sick, never from any illness. Doctor Lundy says that he does not understand, that he is completely baffled, for she defies the odds and must have some inborn mechanism that shields her."

"And she is aware of this?"

"Doubtless."

Chapter 55

THE RAINS had fallen in torrents that spring, delaying the planting of the crops far past usual; finally they halted and the workers took up their toil. Sam Feathers was bed ridden; he couldn't help. Sasha regretted to tell him that he'd be laid up for the full year, yet she did nonetheless. It was the first she'd seen him cry. What she did not tell him was that the effects of undulant fever usually persist for a lifetime. But she hoped his bodily system was strong enough to overcome the illness without lingering aggravations. Adelaide or Sasha, one or the other, brought up Mrs. Van Doke's condition daily.

"She is not improving?" Adelaide would ask.

"Regrettably, I must say no."

"What is your prognosis?"

"She is declining rapidly. I fear she will not endure until Christmas. Her weight loss alarms me."

"Goodness! That quickly?"

"I'm sure. It breaks my heart to think of it."

"Then we must try to see her more often. Is Andre aware of this? And Jim and George?"

"They know."

"When will Andre return home?"

"At the beginning of summer. He said that in his last letter."

Sasha was busier than ever, seeing patients and watching after Mrs. Van Doke, at her side longer than she could afford because there were others who needed her more. She could do little for her other than keep her company. Cynthia attended to her every basic need, bathing and feeding her and doing whatever else. June arrived and Andre came home. Sasha had dropped by to look in on his mother one afternoon who was feeling much better, enlivened enough that she asked Sasha if she'd play something for her, the reply given that gladly she would but felt first she should return home and change into clothes more befitting the occasion. There was mirth in her manner when she offered the excuse that she owed that much to Mozart because he was a class fellow. She would do more than play a mere few pieces; she would do a concert, she thought silently, and would settle for nothing less.

"I'll get back within the hour. Perhaps Adelaide and Mary Tonka will consent to join us."

"The idea delights me. Please ask them. I wish Lucy could be here. She is enraptured when you play."

Sasha looked around for Andre and keenly detecting what she had in mind Mrs. Van Doke explained that he was somewhere helping George with something or the other but was due back shortly.

When she returned, with Adelaide and Mary Tonka trailing close, she started directly to the room where the piano sat, and entering, there found Andre standing barely inside the doorway, waiting, and reached and touched him. She smiled as she saw Mrs. Van Doke comfortably seated in a heavily cushioned chair, waiting for the concert to begin. She seemed as much entertained by the dress in which Sasha was now clad as she was from the expectation of the performance. It was of white expensive silk, together with a figured silk tunic, both caught up in large accentuated scallops and pink double bows. The waist was pointed, the neck square, the dress and tunic finished at the bottom with a purple flaring cord. Adelaide had insisted on this wear for her, and since there was little time for delay, Sasha had given in without resistance or fuss. At the last second she stepped over to Mrs. Van Doke and kissed her brow, then went and stood by the piano until everyone was settled.

"What will she play?" Mary Tonka curiously asked, who sat beside Andre in one of the heavy regal chairs stationed side by side.

"I don't know. I'm purely moronic in my grasp of music. The composer is Mozart. I say that because mother assumed it would be."

With feathery lightness she lowered herself onto her seating. Adelaide studied and admired her every movement. Mary Tonka uttered to Andre. "She's very graceful, don't you think?"

"Yes indeed."

With arms extended to the fullest she balanced the sheet music against the shiny upright of the piano. It was Mozart's *Sonata-Fantasia in C Minor.* From the first note onward she played as if in a dream, not over correctly nor precisely, as she did when she first began to practice under the tutelage of Adelaide, but naturally, sitting serenely upright and immovable, her eyes fixed on the notes of the sheet music, her lips partially open, just barely, which made her all the more interesting, sensual, if one may have an opinion, and on and on she played, her face aglow all the while. She played hard, the hardest she'd ever played, the most intense of her efforts erupting in the last part of the sonata, the part in which, in the midst of the bewitching gaiety of the careless melody, the pangs of mournful, almost tragic suffering, broke in. It must have struck the audience with irony that this last surge of drama came from the soft gentle young woman whose nimble sure fingers had birthed the sound. At the very end, as if it were a summation somehow preordained, her beautiful dark hair came loose where it was not tightly appended and a little lock settled onto her brow. Looking over at Adelaide she fell into playful laughter and stood and curtsied. But as she bowed and thanked them her eyes trailed instinctively over to the grand lady, as she had come to envision her, who too was applauding as animatedly as the rest. She wondered. "Is this the last that I shall do in her honor? Only He can say. If not the last the last is not far away."

Throughout the summer Andre and Sasha were at Mrs. Van Doke's bedside, striving to attend to her every need, to be with her, and that was what she needed and wanted most, yet there were other times when she sought respite, to rest, to be alone, then there were still other times when she felt they were robbing themselves of precious hours of privacy together. She would have none of that.

"I'll do just fine. Cynthia can wait on me. You can't stay here every minute. So off with you. Go fishing, go riding, go to Memphis, go to Brownsville, go spread a picnic lunch under the shade of some towering oak."

The summer had transitioned into fall; Lucy had received a letter from Adelaide, and decided she must avail herself at Mrs. Van Doke's side for awhile. Jim would join her as soon as he had transferred his work load. In actuality, they sensed that the end was near. Brister and Prunelle drove her from Nashville, and stayed a few days, taking residence in one of the rooms in the rear of the mansion. One day before they left to return home they went in to visit her at bedside. Trying not to be a bother they hadn't seen her at any time before. She drew them to her and told them how much she loved them and what their friendship had meant to her throughout the years. Brister left crying, hoping she hadn't seen. Staying by Mrs. Van Doke's side day in and day out began to wear on Lucy and grasping as much the dear lady insisted on her getting out of the house, maybe going to pay call on Adelaide. When she arrived, she found Adelaide home but Sasha was away with Andre tending the sick. Adelaide received her with beaming adulation.

"Glory! I am excitedly happy. How have you been, is Jim with you, I've been intending to come over, you're looking so good, Sasha said you were here." These were the opening phrases from Adelaide Sherette and there were similar remarks that streamed from the lips of Lucy. After conversing generally for awhile they moved to the subject of which they were aware and dreaded and which someone of the family must eventually address.

"Adelaide I am concerned. Mrs. Van Doke's burial site is very complicated."

"Very. How is it to be resolved?"

"I can't say for sure. I think it's up to Jim. A while back he talked with her about this."

"You mean specifically where she wants to be laid to rest?"

"Yes."

"And?"

"It's not in the same plot with her husband. She is strict about that. Ah, as I said, this is very complicated. But that's life for you. No one can possibly imagine when starting out what unusual surprises lie in wait."

Adelaide gave no answer, merely going on to the next question. "Does he have any suggestions at all?"

"One."

"And what is it?"

"The formation of another burial plot nearby among a grove of birch trees. She told him exactly where it is. It's on a little knoll where the sun is sure to settle at mid morning or thereabouts. She says she's always loved birch trees, especially their glitter in the sunlight. I'm of mind that's what he'll do. He put this to Andre and George, he said, and they left the decision entirely in his hands. The gnawing trouble about this is in which plot will the children and wives and their children after them be buried?"

"A perplexity indeed. Who is sage enough to wisely say? None of us know Lucy where we'll end up. So many things can happen over time. People divorce and remarry and move half way around the world. And cemeteries can't last forever. We just think they can. An earthquake could swallow them up over night. Now, about forming a new burial plot. That's the easiest part of all. It's Van Doke land and Jim should do as his mother insisted."

The calendar page revolved to the month of November. The grand lady had lasted longer than anyone anticipated, surrounded all through the fall by family members as well as by Sasha and Adelaide and Cynthia. Mary Tonka visited limitedly. Lucy and Andre had stayed with her more consistently than anyone, but Sasha was with her a great amount too, in and out, offering comforting words and diagnosing her medical condition, encouraging her to take nourishment. Mrs. Van Doke avidly sought her presence.

"Sit my child," she said a day or so before the end. When Sasha had settled on the side of the bed, Mrs. Van Doke took her hand in both of hers. "Look at me dear, don't peer downward. Your face is so lovely. I need to see it." There was pity in this face; it could not have been missed. Sasha said nothing, obeying her wish, and leveled her eyes into those that weakly searched hers.

"Do you remember the first day I met you?"

"I think so."

"I'd come over to see you. You were of the impression that I was there to call on Adelaide. I was there to do that all right, but you were foremost. How lovely you were. You took my breath away." A tiny chuckle escaped Sasha's lips. She looked down, but back quickly. "I still see it so clearly. Your hair was pulled up and you were bedecked in a stylish green cap. I don't believe I've ever seen you since with it done up like that. It's your habit to wear it long I've discovered. You had removed your pretty white coat which had covered your nice blouse, also white, and littered with a swarm of ruffles, if I may exaggerate. I hugged you. I'm not sure you liked it but I did. How lovely were those dark black eyes, I thought, the loveliest I'd ever seen and they still are. You were so young I couldn't believe it. I said then, to myself of course, that I'd give anything if you were my own, and now I say it again. I would give anything my darling if you were. You see, I never had a daughter. I suffered awfully because I did not. I'd gotten used to it after awhile; let me say I'd repressed it. When you came along, when I first saw you that day, it started up all over. You literally lit up my life, you were my bright star, my lovely flower. I craved to see you everyday thereafter. You became my reason for living, you and my three sons. You are still, but as you are aware my days are down to a precious few."

"You're going to be all right. Don't—."

"Shhhh. No need to pretend. Your beautiful sad eyes betray you. Just let me talk to you and touch you while I can and thank you my darling for everything you've been, and if I didn't have a daughter, I finally had you; He sent you to me and that made up for everything that might have been that wasn't."

She breathed heavily, obviously needing to break her words. "I must stop for a second." Shortly she continued. "But come closer; let me embrace you, hold you my child." So Sasha leaned against her, her body pressing against her breast and felt the grand lady's arms close feebly around her, then uncontrollably burst into sobs.

"There, there. You are crying my little sweetheart, but do not grieve. Please don't. I do not I assure you. I leave this life thankful that He gave it to me, and that I have done my best to live it well."

When she died Andre and Sasha were sitting along side her, holding her hands. A life was over, a rare life by any number of measures, one replete with ups and downs, yet the ups were many in proportion to the downs. As he had done for his father, Jim led the way with arrangements, with Lucy and Adelaide providing augmentation. The funeral was to be held in the Van Doke mansion, but that plan was necessarily altered, given the expected turnout for the service. A huge tent would have to be erected.

"Lawrence Sherette is to conduct the service, Adelaide," said Jim when they were finalizing the tedium's of the preparations. "Mother talked to him about it fairly recently. He said he gladly would."

"I said something of it to him myself. He feels honored."

"Good. She knew him for a long while and considered him the finest, even when he was growing up."

The funeral went as funerals go in general, endowed of the usual composites; there was sadness and expressions of sympathy, there were condolences offered to the family, there were exchanges among the congregation that she was a wonderful splendid person and mother, there were men dressed in their finest suits and women attired in expensive black dresses and frocks, and there was the immediate family that sat on the very front row, Jim, Lucy, George, Andre, and Joseph Nomehart and his wife Angeline, who had as hastily as conveyances could transport them traveled from Virginia. Cynthia and Sol sat directly behind Jim and Lucy. Then there were those next to the immediate family who sat across from them, as close as seating allowed, Adelaide, Sasha, Mary Tonka, and Sam Feathers. To Mrs. Van Doke they were indeed precious to her heart and had it understood with Jim that at her funeral they were to be seated as near the family of true blood and marriage as seating allowed.

The tent was large, massive, thrice greater in span than the one erected for the funeral of Jordan Van Doke, for Martha Van Doke was a most venerable person in the eyes of those who knew her, much loved and revered, as much by the slaves as by the planters and other constituents of the community. Therefore, as allowed for, the throng was massive that turned out, which in some way was a demonstration of the goodness of her life. Lawrence Sherette was robed in his Priestly attire, the alb, a long white vestment with liturgical tapered sleeves, together with the amice, which consisted of an oblong piece of white linen that fitted around the neck and shoulders and partly under the alb; and then there was the biretta, a square shaped hat trimmed with blue silk. Upon seeing him dressed in this manner Sasha released the faintest smile which he keenly grasped, his gaze being straightaway at her, yet felt restricted from returning his inner feelings. "You look very nice," her smile conveyed.

In commencing the service he gestured to an old Negro slave woman situated on the front row to sing a religious song, who over a length of many years had sung it in cadence with her brothers and sisters in the cotton fields, a mournful rendition that only a slave and a cotton worker could have yielded forth, a symbol of the trials and tribulations that her soul had endured over the long years of her servitude. The congregation sang with her, this including the families on the front row, and even the swollen crowd, some of them rich land owners and their wives, who had gathered on the exterior, coming late and finding no room left inside. It seemed that the entire slave community was there. Lawrence Sherette spoke softly and reverently and had carefully selected the proper words for beginning the service, and then upon finishing with the preliminaries cited passages from the Book of Ecclesiastes by heart, skipping lines that he liked less and using those he apparently liked more. "There is a time for everything, a time to be born and a time to die, a time to plant and a time to uproot, a time to weep and a time to laugh, a time to mourn and a time to dance, a time to tear and a time to mend." Not lost from observation was his omission of the darker phases of the scripture, such being, ". . . a time to hate," and ". . . a time for war," having done this because of the radiance of the lady's disposition while living, surmising that such words as hate and war were not consonant with her character.

With these citations delivered and laid aside, he next began not what was a sermon for the deceased but an allusion to the many good aspects of her life, an almost personal oration, seeming at once speaking to himself and to the family. He talked; he did not preach. It wasn't his nature to preach.

"All my life," he said, among many other narrations herein omitted, "there has been a Martha Van Doke, our neighbor—wonderful, caring, generous—a loving mother of three sons. We are fortunate to have had her in our midst for so long. Her children will miss her; we will all miss her. The void that she has left cannot be filled, for it is too wide and too deep, yet we shall go on as she would have us do. We grieve, yes, but this is not to be a sad day, only one of rejoicing, a celebration, a celebration for the life she lived and the giving over of her beautiful soul to Him on high, her Maker, who has called her home. For this we rejoice but rejoice as well because she leaves us with untold examples by which we should live. She left her mark. Marha Van Doke was at once an inspiration and a model, which I shall strive hard always to follow. Since I was a little boy she has meant so much. Never will the sun set nor the moon rise without my remembrance of her. And then lastly I wish to relay some lines to you that she gave over to my possession but recently, just days ago, asking that I impart them as she lay here in rest. 'I am quite fond of this poem Lawrence,' she said, 'I have held it for a long while; will you read it at my funeral?' I will do better than read it; I shall cite it, for I have committed it to memory. Will you rise?" At this the congregation slowly began to stand, there emerging at the same time a rustling of dresses and scudding of chairs on the turf.

Do not stand at my grave and weep
I am not there, I do not sleep
I am a thousand winds that blow
I am the diamond's glint on snow
I am the sun on ripened grain
I am the gentle autumn rain
When you awaken in the morning's hush
I am the swift uplifting rush
Of quiet birds in circled flight
I am the soft star that shines at night
Do not stand at my grave and cry
I am not there; I did not die

The body of Martha Van Doke, attired in a blue silk gown that she herself had chosen, was carried to the grave site by a cadre of slaves of the plantation who in their years with her had earned her endearing affection, and there with the briefest of words Lawrence Sherette uttered, "Lord, this is as far as we can come. She is now in your care." At this, the casket was lowered into the grave while the old slave woman again began her intonations, whereupon, at that very moment, the unclouded sun punctually assumed its role, leveling the full intensity of its rays on the noble white birches, the latter seemingly bemused and honored that this august celebrity was now a permanent resident of their colony. She had strolled among them since young womanhood.

No one left for home; they stayed on, Jim and Lucy of a decision not to abruptly depart for Nashville, nor were Joseph and Angeline planning to leave right away for Virginia, someone indicating they might remain for a substantial while. Andre's plans were to leave for Baltimore sometime in mid spring, choosing to linger until the flowers were in bloom.

Life without Mrs. Van Doke was dreary and moods low. In the near days that followed Sasha chose to avoid the piano, and Adelaide and Mary Tonka usually sat in the swing on the portico but with minimal exchange. Once Mary Tonka said it was strange that they, meaning Jordan and Martha Van Doke, went at nearly the same time, only a few months apart, with Adelaide returning that yes it was strange but that things happen in that way.

While in her mind Thanksgiving and Christmas would not be the same, Adelaide, nonetheless, with steely unsoftening grit determined to make the best of things, seeing that the workers were well fed, as always, and suggested tactfully to Jim to shoulder the responsibility at the Van Doke plantation of doing likewise for the slave people. A short stretch before Christmas Adelaide and Sasha decided on a trip to Memphis to buy gifts for the workers, taking Mary Tonka with them because to leave her alone in that huge towering edifice was in Adelaide's view "too much."

"She'd be terribly lonely Sasha and I can't bear the idea of that."

They spent the night with Tahitia and had dinner at Randolph's.

"My, my, my," Randolph let out as they entered the doorway, "you have brought Mary Tonka. I am terribly delighted to see you dear. It's been awhile. Here, let me hug you." Randolph wrapped his arms around her, while Mary Tonka gave off something of a laugh of amusement.

"And Sasha, more beautiful than ever," he blurted with excitement, drawing her to him. "But what's this the grapevine tells me. You're slipping off to Baltimore."

"Not yet, next fall."

"Ah. We will miss you."

"I'll return the next summer. I think of it as a vacation."

"That's good. That's the healthy way to look at it."

At one juncture Adelaide quietly tugged Randolph aside to pump him for his view on what she regarded as the impending war, to which she sometimes alluded as the gathering storm.

"It's unavoidable Adelaide, I shudder to tell you. The hot heads will goad the nation into it."

For Christmas, Adelaide had a ponderous western fir erected on the north lawn, with gifts for the workers laid at the base of it, and in addition she and Mary Tonka prepared a lovely dinner for Jim and Lucy and the Nomeharts. Andre and Lawrence Sherette were there, naturally, and sat to the right and left of Sasha.

"When will you return to Virginia?" asked Adelaide of Joseph Nomehart.

"When? I can't say. Not yet. I'm combing through some management essentials with George. I see no need to rush back, and he may need me. Said he's going to Chicago for a month." Turning to Jim he added, "You and Lucy are leaving for Nashville next week, are you not?"

"Next week. I'd like to stay on Joseph but I can't. Wish I could. Planting is just around the corner and I'd like to see the turning ploughs break ground, but I can't. I'd wish you good luck but you don't need it. You'll have Coon; he's a good man, the best, who has it all under his thumb, just like Sam Feathers."

Chapter 56

GEORGE HAD asked Joseph to fill in as temporary overseer during his absence, despite his awareness that the man was seriously lacking in the methods of grand scale farming and handling the slave hands. Jim worried no little amount about this, but there was something more bothersome that consumed his thoughts, his suspicion that George's jaunt off to Chicago encompassed more than a visit with Elizabeth Edom, his knowledge of his brother's evolving life style telling him that he had fallen prey to sporadic gambling binges in which he had lost rather large sums and more lately had begun to leverage money with a Chicago brokerage house connected with the London Futures Market.

Doctor Lundy promised Adelaide that he would avail himself more frequently beginning in August or September, or any event when Sasha was to depart for Baltimore. She was beside herself. Where was she to find an extra doctor for helping Doctor Lundy and then there was the dread of Sasha leaving. It clung to her as a fever. Several were the nights that they lay in bed and talked of the day it was to come.

"I'll miss you sweet heart."

"And I you."

"I'm about to find out about how hurtful it was to Mrs. Laster to give you up."

"Yes. But it was equally as hard on me."

"But it turned out well."

"You'll never know how well Adelaide. Living here with you has been Heaven, and I have to tell you that I have entertained the idea of not going. A good many times I have. Look at all I'll give up."

"Shhhh. You mustn't devote a thread's worth of regret to that. Look at the promise, not only for you but for all humanity. Look at the people you will help restore to health."

"I do look at that. But also at the people here. Who will care for them?"

"Someone. We'll find someone. We'll have to. But not like you darling."

"I will pray that Doctor Lundy will help you find that person. And just think of this. I'll return every summer to be with you. I'll always come back to you. Isn't that a nice thought?"

"Wonderful."

"As I said to Randolph I think of it as taking a vacation, and besides, you'll visit me on every chance, I hope. Especially in the fall when the harvest has been put away."

"Rest assured. The trains will soon start to run I'm told and that means that I'll pop up at any time."

"Ha, ha, ha. What a lovely idea. And we'll drown ourselves in the operas. Andre says they're fantastic. You'd like that wouldn't you?"

"Immensely. I'm already looking forward to it."

Half rising, Sasha had begun to bash her pillow and smooth it, her lovely fleeces falling about her shoulders, then she sat up and placed her arms around her knees, a look of contemplation on her face.

"I'd make a promise to you Adelaide, but I don't think I'd keep it."

"What's that darling?"

"When I leave I won't cry, but I will. I know I will."

"And I too. So don't make your promise."

Time flew. This lovely landscape, which had wound its way into her heart she would bid goodbye within a few brief months, and passionately set about to enjoy it for the length remaining. Long hours she spent in the fields where the planting was in full swing, sitting on the wagon seat by Sam Feathers looking on, and if not that then helping the workers with the picking of grapes and peaches, often by Thea's side, both using the same basket in which the fruit was dropped. "I need to commerce with mother earth," she spoke silently. "How dearly I will miss all this when I move to the city." Not omitting a single day she rode her sorrel, stopping off now and then to visit Thea, provided she was home, who now was with child, sometimes carrying with her a bundle of clothing for the infant when it was born. The orchards were rife with honeysuckle and fruit tree blossoms, the aroma intoxicating as she passed through, and of these and companion fragrances she was compelled to set down on paper to her dear Mrs. Laster. "One of the delights of the day is to ride through the whereabouts of the orchard. The fragrance is overwhelming, the result, I suppose, of the luring mixture of apple blossoms and honeysuckle acting upon my sense of smell; and there are other specimens that attract me too, the colorful flowers, magnificently gorgeous. You will laugh at this. Sometimes I think of this as my Garden of Eden. I will miss these splendid gems terribly when I move away." Nor did she overlook the infirmary. She looked at it every day, and remembered, recalling a stream of people she had there attended and the exact ailment that beset them as well as the medical application for correcting or relieving it. "Let me see. Yes. Let me look into the journal to refresh my memory of the treatment undertaken. Oh, here it is. The Presley boy. The green thorn in the fat of his hand which had to be slit open to allow relief of the pus which had accumulated in dangerous amounts. He's doing well now. Perhaps I will see him before my departure." And on virtually every evening she sat with Adelaide and Mary Tonka in the portico swing watching the zig zag flight of the fireflies. "See, there's another one. Over there Mary Tonka. See." Near the last all three visited Lawrence Sherette in Memphis, attending early morning mass, then at the suggestion of Adelaide scouted about the city the rest of the day to show it off to Mary Tonka. But all too soon time ran out, the curtain was drawn on the lovely events of the summer past, and fall was there to claim its rightful place. Doctor Givens and Andre had arrived to take her back to Baltimore with them.

Sasha and Adelaide had their final chat while lying in bed the night before, very saddened, but facing up to what was to come to pass. They'd not weaken, they'd remain firm and endure it, they said, but knew they weren't uttering the truth.

"When I say goodbye Adelaide I'll try not to look back, because if I do that will just make things worse. I'll encourage Andre to drive away hurriedly. Once we're on the open road I think I'll be all right. Seeing the loveliness of the countryside will help a lot. But what about you and Mary Tonka? I worry for you. You'll feel awfully lonely in this big home. I know you will."

"We'll do fine," she answered, not really feeling they would but saying it nonetheless, pretending bravery for Sasha's sake.

Finally, after turning over it appeared they had fallen off to sleep; Adelaide had, but Sasha was actively pondering something to which she had returned time after time, all week long, and within moments touched Adelaide on her shoulder.

"Are you awake Adelaide?" she asked softly.

"Uh, uh. Oh. I am now. What is it sweetheart?"

"Something I forgot to mention."

"What is that?"

"I'm about to go on my first train ride, my very first. Isn't that exciting?"

"Ha, ha, ha. I'd say it is. And there's something you left out."

"I did?"

"Yes. Looks like you're making history ahead of me. Remember, I've never ridden a train before, none around here to ride, but that's on the way to changing. I'll have my turn. Pretty soon I'll hear one after another crossing the bridge over the marshes and when they make it up this far they'll set off a blast, like, like, dear me, let me think, oh yes, like you hear on a ship, a fog horn, and I'm told by Prudence Autry that I can catch one at the depot almost any day and ride it all the way to wherever I want. Of course you know where that is, don't you?"

Sasha let out an exuberant laugh. "Oh yes. Where else?"

They were closing the evening on a note of cheerfulness, likewise falling into misty slumber, but with a vagueness of tomorrow's dread.

Next morning as the dawn broke there stood a small assemblage at the portico's edge. The horses were hitched to the carriage, held by one of the workers, while Sam Feathers with the aid of Andre loaded Sasha's belongings. In the gathering there was Adelaide, Mary Tonka, Doctor Lundy, Lawrence Sherette, Thea, Sol, Cynthia, Doctor Givens, Andre, Sasha, and Sam Feathers, a sum of eleven. all visibly saddened, but none so far shedding tears, not yet, all keeping a dry eye until Sasha moved to Sam Feathers, squeezing and patting his arm. "You take care of yourself Sam Feathers. Don't overwork and go to bed early. I'll check you over next summer when I am back home." Sam reached and pulled out his oversized bandana, daubing it to his eyes, summoning up all within himself to retard the basely sobs that wound their way from deep down in his chest. Sasha made her rounds to everyone to say goodbye, each of them holding her for a tender moment, then freeing her for someone else. Lawrence Sherette seemed to hold her a little longer than the rest, though not then shedding a tear. He'd save that for later. On the very last she sank into the arms of Mary Tonka and Adelaide—for they were gathered around her at the same time—who lovingly kissed her. She lovingly kissed them back, and for a moment held them one last time; "Goodbye," she uttered, then turned, and fighting to hold back the tears ran quickly to the carriage where Andre lifted her up to Doctor Givens who helped her into her seat. Andre, who by now had sat down in the driver's position clucked to the horses; the carriage began to move away. As promised, Sasha did not look back.

Lawrence Sherette and Doctor Lundy had decided to spend the night, first, to allow Doctor Lundy to look in on a few patients of minor ailments that so far had not been cared for and second, to assuage the loneliness that was certain to abound in the hearts of Adelaide and Mary Tonka. Adelaide was grateful they were staying. It would help. That night they sat on the portico, as Adelaide and Mary Tonka and Sasha frequently did, none seeming inclined to start into conversation, but each having relatively the same thoughts of mind.

"They're stopping off about half way to Nashville for the night's lodging," said Lawrence Sherette, in all likelihood bringing up the subject to enliven everyone, to lift them up, most especially Adelaide and Mary Tonka.

"About half way. That's right," answered Adelaide. "Andre said they'd stay where Jim and Lucy sometimes put up. That's on beyond the Perryville Crossing where I'm estimating they caught the ferry in the early afternoon. Sasha liked that. She's fond of boats and don't we know she's had her share of experience with them."

"And from Jim's and Lucy's home they're taking the train to Louisville," Lawrence Sherette resumed, "then from there into Ohio, but the routing into Ohio and from there on is a bit unclear to me, except according to Doctor Givens they're in for a raft of changes, in other words, switching from one train to another." After this, Lawrence Sherette arose and walked over to the edge of the portico, there looking up as if studying the Heavens, doubtlessly reminding everyone that this was a habit of Sasha's. A few stars here and there faintly pierced the pale blue of the immensity and playfully flaunted their little sparkles. Sufficiently concluding his reverie Lawrence Sherette came back to his chair and sat down, and disregarding his own melancholy cast a glance of empathy over at his sister.

"You are strong Adelaide; you'll recover to your normal self in no time."

"I will. I always do. But to say that I'll miss her is an understatement. You know it is. I'll miss her terribly, as I am now. When she was around the whole place was aglow; it was always morning."

"Well, sure, she was like that. What a girl. It's like suddenly the lamp is blown out. But it won't stay out. Both of you will inundate the mail system with a ripple of letters in reverse, one from Brownsville, then one from Baltimore, then one from Brownsville, then one from Baltimore. I can see them flowing. Why, I'd bet you'd write her this very night if you had her address."

"I would. I'm certain I would."

☙ ❧

Lucy received them with the utmost of dignity, bowled over with excitement, honored to have Doctor Givens and Sasha in their home, a very fine home it was, and she was thrilled through and through that they were there. "It's your first time here," she breathlessly remarked, looking at one then the other." She beamed. "We are terribly pleased you decided to stop off and spend the night."

"I'm afraid this may be an imposition," said the doctor apologetically.

"No, no, no. Don't say a word of that," said Jim with resistance. "We are honored; we are overcome that you have." The doctor chuckled. Shortly, a few minutes after the greetings reclined to a terminus, Lucy showed the guests their rooms, Andre's next to Sasha's, and the room for Doctor Givens further on down the hallway; then they all retired to the living area, there taking up a hodge podge of topics until the serving of dinner. Jim asked Sasha what she thought about the crossing of the Tennessee. "I liked it very much. The cable was fascinating." She meant that a steel cable tethered to a team of work animals was used for towing a barge back and forth across the river. Supper was served, the aroma of the food sifting from the kitchen having triggered everyone's hunger, especially the travelers. Prunelle was all over herself to wait on Sasha, asking continually if there was anything else she might hand her from the many assortments on the table, keeping her tea glass filled and intermittently could not resist the delivery of a loving pat on her shoulder. Sasha had clad herself in a beautiful green dress which was adorned by a white pearl necklace at her neck. Brister kept looking at her. Prunelle glanced at his staring and drew him aside. "Youse impolite Brister. You'll make her feel uncomfortable. Quit that."

The subject of the train trip ahead arose and Doctor Givens said that Sasha was in for a treat and Sasha added that she knew she was and was fortunate to be traveling with her two splendid companions. Her decorum, thought Jim, was a feature not of ordinary affectedness and remembered from the first time he set eyes upon her that her grace and charm were qualities that readily pulled him in. When they had all settled into bed, Lucy decided to rise and go into Sasha's room and kiss and hug her, understanding that she was naturally saddened and badly missed Adelaide and Mary Tonka. But only the pillow on her bed would know the full measure of her melancholy, for soon after Lucy left the room and Sasha had laid her face upon its softness, the evidence emerged. It felt the tear drops.

The next morning, Jim and Lucy, with Brister driving, accompanied the three travelers to catch their train. Minutes after their goodbyes they were seated. When the fog horn blasted Sasha looked over at Andre, a flushness of adventure showing itself. They were off to Louisville and northern domains beyond. Sasha would write to Adelaide of this experience in some detail.

> The smoke pouring out of the round like cylinder in the top of the engine, the smoke stack, I think they called it, was enormously black, thick and putrid and spread as a pall over the nearby buildings. It seemed unhealthy. Sometimes, when the train had penetrated deep into the countryside the tracks curved to the left or right, to the extent that I could see the engine from where I sat, the smoke still

pouring into the air, whipped into a thousand fragments by the wind. We moved amazingly fast, sweeping by the fence posts and the towering trees; and across the pretty streams too numerous to count. When we crossed a bridge—and there were many—there was a rumble as if lightning had struck and thunder had followed. The wheels sounded of a clickety clack, clickety clack—in something of a rhythm, which lulled me almost into sleep.

Our passenger coach was crowded with people, all finely dressed, and most as carried away as Andre and I. Doctor Givens was far more subdued. I don't know where it was, far into Ohio I'm sure, when Doctor Givens began to converse with a well dressed gentleman whose son was attending theology school at Harvard. It was apparent he was proud of him. The man was dressed in a double breasted brown, very distinguished, and I took it that he was of wealth and had many connections. The gentleman asked Doctor Givens if I were his daughter and Doctor Givens answered that I wasn't, that I was to work with him at Baltimore's principal hospital. He seemed confused. I was glad when they switched to something else because I didn't want to answer a deluge of questions that the man might have had in waiting. He went on to ask Doctor Givens where our journey had originated and Doctor Givens returned that it was from a plantation near Brownsville, Tennessee. This naturally enough sparked the next question, which was how did he feel about the chances of war breaking out. Doctor Givens replied that war was probable, but that he was praying it wouldn't happen. The man said he was too. Somewhere further on he was still with us, and when I opened up the basket of food that Prunelle had fixed and offered to share with him he accepted, seeming to enjoy a chicken leg and biscuit as well as the rest of us. When we had penetrated further north into the Pennsylvania region the terrain turned markedly rugged, quite rugged, high hills and mountains surrounding us and then there were the valleys in between, where the land leveled off and the train ran smoothly and straight. We arrived on the third day, in early morning, before daylight. Doctor Givens and Andre escorted me by way of hired taxi to the dormitory where I was to live and helped check me in with the night clerk. The clerk said he had expected him, meaning Doctor Givens, and asked if I was Sasha, wherein he was given the reply that I was. I hugged Andre and Doctor Givens goodnight, then the clerk picked up my baggage and led me to my room. I offered to pay him a tip. He backed away, holding up the palms of his hands in refusal. "Against the rules." I thanked him for carrying my baggage to the doorway and bade him goodnight. Truthfully I felt worn from the long journey and after hastily inspecting my furnishings, which were nice, not a great many pieces of furniture, but nice, I snuffed out the light and tumbled into bed. I'll write you again in the briefest. You cannot realize my emptiness for you and Mary Tonka.

On the second day of their arrival Sasha had reported to Doctor Givens, whose office was situated off the corridor which intersected with a maze of other corridors.

"This place is complicated," it occurred to her, "and massive. How am I to ever learn my way around?"

When she tapped lightly on the door Doctor Givens answered, "Come in," and at that she pushed it open and made her entrance, seeing her great friend sitting at his desk viewing the chart of a patient. His desk showed signs of recent paper shufflings; the top of it was a bit disheveled. His office was expansive, tastefully furnished, and immaculately clean, with an oversized window that opened to a view of tall handsome oaks and a pretty lawn. Walkways and benches were emplaced among the trees, these accoutrements usually in use by recovering patients and family members.

"Ah, Sasha, there you are. Are you recovered from your long journey?" At this point he was standing. He smiled warmly.

"I am. Isn't it amazing how the body and mind recover?"

"Yes indeed. A little food and rest does wonders. And speaking of food. Have you had lunch?" The hour was passed eleven. "If you haven't you can join me. Then I'll introduce you to the staff, beginning with the hospital administrator."

"Good. I haven't had lunch."

Laying his chart aside he crossed over to the clothes rack and lifted off a shiny white coat and slipped it on, which reached to his knees.

"We could take lunch out some place, but if it's all the same with you we'll take it in the cafeteria."

"Good. That'll help acquaint me more with the hospital."

"You haven't eaten here before now?"

"No. Yesterday afternoon late when I caught up with my sleeping I took supper at the small café on the corner."

"Bancrofts."

"That's the name."

"And you haven't eaten since?"

"I haven't, but I slept late this morning. I'm ready for something now."

"Sure. Let's be off."

Walking down the hallway they turned this way and that until approaching a doorway with wording above the façade that read CAFETERIA—all in capital letters. As they entered, the young doctors, and the older ones as well, fastened their gaze on the young beautiful woman at the side of Doctor Givens, who was attired in a soft blue cloak, and a pretty white blouse accentuated with a fashionable red bow that one might have judged to be of slightly more than ordinary size. Sasha pretended not to notice the flood of eyes descending on her. But Doctor Givens saw them plain enough and did not effort himself to hold back a tinge of mild laughter. "Let them have their moment of gawking Sasha. Oh for sure they like what they see but I think they're also assessing the quality of the young person that's joining our staff. Rest assured they've already heard of you."

They ate and left, Sasha thanking him for lunch, and complimenting the food, a salad, a pork chop, and jello.

"I'm glad you liked it. But no need for the thanks. Meal cost is waived for the medical staff. I merely signed the ticket."

Returning to his office, they sat and chatted for a length then he began to finger through some papers that were left off within the hour by an intern during their break for lunch. "Nothing of immediate importance," he half mumbled, half spoke. She took it that he was talking to himself. "Tell you what Sasha, I'll show you around the hospital a bit, and then we'll meet with the administrator. After that, you'll need to see your office which from here is but a few paces down the hall."

"Fine."

Planning his stops in sequence, Doctor Givens led her first to the nurses stations, then to the surgical room on the first floor, to one of them in any event, and next to the chemical lab on the second, spending but a brevity at each site visited. Leaving the chemical lab they descended the stairway to the first floor, there starting to retrace the corridor that led to the cafeteria, but before reaching it abruptly turned into a narrower corridor and soon came to the whereabouts of the administrator. When Doctor Givens called upon them, who now was chief of staff, every official of the hospital put on hold their present business and gave attention to whatever was on his agenda.

"Doctor Givens, good to see you."

"The same here Mr. Conrad.

"This is Sasha," spoke the administrator. "Doubtless it is."

"Yes. Sasha, this is Gerald Conrad our administrator. Mr. Conrad this is Sasha Duval."

"We're delighted that you're here. I've heard much of you—naturally from Doctor Givens. I have your complete resume."

"Oh!"

"Yes I do. Doctor Givens supplied it. I said complete resume. Mostly I had in mind your medical experience. Most interesting. You have a, a flair for medicine, especially the surgical aspects." Sasha averted a direct response.

"I look forward to working here. It's what I've long hoped for. But it will require some getting used to."

"You'll do that quite well. Doctor Givens has offered testimony to that."

Gerald Conrad spoke in something of a disciplined tone, choosing his words thoughtfully; he was an ex military man and it showed. He most always sat erect, but in this case stood, and smiled vaguely, demonstrating a friendly though business like countenance. Doctor Givens liked him, trusted him, depended on him. He was a doer, an exacting man who could shoulder critical assignments and carry them through with dispatch. He had occupied his position for six months.

"You have an accent sir. Do you mind my guessing that you are British?"

"Ha, ha, ha. You've guessed correctly. Is it that obvious?"

"Somewhat. It easily reminds me of a dear friend who is also British."

"And who is this person?"

"A lady who resides in San Antonio, Texas."

Judging that the introduction had run its proper course Doctor Givens decided to intervene.

"Well, I thank you Gerald for your time; you will see Sasha often in her activities around here."

As they left through the doorway the administrator called out, "Whatever I can do Sasha. Anytime. Anytime."

Chapter 57

THE REST of the afternoon was spent in the introduction of Sasha to the multiplicity of doctors, and to the higher echelon nurses. The hour nearing four, Doctor Givens led her to her office, not a large space by any stretch, but large enough, equipped with shiny oaken shelves housing volumes of medical books and journals of many classifications and a brand new spacious desk. Doctor Givens's eyes followed with satisfaction as she gazed through the colossal window which opened onto the same view that he enjoyed from his own office. He had suggested to Gerald Conrad that Sasha might like this location in particular, "and also, let me stress, it will place her within convenient reach when I need her." Seeing them the second she entered, she did not mention the sprinkling of paintings adorning the walls, one most singularly—a fiddler in tattered costume wearing a straw hat while busily orchestrating his craft. It dawned on her that Doctor Givens might have purposely selected the art piece and had it hung in advance. She was curious as to the whereabouts of Andre's office, but did not ask, though remembering his explanation that it was far removed from where Doctor Givens resided, situated in one of the wings with doctors having only minimal relatedness to the surgical staff. As she would learn, she seldom saw him while at the hospital.

ᘐ ᘎ

Within short while Sasha commenced her efforts to search for a house to lease, given that the quarters the hospital provided was without charge, but not to her liking, excessively crowded with female nurses, as well as those preparing for the nursing profession; and moreover, she was spoiled. She'd had the run of a splendid home of great expanse and décor—in comparison to the hospital dormitory—and found herself in an atmosphere with which it was difficult to blend. Andre, as much as his schedule allowed, started to help her look around, especially running his eyes up and down the for lease listings posted on the hospital bulletin board and logically asked if she could offer more specifics about what she wanted.

"I'd like something like your mother said her father built for his family when she was a young girl. She took delight in telling me of it."

"The chimneys, the gables."

"Yes. I love chimneys and gables."

"And a house that's high up overlooking the sea," he ventured.

"As much as possible. But within the bounds of reason. I don't expect anything perfect."

"No, not perfect. But is there anything else you are seeking in your rental?"

"A little more privacy than at present."

"Understood. Is there anything else?"

"A portico that encircles the house, with a swing on the front and side. I'd especially like those two features."

"We can take care of the swings. First we have to find a house with a portico."

Weeks rolled by, the search continued, and Sasha in the meanwhile had plunged into her work with Doctor Givens. She had begun to slacken in her quest for a house, but refused to quit altogether. In the interim she wrote letters to Adelaide, lots of letters, whereon in the last she'd written she reported her hopes of finding a new living quarters that suited her better than what she had; but that finding something wasn't proving easy. "Guess I'm spoiled. Do you wonder at that? Wish you were here to give me a hand."

Adelaide promptly relayed a letter in return in which she said she couldn't come help her with her relocation search, but in time would be visiting and possibly might then buy a home for her as an investment. "Besides dear, I'll need a place to stay while I'm there. Be patient. Very patient. I understand your befuddlement with the crowdedness, but there are worse things. Do not under any circumstances tap your fund for rent or purchase; the fund is for living and recreational costs and for all other basic needs, clothing inclusive. But keep looking, that won't hurt, and keep me posted. Love you. And oh yes, I'm glad you're spoiled." Sasha smiled and kissed the letter. "Ha, ha, ha. Isn't she a wonder? Sometimes sister, sometimes definitely mother. She is right. I should remain patient, and I shall. After all, the dormitory is not all that bad. Just takes some getting used to."

Andre lived near the hospital, a consolation of a sort, for when he wanted to see her after work it was but a jiffy that he was there, meeting her in the reception room which in all fairness was furnished with an adequate number of couches and chairs of tasteful quality, together with a few books and magazines. The room was pleasant enough, but there was no privacy. To compensate, not infrequently they strolled the streets of the city, stopping off at some quaint boutique where Sasha delighted at browsing the merchandise, seldom buying anything; or spending time in the art galleries viewing the works of mostly foreign artists of the renaissance period, or attending the operas whenever there was a performance scheduled. Not to be left out was their many trips to beach side for which she swiftly developed a yen, where mostly they walked and sat but sometimes swam when the weather was warm. She'd bring along a picnic lunch, never missing, though apologizing to Andre that she was afraid her preparations weren't anywhere near the quality of those of Mary Tonka's. "They're wonderful Sasha. I love your stuffed eggs," he'd take on. Sometimes Doctor Givens joined them and would take on too. Sasha poo poohed their accolades and accused them of embellishing just to please her. Andre sometimes tried his hand at fishing, but with little success, while Sasha chose to gad up and down the sand dunes barefooted, throwing rocks at the angry waves that constantly showed off their temperamental side. Once—and this was terribly embarrassing to her because Doctor Givens sat close by and couldn't have missed the scene—the wind blew with such fitfulness that Sasha's dress flew upward, nearly over her head, thereby illustrating her most excellent form. She shrieked and with frantic quickness pulled it back down while Andre, Doctor Givens, and a host of onlookers stared amusedly, to say the least.

Daily she was at Doctor Givens's side in his performance of the many forms of surgery, some prodigiously serious and others of a lesser classification, it might have been contended. But Sasha was aware without commentary from the doctor, which he not infrequently gave, that any and all surgeries were serious and that it was erroneous to speak of them as minor. For awhile she had observed, assisting when he asked, with the doctor moving her gradually, almost imperceptibly, into the fray; and was affectedly inspired at the keenness with which she followed the minutest of details. Once, when Sasha deemed that he was lost in the most attentive concentration on his patient, as if he were eons away, he looked over and caught her by surprise, "You're stealing my techniques Sasha but that's what I want you to do." On the beginning he had her merely handing over the surgical devices whenever he asked, to which she unhesitatingly responded, vigilantly anticipating which was the one needed, and then from there the application of the anesthesia, and if not this then stitching the incision when surgery was complete. But as months slipped by there were changes, Doctor Givens electing to stand and watch while the young Sasha with infinite exactness and nerves of steel assessed where the blade should cut and matching the proficiency of the august surgeon at her side opened the flesh of the ailing patient and sewed it up. "She is amazingly quick," said he. "She is going to be a great one, which was apparent to me from the start." And so it went month after month, for a year, then a second year, the young Sasha advancing further her skills and knowledge while winning the respect and admiration of the various staff, particularly those who stood observing her proceedings. She was becoming known as the budding young surgeon of brilliance, Doctor Givens's protégé. "You're with me now Sasha and I with you," he once said. Perhaps it was just after they had finished with a procedure. "I am close by your side and will be for a good long while I trust. But someday you'll find yourself alone, the one that all others look to, just you and the patient, and some helpers, the anesthetist and the like. Technical people. The stakes will be critical, life or death possibly, and life will not always win out, as you so well know. By the way," he asked in a tone of casualness, as if he'd had an after thought, "where was the young Negro girl buried that died while giving birth? You told me of it. Remember?"

"I do. In the burial plot on the plantation that Adelaide's father created.

"Hmmm. I've sometimes wondered. Did her death bother you?"

"A little. Well, more than that. But I tried not to let it."

"I'm much the same. You badly regret losing someone. You can't help it. It's something you never get used to."

At the end of the first year in the city, when summer was well under way, Sasha and Andre had packed up and gone home for a short stay, with Adelaide and Mary Tonka showering Sasha with most loving affections the moment she had jumped down from the carriage. They met her in the yard, not waiting for her to reach the portico, and when Andre had dismounted and finished tethering the horses he lost no time closing the distance to them where he too was met with open arms. That night Mary Tonka inundated them with a table of delicious foods, Andre there too because Adelaide and Mary Tonka threatened that they would not eat one bite unless he ate with them. Sasha, during the supper, asked for a report on everyone, Doctor Lundy and Sam Feathers at the forefront, and also inquired about the Nomeharts, who were keeping watch on the Van Doke plantation. She explained that they had stopped off there first, finding Cynthia and Sol as expected, but not the Nomeharts, whereon Sol hitched fresh horses to the carriage for Andre.

"I sho am glad to see you young folks," Cynthia said jubilantly, "I sho am. This place is like a dead old piece of wood without you." She hugged Sasha with her huge arms and kept on hugging her. "Ah Sasha, you ain't done nothing but git more beautiful, you sho has. Don't youse think she has Andre?"

"I do. She does more every day."

Sasha had learned from Jim and Lucy when they stopped off to spend the night with them in Nashville the night before that the Nomeharts were still at the plantation.

"Doctor Lundy and Sam Feathers are well," reported Adelaide, "they're anxious to see the both of you. Sam appears to have just about recovered from his bout with undulant fever. But he says he sometimes feels a bit weak at day's end. You'll need to check him over." Not much mention was made of George, other than he'd announced plans to marry the Edom girl of Chicago at some yet undermined date during the next summer. Not long afterwards Andre begged to excuse himself, with words that there were a few chores he must attend to before turning in for a badly needed night's sleep. He hugged them all and kissed Sasha's lips.

While sitting in the portico swing that evening Sasha breathed in the fragrance sifting across the yard from the garden where a few of her favorite peach trees grew and said that one of the first things she wanted to do the next day was to go pick off one and devour it on the spot. "They are ripening aren't they?"

"They're beginning to" answered Mary Tonka, "and the ones that are have a really melting taste;" and so the next morning, the sun still residing in the mid portion, the dew not fully lifted, they were seen passing through the garden gate, with their bonnets on, going further into the interior.

"Ah, they are of a really rich aroma," said Sasha, "and all of them of any and every variety seem to be racing against one another to see which can bear first." Then she took in a deep breath and closed her eyes, thus intimating that the fragrance invading her sense of smell was of Heavenly sweetness. "They look healthy this year, more than usual. I see no presence of worms that amounts to anything. They have been well sprayed."

"They have," returned Adelaide. "Sam started early. He said he didn't want the worms to gain a toe hold."

"Well, it sure worked. And it does seem the trees will bear heavily. Seems I've arrived just in time to help you with the harvest."

"Not this year dear. Sam will have the workers do that. You're on your vacation. No work for you this time. But you can pluck off that peach that's hanging from that limb just above you. I'll let you do that. Here, take this hoe and tap it. It's about ready to fall. You did want one to eat, didn't you?"

"Yes I do. For a bit I was distracted. Let me have the hoe. Will you catch it in your basket Mary Tonka? I don't want it to hit the ground. Being ripe like it is the impact will bruise it."

As they left and had passed through the gate, Sasha maneuvered between them and reached her arms around their waists and said with very happy voice, "I have missed this; I have missed it badly. I'm glad to be home."

When not encumbered with other pursuits, particularly when she was free of attending her patients, Sasha and Andre found great delight in riding down the idyllic pathway to the gurgling stream with the enchanting bridge. Adelaide's father had built it long ago. They left at noon one sunny day and after traveling for whatever the distance not unexpectedly reached the opening in the woods, the fount of the pathway, and there entered, suddenly finding that the sunlight had vanished, having given way to the shadowy coolness as afforded by the leaves of the lordly oaks and sycamores.

"Pooh. The leaves are too thick. No dappling today Andre."

When they came to the bridge she dismounted and tied her horse to a sapling, there beginning to take pebbles from Andre which she threw one by one into the water as she had once before. Andre leaned against the banister watching her at play.

"Andre," she called out, "do you remember the first time we came here? Do you?"

He laughed a little. "How could I not?"

They stayed a while longer and left, yet not before Sasha pulled off her shoes and splashed about. On their way home she urged her sorrel into a gallop. "He handles just like always," she said to Andre who had reined along side her. "I think he still likes me."

Sasha worked with minimal pauses with her patients for the remainder of time that was left. Adelaide insisted that Doctor Lundy could see after them but to no avail.

"You need rest dear. This is your vacation." But contrarily Sasha insisted that Doctor Lundy needed help, and while on the subject of rest brought up Doctor Givens.

"You are correct Adelaide. Every one needs to recreate, to take it easy at times as you often say. I'm okay. I find work refreshing. But I am concerned about Doctor Givens."

"Why is that?"

"He works too hard, too long, often for fifteen hours a day or more. I'm tempted to tell him that. But hold off on the very last. My good intentions fail me."

At some interval of her stay Adelaide asked Sasha if she'd heard from Mrs. Laster. "I have. I hear from her often. I quickly answer her back. Our exchanges are very nearly equal. She never fails to mention Father Lumas, for which I am gladdened, and many interesting things about San Antonio. But I'm afraid I've let her down. I promised to see her this coming fall. I'm so sorry. I'll have to write that I can't make it. I have a feeling she senses it already."

Of mind that Sasha was unhappy with her current residence Adelaide inquired of her intentions of moving into a different place to live and if Andre was helping her look for one. She answered that she had continued to look and that Andre was faithfully helping. Adelaide promised to travel to Baltimore and see about buying a house as an investment, as she had earlier written. "I cross my heart that I will Sasha."

They went to Memphis twice, while there attending mass at Lawrence Sherette's church and Lawrence Sherette had matched this number in returning home to the mansion. While in Memphis also Sasha bought Thea an assortment of pretty clothes. She had spent as many hours with her as her schedule allowed, quick always on her visit to examine the baby, finding him healthy, and assuring the same to Thea.

"You're the best friend I have Sasha. I've been terribly lonely since you went away. I miss you. I so hate to see you go back."

Her visit was rounded out by one last stroll through the fields, taking the route to where she knew the workers were busy cutting and harvesting early clover and there joined Sam Feathers to sit and watch, who upon seeing her, as she approached the wagon where he sat, let out in very happy raised voice, "Sasha, Sasha," reaching and pulling her up beside him; and then as another last gesture, a short while thereafter, sat down at the piano and played a succession of lovely impromptu melodies while Adelaide and Mary Tonka listened and Thea also, who had joyfully accepted Sasha's insistence on her presence. Time ran out. In mid August Sasha and Andre left for Baltimore.

The war was soon upon them, on the north and on the south, on Sasha and Adelaide and Andre, on all who lived within the nation, but there were other events that came to pass not long before that calamity descended; and here, it becomes necessary first to treat of their existence.

Adelaide came to Baltimore, not one year later as she had promised. It seems to have been a year and a half later, well beyond Christmas and New Years, perhaps well into spring, for mention was made in one of the correspondences of their sailing on the Chesapeake with Mister Conrad the British administrator of the hospital who owned and piloted the vessel. Adelaide spoke in one of her diary entries that "the afternoon was sunny, the wind gusty but not fiercely, and the waves choppy. I could have gone back every day." She spent two months with Sasha. Sailing on the Chesapeake was one of their more avid past times, in which they frequently indulged, going to the theater another, and visiting the boutiques and quaint cafes another, most singularly a little French café. Nothing would do when they were touring the streets downtown but to stop off on every chance. According to the menu, cheese was the French dessert staple, and it revealed further that the French made much use of milk and cream in soups and sauces and that some of the sweet quires of milk and cream were transformed into soufflés, mousses, and crème Anglias; and that the soft pyramids of sweetened whipped cream atop desserts were for special occasions.

"We must try it," said Adelaide, reaching across the small table to touch Sasha's hand, "because this is a very special occasion."

"Yes, of course," answered Sasha, taking in an excited breath, whose eyes had scanned every item listed, "but let us not leave off that delicious *café sucre avec du laite chaud*."[8]

Within the time that Adelaide had allotted for the visit Sasha broke away from her duties at the hospital as much as she could to explore the city with her, particularly the gorgeous green parks, and there were many; Druid Hill, Mount Vernon, Charles North, Reservoir Hill, and then there was the Port of Baltimore, to which Dr. Givens had alluded with bountiful fondness, a blue serene body of water accommodating a congestion of assorted vessels, large and small, on the shorelines as it wound its way to the Chesapeake. Sometimes they sat for an extended length on a small wooden bench on the brow of an overlook which the locals called the promontory, watching the boats come and go. "What a spectacle," cried Sasha. "I wish I were a painter. I would set this very scene to canvas."

Adelaide feigned a disagreeable face. "You want to do everything sweetheart. But becoming an artist! You'd best forget it. I don't doubt you could do it, but where on earth would you find the time?"

Among the endless novelties into which they ventured was the basilica, "the first Roman Catholic cathedral built in this young nation Adelaide," said Sasha one day, this coming after they had attended mass at the splendid facility, whose luring façade of a classical Greek portico with iconic columns quickly caught one's eye. This noted edifice which decades later became a minor basilica, an elevation in recognition by the Pope, was where Sasha took evening mass. More than once they rode the train to Washington, a short distance, there staying for the greater part of the day and returning on the nightly run; and did not pause in their search for the house that Adelaide would buy. "You've waited long enough. Let's settle this necessity while I'm here. After all, you and Andre might marry some day and if so might need it for raising your children." And then with sisterly lovingness let out what she had been wondering, "Do you continue to think of marrying him?"

"I do. I do frequently. He is the one Adelaide, the only one in the universe. Where would I find someone like him, incomparably kind and patient, and loving me infinitely. I

---

[8] Sweetened coffee with hot milk.

hope our children are likened to his qualities. Yes, I plan to marry Andre. In a little while. Not much longer from now. But I don't know when. We'll see."

ᏨᏨ ᏩᏩ

The house was bought and Sasha moved in before Adelaide left for home. But she left soon afterwards, therefore missing the hours and weeks of scrutiny that Sasha devoted to physical and artistic changes. For awhile she moved continually from room to room looking at this or that, her finger to her lips, thinking, her mind going back and forth, then finally settling on what it was she wanted to do. It would need a degree of modification, nothing substantial she figured, but some; and especially pleasing to her was its near resemblance, she thought, to the house in which Mrs. Van Doke had lived when a young girl.

"I love the chimney and gables," she said to Andre, "and the vaulting in the great room. Ooooh! Look at its height. We could hang a chandelier from up there. If it's not too large. And with a wall or two removed this space could easily serve as a miniature ballroom."

"Do you like the floors?" he asked.

"What are they made of? They look to be of oak."

"They are."

"Could you find a craftsman to sand and veneer them? Perhaps he could add a very large window, maybe two, as large as the ones in the mansion back home."

"Ha, ha, ha. We'll see."

"Why do you laugh?"

"You said back home. This is your home."

"No. Not truly. Aurora is my home Andre, and will be always. I grew up there."

"Un hunh. Yes you did. Almost. Well, I'll find a carpenter for the remodeling, which I have a feeling will amount to more than you're counting on."

"We'll see. And if the cost isn't too excessive I'd love to have a second fireplace. It would add so much more."

"Ah. What would it add?"

"Well my goodness Andre. Romance and coziness. That's what. Where is your Amour?"

"We'll work that in too. Likely not now but sooner or later. I'll do my best."

"Is that a promise?'

"I promise." But the undertaking and completion were to run for a much longer interval than either anticipated.

She was happy. The house was what she wanted. Old it was, of antique style from the mid last century, and of towering height from ground to roof, the latter on which, with careful scrutiny, there could have been detected a verdant growth of moss before the house was bought, but this did not matter, for in time, with Andre's faithful help, her iron energy of purpose prevailed. Within a year the house was likened to new; new tapestries, shiny floors, and art works adorning the walls, and the two coats of paint the painter added to the exterior brought change with dramatic effect, even more than the new roof. No one could quibble that it failed to match the attractive quality and style of the houses owned by her comparatively wealthy neighbors.

"If only I had a piano," she lamented. "I have tremendously missed playing. I am rusty; I'm sure of that. I fear that I cannot play at all."

"You can still play sweetheart. I'm confident of that. We'll have to buy a piano. A used one will do if tuned well. If we could transport it you could have the one belonging to mother. She would have thrilled at your ending up with it."

ꟾ ꟾ

At some interlude of her stay Adelaide and Doctor Givens had their private conversation, for which Adelaide was gladdened; she'd had a persistent urge to ask him for a status report on Sasha.

"Ha. You know already Adelaide. She's marvelous. She will lead us one day. And while I am claiming as much I should let you know that we are sending her abroad to study in London. We are figuring a way for her to take her medical degree. She will fly through the exams, as she could this very minute. The staff there will swoon at her intellect and capability."

Indeed, Doctor Givens and certain high level staff of the hospital were contemplating sending Sasha to study under the surgeons of King's College of London, the aim of which was to expose her to some of the renowned medical personages of Europe and, as said, to move her toward securing her medical diploma. These intentions had not as yet been laid before her, but were only a narrow time away. Within weeks Doctor Givens addressed her with the subject, his revelation not in any way striking her ponderously, for Adelaide had already hinted to her of the impending news as Doctor Givens suspected she might. Taking only a brevity to sort it through Sasha accepted the proposal with gratefulness, yet not without inquisitiveness.

"How long will I remain there?" she asked.

"Six months, maybe eight. That isn't long of course, but you're likely to have to return on a trip or two."

Only recently Doctor Givens had sat with Gerald Conrad the administrator to work out the details of her travel, where she would take residence while in England, to whom she would report, and added to this list a plethora of other particulars.

"What an enriching experience for her," said Mr. Conrad. "But I am entertaining in my thoughts whether the staff will be accepting of her. As I have heard you attest she is very well read and self educated, obviously accustomed to listening with profit to lectures on the many aspects of philosophy, and even plays the lute. But as commendable as they are, will these attributes not pose her as an object of resentment, coming off as something of a young uppity shall we say?"

"I have listened to you carefully my good friend, and shall offer this in answer. She is all the excellent things you have enumerated, and without becoming unamiable or pretentious, as sometimes young people are when they pursue those lofty spheres. They will see as quickly as you and I saw that one of Sasha's numerous traits is humility, but fused with a steely resolve, and for these fine qualities they will admire and love her. But let us return to medicine for a moment. To me your question alone, without the other things thrown in, could have been whether the staff at the college will be accepting of her for her medical proficiency and overlook the fact that she is a woman."

"Yes. That is the better question and is what I wonder about. I know how men doctors are."

"Meaning?"

"They are quite generally resentful of women who are attempting to enter their domain. Sometimes they are hatefully resentful. Tell me. What confidence is it that elevates her to believe she can conquer this resistance?"

"First I will respond to your last point. It is that with which she was born; that which is innate. In her silent way she is fiercely determined. And now I will address your observations of men doctors. I am keenly aware of their dispositions Mr. Conrad. At first they will resent her I suppose, as they did here. But it won't be long lasting."

"No it won't. I concur. She is so well steeped in the science of medicine and chemistry that it will show in a flash. What is the age old dictum? Resentment gives way to respect and respect leads to admiration, and that will happen in the case of Sasha. She is too able for that not to become so."[9]

---

[9] It should be here related that Sasha's abilities shone with such brightness to the English staff that through their promotion and recommendation she followed with advanced surgical training in the teaching hospital at Vienna, earning her degree at that institution.

"Ah yes. Who could disagree?"

"I have been enriched," said Mr. Conrad, starting to turn away. "Thank you sir for allowing me to give my considered views and suggestions."

"Gladly I accept your thanks. But before we depart let me correct you on your error regarding the lute. It is the piano on which Sasha performs, not the lute."

"Then I have heard wrongly. My apology. Again, thank you."

Chapter 58

Sasha arranged with Andre to live in her home during her absence, and shortly afterwards hired a Negro maid, whose name was Padgett, to come weekly or as needed and keep house and cook for him, then she sailed for England. This was a week before the outbreak of the Civil War.

"I'll write you often dear Andre, once a week at the least, and if I succumb to loneliness—and already I am about to—I will likely double the number."

"And I will double mine."

With heartfelt reluctance she boarded the ship, waiting until the foghorn sounded before ascending the steps, but she made it and stood atop the deck and cried and looked and waved at Andre for as long as he remained in sight. She remembered all too well that sad day when Father Kestner stood on shore watching her depart for San Antonio. "That seems as only yesterday," she heard herself whisper. She had written Adelaide and Mary Tonka separate letters the day before and mailed them, and had sent one to Mrs. Laster several days prior, portions of which have been copied.

> My dear one. I am soon off to England, to your homeland. You have the place of residence where I'll be staying, a cozy flat near the River Thames. Roomy aplenty for us to share when you come. Did you say I could expect you in three weeks? We will do much catching up; I am greatly thrilled. You recall Doctor Robert Charlatan I am certain, you know, the ship's doctor when we sailed from Corpus Christi to New Orleans. He has been studying at King's College for some time and has now established practice in sprawling London. Somehow, he learned that I was soon to be on my way and sent me correspondence and generously took it upon himself to inspect the flat that the college officials have found for

my occupancy. He reports that it is a quaint little thing. We shall like it immensely, I feel.

She was sailing on the *Great Eastern*, one of the finest on the seas, endowed of speed and size, twenty tons, and lushness. The voyage lasted eight days, or approximately that length, during which Sasha read in her cabin, strolled the decking and looked at the sea, sometimes frothy, sometimes calm. When of mind to visit aloft she clad herself in a stylish top coat that Adelaide had given her when they were last together, a pretty pastel, the coarseness of the fabric suitable for mid climate temperatures, and had arranged her hair in the fashion of braids hanging down the back of her neck. She had selected this style as a means of combating the wind that otherwise would have blasted her locks into an immensity of tangles. Sometimes she frequented the dome shaped diner, the first of its kind, where she sat and soaked in the sunrays bleeding through and sipped tea. And wrote letters. Even one to Sam Feathers. She'd mail them upon reaching shore.

When the ship had entered the London harbor and edged along dockside a Doctor Elton Yorkshire was there to greet and assist her, promptly assigning a porter to gather and carry her belongings to a carriage which he had detained. A young man of slightly past thirty, his eyes were dark as was his hair, his complexion light and smooth. He dressed immaculately. There was a resemblance of Andre in him she thought. He smiled as he talked and seemed to be sizing her up, seemingly shocked momentarily by her youth and beauty, but there was a distinction about her that he saw which told him she disliked being the object of study, and shrinking a bit, he turned his eyes toward the carriage and then humbly back to her.

"I'm acquainted with the location of your residence Miss Duval; you're at 113 Ellington. It's close on the Thames. Not far from the hospital. I'm under instructions from Doctor Alton Fitzgerald, the chief of surgery, to accompany you there and see that you are properly settled." Sasha recognized the name. Doctor Fitzgerald was to be her supervisor of training.

"Thank you. I'm anxious to see it. "

When they arrived at the flat and Doctor Yorkshire had wagged her belongings inside he did not leave momentarily.

"Is all to your satisfaction Miss Duval?" She wished he'd call her Sasha. Seldom did anyone address her as Miss Duval. "Thank you for asking. I find everything very suitable."

"That is good. I will pass word along to Doctor Fitzgerald that it is. He will not delay long in wanting to know."

"When may I expect to meet him?"

"This evening at about the hour of eight, assuming he is not detained by an emergency. He will come here to discuss his thoughts with you. And of course to meet you. His sister Melana is agreeable to staying with you in your quarters here, he said tell you, if you are receptive to the idea. Doctor Fitzgerald, allowing that you are a stranger to the city thinks it wise that for awhile you have someone with you, his sister, as said, on whom you can depend until you are further established. You may rest assured that it is his aim to leave no stones unturned in caring for you."

"I'm grateful. Doctor Givens said he would think of everything."

"Yes. Your Doctor Givens in Baltimore. Doctor Fitzgerald and he have maintained a close friendship for many years I hear."

Thinking that all was said that should be, Doctor Yorkshire bowed with a slight and bade her good afternoon and left, then she began to view every nook and cranny of her new residence, finding it very well furnished and clean—in fact it was new; the hospital had but recently built a cluster of other like dwellings for housing the staff, mainly interns—and she sighed softly when stepping out onto the terrace which overlooked the river. "A very lovely view." There also to her liking, in the near center of the terrace, was a single rounded table, clearly of Italian vintage, which she was quick to observe, devised of ornamental iron and from the looks of its armorial bearing surmised that it might have proceeded through a family of wealth and nobility over the centuries until the members eventually died away. It was equipped with chairs for four. The periphery of the terrace flaunted a serry of decorative uprights, thin metal posts, shaped at the apex in the manner of arrows pointing skyward. Exquisitely placed at various angles there was as well an assemblage of urns and vases with lovely yellow and red flowers implanted in them which showed evidence of the most assiduous care, and were in such redundancy of health that a large number of their tendrils had wreathed over the rim. "Ah, reminds me of beautiful Sorrento." Sorrento is a small idyllic town in Campania, southern Italy, wonderfully located over white cliffs and offers a picturesque view of the Bay of Naples. Her father had taken her there once when enroute to Europe. She wistfully closed her eyes. "I'll spend many a happy hour out here." Upon retracing to the inside she next reinspected the bedrooms, the beds standing high above the floor, the peak of their mattresses measuring almost to her waistline. She laughed aloud. "Two beds. Yes, I remember. But I have long been weaned. I wonder if my dear one will have to struggle to climb up. I'll just have to help her."

Late that afternoon she decided to stroll the narrow street running parallel to the river, which was studded with a charming array of gas lights that had become common to Londoners, and thereby provided safety for strollers and walkers to move about at twilight and after darkness had fallen. Ellington Street was even more thickly endowed with these lights. The river was wide and calm, with boats of many shapes and sizes trafficking up and down it and in the night time the assemblage of lanterns hanging from the mast and sides of the vessels discharged a spray of glitter. She reminded herself not to stay past twilight, that she was a young woman and alone. Soon she returned. She would sit on the terrace for awhile watching the glow of the street lights on the shoreline descend into the waters, there depicting an illusion of glimmer and magic. "How beautiful, how enchanting. But not a soul with whom I can share it. No one. I feel very alone. Dear me, I suddenly do. I wonder. What is my Andre doing this evening; what are Adelaide and Mary Tonka doing; and Sam Feathers; and Cynthia and Sol; and Doctor Givens; and my beloved Lawrence Sherette; and Mrs. Laster? I would give anything if they were here, all of them." She would sit for a while longer, then go inside and make coffee, then come back with a cup in hand and begin to sit again. Eventually she would go back inside and begin to read from one of the medical journals she'd brought along. The subject that greatly intrigued her had appeared in an article dealing with surgeries of the gynecological and abdominal regions, surgeries too often fatal to the patient in that era; and Doctor Givens had increasingly urged her to move further into this realm of medicine. There was once when she quit her reading, laying her journal aside, her thoughts falling on Doctor Yorkshire and his field of specialty. It was not surgery she deduced or else he would have revealed it. She wished she'd asked. She checked her watch. It was half past eight. "He's late. I guess he's caught up in an emergency." She left for the terrace for another look at the lights glistening on the water, then shortly returned and commenced to read once more. There was a knock, a soft one. When she opened the door the light from the inside lamps poured outward and there stood a man of about sixty she guessed with a handsome head of graying hair, a gentleman of distinction at first sight, and a woman at his side who appeared to be near ten years his junior.

"Ah Sasha. I am here to welcome you. Even though I am late."

"Doctor Fitzgerald! I am delighted to see you, to meet you at last."

"The same here. And the same for my sister Melana, I am sure, who is here with me." Melana was not married, nor had she ever been. She was pretty and trim. Sasha would soon wonder why there had not been nuptials in her life.

"Yes, I am very glad to meet you Sasha." Melana's voice was cheerful and bright but there was an air of timidity about her.

"And I you. And thank you for coming along also. Now, let me pull up chairs, or would you prefer the sofa."

"The sofa is fine," replied Doctor Fitzgerald, "just fine."

He then sat down and Melana sat down beside him. Though happening quickly his eyes took bead of Sasha the moment he had occupied his seat, and this continued throughout his visit, as if he were determining for himself the great depth of intellect in her of which Doctor Givens had remarked in earlier and recent correspondence. She is quite young," he thought, "I am a bit astonished." Melana did not appear inclined toward talkativeness, but her brother was, quick with a friendly laugh if appropriate for the subject, and waited graciously for Sasha to respond. Sasha was slow to dive into conversation, using words with measured selection, a tad intimidated by the man, knowing that he was a personage of medical circles across all Europe, whose reputation even reached as far away as America. Upon glancing the features of the interior, or as many as his eyes could catch in a fraction, he continued. "I see your flat is new. The hospital has been adding residences for some time. I've watched them from the foundation upward. A good many interns and their families live in them. I trust that you like yours."

"I do. Very much I do. I did from the start. It's precious."

"And the terrace?"

"It's splendid. Perfectly splendid. I've spent a while on it already. Watching the boats and heavier vessels pass in review."

"Pass in review. What an excellent way to put it."

The doctor was gladdened to see Sasha in good spirits, taking it before seeing her that her long voyage will have affectedly brought on a degree of fatigue and that the strangeness of the city of three million people, the largest city in the world, would have been upsetting, if not overwhelming. He asked if his young associate Doctor Yorkshire had attended her satisfactorily and she complimented the latter with the highest of praiseworthy remarks. When they had talked on a while further, Doctor Fitzgerald uncloaked a sudden seriousness of expression, his face somber as Sasha later learned it could instantly become, that London was a city of three million souls and that one never knew what malignant mind might be watching and that she was a most beautiful young woman and that she must be cautious when on the streets alone, and went on to say that if acceptable, his sister Melana would gladly stay with her through the night time, not that her little place was susceptible to burglary or worse, but because she might feel lonely all alone and that his sister might be of some advantage in keeping her in good spirits. Melana smiled as if to say she would gladly do as her brother suggested, and Sasha, quite happy to hear the suggestion smiled receptively back, then turned to Doctor Fitzgerald.

"I had hoped that you would have ready a provision of this sort," she said gratefully. "Doctor Givens assured me you would think of everything. My answer is a hastened yes."

"Ha. Doctor Givens. My dear friend. Yes I shall do my best to see that you are secure and comfortable. I owe him that. And owe you even more. You have sailed a long way my dear. Across that entire broad sea. I am greatly pleased that you consent to Melana staying with you."

"But where are your things Melana?" asked Sasha. "Are they with you? You are planning to stay this night, aren't you?"

"They are in the carriage," she answered. "Will you ask the driver to set them in?" she said, conveying her remarks to her brother.

"Yes of course." Then Doctor Fitzgerald went to the door and called to the driver to do as Melana had bid.

The driver promptly brought in her encasement, a wrinkle springing to his face that inquired of Sasha if his placement of the equipage was suitable to her.

"Very good. It will do right there."

Doctor Fitzgerald had stepped over to peek through the window at the river traffic, commenting that on this clear night the boats were moving more thickly and that the lighting emanating from the lantern glow was a treat to see. After not more than a brevity longer he announced that he must go. "Well, it's time that I should leave you Sasha. Come the early morning I am at work. You will find Melana delightful to be with and that she knows the neighborhood like the back of her hand. Even the Bobbies who walk this beat are well acquainted with her. You are secure with her around. Ah, I almost forgot. When did you want to see me at the hospital?"

"Tomorrow is fine."

"Tomorrow morning perhaps?"

"If it's satisfactory with you sir."

"It is. Is ten o'clock too early for you?"

"Perfect. I shall see you then."

"Very good. Young Yorkshire will call on you near the hour and transport you to my office. It is no piece. The distance is a mere half mile."

The rain fell that night and was persisting into the morning when Doctor Yorkshire arrived with a top on his carriage. The time was fifteen before the hour. Sasha was waiting, sipping the last of a cup of coffee which had been brewed by Melana, who also insisted on preparing breakfast. Melana had departed already, catching the transit that passed by 113 Ellington each morning at the hour of nine. She worked as a trade specialist in cotton and tea, transacting entries for the brokers of the East India Company, and was officed at the docking area where the great ships came and went.

Doctor Yorkshire met her at the doorway, holding up a parasol as a means of shielding her from the rain, now a mere drizzle, insisting that he keep it raised above her while they narrowed the distance to the carriage. Sasha had selected a stylish green suit, a lovely thing, accentuated by her pretty white blouse of plentiful ruffles. Her bright green tie matched her suit. She had let her hair stay loose, falling about her shoulders and onto her back. The young doctor was obviously swayed to be escorting her and could not help but let his eyes fall upon her at every chance. He felt shy in her presence. On the way he refrained from bringing up the subject of medicine, taking it that she preferred another topic, and spoke instead of the city of London, of its vastness and that it was home to a conglomeration of cultures. She had little to say. Mostly acknowledging his remarks. Something else was running through her. "How busy my dear one and I will be darting here and there in this awesome metropolis. She is immoderately acquainted with it. She will lead me everywhere."

Doctor Yorkshire was accustomed to driving the street on which they were traveling, people moving towards them waving with friendliness.

"They know you," said Sasha.

"Quite well, and I know them. I am on this street often."

In time she would ride the transit, the same that Melana had taken earlier, but for now it was Doctor Fitzgerald's decision to send someone for her until she became more accustomed to moving about. When they entered the hospital and had taken but a few steps down the hallway, Sasha looked over at Doctor Yorkshire, not with a frown but with a wrinkle of her pretty nose.

"The smell of hospitals is always the same, isn't it?"

"All the same. And I don't think I'll ever get used to it."

They had turned here and there, Sasha all along eyeing the doorways and at the names inscribed on the frontage. Suddenly there it was.

"Well, this is where your escort leaves you. This is Doctor Fitzgerald's office."

"I see it is. And thank you very much for bringing me."

She knocked. "Come in," the voice answered that she recognized. She opened the door and moved a slight to the inside.

"Well good morning Sasha. Come on over and have a seat," he said, rising and pulling up a chair to the side of his desk. "I'm glad to see you. I love your beautiful green suit."

"Thank you."

"I trust that you slept well."

"I did. Very well. The rain is opium for promoting sleep."

"Ha. That's me too. There's something about rain that's soothing."

"I almost overslept. But Melana took precaution that I didn't. She had breakfast ready by eight and woke me at seven thirty."

"You had a good breakfast?"

"An excellent breakfast."

"Did she bake you some of her very tasteful Garibaldi biscuits?

"Yes," answered Sasha with a grin of sincerity stealing through," they made breakfast even better."

"I'm quite glad she took good care of you. And in that young Yorkshire has delivered you safe and sound you are now in my hands; so I'll tell you what. I'll review my agenda with you, and we'll see how you fit in. I have patients to see beginning at eleven, routine you know, and would like to have you with me. We'll catch lunch somewhere as we go along, a quickie mind you, and then in the interval between three and three thirty there is a surgery on my schedule. It's a tumor on a lady's neck who's in the vicinity of some sixty years of age; I don't see it as a complicated procedure, but can't be absolutely certain. Of course I can't. But it has to be done either way. I'd like for you to join me."

"I will gladly."

This was the beginning of her medical affiliation with Doctor Alton Fitzgerald, a virtuoso surgeon of his day, and he would soon learn that she as well was a virtuoso. As she had exacted a certain role with her dear Doctor Givens, another virtuoso, she did with Doctor Fitzgerald, starting as an observer, then moving from there as an assistant and with not a great passage of time commenced surgeries herself, with him standing by. She amazed him, as she amazed the two guest surgeons from Vienna and Paris who also stood by, noted for their success with abdominal and gynecological illnesses. When out of her presence Doctor Fitzgerald and the gentleman from Vienna, Doctor Peter Metternich, and the one from Paris, Doctor Pierre Dontonte, would talk.

"You heard of her through the American Doctor Shane Givens."

"I did," answered Doctor Fitzgerald. "He recommended her. He's an acquaintance of mine of long years. I met him in Paris where he was once a student."

"I see," said Doctor Dontonte. "He had good cause for his recommendation; she is remarkably skilled."

"And knowledgeable," Doctor Metternich threw in.

"Indeed," answered Doctor Fitzgerald. "I quickly ran into that. She has read subject matter that goes beyond my limits."

"I have had coffee with her on occasions," said Doctor Metternich. "She is an interesting young woman. I, like you, find that her range of research coverage seems to have no bounds."

"This is a teaching hospital Doctor Fitzgerald," the other doctor entered in, "do you consider her a pupil? Is that why she is here?"

"You'd think so wouldn't you? But how can she be a pupil? She is a skilled surgeon. And I intend to use her in that role, taking care, I should stress, to stand by her in any case; she is not yet a doctor with a diploma. But, beyond her working with me, my plan is for her to venture into other specialties, such as yours, abdominal and gynecological surgeries. She has communicated to me not infrequently that she is keen on delving into the afflictions of the appendix, which causes a prodigious number of deaths."

"Too many, yes."

"I have asked Sasha if she's agreeable to joining you in these spheres of medicine. She lit up. She's quite agreeable."

"We're delighted," said Doctor Dontonte. "I'm glad she lit up. But let me say more of that. When I have conversations with her outside the busy surgery room she is forever sunny in her disposition, but when surgery begins, and she is cloaked in white with a mask on her face she is altogether another person. Cold as steel, and those big eyes—only the eyes you see—seem to be calmly thinking of everything at once. She is a model of control. It's almost strange, and would be if I didn't already know how lovely that face under the cloth that hides it."

Chapter 59

SO SASHA set out with Doctor Dontonte and Doctor Metternich in their specialty of medicine, while staying close to Doctor Fitzgerald and kept her friend and mentor in Baltimore posted. "These are brilliant men," she said in a letter, "and I am profiting awesomely by being with them, although progress at conquering appendicitis is slow; inflammation is troubling and dangerous. No one can speak with certainty when surgery will ascend to a level of preciseness as to make safe, or relatively safe, the opening of the human body to look upon the intestines and remove or treat that frightful persnickety culprit that refuses to stop discomforting the lives of people. More time is needed."

In modern times appendicitis is defined as an inflammation of the inner lining of the so called vermiform appendix that spreads to the other parts. Appendicitis happens when the appendix, a small finger shaped stub that protrudes from the large intestine on the right side, becomes inflamed. Surgery for eliminating this ailment was not successfully developed for another twenty to thirty years from that period when Sasha was studying and practicing with Doctors Fitzgerald, Metternich, and Dontonte, which was an era when appendicitis was generally not treated operatively and reflected a high mortality rate. Not known is the success of Sasha's pursuit of this form of surgery, for Mrs. Eastbrook spoke not particularly or generally of it in her essay, nor was there reference pertaining to it in Sasha's dairies, but her dogged persistence, along with others, surely led to many advances toward its attainment and placed her among the giants who extended their expertise and imagination well into the next century.

In the proximity of three weeks after her ship had docked in London, Mrs. Laster's ship docked too, Sasha standing close by, anxiously looking for her dear friend and pretty soon saw her descending the steps that led onto the wharf. Unable to hold back she waved with abandon, though not yet seen, but when she hastened toward her, yelling out, "Mrs. Laster, over here, it's me, Sasha, over here," her voice sallied above the chatter of the crowd; and Mrs. Laster, dropping her baggage from the effect of excitement moved as fast as possible for her age and physique. Sasha enfolded her into her arms.

"At last, at last," she exclaimed.

Mrs. Laster more or less uttered the same. "Sasha my little darling. You are here. You are here. I must be dreaming. No I'm not dreaming. It's you. I'd begun to believe we had gotten lost from one another forever. You can't imagine the thrill in my heart."

"Of course I can. It's in mine too. It's in mine too. I am happy enough to explode."

The people around looked on at the reunion but with minor watchfulness. They had their own agenda, some aspect of business to attend to or relatives or friends to intercept. After the embraces were relaxed and the tears had subsided, Sasha pointed to the carriage not more than a stone's throw away that she had detained for them, which was owned by a taxi driver who knew the city inch by inch, he had boasted, and in truth was a driver of verified capability, this coming from Doctor Yorkshire who had selected him, explaining to the man that he was to give service to a dear friend, and that his dear friend was expecting a guest from abroad, on the ship *Gargyle,* which was arriving at two o'clock and that he must execute his responsibility with irreproachable punctuality. The driver and Sasha had availed themselves at the docking area a half hour early. The driver went by the name Servies, Ronald Servies in full.

"Mr. Servies you are to drive us to 113 Ellington," Sasha instructed when she and Mrs. Laster had ascended into the carriage with his help.

Mrs. Laster kept repeating, "Imagine this. Meeting up with you here when I had so expected your visit to San Antonio." Then she followed with a discharge of happy laughter, exclaiming, "The Lord works strange happenings, doesn't He?"

"It is strange, and He does work strange happenings."

Mrs. Laster held Sasha tightly to her for the duration of the conveyance, not a long distance, perhaps less than thirty minutes if defined in clock hours. When Servies drew the horses to a halt in front of 113 Ellington, Sasha nimbly let herself down, then helped Mrs. Laster descend.

"Careful dear. We don't want an injury."

Mrs. Laster smiled lovingly. Servies had unloaded the baggage and had transported it to the doorway, standing patiently as a soldier might in anticipation of the key that Sasha would hand him and when she had he opened the door and upon learning from her where he was to deposit Mrs. Laster's belongings set them down, and then accepted the customary fee and left.

"Sasha! This is a grand little place! So exquisitely quaint! You must like it enormously."

"Oh I do. I do. What time I am here, which is at nighttime. I am kept busy during the day at the hospital. Sometimes I'm called in when I'm off duty, if an emergency necessitates it. But don't worry my dear. We will have many hours together."

"You mustn't let me interfere with your work. I shall make out very well. You know, reading and walking about the terrace and the like. Do not worry about me. I will have plenty to occupy myself in the passing hours. I know this city well, remember. I can navigate it with hardly an effort." She would later begin to feel concern that she was robbing Sasha of precious time at the hospital where she was badly needed.

"Do not worry of that. I've talked with Doctor Fitzgerald and he urges that I take some days off at first in allowance of our being together. And Melana has graciously consented to stay with you during some of the hours here at the flat when I am away, and even join you at odd times as you meander about the city. But as I said, you and I will do as much running about as we wish."

"Yes, we will darling. There is so much for me to see again. This is where I grew up and lived. Isn't it the most uncanny thing? Ha, ha, ha. I am visiting you in my own hometown." Sasha answered with laughter and then agreed that it was.

While she boiled tea they continued to busy themselves with a whirl of narrations, jamming one topic on to another. Melana Fitzgerald had been with her the three weeks past, explained Sasha, the sweet sister of Doctor Fitzgerald, her supervising surgeon, who had stayed with her to keep her company but had returned on this very day to her brother's home where she ordinarily lived with him and his wife, and Mrs. Laster rose from her chair and went to view the calm serene river flowing silently by, revealing that when she was but a girl she frequented these very banks to picnic and Sasha said that they could do that too, but was also looking forward to their seeing the dramas of the stages and Victoria Station and the Clock Tower and Windsor Castle and the great ships coming and going and the magnificent homes of the opulent and spending hours shopping in the many splendid stores, especially the famous Harrods of Knightsbridge. It still stands to this day where it was established, and some contend that it is recognized as the world's most luxurious department store on every visitor's list. Piccadilly was a must on her itinerary, the great thoroughfare leading from Haymarket and Regent Street westward to Hyde Park, densely crowded with carriages and horses of every description, from aristocratic chariots to the plebeian's cart. "It's more democratic than Bond Street and St. James's Street I hear," said Sasha. "It's crammed with people of as many different classes as there are vehicles." She then lapsed into silence, taking it that Mrs. Laster was on the verge of responding but she wasn't. She waited for Sasha to continue. Deciding as much Sasha spoke once again. "I would love to visit all these exciting places my dear, while you are here with me. And innumerable others."

"You've seen a few already?"

"I have some. As much as time has permitted. Doctor Charlatan has toured me a bit, but we've hardly scratched the surface. I was intercepted by him in the hospital hallway two days after I was ashore. I was thrilled to no end to see him again and he was me too. He called my name as I was walking down the hallway. Someone had identified me to him. He said he hardly recognized me. He but recently took me to see Westminster Abbey, which I learned is where the British Royal family holds most of its marriages and christenings and funerals; and we went to see a painting of the Queen which hangs in the Gallery of Portraits, and oh yes, to St. Paul's Cathedral. My. So grand and stately. But hardly the way one should speak of a shrine of holiness. Sorry. I don't seem to have better words handy as of this minute."

"That's all right. It is grand. I used to walk by it and never ceased to be awed, perhaps because I knew of its history more than for any other reason. The St. Paul's that now stands dates back to the 17th century but it is London's fifth St. Paul's, all having been built on the same site since AD 604. We will visit again if you like, and all the other sites you have enumerated, not leaving out a single one. We will for as many times as hours will allow. I'll even show you where I grew up, my family home, of which I am still the owner."

"You still own it?

"I do. I lease it. I don't think I can ever let it go. I will keep it for my son to inherit."

"Ah," Sasha exclaimed with tenderness.

In that Mrs. Laster had but two months to spend with her they set down on paper that night an itinerary that specified the sites they were to prevail upon first and those that were next in line, allowing too for visits to numerous others that were not yet in their consciousness. They must hasten. Time would fly.

The larger means of their travel was accomplished by carriage; the other part by train, for trains ran frequently, the tracks reaching their tentacles to every sub town of that enormous cosmopolitan maze. Most generally they boarded at Victoria Station, catching other transports somewhere further along, and Sasha soon learned the meaning of the posted symbols that represented the trains carrying passengers to the various destinations. Being a native, Mrs. Laster already understood the symbols. Apprehensive about traveling at night, they sought and received the accompaniment of either Doctor Charlatan or Doctor Yorkshire, who not only provided security but were abundantly knowledgeable as resource guides, and who now and then purposely swayed them off course, touring them into one of the rackety cafes on the Piccadilly thoroughfare that reminded Sasha of the same flavored little dive in New Orleans where Bryon sometimes took her to early morning breakfast. After this, dropping in on Harrods was an expected stop, if the hour wasn't excessively late, their escort, whichever it was, acting as if he were only too glad to stand by. On one outing Doctor Charlatan thought it a fun idea to tour them through the Soho district, formerly populated by the rich, but now littered with prostitutes and musicians and small narrow theaters where the language of the script was purposely graphic. Mrs. Laster was well aware of this vicinity. Underneath she preferred that Sasha not see it, concluding however, that after all she was grown now, no longer the young girl she had once mothered, and was about to become a renowned doctor. "And besides, she can see first hand where some of her patients live."

"How did Soho come about?" asked Sasha.

"Believe it or not this place was once lush grassland, then the wealthy started investing and building. Supposedly it was to rise to the level of Bloomsbury, Marylebone, and Mayfair," she explained. "But that failed to happen. When the rich moved away, well, you can see for yourself. It's not of your culture my dear, a bit risqué and bawdy if I may say so, but it's part of London and you don't know London until you see it all."

In the time allotted they visited every scene on the list and then some, going full blast, and still their thirst was not quenched, but time ran out. Two months had raced to an end. Mrs. Laster had to depart.

"It breaks my heart darling," she tearfully said. "Even though London is my home, it will seem a great length away, so very far, when I am back in America, knowing that you are still here."

Sasha swallowed and tried to act courageously. "I am here not many months longer, then I shall return."

"You will come to see me soon after you are there?"

"I promise. With all my heart I do."

While they had thrice from the exterior seen Mrs. Laster's fine home in Brighton Heights they nonetheless went for one last look. That night Sasha decided to lie beside her for awhile and talk before they dropped off to sleep. Already she was beginning to give way to occasional yawns. Finally, at the very end, Mrs. Laster spoke what she had saved for last.

"I was thinking Sasha my darling, about all the things we've seen and done during my time here with you, and that if the Lord had tilted his scheme just a little differently you would have been born to me in that big house in Brighton Heights, and would have grown up there and attended school and we would have seen and done all these things in old London town as mother and daughter; but on the other hand, it's pretty well happened like that anyway. You are my daughter my darling and were the first time my eyes fell upon you. I love you. I love you with all my being. You will forever dwell in my heart."

The next day she sailed from the London harbor on the good ship *Gargyle* enroute to San Antonio, Texas. Sasha and Doctor Yorkshire stood on shore watching. He had driven her and Mrs. Laster to where the ship would launch.

With Mrs. Laster no longer there Melana moved back in and Sasha kept on with her usual busy schedule working with the three doctors, a load, considering that they employed methods not always exactly corresponding and views toward a solution which sometimes substantially varied. But as quick as she was she adapted. As in Baltimore the common illnesses flooded the hospitals, hers not spared, many of them disproportionately affecting the poor, therefore sometimes called poor people's diseases, largely tuberculosis, malaria, measles, pneumonia, typhoid, dysentery, cholera, small pox, yellow fever, and diphtheria—the leading offenders—and Sasha was charged with a part in treating them, although her principal activity had to do with patients suffering from abdominal and gynecological disorders and the surgical procedures with which Doctor Fitzgerald was occupied. The women patients, the poor, the less poor, the wealthy, no matter who, seemed to like her better than the men doctors. It was her bedside manner, gentle, comforting, encouraging, which was immeasurably welcomed, as it is today in modern medical practice.

In this period of the nineteenth century Britain was recognized as the world's first industrial society; it also was the world's first urban society, where more than half the population lived in towns. London was choked with human presence. Conditions were dreadful in certain sections, dirty, unsanitary, where rubbish was allowed to collect in piles in the street, and if one dwelt in the southwest or comparable district of the city he lived in a most unfortunate place, for there, numerous factories saturated the atmosphere with noxious products, making the surroundings unsuitable for human health. Was it this specter that John Ruskin saw when he was inspired to write of, "That great foul city of London, rattling, growling, smoking, stinking—ghastly heap of fermenting brickwork, pouring out poison at every pore?" Families of six or seven or eight or more lived in back to back houses, sharing but one toilet of appalling unsanitary condition. Sometimes they formed a queue to await their turn. In the early 19th century poor people often used cesspools, which were emptied with unacceptable tardiness; then eventually commenced to use earth closets, where there was a catch pail with a box of granulated powder suspended over it, so that when a lever was pulled the box tilted, thereby spreading the powder over the human waste. Given these horrid conditions it was not surprising that disease was common and that life expectancy in towns and in the great city of London was low, markedly lower than in the countryside. Infant mortality rate was alarmingly high. Sasha daily empathized with the plight of these poor souls as they lay in their hospital beds, seeing it in their faces, hearing it in their weeping, experiencing it in their tales of hardship as she sat beside them. Suddenly she recalled the joyful life she'd had at the Sherette plantation, drifting into fantasy, again walking the open fields, where the air was fresh and serene, where there were no groans of pain to be heard and the grotesqueness of death was far away.

She and Doctor Fitzgerald had grown close and at times she addressed him with their misery, who answered that he naturally had long pitied the dilemma of the poor, a circumstance which through fate, it seemed, they were destined to endure and said that he, when but a young student starting out, had pledged to do all within his capabilities to alleviate the awfulness of their plight. While he was rich himself, born to powerful landed gentry on both his father's and mother's side, he was in character a pale resemblance to that mold. He gave generously to the hospital where he practiced, and to other worthy causes. Sasha had learned of his benevolence as she became better acquainted with Melana. He chided the rich for not already having instituted change. By rich, he meant the Victorians, who in their callous attitude were great believers in self help, that everyone should be self reliant and not look to others to offer a hand, and also believed that anyone could become successful through sheer hard work and thrift. Logically, that meant if you were poor the fault was yours.

Not all Victorians were of this notion. Eventually, but far too gradual in surfacing, laws were enacted and change was brought about. And it was the Victorians who saw to it, mandating that sewers be dug and piped water supplies created, which made life much healthier. But it is not too unreasonable to assume that the cause that stirred them resulted more from the awful outbreaks of cholera, which threatened them all, rich or poor, than from their generosity. Even though their plush homes were equipped with flushing lavatories they were not immune to the diseases which could spread from one person to another.

To speak of the poor and the hideous conditions under which they subsisted is not to suggest that London was of this state of being throughout, for anyone familiar with the history of the city knows well that it was endowed of great shrines, and canals, and financial institutions, and theaters, and cathedrals, and Windsor Castle, and magnificent galleries of the arts, and world wide commerce, and fashion, and Buckingham Palace, where Queen Victoria, the first monarch, chose to reside upon her ascension to the throne in 1837. In brief, the city was fantastically opulent yet still had its poverty as well as the concomitant diseases and misery to which poverty gave birth.

Sasha left the hospital and returned to her flat each day; if she had not assisted Doctor Fitzgerald she had Doctor Metternich and if not him then Doctor Dontonte, or often all three. Though tired, she was not without vibrancy and so penned her customary lines to Andre weekly.

> My dear Andre,
>
> I will share with you my thoughts this evening. I have others but these are the most prominent upon me.
>
> I have been among the poor this week in that there has been an overflow into our hospital due to an outbreak of cholera. We seem to have it under control. Water contamination is at fault. I feel very certain of that. If they would only boil it. Without being offensive I constantly preach this to them. The governors of this city must take every action to assure fresh water which is free of disease bearing agents.
>
> London is a massive place, of such largeness that I think I need two years to explore it to my satisfaction. Besides the blight where the poor live it is a great city. It is excitingly fashionable. I read just the other day that, "When a man is tired of London, he is tired of life, for there is in London all that life can offer." It's ironical, isn't it, that once a few weeks ago I said to Melana that I would like to get away for the weekend, that I had never set foot on French soil and would like to do that very much. She answered why not and volunteered to go with me. We sailed across the English Channel—a bit choppy; the wind was up—and went ashore at Calais. I bent over and touched my face to the ground, the soil from whence my father sprang. My way of joining him. It seemed spiritual.
>
> Please give Doctor Givens my love, and tell him that I yearn to return and that soon is not soon enough. And tell him to stop working too hard, and that applies to you too. For now I'll leave off, but not before I kiss these lines that I am sending. I love you.
>
> Sasha

Judging from his own experience, Doctor Fitzgerald knew that Sasha needed breaks from her perpetual grind, something cultural, infinitely more than the usual sight seeing and shopping excursions with Melana. He proposed to her that she join him, his wife, and his sister at some of the various operas that appeared regularly in the city. It happened that there emerged a date involving an orchestra from Vienna, which Mrs. Fitzgerald opined would offer much to Sasha's liking, the performance scheduled to take place at the Royal Italian Opera House. The orchestra was to provide the music for the drama which was titled "The Lily of Kilarney," superbly renowned in that era. Mrs. Fitzgerald felt they should attend. They went and Sasha praised it for days, never missing one of the steady continuances of others coming to London while she was there. How proud they were, the famous doctor and his family, to have this young charmer, eloquent and beautiful, sitting with them in their box for four, on which a house of curious eyes were trained, with ready questions when the opportunity availed itself, this happening repeatedly at intermission in the foyer where Doctor Fitzgerald and his wife went to enjoy a serving of punch.

There was once when, "I say my good doctor. Who is that lovely thing sitting with you and your family? I haven't seen her before. Is she Parisian? I swore to my wife she is."

"She is not, I must tell you. She is American. She resides in Baltimore. She is on visit, a student of medicine."

"I am stunned. She is poignantly flavored of French. Perhaps her ancestors were French."

"Perhaps."

Chapter 60

NOT LONG thereafter a ball was held at one of the extravagant homes of the city, and to this affair Sasha was also invited by Doctor Fitzgerald and his wife as their guest. "You must attend Sasha," Mrs. Fitzgerald insisted. "You owe it to yourself. You will love it. It's the Social Season." The Social Season was a distinguished event among the nobility and gentry of England, the season officially starting near the end of December and extending until mid summer. This was a time when Parliament was preparing to open, when England's elite traveled to London for the occasion.

To the gentlemen it meant Parliament, discussing politics, dinners, the theater, and meeting young ladies; and for mothers of the young ladies it was the golden opportunity to show off their finest clothes, and their jewels, and to host the extravagant festivities and above all else to find rich husbands for their daughters. A ball was where the finest society gathered at a private estate for an evening of traditional dining and dancing.

If one could afford it and did afford it, such person's name was lofted to a higher social level and mentioned at every gala before and after the season. Squire Irving Crenshaw had stepped forward to fund, prepare, and orchestrate this ball, the first of a long line of similar occasions that followed. The squire had hosted like events in previous seasons and did not expect higher elevation of status from this one, nor did he need any. He was as high as he could climb.

The number of guests accepting invitations to attend had to be accurately determined by a certain date, and it was necessary to provide enough room for them, as well as their chaperons, their maids, and any other servants that were brought along. Four rooms had to be put into readiness, exquisitely prepared and beautifully decorated, each serving a definite purpose, the first being the dining room, where at midnight the guests sat down to an elaborate eight to ten course meal. The second room was for refreshments, the third for hanging garments, the cloak room, and the fourth for the ladies only, where there were chaises and mirrors that made for an opportunity to relax or fix their hair or have damage to their gowns repaired.

There were certain rules that guests were expected generally to obey and other rules that were strictly to be obeyed. Even though the invitation stated that the ball was to begin at eight, guests were not in actuality expected to arrive on time. Being fifteen minutes to an hour late was taken as fashionable. The ladies were escorted by their husbands and those not married by their mother or another substituting in her place. A lady could not refuse to dance with a gentleman unless she had a prior invitation to dance with someone else. If a lady did refuse to dance without a prior commitment she had to have a reasonable excuse to offer the gentleman, regardless of whether it was trivial or not. It was viewed as an act of politeness, and if failing in this regard, she was looked upon as rude and ill bred.

Doctor and Mrs. Fitzgerald had bought Sasha a gown for the affair, a gorgeous red fabric done in the Victorian genere and all eyes were upon her as her locks, lush and lovely, fell upon her shoulders. She was dazzling; in every sense of the word she was, and every male standing in the wings eagerly waited his turn. Doctor Fitzgerald had his quite early. There was no need for him to put in words that she was spellbindingly beautiful; he said it with adoring eyes, and what man would not have been equally charmed. As soon as was possible Doctor Charlatan and Doctor Yorkshire joined in, occupying her time more than a fair share, and then after them there was a succession of others, young, middle age, and old. Understanding the rules and wishing to do nothing that caused embarrassment to Doctor Fitzgerald and his wife, she turned no one away. So round and round she went, every revolution reminding her of the splendid extravaganza once held at the Van Doke mansion and kept going until she was spent and the hour was late. She thought of Andre. The feeling inside her was not quite right. "I feel guilty, I really do. I'll write him a letter this very night and tell him I cried because he wasn't here; no, on second thought I won't. I'll do it when I'm home and in his arms. I must also enter scriblings into my diary to share with Adelaide and Mary Tonka and Mrs. Laster."

When midnight struck the crowd gathered round the massive dining table where Squire Crenshaw spoke appreciation for their presence, to which there followed a happy and ringing applause. He grinned from ear to ear. Doctor Yorkshire had hoped to sit by Sasha, as did many a young man, but naturally she gave them not the slightest of consideration, gracefully and properly taking her place between Doctor Fitzgerald and his wife. After the blessing there was a scraping of chairs and a rumble of chatter as the guests prepared to partake of the food. The food was wonderful, Mrs. Fitzgerald carrying on over it profusely to Squire Crenshaw as he happened over.

"This is a splendid dinner Squire Crenshaw, positively splendid. You have outdone yourself."

He spilled over at the compliment. "Ha, ha, ha. Why thank you, thank you. I am delighted to hear that."

But they ate sparingly in avoidance of sleeping or trying to sleep on a stomach over fed. When the clock gonged at one Doctor Fitzgerald checked his watch and relayed to friends close by that he and his party had to leave. "I must be at the hospital early." Squire Crenshaw accompanied them to the door and helped the ladies with their frocks, generously thanking them all for their presence.

"And I thank you especially Miss Duval. You have decorated our party radiantly this evening. You must join us again. I would have sought your hand in dance, but couldn't. I was afraid that my trick knee might fail me. It bears a deformity from a hunting accident of some years ago. My horse fell."

"My goodness!"

"No, no, no, no. It wasn't that bad."

"Perhaps next time it will have sufficiently improved and I will have the honor of partnering with you then. I do thank you sir for inviting me to come again. I have greatly enjoyed myself. I look forward to a return." She curtsied. Squire Crenshaw took and kissed her hand.

Three months were left. From there on Sasha worked harder and longer each day than she had the day before, if that were possible, seeing the end in sight, the completion of her internship, if one chooses to call it that, and then the taking of her diploma—and then back to America, to Baltimore and Andre and Doctor Givens. These were happy thoughts. Of the three months remaining she spent one in Vienna with Doctor Metternich participating in high risk exploratory surgeries, in some instances with appendectomies. In what spare time she had she toured the lecture halls drinking in knowledge and studying the methods of varied specialists from near and far who had been brought there because of their heralded achievements. She copied reams of notes. At the end she returned with Doctor Metternich to London.

Knowing that soon she would be leaving she increased her efforts to tour the city with Melana, who now was a never parting friend, and with Doctor Charlatan who had been particularly kind to her over the years. At this stage of their acquaintance her trust in him was complete and when on an occasion he suggested to her that she accompany him to his favorite pub, an unquestionably decent place, though noisy, she took him up on his invitation.

"It's smoky in here; I feel I'll choke."

"That's the English for you. They love to smoke. We won't stay long," he promised. "What'll you have for supper?"

"Corn beef on rye, and tea."

"That's all?"

"That's enough thank you."

"Good. And how was your day at the hospital?"

"Normal. Two surgeries, and the sewing up of a young lad of the alley who was knifed."

"Ah, too bad."

"That's what I think every time it happens. But that doesn't help. It keeps happening."

"Yep."

Doctor Charlatan looked down at the table cloth for a moment, lazily dragging his fingers over it as if he were thinking.

"You know, you'll leave us pretty soon and I'll miss you terribly. It's sad, it really is. It seems I've known you for the longest."

"You have."

"Yes I have. For a while anyway. I remember when I first met you Sasha, a beautiful young thing I must confess, and overflowing with curiosities. You won't believe it, but I said to myself right then that you had something extraordinary going for you, that in due time you'd rise to the top of the heap in the medical world. I'd like to have had what you had, I mean brains and skill and toughness—but I didn't. I'm ordinary, and that's all right. I'm content with ordinariness. But you! You weren't cut out to be that way. I'd wish you well my darling, except you don't need it. Doctor Fitzgerald says you are already reaching for the stars and that he will say one day he was fortunate to have known you. And I'm saying the same myself.

"You over do it. I don't deserve these accolades."

"But you do. And concerning accolades let me pass a good many on to that young Andre Van Doke who's crazy over you, according to what Adelaide says in her letters, who has won your heart and who one day will be marrying you. Lucky dog. Why couldn't it have been me? Don't answer that. You'd be embarrassed to tell me I'm too old and you'd have it right. I am. But if our ages had been closer, oh well, they weren't." She reached across and gently placed her hand on his arm. "You'll find someone. You will. You will soon. Someone you'll love with all your heart. And then you'll forget all about me."

"Forget about you! Who could ever forget Sasha Duval? But of that I've said enough. We'll remain friends and as the years trudge by you'll let me hear from you, won't you, regardless of how busy you are."

She patted his hand assuringly. "I'll never get that busy."

After asking if she'd finished with her food, seeing she had pushed her plate aside, he suggested they depart, to which she remarked she'd like to hold up a second, for she'd let something escape on which he might shed a ray of light.

"You remember Captain Dolby, the Captain of the *Surety*. You do, certainly. Do you currently have any idea of his whereabouts? He had a wonderful affable disposition. He, as well as you, attempted to uplift me when I was at my lowest ebb."

"I will see what I can do Sasha. The last I heard he navigates one of the Queen's ships on the Atlantic. I can trace him I'm sure. Was there anything in particular you wanted in his regard?"

"No, other than he's part of my past and I'd like to hear from him again. I've long retained his kindness in my heart."

❧ ❧

As the days dwindled down, they all sensed that Sasha would soon be leaving and began to express their sentiments variously. Doctor and Mrs. Fitzgerald had her over to their sumptuous home where dinner was served, and to which Doctor Metternich and Doctor Dontonte were also invited, each bringing gifts of paintings, one of the *River Thames* with a cottage on the shoreline and another of the *Communion of the Apostles*, which they hoped she'd hang on her walls in Baltimore. Doctor Fitzgerald and wife also had gifts in mind, already purchased, but preferred to extend them at a later date, a day before her departure. Melana had grown close to Sasha and ached hurtfully to think of her leaving. As of late she had increasingly learned more bits and pieces about Sasha's life, for they had begun to talk every night near bedtime, much as Sasha and Mrs. Laster had done. She had grown obsessively fascinated with what Sasha had said of the Sherette plantation, saying that it indeed must have been idyllic to have lived there and wished that sometimes she could come see it.

"You shall. I insist that you do Melana."

"Mary Tonka. You tell of her so vividly. She is a rarity. Tell me more of her. Why is she a part of the mansion?"

"Adelaide's mother found her. It was through the church. She's Choctaw, as I've earlier revealed. Mary Tonka virtually raised Adelaide."

"I see. And you said that Adelaide attended college in England. Isn't that astounding, in that I lived here all that while? I have a very driven wish to meet her. She is indeed novel."

"She's wonderful. My heart beats faster every time I think of her and Mary Tonka, knowing I'll see them soon after I arrive in Baltimore."

"Oh I wish you hadn't said anything of that city. It seems terribly far from here, and I fear I'll never see you again."

"But you will. You'll come see me and I you. We'll exchange letters too."

At a subsequent near time Sasha asked Melana to ride with her throughout London via the rail system to have one last look, and on another occasion, to attend mass at St. Paul's Cathedral with her, which she had adopted for worship during the several months of her residence in the city.

On the day she set sail for America her friends stood with her on the sprawling wind-blown decking, these including the Fitzgeralds, as well as Doctors Metternich, Dontonte, Yorkshire and Charlatan, each sad, for goodbyes are of their nature sad, and just before she started to ascend the steps to the upper level, the graying Doctor Fitzgerald pulled her to him in what seemed to be a special embrace, a tear or two trickling down his cheeks and told her she could not know the fulfillment of happiness she had brought to him. Melana cried remorsefully; she was losing a roommate and a lovely wonderful one at that, envisioning that for awhile she would miss her badly. They all promised faithfully to write. In the week preceding, Sasha had received her diploma, a scroll of the finest of parchment which bore the signatures of three doctors, Fitzgerald, Metternich, and Dontonte, in that order. The degree was granted by the medical university in Vienna, ostensibly, because the institutions worked substantially close in a cooperative endeavor, and thereby the doctors decided that it was in the best interest of Sasha as well as the institutions that Vienna was selected as the grantor. She was now a European doctor, which in terms of prestige, and likely in terms of capability, afforded a substantial advantage in that age of history.

༻ ༺

When she arrived in the harbor of Baltimore Andre was standing in wait, having stood and watched for most of the afternoon. The time was in the vicinity of four o'clock. It was if he had remained in that exact spot where he stood when she had left for London almost a year ago. As the ship began to pull along side the disembarkation zone he saw her next to the railing moving toward the exit and even though she tried to sort him out she failed. He was camouflaged by the crowded assemblage. He had moved close to where he would intercept her, standing at the last step of the several she would descend and when she was there he lifted her into his arms.

"Sasha, Sasha."

In the midst of the exhilaration many sweet and endearing words rushed from one to the other, a line or two coming from Sasha that it was so wonderful to be home, with Andre answering that he'd wished for her a thousand times. "Or more than that," he added. They were ecstatic. Forgetting the world around them, as if they were the only ones in it, they stood in continual embrace, and laughed and sobbed. He kissed her lips time and again, and her brow and her nose too, even a lock of her hair that had fallen in the way because of the behavior of the unruly wind. Much was he so caught up in the maelstrom of emotion that he was in the semblance of a puppy whose master had been absent for a long while suddenly now returned. But as reunions will, this one in a short while settled into a calmer disposition as happens when emotions start to subside. When he released her she stepped a step back, giving him the once over from top to bottom.

"You've taken good care of yourself Andre. You look vibrantly healthy."

"I feel so. But credit it to Padgett. She's among the best of cooks. I told her that she'd better keep it up when you returned or else you'd sever her employment. "

She let out a lovely laugh and put on a playful pose. "You didn't do that."

"No I didn't. But she is a good cook."

"Well," she said, with no further reference to Padgett and her cooking proficiency, "help me to the carriage and drive me home. We've stood here long enough. We can talk all night sitting on the portico. So much catching up to do. The swing is still working well isn't it?"

"Very well. I've sat in it every night while you were away."

"Every night?"

"Many nights, I meant."

When they had gotten home Sasha climbed agilely down the carriage siding, without holding back for Andre to assist her, aiming for the front door, which he, dashing ahead, opened for her. Once inside she began to look around, at everything, even at the smallest piece of furnishing, even at the tiny coo coo clock mounted in the kitchen, and when she ventured into the east wing she stopped in her tracks, unleashing a happy smile. Now she knew of the surprise of which he had spoken in his letter. Under his supervision the wall had been opened and a chimney and fireplace built into the gaping. Suddenly she pulled up a chair and sat down, extending her feet onto the hearth in imitation of warming them. Looking up at Andre she released a playful laugh, as a girl in her early teens might who was suddenly handed a gift, or had something extraordinary happen to her that evoked a thrill. Pulling him down to her she kissed his ckeek.

"You told me you might do this. I wasn't sure you meant it. Since it was so long ago that you gave your promise I'd begun to doubt that it was to happen at all. You're the sweetest thing Andre. I'm swept away. Now we have two fireplaces."

Padgett was thorough with her latest cleaning; the furnishings and floors sparkled, and cunningly realizing the benefit to her by pleasing Sasha she had prepared dinner and set it out on the miniature side table in the alcove. Sasha lit a candle. She looked magical in its glow and Andre was alive with adoration. "You are more beautiful than ever Sasha." The softness of her smile acknowledged his compliment. He started to say more but she pressed her finger over his lips. "Shhhhhh. That's enough. You'll embarrass me." During their dinner she spoke of Melana, who was a very dear person she said, who went with her on many sight seeing excursions of London, and mentioned Mrs. Laster too, explaining that she owned a fine home in Brighton Heights, and commented on how strange it was that she once lived in the city. "I could hardly bear to see her leave." She went on to say that she worshiped at St. Paul's Cathedral, an Anglican church dedicated to Paul the Apostle, choosing it because Melana worshiped there. "It sits on top of Ludgate Hill Andre, the highest land elevation in the city of London." When they had eaten twilight had descended and faded from view, which beckoned that the swing was waiting for company, and then Sasha changed into an evening cloak, joining Andre on the portico.

"Now we can talk some more. Who is first, you or me?"

"You. How was your voyage? Are you tired?"

"We were a little better than eight days crossing. The weather was mostly calm, except for one day when we were bounced about. The Atlantic is never entirely calm. No I'm not tired. I saw to it that it was a peaceful restful trip, much reading, and studying the waters with my binoculars. Just thinking of home and you my dear kept my spirits reasonably high."

"Ha, ha, ha. I'm glad to hear the last part. But besides Melana, tell me about your other English friends. You brought them up in your letters."

"They were wonderful. I hated to leave them, especially Doctor Fitzgerald, the chief surgeon, who reminded me of Doctor Givens. But he was older than Doctor Givens and graying. I'll tell you more about them in due time. When they naturally pop up to me."

"And London? What impressed you most about it?"

"Hmmmm. That is hard. I'm prone to say their Cathedrals and would were it not for their trains, which run everywhere. They were how I largely got about when I went somewhere. You won't believe it Andre but the train system there is far advanced to ours in America."

They talked on into the night, pouncing on everything that came to mind, at one point Sasha asking if he had heard from Adelaide, whereon he replied that he had and from Jim as well and that Jim was spending more time than usual at the Van Doke plantation, though hadn't said why. Eventually they took up the war, which was in its second year. Sasha had returned in the spring of 1862.

"It's bad Sasha. Looks like it'll worsen. Troops are constantly moving north and south, without either side gaining the upper hand. Did you hear much about it in England?"

"I read the papers and listened to people discuss it. The English stuffed the columns with it. I think the entrepreneurs are worried that cotton prices will soar due to a shortage of supply. Sometimes the doctors brought it up; I don't mean about cotton but about the war, talking low as if they were trying to keep me from overhearing. I don't know why. They knew I read the papers. But that didn't bother me because I preferred not to discuss it with anyone, except sometimes with my dear Doctor Fitzgerald and as you know I said nothing of it in my letters."

"No you didn't. I'm glad you didn't. That would have told me you were worrying." Andre gave the swing a push with his feet against the planking and seemed to be contemplating a further aspect of the subject, seconds later saying what it was. "The hospitals are beginning to overflow with the wounded. Doctor Givens and his staff have their hands full nowadays. You can't imagine how nasty the injuries. I hate for you to be drawn into the turbulence."

"That's beyond question. I must, and soon. You know I do. Tell me, how is Doctor Givens holding up?"

"Frankly, I don't like his looks. He's lost weight and his color isn't good. He works gruelingly long hours. And the stress from dealing with the wounded, well, I guess you can picture that vividly enough."

"Poor man. I'll report in day after tomorrow to relieve him. Dear me. The war. How tragic. No one knows where it is destined from here."

"No. But the signs say it'll only worsen."

The air had grown chilly, Sasha thus opting to the inside for a heavier garment, a robe, coming back in a brevity to sit down and resume her place in Andre's arms, who pulled her tighter to him, and softly began to stroke her hair.

"Let's not talk any more Andre. Not for awhile anyway. Let's just listen to the quietness."

"Sure. Let's do that."

Andre gave the swing a boost now and then. She felt warm and lovely against him. There was something once that he started to mention, though held back, for her obvious quietness and the symphony of her bosom rising and falling told him she had succumbed to slumber. He chuckled. "I figured this was about to happen. She's worn out, which is not much of a feat to understand. She's traveled across the entire ocean." There, at length, he held her, in the tenderest delicate way, hating to give her up. But realizing at last that the hour was late he arose with her in his arms and carried her into the bedroom, where Padgett had turned back the covers, and tucked her in. Kissing her brow he uttered, "Good night sweetheart," to which she was oblivious, and went to his bed across the hallway. The next morning he left early, hours before Sasha awakened. There were people to see at the hospital. Just before exiting the doorway he stopped and ambled over to the small table in the alcove, there writing a note which he left in clear sight, the words saying that he would have kissed her good morning if he had not feared waking her, and added that Padgett was due at ten o'clock and that he would see her again near nightfall. "Save me a seat in the swing." There was also an envelope that he placed along side his own note bearing the name of Adelaide Sherette, the sender. When Sasha had risen and had begun to wander around a bit her eyes fell curiously on the two items, first reading Andre's note and then turning to the envelope addressed to her from Adelaide. She wasted no time in opening it. "Welcome home darling." Sasha burst into laughter. The letter was dropped off by the postman a few days prior and Andre had laid it conspicuously out for her to see.

Chapter 61

THROUGHOUT THE day she stayed busy unpacking her belongings and storing them away, and studying how she might rearrange the interior, definitely the kitchen. She said to herself that the wall to the adjoining room should be torn out and the two combined. "But no touching the coo coo clock. It stays exactly where it is." She wished she had the two paintings from Doctors Metternich and Dontonte. She thought she had decided where she'd hang them. But they were scheduled to arrive later by separate shipment. Sometimes she sat down at the little table in the alcove, doodling with pen and paper, reflecting on the events of the year past. Some of the day she spent with Padgett, going over plans of work and at one point asked her if she'd like the job full time. She had deemed before hand that she needed someone fully engaged to tend to the daily matters of the home, inclusive of the preparation of meals and washing and ironing, for she envisioned, and did so correctly, that her schedule and activities at the hospital would be continually intensive, let alone the courier night messages urging her to rush to the aid of a patient in distress.

"I sho would Miss Sasha. I needs it."

"Good. Then you started as of this morning."

The following day Sasha left early for the office of her dear friend Doctor Givens, who, after enfolding her in his arms, at the same time choking up a slight, playfully addressed her as Doctor Duval. He already had a letter from Doctor Fitzgerald reporting that she had been awarded her degree.

"It sounds very natural Sasha, very distinguished. I have immense gladness in my heart for you."

"I can't thank you enough."

"Bosh! Thank me? You owe thanks to only one person and that person is Sasha Duval. She earned it and I am adding, as did Doctor Fitzgerald, in the swiftest of time."

After they had descended from their cloud of jubilance, and talked a while about her experiences abroad, Doctor Givens sat down at his desk, Sasha sitting down beside him with tablet and pen in hand, and somberly gave her an accounting of what he had so far endured from the war and what he thought to be awful times in the making.

"I will not spare you my darling, nor do you need sparing because your hide is thick. More than mine. Seeing bones shattered and bodies torn open from cannon fire and hearing men scream is not for the shy. I am thankful for you at this hour of graveness. You will greatly relieve my load. And I know this too; you will save many a soldier who will not have survived without you."

When Sasha first arrived in Baltimore from abroad the war had been upon the nation by a year, the first shot ringing out at Fort Sumter, April 12, 1861, in the early morning hours. The monster was let loose that ravaged the land and its people for four tragic years, the social and economic destruction created in its wake staying unresolved well into the next century. The nature and effects of this embattled period have been narrated immemorially by essayists and poets in droves and therefore the intent here is not to add more lines of a similar construction, but to describe limitedly the conditions—the battlefield injuries, the sicknesses, the attempts to save lives—that were a part of the violent furor and thereby show what our dear Sasha and Doctor Givens, and hundreds of other doctors, were medically up against in dealing with them.

The Civil War was fought, claimed the Union Surgeon General, at the end of the medical Middle Ages. Little was known, it should be truthfully said, about what caused disease, how to stop it from spreading, or how to contrive methods and medicines that resulted in a cure or correction. Surgical techniques ranged from the barbaric to the barely competent—though certainly there were exceptions. A Civil War soldier's chances of not surviving was about one in four. These fallen men were cared for by a woefully under qualified, under staffed, and under supplied medical corps. Working against incredible odds however, the medical corps increased in size, improved its techniques, and gained a greater understanding of medicine and disease every year the war was fought.

During the year just before the outbreak of hostilities a physician received minimal training and nearly all the older doctors served as apprentices in lieu of formal education. Even those who had attended one of the few medical schools were poorly trained. Few, if any, were trained in the science of triage, the order and treatment of the wounded which was common in the modern hospital in Baltimore where Sasha practiced; but proportionately few soldiers were lucky enough to be placed under its care. In Europe, four year medical schools were well established, such as those in London, Paris, and Vienna, laboratory training was wide spread, and a greater understanding of disease and infection existed. The average medical student in America, on the other hand, trained for two years or less, received practically no clinical experience and was given virtually no laboratory exposure. Harvard University, astoundingly enough as we look back, did not own a single stethoscope or microscope until after the war. But despite these limitations it must be acknowledged that Civil War doctors, although referred to as butchers by their patients and the press, managed to treat more than ten million cases of injuries and illness in just forty eight months and most did it with as much compassion and competency as was inherent within them. In the manner of the battlefield soldiers the doctors too existed and worked in a living hell. In all fairness, it should be related, every effort was summoned forth to treat wounded men within forty eight hours, most primary care administered at field hospitals, often barns and sheds and tents located at some point behind the front lines. Those who survived were then transported by unreliable and overcrowded ambulances—two wheeled carts or four wheeled wagons—to army hospitals situated in nearby cities and towns. Sadly, but truthfully, hospitalization was often regarded as the equivalent of a death sentence.

Of the approximately one hundred seventy five thousand wounds to the extremities received among Federal troops, about thirty thousand led to amputation. Roughly about the same proportion befell the soldiers of the Confederacy. One witness described a common surgeon's tent this way: "Tables about breast high had been erected upon which the screaming victims were having arms and legs cut off. The surgeons and their assistants, stripped to the waist and besplattered with blood, stood around, some holding the poor fellows while others armed with long, bloody knives and saws, cut and sawed away with frightful rapidity, throwing the mangled limbs on a pile nearby as soon as removed." Contrary to popular myth most amputees did not experience the surgery without anesthetic. Ample doses of chloroform were administered beforehand; the screams heard were usually from soldiers just informed that they would lose a limb, or who were witnesses to the plight of other soldiers under the knife. One cannot easily imagine, or can he, how horrible to have been there watching this scene with his own eyes.

Those who survived their wounds and surgeries still had another hurdle, the high risk of infection. Joseph Lister had not yet discovered the power of the antiseptic; that happened briefly after 1865, the year the war ended, but too late to benefit the poor Civil War soldier. While most surgeons were aware of the relationship between cleanliness and low infection rates, they, it seems, did not know how to sterilize their equipment or know that they should. Due to a frequent shortage of water, surgeons often went days without washing their hands or their instruments, thereby passing germs from one patient to another as they were treated. The resulting vicious infections, commonly known as surgical fever, are believed to have been caused largely by *Staphylococcus aureus* and *Streptococcus pyogenes,* bacterial cells which generate pus, destroy tissue, and release deadly toxins into the bloodstream. Gangrene, the rotting away of flesh caused by the obstruction of blood flow, was also common after surgery.

While the average soldier believed the bullet was his most nefarious foe, disease was the biggest killer of the war. Of the Federal dead, roughly three out of five died of disease, and of the Confederate, perhaps two out of three. One of the reasons for the high rate of disease was the slipshod process that allowed under or over aged men and those glaringly in poor health to join the army on both sides, especially in the first year of the war. About half of the deaths from disease was caused by intestinal disorders, principally typhoid fever, diarrhea, and dysentery. The remainder died from pneumonia and tuberculosis. Camps populated by young soldiers who had never before been exposed to a range of common contagious diseases were plagued by outbreaks of measles, chicken pox, mumps, and whooping cough. The culprit in most cases of war time illness, it should be stressed, was the shocking filth of the army camp itself, badly littered with refuse, food, and other rubbish, sometimes in an offensive state of decomposition. Slops were deposited in pits within camp limits and manure and offal likewise were let heap up close by. As a result bacteria and viruses spread through the camp like wildfire. Bowel disorders constituted the soldier's most common complaint. The Union army reported that more than nine hundred ninety five out of every one thousand men eventually contracted chronic diarrhea or dysentery; the Confederates fared no better. Typhoid fever was even more devastating, one quarter of non combat deaths in the Confederacy resulting from this disease, which was caused by the consumption of food or water contaminated by *salmonella.* Epidemics of malaria spread through camps situated next to stagnant swamps teeming with the *anopheles* mosquito. Although treatment with quinine reduced fatalities, malaria nevertheless struck one quarter of all servicemen. The Union army alone reported one million cases of it during the course of the war. Poor diet and exposure to the elements only added to the burden. A simple cold often developed into pneumonia, which was the third leading killer of the war, after typhoid and dysentery.

Not anytime soon would conditions turn for the better; the war was spreading and discernibly growing more intense. Sasha had prepared herself, steeled but not entirely steeled against the screams of the soldiers and the visible destruction of their bodily parts that Doctor Givens had earlier told her about. After a length of some months Adelaide wrote and asked what she did to lessen the weight of the stress that surely had fallen upon her. "I pray a lot Adelaide," she returned. Keeping stride with the worsening of the war the casualties proportionately mounted and with alarming quickness. Increasingly the medics transported the wounded, sick, or dying to the Baltimore hospital, which had rapidly gained recognition for the triage capability of the staff. Yet, even as conditions worsened, there was a silver lining that shone through, this being the surgical team that Sasha had meshed together, "Sasha's group," they called them, steadfastly adhering to the rules that she had set in place, where, before every surgery there was a washing of hands and arms up to the elbows. "Scrub, scrub, scrub," she instructed, "scrub the patients and scrub yourselves." Removing the slip on coat of white, often blood splattered or smeared of pus, was a policy of iron clad solidness each time a surgery was performed. The rule had to be unvaryingly obeyed, and it was equally incumbent on each team member to come prepared for surgical readiness, which meant to be clad in a radiantly clean shirt or blouse and topcoat. The levying of these strictures profoundly paid off, resulting in fewer infections, fewer soldier fevers, fewer loses of life from gangrene, and while this was so there were other designs of her making that had little or nothing to do with cleanliness and disinfection. They had to do with her heart, her feelings, her compassion for the dear unfortunate soul in her care who sometimes she drew into her arms and said soft words to and squeezed and assured him that he was in the best of hands, promising solemnly to do all within her power to see him through. She asked about family, if there was a sweetheart somewhere and what was her name; and whether he read the scriptures and would he like for her to read a passage or two then and there. This was when the patient's wounds were not serious enough to require immediate surgery. But there were other immediacies of a different cast, and other soldiers, whose prognosis was grave; and then, there was no need for Sasha's sweet comforting words. Not a one would the patient have heard. The savagery of the pain overpowered everything else. The chloroforming was started right away, the battered arm readied for severance without delay. When the team had finished with the preparations, they looked over in anticipation to the person with the mask covering her nose and the lower half of her face, whose eyes, deep and dark and studious, revealed she was thinking of everything at once. "Let us begin," she said, with icy firmness, as she nimbly lifted the instrument that would do without variance what it was told by the poignant mind and flawless hands that guided it.

This one pulled through. Not every soldier was that lucky. At a later stage of the year a youngster of eighteen was turned over to Sasha's group by the medics, suffering from severe abdominal pain owing to a bullet that had penetrated into the intestines. There was no alternative but to operate, to probe and see. The boy was deathly afraid. Sasha remembered this one years later to Andre, seemingly more vividly and more singularly than many others that came under her care.

"I'm going to die doctor. I can feel it."

"Shhhhhh. Don't say that."

"What do you think doctor?"

"I'll do all I can for you."

"I know you will. I was told you were the best for seeing after me. I'm glad they brought me to you." She didn't respond directly. She changed the subject.

"Does it hurt you to talk?"

"Unh hunh."

"But maybe you can talk a little."

"Yeah. Unh hunh."

"Where are you from?"

"Iuka, Mississippi."

"I've never heard of it. Tell me, how did a young man from Mississippi get way off up here?"

"We were caught up with by the Yankees. Not in Mississippi. Not far from here."

"In Maryland?"

"Unh hunh." His voice had become weaker.

Sasha hugged him to her and repeated she would do her best. She didn't want to lie. She didn't want to tell him he'd make it when she doubted it.

"We have the finest team anywhere. That's in your favor." The young man smiled with an effort, and did no better, evincing to Sasha that his pain was worsening. She had intended to ask about his sweetheart back home, but never made it that far, because he had begun to discharge blood at the mouth and spoke no more. That night they operated. He was too far gone for Sasha to expect him to live. So badly was he hemorrhaging that an attendant who was hovering close winced and drew back. When it became clear to Sasha that he was going she dismissed the larger number of the staff who were needed elsewhere and held his hand until life had passed. He never regained consciousness. She asked another doctor, an understudy that she had asked to remain, to sew up the incision and cleanse the body, then went out on the balcony and there alone looked into the night, instantly spotting the Eastern star that shone ever so brightly and held it in her gaze for the longest while, thinking, thinking, thinking. More than once her thoughts fell upon the young girl she once lost in child birth, her first, remembering without pause the dress, even its color and texture, in which she was buried. "It hurt then Sasha," she counseled herself, "as it does now. But this is who you chose to become and what you have become is replete with disappointments and sorrows." And then she said her little prayer. "I lost him Dear Lord. You called his number. But let me thank you for giving him eighteen years on this earth. I will say as much in the letter that I plan to write to his mother, confident that You will approve. Amen."

The next day she sat down with Doctor Givens for an interval of respite, which was badly needed.

"We lose them and it touches us Sasha; actually, it crushes us, takes a piece out of us. Every time it does. I've said this before and I say it now. Things won't change. Next week somebody else around here will feel the same way, or it may be you again or me."

"More of it will come. That's true. But we'll keep on."

"Yep, we will."

"But while we're speaking of the subject, keeping on, let me put in an additional word. You've been at this a good while; I mean, dealing with causalities almost daily without letup, ever since the war started. Don't you think it's time you had a vacation? You need to distance yourself from all this for awhile." She declined to tell him that he looked tired and worn and somewhat emaciated. She worried.

"It's occurred to me Sasha, it really has. Perhaps I will when the pace of things slows down." He realized better than anyone else that he was weakening.

"But things won't slow down. The peak of the wounded and sick is yet to crest. You'll have to force yourself."

"Or have you do it for me."

"Ha, ha, ha. I didn't say that."

"Who would replace me?"

"Someone. There's always someone."

"The question is who."

She had already thought of who, but wouldn't suggest the name at the immediate moment. She'd wait. It was Doctor Metternich. Within a week Doctor Givens asked her again who could step in as his temporary replacement, to which she answered that Doctor Metternich might consent to filling in for a while. Doctor Givens smiled pleasantly, revealing that the doctor from Vienna had crossed his mind also and asked Sasha if she would draft a letter asking him to join the hospital with his services. She penned the wording and mailed the letter before the day had closed.

In the meanwhile life at the Sherette plantation had not stood still. Union troops had arrived and stopped off during their surge to Corinth, quartering in the barns and sheds and in some of the empty small shacks, delivering the wounded to the infirmary, where a Union doctor together with Doctor Lundy, who happened to be there, sought to attend them, neither trained in the science of triage. Adelaide had written to Sasha as to the presence of the Yankee soldiers, wishing fervently that she were there to help with the sick and wounded and with other things as well, which she went into as she laid down one line after another.

Dear Sasha,

You are doubtless covered up. I can see you now, hovering over some patient, most likely severely injured. My heart is with you.

I have much to tell. Union troops are here as expected, bivouacked on the plantation grounds, using the barns and sheds for their lodging and some of the small houses that are empty. We met the man in charge, a Captain Arnold, a nice fellow I will admit. Thank goodness he is of good breeding. I looked for him to ask for lodging in one of the bedrooms of our home, which would have been most comfortable in that he sleeps in one of the barns, yet he made no inquiry for an inside accommodation and I made no effort to offer it. In lieu of this I have twice invited him to take breakfast with Mary Tonka and I and he accepted. He is a friendly person, handsome, with intelligent eyes and is quite talkative. He's a mite taller than Andre. We are getting used to him. He's a gentleman. I invited the doctor to eat with us but for some reason or other he declined.

They are supposed to leave this week, targeting Corinth for their next stop. Their departure causes me a degree of anxiety, for I have heard that when soldiers have left homes of other communities here and there they wreaked utter destruction, tearing down and burning fences, butchering cattle, hogs, sheep, geese, turkeys and stealing hams from the smokehouses, and taking off the horses. When I approached Captain Arnold with my concern that the same might happen to us he said he'd already passed word that everything was to be left as they found it and that he will strictly enforce his orders. I believe him. I think the kindness that Mary Tonka and I have extended may have touched the caring strings of his heart.

I have not seen how LaBelle has fared; very well I presume, for only the officers have occupied it and Cynthia and Sol have fed them lavishly, the soldiers too, who are much fewer in number than the ones encamped here. The Nomeharts left well ahead of the troops. I don't blame them. I feel uneasy myself about their presence here. Cynthia slipped over yesterday and we talked, so that's how I know what has gone on. She said that no one has touched or tried to play the piano. Let's hope they won't. Surely someday it will be yours as a gift from Andre. Cynthia said that a young officer kept devouring your portrait, the one we had done of you in Memphis. You remember that don't you? I mentioned Sol, poor thing. He's not well. Doctor Lundy has examined him but doesn't have a creditable idea of the cause of his ailment. I do wish you were here to make a diagnosis, and after all, you have not been home in a considerable while. I do wish you could come.

I have saved something for last that may jolt you. George, who is now in the Confederate army, as an officer they say, has through laxness and foolish decisions steered the Van Doke plantation onto hard times, starting with piling up huge gambling debts, losing outlandish sums on the British Trade Exchange, and experiencing large scale cotton losses due to the boll weevil because he wasn't around to manage. He should have looked ahead and enacted a design of protection a good while ago. As you know we built three spacious warehouses at our place where we stored cotton from the two previous years, thus we had an ample amount to sell at very high market prices, as high as Harry could negotiate, which was quite good. I ended up contracting with Jim to purchase five hundred acres of Van Doke land just to help out. I am uncertain of the extent of the whole amount of the loss because Jim chose to keep that to himself, and he should have; but it was sizeable, I am sure. And will have to be satisfied. I am also uncertain as to whether Andre is acquainted with these circumstances, for Jim did not mention that either, but if you should bring it up please do it gently.

This is all for now my darling. I have said enough, and so will say goodbye and hope with all my heart that you can find it opportune to visit.

I love you,

Adelaide

The war had crept into the beginning of its last year, 1864, with both sides on the brink of exhaustion. It was late spring, somewhere in the vicinity of April or early May, when on an evening warmer than ordinary Sasha and Andre sat on the doorsteps of the portico, breathing in the freshness of the air. Sasha was off from work early and Padgett had prepared their dinner. Both had had a good day at the hospital; they were in a mood to talk. Andre speculated that the war would end that year, in the latter part, and Sasha said she'd say a prayer every night that it would. Doctor Givens was still on leave, but noticeably improving, so said Sasha who visited him twice weekly. Doctor Metternich had accepted Sasha's invitation to help with the causalities and was still with the hospital, working side by side with her, his expertise helping enormously to fill the vacuum that Doctor Givens created when he took leave. He, in the manner of Doctor Givens, was a prince of a fellow to be around and they had many good visits over coffee in the cafeteria trading talk about the latest discoveries reported in the journals, and in addition took up some of their own. On certain nights of the winter past Andre had built a fire in one of the fire places, a treat to which Sasha invariably looked forward and would have preferred one this very evening had not the temperature been too warm. So they sat on the doorsteps and talked and ate popcorn and drank iced tea that Padgett had brought to them. Sasha said she'd like to spend an afternoon on the beach as soon as they could fit it into their schedules and Andre replied that he'd love to also, and throwing off a playful grin, added that he hoped the wind would blow with an extra force on that day.

Knowing what he meant Sasha tapped his face, and accused him of distasteful behavior.

"Of course," she said, laughing, "I'm just kidding my sweet Andre. Did it hurt?"

They would visit the beach the week after, taking both Doctor Givens and Doctor Metternich with them.

"They're beginning to turn the soil on the plantation Andre, readying it for the early crops, and they should be cutting and raking the winter wheat along about now. I wish I could be there. There's nothing like the smell of freshly cut hay."

"I'm the same way. And I can just see Sam Feathers now. In the middle of it all. 'Hey men. Make haste. Let's get this hay put in the barn before it rains.'"

" Yeah. The hay and Sam Feathers. They kind of go together, don't they? It kind of gives me a touch of nostalgia, kind of makes me want to go home and be out there with him."

"I know your feelings."

"I love Aurora Andre and everything that goes with it. I truly do. I miss it. I miss so many countless things about it. I don't always tell you but I do. I have always loved it. I did the first time I ever set eyes on it."

"When was that?"

"When Sam Feathers was driving us back from Memphis where he'd come to pick us up. Suddenly we passed through the tree line and I saw it, reaching for what seemed to be the great Heavens above, and when we drew closer and wound our way through the giant cedars and I saw it close up I was astounded. It was ponderous and beautiful at the same time."

"Now I'm feeling homesick."

Her eyes danced. "I make myself feel homesick."

"I wish we could go sweetheart. I wish we could leave tomorrow. I really do. What a great time of year for a visit."

"Ah, so do I. But what would you say Andre if I said I really did want to and meant it?"

"I would say I'm glad, except I couldn't seriously consider taking off just now. I have exams to prepare for. My degree, you know. You have yours and I don't. Lucky."

"I'm not lucky Andre, and you'll have yours before you can snap your finger."

After this, Sasha's countenance turned to a more serious mien, as if revolving a decision of exceptional import, and upon noticing Andre interrupted.

"A penny for your thoughts. What are they? Care to share?"

"I was just wondering Andre, what you might think of my going to see Adelaide and Mary Tonka by myself?"

"Going to see them! Ah, do you mean it?"

"I do."

" Ah, well, it's your choice. Could I ask if there is a pressing reason why you want to? I mean besides your just having a yen in your heart to do so."

"There is, and normally I wouldn't even think of doing it. I'm bothered at the thought of leaving the patients, and you. But I have a letter from Adelaide. Among other things Sol is sick. I owe it to him to see what I can do. He and Cynthia are preciously dear. You don't have to go with me if you don't think you can."

"I owe it to Sol too. But he doesn't need us both. You're a plenty. With you caring for him he certainly wouldn't need me. I do wonder about your travel. Soldiers are all over the place. That's something of a worry."

"I'll be all right."

"When are you thinking you'll leave?"

"Ten days from now. I'll have to work it out with Lucy to meet me in Nashville."

"Yeah, you'll need to do that."

"I must soon."

"I guess ten days is enough to allow for preparations and all. Looks like Doctor Givens is refreshed enough to step in and work again."

"I think so. He said the other day when I was with him that he's returning."

"Then he will."

Within the passing of the next several days she had discussed the records of her patients with both Doctors Givens and Metternich who graciously agreed to take them over, blessing her for making the long trip to help a beloved. Doctor Givens had met Sol when visiting the plantations and knew what he meant to her. Andre had gone to the train station to purchase train tickets, there working out transitions from one train to another should that be necessary. Padgett had dutifully helped with her packing, double checking everything, even her toiletries, swollen with pride that Sasha might entrust such an assignment to her. In the fullest sense Sasha hadn't, afterwards checking them off herself just to be sure. But eventually praised Padgett for a job she told her was well done.

The night before her departure she and Andre had their words of goodbye. Very sad words, but both accepting why she was taking the trip.

"I hate to see you leave Sasha, more I think than I did when you sailed for England. I guess it's because I realize you'll be home and I won't. It's hard to imagine you there among everyone when I'm not. It just doesn't seem natural."

With delicate softness she touched his hand. "I wish you didn't feel that way. After all, I'm returning within three weeks or less."

"I know, I know. Well, anyway, let's make the best of it and hope you'll get back when you say."

"I hope."

"You're all packed."

"I am. Padgett has helped me. She's done very much."

"Your train leaves at seven. I've double checked."

"Thank you. You're so efficient darling."

"And you received your letter from Lucy verifying they'll be on the watch for you?"

"I've heard from her. She answered my telegraph two days ago."

Both tried to smile, finding that happiness did not easily avail itself.

But shortly Andre wittingly broke the ice. "You know something Sasha. I might even change my mind and board that train with you," he said, half laughing.

"You're a dear Andre. So good, so wonderful a man. You're the sweetest thing on earth. If I thought you meant it I'd do anything to persuade you." She pressed his arm. They were now sitting in the swing and she merely had to reach to touch him. The dark had recently fallen, accompanied by the rising moon which discharged its enchanting glow.

"Careful. That wouldn't require much effort. But the dye is cast and you must be on with your journey, even without me. But I thank you for the compliment. The sweetest man on earth! Boy, that puts me up there."

"Yes. Where you belong."

"Where I belong," he uttered, then slowly raised his eyes to Heaven and when they were lowered he saw her smiling gently upon him. The smile of a woman in love has a brilliancy which we can see by night.

"Je t'aime Andre."[10]

---

[10] I love you Andre.

Andre did the thing that is as common as breathing the fresh morning air, responding that he loved her too, a thousand times he did, telling her that if he could have spoken the language of the French he would have conveyed his feelings far more passionately; and then went on to remember he'd fallen overwhelmingly for her from the beginning, which was when she had come into the room that day when he was sitting in the presence of Adelaide and thought to himself that he was seeing the most beautiful girl that God could have ever made, and that he was right except for one other thing.

"What was that?"

"You're more beautiful now."

She tried to smother her sigh with her hand. "You embarrass me. But I like it. I hope you will always embarrass me. That's the highest compliment that a husband could bestow upon his wife."

Andre had sometimes wondered if he might ever hear these words, "his wife," or words of the same meaning, and was now jolted with surprise, to say the least, if not by stunning suddenness, with one prevailing thought running through him. Did the woman he so greatly adored have marriage in mind with him?

"Doctor Duval, did you in a vague sort of way just now propose to me?" he asked, sounding of lightness and seriousness at the same time, though in his heart there was infinite seriousness, and that only.

"Silly boy." She leaned closer and nestled her face tenderly against his shoulder. "No, I did not propose to you my dear Andre; I simply opened the door for you to properly do so to me."

Not configuring how he should conduct himself in the whirl of excitement that suddenly had sprung upon him he fell to his knees, and prostrating himself, slowly took the tip of her foot which peeped from under her dress and kissed it. She allowed it in silence. There are moments when a woman accepts, like a goddess somber and resigned, the religion of love.

"Ah Sasha, my dearest," he said as endearingly as his voice could find endearing delicacies, still bent on his knees, looking up at her, her hands in his. "I have waited for this, for the longest I have, wondering if you'd ever open the door."

She ran her fingers through his hair and leaned over and pressed her cheek to the top of his head.

"So at last I have. I will be very happy with you Andre, more than pleased to be your wife for better or for worse, and will consider it an honor to bear your children. I can see it all now. What a rich and wonderful life we have ahead."

"The children. You mentioned children. What will be their names?"

"I cannot say. But I have revolved it for a good long while."

"You didn't tell me."

"Certainly not. An unmarried woman is not supposed to reveal such fantasies. But I have revolved it over and over nonetheless. We'll discover the names, we will in due time."

"But when will we marry, when will it happen?"

"I will talk to Adelaide and Mary Tonka about it. I am bent on the wedding taking place at Aurora. That will mean everything to me."

"Please do talk to them. And I'm supposing that Lawrence Sherette will marry us."

"He alone. Who else? He is my father." Andre placed his fingers to his forehead and squinted. "What is it? Why do you act like that?"

"It's odd, isn't it? Lawrence Sherette will marry you off and give you away too. I don't often hear of that. But I should be serious sweetheart. My apologies."

"No need to apologize. It is rare, and I will always tell of it to our children. They will make much bustle over the story."

Soon thereafter they went to bed, Andre sleeping in the one across the hall, which Sasha had asked of him, for she needed his help the next morning with the assembly of her sizeable packings. She had combed through her wardrobe the whole week previous deciding on whatever she would take with her. Her clothes carrier was stuffed, as well as the huge trunk that once belonged to her mother, where inside some gifts of affection were stored that she had purchased in England for Adelaide and Mary Tonka.

They rose early. The train would leave exactly on time. Sasha sat by her baggage in the massive lobby of President Street Station while waiting for its approach, Andre choosing to stand and pace around, intermittently glancing at his watch. The station teemed with travelers, many of them Union soldiers destined for the fighting lines somewhere or home on furlough, especially those who seemed to be hampered by injury. Sasha was dressed in a handsome red coat that flaunted distinctions of French stylization with rather large shiny black buttons on the front, stringing practically the full length of the garment itself, starting at the neck and terminating a slight above ankle level. She also wore a hat; it was dark and matched the buttons, and anyone glimpsing her sitting there, perfectly erect and sipping occasionally from a cup of hot tea that Andre had retrieved from the station concessionaire would have been at once dazzled by the young woman of singular charm and sophistication.

The foghorn blasted just before the train entered the terminal. They had heard the rumble seconds before. Andre scrambled to gather her belongings and with the aide of a porter set them where they would be taken over by another porter in charge of loading the baggage into a freight car for handling materials marked "caution." Andre and Sasha had moved to the passenger loading zone, close at rail side. A minute more and there was a screech of metal as the great engine suddenly drew to a stop, while letting off a cloud of steam and a frightful hiss that forced Sasha to cover her ears. A porter assigned to the passenger coach opened a door and called out "All aboard." Sasha turned to receive Andre's kiss and gave one in return and then turned again and climbed the steps, thinking to wave one last time as she entered the doorway, there disappearing out of sight.

She had taken along a book to read, a novel by Gustave Flaubert, only recently published, something to keep her occupied while en route. Melana had sent her the book, with prodding's that she should read it without fail. "It's fascinating Sasha, but I caution you. Things turn out badly for the woman."

"I'm curious. I shall see."

The train had pulled slowly away from the station, the people standing in clusters in the disembarkation zone looking up through the windows at the passengers, some waving, some throwing a kiss, then turning to one another to exchange words about something or other. Sasha wished that Andre was there to wave at her once more. The train moved on. Soon they were a good stretch removed from the inner part of the city with its fine cobblestone streets and handsome buildings and parks and theaters and had reached the poorer section, that quadrant which to Sasha was acutely dissimilar to the nice suburbs where she lived. She wondered why she had not come to know of it before. "But there was no cause to. We've always sought the center of the city for entertainment and culture or else gone eastward to the Chesapeake." But there they were nonetheless, squatty pitiful things, shanties, shacks, unsightly, crowded together, unpleasant to sight, such as Sasha had seen in London and Memphis, made of unpainted ugly siding and flat top roofs, virtually windowless. She wondered if this community had a distinct name, such as "shanty town," as was given to the one in London that was situated not a substantial piece from the hospital. She would witness the same in Indianapolis, Cincinnati, Louisville, and Nashville. "Poverty is everywhere," she mused. "Even on the Van Doke and Sherette plantations too, but life is different there than in the cities."

Time passed. She had settled comfortably in her seat, looking now at the landscape, at the pretty lush meadows and streams, and tall slender oaks and elms on the hillsides next to the railway, shanty town far behind, which she had repressed from mind for the moment; and it was now that she drifted back to Andre and the lovely time she'd had with him the night before and the several nights before that. "Isn't it strange? As terrible as it is war does not stop love, nor in the least retard it. Isn't that amazing? It may even help it take root. After all, there's something about war, they say, that's given rise to some of the world's most famous romances. When I am home with Adelaide I shall take this up with her. Ah, war and love and the complexity of. What an intriguing topic. How do they manage to coexist? I'll ask her help with this one. I can hear her as she begins. 'Well Sasha, they just do.' We sat there last night, Andre and I, and said the loveliest words, lost in each other, and even once he kissed my toe, silly boy, but a lovely boy, and war was far away, for we had sent it away, and for the briefest, it seemed not to be anywhere at all. But it was."

Aside from missing Andre, the ride was relaxing and joyful. She read awhile, then looked out at the countryside. Alternating back and forth. At mid morning, she, at the suggestion of a porter, decided to try the diner; a cup of coffee would suit quite well. She'd had breakfast earlier at home. She wasn't hungry but would welcome coffee. She had sat down and was taking her first sip when a handsome tall soldier approached her table and introduced himself as Major Horton of the First Cavalry of the Union Army, apologetically explaining that he had hardly recognized her because when he met her in the proximity of six months ago she was attired in a doctor's uniform. She remembered the occasion. She silently went back over it exactly. She had removed her head cover when emerging from the surgery room, letting her hair fall about her shoulders, which before then was pulled up in mass, there telling the Major that the young soldier had survived the ordeal without complications and that the prognosis looked good.

"You were a surgeon at the hospital in Baltimore. I believe I'm correct about this."

"You are Major."

"I was there when you did surgery on one of my young soldiers. You saved his life."

"I am so thankful that I did."

There were other exchanges, but she declined to invite him to take a seat. She did say it was nice that he said hello, inquiring as well of the present welfare of the young soldier, but her demeanor remained unaffected.

"You're going south?" said the Major. "Louisville perhaps?"

"No. To an estate in Western Tennessee. I'm hoping to help an old friend who is sick."

"I do wish you well. I truly do, and if there's any way that I can lend assistance to making your trip more comfortable and less trying please let me know." He bowed, then turned about and left. Struck by her beauty upon their first interception at the hospital her image had remained indelibly etched in his brain. Of course it had. What man would not have been so affected? He had said a few minutes past, when first coming to her table, that he hardly recognized her. He lied. He had remembered her with crystal clarity. When he was out of sight she arose and returned to her seat in the coach car, there continuing her routine, viewing the streams, the hills, the trees, and some of the small farm houses sporadically dotting the landscape, then reading her novel. She was more than half finished. "Madame Bovary found it not within herself to be faithful. Why? She had everything. A splendid husband of the most gentle kind, and thoughtful, and caring for her every need, much in the manner of my Andre, and he too was a doctor."

Chapter 62

THE TRAIN sped southward and morning slipped into mid afternoon. The Major passed by now and then and smiled. She did not smile back; if so, then it was faintly given, but her disposition was friendly and politely cordial. At one point her thoughts fell on doctors Metternich and Dontonte. She had many thoughts that trickled in and out. "Doctor Metternich is so genteel, much like my elegantly styled Doctor Givens, but Doctor Dontonte, well, he's a tad frivolous, a trifle flirty, come to think of it. But what of it? He's a brilliant fellow, I must acknowledge, and hope to write him sometime. I learned much from the man. I owe him a debt of gratitude. "Unto a friend suffice, a stipulated price," she uttered, a wise maxim taken from the ancient Pittheus which she had come upon in her past readings. And then turned to the Van Doke plantation and Adelaide's letter which had revealed that George had let it slip into troublesome straits. What was happening to it now? Had Jim worked things out to satisfy the debts? Why did George not see after things better? She had not broached Andre with the subject, and speculated that he was as yet without full knowledge of the particulars or else had decided to spare her of these troubling affairs by not mentioning them. "In time it will all come out. Adelaide will tell me everything I'm sure."

Night fell. Sasha took her meal in the diner, then returned to her seating in the coach car, there for awhile looking out the window at the twinkling of the lights emanating from the farmhouses and small towns. At some juncture she collapsed into sleep and slept the whole night through without awakening. The Major happened by once or twice, stopping momentarily to glance upon the beautiful face which was now oblivious to all that took place in its midst, then went on his way. She awakened next morning to the rays of the early sun softly pouring through the windows, hearing a voice say that rain had fallen sometime during the night. "It looks like a lovely day ahead," it occurred to her. "We should reach Nashville by three." At breakfast, which was at nine, a lady of fifty she guessed asked if she might join her in that all other tables were taken, Sasha generously asking her to please sit down. The lady reminded her of Mrs. Laster. She was nice, a very nice lady, who smiled with outpouring friendliness and volunteered that she was on her way to Nashville, but giving no reason why, with Sasha telling her that she'd be stopping there for a visit herself. The lady asked about the origin of her trip. Sasha answered that it was in Baltimore where she had climbed aboard. The lady kept eyeing her black medical bag which was at Sasha's side on the floor, her curiosity finally out dueling the best of her advice to be quiet, that it was none of her concern, but nonetheless she proceeded to ask of Sasha's profession.

"I'm with a hospital in Baltimore."

Sasha decided that that was enough, that to have given her a full accounting would have been useless to either of them and she was correct. It was far beyond the boundaries of the lady's comprehension that the young woman in her presence was a notable surgeon in a hospital in the great city of Baltimore. This having passed, the lady began to pursue other topics that were by and large conventionally social, with no mention of what Sasha did at the hospital, although she kept eyeing the black medical bag resting on the floor. After this, Sasha only saw her once more and that was when she was reading and happened to look up as the lady was passing by. She smiled and the lady smiled back and went on.

The mighty machine kept roaring southward, the mouldering of the fog horn seeming far away, which sounded when there was a crossing, then lapsed into silence and stayed silent until the engineer drew the control rope downward once more, thus resurrecting the low lonesome bellow all over. Sasha closed her eyes and listened, but this time to something else; there was a clickety clack, clickety clack, the ever constant swiftly paced alternating clicketys and clacks rising from the wheels of iron riding hard upon the endless tracks that had been laid atop the gravel packed bedding; and there was something of a sway to the coach car, giving rise not to fear but certainly to apprehension that there was a danger of the train jumping track when attempting to negotiate a curve. Trains were new then; there were defects and there were wrecks and people had heard of them and read of them and anyone utilizing this modern method of travel was understandably ill at ease about the matter of safety. But the trip proved uneventful, or had so far, and would for the rest of the journey excepting an event at the station in Louisville where Sasha was to switch to another train. She had departed from the one on which she was riding, making her way along the station frontage when suddenly her pathway was intercepted by a young Union soldier, a sergeant, who proceeded to inquire about her destination, where she was going and why, and was on the verge of opening her medical bag and other belongings when there was a voice that rang out which was near upon them. It spoke commandingly.

"Sergeant! What are you doing? Put those things down." It was Major Horton.

"I'm checking her out sir, security you know."

"Do you not realize sergeant that you're tampering with a doctor here? Don't you see that's a medical bag? Set it down. You're relieved."

"But I—."

"You're relieved sergeant. Back to your regiment or I'll have you hauled in."

"Yes sir."

"Sorry Doctor Duval. Sometimes these young men lose control of good judgment."

"But he was carrying out his job. Security is an essential element of war I'm sure, however unappetizing it may be."

"You're right. But we're told to be extra careful not to antagonize the citizenry, and to make very good judgments about suspects. I cannot for the life of me figure how the sergeant determined that you were a person of risk."

"Well anyway. That's over. And I do thank you Major for your assistance. I'm glad you happened along."

"Accepted. Please have a good safe journey for the rest of the way. It was my good fortune to run into you again. Perhaps there will be another time as well."

"Perhaps. We do not know about those things, do we? Goodbye."

"Goodbye."

And so the Major walked away, disappearing forever, likened to many men who had fleetingly encountered the beautiful Sasha, silently remembering her face and form for the rest of their lives, and wondering whatever happened to her.

The railroad conductor consistemtly passed up and down the aisle asking the passengers if their ride thus far was satisfactory and hopefully pleasant. When he stopped and inquired this of Sasha she replied that the trip had been fine and then went on to ask of the time he expected their arrival in Nashville. She was imploding with images of the happy faces of Lucy, Jim, Prunelle, and Brister; it had been too long. The conductor's assurance that they would arrive at mid afternoon, meaning three o'clock, varied but a fraction from his prediction and the train pulled in on time, Lucy, Jim, Prunelle, and Brister standing as a cluster at the station. Sasha's feet had no more than landed on the pavement when Lucy, bursting at the seams, hastily crossed over. "Sasha, my darling girl. I am wild at the sight of you. So much time has passed." Then Lucy threw her arms around her and delivered a dozen kisses on her lips and cheeks, and then next was Prunelle who was so carried away that big round tears rolled slowly down her face to her chin. She tagged Sasha with the name "my little one" as she always had, begrudgingly giving her up to Jim.

"Ah, Sasha. I am thrilled, I am through and through. I was afraid I might never see you again. You've gone through so much since I last saw you." And then it was Brister's turn, his large mouth laughing with abandon and he too shedding tears. Sasha took the initiative and held him to her for a little. "Have you been behaving Brister, doing what all Prunelle has assigned you?"

"Sho, sho Miss Sasha. You know I have," he answered, swerving his questioning eyes over at Prunelle for approval.

Brister drove them home in the carriage. The talk that evening was without let up; the mood was high. It was by every definition a reunion. In all of the excitement Lucy found time nonetheless to usher Sasha from room to room to show off her latest alterations, having moved a table here, a desk there, and adding a portrait or two to the ones already hanging, then leading her into her garden on the west side which was flooded with flowers and blooms.

"We live comfortably here Sasha, but it's nothing compared to the plantations. Adelaide is miles ahead of me in nurturing shrubs and flowers."

After dinner Brister brought in Sasha's trunk and clothes encasement, asking where he should set them. Lucy got up and said to Sasha that she knew she'd like to see her bedroom, so, with Brister leading the way they went to see where Sasha would be sleeping and where her possessions would be hung and stored. The room was the same as before, she at once recognized, when she and Andre and Doctor Givens had passed through Nashville on their journey to Baltimore, with the allowance of one striking addition. There was a portrait of Queen Victoria and her husband Albert, Albert standing by the Queen who was sitting in a regal high back posing an affectionate smile. Lucy had avoided leading her to this room until now. It was to be a surprise. "Oh my goodness Lucy. I see you received my letters, definitely you did, and Adelaide's too. I am most sorry that I failed to see the Queen at one of her public appearances. She is a dear lady; they all love her in England. And you are sweet to have done this. I am certain to sleep more soundly than usual because you have."

That evening at the approximate hour of nine Jim managed to wedge in a remark of the travel plans, mainly that they, all of them, would leave Nashville at eight the next morning en route to West Tennessee, journeying south over the Mobile and Ohio Railroad aways, then intercepting another train bound for Medon then Jackson, where Sam Feathers would pick them up in one of the extra load bearing carriages that the plantations kept in storage for transporting five or more persons. Jim was aware that Brister and Prunelle were elatedly counting on going along and would feel muchly hurt should they be compelled to miss the irreverent trip to Big Hatchie country, and had accordingly made arrangements for them.

"Brister, have you ever ridden a train before?"

"No suh, but I'm dying to. I sho am. And I'm not the least bit afraid."

"You're not."

"No suh. I'm too old to be afraid."

That evening at ten they all turned in, Sasha a slight weary; the long trip was sapping. She bathed in the tub of warm water that Prunelle had drawn for her and after sitting and soaking for awhile stepped out onto the flooring and took the towel which was in easy reach and dried away the wetness. Then slipped on one of her lovely nightgowns and took to her bed. Before dousing the light she opened the Bible that lay on the side table and began to read, while at this same intermission there was a tiny soft knock on the door.

"Come in," Sasha invited. It was Lucy.

"I didn't mean to bother you Sasha. I see you're reading from the Gospel. I laid it out purposely for you. May I ask what verses you're reading from?"

"Actually, I'm into the Old Testament. Ecclesiastes. I have read but a few lines."

"I read from Ecclesiastes too. I often do. Would you like to share what lines were of interest to you? Perhaps I have read the same."

"Gladly." She traced her finger under each word, repeating them all, Lucy in the meanwhile looking on.

"Do not withhold from those who deserve it, when it is in your power to act. Do not say to your neighbor, 'Come back later; I'll give it tomorrow—when you now have it.'"

"I am familiar with that passage, and for you it could not be more fitting."

"I don't know. I hope. I try. It is a very wise message."

"You say you hope. Ah, wasted word. My dear, how could anyone give more of themselves than you?"

Sasha merely smiled and Lucy put her hand to her cheeks and hugged her. It was a beautiful moment between two women who loved each other, and it touched Lucy's heart, then she spoke a surprise, which was in her thoughts when she first entered and was the whole reason for her visit.

"May I ask something of you before I leave you my dear?"

"You know you can."

"It is this. You have always said a bedtime prayer with Adelaide or with Mrs. Laster when she was with you, and if you don't mind, I would like to say one with you too."

"Would I mind? Oh dear me no. I'm delighted you have suggested it. Here, let me get out of bed. I am usually on my knees when I pray. Will that suit you?"

"Anything you suggest my dear."

Then they knelt on their knees and prayed, Lucy in the main thanking the Lord for Sasha's safe trip and pleading that He bring to an end the terrible madness sweeping the nation and Sasha thanking Him for the Van Dokes and for their graciousness in receiving her as their guest during her journey.

❧ ☙

Cynthia met them in the driveway; she had waited the whole afternoon. Sol was not with her, not feeling well enough to leave his bed, nor were the Nomeharts there, who had returned to the plantation but were away in Memphis until the next week. They had recovered from their scare of the Union troops, but only after Adelaide had sent a telegraph that she had been treated very well by them and that they should return with no feelings of anxiety. Sam Feathers let everyone off and went on, offering as the reason that he was needed for overseeing chores at the Sherette plantation. Sasha had told him that she would be there a short while later, that she needed to look in on Sol and that Jim and Lucy had promised to bring her. The hour was nearing dusk. As fast as her fat legs could carry her Cynthia came over to Sasha, pulling her to her bosom with jubilant exclamation, "Dear child, we sho has missed you," reenacting a virtual facsimile of Prunelle's welcome the day before. When the embraces and kisses had subsided they all went inside. Lucy and Sasha began together to look around as if they were expecting old familiar faces and voices; Cynthia had followed, not wanting to give up Sasha one second but soon had to break off into the kitchen to start supper, and Lucy, whose thoughts were trained upon the garden with its abundance of luxurious flowers and bright green tendrils, stepped to the door and exited to the outside. "I'll be but a second Sasha. I only want a peep before dark sets in."

There was a lonesome air to the rooms, to wherever Sasha went, who had now wandered into the great ballroom and with a mere glance saw that it was immaculately kept, Cynthia seeing to this, the hardwoods shining as if polished and buffed only that morning. She closed her eyes, taking backward flight. The colorful resplendent ball, Mrs. Van Doke's contrivance, was in full swing, dynamic, wonderful, the music swelling to the vaulting, and she was there whirling round and round, her raven locks flouncing about and over her shoulders, a hundred young men, it seemed, wanting a turn with her. Suddenly the fantasy was over; she smiled disappointedly and sighed as if to say, "It was the most of fun, even if I was play acting. I just had to relive it once more." And then, she found her way into the room of the portraits, where Mrs. Van Doke's collections were largely kept, to which she used to retreat for an interval of respite during the grand lady's last days of illness; and there to one side, in the space where Mrs. Van Doke had had it specifically placed, was the piano. Seeing it, she almost cried. "You have stayed here all alone, all by yourself, haven't you?" she said, as if addressing a flesh and blood sister, while sliding her hand simultaneously across a portion of its smooth shiny veneer. "But here, I shall add cheer to your heart, at least for a minute or so—if I haven't forgotten how." Then she sat down and began to play, her fingers sure upon the keys of ivory, her steel trap mind trained incisively upon the notes of the music sheet from which she had first learned the composition. It was Wiener Walzer's masterpiece, the Viennese Waltz, which, as she fondly remembered, was one among the several to which she had danced when attending the grand extravaganza that took place in the very next room not but a few years previous, an occasion never to be forgotten. She would cut short the composition in full, for only a trial was meant. That was enough. She smiled, pleased with herself. Jim and Lucy were not there with her; they were in another room, yet had heard the sweet rhythmic notes rippling off her nimble fingers, their faces lighting up.

"I knew she'd soon get around to that," said Jim. "I wonder if she has played in a while. If she has, she hasn't said a word about it."

"I don't think she has," answered Lucy, "but she hasn't lost a thing, has she, if my ears are correctly judging?"

Sol was still asleep, so Sasha after finishing with the piano and learning that he would evidently remain that way until the next morning said to Cynthia that she'd better go, for Adelaide would be anxious and that she'd told Sam Feathers to tell her that she could expect her with not a great amount of delay. Cynthia pretended a fret, promising that dinner was not far away but remarked that she understood. "I know my little one how Miss Adelaide is." Sasha went and peeped in on Sol for the second time who showed no signs of awakening. She looked with exceeding intentness into his face, then pulled open his eyelids and had a look there too, then turned to Cynthia who stood anxiously at her side.

"Does he sleep like this a lot or just sometimes?"

"Just sometimes."

Someone had hitched the horses to the carriage in which Jim and Lucy would take Sasha home. It was Coon, who increasingly had taken the lead in running the affairs of the Van Doke plantation, most apparently the activities of farming and handling the workers. Sam had carried her baggage with him earlier. The ride along the narrow tree lined road was quiet, the only audibles coming to their ears resulting from the squeaks of the wheels and the jingle jangle of the trace chains. Sasha was easily drawn to comparing the immediate serenity to her past day and a half travel by rail where there was an unbroken continuance of noises and people bustling up and down the aisles of the coach car. The moon and stars shone brightly down from the Heavens and the lantern that hung next to the driver's seat added to the ambient charm that surrounded the passengers, the accessories affixed to the harness of the handsome horses glittering and sparkling.

Adelaide and Mary Tonka were standing on the portico and from the vantage of the carriage they could be plainly seen from the time Jim reined the horses into the driveway, because the lamps mounted to the portico columns were well lighted. They had risen from their chairs where they had sat watching the play of the fireflies while waiting. The magical little creatures would grow massively thicker as the summer wore on. As they had expected, Sasha bounded from the carriage the second it drew to a halt, and soon was up the steps and into their loving arms. All three sobbed, all three cried, and all three attempted to babble at once. Jim and Lucy had crawled down and were now standing among them, trying to tell Adelaide that they would go on, for Cynthia would have supper ready, and finally, when the commotion had faded Adelaide said she understood but why not have supper with them.

"Oh thank you Adelaide," said Lucy, "but we have to leave. We're going to be late as it is. We'll see you again tomorrow."

But then, as if attempting to alone persuade them, Mary Tonka told of the awesome meal she had prepared, a potpourri of vegetables and meats and pies and cakes and jams of many flavors. She had also churned that afternoon, amassing a heaping bowl of fresh butter. Jim wanted to stay, saying that his mouth had begun to salivate, and so did Lucy, but both begged off, knowing that they had to start their return without further delay or run the risk of upsetting Cynthia. When they had gone, which was briefly, Sasha, Mary Tonka and Adelaide sat down for supper. Adelaide would deliver the wording of prayer.

> Here we are Lord, once again with our Sasha that You have brought safely to us. We deeply thank You for her. There is nothing more precious to our hearts than to have her close. Within a short while we will lose her once more but we are accepting that we must. Where she will be going her load will be hard, You know that it will, so please Lord, take this time to especially bless the food on this table so that it may nourish her and strengthen her and prepare her for the crucial mission she will take up once again when she has gone away. Amen.

"Amen," Sasha extended, and pled before anyone else was able to release one word that she'd like to speak before they did.

"Yes you may dear," replied Adelaide. "What is it?"

"You can't imagine, neither of you, the happiness in my soul now that I am home with my beloveds at suppertime. You can't possibly. I've thought of this moment for days."

"Oh yes we can imagine darling. But you can't imagine how joyous we are that you are here. I've kept my fingers crossed every mile you were in travel that nothing would detain or otherwise disrupt your journey. We both have," Adelaide said with emphasis, looking over at Mary Tonka.

"Indeed we have," said Mary Tonka and then remarked to Sasha. "But I thought you'd never get here sweetheart."

Chapter 63

MANY WERE the topics they would take up, whereas there was one which was cautiously disregarded, the trying circumstances of Sasha's at the hospital in treating the victims of the war. Both Adelaide and Mary Tonka had surmised that these provinces were too delicate to penetrate and that only Sasha should unveil them for elaboration.

"I have not heard from my dear Lawrence Sherette for some time," said Sasha, but adding with a confession that neither had she written him.

"But you're busy Sasha; it's burdensome for you to write letters. You have enough on you." This was Adelaide. "And as for Lawrence, let me give you a late piece of news. He has returned a short time back from San Antonio where he spent some few days with Father Lumas."

Sasha sat erect. "That is news. Incredible. How does he say that dear one is faring?"

"Not very well. He is quite old you know. Lawrence did say that the good Priest's eyes were dazzlingly alive when your name was mentioned, and interrogated him relentlessly in your regard, in short, about how life was treating you. Lawrence said he easily answered that."

"I wish I could have gone."

"I do too, and with you."

"Yes. Yes for sure."

"And we will have to do that very soon."

"Very soon. We should mark it on our calendar of imperatives." Then Sasha turned to the person of Elizabeth Van Doke, about whom she had received limited information and was anxious to hear more about her. "Do you hear from Elizabeth? Jim said on the way down that she had moved back to Chicago to live with her parents until the war is over."

"No I don't. Only from her parents. She wasn't able to cope with things. The war is only a part of it. I don't think she will ever blend in with the life we live on the plantations, not so much because of the people here and their culture but because of—."

"You mean George?''

"Yes, I mean George. He was drinking heavily when he left for the war. And gambling. She actually had left to live with her parents before he enlisted with the Confederacy. I feared she might suffer a nervous breakdown. I'm glad she left. She is in better hands. We'll address this more in detail in the next day or so, when you are settled."

"Where is George exactly? Does anyone have an accounting of his movements?"

"All over I guess. He's a cavalryman I hear, a Captain. He went in as a Captain."

"I see. Well, I feel terribly sorry for Elizabeth. I wish her speedy recovery."

They had moved to the portico by now, there following the erratic antics of the fireflies, Sasha shrieking excitedly when two of the flighty creatures lighted up just as they had virtually flown into one another, and there too was the call and repeat of the whippoorwill, less vociferous at this late hour than at dusk. The workers' houses, a half mile distant, still depicted lamp glow which stole seepingly through the diminutive eye like windows; some of the workers had set lanterns or coal oil lamps on the front porch and had brought out chairs and benches, where they delighted at telling one another tales of kindred deeds and talking of menial abbreviated things that were common to their way of life. Every once in a while their staccato cackles reached the Aurora portico. The hour was quite late; Sasha rose and said she was retiring. She smiled when she saw that Mary Tonka had filled her tub with warm water, quickly disrobing and sinking into it. But she lingered only briefly, sort of splashing about, out in no time, drying herself off, and then plunged into the big Victorian bed with the high back headboard where she had slept many a night. Adelaide laughed amusedly when she entered the room and saw her.

"Now isn't this a surprise. Ha, ha, ha. I knew you'd be here, right where you belong."

"Where else?" she answered. "But please allow me a minute, I must do something. I almost forgot." Then unexpectedly jumped up, her gown dragging the floor, and hastened down the hallway to Mary Tonka's room who was already in bed, the covers pulled up to her chin.

"What is it dear?"

"Mary Tonka, I have to say good night to you, I really do," and then leaned over and locked with her in loving embrace. "Ummph," the gush springing from deep inside Sasha's bosom, who had squeezed her great aging friend with all her might and was starting to turn for the door.

"Goodnight darling. We're glad you're home."

"Me too."

When Sasha had returned she and Adelaide lowered to their knees and prayed, Adelaide saying just afterwards that they'd better call it a day, this thus prompting Sasha to roll over, in a very short while falling into misty sleep. Adelaide grasped that she had because of her nice even breathing. She said to herself that she had had a hundred other things to take up with her but would do that the next day, or the day after, or the day after that. Reaching her arm around her she hugged her with the utmost of tenderness. "It's wonderful to have you home again sweetheart, it truly is. I have missed you awfully. I hope you are thoroughly refreshed while you are here."

The next morning at breakfast Sasha commented that Adelaide's letter painted an intriguing picture of the Captain who had quartered in the barn with his soldiers, and Adelaide picked up that yes, the Captain was intriguing, and quite handsome, with a gentle nature about him. She said they were not afraid of him nor of his men, and reported in the same breath that he kept looking at her portrait hanging in the drawing room. He had sat in the living room where the great chandelier dangled while they were finishing with breakfast and kept getting up and returning to the drawing room where he literally stared at it. She had caught him.

"She's a surgeon in a hospital in Baltimore," she had said to the Captain.

"A surgeon is she? Huh. I am drowned in surprise. Do you mean that?"

"Certainly."

"She's a beauty."

"Yes she is."

"Who is she?"

"My adopted daughter."

After Adelaide finished her story about the Captain, Sasha laughed and said that meeting up with Captains and Majors of the Union Army was something of a contagion, that indeed she had encountered a Major on the train who with clever guise appeared to pursue her, and guessed that was something a woman had to get used to.

"You above all women sweetheart. You will always be pursued. All your life you will. That is what beauty does to you."

"Oh Adelaide!"

"It's true. You will forever attract the eyes of men."

"Well, so be it. So much for their wasted time."

"Do you think Andre is jealous because of the attraction that befalls you? He must see it or hear of it."

"Maybe. But I don't think so. He knows of the depth of my love for him and that no one else could otherwise count. No one. Never."

"It has always been Andre, hasn't it?"

"Always. Well, not always. He grew on me. But there has never been anyone else. He is not the handsomest, nor is he a cavalier, nor a person set apart from the crowd. But he is solid, a rock that I and my children can lean on down through the years and that is the sole criterion that any young woman should employ when setting out on the journey of wedlock."

"I'm glad. He is the finest and is crazy over you. You will make a wonderful couple. A splendid couple. You are intending to marry, oh let see. When did you say?

"I didn't. But we talked of it just before I left."

"But not of when."

"No. I'm undecided. But it's on the way. I did say to Andre that I wanted to wed here at Aurora, and I do Adelaide. This has to be the place. It's my home."

"Of course it is darling. We will talk more of this while you're here. You know, the dress, who will pattern and sew it, and what style. Then there is the matter of who will officiate the ceremony."

"I have decided that already."

"You have?" Adelaide feigned surprise. She knew Sasha's choice without the least of guessing.

"Lawrence Sherette. Who else?"

"Sure. Only him. As you are forever saying, 'who else?'"

Sasha dropped the remark that she did not need more than a wedding of common flavor, an affair not given to the frills of ceremony, very quietly done, and she meant it; yet Adelaide insisted to the opposite, putting it that she had numerous friends and close beloveds that wanted to be there and looked forward to an event that was truly grand and that she could not afford to let them down, "And besides," she said, "you deserve the finest we can create, that which your mother never had. We will make it up to her. I can see you now darling in lovely white, standing face to face with Andre waiting for the next gesture from Lawrence Sherette. You will look so terrific."

There was a partially suppressed smile that visited Sasha's face. "Adelaide, my dearest. You are a wonder."

Adelaide had won out with her persuasive insistence. From that second onward the matter was settled; there would be a grand wedding, each sending a line or two to the other over the next several months of ideas they had about it.

Sasha would have taken to the fields to join Sam Feathers somewhere in the far quadrant of the plantation where the workers were raking and loading wheat for transfer to the storage barns. She could not. Sol was suddenly in her vision and had been off and on before breakfast. Announcing to Adelaide that she was soon off to see in on him she rose and went to her bedroom, there slipping into one of her favorite riding habits, then proceeding directly to the equine stables to saddle up her sorrel. She would not drive the carriage. Holding tightly to her medical bag she in the same maneuver placed her foot into the stirrup and swung with inborn suppleness into the saddle. With one cluck from her lips the obedient steed raised his neck and head in alertness and in accord with Sasha's pull of the reins ever so slightly to the right made toward the Van Doke plantation, the medical bag undulating and shaking about as she held it with the one hand that was free.

Sol was awake and alert, expecting Sasha to drop in, for Cynthia had spoken to him that she would. He smiled as she advanced to his bedside and hugged him, striving in combination with his smile to utter her name, which was grossly slurred; Sasha feigned that she was unaware of his handicap.

"Let me listen to you Sol, my good fellow. Let me roll you over. This will only take a minute." She applied the stethoscope. It was but briefly that she took it away. Sol exerted no effort to inquire of her why she was pressing the strange round metallic to his back. Subsequently she shone a light into his eyes and studied his face and lips with poignant intensity. She took no notes. She would easily remember whatever she adjudged essential. Cynthia looked on with innocent curiosity and concern but asked nothing. Sasha mentioned that she would prescribe medicine which she would administer until returning to Baltimore, each day seeing in on him at near the same hour, performing the same examination time after time without alteration. "Good morning Sol," she would speak cheerily as she entered his room. "Did you like your bacon and biscuit that Cynthia cooked for you?" she inquired, which prompted a twinkle in his eyes and a feeble attempt to yield a verbal affirmative.

"Is Sol progressing for the better Sasha?" Adelaide had once asked after Sasha had gone on a good many visits to see about the dear old man.

"I hate to tell you but must be candid. He has suffered a stroke and even a mild one during my attendance of him. Frankly, he is not to be long with us. At best a few months."

"Oh!"

"Yes. It's a matter of when. And of that I cannot say."

"Nothing else to do for him?"

"Only to keep him happy as much as we can. And keep Cynthia as calm and free of worry as we can."

"She knows doesn't she?"

"Wives always know. She suspected upon his first bout with his illness that it was serious. She doesn't query me. She saves me from giving a painful and awkward answer."

Sasha had brought along with her a painting of a pastoral scene for Mary Tonka, where there was a narrow meandering brook about to spill over its banks; and a book to Adelaide entitled *La Vita Nuova,* a medieval text of works written by Dante Aligheiri, which was a portrayal of the genere of courtly love of that era, secretive, unrequited, and scripted in both prose and verse. Sasha felt that Adelaide might be keenly enthused with the book because of these aspects, but surmised that it might be even more appealing to her in that the soul of it lay in the person of Beatrice di Folco Portinari, a Florentine lovely known as the muse of the poet Dante Aligheiri. Supposedly, Dante first met Beatrice when his father took him to the Portinari house for a May day party. At the time Beatrice was eight years of age, a year younger than Dante, who was completely taken by her and remained smitten by her beauty throughout her life even though she married another man, banker Simone dei Bardi in 1287. Beatrice died three years later, June 1290, at the age of 24. Dante continued to hold an abiding love for the young woman after her death, even after he married Gemma Donati in 1285 and had children. After Beatrice had passed away Dante withdrew into quiet brooding and began composing poems dedicated to her memory, hence the collection of these poems, together with others he had written in his journal in awe of her beauty, which became *La Vita Nuova.*

"Where in the name of rare wonder did you find this intriguing relic?" asked Adelaide a night or two after she had received the token and had read more than half the pages.

"At a London brokerage house that deals in olden creations of text."

"She broke Dante's heart."

"I'm afraid she did."

"Too bad. She shunned him, I venture. What is it they say? The first cut is the deepest. With Dante there was no later cut; the first was also the last. And deep."

Every day Sasha rode into the fields, sometimes to the whereabouts of Sam Feathers who was overseeing the workers, there climbing into the wagon with him, he with the extension of his hand helping her up.

"Sasha, I'm glad you came to see me."

They did not talk much; they did not need to. It was what they felt toward one another that mattered. They mostly sat and gazed and thought. Since ever so long Sam had looked upon Sasha as her surrogate father, something of a stand in for Lawrence Sherette, never forgetting that night in Memphis when he first saw her in the rain holding an umbrella over her person, a mere young beautiful girl with big bright eyes, a child practically. He had adored her at first sight. He had not once ever told her of his feelings; he wasn't equipped with the language or the temperament. But she perceived his feelings. She read them.

Sasha still worried about his condition of health, whether or not there persisted the effects of undulant fever, and while sitting but a foot away from his face subjected him to the most incisive scrutiny, concluding that there were none.

"Do you feel well these days?" she would ask nonetheless.

"Fine. Fine. I feel good Sasha."

She lingered for yet a while longer but when ready to leave would ask, "When will you finish with the wheat harvest Sam Feathers?"

"We have another week at it. We do if it don't rain."

"I will keep my fingers crossed that it doesn't."

"Where are you off to from here?"

"Oh, down to the Big Hatchie. Or thereabouts."

"I see. Well, you be careful."

Sam would make certain that she was, sending his most reliable worker to trail her at a distance to watch after her safety.

Sasha and Adelaide had conjured up plans for a trip to Memphis, there to spend a very limited while with Lawrence Sherette, though more time at the Gayoso House where they would take their night's lodging. Seeing Lawrence Sherette and riding the train together were the thrills that enticed them. They would take mass with Lawrence Sherette the next day and spend an hour after service with him and no more. Adelaide had told Sasha that Tahitia would be away visiting a relative during the time of their stay in the city and that regrettably they would miss seeing her

Toward the middle of the week they left, boarding a train at the depot built on a parcel once owned by the Sherette plantation. Adelaide had sold the plot to the railroad company. Thea promised to spend the night with Mary Tonka at Adelaide's request, the purpose of which was to keep her from feeling lonely. Thea had begun to spend longer hours at Aurora to help Adelaide and Mary Tonka manage the press of daily affairs, showing such proficiency as of late that Adelaide was entrusting to her the business of entering figures into the journals. The bulk of the day was pretty, the sun shining brightly for the greater run of the distance, turning cloudy, regrettably, as they neared Memphis, with rain starting to pour down. When their train pulled into the station the rain was yet falling, and in rather hard torrents, though not deterring Sasha and Adelaide from continuing on to the hotel. They caught a taxi with a covered top, feeling sorry for the horses that were thoroughly drenched, but as Adelaide said, they would dry off. The hour was four o'clock when they registered and checked into their room and unpacked, Sasha's eyes grasping the dinner menu laying on the side desk which read at the top margin Dinner at Six. They were in the dining room exactly on the hour. Sasha was happy when they sat down. She was reminded of good past times. The waiter approached their table and asked if they would take coffee as a beginner, Adelaide answering yes, that they'd like coffee, and after this Sasha looked at Adelaide and Adelaide looked at Sasha and they began.

"It's been a while since I was here," said Sasha.

"It has. And that goes for me too."

"Do you have any idea what I remember from the first time you brought me here?"

"I haven't the slightest."

"The rain. There was a veritable cloud burst. I sat next to the window as I am now, watching the zigzagging of the streamers make their journey to the pavement below."

"A lot has happened since then."

"Much."

"Let's see. Andre was with us. And Doctor Givens."

"That's right. Both were. Andre had an errand to run for his father the next day, something regarding a call on a cotton broker for payment of money owed."

"It was. I recall that." Adelaide would have preferred that reference to Jordan Van Doke had not popped up.

At this intermission the waiter returned with coffee and asked if they were ready to order. Adelaide replied that she was and Sasha said she was also; and so they ordered and continued with their conversation.

"What has Andre been up to as of late? I haven't seen that dear boy in sometime either. Where is he hiding? His presence is badly missed."

"He is not hiding. Soon he will receive his doctor's diploma. He has worked enormously hard for it."

"I am happy for him."

"So am I."

"But I am more happy for him, and for you dear Sasha, because of your impending marriage. You have of course said you were uncertain as to when."

"No I am not certain Adelaide. I'd thought perhaps this Christmas but there are stumbling blocks that I foresee."

"Oh!"

"Yes. There are many loved ones that I'd like to have attend and unfortunately Christmas may be an impediment. I'd love to do it at Christmas. You know, the great spiritual atmosphere and the color of decorations and all. But I doubt that it will pan out; there is my work, the injuries of the war that demand my presence at the hospital. I could not possibly leave and be here for an extended period while suffering is running rampant. I just couldn't." She had an impulse to reveal that she felt a bit guilty for taking time off to come this time, but thought better of it.

"No you couldn't. And therefore, I guess, you have to be thinking that when the war ends you will have your marriage."

"I see no alternative. But I want us to move ahead with plans. Will you agree to help me with that?"

"You know you don't need to ask. Be absolutely assured I will. You know that I will sweetheart. What will you have me do?"

"I have thought that you might prepare a list of invitees. If we start in plenty of time many will attend."

"I will start to work on that. Mary Tonka can help me."

"Of course. And Thea."

"Shall we decide on a dress?"

"Let me think about that."

"Sure."

"But there is one thing that I'm certain of—besides having Lawrence Sherette officiate."

"And what is that?"

"As I earlier said, I want the ceremony to take place in the great living room in front of the fireplace, with my mother looking on from her portrait."

"Oh! How sweet. How touching. She'll see her daughter married. Won't that be something? Left alone I wouldn't have thought of that in eons."

They had now finished with most of their meal. Sasha, thinking it fun to play something of a game with Adelaide, said she'd bet she didn't remember their order for dinner when she first came with her to the Gayoso House. "That was the time that Doctor Givens and Andre were with us."

"Ah. Sure I do."

"What is it? Tell me."

"Veal cutlets and a cut of pork."

"Oh! Ha, ha, ha. You do remember. You are just too clever Adelaide."

"No indeed. I can't lay claim to that attribute. I did remember, as you found out. But I had some degree of advantage. You see, I was the one who conveyed the order that evening."

Then Adelaide abruptly opted to a topic not nearly as light of mood, asking Sasha when she felt the war might draw to a close.

"Heavens! Who can say? I pray that it is not long from now. Andre feels that is the case. In any event he thinks no later than early spring."

Adelaide had more to pursue. Like most, the war was ever pressing in her thoughts in some manner or other.

"Sasha, did you see any soldiers in the vicinity of the railroad on your way from Baltimore? I was concerned that you might."

"You mean fighting?"

"Yes."

"I saw none. Were there galloping cavalry attacking to the right and left, was there heavy concussion artillery on the move, were rifle platoons firing at one another in rapid succession? The answer is no, not where I was. It was a peaceful journey. In fact, I saw not a single soldier other than those in the lobby of President Street Station and on the train and at the stations in Indianapolis and Louisville where we stopped. Yet I must say that there was worry among some of the passengers that one or other of the enemies might for a reason unexplainable attempt to dynamite the rails, but then they started believing that was absurd."

"Why absurd?"

"Because either side, either army, realized that some of their own loved ones were on board, or could be, Northerners or Southerners. The travelers were mixed. That's how it is. This is a strange war."

Chapter 64

THEY RETIRED early. The next morning at seven they were to take mass at Lawrence Sherette's church, spend an hour after this with him then return to the Gayoso House to pull together their equipage and clothes and prepare to catch the train back to the plantation. Lawrence and Sasha literally ran to each other.

"Sasha, Sasha. My little girl. But all grown up I must confess."

"I'm afraid so."

"You look wonderful sweetheart, you are stunning, and it's been far too long."

"I second the latter."

"I would have been at supper with you last evening but was detained. There was sickness in my flock."

"Oh, I hate that."

"When are you leaving to return to the plantation?"

"We catch the ten o'clock train," Adelaide broke in. "So we don't have much time."

"Okay. Sure. Mass starts right away; after that we can visit further."

When at mass Adelaide and Sasha sat immediately in front of the altar, looking up at Lawrence Sherette as he conducted the ceremony. Sasha was taken aback at the growth of his congregation, which necessitated an addition of appreciable footage, plus the installation of more windows with beautifully colored mosaics. Her eyes glowingly traveled up and down each of them until she had thoroughly canvassed the very last, nudging Adelaide once to look at the angelic baby cherubs to which she was fondly drawn. Sasha complimented Lawrence Sherette when mass was over on the progress of his church and lamented that she was not present to see it happening. They went to his office and sat down, whereupon he began to ask her about recent happenings in her life, but skipping her work in the hospital because Adelaide had written him in advance to avoid bringing up the matter, that she didn't think Sasha would be open to discussing the ordeals she had been through.

"Well, tell me what you will about old England."

"London I can. But England I cannot. I didn't explore it very extensively. London is rich, London is poor. London is gorgeous, London is ugly. London is a great city. I am terribly glad I went. As you know, Mrs. Laster was with me for a length of nearly two months and we went everywhere. She owns a home there. Were you aware of that?"

"No. Who lives in it?"

"She leases it. She failed to speak the name of the lessee."

"What else? What else about London?"

"It bulges with magnificent buildings and splendid art. The ships in its harbors are stunningly large and sleek."

"Someone has mentioned the Fitzgerald family. I think it was Adelaide here."

"It was I," Adelaide answered.

"Oh yes. The Fitzgerald family. Doctor Fitzgerald was my supervisor of surgery. A man extraordinary. I attended the operas and theaters with him and his family. They were so very kind to take me along. London is replete with great halls of entertainment."

"Yes it is. It was when Adelaide and I were there doing our studies more years ago than I care to admit."

Lawrence Sherette said he looked forward to hearing more about her visit to the spectacular city when he visited with her within the next few days, regretting they couldn't stay for another night to have dinner with him at Randolph's. Then went on to say that he knew that Adelaide had already told her that Tahitia was in LaGrange, Ezra having driven her there the week before. When they had talked a while longer Adelaide spoke up that they must run along, that they had but an hour left, but would look forward to seeing him shortly. Lawrence Sherette hugged them and said to Sasha with the gladdest of feelings that it was so good to have her back. "I love you darling," he tacked on. As they were leaving, having gone a few paces, he as an after thought called out, "Sasha, tell Mary Tonka to set out my walking boots. We're going into the fields when I get there."

"I will. I will. Wonderful. I'm overflowing at the prospect."

When they stepped off the train that afternoon Sam Feathers was there to transport them over the short distance to Aurora. Upon their arrival Thea was just leaving and on seeing them pull up she paused then moved hurriedly over to the carriage, smiling from ear to ear, her arms outstretched, and so were Sasha's.

"I've not seen you yet," said Thea excitedly. "I've been threatening to come over and twice did, but found you not here. Now you are. You look so good."

"So do you Thea. I guess Mary Tonka has caught you up on what I've been doing since I've arrived from Baltimore. We're just returning from Memphis, where we've been since yesterday. I'm sure she told you that too."

"She has. And a bit more."

"Such as?"

"About the book you've finished."

"Yes. I'm through with it. You should read it. Every woman should. A friend in London sent it to me."

"My goodness. Please let me see it as soon as you can."

"Come in and you can take it with you."

Sasha gave her the book, remarking of some points about it as she did so, suggesting it as a supplement to the other sources that she some time earlier had supplied her, further saying that Adelaide and Mary Tonka, who had been helping her master reading, as well as ciphering, had spoken quite commendably of her progress.

"Someday Thea, you will be of much importance to the management of Aurora. Keep up the good work."

The next day Sasha, Mary Tonka, and Thea went blackberry picking, Sasha wearing a polka dot bonnet on which Mary Tonka had insisted because she felt her face as white and tender as it was surely would get sunburned, and further, rubbed fat back on her hands, arms, and ankles to keep the chiggers at bay. At noon they returned. The heat was intense. Mary Tonka figured that it was unsuitable for Sasha to continue to endure it. When she and Mary Tonka had embarked on like hunts in earlier times Sasha learned what to expect, and found things now the same. Picking the wild fruit was irritable to her hands—the briars pricked them without mercy—and she fell far behind the other two in filling her bucket. Upon seeing her shortage Thea said she was giving what she had picked to her, not only because sharing was the right thing to do, but besides, it made her feel better to do something for someone she loved so dearly. Sasha accepted, though only on the condition that Mary Tonka invite her to one of her fabulous suppers, when blackberry pie was the featured desert.

In keeping with his promise Lawrence Sherette availed himself at the plantation within the bounds of when he said he would, with thoughts fast upon Sasha to see that she was energetically entertained and freed from the strains of her ordeals at the hospital, which she would shortly resume. They would ride, they would ride everywhere, to the extremities of the Sherette boundaries, sometimes crossing over onto the Van Doke property, depending on the roadway, leaving often at dawn when the mist was heavy upon the earth and the sun in the east not yet born. Mary Tonka had made them coffee to take along, pouring it into two separate cider jugs of diminutive size. Some days they walked, sometimes along the way sitting down for a respite, Lawrence Sherette there lying on his side, his elbow extended to the ground, his face tilted sideways into the flat of his hand. Sasha sat beside him. Since the sun was high the Killdeer whose friendship over time she had cultivated was busy foraging close by and had crept close, now anticipating the few grains of corn that she removed from the corner of their lunch basket and pitched to her. "How kind her heart," it ran through Lawrence Sherette. "She is blessed. God surely blesses those who are generous to the creatures he has created. Andre has quit hunting quail because of her. Good for him. I have known him since he was a tot. He is a splendid young man, ever intent on sharing praise for something achieved and skillfully avoiding envy and banishing idleness and expensive living. What fine qualities he has enshrouding him, with which of course he was born or else developed over time. But both, naturally both. He will succeed far. It has been my utmost hope that they will marry. Now I hear that is a certainty." And then his musings turned.

"You know something Sasha?"

Her eyes asked what. Then she responded. "That could be one among a thousand things."

"Yes. But specifically, I was just thinking the other night about when I first met you. I often think of it, as I am now. I've told this to you before but this one has a slightly different twist. I had received this strange letter by special courier from Father Lumas telling me that my dear friend had died or that his demise was expected and in his last behest wished that I would take his daughter in and care for her. Imagine the shock. I had planned to stay two weeks longer in New Orleans. But I didn't. I boarded the first stage I could catch and raced through a fitful unrelenting storm to get to the young girl that our dear Father Lumas had told me was waiting. When I arrived there she was, the most beautiful little thing in the world, and half scared to death. I didn't know it then but He did; she was to become my precious daughter. Is that not astounding? I had to be enormously blessed, for look what a gift He gave me, and it came to a fellow who is likely never to be married."[11]

---

[11] A report was given out in time, or perhaps it was light gossip with no intention to harm, which held that Lawrence Sherette so fiercely claimed Sasha in his heart for his own that he purposely

"Ha, ha, ha. And what a gift you were to me. I will always cherish you Lawrence Sherette."

"Thank you sweetheart. And I will cherish you. But in the bargain let me say that I was the one on whom the greatest profit was bestowed."

"No. It was I."

"No. It was I."

"No, no. It was I."

"No. It was I." And on and on they continued until summarizing with the longest laugh. "But allow me to alter the topic if I may," said he after putting forth the last objection.

"Be my guest."

"When you marry am I the one to officiate?"

"I can't imagine any one else performing it," she teased. "Can you?"

"Absolutely not. It would grieve me irrecoverably if they did."

"Never will that happen my dear. And not only will you marry me off; you will give me away at the same time."

"What joy! A double pleasure. When will it happen? Have you set a date for the ceremony?"

"No I haven't. But it's not long away. We shall have to see. The onslaught of surgeries at the hospital will determine. I had thought of Christmas. But I am doubtful. Who can say?"

"A year from now maybe?"

"Perhaps."

"But sometime close to that."

"I think so."

"Ah me. Here we are talking of your marrying off and then the family begins. Just like that. Children."

"Yes of course."

There was a doubting chuckle that escaped him. "You don't seem old enough to have babies. It's almost like yesterday that you were in your young teens."

"But I am old enough. As you say time passes on."

---

concealed her true parentage, introducing her to strangers as his daughter without clarification. This however is neither supportable nor disputable, but being more I think of legendary fable than of irrefutable authenticity. Mrs. Eastbrook's notes were troublesomely vague, barely touching upon the allegement, but sufficient enough for arousing a smidge of curiousity. So we leave it there.

"Children. My, my, my. But the pity of it darling is you'll be living in Baltimore or some place else far away and I'll never get to see those little tykes."

"Oh yes you will."

Lawrence Sherette had hoped she would have said something else, like for instance that she and Andre might some day return to the plantation to manage the enterprise, and that considering his status as a celibate her future birthing of children would pass to him as a great personal joy; for they in his fantasy, would become his grandchildren, with whom from time to time he would walk and frolic through the fields just as he had with their mother. He had relayed this very idea to Adelaide once in privacy, when she had suddenly let it come to light that she might eventually marry and move to New Orleans.

"They would never do that Lawrence. Never will they return here to live permanently. Their lives are fixed, irretrievably on a professional course."

"I'm afraid you are correct. Nonetheless I will keep hoping."

"It's a lovely idea. We shall have to see, won't we?"

She had stayed long enough. It was time to get back. Sasha took one last look at Sol who now did not recognize her, concluding to Adelaide that it was the last time she would see him alive and urged that Adelaide ask Lawrence Sherette to be prepared to come on a moment's notice to perform the last rites. "But don't act too hastily. He may have a while. A month or so, I hope." With this, and the several goodbyes she said to her loved ones, she left, Sam Feathers driving her to Jackson where she caught the train to Nashville, there spending the night with Jim and Lucy who the next morning saw her off to Baltimore. The trip was largely uneventful, similar to her ride when she traveled south, although there was a stoppage north of Louisville whereon she was transported several miles distant across country by way of carriage to a section of railway where she boarded another train. No reason was given to her for the transfer other than the train stoppage was necessary and because she was a doctor and urgently needed at the place of her destination the officials in charge had figured a way to hurry her on.

The train rolled into President Street Station in the early afternoon of the next day. She was met by Andre, who was jubilant at seeing her. When he had loaded her belongings into the carriage, he with great delicacy helped her up and then they were off toward home. Andre peppered her with an avalanche of questions regarding things back at the plantations and especially for a diagnostic report of Sol's condition of health. She asked him how were Doctors Givens and Dontonte holding up under the extra load they surely had to bear due to her too lengthy absence. The next day she returned to the hospital, this being well into the morning, and was scolded by Doctor Givens for reporting so soon after her trip had ended, who insisted that she should have gotten more rest. Her answer was that she wanted to gain a head start at reviewing the records of surgeries pending and to say hello to her immediate staff. He hugged her fondly and welcomed her back, adding that he was terribly glad to see her. He did not speak it but felt the urge to let her know he was greatly relieved that she had returned, that she was desperately needed. "I trust that you are rested my dear. Take it from me. A brief while away from all of this does wonders for one's constitution. Oh, by the way, how was your friend Sol?"

"Not at all good. I think he will die in the near months, if not sooner. I'm sorry I had to leave him. But it was of no use to remain longer. There was nothing more that I could do."

"I understand. I am sorry to hear of this."

Another day passed and she was into the fray of things as usual, the team happy for her return, anxious for her leadership and savvy. When she took her first meal in the hospital cafeteria the staff from the various departments on seeing her once again in their midst one by one went over to embrace her or shake her hand.

The war wore on, each month alarmingly piling up casualties, August, September, October, November producing relatively the same number, with no end of the turmoil in sight. Sasha wrote letters; to Adelaide, to Mary Tonka, and to Jim and Lucy, telling them she could not reasonably think of returning home for the holidays, supplying reasons which they already understood. She would send Christmas gifts, to many she would: to Mrs. Laster and Bryon and Father Lumas and Sam Feathers and Thea and Tahitia and Doctor Lundy and Cynthia and Brister and Prunelle and Jim and Lucy, and above all to Lawrence Sherette and Adelaide and Mary Tonka. Andre took the endearments to the post office for mailing a good two weeks before Christmas Day, bearing in mind that she had hoped to him that no one would be guilty of opening a gift early, until Christmas Day, and Andre gave to her hopeful assurance that they would not. There was one gift that she would have sent additionally if fate had not decided otherwise and that was the gift going to Father Kestner, to whom she always sent one. Mrs. Laster's letter of some months past had informed her of his demise.

Led by Doctor Givens the medical staff and nurses had pre Christmas together, no gifts exchanged, assembling in the cafeteria for a noon meal of bountiful amounts prepared and set out on large elongated tables abutting each other, which were overlaid with shiny white spreads buttressed with candles spaced periodically from end to end; and napkins with a greenish tint were set under each plate, which along with the brilliantly lighted tree at the room's entrance resulted in an atmosphere which was even more agreeably Christmasy. Sasha thought of the past Christmas gatherings at the plantation, feeling a tinge of homesickness. She said as much to Andre who sat by her. He read it in her face and clasped her hand in an effort to offer comfort and in a way say he also felt the same. Doctor Givens, who sat at the head of one of the tables, the other end occupied by an invited philanthropist, rose and said the appropriate words, particularly emphasizing that all those there were immeasurably fortunate, for there were soldiers now in the ward close by who lay badly injured and whose outcome was in serious question, urging everyone to give their all to uplift those who were lucid enough and well enough to indulge in a spirit of Christmas joy. He hardly said more. It was his nature to be succinct.

That evening when Sasha arrived home she found that Padgett had dinner waiting for her and Andre, Padgett inquiring if Andre planned to be there. She had understood that he would.

"He's due right away Padgett. How nice of you to do this. But you should be home with your family. I'd given you time off."

"It's Christmas time Miss Sasha, or soon will be. I wouldn't have felt right without doing something for you and Mister Andre."

"Good. We'll all enjoy it, all three of us. I'll change clothes and by then hopefully Andre will have joined us." She would slip into the beautiful purple robe with a white collar that the Fitzgerald's of London gad given her.

"Yes, I would especially like to wear it this evening. It reminds me of them. I wonder what they are doing this Christmas. I miss them. I must write."

As it happened Andre knocked within minutes and Padgett let him in, his eyes falling on the sofa situated in front of Sasha's library shelving's where he took a seat and began to read the afternoon paper which he had lifted from the adjoining side table. When Sasha entered they all sat down to the very splendid meal that was now waiting, Andre blessing the food and giving thanks for the Lord Jesus, then they began to eat. Sasha had eaten sparingly at the noon meal and said that she was hungry. To her and perhaps to Andre as well, it all seemed so lonely, only three people there, when both were accustomed to droves of familiar faces back at the plantations—singing, laughing, noisy, happy—where gifts by the hundreds were handed out to children and adults alike. "It was a fiesta, it was a panorama," she thought in her mind. Sasha and Andre together had purchased a heavy fur coat for Padgett's Christmas gift, the box in which it was contained wrapped in colorful red and green crepe with an imposing bow of white on top center. Andre had laid it down in the foyer before coming inside. Very shortly after the dinner, Padgett began to return the dishes to the kitchen, explaining that her uncle was likely on his way to pick her up for a large family gathering at his home later on, which she and her family were to attend.

Sasha insisted that she and Andre would care for the dishes and the setting away of the food, then asked Andre with a nod to retrieve the gift for her which lay out of sight on the other side of the door, which he promptly did, and when Padgett, with great suspense on her face, feigned or otherwise, opened it up and saw the gorgeous specimen inside she let out a shriek that the neighbors might well have heard a half block away.

"You shouldn't have Miss Sasha, Mr. Andre. You shouldn't have."

"Ha, ha, ha." It was Andre's laugh. "Certainly we should have. That's why we did it. It shows our appreciation for you Padgett. You are a very deserving person. And you'll find it to be most handy. We have some very cold months facing us, mind you." They bade her good night. She was singing as she happily stepped the short distance to her uncle's buggy. It was a joyful evening after all. For awhile they sat on the portico swing covered with heavy woolen blankets viewing the twinkling lights of the great city in the distance. After this they left for the inside and kindled a fire in the fire place.

"I hope you're not called to the hospital tonight darling. You need the rest."

"I guess so. I do feel a pinch tired and I'm very sleepy. I think I'll just stay in bed until mid morning for a change." She knew she wouldn't.

Sure enough at eight the next day she was in her office sorting through the records of new patients and some old ones that she intended to see later. Suddenly, there was an unopened envelope from Adelaide which caught her eye that she'd overlooked the day before or else it arrived by courier after she left. The news was not good but not unexpected.

Dear Sasha,

Our beloved Sol has passed away. He realized from the first that he would not get up again. One day when Cynthia was giving him his medicine he began to sob and kissed her hand, and the next day after that he received communion and unction from Lawrence Sherette, who was here, and quietly died. You said he had only a little while. But he lived longer than we thought he might. We are terribly sad and I've tried to do all within my grasp to comfort Cynthia. She's at a loss, in kind of an aimless limbo. They were seventy years together. I will miss Sol dearly; we all will. He loved you as his very own, even mentioning your name on his last day. I think he believed you were still here. I wish you were with me to help comfort Cynthia.

Jim and Lucy were here for the funeral, driving down from Nashville one day before it was held. Lawrence presided; you of course don't need to be told that. Sol was buried in the plot where Mrs. Van Doke was laid to rest, under one of the white skin birch trees. That's where I'm supposing a good many of her family, her sons and their wives will be laid to rest too. I sat with Tahitia and Doctor Lundy and Mary Tonka and Thea and Sam Feathers during the ceremony, and Jim and Lucy sat next after Doctor Lundy and after them Brister and Prunelle and Hallie and Fannie. The Nomeharts sat elsewhere. I was pleased to see the sizeable turn out of white people. I expected it. Sol was loved by everyone.

In the event you're wondering, I'm trying to persuade Cynthia to spend as much time with me here at the Sherette plantation as she will. She says she feels she ought not, that it wouldn't seem right in view of the Nomeharts needing her help at the Van Doke plantation. Mary Tonka and I will go often to keep her company nonetheless.

Goodbye my darling. Please take care of yourself and come when you can.

Love,

Adelaide

Chapter 65

"SOL, OUR beloved old man," said Sasha, in her remembrances. "I loved him at first sight. I don't think he knew quite what to do with me, especially when I went over and hugged him. He had that bewildered look in his eyes, but finally forced himself to timidly wrap his arm around me. Adelaide and Cynthia amusedly watched him struggle, and I'd bet anything Cynthia teased him unrelentlessly when they were in privacy."

Throughout the months of fall the wounded had continued to be brought to the hospital in steady regimen, most surgeries performed successfully, some not, with the bulk of the soldiers released either to return to battle or return home for good. This was the usual pattern Sasha had come to expect, but the steadiness of her routine was bound for interruption, for there sprang one day a most sudden surprise. By feat of the strangest probability George Van Doke was left at the hospital by a union medic in serious if not grave condition. It was believed that he had been wounded by shell explosion in a cavalry encounter with General Grant's army in the upper reaches of Virginia. When was the date? The last day of December, 1864, Christmas barely come and gone, said Sasha's diary entries. No one seemed to have knowledge of where the incident exactly happened, yet it was apparent that his wounds were fresh and that he was transported in the course of a few days from the battle scene by wagon. Since he was delivered to Doctor Givens's ward it was he who first realized the soldier's identity, having actually met George during his first visit to the Van Doke mansion, as he recalled, and fraternizing in discussion with him on subsequent visits. The doctor recognized him by name—which was on the bronze metal tag about his neck and on the papers that the medic had handed him—not by looks. In terms of his physical appearance he was drastically altered from the young man he once knew, his beard grown long and shaggy, his body approaching emaciation, his face demonstrating horrendous pain. At once Doctor Givens went to Sasha to take up the matter. When he had relayed the news she gasped, her hand flying to her lips, and expressed that what she was hearing was near unbelievable.

"But what I tell you Sasha is beyond doubt."

"Merciful Father." She crossed herself. "Why have You chosen this?"

"That is what I asked Him too."

"What is his condition? Is he in a bad way?"

"A very bad way. It's his leg."

"How bad is it?"

"Ripped. Mangled. There is no chance of saving it."

"I fear gangrene."

"Yes. That is a certainty, or worse. Let us go to my ward where he lies. They're cleaning him up."

"No one knows his identity but us. Is that correct?"

"Only the two of us. So far."

"I'm anxious to see him."

When they entered the room, George, though in agony, turned his face to them, his eyes darting with fear and disorientation, failing to recognize Sasha in the least. To him she was only another doctor in white now teaming with the one who had momentarily left him and returned. The attendants had finished with their cleansing procedure, exacting infinite care to be thorough, particularly swabbing the leg with sodium chloride or carbolic acid but refraining from administering morphine, which the patient badly needed. At recurring intervals, which were shorter and shorter between, the shrieks and moans coming from him were ghastly and unnerving but though terrible they were, almost animalistic, Sasha somehow ignored them and bent over the patient, saying the softest soothing words, there repositioning his form by a slight in order to thoroughly examine his leg all the way round. Upon quitting her inspection she turned to Doctor Givens, her face filled with apprehension, thus denoting that the outcome was in doubt, and raising her voice above its usual level instructed with urgency to her number one aide, who now stood at her side, that morphine must be administered at once.

"As you say. We will at once."

"And we need Andre over here in haste," she furthered. "Andre is his brother."

"We'll take care of it," he replied, then motioned for another aide to start on his way to locate him.

The morphine was administered, a low dose at the moment, designed to promote rest and sedation against agitation and fear, as well to reduce the pain. Andre arrived in the quickest of time, finding however, the morphine already taking hold, and then sat down and listened calmly to Doctor Givens and Sasha tell what they knew of why George had ended up at the hospital in Baltimore. "He was struck by cannon fire, we understand," one or the other said, "and transported here by way of wagon. He was in transit at least two days, maybe more. It's amazing that he lived. Someone at the dressing station stopped the blood loss thank goodness and bound up his wound pretty well." Andre was racked with shock, and supposed that they were too, when the news reached his hearing that George Van Doke was in their care.

"Did you talk to him Sasha, I mean before he fell off to sleep?"

"No. His pain was too acute for that. But I examined his leg, which is covered by the sheet. It's all to pieces from the knee downward."

"You will do surgery, naturally. It has to be amputated."

"Either I or Doctor Givens will do the surgery."

"You are the one Sasha," Doctor Givens quickly chipped in. "There can be no question. You are the one."

"Very well."

There was a silence that fell upon them for a moment, each seeming to deliberate the next step, but knowing with certainly what it was.

"He will awaken shortly Andre," Sasha broke in, "and I believe will then recognize you. You talk to him first, then I will follow."

"And after that?"

"Surgery. The team is ready. We have no time to waste."

"When will he awaken?"

"We can arouse him shortly. As I say, you talk to him, then I will, and then we'll take him under again for quite a spell."

"Yes. I know. Is it fair to ask what are his chances?"

"It depends. I hope he's strong. That's the vital thing. We'll do all we can to fight the infection and then we'll see. We're using a disinfectant developed by the medical team in London as of late. It's experimental but we have great faith in it. It's very effective. That is all I can tell you my dear."

"You're the best Sasha. It's not right that I say if anyone can save him it is you, but I am thinking that you are the best. Because you are. That's all I'll say, except good luck darling."

"Thank you Andre. Would you like to stand by during the surgery? You can if you like."

"No. I don't think so. It's best that I don't."

The morphine did its work as Sasha intended, George awakening blurry eyed within the shortness of while looking about with confused searching of the walls and ceiling, babbling words that told the observers of his uncertainty of his whereabouts; but as the minutes ticked away his eyes cleared somewhat and he caught Andre's face of hope and concern beaming down into his. Yet the face was not entirely distinct. Then as additional seconds diminished his eyes fluttered and blinked, and little by little he realized for certain that the man standing by him was his younger brother.

"And, And, Andre. It's you. Oh my Good Lord, it's you." George did not notice the alarm on his brother's face. "Ah yes. Let me see. Where am I?"

"You're in the hospital in Baltimore George. They're going to take care of you."

"Take, take—."

"Yeah. Take care of you."

"Ah, that's good. I've suffered terribly. I was suffering a little bit ago. But a lot of it has gone."

"That's good. You were suffering. But they stopped it."

"Let's see. My leg. Its bad. I'm sure it is. Yeah. I saw it. Will they cut it off? Will they? Will they?"

"Now, now. Don't get excited."

"I'm not excited, I, I just want to know what the surgeon thinks. Oh, oh. There's that damn pain again. I can't bear much of this."

Then George closed his eyes and grimaced, but quickly opened them and looked around. It was as if he were afraid of drifting off. There was a wildness of fear in his short snappy glances.

"Listen to me George. You're in the best of hands here. Sasha is your surgeon. She's here. Over there. She's here to care for you. You remember her, don't you?"

"Sasha. Sasha. Oh yes. I remember her. The brilliant one who went to Baltimore. Where did you say she was?"

"There. Sitting right over there. She'd like to speak to you. To go over some things."

Sasha then moved to George's bedside, and eased into a chair; she softly took his hand into hers, seeming to spread over him an instant calm.

"Sasha, Sasha. Oh yes. I remember you. Funny that we meet here. Funny that we meet here like this."

"People meet in the most unexpected places George. Perhaps the Lord has brought us together."

"I hadn't thought of that. Oh, my pain. It's back. It's bad. Can you do something for it?"

"I can. I will. But let me say a thing or two to you. I'll make it brief."

"What? Hurry."

"Your leg has been badly damaged. I'll have to remove it. I must do it soon. Do you understand?"

"I, I, think I do. I wish it was done sooner. I'd have a better chance."

"Shhhh. No need for you to talk. I'll do all I can. I have a great and competent team to assist me. As of now, I just want to make certain that you know I am planning to remove your leg and that it absolutely must be done. When you wake up it won't be with you. You'll feel no pain, not for a good long while anyway. I'll put you under."

"Under? Let me see."

"We'll give you an anesthetic," which was chloroform. (The use of chloroform was replaced by either at the beginning of the twentieth century.)

"Anes, anes—." Swiftly drifting off that is all he said.

The attendant stepped forward and rolled him into the room where the surgery was to be performed.

"Go ahead, administer the anesthetic," Sasha was heard to instruct her anesthesiologist. "We'll want him out of it for awhile."

༄ ༄

George lay in bed for two weeks, Andre and Sasha together sitting by him, or taking time about, Sasha and her team keeping their fingers crossed that he'd pull through. Sasha and Doctor Givens did not believe his condition of stupor, waking and falling back into sleep, derived from infection, but from shock and a weighty draining of energy from his body following his injury. The stub where the lower portion of the leg was severed was plentifully sprayed with carbolic acid and there were no other wounds of threat. Sasha felt that if he fought vigorously enough for his life he would emerge from danger.

"There was some gangrene that had spread," she had told Andre as they sat watching. "But he can overcome that."

"I'm concerned Sasha. I'd think by now his condition would have elevated."

"I too Andre. But patience."

At the end of the second week Sasha felt George's pulse and checked him for fever, smiling vibrantly at what she detected: his pulse was beating at normal rate and there was no fever. Adding to her pleasure he suddenly opened his eyes and glanced up. "Sasha. It's you."

"Good morning. Yes it's me."

He struggled to smile. Then faintly one broke through. "I'm going to live; I've made it. I'm going to live."

"Yes you will George. You've been through the wringer, but you have made it. We've all been pulling for you. In fact, we've prayed for you, many of us."

"I'm thankful."

"Are you hungry?"

"I feel I am. I know I am. But that can wait."

"Very well. But anytime you want something we'll see that it's here for you."

"How long have I been out of it?" he asked anxiously. "Quite a while I guess."

"Two weeks."

"That's staggering! I've really lost track."

"You have indeed."

"I can't believe these things have happened to me. The war, the —."

"You mean your wound and ending up here in the hospital."

"That's what I mean."

"Well, I can't either but it has happened, so let's do all we can to return you to wellness and feeling good again."

"Yeah. I'm for that. Oh yes. Let me see. My leg. It's heavily bound I can tell. Do you mind if I take a look?"

"Let's not right now. As you say it's heavily bound. You can a little later."

"Did it go well?"

"You're speaking of the amputation?"

"I am."

"The surgery went quickly, within minutes."

"Oh!"

"Why oh?"

"I never felt a thing."

"You were unconscious. And I'm thankful that you were. Well, I must leave you now. Andre will drop in before too long. Lie back and sleep."

Sasha laid her hand on his then stood and left, a smile of long awaited satisfaction on her face.

Over the ensuing weeks Andre found frequent opportunities to be with his brother, Sasha too doing the best she could to visit and certainly keeping a vigilant eye peeled on his progress, though her principal attention was necessarily devoted to the incoming soldiers of serious injury. George had begun to improve daily and was gladdened to no end when Andre stole quietly in from his routine and stayed awhile. George's mind had begun to clear, not altogether, but his improvement was markedly favorable, the pain by now sufficiently controlled; thus he had begun to try to organize everything into perspective, starting with when he was fallen on the battlefield.

"It's like a dream my dear brother. When I got hit by that shell or whatever it was that waylaid me, I thought I was a goner. I do remember that. Actually, I didn't realize much of what was happening from that time on, even while they were bringing me here in that wagon, actually not even until I woke up and Sasha said good morning."

"You don't recall me being with you? At your bed side talking?"

"Vaguely. Though I see it all pretty clear now, or else have figured out a lot of things, especially recalling when Sasha took over with her team and said she'd see me through."

"You didn't just figure it out. You were aware of a lot that was taking place. It'll all come back."

"Oh yeah. Sasha. I'm sure I'm right about this. She bent over me soon after surgery or maybe it was later than I think and said I'd be all right. I think I cried a little. She saved my hide didn't she?"

"She did George. You're lucky. She's the best there is. With anyone else at the helm things might have turned out differently."

"You're right. I'm lucky. Truly I am. She saved me. No one is more aware of that than me."

"No doubt she did. And just as you are, I'm so grateful too. I was worried George, terribly. But you're okay now, doing fine. Improving every day, and eating like a horse. That makes Sasha happy. "

"I'm glad of that. I have to find a way to than, thank her." His words trailed off. Turning his head away from his brother he began to weep.

"Now, now. You'll get around to thanking her. You'll find the opportune moment."

"I will. I intend to soon. As soon as I feel a little better. I'm already trying to figure out the words."

"You will. And they'll be the right ones."

"That's not exactly what I'm driving at."

"Oh! What?"

"As you well know Andre, Sasha and I never saw eye to eye. I guess I would have with her, but I don't think she would have me. I feel for sure she wouldn't have. And it was my fault. I was an ass once, and she put me in my place; that was when she was very young, the first time I ever saw her. She didn't do it with words, but with that look of hers. It cut. When a woman is as beautiful as Sasha the cut is always deeper than ordinary."

"She didn't mean anything by it I'm sure."

"But she did. I remember it well. She and Adelaide were riding in a carriage together on their way back from Memphis. I guess I was a little cocky. I rode up to them and said something that was a bit haughty. And as a result I got what I deserved. That's how we started out. And things didn't improve any over time. And that's the thing I've turned around in my head for the past several days, ever since I began to half way think straight. I want to make up to her Andre. I guess you think it's because she saved my life that I want to and it's true. That's the reason, but I guess I always wanted to anyway and would have done it even if this surgery hadn't come about. As I look back I have to wonder." George paused and began to cry and then looked away, covering his tears with his hands.

"Wonder?" asked Andre, feeling a lump in his throat. George recovered then went on.

"Yeah. It had to run through her when she was on the verge of cutting off my leg to save me from an awful gangrene death that I was a perfect jackass and hadn't been half as nice to her as I should have been through the years."

"No, no, no. She never did that George. She's a doctor. A great one, honoring the highest principle of medicine, to save a life, to heal the patient. To heal you was the only thought in her brilliant head. Her business is the pursuit of excellence, a riveting concentration on medical surgery, with no room left for the ordinary trivia of human emotions."

"Well, I guess. I think I understand you. But I can't help but think of all the thoughts I've just said."

"That's all right my brother. Don't worry about that. I'll assure you that Sasha's not worrying about it. She's too busy. But when you feel like it you might pick your time and tell her how you admire her and how wonderful you think she is. She might just like to hear that from you. But a word of caution. Don't thank her for saving your life. I don't think she'd take that very well. She would have done the same for anyone, no matter who they were. That's the way doctors look at such things."

January had turned into February and February into March, finding in retrospect that General William Tecumseh Sherman had captured the City of Atlanta, November 15, and then marched on to capture the Port of Savannah, December 21, breaking the back of the Confederacy strategically, economically, and psychologically, a monumental victory. Sherman's army had wrecked three hundred miles of railroad and numerous bridges and miles of telegraph lines and seized 5,000 horses, 4,000 mules, 13,000 head of cattle and had confiscated 9.5 million pounds of corn and 10.5 million pounds of fodder. Add to this the destruction of uncounted cotton gins and mills. His accomplishment was nothing less than militarily stupendous, in which he had destroyed much of the South's will to wage war. Turning from Savannah, Sherman had advanced northward to help General Grant's army in Virginia which was at a stalemate against the forces of General Robert E. Lee.

From January onward George Van Doke was in rehabilitative care at the Baltimore Hospital, Sasha seeing him less and less, because she had to devote her time to freshly wounded soldiers, and Andre seeing him more frequently, eventually pushing him around the hospital grounds in a wheel chair, the two of them taking up an exhaustive range of subjects, one of which was the status of the war, about which George was but meagerly apprised. He had heard trickles about the fighting from various freshly wounded soldiers with whom he had recently gained acquaintance, yet such reporting and comments fell short of the facts. But Andre knew much more, telling George of Sherman's ghastly reduction of the State of Georgia in his march to the sea which historians have famously narrated with untiring penmanship.

"That's terrible Andre, just terrible. Where is Sherman now?"

"They say he's joining Grant to fight against Lee in Virginia, or already has."

"What does that mean?"

"The war is practically over. The Confederates have lost. A peace declaration is only days away, a month or two months at best, I hear." George hung his head as if he were struck with deep irrecoverable sorrow at the news.

Chapter 66

ONE DAY when on one of their jaunts George mentioned that Sasha had not let him see his leg, to which Andre offered the explanation that she figured it prudent to allow the leg more time to heal, that she wanted him to see it later on, when it would look better suited to the eye.

"She's only thinking of what is right for you George, that's all."

"I understand. Mind you though, I haven't lately asked her about it. That's why I've asked you."

"She'll decide for you to see it when she deems it best. And not before. Be patient."

George also had begun to use a walker for moving about, but as a supplement to the wheel chair, the latter far more preferred than the former because he loved the exchange with his younger brother and felt that the strenuousness of using the walker stole some of the vitality from their conversations. Sasha was delighted to see Andre rolling him around and pleased to see George using the walker, even if limitedly. The grounds of the hospital were lush and green, gorgeous oaks and firs scattered about and meandering walkways winding over the rolling landscape, which in the spring and summer and fall were bordered with colorful flowers of many species. But she would soon step up the usage of the walker, explaining to Andre that George's increasing use of the device would lead to quicker self dependence.

As they slowly crept along George sometimes recalled the habitual rides he took across both plantations on his black stallion, "clear to the Big Hatchie," sometimes seeing Sasha, he said, galloping her sorrel across the fields, then all at once enticing the animal to burst forward as if she had in mind challenging some other rider who didn't exist. "She didn't know I saw her, cause I was concealed from her view behind a thicket or grove of timbers.

She was a gorgeous thing in that riding habit Andre, and really graceful in the saddle. She rode like a swan gliding on water. You're lucky. She loves you. I can tell. I could always tell. Who wouldn't be lucky to have a woman like that love them." And more than once, no, many were the times that they took up another subject, George's failure to manage the plantation. George was the one to initiate it. He felt deeply ashamed of his record of gambling and drinking and playing the English trade market against worldwide brokers who laughed deep guttural laughs and concocted snide cutting jokes over the sucker they'd lured into their trap from America.

"I was a fool Andre. I'm ashamed. What's more, I may have lost Elizabeth for good."

"Have you written her, made contact?"

"No. I don't think she's aware I'm here."

"She is. Adelaide has stayed in touch with her. She's kept her posted. It would be a good thing if you wrote her."

"You're right. I should have long before. But I kept thinking she might write me."

"Gosh George. You're plenty able to write by now. It's your responsibility to take the initiative. You have some making up to do."

"You're right Andre. And I will. I promise I will."

"Well, I urge that you do. But let's talk about something else for a spell. Okay?"

"And what is that?"

"Where do you plan to settle when you leave here? You should be deciding that."

"Well, I have been a little. The truth is, I've been pondering that I might choose Chicago, if Elizabeth is agreeable. But you probably think I should be saying in my head I'd like to take over the plantation again and grow cotton."

"Are you?"

"No. That's no where in me. Not after the mess I made. But the real reason is my leg. I'm no longer the man I once was. With only a leg and a half to steer me about! Bah. I'd simply be in the way of the others who are doing a whale of a job managing things. They wouldn't tell me to my face but they'd see me as something of a joke, a needless scalawag in the way. The plantation is now in able hands with Adelaide and Sam Feathers and Coon heading it up. Naw, naw, I shouldn't, not even a tiny bit, think of taking it over again. As I say, I'd just be in the way. But there is the matter of my not knowing what I should do with myself, not yet anyway. It depends a lot on Elizabeth."

"Let's hope it works out for you. Write her a letter soon, will you?"

"You have my word."

Andre at this time concluded he had begun to over do the cajoling of George to write Elizabeth and told himself to avoid bringing up the matter again, then without explanation got up from his chair and ambled across the room to look through the large solid glass window at the people moving about on the grounds. Finally he returned to his chair and sat down without comment, seeing then that there was a look of animation on his brother's face. George was gearing up. Andre concluded that it couldn't be about his writing Elizabeth a letter but wondered.

"What is it?"

"Something I was thinking."

"Such as?"

"Well, I was just running it through my head. She hasn't told me, but there's a buzzing around here that you and Sasha before a good many pages of the calendar turn are to marry. Not any time soon, but on down the line. And I was just thinking. Is it in the stars that the two of you might want to return and see after the affairs of the plantation yourselves?"

"Ha. You have the first part right. Yeah, we're going to marry, God willing, and I'm sure He is. As to the second part. Not a chance. This is where we'll live and work for the rest of our lives George. It's what we studied and planned for. It's what we can do best for humanity. Naw, big time farming isn't for us. And there's more to be said about that. When this war is at a dead end the South and plantation life that you and I knew will be turned up side down most likely. Drastically different. Even if it stayed the same or nearly the same, Sasha and I would have no yen for it. But it will be a place to return to that's dear to us. We'll always do that. We talk about that all the time. Sasha is imbued with the idea. She's always saying, 'That's where I grew up Andre, that's my home. I'm forever tied to it, just like you, for as long as I live. He guided me there. I'm sure of it. I can see it all so clearly, the children and I and you romping through the fields, just as I did as a girl, and still do, or riding on the wagon with Sam Feathers or his replacement after he's gone, or saddling up the horses for a ride.' Yeah George, we'll be going back every so often, every chance we get."

The war was rapidly drawing to a close. There would be those that felt sadness, the losers, and those of a mood of elatedness, the winners, but all glad throughout the battered nation that the savage roar of the cannon was at last quiet. Doctor Givens had spoken to Sasha that he thought it proper to call the staff together for a celebration when the peace declaration was official. She echoed his sentiments, and further opined that it should be kept within the frame of moderation and exacted with reverence, but for the time being the war had not ended, thus Doctor Givens and Sasha and the good many other doctors stayed busy without let up.

Adelaide had written to Sasha with regard to the condition of George, to which Sasha replied that she regretted not keeping her more regularly posted, reporting in the same lines that he was progressing very well, in accord with her hopes, and that his leg had healed satisfactorily and that she, during the past week, had allowed him to see it for the first time. She said she was at a loss to describe his looks when he observed it, opting to relay in words of limited detail that he was likened to someone suddenly happening upon a bad scene, his eyes and face momentarily frozen, and that a thousand emotions surely ran through him. When she began to rewrap it, she said, he broke down and cried and that she hugged him and told him that everything would turn out well if he kept his faith and worked zealously to overcome his handicap.

The next day Sasha decided to push George around the grounds herself in place of Andre, who had for the most part rolled him once a day, telling him that it was something she felt she should do because George was soon to leave the hospital and that there was an urge in her heart to spend a few private moments with him.

"I have some thoughts that I want to go over with George, Andre, and he may have one or two to share with me."

"I'm sure he has."

On this morning the weather was pretty, no clouds in sight, only the radiant sun which was accompanied by a lazy breeze. Sasha was clad in a stylish purple cloak, light of wear and suitable for mid spring, with her hair hanging to her shoulders. She had looked with happy countenance to being out in the open, feeling fresh and invigorated as she glanced about. George saw how her dark eyes flitted and danced in the sunlight. He refrained from telling her that his chest was swollen with pride because of the close presence of his future sister in law, who was so beautiful, he thought, and also a person who had attained to such very lofty heights in her professional world, the latter of which he had begun to revolve. "They must be awfully prideful to have her here. I thought of taking up medicine once but I didn't make it. I quit before I started, knowing I'd have to compete against people like her, a fool hardy useless thing it would have been indeed. I would have been like a fish on dry land as the proverb goes. Yeah, against the likes of her that's what I would have been. But that's all right. She was meant to be what she is and I was meant not to be that. But I will I trust be her brother in law and that's a very big something."

As said before, the grounds surrounding the hospital were lush and green at that time of year, the walkway wandering throughout and when they had traveled onward a piece she stopped under a willow tree and took a seat on a dwarf sized settee. It was plentifully supplied with an assortment of exotic sculpturing emplaced around the hard stone rocks from which it was constructed and was limited in size to a smallness that kept it from accommodating more than one person. There was an engraving on the backing that read *THE CHIHUAHUA*. She was often there alone to sit and muse. George sat in his wheelchair nearby and smiled, which implicitly conveyed that he was glad she had decided to pause at that exact place because he and Andre often halted there during their usual strolls. Sasha asked him what Andre had already asked of him some few weeks earlier, which was, where did he intend to settle when his convalescence had run its course, thus ending his stay at the hospital. George replied that he'd try Chicago, provided Elizabeth was willing to take him back and said he thought she would.

"She will George. She's a very gentle person and generous; if you're wise you'll go to her and convince her that you are ready to piece your life back together for good. But a word or two more if I may. She is fragile and delicate and you must take those qualities into account in your relations with her. Whatever you do, do it easily."

He nodded his head seriously which carried the affirmation that he accepted every word of her counsel, then proceeded to say once again that he was of the notion that Elizabeth would take him back and hoped with all his heart she would. He knew well that her acceptance was on the condition that he'd have to live in Chicago, that never did she plan to return to the plantation with a sense of permanence, only to visit. Sasha knew that Elizabeth had suffered bad times there, unlike the romping grand life she herself had enjoyed with Adelaide and others on the Sherette plantation. Elizabeth had said, according to George, that her father might let him help manage the harness business or else the mercantile store. Sasha said encouragingly that this was good news and for him to pursue discussions of these possibilities with vigor and immediacy.

"Don't flounder the opportunity George. Be clear and straight. Elizabeth is a good woman. You need her. You'll need her more so as you grow older."

Sasha had brought along a canteen of lemonade that she had set in the back of the wheelchair, figuring by this juncture that George might like to have a swallow. The morning was turning warmer. She had lifted off her cloak. He took the beverage from her and drank thirstily. When he returned the container he thanked her and cleared his throat, then looked up and confessed that there were some things eating at his brain that he'd like to express while they were alone, since he did not know if ever again he'd have the opportunity.

"Absolutely George. Absolutely you may."

"I don't know where to begin. I guess any place will do."

"I don't see why not."

"Well, it's something my mother spoke to me about more than once, several times. You see, I don't think I've treated you as well as I should have over the years, that I've been a smart aleck sometimes when in your presence and I'm deeply sorry if I came across in that light." There were instances in the past in which she would have claimed that he was no better than a mountebank, yet suddenly, less than the distance of the whole excursion, she began to view him with a vastly altered image. It fell upon her that she had begun to like him.

"Don't give such thoughts a blink George. I might have been as much to blame as you. But I'll accept your apology if you'll accept mine."

"Ha, ha, ha." It was the best laugh she'd heard from him since his arrival. "You don't owe me one Sasha. How in the world could you? You're wonderful, and I admire you more than you can possibly imagine. I always wanted to tell you that but didn't know how. Sometimes a person feels that way about someone else and just can't quite discover the proper words or catch the right moment handy to use them if he does. You know how it is I'll bet."

"I do. I very much do. That's how I was towards Lawrence Sherette for so long a while."

"Ah!"

"I was."

"Well, I guess everybody is somewhat like that. That has to be pretty much the fact. But let me see. Er uh, I've lost my concentration. Where was I? Oh yeah. As I was about to say, my mother often said you were an angel Sasha, that you were the most wonderful thing that ever happened to either of the plantations, and that she believed in a way God had ordained you to light there."

"What an accolade. But she told me that too. I didn't deserve it, but she told me."

"You did deserve it. Everyone loved you. Everyone. And why not. Who could have done more for them? Who could have lifted them as high as you? Even my father used to say that. Poor soul. Before he lost his sanity."

"You don't need to—."

"But I want to. You see, something happened to him. And we don't know what. He lost his mind is a good enough way to put it. He was always fond of you, really fond, for the longest he was, until your mother's portrait started to weigh on his faculties, which by then were sinking rapidly. Deep down I don't think he ever truly believed she was your mother. Anyway, you know what finally happened."

"It's all right. I don't mind how he felt. I suppose that many more felt that way too. As a young girl my father cautioned that I'd run into such curiosities and urged that I try to get used to them."

"Cautioned? About—."

"That as I moved through life people would become increasingly aware of my heritage and wonder about it."

"That you are of Negro blood line."

"Some. Half, one quarter. I don't know. My mother was part Egyptian she always told me. I am part French no doubt. And a dash of Serbian. My father had kindred in Serbia. Naturally, complete verification of these strains would amount to a long and arduous ordeal to establish. But whatever I am George, I am me, Sasha, His creation, and that is the only thing that matters."

Andre kept up his practice of rolling George around the grounds or walking slowly with him if he used the walker; Sasha did not accompany him again, but maintained an unvarying vigil of his recuperation, each day scribbling a note with respect to his progress and passing it on to Doctor Givens. In the meanwhile George anxiously turned the pages of various reports he had gathered from soldier friends concerning the Confederate in the war against the Union, all realizing that Lee's forces were on the brink of capitulation. Andre had virtually quit entering into conversation about it, and Sasha, if George brought up the subject during her examinations of him, said even less than Andre and cleverly opted to another topic.

The war did not end but George's convalescence had come to a halt, his discharge from the hospital imminent. Elizabeth, after repeated exchanges of letters had written that she was hopeful of seeing him in not many days, and Sasha was communicating with a specialist in the city of Chicago about the production of an artificial leg for her patient. She explained to George that the device would necessitate some getting used to, though in a while, quicker than he realized, it would become a natural part of his daily habits. He had let it be known that he would like to stay around until the war was over, which could not be honored because of the rules of the hospital that when a patient was sufficiently healed his discharge was to be administered without negotiation. So, shortly, Andre, Sasha, and Doctor Givens stood with him at the depot awaiting his train, which from Baltimore would transport him to Chicago. A cool wind blew that early morning, with a stream of trains coming and going, creating a mass of steam and crunching screeching noises, the busy activity still relating in the main to the war. Sasha remarked that she'd keep her fingers crossed that the good weather held throughout his travel. Pretty soon his train drew to a halt, the coach on which he was to board nearby.

"Well, George, this is it," said Andre. "You give Elizabeth and her parents my love and best regards."

"Yeah. I will, gladly," George returned, as they warmly embraced. And then it was Sasha's time.

"Goodbye George. You've been a model patient in view of what you had to withstand. I'm proud of you. Good luck and give my love to Elizabeth." Sasha had never met Elizabeth, yet felt that words of sentiment to her was the thing to do.

"Yeah. Sasha. I'll do that. I'm looking forward to seeing her. I really am. And I hope the both of us can attend the wedding. When do you expect it to happen?"

"This summer," she answered, smiling over at Andre, who was looking at her with more than mild anticipation.

"Well, goodbye; I guess I'd better crawl aboard." And then he pulled her to him, his lips close to her ear, and whispered, "You are dear to me Sasha. You can't measure how much. At last I got to know you. And I'll never forget what you've done. God bless you."

"And may He bless you too George. Have a good journey."

On the very last George and Doctor Givens embraced and said goodbyes, wishing one another well. After George had hobbled aboard and the train started to ease away, Doctor Givens recalled casually to Andre and Sasha the first time he had met him, but stopped short of saying aloud how very strikingly he had physically changed from the young flamboyant man he use to be. It silently ran through him that "Time and tragedies take their toll, don't they?"

The great Lee surrendered at Appomattox, as the historians have avidly written, and that he came within a thread of winning the war. Surrender had to be a heart wrenching decision for the grand old man of the South. Yet there was no alternative. General Lee was an incomparable hero to those of his native region, and if not at that moment to those of the North he eventually became so, in time admired by the nation throughout. The greatness of the man is seen definitively in his lines to devoted General G. T. Beauregard a short time after the war had ended.

> After the surrender of the southern armies in April, the revolution in the opinions and feelings of the people seemed so complete and the return of the Southern States into the Union of all the states so inevitable, that it became in my opinion the duty of every citizen, the contest virtually ended, to cease opposition and place himself in a position to serve the country. I need not tell you that true patriotism

sometimes requires of men to act exactly contrary at one period to that which it does to another, and the motive that impels—the desire to do right—is precisely the same.

There is as well a poem in the archives of every sufficiently stocked library that carries the same sentiment, this by Abraham Joseph Ryan, 1838—1886, a Roman Catholic Priest attached to a Southern regiment from 1862 until the end of the war. It was *The Conquered Banner,* inspired by the death of a younger brother in battle and the defeat of the cause in which he so strongly believed.

Furl that Banner, for 'tis weary;

Round its staff 'tis drooping dreary'

Furl it, fold it–it is best;

For there's not a man to wave it,

And there's not a sword to save it

And there's not one left to lave it

In the blood which heroes gave it;

And its foes now scorn and brave it;

Furl it, hide it–let it rest!

Later in her life, when she was becoming old, Adelaide removed this poem from the shelves and read it to Sasha. Together one Sunday afternoon they were sorting through some old memorabilia and had happened upon it unexpectedly.

Abiding by his commitment, Doctor Givens called for the staff at the hospital to assemble in the cafeteria to celebrate, reverently giving thanks to the Lord that the slaughter of lives had ended and that the nation could begin to mend its wounds and rebuild. The room was colorfully decorated, richly embroidered tapestries laid upon the tables, candles burning, flowers of every variegation emplaced here and there; but no food, excepting the pastries in better than adequate supply freshly brought in from the kitchen. And there was coffee and tea. There is no easy way to explain the mood of the staff, for it varied exceedingly: they were ecstatic, they were in the clouds, they were drunk with happiness, they cried and laughed at the same time. They were as the whole nation, greatly relieved.

"It's over Sasha," said Doctor Givens as he came up to her at the instant she was leaving a gathering of fellow staffers, beginning her way toward the service table for coffee. "I don't think we can quite grasp it yet, but it is over. Of course, we'll still have those here undergoing rehabilitation for awhile. But for the most part the wounded sent to us for care will begin to substantially lessen."

"I'm so thankful for that."

"Maybe you'll have more time now to spend on your research and chemical experiments."

"I haven't thought about that much, certainly not recently, but I'm sure I'll begin to."

As they continued on something was said about the difference they could expect in their daily procedures at the hospital, which would be tailored to a peacetime culture. But these exchanges lasted no longer than a fraction. Fellow staffers had suddenly come into their presence and the topic changed. But there was another topic which Doctor Givens was on the verge of addressing to Sasha before they arrived, which he tucked away, there letting it linger until later.

Chapter 67

THAT AFTERNOON Sasha had come into his office to discuss a matter pertaining to a patient she felt they should take up together. It was not a subject of immediacy. Laying down the medical chart that he studied he looked up with beaming face, and not bothering to as ask why she was there revealed what was uppermost in his thoughts. "Sasha. You're just the person I needed to see. I have not forgotten your marriage to Andre. It has dwelled momentously in my thoughts for the past few days. I meant to bring it up earlier but kept getting sidetracked by distractions. Now I am no longer. So let me ask you. What is your intention? You know, the date and so forth. I must put it on my calendar of events as a matter of absolute importance. I love weddings. I will especially love yours."

"Ha, ha, ha," she teased, "you are clairvoyant. Already this morning Andre came by and we went over a sprinkling of particulars. I'm writing Adelaide a letter very soon to request that she help me with the preparations."

"The wedding is to be at the Sherette plantation, I believe you have earlier told me."

"At Aurora. Yes. "

"Unh huh. The perfect place, and I can understand why. And the date?

"July. On the fifteenth I think. I'll confirm this exactly before the week is out."

When Sasha left Doctor Dontonte knocked on Doctor Given's door and went in, the two of them naturally enough taking up her marriage, with Doctor Dontonte unleashing a compliment of remarks that might have tingled her ears had she heard them. "I say good friend, she is a fine one, is she not; as I have forever said, the finest, I have long felt, and the most gorgeous on any side of the great seas. I tell you this because I believe it; no man could ever expect to win a woman so rare without a lengthy pursuit indeed."

"Ha. I should say. No man at all, regardless of the time. But Andre eventually did. I saw that romance begin to bud. Oh, how he drooled over her, though she did not return it, not instantly; she is of that nature, but as time dribbled on she relented. She's very much in love with him. Andre is steady, dependent, with beautiful morals, qualities that a woman of immense strength requires. 'Won't he make the most splendid father of our children,' she said not long ago? What a team they will be."

ꟸ ꟷ

That night the stars shone brightly in the skies over Baltimore, a peaceful calm appearing to settle upon every neighborhood throughout. The carriages on the street that ran in front of Sasha's home crept slowly, heading toward the heart of the city, the horse's hooves sounding a rhythmic clip clop, clip clop on the cobblestone road. The occupants were heard chattering happily back and forth. Andre and Sasha, who could not hear well their voices, assumed they were discussing the ending of the war. They had sat on the portico for an hour after supper watching the traffic flow by, then with a suddenness, Sasha ventured that they should be going downtown too where the crowds were evidently gathering to celebrate, and there also show their own patriotism.

"I don't think it will be dangerous. Harness the horses and let's go Andre."

They did therefore what a throng of folks were doing, climbing into their carriages and driving to the center of the city to be a part of the massive display of happiness. The stores had closed early, but the cafes had stayed open, and in the parks which were but a short distance fireworks now and then exploded. They drove around for awhile, opting to a selection of various streets, finally finding an available hitching post where they left their horses and carriage. Casually they began to walk about, not yet joining the crowd, fascinated by the peaceful twinkling of lights emanating from the windows of the small unpretentious houses, some painted white, some not at all, which in goodly numbers but not necessarily crowded were situated in the heart of the city. These were the dwellings of the laboring class; the rich lived further out. It was but a pittance that Sasha's eyes fell upon the popular museum which she sometimes browsed while shopping downtown. The city officials had ordered that lanterns be set out completely surrounding it, which at this hour threw off a glow both mystical and beautiful. The museum was of an older vintage, Sasha said to Andre, fringed with an array of sculpturing and elongated windows, and there was a headstone set above the entryway. It was a big if not a monstrous assembly contrived by human hands and an inventive mind belonging to some unknown architect of a former period. She did not need to go inside to see the splendor; she had seen it already, not many times but several, and knew that it resembled a Catholic cathedral, which momentarily threw up visions of her forthcoming wedding. As they began to leave the vicinity she judged that the style of the shrine was either of Norwegian or Germanic descent; she didn't know which but would delve into the archives to be certain. On down a ways they had started to drop into a café, yet decided on commingling with the masses which were assembled a few blocks away in the town square where the celebration was largely taking place.

The people seemed calm and happy but bumped into one another with thoughtless abandon, the men hugging the women and kissing their lips, though when trying as much with Sasha she allowed the hug but eluded the kiss, frowning over at Andre as she turned away, who was taking it all in good stead. The mayor and his staff had planned the celebration well, offering a preponderance of things for the people to see and do. Sasha and Andre stood for a while watching a combo of Negro musicians playing a medley of indistinct music whereas some of the folks nearby formed a circle and danced to the rhythmic whining and strumming of the fiddles and banjos, snappily picking up their feet and letting them down. And there was a marching band clad in military uniforms that played with excessive loudness, depending on one's hearing capability, and walked with a quite rapid pace. They were former Union soldiers. One man had climbed to the top of a two story hardware store where he delighted in dumping confetti on the crowd below. At one intermission the mayor stepped from a café onto the sidewalk and delivered an emotional harangue that at last freedom and peace had come. The applause was uproarious. Staying a little longer Sasha and Andre felt they should be on their way. Pushing through the gathering they finally reached their carriage and crawled in and returned home, again taking a seat on the portico.

"You know something Andre?"

"Yeah. You didn't like the way those men behaved."

"No I didn't. Not really. And I don't think you did either. But everyone was in a state of euphoria. That's kind of how crowds are; so I won't blame them entirely."

"Yeah. Okay. But they were a trifle rowdy. And Euphoria. Your creation. That's an apt word. That's what they were, not rowdy but euphoric. Thank you. The whole crowd was I guess."

"Hmmm. That reminds me. My father once said that a crowd has a mind of its own, not given to very much thinking, maybe not thinking at all, just reacting, driven only by emotion. But that is another matter isn't it dear. I'm drifting. Sorry. Let's talk about something else." And for awhile she turned busily from one thing to another, while Andre smiled amusedly over. He loved it when she was talkative; often she was not. Eventually she ceased and seemed to him to be toying with a matter that was seriously thoughtful and meditative. Finally it surfaced.

"Soon I'll start arranging the wedding Andre. My work here will begin to abate a little in a few weeks, hopefully sooner. I'll write Adelaide to help me with it. Of course she is already helping. But she's waiting for the date."

"What have you decided?"

"How is July 15 with you?"

Andre happily echoed his concurrence and wished to her that it could happen sooner and then asked, "Who all is coming?"

"Everyone I can recall. All my friends and then some. But Heaven knows that I don't know who all they are at this very minute, because I can't recall them at this very minute. But I will sooner or later."

"A grand affair no doubt. Every bit a grand affair."

She responded in jest. "Naturally sir. The man that I'm marrying deserves the grandest wedding affair that the Sherette and Van Doke plantations have ever seen. Don't you agree?"

"Why yes. How could I not. Ha, ha, ha."

That night they retired happily to bed, both sleeping well they reported to each other the next morning, though it seemed that Andre slept a bit better than Sasha, for she awakened sooner than he and knocked on his door, calling out that Padgett was there earlier than usual and would he like to have breakfast and a refreshing cup of coffee with his future bride."

"Hmmm. You tempt me. Give me a minute. I'll dress in no time. What is it that she's serving?"

"Ham and eggs, your favorite, capped off with a bowl of oatmeal deliciously buttered and sweetened. And you can have a croissant, maybe two, but no more."

Cupping his hands while looking up into the Heavens, Andre playfully uttered, "Oh my dear precious Lord, she is already laying ground rules for the assurance of my good health. But as You know, she has been at that for the longest."

In thin flawless calligraphy Sasha penned a letter to Adelaide. She began with, "My dearest," then proceeded to say that she would be there very soon to prepare for her wedding, which largely dominated her thoughts these days, especially since the war was over, and that the thrill of it all was beginning to mount. She continued on that she was trying to arrange first things first and knew that she was proceeding likewise, and that she was setting July 15 as the wedding date, which, she figured, allowed time enough to notify the invitees, provided the mailings and word of mouth commenced without letting many days escape. She asked Adelaide to take notice of the invitee list as per attached, conveying in the next line that she knew she had also prepared one, continuing with an urging that if someone had been left off then please set her aright.

"There will be many to attend, I do believe," she spoke, but wondered about their lodging, then exclaimed that naturally, "the Aurora and La Belle will suffice to accommodate a sizeable number, but will that be space enough? Oh! Weddings! They are demanding aren't they?"

Then she got to the gown, proceeding to take up that it might prove excessive for her and Mary Tonka and Thea to pattern and stitch, and did she still think they could; furthering that if the plan were still intact, then she would supply the description and specify the materials from which it should be comprised. She would in fact do that before she fell off to sleep, she added, for the loveliness of the beautiful garment spun fast in her brain and had kept her much awake at night for the past several nights. She had dreamt of it, she said—in the brief span that she was sleeping.

"I must report to you that as of late I have done much searching and looking in the House of Fashion, the most notable in the city, viewing one breathtaking specimen after another—they are plentifully many, a sea of them—but am especially swayed by one lovely thing which I shall tell you about. It keeps recurring to me. Did I not intimate that I have dreamt of it? Yes I did. It will not leave me. Therefore I must very much like it."

The garment of subject, which she described in minute detail, featured a set of gorgeous feminine lace sleeves which accentuated the full blown skirt, a lovely thing in and of itself; then there was the appliqué bodice, the material consisting of English and French Chantilly lace sewn onto an ivory silk tulle. She had recently observed one of the House's displays where there was a bodice that was made from "rose point silk needle lace tulle," the sales brochure read, only slightly different from the other. Either would do, she explained, granted that hers must possess a veil with the sheerest adornments that covered the face and lapped back over the shoulders. And it struck her tastefully that the bodice should be endowed of a row of satin buttons fitted in the back, thus not interfering with or detracting from the high neckline. "I like the high neckline." She could consent to having the buttons in front and opt to a V neckline, but didn't think she would. She had once seen a portrait of Queen Victoria when she was wed, she inserted, and that the Queen had selected the high one.

"And oh yes my dear. I almost left off a vital. I think I prefer an olden tiara crown, a sort of medieval ornament; I like the idea of the olden, and moreover, the tiara in conjunction with the lovely veil piece will lend balance to the volume of the gown. No, I have not forgotten the train, but do allow me to exaggerate. Andre says to make it a mile long. Well, not quite. What a funny boy. We shall have our laugh about that when we are together."

When near the last her lines disclosed that she was aiming to arrive at Aurora by no later than the last of May, whereon they could then debate back and forth with respect to modifications, yet, threw in also that if Adelaide liked, she was positive that she could persuade the management at the House of Fashion to lend her a thorough diagram of the gown, as well as a visual sketch of the attendant accessories; and that this would give her and Mary Tonka and Thea a head start. "Just an afterthought," she tacked on. "I love you. Sasha."

Though trying it would be, Adelaide was on her way to evolving solutions to the rash of obstacles that suddenly loomed before her; the wedding gown was one thing but there were endless other imperatives with which she must concern herself, and repeated silently that Sasha was correct, that weddings were demanding. *"Donne-moi Seigneur, une bonne resistance; je ne dois pas lui manquer."*[12] When she had read Sasha's letter she was alert to grasp her reference to Aurora and La Belle as maybe not having sufficient space for accommodating the guests. "Dear me; isn't that just like her," and speculated that she was likely revolving a hundred other trivial details, but that she could not let her do that, that such was not her domain of responsibility. "She won't have the time. She is yet tied up with a backlog of lingering surgeries at the hospital, helping young soldiers back on their feet. It's up to us here to shoulder the burden of putting things in place, to keep even the lightest load off her." Then she sat down and began running her fingers through her quite full head of lovely hair, revolving a dozen things at once. Mary Tonka saw it building—Adelaide was twitching her face to the left and right while unknowingly biting her lips—so she did what she often did; she brought in a glass of fresh iced tea and set it on the table beside her. "Can I help you my dear?"

"Believe it or not, Mary Tonka, it has suddenly swept over me that you might."

"And?"

"Sasha's letter. It sends me scampering. The wedding calls for a mountain of things to be done. Let's see. Oh. Now that you're here sit with me and let's browse through them. The principal ones anyway."

---

[12] Give me strength Good Lord; I must not fail her.

"I'll take notes as you sort them through. You must have a good many organized in your head.

"I do."

"So then?"

"As I say, let's go through them, the mailings first, the invitations that is. Heaven knows we've sorted through them a dozen times or more. And I think we've accounted for practically everyone, unless Sasha later surprises us with an upshot of unexpected folks. I've studied her list already; it corresponds infinitely close with the copy we've put together ourselves. But then, there are the other essentials. Let's keep going."

Then they turned to the subject of food, the various assortments and amounts of it and who would prepare it and in what manner it was to be served, and then next to the gatherings of the people, to those attending the ceremony inside Aurora and to those who by and large would not, these the workers and slaves assembling on the grounds outside, and then there was the music—of various styles that had to be arranged—a common style of folk music on the one hand supplied by the banjo pickers and fiddlers of the plantations, and the suave violinists of the ensemble on the other who would produce the Heavenly swells and tones at the ball which were to follow the wedding that evening.

"Two kinds of music Adelaide?"

"Sasha would want that."

"On second thought I think she would. One for the field workers and the other for the beautiful folks."

Adelaide burst out laughing. "For the beautiful folks! Well. I guess so, if you're judging by what they wear. Anyway, we can hire musicians for playing at the ball out of Memphis."

"I don't know where else. That's where Mrs. Van Doke always hired them."

"I know. Yes she did. Perhaps Randolph can handle that chore for us. I'll have Sam Feathers drop by and speak to him about the matter. Or Doctor Lundy." She ran her fingers through her hair again. Mary Tonka had seen her do that scores of times throughout the years; she knew it had become one of Adelaide's pet traits. She smiled inside. Adelaide spoke again. "It's a heavy task isn't it my dear, a heavy one indeed, but we'll have to deal with it, won't we, so where will we go from here?

Mary Tonka answered without the least of hitches, as if she'd been following Adelaide word for word and she had, and had done it astutely, as she always did.

"We'll just begin where we are and keep on until we finish. No matter how long it takes."

A very happy and amused laugh leapt from Adelaide's breast and across her lips. And Mary Tonka laughed with her, then they bent themselves to the preponderance of other essentials remaining that they knew had to be thought of and dealt with. One of these was to associate certain persons with a particular task or tasks. "Let's do that as we move along. That will help us be more efficient," Adelaide declared. "Two things in one." They would work late, until close to one o'clock.

Lawrence Sherette was given the first assignment, the first two assignments in fact, the drafting of a letter to Mrs. Laster and Bryon containing the wedding date, including some extras extemporaneously thrown in, and devising and printing the ceremonial brochure. Mary Tonka insisted that she'd take it upon herself to relay to him a note to this end, to save Adelaide from having to bother with it. "I need to send that boy a line anyway." Sam Feathers was singled out for overseeing the setting up of the outside tables under the ponderous oaks and the cooking of the pork over the open fires where everyone would come to off and on and stand and watch and talk and laugh while the meat was little by little barbequed to the nth degree of correctness. The best Negro barbequers were to be selected, the best anywhere, Sam Feathers would tell you, who had overseen some of them for as long as thirty years, or longer.

Staying at their tasks until the clock hand had passed one Adelaide and Mary Tonka retired, waking early at the next dawn with a renewed energy to finish. Much of the day was to be consumed checking and rechecking before they wrote down the last name of the attendees, the jobs that had to be carried out, and the persons who would shoulder them.

Mary Tonka said that she would take it upon herself to organize the group of women, the most reliable and competent on the plantation, for preparing the meals for the inside servings, and others, who would clean and dust and wash windows and the like, not stopping until the interior of Aurora looked spick and span. "I'll put the women together Adelaide; none of that will be left to you." And she would sit with Cynthia to make certain that all went well in the same general manner at La Belle. The Nomeharts were still residing there but neither Adelaide nor Mary Tonka expected them to help significantly, a scant contribution at best. "Cynthia knows how to handle the folks, she surely does. She ought to; she saw a heap of them born. And let me say this too my dear; they'll all do anything for you and Sasha. Anything. They'd break their backs to get to. All they need is someone to let them know what to do, plus a little nudging here and there. But of course you know all this. You've just about been managing the field hands since you were a little girl."

"Bless you Mary Tonka. What would I do without you? Come to think of it I don't know, for I never have."

The dear old woman she had been with practically from the fount of her birth leaned over and patted her cheeks and hugged her and smiled a smile that only a person of age can smile, not a broad one, a subdued one, which perhaps would not have seemed to come naturally, but it started from deep within her heart.

"You have the right idea dear" said Adelaide, "just exactly what I needed to hear. As soon as we can let's sit down with Thea and Cynthia and Sam Feathers and Coon and divvy up the jobs."

"Good. Let's do that."

"But the gown. The wedding gown. That again we must address."

Adelaide had been thinking about it all along; it would not leave her, and began to speak aloud of what had evolved in her head, reasoning that since the other loads were defined and settled she was of mind to visit Baltimore and spend whatever time necessary supporting Sasha with regard to the gown, and that she was of further mind that the House of Fashion should be engaged to make the beautiful garment in that it was wholly impossible for Sasha to come home and get it done there, especially since she would arrive as late as the last of May and that they could not adequately do it for her in the meantime with her so far away.

"Standing for the fittings will eat up hours. Oh yes. Letting the House of Fashion handle the whole bit of it is the answer, the only answer, right there in Baltimore. What do you think?"

Mary Tonka saw that she was determined, and agreed completely. "Very good. When will you write her of this?"

"This very afternoon. I'll send Sam Feathers over to the railroad depot for mailing it. No, I'll saddle up and do it myself. He's too busy in the fields."

Mary Tonka smiled once more. "Fine. I think we're on our way to a beautiful wedding."

When Adelaide had finished her meeting with Sam Feathers and Thea and Cynthia and Coon, naturally Mary Tonka at her side, she then drafted a letter to Sasha telling of her intentions and why, receiving in the quickest a reply, in which Sasha begged, "Do please come on; the sooner the better." Sasha had practically leapt with joy at the message. Adelaide was driven to Jackson by Sam Feathers where she caught the train—there were none on the day of her departure stopping at the Sherette plantation depot—eventually reaching Nashville in a round about way, then without stopping off to visit with Jim and Lucy, she caught another train, and with no additional switches in the remaining distance, rode directly into President Station in Baltimore at mid afternoon. Sasha had learned by telegraph the hour of her arrival and was there to meet her.

Chapter 68

AFTER THE hugs and kisses and the emotions had begun to die away, they climbed into a waiting carriage, with Sasha furnishing instructions to the driver of the routing to her home. Barely had they started to roll away when the subject of the gown was taken up.

"When I read your letter Adelaide, I wasted no time in arranging a session with the House of Fashion."

"And what did they say?"

"It's a deal. They can make it here."

"Great! Wonderful! I knew they could. What all will that entail?"

"Two things mainly. The fittings, and the choice of what I want."

"Ha, ha, ha. I can just see you now. You know, standing still while the seamstress takes your measurements. That's going to be something hard for a wiggle worm to do."

"No it won't. I can stand still. I'll just close my eyes and imagine the end reward."

"Good for you. But the gown. It's a lovely thing that you rather infinitely detailed in your letter. Is that what you want?"

"Very close, very close indeed. And as you say, it's a lovely thing. Very lovely. I can't wait for you to see it."

"When can I?"

"Tomorrow. We'll call on the House of Fashion in the morning. The hour won't matter. They'll gladly receive us."

The next morning at ten they sought out the Charge d' Affaires of dress making, the highest position in the chain of command of the firm. She received them graciously. Right off Sasha asked that they be led to where the dress was displayed.

"This way," she said, motioning with her hand, bowing slightly. Passing through a corridor, then another one of the quite large facility, they soon came to where Sasha said she had seen a sea of gowns, and Adelaide then realized what she had meant.

"I've never seen as many," she cried out.

The Charge d' Affaires was obviously pleased with Adelaide's excitement, smiling broadly, then led them into another room where there it was, a solitary gown, a beautiful thing of white silk and lace fitted on a lifeless but shapely mannequin.

"For goodness sake," Adelaide let out.

Sasha burst into light laughter. "You like it?"

"It's precious. It's gorgeous. I vote for it here and now."

"I knew you would."

"It's practically made already, isn't it?" said Adelaide, her eyes leveling on the Charge d' Affaires.

"Not quite. We'll have to do the measurements."

"And how long after that will your seamstress need in order to complete her work?"

"Two weeks, given that much is done already and that she has a team of rare proficiency with her."

"Two weeks. Ah, that is quick. That is efficient. And when will you have Sasha meeting with the seamstress?"

"Two days from this date."

"How long can you stay Adelaide?" inquired Sasha.

"I have planned on three weeks, maybe a little longer."

"Wonderful. Then you will see how it fits me. And I'm sure it will."

"Oh it will fit you Doctor Duval," the Charge d' Affaires said with emphasis. "Our seamstress is flawless. At both measuring and sewing."

"You mentioned the tiara in your letter," said Adelaide. "Something to the effect that you desired an old fashioned one, perhaps dating back to an era long past. Did you say the medieval period?"

"I did. But I don't think we discussed that," she said, looking over at the Charge d' Affaires. "Is there a problem with what I would like?"

"None. We are entirely complete here. We will find what you want. Could you visit with us next week for an observation of the ornaments that we will display for you? When can you come?"

"Next Tuesday."

"Then I'll write out a reservation card for you. Is ten o'clock suitable?"

"Quite suitable."

While Adelaide was there in the city, Padgett outdid herself at cooking and serving meals, aware, one might judge, that Adelaide was that rich plantation owner from somewhere in the South, and that she was instrumental in Sasha buying the house, supplying a great amount, if not all, of the original funding. Andre was over almost every evening for a visit, leaving soon after supper, if he ate with them. When they went out for dinner he generally went along, and sometimes Doctor Givens and Doctor Dontonte.

The fitting came off smoothly, Sasha not at all squirming around as Adelaide had laughed and implied that she might. The seamstress was a Madam Merkel, a German lady in her fifties with her hair pulled back tightly and rolled up as a bun in the back. She was a no nonsense woman who rigidly concentrated on her job, and seldom spoke, the times that she did amounting to no more than, "Will you stand more erect please, Doctor Duval," or "Will you step to the right (or left) for me please?" Sasha was convinced that she was a superbly capable lady at her craft and grew more pleased with her with the passage of each session. As she said she would, the Charge d' Affaires had laid out the tiaras for Sasha to view, specimens of such resplendency and glitter that both Sasha and Adelaide were at a loss when they were faced with making a final choice. The Charge d' Affaires proved here to be of the utmost value in lending assistance, tactfully remarking that the gown Sasha had selected was a splendid match for the ornament, and that she had constructed many a gown and selected countless tiaras to go with them. And in that they had no hesitation about trusting her Sasha and Adelaide bowed to her recommendation. Near the completion of the garment Madam Merkel showed them the train which she felt was exactly the one to fit with it, but stressed that she could not have the work completed at the end of two weeks. This meant that Adelaide could not see it in finished form, seeing it attached to the gown before leaving, yet agreed that the display on the mannequin, only now underway, was breathtaking, and felt absolutely positive that at the wedding the train would look better by far than what she was viewing as an incomplete exhibit. For the time she had left in the city, Adelaide and Sasha stayed busy gadding about here and there, the theater first, the train rides next, and shopping third, but there was an additional lure, among scores of others, that Sasha could also not leave off; she said she absolutely could not, which was a quaint little diner on the shore of the Chesapeake where the main menu featured shrimp and lobster.

This was next to Adelaide's last night and their last night together out on the town. They were a mite more subdued than they had been over the days previous. "Leaving you darling makes me sad."

"And it saddens me too, terribly. But I'm thankful you've spent the short while that you did with me. We attended to everything that we needed to. Don't worry about the wedding gown train. It will turn out fine. In every aspect of their business I am trusting in the Charge d' Affaires and Madam Merkel."

"So am I."

"Aren't the lights pretty out there?" Sasha suddenly said, breaking away from their preoccupation with the gown, but apologizing that perhaps she too quickly had opted to another topic.

"Don't apologize dear. I was about to do that myself. The lights are pretty. And they in a way take me back to a little café on the edge of the Mississippi."

"In New Orleans?"

"Yes. It's a favorite of Harry's, whose specialty is fish, not shrimp and lobster. When I am with him he usually does the ordering, often the same thing, but for the life of me I don't seem this minute to come up with what it is."

"And what is the name of that quaint little place? Were we ever there?"

"No we weren't. I guess we were too caught up in other things. The name of it is Chalmette."

"I love it. It's Frenchy. And Harry really likes it? Forgive me. You've intimated that already."

"Very much. He's the reason we go."

"Ah, Harry. He is coming to the wedding, isn't he?"

"You couldn't tie him and keep him away."

"Such a nice man Adelaide. I know you'll marry him some day. And you should. He's a catch."

"Ha, ha, ha. We shall see sweetheart. We shall see."

At this, the waiter approached to take their order, then they forgot all about the wedding gown and Adelaide marrying Harry. But had come to terms with ordering; they chose abalone.

The last day of her stay in the city suddenly was there; Adelaide paid one last call on Doctors Givens and Dontonte, thanking them for the hospitality they had shown her, and assuring them that they would be well cared for when they visited Aurora for the wedding. They, in concert with Sasha, were at the railroad station that afternoon when she boarded the train. Andre was obligated at the hospital and could not be there. He had bid goodbye to her at lunch. The weather was pretty and sunny. They stood for awhile, then decided to wander around on the inside of the station, Doctor Dontonte amazed at the height of the ceiling, and alluded to it as an engineering masterpiece. Not long thereafter they returned to the frontage and took seats on the deacons benches running the full length of the building, with spaces in between. Sasha and Adelaide sat together on one bench, Doctors Givens and Dontonte on another. Sasha told Adelaide while they waited that she'd give anything to be going with her, with Adelaide replying that it was of no length when she'd see her again.

"Now, do away with that melancholy cast."

"I will. I will. And you have yourself a good ride, and be sure that the porter supplies you with a nice soft pillow to help you sleep well. You'll be riding throughout the night."

Sasha stood and watched the train until it had vanished from sight at the bend of the tracks a quarter mile away. She then turned and went to the carriage where Doctor Dontonte, waiting to perform the courtesy, helped her up into her seat.

At some time during the weeks before her departure Sasha went into detail with both Doctor Givens and Doctor Dontonte as to the condition of the patients under her care, this including a look at their medical charts and a reflection on the oddities, if any, that affected them. Doctor Dontonte spoke that he was more than glad to assume the extra load resulting from her absence but didn't know what the hospital was to do when they themselves took time off for the wedding.

"We're looking into replacements," remarked Doctor Givens. "We might hire one from Doctor Fitzgerald's surgical team in London. Regardless Sasha, that's not for you to worry yourself about. You have a wedding forthcoming. And by the way, how long did you say you needed off?"

"We agreed earlier on two months."

"Two months. Yes we did. We'll miss you, but you well deserve it. And where is to be your honeymoon, if it's any of my business?"

"Sorrento, that gorgeous seaside resort in Italy. My father once took me there."

"I have heard you say that. My, my. You will be overcome by that idyllic haven."

"Indeed I will. Every since my father took me years ago I've yearned to return."

Sasha had seen Madam Merkel more times than necessary with regard to the wedding train, but Madam Merkel was glad she came, for not only did she want Sasha there to inspect and approve her work, she as well savored her presence. The sessions were lively of exchange, even though as a rule Madam Merkel was much reserved in the matter of conversation. She had many curious questions to ask Sasha with regard to the Sherette plantation. It was obvious she was thrilled at the thought of visiting a place as grand as had been described to her. She planned to arrive with the wedding attire sufficiently before the ceremony, this including her sewing machine and pertinent cutting and stitching devices should they be needed. But added that she expected no adjustments. Sasha and Adelaide would intercept her at the plantation depot, Sasha assured her in their last session together, standing in watch for her without fail.

At some time in their various meetings Madam Merkel asked of her trousseau, meaning her dresses for the honeymoon.

"Who is making them for you Sasha?" Sometimes she forgot and called her by her given name rather than Doctor Duval. Before Sasha answered she proceeded. "I will gladly make them for you at no charge." Sasha replied that she and Adelaide had decided to purchase the clothing in Memphis soon after she arrived home. Nevertheless, Madam Merkel finally persuaded her to let her contrive and stitch three lovely designs and refused to accept not one dime for her services.

Nearing the last of May, Sasha was at the same railroad station where only week's earlier Adelaide caught her train to Aurora. She was carrying with her a very large clothes encasement. Andre could not go with her just then because of his encumbrance with patients at the hospital, promising not to overlook the several articles he was to bring when he joined her three weeks later. More than once they scanned the check off list to ascertain that he missed nothing.

She was dressed in green, a green skirt that flared to her ankles, and a soft silky blouse with full fluffy sleeves extending to her wrists. And adding to this there was a female's vest, also green, yet featured a collar of whitish hue, which was stiffly upright. Tightly fitted around her waistline, trim and shapely and girlish, the lower portion of the vest together with her complete attire made Sasha Duval a most conspicuous figure. The train was late, reported an old porter pushing a stack of boxes on a depot cart equipped with red wooden spokes and a slanted handle bar that he gripped as he forced the vehicle slowly along, squeaking and grating. Andre had asked him if the train's tardiness was expected. "It sho is suh," he answered, drawing his watch from its pouch, astutely studying the hour hands. "Bout twenty minutes from now."

Andre was restless, perhaps the result of Sasha going away without him; or in any event that was as she figured, and asked him to sit by her on the deacon's bench. Without delay Andre slid onto the seat beside her.

Shortly thereafter there arose the oddest occurrence; or what one might take it to be, or perhaps it was not odd at all. The sun, in its mid afternoon trajectory, had suddenly and deftly crept onto Sasha's face, forming a most magnificent luster, throwing at the same time a singular radiance of beauty across and into her eyes. It was one of those infinitely perfect unintended visages that one sometimes sees in another at the briefest glance, only once perhaps in a decade or in a whole life time, realizing that within seconds it will have lapsed into another form, never again to reappear. But Andre saw it and whatever he saw had moved him to the point of amorousness. "You look so lovely sweetheart," said he, "more I think than I have ever seen you before."

Sasha simply looked over at him with a fix of amusement upon her face then leaned and kissed him. Then she laughed happily. She thanked him for his compliment and spoke another word or two, and then suddenly embarked upon a subject which she quite surely had been exploring in her thoughts for at least the past short while.

"Think of it my sweet Andre; I am going on a trip, more than a trip, almost a hallowed journey let me call it, and you will follow, and when we return to this very place, thus completing the circle, we will be husband and wife; then begin to raise our family. So you take care my dear, and do not fall victim to injury or become sick, for you will find me too far away to attend you and Heaven forbid that, for you and I have a beautiful wedding underway and I do not want anything to happen to interrupt it."

"Are you superstitious?"

"No. Not a bit. Just a woman in love and mindful of those precious little babies that I eventually will give birth to and raise."

☙ ❧

When Sasha arrived at the Aurora there was a general stir of excitement among the workers and former slaves, the warmest of love in their hearts for the young woman who had grown up among them, who had attended them when they were ill, delivered their babies, along with Mary Tonka, and also separately, and gone with Andre to their dances and feeds, and given clothes to their young, and walked among them in the fields, sometimes herself pulling a cotton sack. She was theirs; she had grown into them and they into her: she was their daughter, no less, as they saw her in their imagination, and they were marrying her off. As they had listened to Adelaide and Mary Tonka and Thea and Cynthia describe the wedding dress and tell of the lush decorations that were planned for the great living room where Sasha and Andre were to marry, they had become still with wonder and envisioned themselves attending the most magnificent wedding ever performed on earth. Few had ever been privileged to be a part of a wedding of such eloquence and to think of attending it, being part of its magnificence, was quite close to more than they could comprehend. For weeks they had talked with one another, of how beautiful the bride would look in her wedding gown, and wasn't it something that Lawrence Sherette was to perform the ceremony and that Izu would from her portrait enclosure be there looking on as her daughter was wed. And they had heard that Thea was to have a prominent role, something like a maid of honor they told one another. With these visions driving them it was no wonder that they devoted their all to assisting with the deluge of preliminary arrangements, whether on the outside grounds or on the inside of the Aurora. "Sasha, Sasha; she's getting married," the whispers flowed, starting in the several weeks previous, and if anything, these exultations had grown more intense and more often delivered as time passed.

One of the imperatives on Adelaide's agenda with which she wished to dispense up front and early was the contracting of the best orchestra that Memphis had to offer for the reception dance and as soon as Sasha was settled they set out for the city. To Sasha's delight they would ride the train. That would give them the luxury of sitting and riding and talking at the same time.

"I love this Adelaide. I dearly do. It's so good to be out with you again. Do you recall the train ride we took together from Baltimore to Washington and back? Of course I know you do."

"That was fun. So much fun. But now I am suddenly a bit sad."

"Ah. Why is that?"

"You are marrying off my darling and I am afraid that afterwards I'll seldom see you."

"Don't talk like that. Anytime you look up, there I'll be. You'll see me so often you can't stand it."

"Silly. Ha, ha, ha."

Carriages were waiting in droves at the train station, "a new building," remarked Sasha as she looked up at the exterior vaulting high above and at the run of windows installed at near the roof line which admitted a suffusion of outside lighting. Adelaide gestured for a driver, who came quickly and helped them climb up, and upon clucking to his handsome horses the carriage suddenly moved and they were off and soon at the Gayoso. They had set foot on Memphis soil at mid afternoon, planning to have dinner at six in the dining room—naturally; they were addicted to this plush setting—yet before dinner they were to meet with Randolph in the lobby to discuss the hiring of the orchestra which he had promised Adelaide he would secure, and he was there when they entered, ready with papers for her signature.

"It's done Adelaide. You'll love them I'm sure. They're the same musicians that Mrs. Van Doke always used when she had her dinners and dance gatherings."

"Yes, I know. That's the reason I'm wanting so badly for them to play for us."

"And I want them to equally as bad. And Sasha dear, you beautiful girl, congratulations. You are landing a fine young man for a husband, and he is landing the most gorgeous and finest woman of all, I mean anywhere, for his wife. And I shall be there dressed in my best suit seeing it all."

"Yes you will Randolph. My disappointment would be crushing should you fail to attend my wedding. Horrors."

"No danger of that dear."

At this, Randolph hugged them goodbye and promptly left, citing that he had to make double time to be around to ascertain that the formalities were in place for his early evening patrons.

As they were always when visiting the Gayoso, the two women were clad in the most eloquent of clothing. They were among the bold and aggressive pace setters for the evolving fashions subtly departing the Victorian era. A lovely sight, they made tasteful prey for men's eyes, and they knew it, and talked smilingly about it during their dinner; but what man could have missed the sparkling ring upon Sasha's finger. Ah, but that was of no consequence, for beauty is beauty whether the possessor of it is betrothed or not.

In the days before this date Mary Tonka had been patterning and sewing a number of dresses for Sasha's trousseau and Thea was working on two.

"You must have plenty of changes darling," Mary Tonka had said to Sasha. "There's no telling where you'll go and what all you'll do, so we must allow for that. And oh yes. Your hours on the ship. What will you wear then, and will it be gusty, sometimes stormy?" Sasha laughed and answered.

"I'll select from the many things you and Thea are putting together and as to the wind, let me say that I am sure at times it will blow woefully and there could be a storm. We'll just have to see."

Adelaide was taking the clothing into account that Mary Tonka and Thea were devising for Sasha's trousseau, when, the next day they began to shop at some of the finest women's stores in Memphis. By mid afternoon they had selected twelve dresses and suits plus a summer frock or two, Sasha contending several dresses before the twelfth was ordered that they had purchased more than enough, but Adelaide had refused to stop. "No, my darling. I only wish I could see you in them. I will never let it be said that you weren't the best dressed young woman on the ship and in all of Sorrento. Nothing is good enough for my beloved little sister." Sasha merely smiled, knowing that Adelaide was determined to have her way and that it was born out of the inestimable love in her heart for her. That afternoon, with boxes of clothing stacked as high as they were tall, they boarded the four o'clock passenger train for the Sherette plantation, arriving just before sundown at the depot where Sam Feathers was standing by.

"My lands! What all do we have here?" he let out as he loaded the cargo into the carriage.

"Part of her trousseau Sam," said Adelaide, doubtful that he knew the meaning of the term. But he let out no further inquiries, saying only that he figured Mary Tonka would have supper ready when they pulled in front of Aurora.

Chapter 69

NOT LONG after this date Sasha and Adelaide set propped up one night in the mammoth Victorian, with a stack of pillows behind their heads, pouring over a list of the invitees. These were the names of persons that Adelaide had earlier copied down, together with those names that Sasha had sent her from Baltimore. Now Sasha wanted to see the complete list, sort of a last minute inspection and began to scroll down the names with her forefinger, pausing at each, there dropping an abbreviated comment, and with much animation.

"Melana, oh Adelaide, she is such a delightful person. She stayed with me when I was in England. You remember don't you? She's Doctor Fitzgerald's sister. She has never married.

And yes, here is Doctor Robert Charlatan, the dapper young doctor who was on Captain Andrew Dolby's good ship the *Surety*, which Lawrence Sherette and Mrs. Laster and I caught at Corpus Christi, sailing from there to New Orleans. You know Adelaide, I honestly think Doctor Charlatan fell in love with me on that trip, young as I was."

"Hmmmm," Adelaide issued playfully, "you never told me as much."

"Ha, ha, ha. No I didn't, did I?"

And then she continued. "Here is Doctor Dontonte, my cavalier friend, a marvelous doctor, with whom I expect to stay in touch over the long years. He is a very good dancer, a splendid dancer, and talks your ears off while whirling you around."

"And when did you dance with him?"

"When I was in London. Doctor Fitzgerald and his wife took me one night to a most eloquent ball, a beautiful outing, and I think I danced with every young man, and old, in the room."

"Of this I've never heard."

Sasha laughed with gaiety. "But now you have. And before you go one step further I'll reveal to you that I've already told Andre."

"I was just about to ask that."

"No you weren't."

Adelaide chuckled cutely. "No I really wasn't."

And then Sasha proceeded further to examine the list. "Oh, here I see Mr. Prudence Autry and wife Arlene from Louisville. They are coming down. Wonderful. Arlene was involved in fashion wasn't she?"

"Yes she was. Is it all right that I've invited them?"

"Of course. You know it is. I recall Mrs. Autry from the Van Doke dinner, the Christmas dinner. She is much spirited."

"A mite more than that."

"And I see that Mr. Benjamin Donovan, the railroad man is to avail himself. How on earth Adelaide have you kept up with these folks?"

"Oh I just have. But to tell you the truth, I went back and had a look at the register. When I glanced upon their names I knew I had to invite them. "

Sasha offered no response and inched further down the list. "And then I see that Mr. J. Otis Presly and wife Estelle are to be in attendance, and I hope their son will as well. You remember him of course. He's the young man from whose hand I removed an ugly thorn once. How is he these days?"

"Doing well. He's taken over his father's planting business. Mrs. Presly said to me once that he was terribly in love with you."

"Ahhhh. I didn't know."

Adelaide just had to giggle. "Says you."

"And Mrs. Laster, and Bryon, and Doctor Givens, and Doctor Lundy," Sasha let out as she touched their names, "all coming to the wedding, naturally. They are taken for granted. But oh, I see that Paula's name is scratched. She can't be here?"

"No she couldn't dear. She's tied up with her teaching. And as you already know, neither can Doctor Fitzgerald. But Melana can and will represent the family."

"That's what she said in her letter to me of some weeks past."

So on and on they kept at it, until examining the list in its entirety, the gong of the clock down the hall signaling that the hour was late. They had crawled into bed when the night was no longer young, and so after a few more of Sasha's yawns they exchanged hugs and Sasha turned over and Adelaide got up and blew out the lamp flame and then returned and lay down again.

"Goodnight dear."

"Goodnight Adelaide, I love you."

The days marched on and finally Andre stepped off the train at the Sherette plantation depot, where Sasha and Adelaide had stood for an hour wishing he would soon arrive. Sasha rushed over. He hugged and kissed her.

"I am so happy to see you my darling," he said. "One more day of doing without you and I would have quit the hospital." Sasha laughed with hilarity. Andre finally let her go and went to Adelaide. He hugged her tightly and spoke also that it was wonderful to see her. In route to the Aurora Sasha drove the horses, refusing to let Andre take the reins. Among their spirited jabbering and high elation Sasha suddenly said there was something that they must attend to with little delay.

"Andre, we'll have to get into the business of your fitting tomorrow, absolutely tomorrow. We are but a few days away from the wedding."

"Where? Where is my fitting?"

"Jackson."

"That's a relief. I thought you might have in mind Memphis and that is a far piece on such short notice."

"I know."

"Jason's will do your fitting," inserted Adelaide. "They offer the finest tuxedos anywhere and have a wide selection. We've made a reservation."

"Oh yeah. I'm familiar with the place. They're a Jewish store. I'm with you. They have the finest of clothing. My mother used to take us boys there when we were much younger. To dress us up for dinners and such."

"I know. I was at those affairs. All of you really looked so, so debonair."

"Yeah. She insisted on that. What a dear." He then turned to Sasha and slid his arm around her. "I so wish she could be here with us."

"I do too Andre, I dearly do."

The next day they set out for Jackson, catching the early morning train, the hour still dark, the coachmen wagging their lanterns as they hurried up and down the switch yard using an unintelligible train language which only they understood. The air was chilly, prompting the women to pull their capes up tightly. Once aboard Sasha was bent on their having coffee in the diner. But suggested that they delay breakfast until reaching Jackson. Andre gave a salute of approval and Adelaide had started to rise from her chair. Too sleepy to do otherwise they sat at first talking limitedly while savoring their coffee, vaguely listening to the screeching and rumbling from underneath which gave off something of an unvarying rhythm that was more noisy than rhythmic. Sasha every once in a while pressed her face against the windows to try to see the trees racing by which she knew were there but could not yet make them out. Andre had continually yawned and now, after receiving Sasha's blessing, had returned to his seat in the passenger coach, soon falling off to sleep. The porter was trooping up and down the aisle of the diner handing out hot pitchers of coffee and stopped at Sasha's and Adelaide's table.

"Would you like a refill madams?"

"Yes, thank you," the reply came from one or the other.

Sasha lifted the vessel and poured her cup full, Adelaide's too, and then took a sip, while reclining back in her seat. She sighed softly.

"J' aime le matin tot. Il est quand l'esprit est le plus frais et a' la crete de sa cre'ivite."[13]

Adelaide smiled at Sasha's usage of French. It never failed to amuse her, especially this early in the day. "That's the way it is with me too Sasha. The early morning has always been my best hour."

The train kept rolling onward. In a while the passengers could feel it slowing and shortly it rolled to a stop altogether, suddenly discharging a volley of loud hissing steam. There then ensued a heavy coarseness from a Negro porter standing at the doorway, "Jackson, Jackson. All out for Jackson."

They would have breakfast at a small café in the city that opened early. After eating, they sat around for awhile doodling with their coffee which neither any longer wanted, merely killing time, waiting for Jason's to open. When entering the store there was a sea of tuxedos mounted on hangers whichever way they looked, beautiful raven black garments that depicted a slight of glimmer. Sasha fell in love with every one she saw, finding it almost impossible to narrow her thinking to a single choice, having Andre try on at least twenty, he later greatly exaggerated. At last, Sasha and Adelaide huddled off to the side in discussion of a final choice. Andre wisely stayed free of the selection process, realizing that to go up against two women was unwise and futile and concluded that even if he had a view it likely wasn't as good as theirs. It was his inclination that the matter of clothes fell into a domain that altogether belonged to the female gender. In any event, when Sasha told him that they had decided on a garment, the most attractive in the

[13] I love the early morning. It's when the mind is freshest and at the peak of its creativity.

house, she said, he was indeed happy and relieved and ready for the measurements which they were told would be initiated promptly. The person performing this function had been shifting around watching Sasha and Adelaide painstakingly attempting to conclude a choice. He was a man of dark complexion, of medium height, and quite handsome. He moved with a snappy confidence. Adelaide leaned close to Sasha and whispered that he appeared to her as someone well versed in the clothing industry and soon had reinforcement that her observation was correct. The owner of the enterprise introduced him as a recent Russian émigré of Jewish extraction, emphasizing that the gentleman was expertly proficient at his trade.

"This is Alex, Alex Zorosky," he said proudly. "He's the best. He designed and stitched in the old country. He's only shortly here from abroad. He'll take care of your needs from here on." He had said as much while looking squarely at Andre.

After the measurements, Alex said that he personally would make the necessary adjustments, assuring that his work would not exceed more than an hour, and asked if they cared to sit during the interim in the receiving room up front which was excellently furnished with heavy fluffy sofas and a supply of magazines and the local newspaper. Sasha replied that they preferred to leave and return within the hour, or not far beyond, and walk about the streets sightseeing, for it had been a while since she was in the city. An hour later they returned to find the tuxedo neatly arranged and packaged and ready for transport. During their ride back Sasha seemed to smile practically all the way. It was the vision of Andre in her head, the sheik Andre Van Doke standing in anticipation of his bride, looking fantastically handsome in the lush tuxedo that she had personally picked out. She too envisioned herself moving nimbly toward him in her gorgeous white gown with the lovely sweeping train proportionately adding luster in its position at the rear.

Closer and closer the wedding date approached, and little by little the guests trickled in, Elizabeth Van Doke first.

"Ah Elizabeth! At last I get to meet you. I am so happy."

"And I too Sasha. I've even dreamed of seeing you in person. I have so wanted to." This was the first time that the two women had laid eyes on one another, though each had seen a portrait of the other. Sorrowfully, Elizabeth reported that George was unable to attend the wedding because of his leg, which was not a serious bother she assured but enough of a handicap to prevent his traveling the distance from Chicago.

"He fretted that he wasn't able to be here Sasha. He would have attempted it but I advised to the contrary. You understand I hope."

"Yes I do Elizabeth. I do fully. I mentioned to him before he left the hospital that for awhile he would be plagued with an inability to move about freely. Do not worry dear. I fully understand, as I said, and I am so glad that you are here."

"And I too."

The next day there was the arrival of Madam Merkel, Doctor Dontonte, and Doctor Givens, met by Sasha, Andre, and Sam Feathers, the latter two very slowly and carefully loading onto the carriage the boxes which contained Sasha's wedding dress and train. As excitedly as she had met Elizabeth the previous day she greeted this party with similar likeness. If one had watched carefully, Sasha would have been seen to embrace Doctor Givens with particular affection.

"My oh my Sasha," Madam Merkel let out, "I've never set foot on a plantation before. I am struggling to believe all this. But Doctor Givens has done his best to tell me all about it on the way down, therefore, in a sense I have a reasonably good understanding of how everything is here."

"And I will add to all that he's told you by giving you a personal tour as soon as we can work it in."

Doctor Dontonte would take residence at the Van Doke plantation and Doctor Givens and Madam Merkel were to stay at the Aurora.

Sasha was anxious to see at the earliest how her wedding adornments fit and looked upon her, which happened at ten o'clock the next morning.

"How lovely, how stunning, how beautiful," Adelaide erupted with praise and commendation as Sasha moved gracefully into the great living room clad in her wedding gown. Madam Merkel held up the tip of the train as she proceeded from the rear. She was ecstatic at hearing the superlatives that Adelaide had just uttered, smiling from ear to ear and judged then that her work was a complete success in the eyes of the others. Mary Tonka and Thea clapped vibrantly as they sat off to the side observing.

"Do you like it?" asked Adelaide, doubtlessly aiming her inquiry at Sasha.

"I love it. It's beautiful." She then turned broadside, looking at herself and the gown in the mirror that had been moved from the room where the bulk of the art work was displayed.

"Oh yes. Madam Merkel, you are fantastic. It was my lucky day when you committed to pattern and stitch this most lovely garment. I can never thank you enough." Perhaps in Sasha's thoughts she was correct, but the sum that Adelaide paid to the House of Fashion in Baltimore and to Madam Merkel as a commission was staggering in comparison to the standard price for like work in that era and was thanks enough many times over. Seeing that all were pleased Madam Merkel retreated with Sasha to the drawing room where she meticulously slipped off the gown and after looking at it inch by inch as if undertaking a last minute inspection, hung it with delicate affection in an armoire bought in Paris by Adelaide's mother near the turn of the century, where it was to stay, along with the train, until the day of the wedding. There is little surprise that on frequently repeated occurrences thereafter, Sasha, Adelaide, and Mary Tonka stole into the room where the gown was stored and opened the fixture and peeped in.

The guests next to appear were Mrs. Laster and Bryon.

"How was your trip," she rang out excitedly, dashing to meet them? "Was it tiring?"

"Fine. Pretty weather all the way. And we aren't tired." This was Bryon's voice, but Mrs. Laster spoke the same meaning. Then Sasha exchanged embraces with the both of them, Bryon seeming to hug her especially tight and slow to let go. He even kissed her lips, which she did not return but smiled and looked into his eyes vibrantly as if to say, "That was okay, that was nice and entirely appropriate," and then took each by the arm, leading them inside to the dining room where Mary Tonka was pouring iced tea. When they had sufficiently relaxed Adelaide laid out their lodging accommodations, this being that Bryon was to reside at the Van Doke plantation and Mrs. Laster at the Aurora.

Doctor Lundy and Lawrence Sherette appeared the day after, and after that, there was a stunning surprise that landed not only on Sasha but also on Lawrence Sherette and Mrs. Laster. I shall tell of this with singular emphasis. Doctor Charlatan had taken a ship from London to Baltimore and from there by way of train to the Sherette plantation, bringing with him his former boss and Captain of the *Surety,* Andrew Dolby. They had sailed from England together. Knowing how precious it would be to Sasha for Captain Dolby to be at her wedding Doctor Charlatan had persuaded him to "attend one of the truly spectacular wedding affairs of the region" and that he was certain that he, Captain Dolby, would be amazed at how Sasha had blossomed.

"She is truly a great beauty Captain."

"That, I don't doubt my good friend. She was already as a girl when she was aboard the *Surety* bound for New Orleans."

When they stepped onto the portico, Sasha and Adelaide were moving through the front door, with Adelaide exclaiming, "My goodness, there is Doctor Charlatan and who is the gentleman with him?"

"I don't know," said Sasha, her eyes narrowing in wonder, and then she gasped. "Mercy, it's you, Captain Dolby. The Captain of the *Surety*. Oh!" Then she threw herself into his arms with a little tear trickling down her cheek. "I had begun to believe that I would never see you again. But here you are."

"Oh yes. Here I am. And my, you are different."

"Some, I'm sure. But not all that much."

"But you have changed. Such a gorgeous woman. Yet you always were, even as a girl. And you are marrying a Doctor Andre Van Doke I understand. A doctor, just as you are. I hear from Doctor Charlatan here that you have become famous as a surgeon."

"Not really. He exaggerates."

In this moment she reached and took Doctor Charlatan's hand and then hugged him. He had had to wait; but not in the least minding.

"I don't exaggerate Sasha. I assure you Captain Dolby I do not. She is quite famous."

"I believe you Doctor Charlatan. I never dreamed once back there that she would rise to such heights, although I had a certain feeling about her that she was heading somewhere lofty."

Sasha shushed the accolades. And then reminded Captain Dolby and Doctor Charlatan that they had already met Adelaide who was standing by her side.

"Adelaide," said Captain Dolby. "My stars, I have met you before. It was in New Orleans."

"Of course. We all went to dinner together."

"I have kept track of both you and Sasha through my friend here Doctor Charlatan, who was in New Orleans with us at the same time."

"Yes of course. I recall that well." Here she broke off, then picked it up again but with a different slant. "And we are floating on clouds that you have sailed the ocean to be at this most special affair."

Doctor Charlatan exclaimed that for all the gold anywhere they wouldn't have missed it. And Captain Dolby said that throughout the years, which hadn't been all that many, he had wondered how Sasha would look when she was grown. And that now he knew. In actuality, and much to Adelaide and Sasha's surprise, the Captain was not very much aged in appearance.

Shortly they all went inside where Adelaide laid out arrangements for their lodging. They would take residence at the Van Doke plantation under the care and guidance of Andre. In the brief interval before the wedding, Sasha on every chance sat with Captain Dolby on the portico and relived her journey on the *Surety* with him and Doctor Charlatan.

"The cake, Sasha. Do you remember your dividing it with us? I think you said some young friend of yours had baked it at the cathedral, especially for your journey. Is that right?"

"It is. The girl's name was Chenelle. She was Father Lumas's maid at the Rectory."

"So she was. That's what you told me at the time."

"May I ask you Captain, have you run across Captain Eric Johansen over the years? Actually visited with him? He was most dear and kind to me on my journey from the Canaries."

"I have talked with him, but not recently. He is widely known and is much revered by the people of the high seas. My appreciation of a man of that sort has no bounds. I do hear that he has retired in London, as you too might have heard."

"I have, through my wonderful friend, my angel Mrs. Laster, who has traded letters with him sporadically and I too have communicated with him off and on. I plan to see him when I next visit London."

"You will go there? You have plans to? But why do I ask these things? Naturally you will be going. Doctor Charlatan tells me of your experience there and that you are held in high esteem by the medical staff at Kings College."

"No immediate plans. But I am likely to receive an invitation and if I do I will accept. I maintain close affiliations with some of the physicians on the Kings College staff. One such person is Doctor Pierre Dontonte, from Paris, but an affiliate of the college, who is also attending my wedding. You will meet him."

"I hope to, indeed."

Chapter 70

THE ENERGY and effort spent on the preparations were enormous. Adelaide and Sam Feathers shouldered a heavier load than anyone else. Sam had supervised the digging of the pits for barbecuing the pork, seeing that the meat was cooked with infinite properness and that the tables were set out under the giant oaks for accommodating the gathering of folks who would be served after the wedding. These folks, the masses, would not occupy an inside seat in the mansion for the actual ceremony; but rather, would stand on either side of the pathway on which Sasha would proceed to the interior of the Aurora. Sam and Adelaide had given consideration to erecting a huge tent for their shelter, one of gargantuan width and depth, deciding in the end however that there appeared to be insurmountable obstacles associated with a contrivance of this vastness. As it happened, Sam had a much smaller one built, a mere dot in comparison to the giant structure they had originally conceived and it would be here that Sasha was to emerge and begin her wedding procession.

"The tent," thought Adelaide. "What a distasteful flat sounding name, especially in view of its use." When she asked Sasha what she thought Sasha instantly agreed, volunteering that a slight modification of the word might be substituted, suggesting simply the addition of one tiny letter. "Let us call it not a tent but a *tente*."

"You are right. *Tente* is the word. Isn't it amazing. The language of the French! How adaptable and handily useful! When the newspaper over at Jackson writes of this gorgeous event they must absolutely say *tente* and I will see that they shall."

The good folks, standing in the open, under no shelter except that of the overarching branches and boughs of the trees, would know when the procession was about to begin, for it will have gotten about beforehand that there was to be an organ emplaced on the grounds in the immediate vicinity that someone was suddenly to start playing when the bride was on the verge of her debut.

Among the masses there would be a substantial presence of white wealthy land owners who because space inside was necessarily limited to forty, could not be a part of those witnessing the principal affair. But no one would mind the exclusion. This was Sasha Duval who was about to be wed, their Sasha, the young woman they had come to know and adore, the mysterious girl who once had suddenly sprung into life at the Sherette plantation, once their doctor or doctor to members of their family. They would be content to stand in line just to have a glimpse of her in her lovely gown, even if they could not see more.

The interior of the great living room was adorned with flowers of numerous assortments, red lovely roses predominating, and Adelaide, with Sasha's approval, had moved Izu's portrait to a higher level than it was before to engender the effect of having her look more directly down at her daughter during the ceremony. There was a deep green baize, a carpet of woolen fabric, that extended from the doorway over which Sasha was to pass on her way to the edge of the altar, the latter of which was wrapped in a tapestry of golden hue. The wrapping fell loosely over the front of the holy ornament until it reached the kneeling ledge below. Lawrence Sherette, who had seldom spoke up with suggestions, had inspected it and given his blessing. He had, as well, taken notice of the more than conventional size Bible emplaced on the lectern and remarked that he was well pleased. "I like oversized Bibles; I always have. Not that they're anymore holy; it's just as I said; I like them large. And I will be especially glad to lift from it a selection of passages that I'll read at the ceremony, for it belonged to our father and mother. By the way Sasha, do you and Andre have a favorite verse or two that you wish to be read aside from my own choices."

"We have talked of it. But prefer to leave you with that decision. I could just about guess which you'd select anyway. If we change our thoughts we'll let you know in plenty of time."

"Very good."

Candles were situated in the shiny sconces that encircled the walls, excluding the one wall at the end of the room where the altar was positioned, and were to be lighted at sunrise on the day the wedding was to take place. Adelaide kept repeating that "The wedding is practically upon us. Can anyone think of anything we've left undone?" She was speaking to Cynthia, Tahitia, Thea, Mary Tonka, and of course Sasha. But not to Lawrence Sherette who was present but disregarded by his sister as an official part of the planners and doers. No one said a word, save Sasha, who said she felt that all was well in place, even though they were likely overlooking some minor things which they'd later discover.

"The wedding will proceed just fine dear. Let's not try to make it too perfect."

Before the small grouping disbanded Lawrence Sherette suddenly asked, as if it were an afterthought, who they had selected for escorting Sasha down the aisle for her marriage, to which Adelaide replied, "Doctor Lundy," as if she decided the matter sometime ago. The truth was that she and Sasha had done it together.

"Oh. Very good. He's the perfect one."

"Lawrence, I realize" said Adelaide, thinking now of another aspect of things, "that you are wanting to give her away and truthfully there is no one for that other than you. As her father you should. At the same time, how can you give her away? You'll have your hands full with other demands. Sasha and I have talked of this. We are suggesting an alternative, if it pleases. Simply take time out in the ceremony to explain that you are giving her away, but that you are in spirit without going through a procedure of physical formality." Looking over at Sasha, he saw her approval by way of expression, replying to his sister that what she'd just suggested was completely agreeable.

Melana arrived the next morning with Sasha and Mrs. Laster meeting her at the depot. Sasha hugged her tenderly. "I am so glad you are here. I had begun to worry." Mrs. Laster and Melana met each other seconds later with an embrace, with Mrs. Laster delightedly uttering that "It's so nice to see a Brit again." Sasha took Melana's baggage and loaded it into the carriage. The countenance on her face betrayed her inner amusement when Sasha climbed into her seat and took the reins. "Ha, ha, ha." Melana was unable to longer restrain herself. "Gracious. You can drive these horses? My brother would be seized with astonishment. 'One of my prize surgeons doing that!'"

"It's nothing Melana. I was taught some time ago by Sam Feathers to drive a team."

"Sam Feathers?"

"Yes. Sam Feathers. He's the foreman, and was long before I arrived here."

She assigned Melana a room at the Aurora, telling her that lunch would be served at noon and that she would show her about afterwards, but for the time being Madam Merkel had a question to take up with Sasha and as a fill in Mrs. Laster would assume the charge of introducing her to Mary Tonka. And to Adelaide when she returned from the Van Doke mansion, who was shortly due.

That afternoon, in the latter part, the women, led by Sasha and Adelaide left for the Van Doke mansion to inspect together the grand ball room, which was colorfully decorated with banners and garlands and urns stuffed with various bright flowers. The floors were immaculately shellacked, and buffed to the point that one's shadow was practically visible upon them. "It's as resplendent as the first time I ever attended a ball here," thought Sasha,

"Mrs. Van Doke's ball, may God bless her. Little did I realize then what she meant to so many. And just think of it. On that same evening I was on my way to becoming her daughter in law and her son's wife. In my heart I badly miss her. In her honor I will strive with all that is within me to see that this dance unfolds with the uppermost of civility and grace."

"I see the tables are covered in the most brilliant of linen Adelaide," she said aloud, "and I adore the candles."

"Yes. I know how you love candles."

Cynthia and Mary Tonka had tried themselves at putting the ballroom into readiness, and Sasha knew that they had; they had conferred with her endlessly throughout the past week about the suitability of the assortment of decorations and the condition of the floor. She confessed that she couldn't thank them enough.

"Don't say that," Mary Tonka spoke up. "We would do it many times over if need be. It's your wedding darling, your wedding, ah, Sasha's wedding, and as far as we're concerned there has never been one of its resemblance. We are blessed that we are a part of it. No. A hundred times no. Do not thank us. We are the ones to be thankful."

The day of the wedding was finally there, with Mrs. Laster waking Sasha at eight to glance over her schedule with her. Sasha had begun to worry that Harry Lancaster, who was to hold the rings in his possession until requested by the Priest, had not arrived, and when she asked about him she was told that he had gotten off the early morning train. She sighed a sigh of relief. By nine o'clock Sasha had bathed and shortly thereafter breakfasted, eating a parcel of toast with jam and having one cup of coffee. Mary Tonka scolded her for not eating enough.

"You need more my dear, you really do. Think of the whole day before you, and the dance tonight. You're a doctor and should know better."

Sasha merely smiled and kissed her cheek. "I'll eat after the ceremony Mary Tonka. Don't you worry. I'm fine."

Madam Merkel was on edge with regard to keeping Sasha from view of the public until the time was appropriate. "What are we to do?" she asked Adelaide. "The people should not see Sasha on her way to the *tente* to dress; they must only see her when she comes forth in her lovely gown. Otherwise, all the suspense is spoiled."

"Yes, yes. I understand. But that has been allowed for. The people are not to arrive until one hour before Sasha is to emerge. That's what they have been told. And Sam Feathers has posted sentry's to keep them at bay. They won't see Sasha until she all at once comes forth from the *tente*."

"Good. I hadn't heard that."

"Anything else?"

"Thea's two little daughters. They are to trail behind holding up the tips of the train. I will need to coach them before hand."

"Please do. And I'm sure you'll fall in love with their Easter pink dresses. And them. They're the sweetest little things."

When Sasha left the Aurora for the *tente,* the time was thirty minutes of eleven. Madam Merkel was close behind carrying the encasement that housed the wedding gown and Sam Feathers carried the train, tediously obeying the rules of care as laid out by Madam Merkel. This was Madam Merkel's hour and she was determined to see it through without fault. Early that morning a collection of women had over spread the *tente* with a fine material of golden silk, the appearance of which had now become in the illusionary sense expensive and regal, "such" said Adelaide, who was present, "that it almost seems as if the marriage of a medieval princess is about to take place." The silken walls of the *tente* quivered and billowed in the breeze and the curtains serving as the doorway were no less aroused. When Sasha entered she found two women standing with very broad fans in their hands which they would move to and fro as a means of keeping her cool and fresh. For a while she rested on a layer of pillows that were emplaced on the ground floor, amused at the attention she was getting, but laughed inside and in no way objected. At eleven thirty Madam Merkel began to slip on her gown. When she had finished Sasha reached into her purse which lay on a nearby stool, there withdrawing a shiny spangle which she appended to her waist.

"You will adorn yourself with that," exclaimed Madam Merkel, "on this beautiful gown?"

"Surely."

"I don't understand."

"But you will. You see, I am Spanish in origin, by custom that is, not by blood. I was born and raised on the Canary Islands before arriving here. My mother dressed me particularly in the fashion of the Spanish and born from earlier habit the style and taste is still fast with me. "

"Oh I see."

After this, she began to do Sasha's face, saying no more about the spangle, seeming to have forgotten it altogether. But quickly there was something else that engaged her.

"You look so lovely Sasha. Even more so when one is close up to you. Your skin is the smoothest I have ever seen and your eyes, if you allow me to say it, are rapturously beautiful, the result I think of that slight tinge of mystery that lies deep inside them."

"Thank you. I don't deserve it. I really don't."

"Ah but you do. You are too gracious."

At fifteen minutes of noon Madam Merkel showed once again Thea's daughters how they were to hold up the tips of the train and was well pleased with how quickly they caught on and how very pretty they were. Sasha stood ready; someone would open the curtains when the organ began to play which was to happen at any moment. "Oh, I have never been a part of anything like this, never," uttered Madam Merkel. It was then that the first note of the organ was struck. Madam Merkel took a deep breath and then the curtains were drawn. As Sasha emerged, stepping softly onto the lush green grass that had been watered and groomed for weeks, the crowd responded with a low murmur and she began to move as if walking on air along the designated pathway.

In the few minutes before, a short distance away, the little flower girl had wafted down the aisle of the great living room clutching a bouquet of roses and orchids which Sasha was to take and place at the base of the Virgin Mary after she and Andre had spoken their vows. After her, the maids of honor, Thea and Lucy, walking side by side, made their approach and came to rest at the right of the altar. Adelaide and Mary Tonka sat with eyes darting on the front row, Adelaide holding her hand to her mouth as if to muffle her words as she whispered to Mary Tonka, "Don't they look simply divine? I've never seen Thea in a gown before, and to think that she made it herself."

Sasha had wanted Adelaide to be the maid of honor but Adelaide had begged off, rationalizing that she didn't want to miss a thing and that if she were in the crowd occupying a front row seat she wouldn't. "Thea and Lucy will be enough my darling, and besides, I'm kind of your mother. That's the role I should play."

"And my sister," Sasha added coquettishly.

Next proceeding were Sam Feathers and Jim, the two best men, taking their places to the left of the altar. Lastly, there was Andre, appearing as if he were bursting with happiness, but holding it in, advancing with soft tepid steps until reaching the place where he was to stand in wait, there glancing upward into the face of Lawrence Sherette with a subtle smile. Lawrence Sherette released one back to him, and then Andre turned to face the audience. He stood dead center of the aisle, directly in front of the altar, where Sasha was to join him in a matter of minutes. Andre looked a handsome figure in his fashionable tuxedo, and one had to wonder, especially Adelaide, who viewed him with keen studious eyes, how awed Sasha might be when she once saw him attired in this splendid garment.

The crowd situated on both sides of the pathway was standing; there were no chairs for them. They were too numerous, and chairs for that many were no where to be found. But no one complained. They were seized by a joy that pushed the discomfort to their legs and feet far out of thought, releasing low audible sighs that swelled from the heart, something of a sound that denotes admiration and love. Without the least of any suggestion from Adelaide and Mary Tonka they on their own had gathered flowers of many carousel colors for this hour, the women cradling them in their arms as Sasha passed by. All eyes were encompassing and examining, studying every movement of this beauty in their midst, the women, especially the women, leaning over to someone near with reference to a particular aspect of the gown. A few waved at Thea's little girls, a kind of quiver with their fingers, but quickly got back to Sasha. Once when coming abreast of an old Negro woman, for which someone had retrieved a chair, Sasha paused and bent over and kissed her brow, and then the old woman momentarily took Sasha's hand in hers, there pressing it to her cheek. In the past Sasha doctored her when she was sick. Seeing this, some of the women cried. All the while Sasha had moved steadily along, looking mostly straight ahead but with a gentle smile on her face, as if to say, "I love you, everyone of you, and you are here because you love me too, and I am grateful." She moved on, at last leaving them behind—some groaning in disappointment that it was over—and with the assistance of two attendants stepped lightly and slowly onto the carpeted portico, and into the foyer. As she approached the entrance of the great living room, Doctor Lundy, who was waiting for her, extended his arm which she gingerly accepted and then they proceeded through the passage of the heavy twin doors which had been suddenly opened; and from there moved with creeping slowness toward the altar while the choir hummed a holy refrain. Sasha smiled radiantly and happily as she stole glances at the people whose gazes were fixed unmoving upon her. The tiny spangle affixed to her mid waist sparkled and twinkled, but not nearly as brilliantly as those dark exotic eyes that danced and flitted as she leveled them ahead at the beaming Andre.

When Sasha had reached the altar, she turned and faced him. Lawrence Sherette motioned to the acolyte to come forward and light the candles, five on each side of the altar, the lad coming directly over and lighting them, then fading into the vicinity of the choir. At this point Lawrence Sherette delivered greetings to the audience, telling them that he had known the bride and groom for a long while, and knew that the Lord was especially blessing them in this hour. There was a pause that was followed by the choir singing Holy, Holy, Holy, which was specifically selected by Sasha, and after this Lawrence Sherette looked down and smiled at her, with love pouring out of his face and then went on to something else that was on his agenda. He had written a note to himself that absolutely he must not forget it.

"Before going further my dear friends, I wish to share with you a letter that was recently handed to me to read by our beloved Sasha. It is to her from Father Sisco de Endera Lumas of the San Fernando Cathedral in San Antonio, a dear one to both Sasha and I, and in some ways is responsible for both of us being here today. I shall read.

My dear Sasha,

You are marrying. I wish I could be the one to perform this holy ritual as I once performed the union of your father and mother. But Lawrence Sherette will have the honor of doing this for me, and how fortunate I am; you are both mine and I love you each beyond the reach of words.

I have reflected a thousand times on the hour you first came into my midst and on the circumstances that brought you to me. You will never forget your father and mother, and neither can I. Losing them so early in your young life was almost unbearable I am sure. There was great sadness in your heart, as there was in mine for you. I cried secretly. But as the Lord taketh away He in turn giveth. He led you to me and then to our dear Lawrence Sherette, who took you under his wing with tender loving care and the rest we both know. You have climbed fast and high in this world, doing rare things for humanity's sake. The Lord blessed you; He showed you the way.

And now, as I have said, you are marrying and to a fine young man, or so Adelaide and Mrs. Laster tell me, and you will have children by him and will, I predict, enjoy many happy years with them as you nurture them into maturity. Though not in the flesh I will be there in spirit and in my mind what a beautiful and holy wedding you will have. May God bless you my dearest—and He will; He has—and may He see to it that there is in your life, all the way through, as much joy as there has been in my heart for having known you.

I love you.

Father Sisco de Endera Lumas

There was a pause once again, lasting but for a brevity, while Lawrence Sherette's eyes met Sasha's in solemnity as if to say, "The words touched my heart. He means everything to the both of us. I am moved to sorrow that he is not here." Then following the pause, the choir sounded, "Alleluia, Alleluia, Alleluia."

Lawrence Sherette began with the core of the ceremony, citing from memory certain lines that he had used over the years. The crowd was so silent that it seemed they were not even breathing. "This marriage," he announced, "is a covenant made before God and before all of us as witnesses in acknowledgement of its holy purpose and the power of the occasion, so let us pray:

> God of Love, who stirs the longing for, and capability of loving, we give you thanks for Andre and Sasha, for their open hearts and willing spirits and for the example of purity and goodness that they have embodied in the years that we have shared with them. Be with them on this joyous occasion of uttering their vows; and be with us, their witnesses, and may we all oh Father be reminded that you have created the bond of marriage a mystery, an irrevocable symbol of Christ's love for the church. Amen."

"And now my dear ones," he said, turning to Andre and Sasha, "in the presence of the church and with Christ our Lord looking down upon us, I am to ask you to state your intentions. Will you hold one another's hand and answer as I direct.

Have you come here freely and without reservation to give yourselves to each other in marriage? Andre, you first."

"I have."

"Now Sasha."

"I have."

"And will you love and honor each other as man and wife for the rest of your lives? Andre."

"I will."

"And Sasha."

"I will."

"Will you accept children lovingly from God and bring them up according to the law of Christ and his church? Andre."

"I will."

"Sasha."

"I will."

"Now, since it is your intention to enter into marriage, will you join your right hands and declare your consent before God and his church? In that I know that both of you can recite this holy declaration, without my repeating it for you to follow, I shall therefore not repeat it. Andre, you first."

"I Andre Van Doke take you Sasha Duval to be my wife. I promise to be true to you in good times and in bad, in sickness and in health. I will love you and honor you all the days of my life."

"And Sasha."

"I Sasha Duval take you Andre Van Doke to be my husband. I promise to be true to you in good times and in bad, in sickness and in health. I will love you and honor you all the days of my life."

At this, Lawrence Sherette, realizing that what he was about to do broke somewhat from the usual protocol, nevertheless stepped from the altar to the floor beside Sasha and Andre and gathered them in his arms. "My heart is overflowing for you," he whispered, and then faced the audience and said, "I just had to do this; these two are just like my son and daughter." A buzz of light laughter sallied throughout the room. "Yet I am not quite through. Allow me to go further. You noticed I am certain our dear Doctor Lundy escorting the beautiful bride down the aisle only minutes past. You would think that he was to serve to give her away, but he cannot, for I am essentially her father and have been for the longest. I could not, I reasoned, perform the functions that bear upon the officiating of this splendid ceremony and give her away too. But in spirit I can; so please accept my fullest acknowledgement that I hereby give my Sasha away, not begrudgingly, but wholeheartedly to a young man whom I have known since his birth, and that she could have looked the world over and not found one his equal."

To this, the crowd laughed once more, at the same time letting out a controlled and light applause, taking it that if he could alter protocol so too could they.

When the laughter had subsided Lawrence Sherette grew solemn once again and began to cite while still holding them in his arms, looking at one and then the other: "You have declared your consent before the church. May the Lord in his goodness strengthen your commitment and fill you both with his blessings. What God has joined, men must not divide. Amen."

"And now the rings. Who holds these holy ornaments?"

"I do," said Harry, rising from his front row seat, moving into the presence of the ceremony, holding them out. Lawrence Sherette faintly made acknowledgement with a tilt, and began to utter his blessings of them.

"Lord, bless these rings which we bless in your name. Grant that those who wear them may always have a deep faith in one another. May they do Your will and always live together in peace, good will, and love."

With this said Harry handed Andre the ring for Sasha, which he took and with tender delicacy slid it on Sasha's finger, saying, "Sasha, my beloved take this ring as a sign of my love and fidelity, and in the name of the Father, and of the Son, and of the Holy Spirit." Next, Harry handed the ring for Andre to Sasha, which she took and with the most loving care put it on Andre's finger, uttering, "Andre, my beloved, take this ring as a sign of my love and fidelity, and in the name of the Father, and of the Son, and of the Holy Spirit."

"You are husband and wife and you may now kiss each other's lips," Lawrence Sherette was heard to say. But by the time his words had ended the newly weds in their eagerness already had. With a heavy crescendo the single combined voice of the choir swelled to the vaulting, much higher than earlier, "Alleluia, Alleluia, Alleluia."

Chapter 71

WHEN THEY pulled back and released one another, Harry and Lawrence Sherette came over with embraces and congratulations, then Sasha took Andre's hand, and that of the little flower girl, who held the bouquet with the other, and led them to the statue of the Virgin Mary, lowering herself on her knees, with the little flower girl and Andre duplicating her movement and intent of ceremony. Sasha took the bouquet and laid it at the foot of the Virgin, crossed herself, and commenced to pray, Andre and the little flower girl following likewise. Those in the audience who sat watching were mostly Catholic, and felt an incumbency to cross and also pray. Shortly, Sasha, who was now engaged by a circle of well wishers felt Adelaide touch her shoulder. Adelaide knew that Sasha was flooded with thoughts in consideration of the people she knew she was to greet, whom she ventured might take it as a slight if not given sufficient time and attention.

"Dear," she whispered, cupping her hand to her mouth, wishing to keep other ears from hearing, "you'll need as soon as you can to change your clothing. The pieces are already laid out for you. The people on the grounds are hungry I am sure but will not start unless you are there."

"I know I can't hold them up for long and won't. I'll join you just as soon as I can mingle a bit with everyone here who wants to speak with Andre and me."

"The room was jammed. And it was a most beautiful wedding darling." She hugged Sasha, and then Andre who stood close by, leaving instantly afterwards with Mary Tonka who would help her refit Sasha when she was free to join them. Sasha would not break away suddenly, the effort taking a while, with everyone wanting to shake hands or hug, mostly hug, offer well wishes, and if not a part of the inner circle, who knew already, inquire of the destination of their honeymoon. On the matter of the honeymoon she held up a finger in the semblance of saying, "naughty, naughty, naughty," without saying it and with a melting smile cleverly teased that that was a subject of confidentiality.

Finally, the crowd began to dissolve and with Harry and Doctor Givens escorting her, Sasha left for the master bedroom where Adelaide and Mary Tonka were waiting with the attire that she was to wear at the serving. Andre, ever the suave statesman, stayed behind to visit with those who had not concluded with their praising of the beautiful affair and generous outpourings of well wishes for a future just begun.

"And what clothing have you laid out for me?" Sasha curiously asked as she entered the room, surmising that whatever it was would be pleasing in every aspect because where the selection of clothing was at issue, as well as almost anything else, Adelaide was her undoubted ego alternate.

"You'd never guess. But it is something of most extraordinary comfort and flavor." Adelaide then said that the attire had never been in her wardrobe until early that morning, but did not yet tell that Madam Merkel was the creator of this rich colorful masterpiece.

"She will love this attire Adelaide," Madam Merkel had said. "It's of European design, light and airy, the ideal costume for her as she mingles with the crowd."

"Let me see it." Then Madam Merkel led her to the closet in which it was set aside and opened the door and showed it to her.

"I hope that she'll wear it," exclaimed Madam Merkel with a shade of both doubt and hope in her voice.

"Oh my goodness. Mercy. It's adorable. She will wear it Madam Merkel. Yes, she will wear it. She will love it."

"The suspense is killing me," exclaimed Sasha. "Where is this precious thing?"

It hangs behind this blind," answered Adelaide, pointing her hand outward. And drawing back the curtain there it was, an adorable colorful costume. Much of Spanish flavor. The skirt was a cut of orange and blue, but trimmed in delicate embroidery of white, full at the lower portions, though not greatly full, and drawn in tight at the mid waist. The torso region consisted of a vest of purple spread over a blouse of silk whose sleeves were of such fineness that literally they fluttered and trembled upon the minutest activity of the wearer's limbs. This was the attire which Madam Merkel had drummed up in her fantasy and which she had converted into a substance of reality; and so Adelaide and Mary Tonka slipped these lovely pieces upon our Sasha, then Adelaide stepped back, momentarily taking measure of what was before her. But her thoughts ran further than the attire itself. They were on the face too, on her complexion, strangely deep and brilliant, perhaps brought on because of the fantastic costume that Madam Merkel had created. "I am wondering," she thought, "if some fresh rich flowers appended to her hair might enhance her even more." But then upon wrinkling her brow shrank from the idea. "No. She needs no flowers. Why try to make her better than she is; why try to accomplish the unattainable."

Sasha concluded that she was spinning some such fantasies in her head, though she did know what, and interrupted her ponderings. "Everything is fine Adelaide, just as I am. I need no more embellishments. These clothes I have on are fine. I love them."

"Totally. I agree. But your slippers. Will the ones with the silver toning do?"

"They are perfect. The heels are neither too high nor too low. They are just right for my getting about. They are comfortable and that is what I need now more than anything else. But I am left wondering. Who has constructed these beautiful clothes? I've not seen them before. They are so, so, so exotic."

"Madam Merkel."

"Madam Merkel! When?"

"Last night. She spent the whole night patterning and stitching them. She made them from some never used uncut material of my mother's that I have kept. Isn't she a genius?"

"Mercy," she said, crossing herself. "That dear woman. I shall hug her unrelentingly when I see her."

"You'll see her. She will be among the crowd watching you."

They had expected Andre to knock at any minute. He and Sasha had decided beforehand that he was to escort her to where the crowd was gathered for the feeding, and be with her at the serving line. It was not long that he did as they expected. He knocked. Mary Tonka opened the door. Andre peeped in, and seeing Sasha in her costume of such drastic change from her gorgeous wedding gown was taken aback. "Oh my! What a transition. One minute a swan, the next a peacock. What colors. You look radiant my darling, you really do. Do you like it?"

"I do. It's just the thing for me to wear while being with the crowd. It's very casual, wouldn't you say?"

"Very casual. And very different."

"Now, my husband, may I take your arm as we proceed to the reception?" Although Sasha called it the reception, it was more accurate to allude to it as the peoples' reception, for it was held in honor of the workers and former slaves. But everyone thought of it as merely the reception, referring to it by that name.

As they neared the crowd Sasha mentioned to Andre that since she was so close to the women, having been their doctor and the doctor of their children, she was necessarily obligated to spend a disproportionate time with them.

"I understand sweetheart. I had counted on your doing that. You have to be with the women and their children. Naturally you must. I'll be careful to stay out of the way."

"But start with me through the serving line; they all expect to see you with me there. They're honoring us."

"Oh yeah. I know. But far more you than me my darling. And it shouldn't be any other way."

"But they love you too Andre. They do. I know they do."

"But mainly you. And I wouldn't have it any other way. You're their shining star. You have been for the longest. That's what my mother said of you."

Sasha merely looked up at Andre with pensive eyes. "This is not the time or place to shed a tear," she told herself silently. While on their way to the serving area the crowd caught her in their sight, with someone calling out, "There she is, there's Sasha," at which time there arose an "Ooooooh," as if released by one giant synchronized breath, a sound of unified awe and adoration and love and an expression that at last she had come. Sasha broke away from Andre by a step or two and proceeded directly to them—smiling the most beautiful open smile—to the women and children especially, but to the men as well. Randolph had sat through the wedding but had not yet had word with her. She saw him and hurried over.

"Randolph, it's you. You came."

"Sure I did. I wasn't about to miss it. It touched my heart Sasha. It really did. Never have I seen a bride as lovely. Not even close. I swear that. And I was so happy. But I was saddened a bit also. I felt that I was giving both of you away," he said, glancing over at Andre who had caught up.

"You're sweet Randolph. Thank you for coming," she added.

Sasha would have talked on but Randolph, aware that she was obligated to mingle with many others and was stretched for time, said that he would not detain her longer.

"They all want to be with you Sasha. I'll have to let you go."

Realizing that everyone anxiously awaited her to take her place at the head of the feeding line Sasha accepted a tray that was handed over by an attendant who began to heap food upon her plate in great amounts. She laughed and stopped him. "Oh dear me. That's enough. Thank you. I cannot eat half this. It's wonderful," meaning the pork, "but I must not allow my appetite to lure my stomach into a state of indigestion."

With her husband, Thea had moved to a position near Sasha's side and had laid her hand on her shoulder. Sasha turned around and seeing who it was kissed her brow. Andre struck up a conversation with Thea's husband, the both of them, after their plates were filled, finding empty seating at one of the tables, there sitting down and beginning to eat and talk. Sasha and Thea had continued their exchange, some of which, as could be expected, reflected on the wedding. Sasha told Thea she could not thank her enough for consenting to be one of the bride's maids, which warmed her heart. They went from there to one piece of conversation after another, one subject having to do with how they'd enjoyed each other's presence and company over the month past. Thea said she hated the thought of Sasha leaving, that life would be terribly empty without her. "I'm like that too Thea; I'll feel lonely for awhile but I'll have to brush that aside. We're leaving for Sorrento on our honeymoon after a day or two in Baltimore."

With Thea understanding, Sasha left her to join a collection of women nearby who were anxiously looking over, hoping that she'd soon finish and come sit with them. Sasha went to them and sat down and began to chat, which was of immense pleasure and joy to the women she had joined, for most had never been around her close up and had never heard her voice utter a word nor look into her lovely eyes with so little distance between them. Yet she soon had to excuse herself to be with others. What seemed to excite the chords of Sasha's happiness most occurred when she kneeled down to kiss a child's cheek, knowing she'd receive one in return. Sometimes the children, of three or four or five years, liked to touch her face and rub their fingers across its smoothness and tell her that she had pretty skin and that they liked to look into her eyes. Sometimes they ran their fingers through her hair, giving it a mild gentle tug, which brought her to laughter.

And all this was seen and watched by the smiling drooling mothers who supposed that one day they would describe these scenes over and over to their children who by then would be grown, to whom such occurrences will have become mere blurs or altogether blotted from memory. But they at least hoped that their children, as grown ups, might recall that there was once a grand wedding of young Sasha Duval and Andre Van Doke on the Sherette plantation and that they were there as guests.

Time had run out, and Andre came to Sasha's rescue, who likely was to have stayed on indefinitely; "Sasha, you need to lie down. You need to sleep awhile. You'll need to be ready for the ball this evening."

ꟿ ꟿ

That evening at the hour of thirty minutes until seven Andre and Sasha took their positions at the entrance of the Van Doke mansion. Likened to Andre's mother and father of some years past, they now were themselves the powers of the throne, in any event, the chosen ones of the family of Van Dokes to stand greeting the guests. Both Andre and Sasha tried gamely to persuade Jim and Lucy to assume that role, yet things did not pan out as they hoped. Jim objected.

"Destiny knocks Andre," said he. "It's clear to everyone, and certainly to me, that you and Sasha are the crown bearers of La Belle, and will be for years to come. You two are much younger and have the energy and fortitude for it. Lucy and I feel we don't."

With Andre again dressed in his handsome black tailcoat, but not the tuxedo that he wore at the wedding, and Sasha clad in a lovely gown of pale yellow, which literally dropped to the floor, they were the epitome of elegance.

"How do you do Mr. and Mrs. so and so," Andre, with charming charisma would greet some couple, with Sasha close at his side, beautiful and serene and smiling, often adding, "We are most delighted that you came." She recalled the first ever dinner that she attended at the Van Doke mansion. "Adelaide and I were met by Andre, who helped us from our carriage and escorted us to the frontage where we were greeted by his mother and father, Mr. Van Doke appearing a bit pompous whereas Mrs. Van Doke was reserved and graceful. I thought then that they were profoundly rich and lordly, a little intimidating for a young girl for sure, but in another sense they were down to earth and both quite nice. I believe she liked me at first blush; in her on subtle way she showed it, and later proved it, and God rest his soul, I believe that Mr. Van Doke did too. Well, here we are, Andre and I. Doesn't the passage of time create unusual if not strange circumstances."

There were two young men of age twenty years, American Germans, Charles and Whitney Enzor, sons of a rich landowner on whom the honor was bestowed to escort the guests to their tables, which were situated on the periphery of the ballroom floor. To be chosen for this prestigious responsibility was indeed a feather in the young men's caps and as they went about with this or that lady clinging to their arm, their parents sitting at a table not far removed were overwhelmed with pride. A barrage of guests would attend. A wedding ball of this magnitude and esteem was an event that simply could not be missed by people of the region of opulent means. One by one they arrived in black sleek coaches or carriages, a Negro driver at the reins dyked out in a coat of bright red with yellow tassels at the shoulders, and clad in dark shiny trousers. Of especial notice was his posture, which was at all times soldierly erect, or was until he promptly dismounted to open and hold open the door for the occupants who were about to lower themselves to the pavement. The horses that pulled the vehicles were magnificent animals, for the most part harnessed in leather strapping with golden rivets holding the gear together. As had always been the custom, a tradition originating with Mrs. Van Doke, a lady was assisted by an escort at the point of departing from her transport who cavalierly offered his arm and led her to Andre and Sasha, her silken gown swishing and rustling with every step. The order of procedure from this point on was thusly: the usual greeting occurred, of course, a few exchanges following, and then the escort extended his arm once more, leading the lady the rest of the way to her table, her husband, or gentleman friend if she was unmarried, trailing by two paces in accord with the rules of etiquette. When catching up, it was this person's obligation to pull back her chair and take his place beside her when she was properly and comfortably seated.

At the hour of seven thirty precisely the first chords of the orchestra were struck, the beginning of the preliminary music. No slippers were to touch the floor this evening until after dinner, whereon, after this, Andre and Sasha were to rise at the appropriate gesture of the orchestra leader and begin their wedding dance. When the music sounded they had left their post at the frontage for the inside, leaving the formality of greeting to an old seasoned Negro doorman who was trained to carry out the protocol of receiving guests arriving late. There were two modes of seating; there were the small round tables designed to accommodate two, then there were the much larger tables, which could care for persons of eight in number and it was here that Andre and Sasha elected to sit, feeling that to sit alone might signify snobbery, and equally as bad, result in the loss of shared group conversation. Sitting at this table as well were Rudyard Shaw, presiding judge over the district of Jackson, his wife Nadine with him; Whitney Enzor, rich landowner, as earlier relayed, his wife Ingrid by his side; and Prudence Autry, the banker from Louisville, and his wife, the vivacious Arlene. Whitney Enzor and his wife had met Andre of some years past, the introductions coordinated by his father, yet neither had met Sasha. The same could be said with respect to Judge Shaw and his wife Nadine. They were acquainted with Andre but not with Sasha, not until this evening at the frontage where she stood with her husband welcoming the guests. Now that the Shaws and Enzors were sitting close up to her they easily got an eye full and would continue to for the duration of the evening. A candle was emplaced in the center of the table, which was covered by an exquisitely fine tapestry. The surface of the material was thickly indentured with irregular arabesque forms of encapturing colors, the symbolic meaning of which Mr. Enzor kept attempting to decipher. On seeing that Sasha had become aware of his complexity he gave up.

"Ha, ha, ha. Doctor Duval, I'll confess that I find myself in a stew of ignorance in trying to understand the meaning of these unusual patterns that I see on the table cloth here. Can you help me?"

"I can try. But confess that I'm no authority on the subject. Arabesque, sir, is a form of artistry as I understand it, consisting of surface decorations, such as what you are seeing on this tapestry, which I shall call motifs. As I said, it's an art form, originating from the Arab culture centuries ago. I am very certain that it did, but arabesque art is prominent in Europe as well, though it is inconsistent and confusing. You can tell at a glance that it is not of Islamic descent. But back to your original question. What do the symbols mean? Sorry. I cannot say."

He was surprised at how simply she had responded. "How genuine she is, how sincere, how clear," he said to himself. Whitney Enzor had asked for Sasha's explanation because it was a means of breaking the ice, a way of getting to know her a little better and at the same time it helped him feel more comfortable in her midst. At base, he had felt intimidated by her in the sense that she was so eruditely intelligent and schooled in the academics and by now a surgeon of eminence. He instantly liked her; he had found that she in no way was uppity. To the contrary. "She is sweet and gentle and very, very beautiful," he thought. You could tell also that his wife Ingrid was of a similar impression.

Judge Shaw and his wife Nadine liked her too. It was evident. They repeatedly looked across at her but tried not to over do it, Nadine smiling ebulliently, the Judge more with his eyes than with his mouth. He was not as inherently friendly as Whitney Enzor, or perhaps it was his deep coarse voice together with his somber seldom smiling face that portrayed this disposition. His wife Nadine, a gentle lady, liked by everyone, at times counseled her husband about his abrupt and too straight forward remarks when in public gatherings such as the one this evening. On every chance, when seeming appropriate, Nadine sought to draw Sasha into conversation, and others too, but Sasha more so. Sasha intrigued her. The Autry's were still themselves, as Sasha remembered, Prudence Autry reserved and guarded with his words and Arlene, flamboyant and talkative, the liveliest of all by far. The three men were clad in expensive suits of tailor made style and quality, as did virtually any male in attendance of over fifty, whereas the younger generations opted in favor of flashy tuxedos. Yet these were not the styles exclusively; the styles were many and various. One young man had decided to sport a civil war soldier's uniform, a striking gray fabric with bright red tassels affixed to the shoulders. His older brother had served in the Southern military army under Nathan Bedford Forrest's command.

Besides Andre and Sasha no one at the table danced except Arlene. She liked to dance very much, and often; knowing this, Andre devoted as much time as he took to be reasonable to honor her with a round now and then, but arranging also for Jim or Doctor Dontonte or Bryon, in addition to certain others, to pick up where he left off.

There was also a rule of etiquette in effect that evening that allowed and encouraged the guests to move about from one table to another, provided that such activity was kept in moderation. Andre and Sasha liked this, for there were many friends they wished to visit as the evening wore on, as well as having others come to them. They were delighted with their table neighbors and intermingled with them nicely but from time to time welcomed an escape.

When the dinner was served and the guests by and large finished with their meal the orchestra leader waved his baton and the musicians began. Andre stood quickly and pulled Sasha's chair away, then they left hand in hand for the ballroom floor, but with her a slight in front. Their smiles were lavish, their smiles were happy. They beamed. "Our wedding dance, it's our wedding dance Andre," she whispered lowly, excitement darting from her eyes. As they moved to the dance floor Andre looked over as if to ask, "Are you ready?" There was no reply; there was only the trained soft touch of her hand on his shoulder, the other held tenderly up and taken by his, and when the music swelled once more they moved smoothly with it. It was a waltz; Bom bom bom bom bom/bom bom–bom bom, the sounds of the bassoon, the Heavenly strings, and the oboe a bit jammed in the forepart but retarded and spaced more in the latter.

"They're the most beautiful couple I've ever seen," said Ingrid Enzor, speaking to her husband, who hardly heard. He was too caught up in the enchantment. People had clapped lightly when the dance was commenced but more vigorously as Andre and Sasha came to the half way point, half way around the room, where the lights poured more radiantly down on the dancers than at any other place, where the suffusion of the glow was most prominent. Lawrence Sherette, who sat next to Mary Tonka, said they were as "flamingos or swans floating on a velvet fog."

"They are gorgeous Lawrence, they really are," replied Mary Tonka, wiping a tear from her cheek.

So on they went, round after round, in no manner feeling the result of effort—they were too young and too filled with physical strength for that—only vaguely aware of the number of times they had circled the room, but glancing over Sasha noticed that Adelaide had raised her hand slightly upward with her thumb and fingers extended, which, if interpreted said, "Five times. That's what we agreed to for the opening." The end had come to their first dance, their wedding dance; so, holding hands, Sasha and Andre returned to their table where Whitney Enzor had as a gesture of courtesy pulled back her chair.

"Ah, you two were a sight to see. Beautiful. My! And what energy! And you're not even breathing hard. Must be nice to be young."

Sasha answered that it was more taxing than he might believe, and thanked him for the compliment.

Andre and Sasha had gone through the first dance, soon to be followed by scores of others. When the orchestra struck up another waltz the floor was suddenly crowded with ladies in their colorful expensive gowns and gentlemen in their dark tail coats and black or white ties. The women were attired in opera gloves as was Sasha in her first dance, which was the dress code for the evening. From above, from a God like view, the scene below was a magnificent panorama, a carousel of whirling figures, the ladies' gowns in the lower half fanning out like open spinning umbrellas, or in the resemblance of a merry go round. At this stage few of the older couples took part in the dance, electing to sit it out. When this dance ceased another began, some of the dancers leaving for their tables, others quickly filling their places. The orchestra switched from one form of music to another, to the valse, to the quadrille, to the mazurka, and sometimes to a southern hoedown. The crowd was caught up in a spirit of disquieting gaiety and seemed to love one dance as well as another. Andre and Sasha did not participate in these latter dances as frequently as they did the free style. Sasha had always enjoyed a single partner more than the group configurations, and besides, her day had already grown quite long. She would pace herself, but would devote time unlimited to her favorites, starting with Jim who had approached her once after she and Andre had just sat down. He sat down beside them, but allowed Sasha to catch her breath, then began with an allusion to something that he thought he had failed to cover much earlier. "

"I failed to do it today Sasha, that is I think I did. If I did forget it I had meant earlier to tell you my dear that I am so greatly happy that you are a part of the family."

"So am I Jim, and I am very glad that you are now my brother in law."

"Yep. That finally came true. I guess I always figured in the back of my mind that it would happen one day. I even thought of that when you were a young girl. And it was only yesterday it seems that you were precisely that—a young girl.

"But I am no longer. And I agree with you that time does fly, but speaking of time, you'd better take my hand and claim me for the next round before someone else does. You did intend to dance with me didn't you?"

"Oh. Indeed. Shall we?"

"We shall." She extended her hand.

The dances kept going, and the night kept wearing on. Sooner or later Sasha had danced with Doctor Givens and Bryon and Lawrence Sherette and Doctor Dontonte and Doctor Charlatan and Captain Dolby at least once and with Captain Dolby twice. Captain Dolby was an exceedingly fine dancer and partner but she felt that Bryon, tall and stately, was the better of the two.

"My. This is my first time ever to dance with you Bryon. I never dreamed you were so artful. May I offer my commendation?"

"Ha, ha, ha. You just did. Thank you."

"When I was living in San Antonio way back you know when did you dance then? I don't remember. Did you?"

"I did. I loved it then as now and I would have had you as my partner, but you were too young."

"And now I'm not."

"Absolutely."

"But when you went dancing back then would you have taken me if I had wanted to go along?"

"My Lord no. They wouldn't have let you in to begin with."

"But suppose they had. Would you have danced with me?"

"No. But you could have watched."

"Watched you dancing with those other girls?"

"Yep. Would that have made you jealous?"

"Maybe. You know how a young girl's heart is don't you?"

Chapter 72

WHILE LAWRENCE Sherette and Doctor Givens saw to it that Mrs. Laster was entertained and kept busy, Sasha began to feel that Melana was less cared for and so she and Andre went over to her table at every opportunity. On this occasion there was but one couple sitting at the table with her. The rest were on the dance floor. Sasha urged Andre to extend his arm at the onset of the next number. When they returned she and Melana began a busy exchange.

"I will never forget my time in England Melana, and how thoroughly and kindly you helped see after me. There is no way I can thank you enough."

"Oh my dear. You owe me no thanks. You were a great joy. The most I ever had. I cried for days after you left. And I'm immensely glad you invited me to your wedding. It makes me feel that I am special."

"You are. You are very special. And I am regretful that I have not had sufficient time to show you around more. I've hardly done that at all. But judging from what you have seen of the Sherette plantation, what do you think of it?"

"Ooooooh, it's huge; it's grand. I can hardly fathom it all. So much unlike London."

"Yes. Totally unlike London. The Sherette plantation is spread out, expansive, open. London, well. It's huge but crowded. Really! But it has the most magnificent things to see. Its cathedrals, and the clock tower, and the harbors running over with tiny boats and ships of enormous length and breadth. They are everywhere. They're virtually uncountable. No wonder they call London the center of the world's greatest empire."

"You must come back as soon as you can Sasha. We'll visit Paris next time. I promise."

"I know you mean it. I do hope I can. And suspect that I'll find the opportunity to do that very thing."

Andre then reached his arm to Melana and they were away once again; and Sasha began to speak with whoever was sitting across from her.

Madam Merkel was cared for with as much thoroughness as were Mrs. Laster and Melana, Sasha and Andre joining her at every opportunity, Andre always extending his arm to invite her for a round. Madam Merkel had watched Sasha all evening. She was her pride and joy; after all, Sasha was married in the very beautiful wedding gown that she with her own hands had fashioned and pieced together. But there was more than this that occupied her. The room was filled with southern beauties, though in her eyes none as rare as Sasha Duval.

"I cannot quite place her," she revolved in her head, "she is of a beauty uniquely strange. I thought that the first time I ever saw her. I mean to say, perhaps rather than strange, that there is an indefinable air and expression about her that I cannot readily identify. Pray tell me, from what sphere of God's people does this enchanting daughter evolve, her complexion above all, so much deeper and more brilliant than any of those southern beauties assembled here to flaunt their charms. I did not construct that lovely gown attired upon her, but she looks as gorgeous in it as the one I devised myself. But then, Sasha's looks and form would breathe life and beauty into a dress of the shabbiest."

Continually throughout the evening words flowed to the ears of Andre and Sasha whenever they were caught still at their table welcoming guests, words which wished them a happy and joyous marriage and heaped upon them that each was the perfect ideal for the other. These were kind and well intentioned phrases, and warmly received but conventionally expected.

"Thank you Mrs. so and so," Sasha returned, smiling with natural civility and charm, "you are most kind and thoughtful and may I also thank you for attending the dance with your husband. I trust that the both of you are enjoying yourselves."

"Oh, we are, we are."

As the clock hand struck half past midnight Jim stepped onto the floor during a momentary pause and raised his voice to a level that he felt was suitably heard throughout the room. It was suggestive that the splendid ball was winding down.

"Ladies and gentlemen. I have the honor of making a few remarks on behalf of my dear brother Andre and his lovely wife Sasha. Aren't they a beautiful couple?" The crowd stood and roared unanimous approval. When they had settled back into their chairs Jim went on. "But I wish to say more than this. I have known Sasha for a good many years. I have watched her grow up, hoping, I confess, that some day she would consent to marry my brother when he asked for her hand. I don't know that I ever told Andre how fervently I wished he would, but he did, and with the Lord working in his favor she answered yes.

Many of you know Sasha and practically all of you, I am confident, know Andre. They are both doctors and now they are married doctors. Isn't that something? I wish that they would establish practice right here on the Van Doke and Sherette plantations, but that isn't their choice. It looks like they've done that already in the city of Baltimore. But no matter, we'll continually remember them and hope they'll return for a visit on every chance. So with this said, Andre and Sasha, I say also, may you bask in great happiness as you go along your way, and may children come to you fruitfully and in health, and lastly, because to me it was the best of Homer's lines, 'may you grow old on one pillow.'"

Few minutes had ticked off when the orchestra struck up again; it was a signal to the dancers to return to the dance floor. Those that were in the foyer having a glass of punch hastened back. This time the music and tempo would be for the quadrille, perhaps the most popular dance of the evening. Those intending to participate had begun to congregate into formation. As Sasha suddenly glanced half the length of the floor from where she sat her gaze caught sight of a man clad in a dark black tail coat that dropped an inch or two below his knees, with his white stockings covering the bottom half of his legs. At his collar there was a stylish white tie. He walked briskly, as if racing with the clock to meet a deadline. Lawrence Sherette was with him. Before this, very briefly before, he had interrupted Lawrence, who had been compellingly amused by the dancers busily scurrying about.

"Kind sir," the man addressed him, "I am Alex Zorosky. The groom, Andre Van Doke, purchased his tuxedo at our store some few days ago for his wedding. His lovely wife, or wife to be, was with him when he paid call. I did the alteration. I hear that you are more than ordinarily acquainted with him and his wife. Would you not suppose my actions inappropriate if I asked her, the lovely Sasha, to dance the quadrille with me? Do you suppose her husband might object?"

Lawrence Sherette was tempted to laugh, but held back, disallowing himself even the thinnest smile.

"Not at all. Not at all. The bride, the lovely Sasha as you called her, is open to a turn with any and all if the time permits. You simply have to step forward and offer your arm. But if you feel my presence will put you more at ease when making your approach I will accompany you."

When they reached Sasha's whereabouts Lawrence Sherette pulled her to him.

"Sasha, this dear man wishes to dance with you. His name is Alex Zorosky."

She recognized him right off. Sasha had decided not to dance to the quadrille, for the hour was late and she felt she should save herself for the last dance with Andre, to be fresh and ready. But she could not refuse the request. Alex wore such a hopeful look.

"Oh, Alex. The alteration man. I am inexpressively excited that you are here. When they sent out the last invitations I caught a glimpse of your name, hoping very sincerely that you would make yourself present. Yes, by all means I shall dance with you. That is why we are all here. To dance. Take my arm. I will be more than happy for you to partner with me to the quadrille."

Alex was more than a good dancer. He was superb, which prompted Sasha to comment of it. "Many excellent dancers are here tonight Alex and I can offer testimony that you are one of the best among them. Tell me. Where were you schooled, and you were schooled? Of that I am certain. Your finesse cannot allow me to believe otherwise."

"St. Petersburg. It is the leading city of Russia at teaching the art of dance. Their evenings are filled with the most magnificent balls. I miss them awfully. When I heard of this one, that is, received the invitation, I knew that I could not miss it and now I am here and my reward is much greater that I could have ever expected."

"Meaning?"

"I am dancing with the bride at her reception affair. I am immensely moved and honored. I am near speechless."

"You are too kind Alex."

"No madam, I am not. I am not kind enough, and you would believe me if I told you that tonight I am very much reminded of that great old city of culture, St. Petersburg."

"Hmmmm. St. Petersburg. Forgive my curiosity. Why did you leave your native Russia?"

"The revolutions."

"What revolutions?"

"Any. They occur incessantly, or shall I say they are all the time in the making. I'd had enough, therefore I left. But there was another reason also. My uncle migrated to America twenty years ago and strange though it may seem ended up in your neighboring town Jackson. He sent for me. I leapt at the chance. And here I am."

"How interesting. Russia does have its share of revolutions if my reading of history is correct, but they are often mired in widespread wars. Do you know much of Napoleon and his skirmish with Emperor Alexander?"

"Much. Through my father."

"Did he fight against Napoleon?"

"No. He was too young. But his father did. At the battle of Borodino, a bloody thing that virtually sapped both armies."

The music ended, Alex led Sasha to her table, bowed and kissed her hand and then bowed to Andre, who had risen from his chair and was now standing. Andre bowed in return, thanking him for his excellent work on his tuxedo. Then Alex in something of a pose of nobility drew to attention, clicked his heels, did a snappy about face, and faded into the mass. "Small world," thought Sasha. "Dancing with a gentleman from far away Russia. How unlikely. But you never know who you'll next meet, do you? He was a most interesting man."

The dance with Alex was the last that evening other than the one upcoming for her and Andre. One o'clock was creeping ever closer; that dance was close upon them. At the previous intermission Adelaide had gone over with Sasha once more the lodging arrangements she had negotiated for her and Andre at the mansion of an old friend who lived but a few miles distant from La Belle. His wife had died some years ago. He lived alone. The old friend and his wife were like family to Adelaide and Lawrence Sherette starting from the time they were children, and Sasha, not many years before, had performed a tonsillectomy on their grandson. The old friend was carried away that he was asked to render the favor. "Andre and Sasha will spend their first night together in my home! How joyous! I am blessed."

With gladness in his heart spilling over he had mingled closely with his servants over the next several days to ensure that the walls and floors and all other parcels of his home glittered. On the day of the expected arrival of his guests he had instructed the two older servants to greet them and ask of their needs, but afterwards to stay well out of sight in their quarters, unless called upon, until the couple had gone away. Then near sunset he climbed into his carriage and left for the home of a grandson where he would spend the night.

It was understood by everyone that when Andre and Sasha were finished with their dance this was the last of the gala occasion, at which time the escorts would begin to help the ladies with their capes and see to it that the carriages and coaches would soon arrive at the frontage for transporting them home. The crowd had shuffled to the edge of the ballroom upon hearing the orchestra commence, forming a circle. Andre and Sasha had located to where they would start, Sasha raising her hand to his shoulder and he taking her other in his. It was again a waltz. Indeed they were splendid young figures as they moved onto the shiny surface of the flooring and into the stream of ambient lighting. Upon completing their third pass the crowd began to applaud and the orchestra played a little softer and Andre and Sasha danced a little closer. Their faces but an inch apart she smiled and kissed his lips. Then the music suddenly slowed, the orchestra leader surmising that the newlyweds welcomed the change. The melody had changed too. It was a melody of love that now played, Andre and Sasha seeming to dance even closer, oblivious to the crowded room of admiring and fascinated eyes upon them.

When I was a young man, years far removed from the splendor of that evening, I would listen to a song that reverberated over and over, which to my discovery had later vacated my sense of remembrance, though as I sat reading through Mrs. Eastbrook's scribblings one day I suddenly recalled two lines of it, no more, only two; "Let us dance on forever, its so romantic this way," and have ever since kept those lyrics in my head and have heard incessantly over the years the lilting sweetness of the refrain. In the play of my mind the images of that moment are yet indelible, Andre, trim and erect, leading, Sasha, following, her enchanting face uplifted to his, her hair of raven loveliness floundering about her shoulders. They dance on and on, unvaryingly in sway with the rise and fall of Strauss's eternal waltz.

As the crowd began to disassemble Andre and Sasha passed quietly through an exit that led to the carriage awaiting them, the driver of the vehicle personally selected by Sam Feathers. Dismounting, the driver sought to assist Sasha with her climb to the inside seating. Sam Feathers waved him off. It was his job to do that. When he had lifted her up and saw that she was secure he backed away and looked skyward. "The moon is in your favor," said Sam to the driver. "A glow like this one I've not seen in a while. You should get there in a little over an hour, hunh?"

"Bout that."

The driver then climbed aboard and clucked to the handsome horses; the trace chains tightened, and the wheels with shiny red spokes began to roll over. Sasha sighed and leaned into Andre's arms, while the carriage moved steadily in the moonlight night toward their destination. When they arrived the driver asked Andre if he could help with anything, perhaps carrying the encasement of Sasha's attire for them. Andre answered no and thanked him. Then the driver left. The portico was lighted with lamps strewn around it for the entire distance. One of the servants was standing at the door that lead into the foyer, who revealed his identity and asked of their needs. Andre said they had none but would call on him should any arise. The servant turned and left. Then Andre deftly pushed upon the door and suddenly they were on the inside, the servant having left the door unlocked for them.

"Look," said Sasha upon their entry. "What taste! Look at the paintings adorning the walls and the flowers there on the table. Freshly gathered too. I can tell by the fragrance."

"They were picked this very morning."

There was a note left on the table on which the flowers were set out and Andre picked it up. "You are to sleep in the huge bed. There's no other in the house like it; so you won't have trouble deciding which it is." Sasha came over and read the note too.

"What a dear sweet man."

At short length, after they had toured part of the mansion, they opened the door leading into the room where they thought the bed might be and there it was, a huge Victorian much in the manner of the one belonging to Adelaide and the other at the La Belle which once belonged to Andre's mother. She'd left it to him in her will. The woodwork was heavy and ornate, gilded with scrolls and curlicues. A velvet coverlet was spread upon the bed that very day, laid there in honor of the guests by the old man and his servants who had tried in every way they knew how to prepare for them.

"Do you like it," Andre asked?

"How could I not. I am awed."

Sasha bathed first, then after doing her face changed into the golden silken nightgown that she had removed from the encasement, then after this went over to the huge Victorian and got in and pulled the covers upward. Andre was only briefly behind, crawling in beside her after dousing most of the several lamps on the portico which had been casting a soft faint glow into the room. The only glow that shone now, other than that from the full moon, was from the single lamp on the portico that Andre had allowed to remain burning.

And there they lay by each other, at last, joined by the blessing of Heaven. In the dimness she looked at him and he at her. She reached her hand to his face, with the softest tenderest touch, a prelude to the kiss that was in the making,

A long, long kiss, a kiss of youth, and love,
And beauty, all concentrating like rays
Into one focus, kindled from above;
Such kisses as belong to early days,
Where heart, and soul, and sense, in concert move,
And the red blood's lava and the pulse a blaze.[14]

The next morning the same driver was there to pick them up. They would pull up in front of Aurora between the noon hour and one o'clock, finding a good many of their beloveds gone, practically all. One by one Adelaide had seen them off. The trains had begun to run early. Among the last of the few to leave were Bryon and Mrs. Laster, who could have left earlier, but declined. They had hung on, waiting at the depot for the last

---

[14] Adapted from Lord Byron's *Don Juan*.

train run of the day, Adelaide with them. Prompted by Mary Tonka, Andre and Sasha had rushed to say goodbye, hoping they were still there. Another ten minutes and they would have been too late. The engine was beginning to discharge its spray of noisy white steam.

"I just had to wait for you Sasha my darling," Mrs. Laster said wistfully, "it is still terribly hard to leave you. When will you come?"

"Next year."

"Promise."

"You have my word. Straight from my heart. Take care of her Bryon."

☙ ❧

The wedding was over; the grand wedding it should be fittingly remarked, almost royal in its aspect and never to be forgotten by those who graced it with their presence. It was the perfect ending to a story of uncommon length and the usual penman might feel well inclined at this intermission to draw the curtain and let it fade imperceptibly into the mist. I acknowledge that I am approaching the finale; but there is more to tell, taken from Mrs. Eastbrook's accounts, which at this date have markedly diminished, and then from my own, fairly lately determined, this latter effort undertaken because there was an unrequited curiosity in my being to learn of whatever happened to the persons' lives I have intercepted in my endeavors, and most singularly to our beloved Sasha Duval. I take the liberty here to address her by her family and not by her married name purposely, I so explain, for interestingly, throughout her lifetime, she continued to use the original in her medical pursuits, not in any manner objectionable to her husband, the kind and gentle Andre.

Two days had gone by when Andre and Sasha happily boarded a train to Baltimore, where they would catch their breath, pack up the belongings indispensable for satisfying their needs while away and set sail for Sorrento. Their ship was the *Alexis,* a sleek steamer that ran to and from Europe at near record pace, the city of Naples a select anchoring port for its passengers which seasonally visited in crowded numbers. I believe that I am correct in contending that Sasha and Andre sailed directly to Sorrento shortly after the wedding, with no diversion other than the stopover in Baltimore. But take pause that I am not entirely certain, for there was talk, as reported in the diaries and letters that I reviewed, that Sasha felt strongly compelled to visit New Orleans for a short stay, and then travel on to San Antonio to see Father Lumas, a yearning that had begun to tug unrelentingly at her heart. She had not seen him since she was a girl. She should see him soon, she had said in a tone of urgency. She and Mrs. Laster had spoken of this during the wedding festivities. I am not of the notion that she made it to either New Orleans or San Antonio that year, despite the prior urge to go through with it, although the records indicate rather indisputably that she and Andre got around to it in the year that followed.

The *Alexis* was a marvelous ship that paid call on many of the well known ports of England, France and Italy. On this trip it would anchor first in Naples, the city about which songs have been written and stories told for centuries, lying but a brief stretch from Sorrento—thirty miles by road—both cities facing the Mediterranean. On the outset the weather was pretty, the Atlantic calm, with only limited clouds in sight. They had set sail from Baltimore harbor that morning. The good weather continued throughout the day, making it pleasant for the newlyweds to stand along the railings watching and feeling the waters rise and fall, Sasha faking a gasp when the sea gulls swooped low, and trying their hand at shuffleboard. On the second day, the weather shifted, beginning in the early afternoon, low billowing clouds threatening to enshroud the vessel. Sasha went and retrieved her raincoat and put it on, covering her head with a cape which lapped over the greater area of her face. Andre laughed at the way her eyes peeped out. Not wishing to remain on deck in the wake of the approaching downpour, they took to the shelter of their cabin and settled in. Sasha had commented when they entered, as she had the day before, that the interior was the epitome of quality. She was well pleased, relaying to Andre that the furnishings were of a fine exquisite flavor, and that their origin of style was a mix of Italian and French. The rain fell steadily that night, with hardly a sign of slowing, while they sat and read and talked and had dinner in their room, a serving of wine supplied as a compliment of the Captain, and when the hour struck eleven they rolled back the covers and retired to bed. The sun rose with a flourish of red and orange the next morning, the rays pouring through the porthole windows onto Sasha's face, who upon seeing the clock on the side table which was smothered with pretty flowers frowned and went back to sleep. It was only six. At nine she awakened again and nudged Andre that it was late and likely past time for breakfast. Andre rubbed his eyes and rolled out. They dressed and went to the diner. When they had eaten—the diner was open until ten—they clad themselves in clothing which was suitable for deck side then went out to bask in the morning breeze.

"When are we to arrive, Andre? Did you happen to ask the Captain?"

"I didn't. Maybe the first mate's estimation is dependable. He said seven days."

On the third day, or the fourth, or the fifth—I cannot be certain, for the information on which I had to depend was unclear and confusing—they were invited to lunch at the Captain's table, his young officers in their sleek white coats with him, so enchanted with Sasha that they uncontrollably flitted back and forth upon her lovely face while attempting to eat their food. The Captain, who could not have missed the commotion that she had ignited simply smiled and did his best to distract them for fear that Andre might be offended. But Andre, who saw and understood the scene before him merely smiled as well and placidly kept at his food. Sasha's tactic was to pretend that she was wholly unaware of the goings on.

The remainder of their trip is best described as routine, strolling on top side, dining in the Captain's diner, relaxing in the chaises sitting about from stem to stern, and reading. They said but little of the wedding to one another; there was no need to say more, because each knew that the other felt that it was a beautiful ceremony. Sometimes Sasha stood against the railing looking out to sea, lost in memories. Andre chanced to ask her what could she be thinking.

"Captain Johansen, Andre, and my trip from the Canaries. He was the kindest man. I'll never forget him. I think of him every day. This voyage so much calls him into my impression."

Chapter 73

THEY SAILED on, by the hour nearing their destination. Daybreak had stripped away darkness a short while before they pulled into dockside in Naples, a tour guide alert to help them rent a carriage and hire a driver for their journey to Sorrento. The driver would gladly lend Andre a hand at loading their belongings. He was exactingly knowledgeable of the hotel where they were to stay and estimated their arrival time to be in the late afternoon. It is at this intermission that I now fall upon the letter that Sasha wrote to Adelaide some few days after their return to Baltimore to her hospital duties. I retrieved it not too many years ago from someone of Jim Van Doke's family tree who had read the letter and was fascinated by it. Yet was only vaguely aware of the heritage of Sasha Duval and the rich variations of her life. He lent it to me long enough for reproducing a copy.

Dearest Adelaide,

I am now returned to Baltimore, back busy at work, yet must take time tonight to sit at my little side table and scribble down the wonderful experiences of our trip abroad.

I will tell you as much as I can of it all, starting with the time the ship docked at the port of Naples, where there we took a carriage for our coverage of the not many miles to Sorrento. The road wound and twisted in the manner of a serpent, I must report, for there is no better way to describe it. The concept of straight is not in the vocabulary of the Italians when they speak of this route way. Needless to say, it was an exhilarating journey. High towering cliffs overlooked the road and the sea from the west, sheer rock walls, whitish and gorgeous, and the sea, the Mediterranean, lay to the east, serene and blue and that was the image as far as the eye could penetrate into the great obscurity. We stopped ever so often just to look.

When we arrived in Sorrento, we took a deep breath—sooooo beautiful. Sooooo romantic. They say if you have not fallen in love before you get there you most certainly will when you do. The city resides atop white steep cliffs and offers a fantastic view of the sea and the harbor. Our hotel was high up, I mean quite high up, and we could see the mass of small sail boats in the bay down below glistening in the afternoon sun. Andre said he figured everyone in Italy owned one. The mayor, plump and jolly, soon happened along to greet us, explaining that for almost two thousand years people had been journeying to that lush place with its breathtaking sunsets and fragrances of orange and lemon gardens and because of a hundred or more other attractions. I wonder of the appearance of it in the years to come; if it will change. What a pity if it does. I hope not in my lifetime.

I mentioned our hotel, high up on the cliffs overlooking the sea, surrounded by mountains with white fluffy clouds covering the peaks. The fog mainly appeared in the morning hours, very soon lifting. In front of the hotel there was a plaza made of nice pretty rocks and equipped with rounded back chairs and small cute tables scattered about, and that was where Andre and I spent a good many hours, especially at night time, sipping wine now and then and immersing ourselves in the twinkling lights down in the harbor. We'd talk about everything, the gorgeously posh surroundings lending spice to the conversation, and Andre was such an interesting and enjoyable conversationalist, more active at it on our trip than ever before it seemed. As I said, we talked about everything, and everybody, about you, Lawrence Sherette, Sam Feathers, Mary Tonka, Thea, and Andre's mother Mrs. Van Doke. Ah, Andre's mother. She was so affectionately inclined toward him. I think more than she was toward Jim and George. Don't you? But of course she was. He was the youngest, her baby. Out of the blue one night he asked if I realized the depth of her love for me and I answered that I did and then he asked me—and this will touch your heart—if I knew how much she wished that I could have been her daughter and that often when she had just gone to bed she wished that she could have held me the way you always did while waiting for me to drift off to sleep. I could not hold back the tears. I told him I grievously regretted that her wish did not come true. She must have been terribly lonely at that hour of night when oft times there was no one with her.

At a certain period during the day we went swimming; the temperature was warm and nice and the water mirror clear. We went just about every day. Andre delighted at ducking me under, but I held my patience and when the opportunity availed itself I repaid him. My father took me swimming years ago when we visited Sorrento. I am supposing it was in the same vicinity in which Andre and I swam and beached out. My mother wasn't much for swimming. She just watched.

We kept on the go, day and night, staying up late and sleeping into the morning. But not sleeping too long. I was afraid we might miss something. In the daytime we joined the crowds in the narrow streets between the high buildings, so many people there that you constantly bumped into someone, or they did you. I loved the shops and the cafes were wonderful. There were plazas at every turn, where benches and tables were literally swamped with vegetables and fruits of the many sorts, grapes and lemons leading the way. Sorrento is noted for growing both. They make what they call lemoncello, a very tasty lemon liquor, which we found in every café in which we set foot.

And speaking of cafes. The city was spilling over with choices. I think I liked the one where late at night they featured the mandolin players. You know what they say. 'What could be more the soul of Italy than the sound of a mandolin?' We were there practically every night. It went by the name Antolini. Andre and I sat at a small table with a candle atop it. Sometimes we ordered food, sometimes only a small glass of wine, and listened to the mandolin players. They always came to our table playing music that was not in my sphere of knowledge. That was of no matter. I loved it just the same. It was very pretty and when I closed my eyes it took me back to my piano and Mozart and Beethoven. Without fail, the lead player, quite a handsome young man, moved close to me and looked down into my face and played very delicately. Softly I mean. I felt embarrassed. I told Andre afterwards that was when the young musician seemed to play most romantically and Andre answered that it was obvious he was in love with me. 'You know how young Italian men are, don't you?' he teased. I laughed and asked if I should leave him a note that I was already claimed. He said no, that the young man would figure that out soon enough if he hadn't already.

There was another café which also had its unordinary features. The wine was the best, and was made especially attractive by the glass in which it was served. It was perfectly round for a ways downward from the rim, then it blew out in the shape of a ball or balloon. Then after this there was only the small round stem and very large flat saucer like support on which the glass rested. They also had an artist who was there nightly with canvases and colors and brushes. He asked if he could paint us. We nodded yes. He did a sketch and said that was a sample, only that. It was very good. We let him finish. Andre insisted on buying it. It's a keepsake for our children and grandchildren. I'll show it to you when we see one another again.

The flowers were astonishingly gorgeous, seen everywhere you looked, in pots set out on the winding walls of the street ways and roads and in urns arranged in something of a symmetrical pattern in the plazas and on the rooftops which were visible from our higher hotel elevation. And you will like this: I learned to pronounce a good many names of the flowers in Italian, for example, Daisy; *La marsherita,* Lily; *Il giglio,* Tulip; *Il tulipano,* Daffodil; *Il narciso,* Rose; *La rosa.* Many more.

Near the last of our stay we went to a Sicilian dance, which is called a tarantella. So fascinating. We stayed for hours. Their style resembled an American square dance or a French quadrille. The men and women paired off into couples, all dressed in white and red, with lace heavily populating the upper region of their attire. The women wore a material of silk over their heads, something of a cravat, soft and golden, a very thin effeminate fabric, and I was amazed at how they kept it from falling off. The whole affair carried me back to a book I once read of Czarist Russia. The Russians have the most beautiful dances, none of them less than grand.

The evening before we left for home we celebrated mass at The Cathedral of Sorrento, Santa Fillip e Gina Como. Andre prayed a prayer for us, asking the Lord to bless and protect us from harm on our return voyage. The Cathedral was built around the eleventh century and rebuilt in the fifteenth century. And I learned some other particulars which I will share. Its bell tower is endowed of a height of three stories and is decorated with a profoundly huge round clock which sounded each day across the city, sometimes before noon and sometimes after. I did not understand why the variation but failed to ask. Sorry. That isn't like me. The belfry's base dates to the time of the Roman Empire. I was thrilled and felt blessed to have gone there with Andre for worship.

We sailed for home the next day, catching the *Alexis* once more which was moored just off the coast. When we went aboard the mayor was there to see us off, speaking out happily to everyone; 'Remember the old adage,' he said, 'when one visits Sorrento he cannot leave without forever wanting to come back.' And I am determined that I will.

Goodnight dear, I love you.

Sasha

A year passed, finding Sasha busily submerged in her work at the hospital, her dear friend Doctor Givens associated with her in the bulk of her endeavors. Doctor Dontonte had long gone, leaving upon her return from Sorrento. That year, as they had planned, she and Andre finally took a trip to San Antonio, there intercepted by Mrs. Laster and Bryon who took them directly to the San Fernando Cathedral. "My darling girl," Father Lumas said with quivering voice, "is that you? You are remarkably sophisticated in your looks. I had given up on ever seeing you again, convinced that I would die before you returned." Sobs by both poured forth and tears rolled down their faces as she grasped him with both arms while he tried valiantly, though feebly, to bundle her in his.

"Yes. Yes. My dear one I have delayed until now, too long I know, which is unforgiving and I am very sorry that I have."

Shaking his head no, he answered that she should not be sorry, for he had heard of her marvelous successes, which had kept her away, then proceeded to bring up that Father Kestner had passed on.

"Yes. I know. Someone wrote me. And I am sorry for that also. I have wished ceaselessly that I could have gotten back to him before he left us."

"But that is the way of life my child. Do not grieve, do not fret. He would have counseled that you not."

Andre and Sasha took their lodging in the Rectory, during the day hours touring the city, Mrs. Laster with them, and sometimes Bryon. Chenelle was still in the employ of the Cathedral and Sasha was beside herself to be with her once more. She inquired of Paula, learning that she was a teacher in a nearby town and on an occasion convenient to her schedule met her for lunch in the city and a few times they had mass together. Sasha and Andre's stay was far too brief, but it had to end. She had to return to her work. When she embraced Father Lumas on the morning of their departure she felt that it was her last to see him alive and kissed his cheeks with tender loving sweetness as if it were a final goodbye.

Another year faded away and Sasha gave birth to a baby boy. The nation had begun a surge of rapid social and economic change, railway expansion happening at a frenzied pace, people traveling in droves to places they had never before seen. When the baby was age three Sasha and Andre went back to Sorrento, finding it as lovely and alluring as they had when first going, though the conditions were not the same. Babies will do that. Their night life was drastically curtailed, in fact cut off, but beaching out was not. I found evidence of this, not in Sasha's diary but in Andre's, who detailed with some measure of hilarity that once when they were strolling on the edge of the sands in a secluded cove, which was away from all other humans, the child began to cry for one or the other to lead or carry him into the waters, but as it was, they were dressed in street attire, and without bathing suits. Neither saw, therefore, any hope of lessening the child's wailing. But finally, Sasha's heart was so distressed at her little one's torment that she removed her clothing, all of it, cradled him in her arms and waded in up to a level just below her bosom. "If someone nearby had chanced to come up on us," said Andre, "what an eyeful they would have gathered. My wife is endowed of a stunning form, even if I do say so myself."

Then there emerged the seventies. The nation the year before had voted into office a new president, Ulysses S. Grant, and on the international stage France and Prussia were at war. And to Sasha and Andre there was born a second and third baby. The business interests of the nation were vigorously promoting and financing the laying of railroads into the western plains, particularly into Texas, and with this medium at their disposal, Sasha and

Mrs. Laster found it relatively easy to make repeated visits to and from Baltimore and San Antonio. At the advent of the eighties Sasha joined Doctors Metternich and Dontonte in London in a medical venture concerned with the as yet unconquered affliction of appendicitis, the undertaking centered at King's College. Doctor Fitzgerald had retired. Doctors Metternich and Dontonte had aggressively insisted on the European medical society inviting Sasha to be there. Mrs. Laster went with her, but not the children. Andre faithfully kept them. Sasha returned home in a month. While I do not know in which decade it occurred, the late eighties I believe, Sasha stayed for awhile in Vienna working again in concert with Doctors Metternich and Dontonte. Soon afterwards Doctor Metternich retired.

The Van Doke mansion burned during that era, a strange fire they said, brave efforts exerted to remove and save many of the furnishings, and several were, this including Mrs. Van Doke's Victorian bed and her piano, which had been left intact in the mansion throughout the years. Some folks supposed that the rescue of the piano was something of a divination for Sasha, because after it was moved into one of the spacious rooms of Aurora she was suddenly again in love with music, which lately had waned, and once more passionately took up playing. Over the years the grand balls had continued to be held at La Belle, Sasha then still young and vivacious, dancing with every male dancer that asked for a turn, and stayed until the orchestra had struck its last note.

I cannot attest with certainty as to the demise of Mary Tonka. Some pieces of script led me to believe that the year of her passing occurred in the seventies; whereas others make mention that her death was near the start of the next decade. But whichever was the instance, a letter spoke of Sasha staying with Adelaide for a full month after the funeral to help alleviate her loneliness, which was profoundly hard for her to endure. Cynthia too passed away, the imbibing on her headstone reading 1883, with no month given, and was laid to rest beside Sol in the Van Doke cemetery where Mrs. Van Doke lay. I am without knowledge of what happened to Tahitia Lillian. There are no records of substantiation. Nor can I do much better with respect to Mrs. Laster, who in her aging years seems to have gone back to England to live out her life, or at one time was considering that she might as hinted in one of her letters to Sasha. Sasha returned to the Canaries once when she was visiting Doctor Dontonte in Europe and then again with Andre much later in her life, on each occasion laying flowers on her parents' grave as well as on Father Kestner's, which she also visited during her journeys.

What happened to Adelaide and Lawrence Sherette? And in the same breath one is inclined to ask also what happened to the Sherette plantation? I wish I could supply more than I possess which is regrettably brief, but I will provide the most I have to offer. It appears that Lawrence Sherette left Memphis for New Orleans on an assignment by the Catholic Church in the 1890's, when he was beginning to show the effects of aging and declining health; and before that, Adelaide had moved to the same city, who supposedly opted to take up residence there to care for Harry Lancaster, her apparent lover in younger years, also in ill health, returning to Aurora for short intervals to confer with Thea and her husband who were managing the enterprise of planting and harvesting. But the plantation was sliding into degeneration, the glory years gone, and eventually it was posted on the block for sale and sold to a corporation.

What can I say about Sasha, of whom I seem to harbor nothing regarding her waning years; where she lived and how long she lived, though assuming that her residence was Baltimore, and that given her vigor and vibrancy, not once ever sick or diseased, if my knowledge is dependable, she could have easily succeeded beyond World War I and even into the 1930's.

Throughout the years I have continued to retrace my search, reexamining the vestiges of the persons that I have heretofore mentioned, reading line by line words that pertained to them in the literature—in the dairies, in the letters, and in the front and back of family Bibles—and in conjunction with this have traveled to various cities and places, finding but a speck beyond that which I already had at my fingertips. What I have most recently sought, and I have striven at it avidly, was whether there was someone in the family lineage who could tell me about Sasha Duval. I have looked for a trace of her in the city of Baltimore as of a few months past when I was there visiting, discovering nothing in the deeds of records of her ownership of property. I did learn through the antiquated medical records of the system of hospitals that there was a Doctor Sasha Duval. And as well I pursued, even if by the wildest of chance, the tactic of telephoning persons in the city directory listed under the name Van Doke, hoping that they might divulge knowledge of certain families of old that were their forebearers. But I was luckless.

Finally, on the very last, when I had exhausted the extent of my efforts in trace of her, I drove westwardly from my native town by a hundred miles to a vast area of land known by the locals as the old plantation. It was my first time ever to set foot on it, to ever see it. Why I did not do this at some date before may seem strange and illogical, as I reflect back, to which I can only reply that things simply happened this way, and go no further, except to suppose that in the end, strange as it was, my Maker arranged for my search to be brought to a satisfactory closure and that I at last was content.

At first sight I knew that this land was once owned by Adelaide and Lawrence Sherette, even knew it before checking the deed of record in the courthouse of the county seat, which told me of a fact that I did not know. Now it was owned by a conglomerate, as I have previously divulged, where giant tractors ran, pulling ploughs and cutters that tore into the soil quicker than those of former generations could have remotely dreamed. There was a foreman managing the enterprise, I learned, who lived in a small frame dwelling on the edge of the premises. He introduced himself as Carlos Randall. Gladly, upon my asking his permission to browse around—for I was familiar with the history of the plantation, I explained, and that it meant much to me nostalgically—he gave it with the motion of his hand and words that I should exercise care lest I stumble and fall, or worse still, step on the hidden pieces of shattered glass that lay beneath the gnarled patches of overgrown vegetation. His cautioning tones revealed that he aspired to be protective of the man in his presence who was obviously no longer young. Uncertain exactly of the whereabouts of what I was searching for I followed the roadway that the man had described, feeling that it was leading me on a dependable course, stopping after a brevity to pause and study the surroundings, most singularly the tree line, then moved on until I had covered a short distance, shorter than I had come already, then halted once more, my senses telling me better than my intellect that I was close. Suddenly, as I looked about I saw the stately cedars, as if in the attitude of a wisp they had decided to pop into view, and then a meager piece beyond there it was, Aurora. "Aurora," my lips excitedly murmured. I cannot adequately describe the feeling, except to say that there was a thrill that surged through me with ecstasy and awe. It was Aurora—I had found it; I assured myself of that—once an emblem of proudness and stately beauty where life literally teemed with joy and creativity, as well as struggles, and I had read and heard of the people who occupied the interior of its walls, even knew them by name. But Aurora was now a mere ghost compared to its former stature, reduced over time and through neglect to shambles, crumbling slowly to earth. There was a sickening in my stomach and my heart sank. I moved closer for inspection, peeping into the glassless windows, seeing as I glanced upward that the roof had largely given way, admitting the rain unobstructedly. I could even smell the effluvium lifting from the once shimmering hardwood flooring presently sunk in a condition of wet decay.

Chapter 74

SOMEWHERE IN these ruins and around the edifice, and out in the vast open fields where the cotton still grew in prodigious abundance, I felt that the vestiges of the person I sought to learn more about lay dormant and quiet. "Surely I will find something here in Aurora and if not in this realm then in the tales of the locals, more so from the Negroes than others."

I had decided to stay two days, checking into a lodging accommodation close on the main highway, traveling to and from, using part of my hours to sort through the accumulation of decaying mass, afraid all the while that a rotting piece of material might abruptly dislodge from above and fall smashing down on my head and shoulders. My search revealed nothing. I had especially hoped to uncover bits of personal endearments, jewelry, bracelets, earrings, and such. Ah! Futile hopefulness. Quitting this, I made my way to the Negro settlements of Yanceyville, which lay south of the highway to Memphis, inquiring of the older of these folks if it was in their knowledge that decades ago there was once a beautiful white girl of some Negro blood in her veins who lived on a plantation nearby. I was met by and large with countenances of blankness. One, however, had heard when she was young, her grandmother and two aunts discussing a white girl that lived for a while in a house that stood upon the land of which I spoke. A very grand house, she said, tall, with many chimneys and a rounded porch.

"Was it the one north of the highway that's falling down?"

"That's it."

"Was it known as Aurora?"

"Aur—."

"Aurora," I repeated distinctly, heading off her stammer.

"I don't know."

It hardly mattered that she was unfamiliar with the name. I was certain that it was the one her grandmother and aunts had long ago taken up for discussion in her presence.

"Did the white girl have a name? If so, was it Sasha?"

"No. If they did speak it I forgot it."

"Too bad," I uttered with a shade of disappointment. "But are you sure? Think back."

She rolled her eyes as if struggling to recall.

"No Sasha. I'm sure."

I had decided to extend my two days into a third. It was a Wednesday. At approximately mid afternoon, the sun slowly descending into the west, I returned to the white frame house where the overseer lived, luckily finding him home, who upon hearing the noise from my vehicle stepped out onto the front porch. His greeting was cordial, blended with an expression that he hardly expected to see me back; he asked if there was anything unfinished about which he could offer assistance.

"I'd like to explore the fields, even as far as the Big Hatchie, but I'm afraid I can't. It seems a mite late for that."

"Can't?"

"Yes sir. I've never gone out into the fields before except through what I've read. I'd hardly be able to find my way."

Upon this admission I was met by surprise and undeserving kindness.

"Ah, that's no trouble. If you really want to. And I guess you do. I'll take you."

"That's too much to ask."

"No it's not. I think I know what's gnawing on you. You're going way back and I ought to help you."

"You're too kind."

"No sir. Not a splinter's worth. We'll crawl into old Sally. That's my truck. We'll have to drive. It's too far to walk. And I promise to poke along as slowly as you like."

In response to his out of the way generosity I uttered that I could not sufficiently express my gratefulness, and when he shushed it off without a word—his facial action said it was nothing—we crawled into the vehicle, which was not in the least old, but modern and new, and commenced a trip across the terrain which in my imagination I had covered times innumerable.

When we drove by a very small number of fruit trees scattered here and there I asked if there was once upon a time a sizeable orchard in this immediate locale and was this the remnant of it, he answered yes, sort of, because the site was the same he'd been told, but that the orchard I had in mind had vanished decades and decades before, and that the peach and apple trees, few in number, that I presently beheld were of quite a relatively young age, set out not more than ten years in the past. He must have read the reminiscences of my face.

"You seem to be thinking of something back yonder."

"I am. I can see them as clearly as if they were right over there," I said, pointing.

"Who?"

"The women. An older woman, quite old, and one just passed thirty, and a young one. The young one is less than twenty. They have on their bonnets and they're carrying their fruit picking baskets with them. They're about to knock down the apples with a chopping hoe."

"Ha, ha, ha. Mister, you've got a heck of an imagination."

Then we drove on, slowly, creeping, as he said he would, me looking at the cotton fields, much of the cotton still in the bolls, but the greater amount had been picked, and when we left this domain we crossed over to the hayfields, wide and endless, the hay already cut and harvested, only the stubble now remaining. No matter. I closed my eyes and took myself back. The mowing was in full swing. There he was, Sam Feathers sitting on his wagon supervising the workers, Sasha sitting beside him.

"Where next," he asked, and I said to the Big Hatchie, for the sun was swiftly sinking; so without waste we moved on, reaching the river when the sun had dropped below the horizon. Dark was closing. We were at the water's edge. I could see it. It had risen close to the rim of the banks. The rain had fallen the night before in torrents. At my mentioning that I thought we were at the right place for my starting to look around he stopped and I eased out, hearing him caution that I shouldn't venture too close to the shoreline because the earth was soft and that it might cave in. Then he suddenly slid out of his truck and brought over a flashlight, saying that he would just lean against the truck fender and wait, but to keep the flashlight on and shining. I didn't particularly need it, I thought, for the moon was full.

"I'll go with you if you want me to."

"I can make it. But thank you."

I think he understood. I wanted the next short while to myself. I went on for a piece, careful not to venture too far, and sat down on a log and began to listen to the rumble of the water, the same rumble that Sasha and Andre heard when they were on these banks generations ago. It was their first time together, it dawned on me, and as they trod onward Andre held back an overhanging branch to keep Sasha from running into it. They must have had a lantern I reasoned. Surely they did.

I lifted myself up and walked a few steps, taking care in the twilight not to move too close to the precarious edge of the river, then returned to the log where I had been sitting. It was but of brief duration that I heard it, which I had begun to anticipate—, the hoot, the same one that Sasha and Andre heard in the proximity of one hundred and fifty years ago, a replica of bubo's, the sound of his off spring, who had ascended successively from an unbroken lineage of progenitors during all this while. A smile of amazement settled softly on my face. "How remarkable that now I have heard it too." I recalled vividly the story that Sasha told to Andre concerning a Jewish man named Agrippa who was leaning on a tree bemoaning his fate at the hands of the Romans and that there was a strange bird whose name was bubo stationed upon one of its branches; and that there was a man of Germanic descent who spoke to him that he should not grieve over his misfortune, for soon he would be relieved of it and promoted thereupon to the highest dignity and power, reigning for many fruitful years. But that he shouldst remember that when he seest this bird again he would have but five days longer to live.

When we neared the mansion on our return, the vestige of it I should add, the headlights of the vehicle swept across the contour of the giant cedars that resided even yet on the periphery of the once magnificent serpentine stretch that led to the portico. The moon, which at this hour was at the peak of its enchantment, shone down with a splendor and I think figured prominently in what I did next. I asked Carlos to stop and let me out for a moment if it wasn't excessively troublesome, the answer coming that it wasn't, not in the least. "I just want to look around at something," I said. "I won't be long."

"Take your time."

With exceeding slowness I then commenced to walk toward the mansion, beginning at the exact fount of the drive, where it commenced at the greater road, the pebbles beneath my shoes sounding of a crunch, crunch, crunch, which had laid virtually undisturbed throughout the long aging years, presently overgrown with vines and sedges and tendrils that extended as an entangled mass in every which way. But it was once magnificent, I knew that, and was the artery that led hundreds of splendid carriages to the Sherette plantation home for one grand function after another. I envisioned in my creation that Sasha had ridden over it for times uncountable on her sorrel, or had walked it just as many by foot.

As I strode further, half the distance at this point, the moon seemed suddenly to yield an even more luminescent glow, I could have so sworn; and the soft evening wind which before that very instant had been whisking gently across my face suddenly turned brisker, sending a flutter through the branches and boughs, and then there was a low delicate sigh—I could have sworn to it—and this was followed by the loveliest softest effeminate murmuring that ever descended on one's hearing. Sasha, Sasha, Sasha, the wind seemed to say. Was this a phantasm that had fallen upon me, or some shadowy aspect of nightly trickery? Of course it was neither I answered, only my imagination running rampant, fed by the wind and the branches and the boughs. What an influence on one's mental faculty when particular combinations gather in assemblage to play upon it, and especially if one is wishful for a certain effect to become reality, if only vaguely. With this over, I decided to proceed a little further, but then after a few steps paused and turned around and began to retrace my steps toward the vehicle. Suddenly I stopped once more, enveloped by yet another fantasy, equally as fantastic as the first. "Suppose," I said to myself, "that you had lived one hundred and fifty years ago and that by some stroke of Heavenly creativeness the lovely Sasha were walking here beside you."

"That indeed is a wonderful fantasy," I replied. "I find myself wishing that it could be so."

When he let me out in front of his house Carlos did not at once pull away, asking in the delay if my visit was ending. I replied that I did not think it was, that there was something inside goading me to stay on another day, my fourth, that I'd like to peep inside Aurora once more. And then, somewhat to my surprise, he said that he'd intended to tell me something previously, beginning on the day we first met, but that it had slipped him. He'd like to share it with me now, he said, whether or not it was of worth.

"Ah! What is it?"

"Well sir, there's a lady, a young lady of less than thirty, a fine looker if I ever saw one. Educated no doubt. She's been coming here for the past few years, before I was hired on as foreman. Come to think of it she seems to be looking for the same thing you are. That's the way it seems. She asks a lot of things I can't answer. She's here now, been here for about a week. She always turns up in the late fall like this. She says she likes the leaves when they're starting to take on a color of gold. "

"Ah! There's a good feel to this. When is she due back?"

"Tomorrow I guess. She's been here every day. Didn't say a word about leaving."

"Where is she staying? Could I telephone her?"

"Sorry. I don't know that."

Admittedly, my curiosity was aroused, but in truth reasoned that it was too remotely far fetched to believe that her purposes were kindred to mine. I bade him goodnight, with a clause tacked on that I planned to return the next day near the noon hour to have another look at the aging Aurora. I added that I might venture inside.

"You be careful. You could get hurt in there."

"I'll watch myself."

True to my intentions the next day I returned, arriving before the noon hour and sat down for lunch underneath one of the noble oaks whose massive branches spread like octopus tentacles over the grounds. I had brought sandwiches and a vessel of water. As I ate I gazed curiously around, picturing that here on this exact piece of earth, or close by, was where Sam Feathers had the workers dig the barbeque pits and where the long crude tables sat overspread with ivory white tapestries and by which the people passed with plates extended, the servers piling on heaps of barbequed pork. As soon as my lunch was finished, I arose and strode over to the portico, or to what was left of it, then cautiously entered the front doorway, turning right into a room of unordinary space, large, quite large, the living room I presumed, where Izu's portrait once hung, or where I thought it did, and where Sasha and Andre were married. And it was in this same room, I recalled, where Sasha played the music of the inimitable composers. I smiled. I wished I had been there to hear. Then next, I ventured into what must have been the drawing room, where Sasha first met Andre, and then entered the infirmary. It had to be the infirmary, for it was of substantial length and equipped with decaying shelving which I surmised once accommodated medicines and medical equipment and a miscellany of various supplies. My mind literally spun, and I found myself traversing from room to room, time and again. Sometimes I even heard Sasha's laughter floating from the portico on a summer night or her footsteps falling lightly down the hall. It was but natural for me to do these things. I had lived them already. Once, when I was in the kitchen, I looked through the glassless windows, hearing Mary Tonka speak to Adelaide as plainly as if I were back in time with them.

"There's Sasha on her sorrel Adelaide, she'll be hungry. She's been out all afternoon."

"Yes she will. Is supper ready?"

"It's ready. All I have to do is set it out."

The hour was nearing mid afternoon when I noticed a shiny automobile making its approach, the driver, a woman, bringing it to rest within a short distance of Aurora. It struck me that she was familiar with the driveway and had traveled over it with some considerable frequency, enough, in any event, that she now felt comfortable driving this far. Before this day I had not dared do as much, leaving my vehicle on the roadside in front of the foreman's house, walking the rest of the way. But today I had driven it the full distance, parking it on the south side of Aurora. From my seat on the edge of the portico I had viewed her as she drove onto the premises, rising only when she left her car and began to narrow the footage between us. She was not in the least apprehensive or hesitant; Carlos had told her as she stopped to speak with him that I was at the mansion, or nearby, and in all probability was expecting her. Smiling as she approached, she closed the gap with a few more steps and introduced herself: "I'm Rachel Duval Swanson," and I followed: "I'm Mark Andrews," I said. Not just then did I grasp her middle name. But later, and with good reason, I began to wonder about it. She eyed me up and down, understandably unsure in all appearances of why I was there, but would get around to asking with little passage of time. In every aspect she was a beautiful woman, with glowing dark eyes that bore fast upon you as she talked, her hair hanging about her shoulders. She was clad in a lovely pink dress which was covered by a stylish fall cloak that hung to below her knees. She had chosen to let it stay unbuttoned. It was apparent that she was possessed of the finest of training and culture. She did not have to explain that she was out of state. There was a Maryland license plate affixed to her automobile. Somehow, she made me feel uncomfortable; I didn't know why but she did. I supposed her beauty was at fault. Whatever it was I hastened to alleviate its effect by beating her to the core of why we had come together.

"I take it you're reviewing the remains of this old mansion, or have been since you arrived a few days ago."

"I am. And you?"

"The same. It was once a glorious structure; much life was lived here."

"I've heard," she said. "You speak as if you are an authority on the subject. Did you have relatives here long ago?"

"No. No relatives. But I got to know them."

There was something of a piquancy that vaguely invaded her face and she sort of laughed. "Now you must explain that for sure."

"I will. I'm writing a story of the people who once resided here. Or I should say I think that I've written it already, and that I've been at it for years. Yep. I know them. I know them all by name and a great deal about their personalities and how they mixed with one another."

"A book? You've written a book?"

"I have."

"Perhaps you'll send me a copy."

"Gladly. But why your interest?"

"My relatives lived here once."

Her relatives! Blood kin! I could have fallen over. "Your relatives? What was their name?"

"Van Doke."

"But the Van Doke mansion was over there a ways. This was known as the Sherette plantation."

"Yes, I know. But there was a girl who lived here that married a Van Doke. The Van Doke mansion burned I am told; so there's nothing to see of it but raw land."

"And who was it she married?"

"Andre, Andre Van Doke. The youngest son. That's according to the genealogical records. And the girl he married was Sasha. Sasha. Isn't that a lovely name? But I am sure sir that all of this is locked into your repository of knowledge."

"It is."

"She was a doctor; a beautiful thing, if legend about her is true."

"It is. I assure you it is. I've named my book after her."

"Oh you have? And what is the title?"

"The Atonement of Sasha."

"Ah. How alluring. But it also leaves me wondering. What was there that she had to atone for?"

"Nothing. Nothing at all except that which she owed to her Maker. You see, as I thought about it, Sasha was a creature of our Almighty, as we all are, yet born into this life to do astonishing things. That was His gift to her, His expectation, her debt, which she owed for her birthright. He was the first to proclaim, I dare say, that upon her last breath, whenever and wherever that was, she had fully repaid it."

"I see. I love that. You said you'll send me a copy."

"Give me your address and I will."

At this, she wrote it out on a pad that she retrieved from her purse, then handed it to me and from there wandered over closer to the decaying Aurora, wistfully peeping inside through one of the window openings. She then turned and began to walk around the structure, twice circling, seeming to focus on every detail—every broken brick, every missing board, the decaying roofline, the heaping pile of rubble that lay at the base of the chimneys, just as I had, eventually returning to where I stood looking on.

And then we sat down on the edge of the portico and poured out a stream of questions to one another and talked, which eventually included something that was bound to surface. "The grave site! Have you seen it?" she asked, suddenly springing the subject out of the blue.

"No I haven't. I've wanted to. But didn't know where it was and neither did I feel that I should bother Carlos by leaning on him to take me."

"He would have gladly done it. I think you should see it. I'll go for him. He'll drive us in his truck. The way there is too difficult for an automobile."

"You needn't do that."

"But I should. It will only take a jiffy."

Then she slid into her car and drove off, while I stayed behind combing through the inside once more. After this, I left for the portico, and stood viewing westwardly where I thought the horse stables were once situated. There were none anymore and I knew as much, for I had looked for them my first day there. By this time Rachael and Carlos had arrived, ready for a visit to the Sherette family cemetery. I crawled in beside her and Carlos soon had us there. It was no piece at all. The cemetery was not large. I had concluded in advance that that was how it would be. Besides those for their parents, headstones were marked separately for Adelaide and Lawrence Sherette, one also for Mary Tonka and one each for Sam Feathers and his wife and children and one for Thea and her husband and children. The elegies inscribed upon the headstones were partially eaten away by the weather, the cold, the heat, the harsh rains and relentless storms. And green moss had crept upward over the years to partially cover the names, cleaned away at times by someone's loving unknown hands, but nature will not be denied and so the moss, undaunted, eventually returned. I would have sworn that there would have been a headstone for Harry, but there wasn't.

"I had half way expected to see one each for Sasha and Andre," I said aloud. "I suppose they lie in the Van Doke cemetery."

"No they don't. They were buried in Baltimore. I know, because I am at the cemetery now and then."

"You are! I'll declare! When I was there once looking for a trace of them I found nothing; only the genealogies, just as you have found."

"The genealogies. But if you had had possession of the old Bibles of the succeeding families and where according to the entries they were laid to rest your mystery will have been solved."

"I'll declare," I let out again.

Time was dwindling fast, the sun not far from making its adieu and Rachael mentioned that she'd need to leave pretty soon. I looked quickly around for one last glimpse and I think she did too; and then we crawled into Carlos's truck and left. He let us both off at the Aurora and drove on.

"I've learned from you Mr. Andrews; I've learned a great deal. You've worked at your tasks. You've uncovered many things about the family. It took some time, didn't it?"

"Time and effort, but it was pleasurable for the most part. Sadly, however, there's one thing of inestimable importance to me that I failed to accomplish."

"What is that?"

"Sasha's portrait. I have hoped to run across it sooner or later. But have had no such luck."

"Her portrait. Perhaps I can help. I should have mentioned it before now."

"You can. My goodness. How might that be?"

"Several years ago, when I was barely starting into my teens, my grandmother showed me a portrait of a beautiful girl in a wedding pose. It was Sasha. She said it was. She even told me a few things about her. 'You must remember her,' she said, 'she was an unusual person, a most unusual person according to earlier forebears on the Van Doke side who talked about her in their various scribblings, and you will be very glad one day to claim her as a relative.'"

"My goodness!" I cried out again. My heart beat fast. "Do you have the portrait in your home in Baltimore?"

"No. Not in my home. When my grandmother showed it to me she said she had borrowed it from another relative and was keeping it for awhile. The name of the lender, the relative, escapes me, but my mother will know in whose hands it is currently secured."

"Fantastic. I find this quite hard to believe. Suddenly I am astoundingly fortunate. Will you have a photo duplicate made, in color if you can, and send it to me? I'll happily overpay for the shipping and the work of the photographer."

"I'll do that. Glad to."

"But one last question, please. It's just now registered. Sometimes legends are exaggerated and made to be more than they are; but sometimes they're above and beyond the image we have of them. What do you think I will adjudge when I see the portrait?"

She answered without hesitation. "There is no question about that. She's incomparably adorable. I only wish I could be around to see your face when you unveil it."

This said, she slid into her car and turned the key, the powerful motor beginning to purr. She extended her hand through the open window and I met it with mine.

"I have immensely enjoyed meeting you Mr. Andrews."

"And I you."

"We'll correspond won't we?"

"Absolutely."

It was so strange that she came, I thought, as I watched the car turn on to the main road. It was the oddest occurrence. Was it an event of coincidence, I asked, or was there a reason insoluble within my sphere of understanding that she appeared, likened to the intervention of a power superior to man, a divination coming to bear? But I chuckled at my fantasy and told myself to quit such nonsense, that the thing of essence was my having met her, and that she had revealed many intriguing aspects of the family's history which otherwise would have forever escaped me.

It was late. The sun was about to set, the shades of evening deftly falling. Early the next morning I planned to leave for home. I had stayed four days and had accomplished everything and more that I had set out to do, seeing with my own eyes where Sasha grew up and had spent enumerable hours; who in her time was the bright glowing star among the people living on the two plantations. Greatly loved. I turned to acquire a better grasp of the scene before me—of the fading Aurora one last time. "Goodbye Sasha; we've had a wonderful journey together, haven't we," I murmured wistfully, then went to my car and crawled in and drove slowly away.

About the Author

Joseph W. Morris, a native Tennessean, was educated in Texas, Tennessee, and Mississippi; he attained the Ph.D at the University of Mississippi. His bent of reading and writing interest obviously resides in the sphere of classical literature; the authors that he continues to admire most are those in the likeness of William Faulkner, Leo Tolstoy, and Nathaniel Hawthorne.

Not by any measure does his style and choice of titles insinuate that he is regional as a writer as one might suppose, for his two recent works, Little Valley of Germania and Cowboy are clearly universal in terms of geography and character selection. But arguably a good many of his most poignant experiences were singularly connected to his farm life in the South, where as a lad he picked the cotton and sang the songs that old field hand Negroes picked and sang, toiling with them side by side, there increasingly sensitized to their mode of culture. Such impressions are vividly reflected in The Atonement of Sasha.

Doubtless his range in terms of depth and substance springs in part from his adventures in the western sector of the nation, this starting when he went off to Texas for college, soon, in need of money, wandering into the oil fields seeking part time employment and finding it on the oil slick drilling rig platforms of North Texas: and upon graduation left for the vast fruit growing region of the San Joaquin and Sacramento Valleys of California, where the crops were planted and harvested by scores of ethnics, then by and large Mexican, Japanese, and Philippine. Here he was hired as a management trainee by one of the nation's largest soup producing corporations. Within a short while he left for the University of Mississippi where he met up with the renowned William Faulkner.

www.ingramcontent.com/pod-product-compliance
Lightning Source LLC
Chambersburg PA
CBHW081131300726
48982CB00005B/922
* 9 7 8 0 6 1 5 2 6 9 4 7 4 *